The Day of the Scorpion

NOVELS BY PAUL SCOTT

Johnnie Sahib

The Alien Sky

A Male Child

The Mark of the Warrior

The Chinese Love Pavilion

The Birds of Paradise

The Bender

The Corrida at San Felíu

The Raj Quartet:

   The Jewel in the Crown

   The Day of the Scorpion

   The Towers of Silence

   A Division of the Spoils

Staying On

The Day of the Scorpion

PAUL SCOTT ∗ THE RAJ QUARTET: 2

THE UNIVERSITY OF CHICAGO PRESS

The University of Chicago Press, Chicago 60637
Copyright © 1968, 1976 by Paul Scott
All rights reserved. Originally published 1968
University of Chicago Press Edition 1998
Printed in the United States of America
03 02 01 00 99 98   6 5 4 3 2

Library of Congress Cataloging-in-Publication Data

Scott, Paul, 1920–78
     The day of the scorpion / Paul Scott. — University of Chicago Press ed.
          p.   cm. — (Raj quartet ; v. 2) (Phoenix fiction)
     ISBN 0-226-74341-1 (alk. paper : pbk.)
     1. India—History—20th century—Fiction.   I. Title.   II. Series.
III. Series: Scott, Paul, 1920–78   Raj quartet ; v. 2.
PR6069.C596D3   1998
823' .914—dc21   98-10781
                                                                                                    CIP

∞ The paper used in this publication meets the minimum requirements of the
American National Standard for Information Sciences—Permanence of Paper for
Printed Library Materials, ANSI Z39.48-1992.

To FERN and JOHN
with deep affection and regard

Contents

Prologue

THE WRITER encountered a Muslim woman once in a narrow street of a predominantly Hindu town, in the quarter inhabited by money-lenders. The feeling he had was that she was coming in search of a loan. She wore the *burkha*, that unhygienic head-to-toe covering that turns a woman into a walking symbol of inefficient civic refuse collection and leaves you without even an impression of her eyes behind the slits she watches the gay world through, tempted but not tempting; a garment in all probability inflaming to her passions but chilling to her expectations of having them satisfied. Pity her for the titillation she must suffer.

After she had passed there was a smell of Chanel No. 5, which suggested that she needed money because she liked expensive things. Perhaps she had a rebellious spirit, or laboured under a confusion of ideas and intentions. On the other hand she may merely have been submissive to her husband, drenching herself for his private delight with a scent she did not realize was also one of public invitation – and passed that day through the street of the moneylenders only because it was a short cut to the mosque. It was a Friday, and it is written in the Koran: 'Believers, when the call is made for prayer on Friday, hasten to the remembrance of Allah and leave off all business. That would be best for you, if you but knew it. Then, when the prayers are ended, disperse and go in quest of Allah's bounty.' Perhaps, when the service was over, it was her intention to return by the way she had come.

If she was going to divine service then she was bound for the Great Mosque, which lies in the heart of the city. Its minaret is not the only minaret in Ranpur, but it is the tallest and the only one from which the call to prayer is made nowadays; the other mosques of Ranpur are no longer in use as houses of worship. Some of them have decayed, others less ruinous are used as storerooms by the municipality. There are still Muslims in Ranpur but the days are gone when the great festivals of the Íd al-fitr and the Íd al-Adzha

[1

could fill the mosques with thousands of the faithful from the city and the surrounding villages of the plain. The days are gone because thousands of the faithful are gone. Some of those that remain still mourn friends and relatives who chose Islam but never reached that land of promise, having died on the way, some of illness, many by violence. Sometimes a train they travelled on would pass one coming out of Islam, laden with passengers who had neither chosen Islam nor been content to stay when they found themselves living there, in the houses they were born in. These people mourned too for what they had left behind and for friends and relatives who started on the journey with them but did not live to finish it. Some of the survivors settled in Ranpur which was, still is, a sprawling city, seat of the provincial government. There are temples and bathing places on the banks of the sacred river, with steps and burning ghats. Bridges connect the north to the south bank which is less densely populated than the north where lateral and tangential industrial development has broken the landscape with chimneys taller than any minaret. From the air this expansion outwards from the ancient nucleus falls into something like a pattern. From the ground no pattern can be seen (except to the east in the military precision with which the roads and installations of the cantonment were built by a people who are also gone) and the nucleus itself is a warren of narrow streets and chowks in which one may too easily get lost and, being lost, marvel that anyone could know of a short cut to the mosque or to anywhere, let alone find it. Here, you might think no experience would be long enough to acquire such knowledge, in fact the confusion seems to be almost deliberate, the result of recognition of a need to huddle together in order not to be destroyed by a land that seems at best indifferent, at worst malignly opposed, to human occupation.

To leave the narrow streets and crowded chowks behind and enter the area once distinguished by the title Civil Lines, an area of broad avenues and spacious bungalows in walled compounds which culminates in the palladian grandeur of Government House, the Secretariat and the Legislative Assembly; to continue, still in an easterly direction, past the maidan, the government college, the hospital and the film studios and enter the cantonment, which someone once described as Aldershot with trees planted to provide shade instead of cut down to make room, is to pass from one period of history to another and to feel that the people from the small and

2]

distant island of Britain who built and settled here were attempting to express in the architectural terms that struck them as suitable their sense of freedom at having space around them at last, a land with length and breadth to it that promised ideal conditions for concrete and abstract proof of their extraordinary talent for running things and making them work. And yet here too there is an atmosphere of circumscription, of unexpected limits having been reached and recognized, and quietly, sensibly settled for. Too late to reduce the scale and crowd everything together, each road and building has an air of being turned inwards on itself to withstand a siege.

If you look in places like Ranpur for evidence of things these island people left behind which were of value, you might choose any one or several of the public works and installations as visible proof of them: the roads and railways and telegraph for a modern system of communication, the High Court for a sophisticated code of civil and criminal law, the college for education to university standard, the State Legislature for democratic government, the Secretariat for a civil service made in the complex image of that in Whitehall; the clubs for a pattern of urbane and civilized behaviour, the messes and barracks for an ideal of military service to the mother country. These were bequeathed, undoubtedly; these and the language and the humpy graves in the English cemetery of St Luke's in the oldest part of the cantonment, many of whose headstones record an early death, a cutting-off before the prime or in the prime, with all that this suggests in the way of unfinished business.

But it is not these things which most impress the stranger on his journey into the civil lines, into the old city itself (where he becomes lost and notes the passage of a woman dressed in the *burkha* in the street of the moneylenders) and then back past the secretariat, the Legislative Assembly and Government House, and on into the old cantonment in a search for points of present contact with the reality of twenty years ago, the repercussions, for example, of the affair in the Bibighar Gardens. What impresses him is something for which there is no memorial but which all these things collectively bear witness to: the fact that here in Ranpur, and in places like Ranpur, the British came to the end of themselves as they were.

*

More than two hundred miles south-west of Ranpur but still inside the boundary of the province of which Ranpur is the principal city lies the town of Premanagar, and – some five miles farther, marking the site of an earlier town of that name – the Premanagar Fort.

Premanagar is most easily pronounced Premman'ugger. Old-style British used to call it Premah'n'gh, strongly accenting the second syllable and all but swallowing the third and fourth, which gave the Fort status of the kind enjoyed by a tent when it is called a marquee. Originally built by the Rajputs, the Fort was partially destroyed and patched up by the Moghuls who held it against the Mahrattas but lost it to the British. In the mid-nineteenth century it was for a time the seat of an English freebooting gentleman of doubtful origin called Turner who raised a company of mercenaries which he styled Turner's Horse. His men terrorized the countryside and were said to be devoted to their leader. Apart from his Horse Turner had six wives, and a modest fortune which he lost gambling in Calcutta trying to buy a seventh. He died in a skirmish which most historians of the Mutiny of 1857 overlook, probably because so far as one can see nothing led up to it and it led nowhere itself. An old daguerreotype reveals Turner as a man with side whiskers and fixed, pale-looking eyes that were probably blue. One suspects that he was murdered. His irregular cavalry either died with him or disappeared in search of further adventure, so no Turner's Horse lived on to perpetuate his memory. He was, it is said, a press-ganged sailor who deserted in Madras and sought his fortune up-country. But no matter. He is a body buried as it were in the foundations of that other ruined stronghold, the British Empire.

Real bodies were in fact buried in the foundations of the Premanagar Fort. It was a fashion of the times, but the parents of young men (and sometimes the young men's wives) who were bricked up alive to give a fort an auspicious start in life were handsomely rewarded. It is said, though, that the misfortunes of this particular fort were once traced to the fact that the treasurer at the court of the Rajput prince who built it – and bricked up a promising young man and his child wife – pocketed the bereaved family's pension for the five years it took the boy's father to pluck up the courage to go over the treasurer's head and hint at injustice. It is not known what then happened to the treasurer, or the complainant.

And anyway it is all conjecture. It has the sound of a myth devised later to explain or anyway celebrate misadventure. The British – as usual – had the best of it. They inherited a partial ruin and preserved it with reverent determination as if awestruck at the thought of changing anything that might then be turned to their disadvantage. Until 1939 the Fort was a detention barracks, and a magnet for military schemes run by grey colonels who had forgotten that as rosy subalterns they had always found such exercises distracting to their sense of what one was in the world to do.

After 1939, the Fort became a prison – a place of civil instead of military detention. It comprised the foundations of the old outer wall, a broken-down despoiled Hindu temple in what had once been the precincts of the South Gate, a still stout inner wall, a pretty mosque, two wells, a flagpole, and a walled courtyard of red earth. Here, in the courtyard, between August 1942 and the date of his release, the Fort's most distinguished prisoner created a garden to pass the time. Traces of it still remain. Given better luck than Turner his memory might have been perpetuated by the habit, dear to Indians, of naming a place after its founder or its most illustrious inhabitant. But it is not known now as Kasim's Garden. Besides, it was only a patch.

Below the hill on which the redstone Fort rests in the massive immobility of its functional decline are other ruins, the site of excavations in 1926 by a team of Frenchmen whose leader became *persona non grata* with the Deputy Commissioner and the Provincial Governor when a complaint was lodged by an English lady, a Miss Frayle, that Professor Lebrun had made an improper suggestion to her while pointing out a recently uncovered frieze of Hindu erotica. The expedition departed for Pondicherry in amused, Gallic disgrace, collectively shrugging its shoulders; and the inquisitive English who subsequently took an archaeological interest in the diggings at Premanagar found the erotica disappointingly mild, so mild in fact that Miss Frayle's reputation suffered and she packed her bags and left for Persia.

Beyond the ruins is the plain, eroded by time, low rainfall, occasional floods and poor husbandry: a complex of old dry riverbeds (nullahs) and scantily grassed hummocks over which herds of goats tinkled and still do, seeking the shade of infrequent trees and of bushes whose exhausted-looking leaves become yellowed by the dust blown up from the unmetalled strips on either side of the trunk road. This road stands out in the arid landscape, a hardened artery. The lifeblood of the country, traffic, flows along it thinly and irregularly. Even today you can stand on the roadside and hear nothing for an hour on end except sometimes the goatbells and the wind in the telegraph wires. The wind is hot. At midday the Fort's outline is distorted by the shifting, shimmering air. At a suitable distance it takes on the look of a mirage and at certain times of the year, when climatic conditions are right, actually produces one – a replica of itself, hovering above ground, sometimes upside down. English people, observing the apparition, used to find themselves thinking of Kipling or A. E. W. Mason, and looking forward to sundown, at which hour it was customary to refresh the body and relieve the spirit of the otherwise oppressive burdens of their duty.

Ranpur and the Fort at Premanagar are the first two images in the story to be told.

Book One

The Prisoners in the Fort

Part One 🌿 An Arrest

Ex-CHIEF MINISTER Mohammed Ali Kasim was arrested at his home in Ranpur at 5 a.m. on August 9th 1942 by a senior English police officer who arrived in a car, with a motor-cycle escort, two armed guards and a warrant for his detention under the Defence of India Rules. The officer waited for ten minutes on the wrong side of the locked iron gates while the chaukidar went off to rouse one of the servants who in turn roused another who roused Mr Kasim. By the time the officer gained the entrance hall Mr Kasim was standing there in his pyjamas.

'Good morning,' the ex-Chief Minister said. 'I'm sorry they've dragged you out of bed. Is that for me?'

'I'm afraid it is,' the officer replied. Mr Kasim glanced briefly at the warrant, asked the Englishman to step inside and promised not to be long. Mrs Kasim came out and offered him an early morning cup of tea which he felt he had to decline in the circumstances. She nodded, as if she quite understood, and then returned to help her husband get ready.

Ten minutes later Mr and Mrs Kasim came into the vestibule together.

'Where are you actually taking me?' Mr Kasim asked.

The officer hesitated. 'My orders are to drive to Government House. Beyond that I can't say.'

'Oh well, that's just an initial formality. They'll hardly put me up there for the duration. I hope it's not going to be the Kandipat jail, though. It's so damp and depressing.' He turned to his wife, to embrace her, and the officer moved away and looked at one of the many portraits on the wall, a head and shoulders study of an elderly Indian wearing a number of rather splendid-looking decorations: the ex-Chief Minister's father, probably. He noted a likeness. The Kasims had always been rich and influential. The house was large and richly furnished, but had the spicy smell of Indian cooking and Indian perfumes which the Englishman always found disturbing, not quite civilized, or civilized in a way that suggested there was no distinction to be made between ancient and modern societies.

'I'm ready,' Mr Kasim said.

'Haven't you a bag?'

'Oh, that's here.' He pointed to a suitcase and a bedroll standing against the wall. 'I packed last night when I had news of the Congress Committee vote in Bombay. I thought it would save us time.'

The officer looked at the luggage and disguised his reaction – one of surprise and slight annoyance – by pursing his lips. Lists and arrangements for the detentions had been made secretly for some time, but the arrests, if they had to be made at all, were supposed to come as a surprise.

Saying nothing the officer stooped, picked up the suitcase and bedroll and carried them out to the waiting car where they were taken from him by one of the servants who had now all been alerted and stood around in the forecourt to see their master off to jail.

It was still dark. Mrs Kasim did not come out of the house. The Englishman waited until Mr Kasim was settled in the back seat of the car, gave a nod to the motor-cyclists and as they kicked their machines into life entered the car himself and closed the door. Now that the most embarrassing part of his job was done he would have liked a cigarette. He put his hand in his pocket. He would offer one to Mr Kasim to show him that he appreciated his co-operation. The last time he had arrested a member of Congress there had been a most objectionable scene: sarcasm, abuse and a lecture all the way to the jail about the iniquities of the *raj*. Mr Kasim was a model of restraint and good behaviour. But then he was a Muslim, and the Muslims were men of action, not words. You knew better where you stood with them and they knew when to bow with dignity to the inevitable. Remembering Mr Kasim was a Muslim, though, the officer realized he probably didn't smoke, and realizing that, he thought it would be better manners to deny himself as well.

*

'I'm sorry, Mr Kasim,' Sir George Malcolm said.

They were in the large lofty-ceilinged room where in 1937 Mr

Kasim had presented himself to the preceding Governor and listened to formal and rather grudging words of invitation to form a ministry, and in the October of 1939 presented himself again to hand in his written resignation and the resignations of his colleagues. He had been in the room on many other occasions, but these were the two that came most significantly to mind.

'Please don't apologize,' he said. 'Are they arresting Gandhiji too?'

'Yes, so I understand.'

'And the Committee in Bombay?'

The Governor nodded, then said, 'Rather a broad sweep this time, as a matter of fact. Even chaps in your district sub-committees are going into the bag.'

Through one of the tall windows light was now showing. Kasim could just make out the distant bulk of the Secretariat. During his own ministry the lights had often burned there all night. A tale was told that on the occasion of his resignation the preceding Governor had waited until he was alone with his ADC and then said, 'Thank God, now for a bit of peace.' An English wit in the Secretariat had commented, 'Well, why not? The war is nearly two months old,' and like the rest reverted to the habit of leaving the office at 4 p.m. to get in a game of tennis and a drink at the club before going home to dress for dinner.

The Governor said, 'I gather you packed last night. Did your colleagues do the same, d'you think?'

'Perhaps. I don't know. Should they have?'

'Most of them.'

'Are they in the building?'

'No. They're elsewhere.'

'In Kandipat?'

The Governor did not answer. Kasim did not expect him to. In a case of mass arrests like this the British would be absurdly secretive about the places where leading Congressmen were to be kept under lock and key.

'If they are in Kandipat or elsewhere, why have I been brought here?'

The Governor took off his spectacles, dangled them, then placed them on the blotter. His desk was untidy. In his predecessor's day it had always been unpleasantly immaculate.

'I wanted to have a talk,' he said.

'Before sending me to Kandipat?'

'I think not Kandipat. Don't you agree?'

Kasim smiled. 'Do I have a choice, then?'

'Possibly.' The Governor leaned back in his chair and put one arm over it. With his other hand he played with the spectacles. 'What a damn' silly thing, isn't it? What did your people expect us to do? Sit back and let you bring the country to a standstill? Did anyone in his right mind really expect us to be blackmailed into granting independence just like that in the middle of a world war, with the Japanese preening themselves on the Chindwin?'

'Does anyone in his right mind think that arresting us all from Gandhi down will help?'

'If it stops you from inciting the factory workers to strike, the railways to stop, the ports to close, the soldiers to lay down their arms. That's what you voted for in Bombay yesterday.'

'I did not vote, Governor-ji.'

'No, you did not vote because you resigned from the Congress Committee last year. On the other hand you haven't resigned from the Congress Party. There have been rumours that you were considering it.'

'They are unfounded.'

'Are they? Are they, truly?'

Kasim folded his hands.

'They are mostly the result of one-time wishful thinking on the part – for instance – of Mr Jinnah.'

The Governor laughed. 'Yes, I heard about that. Is *that* true? That Jinnah promised you a portfolio in Bengal or Sind if you'd go over to the League?'

'Let us just say that his interest was aroused by my resignation from the All India Congress Committee. A certain gentleman was commissioned to ask what my further intentions might be. It is true that there were hints about a rosy ministerial future in one of the Muslim majority provinces, but nothing specific was promised.'

'And your reply?'

'Merely the truth. That I resigned from the committee in order to devote more time to my legal work and that in any case I was not an opportunist. Perhaps I should emphasize that I am not before we go further. You are thinking of offering me a loophole through which I could escape going to prison, I believe.'

'Not a loophole. But it would be an awful waste of your time

12]

and talent if you went to jail just when you were seriously considering resigning from Congress, wouldn't it?'

'I am not seriously considering it, Governor-ji. I am not considering it at all and have never considered it.'

'Will you consider it now?'

'Will you give me reasons why I should?'

The Governor sat forward, replaced his spectacles and picked
up a pencil. 'Yes, Mr Kasim. I'll give you reasons, although as I
see it they all point to one reason only -- that you are no longer in
sympathy with Congress policy. You haven't been in sympathy for
a long time and grow intellectually and emotionally further and
further away from Congress with every week that goes by. You
were impatient with Congress when they won the provincial elec-
tions in 1937 but dithered about taking office. You were impatient
with the face-saving formula which allowed them to pretend to take
office just to show that the scheme for a federal central government
wouldn't work. You were alarmed when you found yourself unable
to form a provincial ministry which would have more accurately
reflected the wishes of the electorate. The Congress majority in the
province was slim enough to warrant a coalition. You wanted
Nawaz Shah in your cabinet but none of your Congress colleagues
would agree because he was a Muslim Leaguist. You were enough
of a realist to bow to the inevitable, and a good enough party
disciplinarian to make sure that on any major point of legislation in
the Assembly your compromises were with the Muslim League
and not the Hindu Mahasabah. You were criticized for that. People
said scratch Kasim and you'll find one of Jinnah's men underneath.
But you preferred to run the risk of that sort of criticism and to
invite defeat in the Assembly than adjust your programme to ensure a comfortable majority of Congressites and Hindu right-
wingers.' The Governor smiled. 'You see, I've done my homework.
So let me continue. You knew what was going on in the districts,
and knew that most of what the Muslims said was going on was
gross exaggeration, but you recognized the dangers and were
appalled at the evidence you had of what actual communal intimidation did exist. You saw that whatever the Congress professed to be,
a national party, a secular party, a party dedicated to the ideal of
independence and national unity, there were people in it who could
never see it as anything but a Hindu dominated organization whose
real motive was power for the Hindus and who were coming into

[13

the open now that they'd got power. That alarmed you too. Every instance that came to your notice of a Muslim being discriminated against, of an injustice against a Muslim, of violence done to a Muslim, of Muslim children being forced to salute the Congress flag or sing a Congress hymn in school, you saw not only as reprehensible in itself, whatever the provocation might have been, but as another nail in the coffin, another wedge driven between the two major communities. And something else alarmed you, the realization that you were a man not with one master but two, the electorate to whom you were responsible, and the Congress High Command. It alarmed you because the High Command itself wasn't administratively committed. It wasn't answerable to an electorate, but it controlled and directed you who were. So when Britain declared war on Germany and the Viceroy declared war on Germany and the Congress High Command objected to having war declared over its head and called on all Congress ministries to resign, you resigned. You resigned at the dictate of a political organization that had no electoral responsibility to the country, except in the provinces through men like yourself. You saw the constitutional absurdity of this, but you handed your resignation in, handed it in here in this room to my predecessor, and he was a man who welcomed it because he was a man of the old school who thought India ungovernable except by decree, a man who'd sat back and laughed up his sleeve for two and a half years as he watched the farce of a ministry trying to serve both its electorate and its political bosses, and who sat back now, breathed a sigh of relief and assumed Governor's control which I've inherited. And it wasn't just the constitutional absurdity that struck you, it was the political folly of resigning, of having to resign. Without power, politics are so much hot air, and power is what your party got rid of. You knew what would happen and have seen it happen. How many seats in the Legislative Assembly reserved for Muslims were won in 1937 by non-League Muslims? A tidy few including your own. How many would be won now if we had an election tomorrow? Any? Where would your slim Congress Party majority be with most of your non-aligned Muslims and even some of your Congress Muslims gone over to the League? Repeat that picture all over India and where is your party's proof of speaking for all India? Where is it, Mr Kasim? Where has it gone? You know the answer as well as I do. Up the spout. Down the creek. Sunk. Why? Because your party overlooked the fact that

14]

on the first assumption of political power the old battle was won and the new one begun. The old battle was for Indian independence and although you may not think so now, Indian independence became a foregone conclusion in 1937 when men like you became provincial ministers. Getting rid of us was still part of your programme but getting rid of us was no longer the battle. The real battle was to maintain and extend the area of your party's power. I've no patience with people, and they're chiefly my fellow-countrymen, who profess horror at what they call the sorry spectacle of the Indians squabbling among themselves because they're unable to agree about how the power they're going to inherit should be divided. Of course you must disagree. Of course you must squabble. It's a sign that you know you're no longer fighting for a principle because you know the principle has been conceded. You're fighting for political power over what has been conceded. It's logical. It's essential. It's an inescapable human condition. When you all resigned the power you'd got, in the belief that you were striking another blow for India's independence, you weren't striking a blow for that at all. You were striking a blow at your own existing and potential political power. You were narrowing the area you could hope to exercise it in. It isn't so much what you all did between 1937 and 1939 to make a lot of Muslims believe the League had been right and that a Congress ruled India would mean a Hindu India that has made eventual partition of this country almost certainly inevitable, it's the fact that you relinquished power, and you relinquished it because you didn't understand the importance of keeping it. I say you, but I don't mean you, Mr Kasim. You well knew its importance and the folly of giving it up, just as you well know the latest folly your party has committed, the folly of not admitting the consequences of the first idiocy, of thinking you can put the clock back to 1939, ignore Jinnah and pretend the real quarrel is still with Britain and that the British are just playing that old game of dividing and ruling and hanging on like grim death. You well know that when Cripps came out in April your party had its last chance to retrieve its position. You well know that for the first time in all the long melancholy history of conferences, working parties and round table negotiations the Cripps Mission wasn't just *us* going through the old motions of palming you off with as little as possible. It was us again, but us under pressure from outside, from our allies, from America in particular, and I think you understood the peculiar

[15

advantages of negotiating with people under that sort of pressure. I think you understood too that the Cripps proposals were the best you are going to get while the war is on and that this was the last chance you had to contain Jinnah. But what happens? Your party shies like a frightened horse from the mere idea that any province or group of provinces should have the power to secede from a post-war Indian constitution and set up a constitution of its own. What does it mean, they ask? What but Pakistan? But who even a few years ago had ever heard of Pakistan let alone thought of it as practicable? Well, it's more than practicable now. It's damn' well certain. It needn't have been if you'd agreed to the Cripps proposals, come back into office, got on with the war and at the end of the war gone to a country you'd helped lead to victory and independence and trusted in the good sense of those people not to let their country be split down the middle. Instead of which you walk out on Cripps, spend the whole summer in cloud cuckoo land working up some absurd theory that if you make India untenable for the British they'll leave and the Japanese won't walk in. And while you're producing this ludicrous scheme you allow Jinnah to continue to extend the area of his power because in the Muslim majority provinces Jinnah's men have remained in office. And now comes the crowning folly, a resolution that's as good as a call to nation-wide insurrection. And you don't agree with that either, do you, Mr Kasim? You know the British simply aren't going to forgive all this Quit India nonsense going on while they're trying to concentrate on turning the tables on the Japanese, not – mark you – just to save themselves and their country but you and your country. You know all this, Mr Kasim, but you're still a pillar of the Congress Party, one of its most famous favoured Muslims, good propaganda and apparently living proof of the truth of their claim that they're an all India party, the sort of man who's influential enough in this province for me not to think twice about locking you up as a potential inciter of riots and strikes, because your party, your party, Mr Kasim, yesterday committed high treason by conspiring to take steps calculated to aid and comfort the King-Emperor's enemies. And the one big question in my mind is why is it still your party, Mr Kasim? What official policy or policies has it adopted and pursued in the last three years that you have honestly felt to be either wise or expedient?'

'Perhaps none,' Kasim said.

16]

'Exactly. And so, my dear Kasim, don't go into the wilderness with the rest of them this morning. However long it is, and my guess is it's for the duration, what a waste of your talent, what misplaced loyalty. Get out now. Write to Maulana Azad. Write this morning, write here and now. Send in your resignation. What more suitable moment? And the moment you write your resignation I tear up this stupid document authorizing your arrest. There's not a single act committed by you since you resigned office in 1939, not a speech, not a letter, not a pamphlet, not a thing said in public or overheard in private that warrants your being locked up. All that warrants it now is your continued allegiance to the Congress, your continued standing as a leading member of an organization we're outlawing.'

'I quite understand, Sir George.'

The Governor studied the expression on Kasim's face. Then he got up, walked to one of the long windows, looked out, and came back again, pacing slowly. Kasim waited, his hands still folded on his lap.

'I want you on my executive council,' the Governor said. 'If it were constitutionally possible for me to re-establish autonomy in this province I know whom I'd invite to head the administration. Short of that I want you *in*, I want to use your talents, Mr Kasim.'

'It is very kind of you, Sir George. I am immensely flattered.'

'But you refuse, don't you? You refuse to resign. You insist on going to jail. Forgive me, then. I hope you don't feel insulted. That wasn't my intention.'

Kasim made a gesture of dismissal. 'Please. I know this.'

The Governor sat down, took off his spectacles and played with them as before, but with both hands, leaning forward, with his elbows on the desk. 'Waste!' he exclaimed suddenly. 'Waste! Why, Mr Kasim? You agree with everything I've said, but you don't even ask for time to consider my suggestion. You reject it out of hand. Why?'

'Because you only offer me a job. I am looking for a country and I am not looking for it alone.'

'A country?'

'To disagree about the ways of looking for it is as natural as you say it is to squabble about how power will be divided when it is found. And as you say, I have disagreed many times about these ways, and people have many times expected me to resign and change

[17

my political allegiance. And if ways and means were all that mattered I expect Congress would have seen the back of me long ago. But these are not what matter, I believe. What matters is the idea to which the ways and means are directed. I have pursued this idea for a quarter of a century, and it is an idea which for all my party's faults I still find embodied in that party and only in that party, Governor-ji, nowhere else. Incidentally, I do not agree with you when you speak of Indian independence having become a foregone conclusion. Independence is not something you can divide into phases. It exists or does not exist. Certain steps might be taken to help bring it into existence, others can be taken that will hinder it doing so. But independence alone is not the idea I pursue, nor the idea which the party I belong to tries to pursue, no doubt making many errors and misjudgements in the process. The idea, you know, isn't simply to get rid of the British. It is to create a nation capable of getting rid of them and capable simultaneously of taking its place in the world as a nation, and we know that every internal division of our interests hinders the creation of such a nation. That is why we go on insisting that the Congress is an All India Congress. It is an All India Congress first, because you cannot detach from it the idea that it is right that it should be. Only second is it a political party, although one day that is what it must become. Meanwhile, Governor-ji, we try to do the job that your Government has always found it beneficial to leave undone, the job of unifying India, of making all Indians feel that they are, above all else, Indians. You think perhaps we do this to put up a strong front against the British. Partly only you would be right. Principally we do it for the sake of India when you are gone. And we are working mostly in the dark with only a small glimmer of light ahead, because we have never had that kind of India, we do not know what kind of India that will be. This is why I say we are looking for a country. I can look for it better in prison, I'm afraid, than from a seat on your Excellency's executive council.'

While Kasim was talking the Governor had searched for and found a folder from which he now took a paper. He handed it across the desk. Kasim unfolded his hands, took the paper, felt in his pocket for his spectacles.

'As you will see, Mr Kasim, that is a very short note which, if signed, will be your undertaking not to commit or cause to be committed any act whose effect is to disturb the peace or to hinder the defence of the realm. The undertaking would be valid for a period of six months from the date of signature. As you'll also see there's a rider to the effect that the signatory would, if called upon, use his best endeavours to inhibit the effects of any such acts committed within the province by others. You'll notice the paper says nothing about resigning from Congress. But sign the paper and I'll still tear this other paper up.'

'Yes, I see,' Mr Kasim said. He put the note back on the Governor's desk and replaced his spectacles in their case. 'You are expecting trouble, then. You have realized the disadvantages of having to lock us up to stop us rousing what you call the mob. But the mob perhaps rouses itself. And it is uncontrolled. It wants to know what you've done with us. All kinds of undesirable elements emerge. You want me therefore to become a sort of *ex-officio* peacemaker, armed with soothing words and no integrity. As you say, the paper says nothing about resigning from Congress, but it need not do so, of course. If I signed it I would be expelled. To sign it is tantamount to resignation. I could not sign it. You didn't expect me to, but I suppose you thought it was worth a try. I'm afraid you must cope with the mob without me.'

'Well we can do that and will.' For a while the Governor was silent, watching Kasim. Then he said, 'You are in a curious position.'

'I do not see it as curious.'

'I was thinking of your private position. Of your elder son, for instance, who holds the King-Emperor's commission. He fought in Malaya, and now he's a prisoner of war of the Japanese. It has always puzzled me why you allowed him to join the army.'

'Allow? He was under no obligation to seek my approval. It was his wish. India must have an army as well as a government. He became an officer. I became a minister.'

'And you both served under the crown. Quite. But you no longer do. He does. No doubt you have heard rumours of the pressures being put on Indian prisoners, officers and men, to secure their release from prison camp by joining units that will fight side by side with the Japanese. News of your imprisonment might well be used by the enemy to add to those pressures in your son's case. He was an excellent officer, I believe. He would be useful to them. His loyalty as an officer might be subjected to severe strain if he hears that we have put his father in jail. In his present circumstances he cannot simply resign his commission as you resigned your ministerial appointment. That is the difference, isn't it?'

'I think it is a difference he will appreciate. Just as he will appreciate that I cannot let personal considerations affect my political judgement.'

'Yes,' the Governor said, 'I expect it is,' and stood up in a way that conveyed to Kasim that the interview was at an end. He stood up too. In the pit of his stomach he felt the old familiar hollowness. He did not want to go to prison.

The Governor held out his hand. Kasim took it.

'I'm afraid that for the time being at any rate your whereabouts aren't to be made known, and this restriction must unfortunately apply in the case of your family. They will write to you care of Government House, and your own letters will automatically come here. I hope, Mr Kasim, that occasionally you will think of writing personally to me.'

'Thank you. Am I to be allowed newspapers?'

'I shall give the necessary instructions.'

'Then I'll say goodbye.'

'Goodbye, Mr Kasim.'

Kasim bowed his head, hesitated, and then walked towards the double doors behind which, he knew, the young police officer to whom the senior man had handed him over, and two British military policemen, would be waiting. But just before he reached the doors he heard the Governor call his name, and turned. The Governor was still standing behind the desk. He made a gesture with both hands, indicating the desk, the papers on it.

'May I send you away with an interesting thought that has suddenly struck me?'

'What is that, your Excellency?'

'That one day this desk will probably be yours.'

Kasim smiled, looked round the room. The thought, just at that moment, was almost sickening. He said, 'Yes. You are probably right,' and, still smiling, turned and took the last few paces to his more immediate prison.

*

At dusk Mr Kasim was taken from the upstairs room where he had been kept all day and driven to the sidings of the railway station at Ranpur cantonment. Here he was transferred to a carriage of the kind used to transport troops, most of whose windows had been blocked by steel shutters. The young officer in charge of him was joined by another. An armed sentry stood guard at the only door of the carriage that was still in use. When approaching the carriage Kasim saw that it was uncoupled. There were other soldiers and police in the vicinity. When he entered the carriage he expected to find other occupants, friends, ex-colleagues; but he was alone. The two young officers talked to each other in low voices and mostly in monosyllables. He made up his bed on one of the wooden benches. A tray was brought in with his dinner: soup, chicken and vegetables, and rice pudding with jam – obviously chosen from the European style menu at the station restaurant. While he ate it one of the officers went for his own dinner. Half an hour later he returned and his companion went for his. Kasim's tray was taken by a British MP. Another armed sentry joined the first. At about nine o'clock the carriage was coupled to others, and the other officer returned from the restaurant. The two officers settled in the middle of the carriage leaving the guards at one end and Mr Kasim at the other. The train started. Kasim read. The officers continued to talk in low voices. They smoked cigarettes. Occasionally they shared a joke. At ten o'clock while the train was still moving slowly, uncertainly, picking its way across points and iron bridges, Mr Kasim gave the officers a start by rising suddenly and opening his suitcase. He sensed that they touched their holsters to make sure their revolvers were still there. From the suitcase he took out his prayer mat, then turned to them.

'I suppose neither of you can tell me which direction west is?' He smiled, was rewarded with vague, uncomprehending but not totally unfriendly negative replies, and then unrolled the mat on the floor, stood for a moment and composed himself in order to begin saying his Isha prayers in a peaceable frame of mind. He then performed in full the four Rak'ahs prescribed.

During the night he woke several times. The officers and the guards were taking it in turns to doze. He observed their faces: slack, remote in the dim pools of light from the overhead bulbs that had been left on. The light scarcely reached the end of the carriage where he lay and once, because he had moved and attracted the attention of the officer whose turn it was to keep watch, he returned the man's incurious, dispassionate, half-dreaming gaze for what seemed like an age before the man suddenly realized that Kasim's eyes were also open and looked away, stared down at his folded arms. When Kasim next awoke this man was asleep, his companion sitting forward, elbows resting on his knees, contemplating his clasped hands in one of which a cigarette was burning. Kasim raised his arm and looked at the luminous dial of his wrist-watch. Nearly five o'clock. The train was not moving but presumably wasn't at its destination. Distantly, through the silence, he heard the cry of jackals. He rose, aware of the sharp movement of the wakeful officer keeping a check on him. From his suitcase he took the waterproof bag, leather toilet case, soap-box, towel and shaving kit that he had packed the night before last, and went into the cubicle. There was no lock on the door. A single bulb illuminated dirty green tiles and old, cracked porcelain. Iron bars were set in the window. Behind them was a pane of frosted glass. He showered and shaved, put back on the clothes he had travelled in. The train had begun to move again. The motion set the door swinging open and shut. When he came out both officers were awake. He nodded good-morning to them, returned his things to the suitcase, got out his prayer mat and performed the two Rak'ahs of the Fajr prayers. Making the last prostration he repeated to himself a passage from the Koran. Oh God, glory be to You who made Your servant go by night from the Sacred Mosque to the farther Mosque. Praise be to Allah who has never begotten a son, who has no partner in his Kingdom, who needs none to defend him from humiliation.

Kneeling he rolled the mat up again, returned it to the case and snapped the locks shut. He made up his bedroll and secured the straps. Then he sat on the hard slatted bench. The officers went in turn to the cubicle at the other end of the carriage. The sentry who squatted at the door rose and woke the sleeping sentry, and then lowered the window and looked out. The train came to a halt. Rain was drumming on the roof. Kasim wondered whether his wife was yet awake. He thought of his married daughter in the Punjab, of his son Ahmed in Mirat, and of his elder son Sayed who was God knew in what hell-hole of a prison camp.

The train was, almost imperceptibly, once more in motion. Both officers had completed their ablutions. Now the sentries took it in turns to go into the farther cubicle. The officers mumbled at each other. One of them looked at his watch and stretched, went to the open window. The first light must be beginning to show, Kasim

22]

thought. The officer stayed at the window for some time. The overhead bulbs went out. The carriage was permeated with a grey mistiness that brought with it the notion of early morning chill, and the faces of his guards were suddenly like those of strangers. The officer left the window and joined his companion. He must have made some sign. They began to adjust their belts. One reached for his cap. Kasim looked away, feeling the hollowness again. A few minutes later the train came to a halt. For a moment, because of the quietness, Kasim imagined they were held up by signals, but the silence was then broken by a voice speaking outside. Turning to look Kasim saw one of the officers at the window. He spoke to someone well below the level of the carriage. A moment later he opened the door and got down. His companion stayed in the carriage but stood at the open door. He lit a cigarette. One of the soldiers slung his rifle over his shoulder and studied the palm of his left hand as if he'd got a cut or a splinter. The carriage echoed metallically. It was being uncoupled. The rain had stopped falling. There was a whistle from up ahead. Kasim stood. The sentry stopped looking at his hand and the officer in the doorway glanced round, then back through the doorway again. He answered a voice from below and came away from the door. An officer with an armband round his sleeve hauled himself up into the carriage.

'Mr Mohammed Ali Kasim?' he inquired, as if making a formal identification.

'Yes.'

'This way, please.'

Kasim picked up his suitcase and bedroll. The others stood aside for him. At the doorway he looked down into the face of the officer whose eye he had held during the night. He said, 'I'd be grateful if you'd help me with my baggage.'

Standing below, near by, were two military policemen. The carriage was in a goods yard. A 15-cwt truck was parked at the shuttered entrance to a warehouse. Kasim smelt coal dust. The officer reached up and Kasim nudged the suitcase forward until he felt its weight taken. The bedroll followed. The officer set both down on the cinders. Kasim turned round to face inwards as he climbed down the narrow, perpendicular steps; then stood waiting. The officer with the armband came down. He indicated the luggage.

'This is all your luggage?'

'Yes.'

'Very well. My men will take you to the truck. Go with them, please.'

'May I be told where you are taking me?'

The officer with the armband hesitated.

'To the Fort,' he said abruptly.

'The Fort?'

Again the officer hesitated. Kasim thought he was surprised. 'You're in Premanagar,' he explained.

'Thank you. I didn't know.'

He glanced round. One railway siding looked like any other. He had not been in Premanagar since his tour of the province in 1938. He had never visited the Fort, but he had seen it from a distance. He had no clear visual recollection of it. Premanagar, he remembered, was not far from Mirat where his son Ahmed was. If they ever told his family where he was, and allowed him visitors, perhaps he would see Ahmed.

II

MAJOR TIPPIT was a small man with very little hair. What was left of it was yellowy white. His face was lined and wrinkled. He had a high complexion. 'I'm a historian really,' he explained. 'I retired from the army in 1938, but they dug me out. It was decent of them to give me the Fort, wasn't it?'

Kasim agreed that it was.

'There's a lot of history in the Fort. I'm writing a monograph. Perhaps you'd like to read some of it and give me an opinion, one day when you have a moment.'

'I have a great number of moments.'

'I'm sorry I wasn't here when you arrived. Let us see, now, how long has it been?'

Major Tippit glanced at the papers on his desk but did not make any effort to find one in particular.

Kasim said, 'Nine days.'

'And you are comfortable?'

'I am comfortable.'

'Have you any complaints?'

'Several.'

24]

'Oh yes. Lieutenant Moran Singh told me he'd made a note of them. It's here somewhere I expect. I'll look into them.'

'Can't you look into them now?'

Major Tippit had very pale blue eyes. He gazed out of them at Kasim as if he had reasons for not dealing with complaints but couldn't remember what they were. He clasped his bony little hands together on the desk – the kind of man, Kasim guessed, who, lacking skill, energy or resolution, would make up for them with a mindless, vegetable implacability. The unpleasant young Sikh, nominally under Major Tippit's command, would know exactly how far he could go, what would be allowed to him by way of license, and what disallowed.

'First of all,' Kasim said, 'is it really Government's intention to keep me in solitary confinement? I understand the Fort has a number of civil prisoners like myself. We are not criminals. We shall probably be here for some time. The others seem to mix quite freely. I can see them in the outer courtyard from the window of my room. But since coming here I've been kept isolated and have spoken to no one except my guards and Lieutenant Moran Singh. Is this state of affairs merely temporary or is it to continue?'

'Yes, I see.'

Kasim waited.

'I am sorry you feel like that. The old zenana house is extremely interesting. I must come over one day and point out some of its more remarkable features.'

'Some of my fellow-prisoners would be interested in it too.'

'Oh, I don't think so. If I may make bold, they are not of similar intellectual calibre. The other prisoners here are very much from the rank and file of your movement.' A look of almost intense disappointment came on to Major Tippit's face, as if he had only just realized what they were talking about. 'We were told several weeks ago that we might have to provide accommodation for a VIP detenu. Of course we immediately thought of Mr Gandhi or Mr Nehru. At first I believed we had nothing suitable. Amazing how you can overlook something that's right under your nose. I had become so used to sitting here and looking through the window and seeing the zenana house, so used to going over there and using it for my own private purposes – I did a great deal of reading and writing and studying there – that I came to think of it really as an extension of my office. Then of course it struck me how eminently suitable it was. In the heart of the citadel, and if I may say so, constantly under my eye. One has that kind of obligation if one takes one's duties seriously. I made the necessary arrangements at once. It was the last thing I did before going on leave. One has to be prepared. I knew I would miss using the little house. I always found it so conducive to meditation. I confess I was a little sad when I returned last night and Lieutenant Moran Singh said that the zenana house was now occupied. However, I was most interested when he told me who you were. A member of the ancient house of Kasim. The Fort was once within the territory administered by the Kasim who was a viceroy of the great Moghul. But you know that? Your kinsman, the present Nawab of Mirat, is directly descended from him. I thought last night how interesting it was that a Kasim should have come back to stay in Premanagar. And frankly I was rather relieved that the occupant of the zenana house was of the Faith. Tell me, are you a Sunni or a Shiah Muslim?'

'Major Tippit, you have not answered my complaint. My impression is that the officers who conducted me from Ranpur brought a letter to you from Sir George Malcolm. Is there anything in that letter that suggested I should be kept isolated?'

'A letter?'

'I think the one near your left elbow. I recognize the heading.'

Tippit looked down, picked the letter up, glanced at it.

'Oh yes. Lieutenant Moran Singh mentioned a letter. I have not read it yet.'

'Would you do so now?'

Tippit looked down again, stared at the letter. His eyes showed no movement of reading. After a while he replaced the letter near his left elbow.

'Well?' Kasim asked. 'Is there anything that suggests or orders solitary confinement?'

'No.'

'Is there anything about newspapers?'

'You have permission to read newspapers.'

'Good. But I have not been given any. That is my other complaint.'

'I will speak to Lieutenant Moran Singh about it.'

'I've spoken to Lieutenant Moran Singh about it several times. I've given him a list of the newspapers I want. I've also written to

26]

my wife asking her to send newspapers. That letter and several other letters are still here. They are on your desk.'

'I'll read them as soon as possible. You understand that they must be read?'

'I understand nothing of the sort. They will be read in Ranpur, either in the censorship office at the Secretariat or by a member of the Governor's staff. Sometimes by both. I have not so far written personally to the Governor as he requested me, but I shall be doing so presently. I should like to be able to make some comments to him on whatever the current situation is.'

Major Tippit glanced up – not, it seemed, recognizing a threat. He said, 'Things have been very distressing, haven't they?'

'Major Tippit, how can I tell how things have been? I have no radio, no newspapers, my guards tell me nothing, Lieutenant Moran Singh tells me nothing and does not even post my letters. No letters have been given to me either. By now I should think there would be several.'

'Such senseless violence. It is difficult to know where to apportion blame. And that poor girl, that unfortunate woman. It has incensed people. Looting, rioting, burning. Yes, yes. One expects. Deplores but expects. But these other things . . . I was delayed because the railways have been so uncertain. In Ranpur feeling is running high. In Mayapore the civil have handed over to the military. The whole country is seething. Will you have some tea?'

'No thank you.'

'It is ten o'clock. I always have tea at ten o'clock. A regular régime. While I'm away things get out of hand. It is five past ten.' He said this without looking at his watch. He made no effort to have tea brought in. Chapprassis were waiting on the bench outside, but he did not call one of them. He said, 'But they will be better now that I am back. Lieutenant Moran Singh has conducted everything with precision and now that I am back to say the word everything will fall into place. I'm afraid I cannot change the arrangements for your accommodation. Have you any other requests?'

'I should like further supplies of pen, paper and ink.'

'I will tell Lieutenant Moran Singh. He will arrange it with one of the clerks.'

'There are two habitable rooms in the zenana house, the one I

[27

have as a bedroom and the one I use as a study. I should like to share these rooms with one of your other prisoners.'

'Which one?'

'Any one. I don't know who you have got here.'

'As I said, rank and file. I cannot allow it. It is against my principles. I am surprised that you wish it. You are a man who has been in a position of authority. Well, well, that is a lonely business. I too am living alone in this fortress, Mr Kasim. I am glad you are here. We can talk together sometimes. I am interested in Islamic art and literature as well as in history. The early eighteenth-century Urdu poet, Gaffur, was also of your ancient family, so I understand. I have translated some of his verses into English. You might like to have a look at them.'

Kasim bowed his head.

'In one or two cases I believe I have managed to convey something of the splendour and simplicity of the original. You are well acquainted with the poems of Gaffur, Mr Kasim?'

'At one time, yes. As a boy. Since then other things have tended to occupy my mind. You said that the country is seething.'

'Looting. Arson. Sabotage. Policemen have been murdered. Track has been torn up. Magistrates imprisoned in their own jails, Congress flags run up. Troops called out. Inevitable loss of life. Waste. Violence. Terrible violence. To no purpose. It's being stamped out. It's best forgotten. I should not talk about it.'

'You said something about a girl.'

'She was raped. Another woman was attacked. An elderly woman. The Indian who was driving her to safety was murdered.'

'Were they Europeans?'

'English. The woman was a mission school teacher. The girl who was raped was of good family. They have arrested the men.'

'Was this in Ranpur?'

'No. In Mayapore. The military have taken over. Your people have done terrible things. I do not understand you, Mr Kasim. Over this we are in opposite camps. We are enemies. But I am a humane man.' Major Tippit paused. 'I'm a historian, really. The present does not interest me. The future even less. Only through art and contemplation of the past can man live with man. I hope you will be content. Think upon the Fort as a refuge from life's turmoils and disappointments.'

Kasim waited, then when he saw that for the moment Tippit had no more to say, he rose, thanked his jailer for the interview and said, 'I have your permission to return to my quarters?'

*

He walked alone across the space that separated the Fort commander's office and the zenana house, under the eyes of the chapprassis and the armed sentries who patrolled the colonnaded veranda of the old barracks. In the centre of the courtyard a neem tree provided some shade. Puddles in the red earth reflected the blue of the sky. Puffs of cloud too light to cast shadows moved quickly, driven by the prevailing south-west wind. By midday it would probably rain.

The courtyard was enclosed to the east by the barracks, to the north, west and south by high crenellated red brick walls with bastions built into the angles. In the west and south wall there were gateways closed by studded wooden doors. Close to the southern wall was the square pavilion where Major Tippit lived. Abutting on to the northern wall was the old zenana house, a two-storey construction of stone and brick with fretted wooden arches shading the upper and lower verandas. A wooden stairway gave access to the first floor. The rooms below were in use as storehouses. The dry smell of grain and sacking pervaded the place. Above, the veranda gave on to rooms all but two of which were ruinous. The farthest of these were boarded in. The two which were habitable were closest to the wooden staircase. Inside, they were lit by the open doors and by windows in the outer walls. These windows were blocked by fretted stone screens that gave the occupant views, through any one of their many apertures, of the outer courtyard and the inner and outer walls of the Fort. The courtyard where the zenana house stood had obviously been the women's. The barracks must have been servants' quarters. He could not see what lay behind the southern wall, other than the dome of the mosque, but from the outer windows of his rooms in the zenana he could see beyond the farther walls to the plain.

The walls of his two rooms were whitewashed. In one room there were a bed, a chair and a wardrobe; in the other a table, a chair and a calendar. The calendar was Kasim's own. He did not mark off the days. There seemed no point in doing so when the period of his imprisonment was not determined. 'I rise at six as usual,

waking by habit,' he wrote now to his wife. 'They give me breakfast at eight. The two hours are spent bathing and dressing and
reading. After breakfast I walk round the compound, unless it is
raining, then write in my journal, and letters, until lunch. After
lunch I doze for a while, then read until four, when they bring me
some tea. After tea I walk again. After that I bathe. Then read.
Then supper. Time of course hangs heavily. Today I expect letters
at last. Please give my love to the children when you write to them.
I am told there has been some unrest. I hope you are safe and
unharmed by it. There must be a great deal for you to attend to.
Do not write more often than you can well afford to. One thing
I dislike is not being allowed to shave myself. They have taken my
things away and send a barber every other day. Today is a bristly
morning. I suppose they are afraid I might hurt myself with the
razor. Even my little mirror is gone. I shall forget what I look
like, no doubt. They have let me keep your and the children's photographs, because they are only covered with mica. I have the portraits
on my desk. Pray remember every morning and night Ahmed
Gaffur Ali Rashid. Our noble but eccentric ancestor! Looking at
the photographs has reminded me of him.'

There was no such person as Ahmed Gaffur Ali Rashid. His
wife would therefore see at once that this particular sentence contained the simple code message – an anagram – they had agreed
upon to tell her where he was being held. He hoped the censors
would not see it first. They would look for such codes in his first
few letters to her. This was his fourth. He ran his hand over the
stubble on his chin and then over his cheeks, wondering whether
prison fare had made his face thinner.

*

So: Kasim's face. There was history in it; the history of Islam's
holy wars and imperial expansions. He traced his genealogy back
to a warrior-adventurer called Mir Ali who came from Turkey in
the heyday of the Muslims' Indian empire just as years later young
Britons came out in the heyday of their own. Mir Ali married a
Hindu princess and they both adopted the new religion the great
Moghul Akbar had devised in an attempt to establish a cornerstone
on which to build the fabric of a dream, an India undivided by
conflicting notions of God and the ways to worship God. Akbar

wished his fellow-Muslims and the conquered Hindus to feel equal in one respect at least. But in the reign of Aurangzeb the Kasims re-embraced Islam. The empire was already running down but the Muslims still held the keys of the kingdom and under Aurangzeb the old proselytizing faith in Allah and his prophet was re-established as a buttress for the crumbling walls of state. A new wave of conversions, even among the proud Rajputs, showed that when belief is at odds with worldly ambition the former is the more likely to bow its head.

The reward for one of those Kasims who re-embraced Islam – the eldest grandson of Mir Ali – was the vice-regal appointment over a territory that stretched from Ranpur to Mirat. He was murdered by his son who had been one of his deputies. Internecine war, war against rebellious Hindu rulers and chieftains, war against the invaders from the west – the Mahrattas – marked the final years of the dying Moghul dynasty. The deputies of the great Moghul were carving out principalities and scrambling for power in the gathering darkness, unwittingly opening the gates that would let in the flood that was to swamp them: the flood of ubiquitous, restless foreign merchants whom they thought at first easy sources of income and personal riches, French, British, Portuguese merchants who came to trade but stayed on to secure their trade by taking possession of the source of wealth, the very land itself. The merchants fought each other too, and there is no honour among thieves. A self-appointed prince, leaning on one of the foreigners to help him subjugate a neighbouring pocket-kingdom, too often found he was subjugated himself, imprisoned, then released by the forces of a different foreigner, set up as their puppet and in the end manipulated out of existence. By the beginning of the nineteenth century, of all those principalities that had been carved out of the territory administered by Mir Ali's eldest grandson, only one remained, and this was the tiny state of Mirat whose ruler, also a Kasim, had by wit and good fortune failed to arouse the acquisitive instincts of the British, had helped them at the right time rather than for the right reasons, secured his jagir and their recognition of his claim to be called Nawab. And since there was now no princely neighbour near enough for the British to look upon the Nawab of Mirat as a threat to their own peaceful mercantile and administrative pursuits he was allowed to continue, to blossom as it were like a small and insignificant rose in the desert of dead Moghul ambitions.

All this was in Kasim's face: a face of the kind that could be celebrated in profile on a coin – a forehead sloping to a balding crown, a fleshy but handsomely proportioned nose which stood on guard with an equally fleshy but handsome chin over a mouth whose lips were by no means thin, but were firm-set, determined, not unsensual. Full-face there was a broadness of cheek and jowl and neck, suggestive of a thyroid condition. The black hair that fringed his temples and the back of his head was flecked with grey. These, the thickness and the baldness, conveyed a different idea of Kasim; of a Kasim bearing the marks not of proconsular dignity and autocratic power but instead the marks of centuries of experience of duller but not unworthy occupations. This was a middle-class Kasim, a Kasim – as indeed Mohammed Ali was – of the branch that traced its connexion to Mir Ali through the younger son of that Turkish warrior and his Hindu bride, and this was a branch that had rooted itself more modestly but more deeply in the adopted country. It boasted no viceroy, no Nawab, no captain of armies. It had prospered in other ways, in trade and in the professions. It might be called the Ranpur branch, and it had provided India with merchants, imams, scholars, lawyers, officials, philosophers, mathematicians, doctors, and a poet – Gaffur Mohammed whose verses Major Tippit admired. It had provided her more recently with a member of the provincial Governor's council, Mohammed Ali Kasim's father whose portrait an arresting officer took a moment off from duty to study, and with the first chief minister of the province, Mohammed Ali himself, a man in whom perhaps could be detected yet another inheritance, Akbar's old dream of a united sub-continent. For this he had come to prison. For this he had incurred the displeasure of Mr Jinnah whose name was also Mohammed Ali, who now had visions of a separate Muslim state but whose forbears were converts from Hinduism and had not come from Turkey.

One month after his incarceration in the Fort at Premanagar Mohammed Ali Kasim (known to the newspapers usually as M.A.K. and to free and easy English as Mac) sought and obtained Major Tippit's permission to make a little garden in front of the zenana house. He also wrote his first letter to the Governor.

*

It took a little while (he wrote) for newspapers and letters to reach me, but presently I was inundated. Having caught up in quite a short while (since there was little else to occupy me) with the events (as reported) that followed the news of the nation-wide arrests, my immediate desire was to address you on the matter, because the newspapers invariably sought to establish that the rioting and disturbance only just now coming to an end were planned by Congress and indeed led by Congress in the shape of mysterious underground leaders people such as myself are thought to have chosen and briefed to carry out the job if we were arrested and couldn't carry it out ourselves. I recalled what I said during our interview about mobs that rouse themselves and, needing leaders, encourage the emergence of all kinds of undesirable elements. By and large I should say this is exactly what happened, although some of the incidents (in Dibrapur for example) show evidence of forethought. Those undesirable elements I mentioned do not of course come into existence overnight, but they are not underground elements of Congress. Neither can they be Communist-inspired, because the Indian Communists have become pro-war minded ever since Hitler invaded Russia, and would hardly do anything to disrupt the war effort against Fascism. They are inspired surely only by themselves, and are a danger to all of us.

There seems to be a general belief, however, that Congress had the wind taken out of its sails by the sudden arrest of so many of its leaders. The point is made that Mr Gandhi probably expected the Quit India resolution as it is now called to lead not to prison but to serious talks with the Viceroy. I am in agreement. (My own act of packing my bags directly I heard the resolution had been endorsed was the result of purely personal logic, and I confess I hoped it was an act I would look back on with that affectionate self-mockery we reserve for those of our fears which subsequent events show to have been groundless.) What I cannot see is how the two views can be reconciled. If the arrests came as a surprise (as I'm sure they did to most of us) surely the men who were arrested and surprised were not men who had planned for rebellion in their absence? Gandhi, you know, never said *how* the country was to be organized to withdraw from the war effort. As you know he has never been much of a chap for detail, and even those closest to him have often been puzzled to know exactly what it is he has in mind. People on your side who don't like him accuse him of

[33

deviousness and of course the general impression now is that his latest and most devious scheme has backfired. You yourself used the word blackmail, and the British in general have met the recent threats to their security in precisely the frame of mind of chosen victims of blackmail who refuse to be victimized. I hope that on reconsideration you will reject, if you haven't already done so, the blackmail theory. It's a theory that works two ways in any case. We could accuse the British of trying to blackmail us into putting everything into the war effort with false promises of independence when the war is won. You would answer that by saying they are not false, although you cannot prove that to us, and Churchill has made it clear that the rights and freedoms embodied in the Atlantic Charter do not apply to India so far as he is concerned. We, for our part, would answer your charge of blackmail by pointing out that the war is irrelevant to the situation because we are demanding nothing that we have not been demanding for years. The war perhaps has made us demand it with greater insistence and has strengthened your hand in not granting it yet, but it has not changed the nature of the demand, nor the nature of the resistance. It has merely added a different emotional factor and a new set of practical considerations; and on these our natures and our views widen our differences. What I hope you will be in agreement with me over is my belief that had we been allowed to continue at liberty the violent events of the past few weeks simply would not have occurred. You would have been faced with the far more onerous task of seeking a way round the deadlock created by a co-ordinated, peaceful, passive end to the co-operation of the Indian people in the war effort. This would have been the type of 'sabotage' Congress leaders, and Congress leaders only, could have directed. Perhaps it is Machiavellian of *me* to glimpse in Government's prompt arrests of leaders a Machiavellian intention: the intention of turning the onerous task into the simpler one of strong-arm tactics. It is easier to fire on rioters led by undesirable elements than to force resisting workers back into an arms factory, dockers back to the docks and engine-drivers back to the controls of their locomotives. And Government must have realized that the people of India would be incensed by the wholesale arrests and imprisonment of their leaders: incensed, at a loss, anxious to perform what their leaders wanted them to perform, but prey to anger, fear, and all the passions that lead to violence. I find it not at all difficult

34]

to accuse Government of deliberate provocation of the people of India: either that or of holding the insulting belief that the people of India are so spineless and apathetic that the disappearance from their midst of the men who have risen to positions of responsibility to them would at once leave them as malleable and directable as dull and unimportant clay.

That they are neither spineless nor apathetic has been proved all too well. I have read the accounts of the riots, burnings, lootings, acts of sabotage, acts of murder, the accounts of crowds of men, women and children attempting to oppose unarmed the will and strength of Government, and accounts of the firing upon these crowds by the police and the military, of deaths on both sides, of attempts to seize jails, derail trains, blow bridges, seize installations; accounts of what amounts to a full-scale but spontaneous insurrection – but with what a sad difference – for most of it has been conducted with the bare hands or with what the bare hands could pick up. There are Indians, I do not doubt, especially among those of us in prison (and our numbers have been considerably swelled since the morning of August 9th) who are proud of what the nation attempted. I cannot be one of them, for my chief reactions are anger and sorrow, and an emotion that I can't easily describe but which is probably due to a special sense of impotence, of powerlessness to do anything that will help to alter things in any way.

The reactions of sorrow and anger are by no means partisan. I feel them for and on behalf of people quite unknown to me, the young men for instance who are out here as soldiers, young Englishmen who as we all know have absolutely no idea about India except that it is a long way from home and full of strange, dark-skinned people. In many cases soldiers like this have found themselves acting as you call it in aid of the civil power. Their principal feeling must have been one of bewilderment that changed swiftly to deep and burning resentment, because all they would understand was that the country they have come all this way to defend apparently didn't want them and was bent on getting rid of them. There was the terrible affair of the two Canadian Air Force officers who were literally torn to pieces by people from a village that had been bombed and who thought these men had flown the aeroplanes in question. Even if they were, the situation as I see and feel it is not changed. It is one that involves us all, as does the bombing, the entire scene and history of this lamentable business. In our own

[35

province I have been especially distressed by the two incidents involving English women, the attack on the Mission School Superintendent near Tanpur, and the rape of Miss Manners in the Bibighar Gardens in Mayapore. In this latter case I do indeed feel a personal involvement over and above any other. I knew, of course, Miss Manners's uncle, Sir Henry Manners, from the time in the early thirties when he governed the province and I sat by his invitation on several of the committees he set up in an attempt to break down some of the barriers between Government and people.

Manners was a Governor of great skill – tolerant, sympathetic, admirable in every way. His term of office in Government House was one of hope for us, a bright spot on a rather gloomy horizon. What enemies he made were reactionary English and extremist Indians. Perhaps without the opportunity he gave me, to make whatever mark I did make on those committees, my own party would not have given me the greater opportunity that led to office. You will understand then the weight of my personal distress at the news of the criminal assault on the niece of a man like that. It is an incident that seems all too understandably to have added fuel to the fires of violence in Mayapore, and perhaps in the rest of the province. The first reports I read, which did not disclose Miss Manners's name – referring to her merely as a young Englishwoman, victim of sexual assault by six Indian youths who had all been promptly arrested – struck me possibly as exaggerations because the reports were hysterical in pitch, and of course I hoped that they were not true. But it seems they were, at least in regard to the fact that the girl *was* attacked, and criminally used; and the eventual disclosure of her name and her connexion with the late Sir Henry Manners came as a considerable personal shock.

I have since, however, become puzzled and vaguely disturbed by what I can gather of the consequences of this affair, and the piece in the *Statesman* yesterday, referring to the rape of Miss Manners (although mercifully omitting her name again – a first step towards some sort of privacy for the poor creature) does bear out my own feelings that some quite extraordinary veil has been drawn over the whole unfortunate business, but a veil that does not satisfy the lawyer in me. I had been reading the papers daily in expectation of further news about the six men who according to the early reports were arrested. Now, according to the *Statesman*, it seems that these six men were not charged with rape. The *States-*

man refers to a very brief paragraph in the *Mayapore Gazette* of one week ago which gave the names of two or three men recently imprisoned under the Defence of India rules, without trial of course. According to the *Statesman*, these men were among the six originally arrested as suspects in the rape. Again, according to the *Statesman*, which has been ferreting about, *all* six have been imprisoned under the rule. Quite justifiably, the *Statesman* asks whether the original reports that 'the suspected culprits have been arrested, thanks to the prompt action of the local police under their District Superintendent, were the result of wishful thinking or confusion on the part of the reporter, or whether subsequent investigation showed them to be innocent. If they were innocent, then as the *Statesman* again properly asks, is it not curious that six men suspected of rape should all turn out to be men whose political activities earned them imprisonment as detenus? Clearly now, there is unlikely to be any arrest or trial in connexion with the rape itself and one must assume the real culprits have gone free. The question raised by the *Statesman* comes to this: Have six men been arrested for rape, found to be innocent either because they are or for lack of evidence that would hold up in a court of law, but have been put away under this convenient act because someone still believes them to be guilty, or is determined to punish them for some reason or other? I doubt that anyone will provide the answer the *Statesman* seeks and presently – although the affair itself will be a long time fading from memory – the legal aspects will quickly be forgotten; as will the curious side issues that stay in my own mind from my reading of the reports and collection of casual data: for instance the apparent fact that one of the arrested men, a man called Kumar, was a friend of Miss Manners; and the fact that Miss Manners (if the *Statesman* has interpreted correctly) declined, according to gossip, to give evidence because the men arrested were not the kind she remembered as the type who attacked her.

I imagine that the details of this distressing affair – which has exacerbated racial feeling throughout the country – have had something of your personal attention, more particularly in view of the victim's family connexions in India. I presume she is the daughter of a brother of Henry Manners. One of the reports gave her address in Mayapore as The MacGregor House, which I remember as the home of Sir Nello and Lady Chatterjee who were friends of Sir Henry and Lady Manners. I take it Miss Manners was staying with

Lady Chatterjee but that otherwise she normally lives with her aunt whom I knew fairly well and who, I believe, still lives in Rawalpindi. I have written a brief letter to Lady Manners, which I enclose. I should be most grateful if you would forward it. I have left it unsealed so that you can quickly assure yourself that I have written nothing to her apart from words of sympathy and regret for the terrible thing that happened to her niece. I cannot, I realize, expect any particular comment from you on the points I have raised in this letter. I offer them as someone whose enforced position as a mere spectator has in no way diminished his sense of involvement, curiosity, and concern with justice.

＊

'His Excellency thanks you for your letter' (one of Sir George's secretaries wrote a month later), 'and wishes me also to convey to you Lady Manners's thanks for your personal message which his Excellency communicated to her.'

Kasim looked up. Lieutenant Moran Singh who had brought the letter over to the zenana house still stood in the doorway, smiling.

'Such influential people you are knowing,' Moran Singh said. 'Letters from Government House and such-like.' He turned and went out. Presently Kasim heard him shouting at one of the sentries. Moran Singh had relatives in Ranpur. He had offered to convey private messages to Mrs Kasim through those relatives, for a consideration. He took bribes, he sold Government stores. He had said to Kasim, 'Major Tippit is mad,' and had hinted that – again for a consideration – he could persuade Tippit to allow Kasim to be visited regularly by selected fellow-prisoners. Moran Singh represented everything in India that Kasim loathed. He had declined these offers.

Kasim wrote in his journal: 'A reply from Government House, which makes it clear that the Governor's request that I write to him occasionally wasn't really the friendly gesture I believed it to be. It is apparently to be a one-sided correspondence. He wanted me to commit my thoughts to paper but won't commit his own. He wants to keep track of me. I am a specimen under observation. They must be his orders that keep me isolated from other prisoners. He thinks isolation will give me time and opportunity to re-assess my position. Underneath that liberal man to man exterior is the

38]

indomitable public servant. Perhaps he is waiting for me to crack under the strain. I could be out of Premanagar by Christmas if I wrote to him and said I'd changed my mind and was willing to resign from Congress and accept nomination to his executive council. And God knows I might do useful work. But I must not be hard on him. They are only spiritual hardships I suffer here, and his policy in regard to me is dictated by good intentions and the determination to do everything he can to govern the province successfully and ease the condition of the people. The Governor buries himself neither in past nor future but in the present. It is an English trait. They will only see that there is no future for them in India when India no longer fits into the picture they have of themselves and of their current obligations. When that time comes they won't particularly care what happens to us. Sooner or later the Governor will find that I don't fit in to whatever picture he has of the current problems of this province. Perhaps I am already beginning to fade out of it. He would have written, I expect, if he had seen an immediate way in which I could be useful to him. One can't help admiring this barefaced attitude. We might learn something from it. There is too much emotion in our own public life. The English could never be accused of that. They lock us up, release us and lock us up again according to what suits them at the time, with a bland detachment that, fortunately or unfortunately, is matched by an equally bland acceptance on our part. They act collectively, and so can afford detachment. We react individually, which weakens us. We haven't yet acquired the collective instinct. The English send Kasim to prison. But it is Kasim who goes to prison. The prisoner in the zenana house is a man. But who is his jailer? The jailer is an idea. But in the prisoner the idea is embodied in a man. From his solitude the man reaches out to others. He writes to Sir George Malcolm. He writes to old Lady Manners. But he cannot reach them as people. They are protected from him by the collective instinct of their race. A reply comes, but it is not from them. It is from someone speaking for them. It has not been expedient for either of them to write. I understand in both cases why this should be. But to understand does not warm the heart.'

*

Several months later, the May of the following year, the prisoner

[39

in the zenana house saw two notices in the same issue of the *Times of India*. Under Births there was this entry: *Manners. On May 7th, at Srinagar. To Daphne, a daughter, Parvati.* And under Deaths, this: *Manners. On May 7th, at Srinagar; Daphne, daughter of the late Mr & Mrs George Manners, beloved niece of Ethel and the late Sir Henry Manners.*

There were times, Mr Kasim told himself, when he thought he would never understand the English. What curious brand of arrogance and insensitivity could lead an old lady to announce to the world the birth of an obviously half-caste child to the unmarried niece who, nine months before, had been raped by Indians in the Bibighar Gardens? 'It is as if,' he wrote in his journal, 'old Lady Manners were flinging an accusation into our faces, to make sure we know that this is an incident that cannot be forgotten and is one we have a continuing responsibility for. I do not remember her as the sort of woman who would make this kind of gesture; but of course the girl has died, presumably in childbirth. I suppose she is telling us that she will never forgive us for what a handful of our men did on that particular night. Or do these announcements mean that she has forgiven us now and taken the child, so tragically and violently conceived, to her heart, for India's sake? One cannot tell. The English have a saying, "He wears his heart on his sleeve," but this is something they never reveal except very occasionally to each other.'

Part Two ✤ A History

I

'So IT WAS with Henry, and so now with poor Daphne,' Lady Manners murmured. And handed her niece's diary to Suleiman to lock up in the black tin box as he had locked up some of her husband's private papers, years before, with an air of reverence or anyway forbearance; but he took Daphne's book as if it were nothing special, put it in the box – whose lid was open – and stood, waiting, not catching her eye, still wearing the old astrakhan cap he had complained of months before in 'Pindi and had had money off her to renew.

Well, he is jealous, she thought, and still resents being sent for, travelling alone and uncomfortably on the bus all that way from Pindi to Srinagar, just to order the household for the journey back in the same direction, a beast-of-burden who has no burden worthy of the years, the centuries, the everlastingness of his service. He is an old man. His hair has gone grey, like mine. Why has he never grown a beard? If he grows a beard I must watch for signs of it and be prepared for the morning he will come to me and say, Mem-sahib, let me go, I am an old man. Before I die I must see Mecca, and having seen it dye my beard red, come back and live out my remaining years in peace and honourable retirement with the bless-ing of Allah the Merciful.

So, too, I would go, but not to Mecca. Where then? And how? I do not know how or where. Nor who has mercy to spare.

And she looked out of the window on to the placid waters of the lake, and heard the crying of the child. She made a gesture and said a word, both meaning the same thing. *Khatam*. Finished. Sulei-man closed the lid of the box, turned the key and handed it to her. His old brown fingers were still supple from a lifetime of manipula-tive care of her property, and Henry's property, which were his gods, his ikons, but to care for Daphne's was nothing to him. It was all gone. But what? Well, it has gone, she thought, whatever it was. And took the key from him, and put it in her handbag, aware of the finality of the gesture without understanding why she should think of it as final. You were handsome once, she told Suleiman without speaking. You had one wife we knew about and two concubines you pretended were your wife's sisters. And were a rogue and a rake, and had children, God knows how many, by whom, nor where scattered. Now you are alone and I am alone, and we cannot speak of it even yet as a man and a woman might speak who share recollections. But if you were to die I should weep. And if I were to die you would cover your head and speak to no one for days. But here in the world where both of us live – poised between entrance and exit, or exit and entrance – we still maintain the relationship of mistress and servant, although we have grown far beyond it and use it simply as a shorthand to get through the day without trouble to one another.

Suleiman took hold of the box and carried it through into the passage that ran along the side of the houseboat – the side adjacent to the bank of the island to which the boat was moored – from her bedroom, with its single bed, past the empty guest bedroom with its two beds, and into the dining-room, up the two steps into the living-room beyond which was the veranda with its view on to the water and the opposite bank where the tongas waited, ready to transport the passengers from the shikaras to the square where the buses and motor-cars halted.

In the water immediately below the veranda there was a cluster of shikaras – one for the luggage, one for the passengers, and upwards of half a dozen laden with Kashmiri art: woodwork, shawls, carpets, flowers; and even a fortune teller – although it was only 7.30 in the September morning, and the mist through which a future might be seen to have substance had not yet cleared. But in the last half-hour before a departure there was always the possibility of a sale. From her room, Lady Manners heard the cries of the vendors offering inducements, bribes, to persuade Suleiman to go back in and bring her out to be tempted.

And today, she thought, I am going to be tempted. And followed Suleiman through to the veranda where he was standing, a thin, frail, stoop-shouldered man, in a moth-eaten fez and floppy pyjamas, with Henry's old Harris tweed jacket hanging on him to keep out the early morning September chill, showing his shirt-tail, blue against the baggy white trousers: and holding the box to his breast, like a reliquary, saying nothing, but watching the opposite shore, standing on guard over the piled luggage. Aware she had come, he spoke to the khansamar, ordered him to have the luggage stowed, and the khansamar beckoned to the men below who came scrambling. The vendors, seeing that departure was imminent, set up a new cry, making their appeal directly to her, holding up whatever it was they most wished her to be tempted by. She beckoned to the man who had sold her a shawl three years before, and had ever since been hopeful. She beckoned to him because of this, not because his shikara was closest (although it was, having been paddled into position early). He clambered, laden, across her own empty shikara and the luggage shikara, elbowing the men who were dealing with the luggage, reached the houseboat veranda and laid his bundle down, salaamed, untied the knot, opened and released a cascade of fine woven wool, with gold, silver and coloured embroidery. The khansamar had brought out a chair. She sat on it and watched the man – his skull-cap, and his touchingly dishonest eyes whenever he looked up to emphasize the truth of the lies he was telling her.

But Suleiman (she thought) stands detached from this foolery. Well, there was a time when he protected me from rogues, for he was our rogue, our beloved rogue, who never cheated us but knew rogues, being brought up with them; and their ways, being brought up in them; and saw lesser rogues off, and equal rogues, and bigger rogues. He taught me all I know about the ways of the bazaars and what he taught me is all that he knows too. He stands, holding the reliquary, anl lets me get on with it as if I were a pupil old enough to know better, too old to be corrected. And does not look, but listens to the crying of the child.

And I choose this one, to warm my shoulders on a frosty night, for I am of an age that can grace a faint vulgarity, am I not? So much silver-thread, and too much scarlet silk. Shall I ever wear it? Perhaps that is doubtful. Or even this one? The green is a bit bilious, after such an early breakfast. Well, any of them? Am I too old, then, for this kind of gesture? For whose sake am I making it? My own? Henry's? Suleiman's? Daphne's? Or for Kashmir's because after all these years of arriving and departing I feel it in my bones that I am going this time never to return? Or is it an insurance? To buy believing it the last, to ensure that it is not? Perhaps I buy for the child, for Parvati, whose crying Suleiman listens to and will not speak of. Has Suleiman yet looked at the child?

She chose a shawl that could have offended no one. But when she had paid for it and gone back inside after repeating the word and the gesture: Khatam: she regretted buying something that would give her neither pleasure nor pain, and wondered at the marvel of losing an opportunity to make a gesture others and she herself could have described later as out of character. In the end, she saw, habit became a vice, and good taste an end in itself: nothing could ever come of it.

Fifteen minutes later the khansamar knocked at the door of her room where she sat alone staring through the little window at the lake, her old-fashioned veiled topee already on her head, gloves on her hands, repeating to herself, with no outward sign that she was doing so, the little prayer she always offered up at the beginning of a journey. The khansamar told her that all was ready. She rose, thanked him for his service, and went out. She had distributed tips the night before. The staff of the houseboat, and of the house she had lived in from the November of 1942 all through the hard winter to June when she had come down to the lake, were gathered on the forward veranda and on the sunroof. Fifteen of them all told: twelve from the boat, and three from the house. She stood for a moment. They watched her in silence. Then she said, 'Thank you,' and allowed the khansamar to help her down the steps into the shikara which had an embroidered canopy and a spring mattress – the kind of shikara Henry once said made him feel when with her like Anthony making himself at home with Cleopatra on her barge. At the foot of the mattress, the young ayah already sat, veiled for the journey from the valley she had never left before, nursing the child. When Lady Manners was settled Suleiman stepped aboard and sat in the narrow prow, still holding the reliquary. Behind her the three boatmen raised their pointed, elongated, heart-shaped paddles and began to negotiate a passage between the clustered boats of the vendors. She turned to wave, but the outline of the houseboat had become infuriatingly unclear. She realized, too, that she had forgotten to look at the flowers in the vase by her bedside, to make sure they were quite dead; and thinking of those flowers thought as well of Daphne's rhetorical question, written down while the snows still held, when the summer that had somehow never been was yet to come:

'Shall we go down to the lake, then, Aunty, and live in a houseboat and fill it with flowers, and have our fortunes told?'

*

I am leaving in two days' time (she had written to her old friend Lili Chatterjee in Mayapore), and so ends, as they say, a chapter – the burden of which you know and have lightened, not only by your too short visit this summer but by your wise counsel, and by the opinion you were able to express, after seeing the child. When I am re-established in Pindi, at Christmas-time for instance, perhaps you would come up and pay me a visit? I do not expect to be much invited out. My own race hardly knows any longer what to make of me and the existence of the child under my roof no doubt ranks as something of a scandal, such a lively, vocal repository for memories of events my countrymen are pretending it is best to forget – or if not best to forget at least wise to consider over and adequately dealt with. I don't make my appeal to you, or invitation, from any sense the last few months may have given me of isolation, but from that other more important sense of contact with a friend who speaks my language and with whom, over Christmas, I should so dearly love to exchange gifts of conversation, plans and recollections.

Today we are moving the houseboat down the lake from the isolated position you thought so pretty to its winter berth, to shorten the distance for the luggage shikaras the day after tomorrow. Since you were here I acquired neighbours. They are now gone back to Pankot where they are stationed. Their boat has been moved away and this last few days I have been alone again, which on the whole I prefer. These people who came and moored near by were punctilious about sending cards across when they arrived. I had Aziz return the compliment. Result: an almost tangible air of embarrassment and curiosity emanating from their boat; cautious nods if we happened to cross one another's bows when out in the shikaras. But no visit, except towards the end of their stay, and that by one of them alone, one of the two daughters, when the rest of them were out enjoying themselves one afternoon. She saw me reading on the sun-deck as she went past alone in their shikara, and waved, then had the boatmen come in close and asked whether she could come on board for a few moments. I couldn't very well refuse, although I thought it a bit offhand after the days that had gone by without a word exchanged. She came straight to the point and said it was embarrassment really that had kept them away, not knowing what on earth they'd be able to say to me that wouldn't make it obvious they were all avoiding any mention of poor Daphne ('the

[45

awful business of your niece' she called it). But they were going back to their station soon and she said she didn't like the idea of leaving without speaking to me. I thought it a rather thin excuse but not an uncourageous thing to do. She said she often heard the baby crying and would very much like to see her. So I took her down into the cabin where little Parvati has her cot. The girl – her name is Sarah Layton – looked at her for quite a long time without saying anything. Parvati was asleep and the ayah was adopting her possessive, on guard attitude, which probably added to the girl's uneasiness. I think she'd expected the baby to have the kind of pale skin that makes the mixture of blood difficult to detect unless you're looking for it. Eventually she said, 'She's so tiny,' as if she had never seen a four-month-old baby before, then thanked me for letting her see her. I invited her to stay and have some tea under the awning on the sun-deck. She only hesitated for a moment. On our way out she caught sight of the trunks with Daphne's name on them and hesitated again. She puzzled me. Nice young English girls in India don't usually give an impression of bothering their heads with anything much apart from the question of which men in the immediate vicinity are taking the most notice of them. Of course, they do go broody every now and again, but Miss Layton's broodiness struck me as odd and intricate, not at all the result of simple self-absorption.

The name Layton had vaguely rung my bell at the time of the exchange of visiting cards and directly she mentioned Ranpur and Pankot I remembered it as a name quite well known there but couldn't recall ever having met one of them. Henry and I were there for the five years of his appointment as Governor but one's social life was fairly crowded. Over tea she told me that she and her sister and mother were sharing the houseboat with an aunt and an uncle. Her father, Colonel Layton, is a prisoner of war in Germany. He commanded the 1st Pankot Rifles in North Africa. He was in prison camp in Italy for a time but as we've advanced from the south a lot of the prisoners have been moved back, so our recent successes there haven't brought Colonel Layton's release and return any nearer. The revelation that her father was a prisoner of war went some way to explain her sudden visit and attempt at apology. In her father's absence she was probably trying to do what was right and thought that coming to see me made up for the rudeness of the rest of the family. They may have believed that story themselves about not wanting to intrude on my privacy, but of course underneath this apparent delicacy of feeling is the deep disapproval I meet everywhere now and am used to. Perhaps dismay is more accurate a description, dismay that I should have stood by and let Daphne bear a child whose father might be any one of half a dozen ruffians, dismay that instead of bundling it off as unwanted to some orphanage when Daphne died bearing it, I take care of it, and have given it that name, Parvati Manners.

I asked Miss Layton whether she was enjoying her holiday. She said it was the first real one they'd had since the war began. Both girls have joined the WAC(I) and work in Area Headquarters at Pankot. They decided to come to Srinagar this year because the sister – the younger of the two – is to be married soon. I'd seen the usual crowd of young men visiting their houseboat so naturally I asked if the sister's fiancé was also in Srinagar. Apparently not. The engagement took place when he was stationed in Pankot, and originally the wedding was to have been there, towards Christmas of this year. But he was suddenly posted to Mirat and has written to say that the wedding must be brought forward and has to be in Mirat, the sooner the better, and the honeymoon can't be for longer than two or three days. Which means, of course, that he expects to be going back into the field (he was in one of the regiments whose remnants managed to get out of Burma in 1942). So the young bride will be a grass widow almost directly she's married. This is why the Laytons have gone back to Pankot earlier than they planned. They'll be off to Mirat soon after they arrive and it seems they hope to stay in the palace guest house so the younger Layton girl is very excited. I told Sarah Layton she'd like Mirat, especially if they stayed there as guests of the Nawab, who entertained Henry and me when we were on tour in that area. Lending the guest house to service people who can't get accommodation in the cantonment is probably part of the Nawab's war effort. He must be getting on a bit, now, and so must his wazir, that extraordinary Russian *émigré* Count, Bronowsky, or whatever his name was, whom the Nawab brought back from Monte Carlo in the twenties, at the time of the scandal over the Nawab's relationship with a European woman. I told Miss Layton to look out for Bronowsky, and how all the English used to hate him until they realized what a good influence he was on the Nawab. She asked whether I had any idea what they ought to take as a present, if the Nawab let them stay in the guest

[47

house. Apparently they've been arguing and discussing it for days. I told her the Nawab was distantly related to ex-chief minister M. A. Kasim, and that the famous classic Urdu poet Gaffur was an eighteenth-century connexion of both; and suggested that the most flattering gift might be a specially bound copy of Gaffur's poems. She was very pleased by the suggestion and said she'd tell her mother and aunt and try to get hold of a copy. I told her she could buy one in Srinagar and might even get it bound here, in a few days. Alternatively that there used to be a shop in Ranpur, in the bazaar, which did excellent leatherwork and gold-leaf blocking.

After we'd finished talking about the book she looked at me with the most extraordinary expression of envy that I've ever seen in a girl so young. She said, 'What a lot you know.' I laughed and said it was one of the few advantages of old age, to be a repository of bits and pieces of casual information that sometimes come in useful. But she said she didn't really mean that, she meant know as distinct from remember. She couldn't properly explain it and got up and said she mustn't take up any more of my time. I told her to come again, and she said she would if there were an opportunity. I took it she meant there probably wouldn't be and as it turned out I never saw her again, except to wave to. I didn't see their departure but after they'd gone one of the boys who'd been on their cookboat brought round a little bunch of flowers with a card 'With best wishes and many thanks from Sarah Layton'.

I have been thinking over what she said about knowing as distinct from remembering. Perhaps all it amounts to is that as we talked and I trotted out these little bits of information I gave the impression, common in elderly people, not only of having a long full life behind me that I could dip into more or less at random for the benefit of a younger listener, but also of being undisturbed by any doubts about the meaning and value of that life and the opinions I'd formed while leading it; although that suggests knowingness, and when she said, 'What a lot you know' she made it sound like a state of grace, one that she envied me in the mistaken belief that I was in it, while she was not and didn't understand how, things being as she finds them, one ever achieved it. It would be interesting to meet the rest of the family, who from their general appearance and conduct I would describe as typically army if I hadn't learned that people are never typical. But what I mean is that one could probably plot a graph of typical experience, attitude, behaviour and expectations of an army family in India and find it a rough but not inaccurate guide to that girl's background and the surrounding circumstances of her daily life. I was touched by the flowers – and by the fact that they have not lasted and will be dead by the time I leave and go down to Pindi.

*

Picture her then, an old lady dressed in a fawn tweed jacket and skirt, a high collar to a cream silk blouse that is buttoned with mother-of-pearl. No longer agile she scarcely welcomes the luxury of the embroidered mattress in the shikara which she finds it difficult to get down to and stretch out on; difficult but not yet impossible for someone trained to the custom of not inviting sympathy, or causing amusement, with evidence of weakness or infirmity; so that now, reclining safely, propped against the back rest, her topee-covered head turned at an angle of dignified farewell, one hand raised and the other seeking and finding some kind of old woman's reassurance from the pleats and buttons just below her throat, there is an air about her of faded Edwardian elegance, Victorian even, for Victorian women were great travellers when they bothered to travel at all; and the early morning mist swathed in the mountains and above the lake, the movement of the boat, the pointed paddles dipping and sweeping, the totem figure of Suleiman, the huddled permissive attitude of the Kashmiri girl nursing the child, all combine to make, as it were, a perpetual willow-pattern of the transient English experience of outlandish cultures.

II

IF ENGLISH people in India could be said to live in (in the sense of belonging to) any particular town, the Laytons lived in Ranpur and Pankot. Ranpur was the permanent cool weather station of Colonel Layton's regiment, the 1st Pankot Rifles. Their hot weather station was in the hills of Pankot itself, a place to which the provincial government also moved during the summer. It was from the hills and valleys around Pankot that the regiment recruited its men: sturdy agriculturalists who had a martial tradition going back (it was said) to pre-Moghul times. Somewhere round about the sixteenth century the hill people turned their backs on the old hill gods, embraced Islam and intermarried with their country's Moghul conquerors. So far as the British were concerned they ranked as Muslims, although it might have been more accurate to describe them as polytheists. In the hill villages images of old local Hindu gods were still to be found. To these the women liked to make offerings – at sowing and harvest-times, when they were in love, when they were pregnant, after the birth of a son or the death of a husband. The men held aloof from such things, unless they were going a journey, when they made sure that a female relation left a bowl of curds and a chaplet of flowers at the local wayside shrine the day before.

The only mosque in the entire hill area was in Pankot itself. Many of the boys who made the trek from their village to Pankot to offer themselves as soldiers at the recruiting depot were unable to distinguish between the mosque, the Kali temple, and the Protestant and Catholic churches. They knew the names of Allah, and of their tribal gods, they accepted that Allah was all-knowing, all-seeing and all-merciful, more powerful than the gods of the hills; so powerful in fact that it was better not to involve him in everyday matters. When you died you would go to his abode. While you lived here on earth it was necessary to be honest, industrious and vigorous. If you lived a good life, did not drink or smoke, practised good husbandry, took wives, procreated, did not cheat or steal, kept your roof repaired, your family fed, then you would please Allah. To live such a life, however, it was necessary to please authority as well – to pay your taxes, to offer gifts of money to minor officials and of loyalty to senior ones, to propitiate the gods of the hills who, being less powerful than Allah, had both the time and the inclination to make things difficult for mortal man by withholding rain, sending too much, making the earth sour, turning male children into female children in your wife's womb, poisoning your blood with sickness, filling the air with bad vapours. Since Allah was all-knowing obviously he understood this. To feed and flatter the hill gods was something you did to help in the business of making your life pleasant for Allah to look upon. All the same such things were best left to the women, because women did not really understand about Allah: they did not need to. For a man it was different; Allah was a man: the perfect husbandman, the supreme warrior. He blessed ears of corn and strengthened your sword-arm. To die in battle, fighting his enemies, was the one sure way of going to Heaven. There were people living on the plains below the hills, and even in Pankot, who did not understand about Allah either. Such ignorance meant that their men were not much better than women. The white man, however, understood about Allah. In Pankot there were white men's mosques. There was also Recruiting Officer Sahib's *Daftar*, where a boy could go to become a sipahi, a soldier. The white man's enemies were also Allah's enemies. The white man called Allah God-Father, but he was the same Allah. They called the prophet Jesuschrist, not Mohammed; but then did not the same sky cover the whole world? In Pankot did it not cover the mosque, the Hindu temple, the two churches, the Governor's summer residence, Flagstaff House and Recruiting Officer Sahib's *Daftar*? To the boys coming in from the Pankot hills these places were all seats of mystery and authority. And of them all Recruiting Officer Sahib's *Daftar* was the one they recognized as the most important in practical as well as mystical terms.

Not one of them made the journey from his hill or his valley to Pankot who was not forewarned of and rehearsed in the incalculable mysteries of the *Daftar* by an older male relation. To make the journey to the *Daftar* was the first test of manhood. To be rejected was thought by some to be a shame a boy could never recover from. In Pankot bazaar there were men – it was said – who begged or starved because they had been rejected and were afraid to go home. To be accepted was imperative if – having chanced one's arm – one were ever again to look another man in the eye. And so they came, year after year, with stern faces (that in a moment could crack into a grin, because the Pankot people were of a happy disposition), blanket over shoulder, bare-foot, each – inevitably – wearing or bearing some token of an earlier family connexion with the Pankot Rifles – a pair of carefully mended khaki shorts, a row of medals, a chit from an uncle who had risen to the rank of Havildar or Jemadar and who begged the favour of offering his nephew in the service of the King-Emperor (whom they confused, vaguely, with the great Moghul and Allah) and gave, as reference, the name of an Englishman who more likely than not turned out to be retired, or dead, although not forgotten. The *Daftar* had a long memory.

*

The main recruiting season extended from the beginning of April until the end of September and coincided with the civil and military retreat from the plains to the hills which – in the old days – brought to Pankot not only the Governor, his administrators, their clerks and their files from Ranpur but detachments of the Pankot Rifles and the Ranpur Regiment from Ranpur.

From April to September Pankot lived a full social life. One met the same people as in Ranpur but in different, more delightful surroundings. Receptions at the Governor's summer residence (built in the Swiss Gothic style, with a preponderance of wood, instead of as in Ranpur in stone and stucco in Anglo-Indian palladian with a preponderance of colonnaded veranda) were less magnificent but no less formal. The important clubs had Pankot duplicates (wood again, instead of stone) and there was the Pankot Club itself which subalterns and junior civilians preferred because there you met all the girls recently out from home who might turn out good for a lark.

Pankot was a place to let off steam in. It was thoroughly English. The air was crisp, the trees coniferous. India, real India, lay below. To the north – defining the meeting point of heaven and earth, distantly, was the impressive jagged line of the Himalaya (usually invisible behind cloud, but occasionally revealed, like the word of God). Summer in Pankot was hotter than summer in England, but the mornings and the nights were cool and the rains fell with nothing like the fury they fell with in the plains. Winter, during the hours between sun-up and sunset, was like an English spring.

As hill stations went Pankot ranked as one of the second class. It attracted almost no tourists and few leave-takers (who preferred Darjeeling, Naini Tal and Kashmir). There was a rail connexion from Ranpur, narrow gauge and single track. The journey took eight hours up and six hours down. There was also a road which was used by the Indian bus and by the military who sent soldiers of the Pankot Rifles and the Ranpur Regiment up and down by lorry. In places road and rail converged, passed under or over one another or marched parallel. The ascent was slow. Embankments gave way to cuttings. Signs of habitation became fewer. The characters of villages changed. There were fewer water-buffalo, more white-humped cattle; many more goats. Rocky outcrops appeared; and then the road began to wind into the foothills, a dusty coil connecting the parched plain to the green-clad heights.

52]

Sound was muffled, amplified, thrown back – depending on the formation of hill-face, precipice, re-entry. There was a scent of timber.

Pankot was built upon three hills and their conjoint valley. The railway ended against a rocky face that the road found its way round, through a tunnel of trees, up, over the top and down into the enclosed vale – grassed acres scattered with hutments that bore the unmistakable signs of military occupation. Here, mists gathered in the evening and the early morning. Out of such mists, a mile ahead, emerged the Indo-Tyrolean architecture of the Pankot Bazaar – a V-shaped township of three-storey wooden buildings with fretted overhanging verandas above open-fronted shops where they sold embroidered shawls, beaten silver, filigree wooden boxes inlaid with brass lotus designs. There were Indian coffee shops, fortune-tellers, the local branch of the Imperial Bank of India, a garage, a bicycle shop, the Hindu Hotel, the Muslim Hotel. At the tip of the V the buses halted. Here there were ponies and tongas for hire, even a taxi or two. This was the favourite place of pedlars and itinerant Holy men and small boys in rags and moth-eaten fur caps who competed with each other to shine the visitors' shoes. There was a smell of petrol, horse manure, cattle dung, incense and sandal-wood, of spicy food being cooked in the open over charcoal fires. The shop signs were in English and in the vernacular in both the Nagari and the Arabic scripts. Here, too, were the Kali temple and the mosque. In the centre of the square formed by the lower tip of the V, the temple and the mosque, stood a phallic stone monolith, erected in 1925, a memorial to the soldiers of the Pankot Rifles who had given their lives in the Great War. In November it received a wreath of poppies, offerings of ghi, buttermilk and flowers.

The arms of the V mounted quite steeply, reaching up into the hills behind the bazaar. The right-hand fork from War Memorial Square was the less steep, but it led finally to the majestic heights dominated by the Governor's summer residence. The left-hand fork led more abruptly to a lower area where rich Indians and minor princes owned chalet-style houses (a few of which had 'Mahal' in their names, to denote that they were palaces). This was an area the generality of the English had little knowledge of. To them Pankot was properly reached by taking the right-hand fork. Here were the clubs, the administrative quarters, the golf course, the bungalows and houses of seasonal occupation; most of them hidden by pines, marked by roadside posts at drive-entrances. And yet there was no feeling of enclosure. The road, at every turn, gave views. There were English people who said they were reminded of the Surrey hills near Caterham. Upon retirement from the civil or the military some of them came to Pankot – not to die (although they did – and were buried in the churchyard of St John's – C of E – or St Edward's – RC) but to enjoy their remaining years in a place that was peculiarly Indian but very much their own, and where servants were cheap, and English flowers could be grown (sometimes spectacularly) in the gardens, and life take on the serenity of fulfilment, of duty done without the depression of going home wondering what it had been done for.

It was in Pankot that Sarah Layton's childhood memories of India were chiefly centred. She and Susan were born there (in 1921 and 1922 respectively). Their christening was recorded in the parish register of St John's Church (Sarah in March, an Aries, and Susan in November, a Scorpio). The register also recorded the marriage in 1920 of their father John Frederick William Layton (Lieutenant, 1st Pankot Rifles, son of James William Layton, ICS) to their mother Mildred Rose Muir, daughter of Howard Campbell Muir – Lieut.-General (GS). Neither James William Layton nor General Muir was laid to rest in the churchyard of St John, Pankot, but there were headstones there that celebrated both names, those of General Muir's unmarried aunt and James Layton's great-aunt – the former dead of fever, aged nineteen, the latter in childbirth, aged twenty-three.

Sarah and Susan's father, John Layton, was in Pankot for the second time in his life in 1913. He was then nineteen years old, newly returned from Chillingborough and Sandhurst. His choice of a military instead of a civil career was his own but his choice of regiment had been dictated by a sense of family connexion. To begin with, Pankot had lain within his civilian father's first district. Layton had no personal recollection of the place. He had spent one summer there with his parents as a child of three, when his father was working at the secretariat in Ranpur and went up to Pankot with the provincial government when it took its annual breather in the hills. Afterwards the Laytons went down to Mayapore where Mr James Layton had been appointed assistant commissioner and joint magistrate. A later appointment still, as acting deputy commissioner took the Laytons down to Dibrapur and when that job was finished young John Layton was eight and due to go home to England to school. His parents, taking their long leave, accompanied him. During school holidays he lived with his paternal grandfather in Surrey. His parents returned to India. Shortly after their return Mr James Layton was appointed Deputy Commissioner for the Pankot District. During his tour of office there he made a name for himself with the people of the hills. He had certain eccentricities which endeared him to them. He used to escape from his office and his staff and his wife and ride ten or twenty miles on his pony between sunup and sunset to talk to the villagers.

In India, as a child, young John Layton was inclined to be sickly. He inherited his mother's constitution. Even in England his health gave some cause for anxiety. There had been a plan, indeed a promise, that in the long summer holiday of 1907 when he was thirteen he would spend a month in Pankot with his parents. His England-based grandfather advised against it and suggested that instead his parents should take long leave and come to England. Only Mrs Layton was able to make the journey.

Sick before she set out (the ill-effects of life in places like Mayapore and Dibrapur had become too deep-rooted for the healthier climate of Pankot to have made much difference) she was sick when she reached home. She was not the mother young Layton remembered. In later life he found it difficult to recall the conflicting emotions the sight of her actually aroused in him. As he said to his daughter Sarah (in a rare moment of confidence – rare but perhaps not unexpected because Sarah was her father's daughter while Susan was her mother's), 'I suppose I was disappointed. My mother looked old in the wrong sort of way. Well, I mean like someone on the stage made up for it. When she died it was like part of an act. I felt my real mother was still in Pankot, thousands of miles away, and this one was a feeble impostor – so when father married again and came back to England with his new wife Mabel in 1909 she was more real to me than my own mother had been. Why am I telling you this?'

＊

Sarah's paternal grandmother, the first Mrs Layton, died in England of double pneumonia in 1907 after a bout of malarial fever six weeks after returning home to visit her son. Young Layton was then back at school, in his first term at Chillingborough. He went home to Surrey for the funeral and wrote a letter to his father in India saying he was sorry, and describing – with his grandfather's help – the headstone that was going to be erected on his mother's grave.

His father's second wife was the widow of a major of the 1st Pankot Rifles who had died heroically on the North-West Frontier. Young Layton met her in the summer of 1909 when his father brought her home on long leave. He liked her. In a curious way she reminded him of his real mother – the one he'd had a picture of. She treated him as if he were already a man, which in a way he was, being fifteen, a promising classical scholar, not bad-looking and growing out of childish debility. He was still thin, but he had bones, and his voice had broken. He was startled by his resemblance to his father, and flattered when his stepmother mentioned it. He had his father's eyes, she said. She was well-fleshed, heavier than he, but she often made him offer her his arm and when he did so she leant on it. She made him feel gallant. She asked him to call her by her first name, Mabel – a name he had not liked but liked now.

To his father's eventual question, 'Well, John, what do you think of her?' he could only say in fullness of heart, 'Oh, she's topping,' and was amazed then when his father took his hand, as a woman might have done, and exerted a momentary pressure. They were lying on this occasion in his Surrey grandfather's orchard under an apple tree whose fruits were suspended in the branches – midway between their summer green sour and their rosy autumn ripe.

'What will it be, John,' his father asked presently, 'the administration or the army?'

'Oh, the army,' he said, thinking of his stepmother's first dead hero husband. 'The Pankot Rifles,' and then half sat up as if to apologize. His father lay back – eyes closed, smiling. 'I mean,' young Layton continued, 'if you agree. I'd like to, well, you know, not make capital out of your standing in the civil, but make a go of it on my own in something different. Do you mind?'

His father said, 'Not in the least,' then smiled more broadly and repeated: 'Not in the very least.'

*

When young Layton returned to India in 1913 his father was member for finance on the provincial governor's executive council. He and Mabel lived in a vast old bungalow in Ranpur. Layton stayed with them for a week and Mabel gave a dinner party for him at which he met the commanding officer of the 1st Pankot Rifles and the adjutant, and their wives. Before the guests arrived Mabel inspected him to make sure that the tailor in London had made his uniform correctly and that he was wearing it properly. It consisted of tight dark blue overalls that were strapped under the heels of wellington boots, a white shirt with a stiff narrow winged collar, a narrow black silk bow-tie, a black silk cummerbund, a waist-length jacket of dark green barathea frogged with black braid and clasped at the neck by a little silver chain. It was hot but not especially uncomfortable. He was proud to be wearing it and not put out when Mabel tapped his chest with her fan and said, 'Let it wear you, then you'll grow into it,' and kissed him and raised her arm in the way a woman did in those days to command the support of a man she approved of.

A week later he joined his regiment in Ranpur (the month was October) and a week after that went up to the Pankot Hills to the depot where he was initiated into the lore of recruitment, initial training, and transportation back to Ranpur of men returning from leave in their villages. In October and November boys still came down from the hills to Pankot to present themselves at the *Daftar*, often accompanied by an elder brother who had come up with his battalion in April from Ranpur and later gone on leave. The recruiting season was also the leave season. 2/Lieut. John Layton sometimes sat with the senior subaltern in the *Daftar*, learning the technique of selection and rejection. At others he watched the boys drilling under the depot Subahdar-major, or took command of the morning and evening parades. Apart from the subaltern appointed as Recruiting Officer Sahib there were two other British officers permanently at Pankot, the depot commander and his adjutant. Layton lived with the senior subaltern in a bungalow near the golf course. His military duties took up little time, but he had social duties. Social duties included calling (by leaving his card) on European officials and civilians (usually retired) and their wives, in order of seniority. Pankot was never empty but in the winter there was an air about the place of almost cosy relaxation. Wherever he went in Pankot he was known as James Layton's son and as Mabel's stepson. He did not mind having no special identity of his own. Life, in its fullest sense, was a question of service. He had an idea that his real mother, from ill-health rather than any other cause, had not fully understood this. In Pankot she also was remembered but as someone who hadn't been quite up to meeting the demands the country made on white people – certainly not up to meeting them in the way her successor, Mabel Layton, met them.

He was careful to take plenty of exercise. He rode and played tennis and at weekends went for long walks by himself; but solitariness, to Layton, was attractive only in prospect. He found the lonely hillpaths disturbing.

The house in which his father and Mabel lived during the summer was shut up. He looked forward to 1914 and hoped he would not have the bad luck to be left in Ranpur. He would have liked to spend at least one hot weather in Pankot while his father and Mabel were on station. By 1915 he would probably be on the North-West Frontier, because the 1st Pankots had not been there since 1907, the year Mabel's husband was killed and his own mother died in England. He also looked forward to the time – still further in the future because peace-time promotion was slow – when as senior subaltern he would live for a whole year in Pankot in charge of recruitment. Perhaps by then his father would have retired and come to live in Pankot permanently. Some people said that India was ruinous to familial devotion, because of the long periods when children were separated from their parents. Some people even tried the experiment of educating their children at special schools in India, but that didn't work very well. The children were marked, for life, as of the country. So far as young Layton was concerned, the years in England had only served to strengthen his devotion to his father, his stepmother, and the country they served.

*

In November he returned to Ranpur. He did not see Pankot again until the summer of 1919. In the hot weather of 1914 he was, as he had expected, left behind in Ranpur. By the time his parents came back from the hills war had been declared on Germany. In 1915 the 1st Pankots moved to Dehra Dun and then to Poona. There was some uncertainty about what role they were to play, and where, but eventually they were brigaded and sailed for Suez. They were in action in Mesopotamia. Subahdar Muzzafir Khan Bahadur was awarded a posthumous VC. The Colonel collected a DSO and two officers, one of them Layton, collected MCs. In 1918, somewhat depleted, they went to Palestine and in 1919 sailed back to India, where their return to Ranpur was temporarily held up because their arrival coincided with civil unrest in the Punjab, the consequence (according to the Indians) of the Rowlatt Acts which were intended to enable the Government of India (in spite of the 1917 declaration of Dominion status as its long-term political aim) to continue to exercise in peace-time certain war-time measures under the Defence of India Rules for the protection of the realm against subversion. These means included imprisonment of Indians without trial. According to the English the disturbances were simply a disagreeable sign of the times, proof that the war had ruined people's sense of values and let reds and radicals – white as well as black – get above themselves.

But the action of General Dyer in April in Amritsar in the Jallianwallah Bagh, where he personally led a detachment of Gurkhas who fired on an unarmed crowd of civilians who were defying his order not to hold a public meeting, killing several hundred and wounding upwards of a thousand, nipped the anticipated revolution nicely in the bud and in May the 1st Pankots left the staging camp where they had been halted and held in reserve, in case further troops were needed to act in aid of the civil power, and continued their journey home.

Pankot gave the regiment an official welcome – a full-dress military parade attended by the Governor and members of his council and by the General Officer commanding in Ranpur, Lieut.-General Muir. Subahdar Muzzafir Khan Bahadur's seven-year-old son and his widow (an unidentifiable figure dressed overall in a black *burkha* that made her look like an effigy) were presented to the Governor and the General (the widow through the medium of those officers' wives) and the son received his father's medal from the Governor. The officers who had been decorated stood on the saluting platform with the Governor and the General while the battalion marched past with fife and drum, followed by the 1st Ranpurs (second-in-command, Major A. V. Reid, DSO, MC) who had also seen service in the Middle East but had returned home sooner, and the scratch war-time Pankot battalions, soon to be disbanded. The rear was brought up, proudly, by the 4/5 Pankot

Rifles who were destined to live on and go down to Mayapore and make it their permanent cool weather station.

Young Layton, as was his due, stood with the other decorated officers on the saluting platform.

'I remember thinking,' he told Sarah, 'that there was something wrong, something that meant all this pomp wasn't what we wanted, and that something irretrievable had been lost. Innocence I suppose. Perhaps I felt this only because father was dead, the war had been a mess and I'd done nothing to deserve my MC, or because Mabel was crying. Well, it was all splendid enough, I suppose.'

*

Layton's father had died unexpectedly in 1917 after a short illness caused by an abscess on the liver – the end result of a long-standing amoebic infection which had never been properly diagnosed or treated.

He died in the Minto Hospital in Ranpur and was buried in the churchyard of St Luke's. If he had lived another year, Mabel said, he would have got his KCIE. Since his death Mabel had altered, her stepson thought. There had always been a hard streak in her. Without it her gaiety would have seemed shallow. Now the gaiety had gone and the hard streak emerged when it was least expected: in private rather than in public. She cried at the ceremonial parade. But when she took her stepson to St Luke's to show him his father's grave her behaviour was off-hand. She seemed to have lost the knack, or the will, to make people feel at home in her company.

A year later, after her stepson's marriage to Mildred Muir and after there had been a committee of inquiry into the massacre in the Jallianwallah Bagh, a report by the Indian National Congress, a debate in the House of Commons on the findings of the Army Council, and General Dyer had been retired on half-pay (disgraced, whereas twelve months before he had been hailed as the saviour of India and was still thought of as such by all right-thinking people), Mabel Layton surprised everybody by refusing to identify herself with the ladies of Pankot and Ranpur who busied themselves collecting money for the General Dyer fund. These ladies had misinterpreted the tears at the ceremonial parade and the stony face over tea and coffee for patriotism of the most exemplary kind, and were shocked when by refusing either to contribute or help to collect money that would keep the wolf from the old General's door she appeared in an entirely different light: widow of a soldier who had died for the empire, widow – for a second time – of a civilian whose work for the empire had killed him, stepmother of a young officer who had fought for his country gallantly, step-mother-in-law of the second daughter of General Muir, but who was, it seemed, nevertheless insensible to the true nature of what the men in her life (including her father, who had been an admiral) had stood or still stood for.

When the total sum collected for General Dyer was heard to have reached the substantial figure of £26,000 the ladies of Pankot and Ranpur felt vindicated, justified. But Mabel Layton's comment was 'Twenty-six thousand? Well, now, how many unarmed Indians died in the Jallianwallah Bagh? Two hundred? Three hundred? There seems to be some uncertainty, but let's say two hundred and sixty. That's one hundred pounds a piece. So we know the current price for a dead brown,' and sent a cheque for £100 to the fund the Indians were raising for the families of Jallianwallah victims. But only young Layton and the Indian to whom she entrusted the money knew this.

'I'm keeping it dark for your sake,' Mabel told him, but with an edge in her voice that made it sound as if she felt he had person-ally driven her to secrecy. 'People would misunderstand. They usually do. You have a career to think of. You can't have a step-mother who seems to be going native, which is the last thing I'd do. I hate the damned country now anyway. It's taken two husbands from me. To me it's not a question of choosing between poor old Dyer and the bloody browns. The choice was made for me when we took the country over and got the idea we did so for its own sake instead of ours. Dyer can look after himself, but according to the rules the browns can't because looking after them is what we get paid for. And if it's *really* necessary every so often to shoot some of them down like ninepins for their own good the least we can do is admit it, just say Hard Luck to the chap who shoots too many, and see to it that the women and children who lost their menfolk, or the children who lost their parents don't starve. There were kids who got shot too, weren't there, at Amritsar? What do we owe them?'

She paid the £100 to one Sir Ahmed Akbar Ali Kasim, a wealthy Ranpur Muslim, one of her late husband's Indian colleagues

on the provincial governor's executive council, whose son Mohammed Ali had already shown brilliance in his chosen profession, the
law, and was inspired that year of the Jallianwallah Bagh massacre
to join the Congress Party whose aim in that same year and for the
same bloody reasons and under M. K. Gandhi's leadership was
reversed from independence by peaceful co-operation to independence as soon as possible by non co-operation.

'You are young,' Sir Ahmed Akbar told his son. 'Your heart is
stronger than your head. When you are as old as I am you will not
be so confused by these emotional issues. You think Jallianwallah
was a new experience? You are wrong. You think the Indian
Congress can ensure that it will be the last episode of this kind?
You will be wrong again. You think Jallianwallah proves that the
British are lying, talking freedom but acting tyrannically and dealing destruction? Again you are wrong. Jallianwallah could never
have happened if the British who talk freedom were not sincere.
It happened because they are sincere. They have frightened their
opponents with their sincerity. I do not mean us. We are not their
opponents. Their opponents, the ones who matter but who will
matter less and less, are also British. They are men like General
Dyer. Why do you call that man a monster? He believed God had
charged him with a duty to save the empire. He believed this sincerely, just as he believed sincerely that in Amritsar there was to be
found an invidious threat to that empire. Why do you repeat parrot-
fashion that the English are hypocrites? With this you can never
charge them. You can only charge them with sincerity and of
being divided among themselves about what it is right to be sincere about. It is only an insincere people that can be accused of
hypocrisy. Sometimes I think we are the hypocrites because we have
lived too long as a subject people to remember what sincerity
means, or to know from one day to the next what we believe in.

'Look' (the old man said, and showed Mohammed Ali a slip of
paper), 'do you know what this is? It is a cheque for the rupee
equivalent of one hundred pounds made out in my name by an
Englishwoman. In exchange for it I am charged to send my own
draft to the fund for the Jallianwallah widows and orphans, and not
to reveal the name of the donor. Perhaps you think this smells a bit
of hypocrisy. To me it smells only of sincerity. It is a straw in the
wind which proves to me that for a long time I have been correct
in my forecast of which way the wind would blow.

'You look at the English people you meet. Some of them you like. Some you hate. Many you are indifferent to. But even the ones you like do not matter. The ones who matter you will never see – they are tucked away in England – and they are indifferent to us as individuals. You think these officials over here rule us? These viceroys, these governors, these commissioners and commanders-in-chief and brigadier-generals? Then you are wrong. We are ruled by people who do not even know where Ranpur is. But now they know where Jallianwallah Bagh is and what it is, and many of them do not like what they know. Those of them who *do* like what they know are the ones you hear about and hear from. Like the General at Amritsar they are frightened people and frightened people shriek the loudest and fire at random.

'Ah well, they were Indians who actually died at Amritsar, but the Jallianwallah Bagh was also the scene of a suicide. There will be other such scenes. It takes a long time for a new nation to be born, and a long time for an old nation to die by its own hand. You will hasten nothing by failing to distinguish between the English who really rule us and the English who interpret and administer that rule. Haven't you yet understood that we are part and parcel of the Englishmen's own continual state of social and political evolvement and that to share the fruits we must share the labour and abide by the rules they abide by?'

'You mean,' Mohammed Ali said, 'submit to being shot down for protesting the freedom to speak our minds?'

'For this they have shot down their own people, and not so long ago. Out here we shall always be a step behind whatever progress the English make at home.'

Mohammed Ali smiled. 'No,' he said, 'we shall be several steps ahead.'

For a while the old man was silent, not because his son had stumped him. He was merely considering the violent landscape so casually mapped.

'Perhaps I am too old,' he said eventually. 'I can't see small print without my spectacles and even then I get a headache. I think the lady who donated this money also finds it difficult to read the small print. She is anyway only concerning herself with the capital letters of an ancient contract. In *your* contract is *everything* writ large, or is it that your eyesight is superhuman?'

•

John Layton was in his twenty-sixth year when he came back to India in 1919. In the last year of his service abroad he was acting adjutant of the battalion. On returning to Ranpur he relinquished the appointment to an officer of the 2nd Battalion who was senior to him. Temporarily he was without regimental employment. He was the natural choice for the role of Recruiting Officer Sahib. He went up to Pankot in May, with Mabel. They lived in the bungalow near the golf course that he had shared with the senior subaltern in the October and November of 1913.

Both Mabel and his father had talked of retiring to Pankot when the time came. They had had their eye on a place called Rose Cottage, inconveniently placed on the other side of the main hill dominated by the Governor's Summer Residence but to them the most attractive of the few privately owned houses and bungalows: attractive because of its garden, its views, and the fact that it was owned by an elderly widower who had been in tea in Assam and couldn't be expected to live much longer.

Layton's father had not been a rich man. What little he left Mabel inherited, but she had money of her own and money from her first husband who had died well-breeched in spite of having lived extravagantly. Since Mabel was childless he would eventually inherit everything. It would be useful. In peace-time an officer found it virtually impossible to live on his pay – he was not expected to – few attempted to however simple their tastes – he found it quite impossible to save. To serve the empire he needed money of his own. For the moment Layton had no worries on this score. Until his death his civilian father had paid sums of money into his account whenever he could afford them; and Layton suspected – surprised at the amount standing to his credit – that Mabel had contributed regular sums herself. Furthermore she declared her intention of handing over to him in full the principal she had inherited from his father, and the accumulated interest, directly he got married. Such funds together with what he had been able to save while on active service represented the kind of basic security without which a man of his kind would feel at a disadvantage when it came to thinking of the future in terms of fatherhood and of a proper education for his children.

When his Surrey grandfather died – and the old boy surely couldn't go on much longer – he imagined he would inherit the Surrey property into the bargain. His own children might spend

64]

part of their childhood there, with their mother (whoever she might be) or their grandmother Mabel, or some relation of their mother's. The long-term plan looked sound. In his twenty-sixth year he felt it was time to be thinking of marriage.

III

THE GOC RANPUR, Lieut-General Muir, had three daughters, Lydia, Mildred and Fenella. They were known as Lyddy, Millie and Fenny. 1919 was their first Indian season – the war had postponed it. It was Mildred to whom Layton was most attracted. Fenny was boisterous and silly. Lydia had been engaged to a naval officer at home who was lost in the Atlantic. She bore her loss rather bitterly and Layton distrusted the element of sympathy that would initially enter any relationship a man could have with her. With Millie he felt at ease, even when they were alone and ran out of things to say to one another.

Mrs Muir was an expert chaperone. Opportunities to be alone with any one of her daughters were neither too few nor too many. It was said that she kept a list of eligible men and that a sign of being on it was the sudden myopia that afflicted that regal eye when you danced out of the ballroom on to the terrace of Flagstaff House and sat one of her daughters down in a place where the artificial light from the crystal chandeliers just failed to illumine the stone flags and the balustrade, but (ideally) lit her eyes and caught some of the facets of the jewellery she was wearing.

He decided after several such meetings that he was in love with Mildred Muir and – which was more important – that she was attracted to him. Eventually he declared his love, proposed to her and having got her acceptance asked the general for an interview, addressed himself to the older man with painstaking old-fashioned formality which (Mildred later told her daughter Sarah) swept the old boy off his feet.

The engagement was announced in September. The May of 1920 was chosen as the ideal time for the marriage. Layton would then have finished his twelve-month tour as Recruiting Officer, and he would be due for long leave. He and Mildred would honeymoon in Kashmir and then take a trip home to England to visit his grandfather in Surrey.

Of these plans his stepmother Mabel seemed to approve although he could not actually get her to talk for long about them. In November he took her back to Ranpur. On his return from the war he had found her living at Smith's Hotel and to this place she returned now, refusing an invitation from General and Mrs Muir to stay at Flagstaff House. After a weekend with the Muirs Layton went back to Pankot alone and this time found that solitude came easier to him. He rode and spent weekends walking in the hills. News of his progress on such occasions passed from village to village and wherever he went he found himself pressed to accept hospitality and knew that it would not do to refuse it. He was the only son of Layton Sahib and also the sahib who knew best how to tell the story of Subahdar Muzzafir Khan Bahadur's gallantry. Old and young men gathered round him in the evenings – and beyond the light cast by the flickering oil-lamps he was often aware of the veiled presence of listening women, and afterwards would sleep the sound sleep of satisfied appetite for food and drink and human correspondence that left in his mind an impression of the hill people's grave simplicity and cheerful dignity so that he thought 'Well, home is here,' and knew that for English people in India there was no home in the sense of brick and mortar, orchard and pasture, but that it was lodged mysteriously in the heart.

*

Late in the August of 1920, newly returned with his bride from England, he found Mabel still lodging at Smith's. They stayed with her there for a week before going on up to Pankot to join General and Mrs Muir and Fenny. Lydia had gone back to England with them after the Kashmir honeymoon and had stayed there, declaring that she would never go to India again. She never did. She took a job as secretary to a Bayswater physician, and later married him.

In October Mildred returned to the plains with her husband. Her first baby was due in the second half of March. By then it would be hot and she expressed a wish for the baby to be born in Pankot. There was a nursing home there, part of the hospital and convalescent home that was the Pankot extension of the general hospital in Ranpur. Still without regular regimental employment, Layton acted variously as his father-in-law's aide and as adjutant of the 1st Pankots, filling a leave vacancy. He sat on courts of inquiry and went on courses. In February 1921 he took Mildred up to Pankot. Mrs Muir accompanied them and so did Fenny. They stayed in the GOC's summer residence, a section of which was opened up for this unseasonable occupation. Five weeks later, on March 27th, Sarah was born.

Layton was only momentarily disappointed that his first child was a girl. She was a delicate rosy-cheeked image of Mildred and himself with none of that red ancient wrinkled look of the new-born baby. All that lacked to complete his happiness was a home of his own to bring her and her mother back to when they came out of the Pankot Nursing Home. They stayed throughout that summer in Flagstaff House. He wrote to Mabel asking her to join them, but she seemed to have no liking for the hills now and stayed in Ranpur. She did not see her stepson's first child until late in the following October, when the Laytons went down to Ranpur. They now had for the first time what could pass as a permanent home – permanent in the transient, military sense. The adjutant of the 1st Pankots had gone to the staff college in Quetta and Layton succeeded to the appointment. He moved his family into the bungalow that was to be their home for the next few years, No. 3 Kabul road, Ranpur: a stuccoed colonnaded structure, well shaded by trees in a large compound with adequate stabling and servants' quarters, and a lawn where Sarah and Susan (born in Pankot, in 1922) played – mainly under the eye of Dost Mohammed the head *mali* who knew the ways of snakes and scorpions so well that neither child ever saw a live snake and only one living scorpion in the moment when, encircled by a ring of fire created by Dost Moham-med, it arched its tail over its body and (so he said) stung itself to death.

*

Sarah remembered the scorpion (she watched what Dost Moham-med called its suicide with the detached curiosity of a child) and the garden at No. 3 Kabul road – the shadowy veranda, a dark retreat from the intensity of sunlight; the high-ceilinged bedroom which she shared with Susan, twin child-size beds under twin mosquito nets, and slatted doors which Mumtez, their old ayah, closed at night and guarded, making her bed up against them, sleeping across the threshold. Sarah remembered being woken in the early mornings by the hoarse screeching of the crows. She confused these memories of the old bungalow in Ranpur with other more clearly sustained memories of Pankot; but neither Ranpur nor Pankot struck her when she came back to them, a young woman, as having survived the years of her growing up in England in the way she herself survived them: to her eighteen-year-old eye, in the summer of 1939, their reality was only a marginally accurate reflection of the mind picture she had of them. There was too much space between the particular places she remembered – places which were strongholds of her childhood recollections – and the strongholds themselves had a prosaicness of brick and mortar that did not match the magical, misty but more vivid impression they had left on her when young, so that returning to them, Pankot and Ranpur – Ranpur particularly – seemed to have spread themselves too thin and yet too thick on the ground for comfort.

The sensation she had was one of insecurity which from day to day, and from moment to moment in any one day, could be cushioned by a notion of personal and family history. India to her was at once alien and familiar. The language came back slowly to her, in stops and starts. She was surprised by what she remembered of it, puzzled by what she seemed to have forgotten, but realized then that what she had ever learned of it was the shorthand of juvenile command and not the language of adult communication.

And yet (Sarah thought) over here in an odd and curious way we *are* children. I am aware, coming back, of entering a region of almost childish presumptions – as if everything we are surrounded by is the background for a game. But Susan and I are somehow left out of the game, as if even now we are not old enough to be depended upon to know the rules and act accordingly. Before we are allowed to play we have to know the rules. Without them the game can be seen to be a game, and if it's seen to be a game someone will come along and tell us to put our toys away. And this of course is what is going to happen. This is what I feel, coming back here. And directly it happens all the magic of the game will evaporate, the Fort will be seen to have been made of paper, the soldiers of lead and tin, and I of wax or china or pot. And Mumtez will not lie across the threshold, keeping our long night safe from ogres. Mumtez is gone long ago anyway. Where? Mother scarcely remembers her, which means perhaps that she was in our service for no longer than a year. She remembers Dost Mohammed but not the day of

68]

the scorpion. Instead she remembers the day of the snake which neither I nor Susan remember – I suppose because mother and Dost Mohammed between them kept the day and the snake well away from us.

But older children forget the toys that have been put up into the attic; only the younger ones remember and then they too in their turn forget and play games as if they were not games at all but part of life. But it is all a business of cobwebs and old chests and long days indoors that find us thrown back on our own frail resources, because we are afraid to go outside and wet our feet and catch a chill. Pankot is such a place. Pankot is a retreat. So is Ranpur. Not the real Pankot, not the real Ranpur, but *our* Ranpur and Pankot. We see them as different from what they really are which is why when we come back to them we are aware of the long distances that separate one place of vivid recollection from another. In Ranpur we become aware of the immensity of the surrounding plain and in Pankot of the very small impression we have made on hills which when we are away from them we think of as safe, enclosed and friendly but which are in reality unfriendly, vast and dangerous. That is our first shock when we return. It's not something we like to see or think about, so after a time we don't see it and don't think about it.

*

The house in Pankot and the bungalow in Ranpur which their parents were living in during summer and winter respectively when Sarah and Susan returned to India in 1939 were not places either of the girls remembered. To begin with each was larger than its predecessor because Layton had now assumed command of the 1st Pankots after a fairly humdrum but not unsuccessful career, which during their daughters' absence at home had taken him (and his wife) from Ranpur to Lahore, and Delhi, Peshawar and Quetta, but since houses and bungalows were built very much to the same pattern neither girl was particularly aware of what made these homes different from those they lived in as children.

Sarah and Susan came back to India accompanied by their Aunt Fenny and Uncle Arthur – Major and Mrs Grace who had been taking home leave in 1939 – the year Susan finished with school, and Sarah, who had finished with school one term before, had come to the end of the short secretarial course she had insisted on taking, determined anyway to be prepared to be of some use to someone, somewhere.

Aunt Fenny, the youngest of the Muir girls, had married Arthur Grace in 1924. Her marriage coincided with her father's retirement. It had surprised people at the time that Fenny took so long to make up her mind between the several officers who from time to time laid siege to her affections. And her choice, coming when it did, in – as it were – the last year of her Indian opportunity (General and Mrs Muir having decided to retire to England) and lighting upon Arthur Grace, left an idea in people's minds that she knew she had delayed too long. Arthur Grace was possibly the least eligible of the subalterns who wooed her, and the gossip was that at this last moment she panicked and said yes to his proposal merely because he happened to make it on a particular day, at a particular hour, when she was especially concerned about her future.

His career had not been successful; they had not managed to produce children, and Aunt Fenny had become year by year more and more unrecognizable as the pretty but shallow girl who had had a good time in Pankot in 1919 and 1920 – a bridesmaid who had caught her sister Mildred's bouquet when Mildred and John Layton were married in the church of St John in Pankot early one May morning, and who had been so solidly surrounded by interested young escorts at Pankot station later that day that she scarcely had time to wave her newly-married sister off on her honeymoon.

Youngest daughter, bridesmaid, a godmother to Susan and Sarah – these were the happy stages Fenny passed through before joining the company of honourable matrons as the wife of Arthur Grace. And then, in her turn, Sarah – being then but three years old – acted as a bridesmaid to Aunt Fenny; although of that she had really no recollection whatsoever beyond what was evidenced by the family iconography, a photograph in Aunt Lydia's house in London and the same photograph in her mother's album in India.

It showed the Layton and the Muir families gathered together in slightly self-conscious but handsome, well-dressed and orderly array around a younger Aunt Fenny and a thinner Uncle Arthur with Sarah standing there, a little to one side, in front of Aunt Fenny, holding a nosegay whose scent she almost thought she could reconjure (in isolation from the unrecollected event that caused her to be holding it) and by her side the image of a five-year-old boy in satin page-boy rig whom she could not reconjure at all but whose name, apparently, was Giles, and who was the son of her father's commanding officer.

Perhaps the group portrait was most notable for its inclusion of Mabel Layton who stood next to her first husband's old comrade-in-arms, by then the commanding officer of the 1st Pankots, Giles's father, with on her other side an elderly Indian civilian who was present at the wedding because of his connexion with the Governor who was also there with his wife shoulder to shoulder with General and Mrs Muir. The photograph was taken in the gardens of Flagstaff House at Pankot and in the background there could be seen the wooden balustrades and the kindly wistaria. Mabel Layton wore a wide-brimmed hat that all but hid her face, except for the mouth – held midway between repose and a smile.

As a child in India Sarah was afraid of Aunty Mabel (as she insisted on being called). This may have had something to do with the fact that Aunty Mabel was not really her grandmother, but her father's stepmother, and stepmothers were never nice people in story books. She liked Aunty Mabel in England better than she had in India, perhaps because she herself had grown up a bit. Mabel came to England with Major and Mrs Layton in the summer of 1933 when Sarah was turned twelve: the year great-grandfather Layton in Surrey was dying at last at the age of ninety-four.

Although in that long period of exile in England as schoolgirls, she and Susan lived in London with Aunt Lydia, they usually spent several weeks of the summer holidays with their great-grandfather. A casual observer might have thought that Susan was the old man's favourite child. It was Susan who sat on his knee to listen to his rather gruesome fairy-stories and his stories of their father's and grandfather's boyhoods in Surrey. Sarah did not mind this apparent favouritism. Between herself and her ancient relative there was a silent understanding that Susan needed looking after because she was the baby of the family. His stories either went over Susan's head or bored her, or frightened her. Towards the end of great-grandfather's life Susan decided that she was too old to sit on his knee although she enjoyed the preferential treatment his invitation – increasingly reluctantly accepted – always gave proof of.

Susan did not cry when great-grandfather Layton died; neither did Sarah but she felt they didn't cry for different reasons. He died towards the end of the summer of 1933, shortly before Sarah's and Susan's parents were due to go back to India with Aunty Mabel. Sarah believed Susan did not cry because Susan had never thought of her great-grandfather as a person, but as an old and rather smelly piece of furniture that had to be put up with in the summer and sometimes came to life in a way that was personally disagreeable to her but reassuring to her sense of self-importance and of everything in the house being at her disposal. In the summer of his death Susan had acquired other reassurances: her father's instead of her great-grandfather's knee, her mother's arms. It was the first reunion since the year of separation, 1930, when their mother, accompanied by Aunt Fenny, had brought the girls home to settle them at Aunt Lydia's and at school before rejoining their father in India; and Susan – in the few weeks before great-grandpa died – now tearfully seized the opportunity to tell her mother she hated everything in England. This puzzled Sarah. Sarah had stifled her own unhappiness in England because she didn't want it to rub off on to her sister who had seemed to take the uprooting and replanting (in what their parents always referred to as home – but which was as outlandish at first as Iceland would be to a Congo pigmy) as if nothing much had happened to her at all. The tears Susan now shed were counterfeit of those Sarah had kept in, and Sarah pondered the unfairness of it, the sudden inexplicable emergence of Susan as a little girl with a secretive side to her nature, who had not repaid Sarah for looking after her by trusting her enough to confide what was really going on in her mind but instead saved it all up to confide to her mother. From her state of puzzlement Sarah passed into one of distrust herself. Susan's outburst about the hatefulness of life in England, at Aunt Lydia's, at school, at great-grandpa's, was surely a pose, a bald-faced bid for the bulk of everyone's attention at a time when it should have been concentrated on great-grandpa who was dying, and it did not escape Sarah that she herself was being accused – although of what she wasn't quite sure. She felt out of things, cut off from her family by Susan's emotional claims on it and her implied criticism of the way she, Sarah, had tried in exile to represent it by looking after her sister as much like a grown-up person as she was capable of. And so when great-grandfather died, Sarah did not weep, because she felt – not necessarily understanding it – the final uselessness of giving way to an emotion: a life, well-spent, was over. It happened to everyone. It would happen to her mother and father, and to Aunty Mabel – to Aunty Mabel sooner than any of them, unless there were an accident or a war, or some special kind of Indian disaster such as cholera or unexpected illness. Susan, though, stayed dry-eyed – Sarah thought – because the death of anyone as old as great-grandpa was remote from her, relevant only to the extent it disrupted other people's concentration on matters she thought of as really important.

Susan did not want to go to the funeral. There was no difficulty about that. The difficulty that arose was over Sarah's resistance to the suggestion that she should not go either but stay behind and look after Susan.

'No, I want to go,' she told her mother – with whom, after the years of separation she had not yet established an easy relationship. 'Great-grandpa was very good to us. Mrs Bailey can look after Susan.' Mrs Bailey was the old housekeeper, who had been left three hundred pounds. 'In fact Susan can help her with the funeral meats.' Funeral meats was an expression Sarah had picked up in the last day or so from Mrs Bailey herself. She thought that as food it sounded unappetizing to eat and doleful to prepare and that it might do Susan good to be made to take a hand getting it ready. She hoped as well that the baking of funeral meats would get rid of the sweet odour in the house that reminded her of cut-flowers going bad in vases.

On the day of the funeral she shared a car to the parish church with Aunty Mabel and two of the elderly Layton relatives who had turned up earlier, had had to be met at the station and on the way to the church talked to Mabel about people Sarah did not know unless they were referred to as Mildred or John, which meant her parents. She did not cry at the service (no one did) nor later in the cemetery, standing by the amateur-looking grave that after a certain amount of necessary palaver received the coffin with great-grandpa in it; nor on the journey back. She cried later that night, in the dark, when Susan – who was not speaking to her – had gone to sleep. What made her cry was the thought that great-grandpa had put off dying until her father and mother and Aunty Mabel could get back home from India, but had not spun it out to put them in a position of having either to postpone their departure or leave England again still in a state of uncertainty. It seemed to be a thoughtful way of doing what the doctor had called 'going out'. No one's plans had been messed up. It struck her that he had deliberately stayed alive long enough to give them the satisfaction of believing they had made the last weeks of his life as jolly as they could be, confined to bed as he was, and then 'gone out' soon enough to give them time to do everything that had to be done, get over doing it, then pack their bags and catch the train and the boat their passages had been booked on months ago.

She cried at this evidence of consideration for others; and then at the thought that in some way she had failed Susan as an elder sister, because Susan obviously hadn't been as carefree as her behaviour had previously suggested, didn't feel enough consideration had been given to *her*. Sarah cried, too, because more than anything in the world at that moment she wanted to go back to India with her parents and Aunty Mabel and Susan. Without great-grandpa and the Surrey summer, England again looked to her like the alien land in which she and her sister had been sentenced to spend a number of years as part of the process of growing up. She felt grown-up enough now; quite ready, aged twelve, to tackle the business of helping her mother to look after father; quite ready to take Susan back, even alone, to the old bungalow in Ranpur where Mumtez guarded them against the dark and mysterious nights (for as such they now came at her). The knowledge that her parents no longer lived at No. 3 Kabul road, that Mumtez had long since gone, even been forgotten, that her mother and father were going back to a place called Lahore which was quite unknown to her, did not diminish the vividness of the picture she had of what a return to India would be like. She did not mind, either, that according to Aunt Lydia India was 'an unnatural place for a white woman'. In any case she did not believe it. Her mother was natural enough for anyone, and so was Aunty Mabel if you thought about it and didn't let it upset you when she averted her face when you went to kiss her (so that your lips merely brushed the soft part of her cheek near the earlobe). Aunty Mabel never let anyone get really close to her, but sometimes you found her looking at you, and felt the challenge of her interest in you; in what you were doing or thinking and in why you were doing and thinking it.

*

It was Mabel who told Sarah the truth about the scorpion; two days after great-grandfather's funeral (and Susan still not talking

74]

to her, so that she was alone in the orchard until Mabel, also walk-ing alone, came upon her and said, 'Well, if you're doing nothing, take me for a walk').

They went through the orchard and through the gate in the iron rail fence that enclosed it from the meadow. This meadow sloped down to a brook and a spinney. There was a path, worn by custom. The meadow was let to a man who kept cows there. Susan was afraid to walk down to the spinney unless the cows were all bunched together at the far end of the field, but Sarah liked cows. In India they were sacred. In England they weren't, but they were warm and sweet-smelling. She liked the way they tore at the tough grass with their thick curled tongues. She wondered how they avoided pulling it up by its roots and what they thought about when they looked up from their tearing and munching, flicking their ears and striking their flanks with their fly-whisk tails, and watched you watching them. Sometimes they took no notice of you at all, but cropped their way with ragged herd instinct from one part of the meadow to another without pausing to look up as you passed near by. At other times they all held their heads up or turned them to watch you pass behind their rumps. Now, as Sarah walked with Aunty Mabel towards the spinney they were pulling up grass on either side of the path. She could smell their breath and thought Aunty Mabel hesitated to pass through their midst. 'They're quite docile,' Sarah said, and took Aunty Mabel's hand, partly to re-assure her and partly because just here the track was ridged and rather difficult for an elderly lady to negotiate. 'They're not great-grandpa's,' she said, forgetting for the moment that nothing was great-grandpa's any longer. 'They belong to Mr Birtwhistle. He lets us watch them being milked sometimes.'

'Do you enjoy that?'

Sarah thought. 'No. But I'm interested in it. I mean enjoy is how I'd describe liking something artificial like a book or a game. But milking is to do with actual life, isn't it, so I like it but I don't enjoy it. Does that make sense?'

'Of a kind.'

When they reached the brook Sarah showed Aunty Mabel the stepping-stones which gave access to the opposite bank and the woodland. 'It used to be our private wood,' she explained, meaning her own and Susan's, and private in the sense of pretend. 'There's a fence on the other side of the spinney. The land on the other side of that belongs to Mr Birtwhistle but it's all right to go in so long as you keep to the edges. I mean it's all right for me and Susan. Or has been. I suppose everything will undergo changes now. It's probably our last summer. Daddy's going to let the house and might even sell it.' She stopped, realizing that she was talking to Aunty Mabel as if she were a stranger instead of a member of the family who probably knew far more about her father's plans than she did herself. And she kept forgetting that Aunty Mabel had visited great-grandfather years ago, long before the 1914–18 war, with grandfather Layton, to meet her stepson, Sarah's father, and so must know the brook and the stepping-stones, the spinney, and the neighbour's land on the other side, and that this might be the last summer of all that any Layton would come here.

'Shall you miss it?' Aunty Mabel asked.

'I expect so, although we only ever come in July and August. I probably wouldn't mind not coming if I knew I could and had simply gone somewhere else for a change. It will be knowing I can't come that will make it seem sad, as if a phase of my life has ended for ever.'

They stood looking at the brook. Sarah didn't sit on the bank because Aunty Mabel was much too old for that sort of thing. Near the water the earth was always damp. It was a hot day, but shady here. Aunty Mabel had a coat on though. She was cold in England. Three years ago Sarah had felt the cold too but had got used to it. She had dreams sometimes, in colour, like in a film, of herself in sunshine in Pankot. The brook babbling over the stones reminded her of Pankot in miniature. But then everything in England was on a miniature scale. She thought this had an effect on the people who lived there always. In comparison with her mother and Aunt Fenny and Aunty Mabel, for instance, Aunt Lydia – although taller than any of them – seemed to Sarah to lack a dimension that the others didn't lack. Lacking this dimension was what Sarah supposed came of living on a tiny island. She felt this, but also felt she hadn't yet developed the reasoning power to work it out in terms that would adequately convey what she felt to other people. So she kept quiet about it and was conscious of Aunty Mabel keeping quiet about something too, and noted this down mentally as one of the things she'd not noticed before that distinguished her Indian family from her English family – distinguished her father, mother, Aunt Fenny and Aunty Mabel from Aunt Lydia, Uncle Frank (Aunt Lydia's physician husband) and poor old great-grandpa. Her English family kept quiet about nothing, but were always speaking their minds. Aunt Lydia sometimes presumed to speak other people's too. And all at once she saw the correspondence between (in particular) Aunty Mabel who never said very much at all and her sister, Susan, who said a lot, but hoarded important things up until someone came along (their parents for instance) whom she judged to be worth speaking her mind to.

Sarah did not understand this unexpected connexion between her sister and Aunty Mabel but knew it was an Indian connexion. The English who went to India were different from those who didn't. When they came back they felt like visitors. And the people they came back to felt that the connexion between them had become too tenuous for comfort (tenuous was one of Sarah's favourite new words). There were areas of sensitivity neither side dared probe too deeply.

Sarah said, 'I think we'd better go back otherwise we'll be late for tea and make things difficult for Mrs Bailey.'

'If you think so,' Aunty Mabel said.

On their way to the house Sarah had what she secretly called one of her funny turns. All that happened in a funny turn (nobody ever noticed them because obviously there was nothing to see) was that everything went very far away, taking its sound with it. It was rather like looking through the wrong end of great-grandpa's field-glasses and at the same time getting the wireless tuned in badly. Sarah had decided that her funny turns were all to do with growing up. At any given moment (she imagined) her bones and flesh expanded a fraction beyond the capacity her blood had to pump itself into all the crevices it was supposed to get at, leaving her brain briefly deprived of nourishment and her eyes and ears in consequence fractionally just incapable of making an accurate recording of what was really going on. She had worked it out that there was no common factor to the turns. It wasn't a question of how cold or hot the weather was, or of how much or how little she had been exerting herself, or of how hungry or how overfull she was, or how she felt. She found the sensation very interesting, but if it happened while she was talking to somebody, she worried a bit about talking sensibly. When it happened now, as they went back into the orchard (Sarah taking care to shut the gate properly) she also worried about making sure that Aunty Mabel didn't fall on one of the hummocks in the rough grass. She was never certain of her own balance during a funny turn because balance depended on getting your sense of perspective and distance right.

So she took her time closing the gate, hoping that in a few seconds she would stop feeling like a giant in a tiny landscape, that Aunty Mabel would come back into her proper proportions, bringing the orchard with her. She said (in a voice that rang in her head but gave no impression of being loud enough for Aunty Mabel to hear), 'I think there's a stone in my sandal.' Sometimes it helped to bend down, because that sent the blood into the head where it was needed. She bent down. A little to one side of her feet there was a fallen apple. Her feet and the apple were tiny, far away. One of the things about a funny turn was that although you felt gigantic in relation to everything else any part of yourself that you looked at was small and far away too. When she had fumbled with her sandal she touched the apple, fascinated by her distant hand; picked the apple up, and was stung by the wasp that was searching its soft bruised underside. The pain was sharp. Her brain recorded the message accurately, but there was still a layer of insensitivity separating her recognition of the pain and her realization that the pain was happening to her. She heard herself cry out. She stood upright.

'What's wrong?' Aunty Mabel asked.

'I've been stung.'

She was all right then – the funny turn was finished. Her little finger hurt. Aunty Mabel took the stung hand and looked at the tiny red puncture – the originating centre of the swelling and inflammation that was already beginning to show.

'A wasp or a bee?'

'Oh, a wasp. It was having a go at the apple.'

'Have you been stung by a wasp before?'

'Yes, twice.'

'That's all right, then. We'll get back and put something on it.'

'Mrs Bailey recommends lemon juice.'

'That will do.'

'Why is it all right that I've been stung before?'

'Because some people are allergic.'

'Does that mean they could die?'

'Yes. But it's very rare.'

'I thought only snake bites and scorpion stings were fatal.'

'No. And not always they.'

They walked side by side through the orchard towards the lawn and the house. On a day like this tea would normally have been in the garden in the shade of the cedar. Not having tea in the garden was one of the family's concessions to the formal discipline of mourning, or a sign anyway of their respect for the feelings of people like Mrs Bailey. Sarah was glad that none of her family seemed to believe in God. She didn't really believe in God herself. She didn't like religious people; rather she did not like them directly they stopped being ordinary and started to be religious. Truly religious people, like nuns and monks and saints were a different matter. She thought of them as truly religious because they gave up their lives to it, and giving up your life to it struck her as the only thing to do if you believed in it. If you didn't believe in it the most you could do was to be charitable and try not to be selfish.

She was worried because Susan had never been stung either by a wasp or a bee. Susan led a charmed life. Aunt Lydia said Susan would always fall on her feet. Sarah could not remember Susan hurting herself badly – not badly enough to leave a scar. Susan did not remember the day of the scorpion, although she had knelt by Sarah's side, watching Dost Mohammed build a fire round it.

'Is it true,' Sarah asked Aunty Mabel as they crossed the empty sun-struck lawn, 'that scorpions kill themselves if you build a ring of fire round them so that they know they can't get out?'

'No.'

Sarah was not surprised, in spite of having once seen what looked like proof that they did.

Aunty Mabel said : 'Their skins are very sensitive to heat, which is why they live under stones and in holes and only come out a lot during the wet. If you build a ring of fire round them they're killed by the heat. They look as if they sting themselves to death because of the way they arch their tails over their bodies. But it's only a reflex action. They're attacking the fire, and get scorched to death by it.'

After a few moments Sarah said, 'Yes, I see,' and was sorry it wasn't true that they committed suicide, even though for some time now she had ceased to believe old Dost Mohammed's story and in the practical experiment he conducted in support of it. She admired intelligence and courage because she often felt herself to be lacking in both; and it had always seemed to her that the small black scorpion found in the servants' quarters at No. 3 Kabul road,

[79

Ranpur, had shown intelligence and courage of a high order; intelligence enough to know that it could never set about escaping without burning itself painfully to death, courage enough to make a voluntary end of it by inflicting on its own body the paralysing stab it knew would kill it. Sarah admired soldiers of ancient times who fell on their swords because they had lost a battle. She had a childhood nightmare of her father losing a battle one day and deciding to fall on his, or shoot himself, to avoid being captured.

Now that Aunty Mabel had confirmed what she already suspected about the death of the scorpion she was able to link one truth with the other: which was that the last thing she would want her father to do if he lost a battle was fall on his sword. It was an awfully impractical thing to do. And it would be impractical of the scorpion to kill itself. After all the fire might go out, or be doused by rain. It was more practical of the scorpion to attempt to survive by darting its venomous tail in the direction of what surrounded it and was rapidly killing it. Just as brave too. Perhaps braver. After all there was a saying: Never say die.

In the kitchen where Mrs Bailey was cutting cucumber sandwiches and watching the kettle Sarah had her hand seen to. After tea, which the family had in the drawing-room with all the windows open on to the flagged terrace that overlooked the garden, Susan sat in the window-seat reading one of her mother's magazines, and Sarah went upstairs to their bedroom. She sat in a window-seat too, which had a view across to Mr Birtwhistle's meadow. She had a pencil and an exercise book and drew a family tree, beginning with great-grandpa.

She had no idea why she drew the family tree but doing it made her feel better. It gave her a sense of belonging and of the extraordinary capacity families had for surviving and passing themselves on and handing things down. She extended the tree by mapping in what she described to herself as the Muir branch: giving her mother the two sisters Mrs Layton was entitled to (Aunt Fenny and Aunt Lydia, with their respective husbands, Uncle Arthur and Uncle Frank) and the parents they were entitled to, General and Mrs Muir. She and Susan were entitled to them too. They had Muir blood in their veins as well as Layton blood. At Christmas Aunt Lydia and Uncle Frank always took them up to Scotland where General and Mrs Muir lived in retirement. Sarah did not like

Scotland. It was cold and craggy. Before her mother and father sailed back to India they were going up to Scotland too, but she and Susan weren't going with them. They were going back to Aunt Lydia's in Bayswater. Aunt Lydia and Uncle Frank had not come down for the funeral but had sent flowers. In her heart of hearts (as she put it to herself) she had never really taken to Aunt Lydia but had done her best not to show it because Susan didn't like Aunt Lydia much either and between them, Sarah felt, they could have made life miserable for themselves by exaggerating the things about Aunt Lydia they didn't like and were in mutual agreement about, and minimizing the things about her which they – Sarah anyway – did like.

When she analysed the pros and cons of Aunt Lydia she knew that it was Aunt Lydia's dislike of India that stood in the way of her feeling affection for her. She took a red and blue pencil and drew a red ring round her Indian relatives on the family tree and a blue ring round her English relatives. Great-grandpa had a blue ring and so did Uncle Frank and Aunt Lydia (although Aunt Lydia had spent eighteen months in India after the war). There was a warming preponderance of red crayon on the tree.

'That is my heritage,' Sarah said, then noticed that so far she had put no ring at all round Aunty Mabel. She put down the red pencil to pick up the blue and then paused.

'Why ever was I going to do that?' she asked herself. And retrieved the red pencil, ringed Aunty Mabel firmly with that fiery colour; the one denoting the Indian connexion.

*

Six years later in the July of 1939 she came across the exercise book among other relics of her childhood that had been packed in a leather trunk and stored in Aunt Lydia's glory-hole. She sorted the trunk out now to make sure that nothing was worth saving from the bonfire – an incinerator, actually, at the far end of the untended weedy walled enclosure that Aunt Lydia called a garden – worth saving from the holocaust into which her English years were being thrown and causing her a degree of pain at separation she had not expected.

She sorted the contents of the trunk on a day when Aunt Lydia was out shopping with Susan and Aunt Fenny who was back again with Uncle Arthur from India. Susan was buying clothes for the tropics. Sarah thought that buying clothes for the tropics in Kensington was a waste of time. But Susan had set her heart on a topee with a veil swathed round its crown and hanging over the brim at the back to give extra shade to the neck; and on white shirts and jodhpurs to complete the outfit. Wearing these she would look like the heroine in The Garden of Allah. She also wanted some dresses in silk and georgette (which would be sweaty). And a shooting stick. And anything else that caught her eye and further excited the image she had of herself as a young girl – dressed and ready for a romantic encounter in an outpost of empire – whose father was a lieutenant-colonel, recently appointed to the command of the first battalion of his old regiment, the Pankot Rifles, and destined, no doubt, if there were a war – which seemed likely – to become a brigadier and then a major-general.

Possibly, she thought, the difference between herself and Susan was that Susan was capable of absorbing things into her system without really thinking whether they were acceptable to her or not; whereas she herself absorbed nothing without first subjecting it to scrutiny. Perhaps this was wrong. Perhaps she tried too hard to work things out. She didn't relax. She didn't have a talent for just enjoying herself, which was a pity because she must miss a lot that Susan never missed.

Finding nothing worth saving from the trunk she took the contents in several batches and several armfuls down the two flights of stairs and down the half-flight into the semi-basement and the kitchen whose door gave access to the garden.

There, on a warm July evening scented by warmed brick, bruised grass and the fumes of traffic in the park and on the Bayswater road, she set fire to the relics of a youth she did not understand but felt had given a certain set to her bones, a toughness to her skin, and caused her now (half-shielding her cheeks from the heat of the fire in the incinerator) to stand watching the conflagration as it were in her own right as a person who now inherited the conflicting attitudes of the Laytons and the Muirs, and of Aunty Mabel, and of great-grandpa who had 'gone out' on an August morning to the scent of cedars and stale flowers in vases, so that she had a vision of herself and her family as the thing she was burning, and of that thing, of that self, as an instrument of resistance and at the same time of acceptance. She could feel the heat on her bones, the heat on her skin. Within them remained the nub, the hard core of herself which the flames did not come near nor illuminate.

So I am really in darkness, she said, and this truly is the difference between myself and Susan who lives in a perpetual and recognizable light. The light that falls on Susan also falls on Aunt Fenny and Uncle Arthur. It falls, but in a way that makes different shadows, on Aunt Lydia and Uncle Frank. I do not know how it falls on Mother and Father – it is a long time since I have seen them – and I do not know who is in darkness except myself.

Two weeks later, accompanied by her sister Susan, her Aunt Fenny and her Uncle Arthur, Sarah Layton sailed back to India on the P & O.

Part Three ❦ A Wedding

HAVING HANDED young Kasim a glass of the forbidden whisky Count Bronowsky said, 'So Mrs Layton drinks, you say. Do you mean in secret?'

Ahmed, taking the glass, held it well away from his nose. He disliked the smell of alcohol. In the palace there wasn't a drop to be had except what his servant or he himself managed to smuggle into his room there. He smuggled it on principle and had trained himself to drink a certain amount every day. It disappointed him that regular tippling hadn't yet given him a real taste for it let alone made him a slave of habit. A serious drinker, and finally an alcoholic, struck him sometimes as the only thing really open to him to become in his own right.

'I don't know about in secret,' he said. 'But she begins first, finishes last and has two drinks to anybody else's one. Also I've noticed that her behaviour is erratic.'

Bronowsky limped from the liquor trolley to the larger of the two cane armchairs that had been placed on the veranda, with a view on to the dark garden. He sat, settled his lame left leg on the footstool, raised his glass and looked at Ahmed with his right eye. The left leg and the blind left eye – covered by a black patch whose elastic, pitched at an angle, was countersunk by long use in a ring round his narrow head – were said to be the result of getting half blown-up in pre-revolutionary St Petersburg by an anarchist while driving along Nevsky Prospect to the Winter Palace.

'In what way erratic?'

Ahmed sat in the other chair and watched the Count select and light one of the gold-tipped cigarettes that came in rainbow colours from a shop in Bombay.

'She is irritable one moment, almost friendly at another. The almost friendliness occurs when she has a glass in her hand.'

'Her husband is a prisoner of war in Germany, you said?'

'Yes.'

'Is she still attractive would you say?'

'Her hair is not grey. She frequently powders her nose.'

'Ah — Her sister, this Mrs Grace, she is also erratic?'

'No. She is perfectly predictable. You can depend on her to be rude at any time. And she does not trouble to lower her voice.'

'Dear boy, what have you overheard her saying about you?'

Ahmed smiled. 'It seems I am quite efficient for an Indian.'

'But it was a compliment.'

'I would also make a good *maître d'hôtel* if I didn't stink so abominably of garlic.'

'I doubt Mrs Grace would know a good *maître* from a bad one. The English seldom do. But she meant well. And you *do*.'

'Garlic strengthens the constitution. My father used to carry an onion in his pocket to ward off colds. But that was mere superstition. Eating garlic is scientific. Also garlic is stronger on the breath than the smell of whisky. So you see it has its religious and social uses too.'

From a quarter mile or so away the drumming resumed. A Hindu wedding feast. Ahmed kept time on the arm of the chair with the fingers of his free hand. During Ramadan such a noisy manifestation of Hindu gaiety could cause communal trouble. He almost welcomed the prospect.

Bronowsky eased and re-settled the stiff lame leg. 'Tell me about the two Miss Laytons. Are they more to your taste? The one who is to be married – begin with her.'

'What an inquisitive man you are!' Ahmed thought. He was not inquisitive himself. To him people were remote, people and things and the ideas they seemed to find electrifying. But he quite enjoyed these regular sessions with Bronowsky, partly because the old wazir had taken him up as if he were someone worth giving time to, but mostly because Bronowsky's endless curiosity about other people helped him to form opinions about them himself, to consider them with greater objectivity and interest than he felt when actually dealing with them. The exercise, he found, enabled him to peel off a layer or two of his own incuriosity. True, when the sessions were over, he usually felt those layers thickening up again and was likely to tell himself that Bronowsky encouraged him to call and chatter mainly because he preferred (or was suspected of preferring) above all other the company of young men. Nevertheless each session left a residual grain of involvement.

'Oh, Miss Layton,' he said, and conjured a picture of Susan Layton holding a length of white material up under her chin and hectic-coloured cheeks. 'People do things for her. She must have trained them to think she can't do them for herself. Every time she lifts a finger to do something on her own she makes it look like an attempt at the impossible. People come running. It's not just the wedding, I think. She has probably always been the centre of attraction.'

'Is she fond of this Captain Bingham?'

Ahmed thought. How could he judge? He did not really know what fond was. His father was fond of his mother. His brother had been fond of the army. He himself was fond of chewing cloves of garlic. Bronowsky was fond of gossip. Fond seemed to be a combination of impulse, appetite and gratification. But even that didn't define it properly. He himself, for instance, had an impulse to make love to girls. He visited prostitutes. He had acquired a taste for sexual intercourse and had gratified it not infrequently. He was therefore, he supposed, fond of copulating as well as of eating garlic, but this was not what the world meant by fond or Count Bronowsky meant when he asked if the younger Miss Layton was fond of Captain Bingham. That kind of fond hinted at a capacity for denying yourself if self-denial was for the good of what you were fond of. He did not think Miss Layton had this capacity.

He said, 'No. I don't imagine she is really *fond* of Captain Bingham.'

'You mean it is merely a physical attraction?'

'On his part, yes. He is more attracted to her than she is to him.'

'How do you know?'

'I think, when he touches her, instead of being agitated she is irritated. Especially if she has her mind on the cut of a dress.'

'Embarrassment,' Bronowsky said. 'Obviously, what you saw was her reaction to a tender gesture made in front of others. The English are very shy of their sexuality. If you were a fly on the wall and saw Miss Layton and Captain Bingham together you might be surprised. Even shocked.'

Ahmed said nothing. He had been a fly on the wall; or rather an un-noticed figure rounding a corner of the guest-house veranda where Miss Layton stood, holding up the length of white material, reacting rather violently to Captain Bingham's two waist-embracing arms and saying, 'Oh, Teddie, for God's sake.' Which was interesting and quite contrary to Bronowsky's supposition, because in public Miss Susan Layton submitted to Captain Bingham's protective and possessive touch with equanimity, even with approval, in fact with an air of demanding it quite frequently as if it were due to her at regular intervals. And she was no less eager in such circumstances to give as well as receive a caress. Only when they were alone, apparently, did the exchange of caresses become distasteful. Fortunately for him he had not been seen on the occasion of the breaking away from Captain Bingham.

'What are you thinking?' Bronowsky asked.

Ahmed smiled, took another sip of the whisky, and said, 'Of being a fly on the wall.'

'Does the idea appeal?'

'Flies on walls sometimes get swatted.'

'Every occupation has its hazards. Tell me about the younger sister, the Miss Layton who isn't to be married.'

'But she isn't the younger.'

'Ah. That is always interesting. I imagine she isn't as pretty. But perhaps more serious-minded?'

'She asks a lot of questions.'

'Questions about what?'

'The administration in Mirat. Native customs. Local history.'

'Is she so very plain then?'

'I find all white girls unattractive. They look only half-finished. When they have fair hair they look even more unnatural.'

'She is fair, then?'

'Yes. And to an Englishman probably as attractive as her sister. And she is better-natured. Is that dangerous?'

'Why?'

'I understand it can be. This kind of English person invites our confidence. They ask questions, at first of a general nature, then of a more intimate kind. You think, well, he is interested, she wishes to be friends. But it is a trap. One wrong move, one hint of familiarity on your part, and snap. It shuts.'

'So says Professor Nair no doubt.'

'But don't you agree? I am asking you. I have no experience. It is what I've been told, not only by Professor Nair. Snap.'

'What are you really asking me? Whether you should be careful how you answer these fascinating intimate questions you anticipate Miss Layton asking you?'

'No. I am always careful. I was only asking your opinion of the belief generally held.'

'What belief?'

'That the friendly English are more dangerous than the rude ones.'

'Are you sure you mean English? Not white? Am I dangerous?'

'Oh, you are the most dangerous man in Mirat. Everybody says so. It goes without saying. One risks everything just talking to you. But then you are exceptional in every way, and I meant English, not white. If we had been subjugated by the Russians I would have said Russians. It isn't the whiteness that matters. It's the position of the English as rulers that makes their friendship dangerous. Dangerous on two counts. It weakens our resolve to defy them and it is against their own clan instincts. They are consciously or subconsciously aware of weakening their position by friendliness, so this friendliness always has to be on their own guarded terms. If we unwittingly think of it as mutual and go too far they are doubly incensed, first as individuals who feel they have been taken what they call advantage of, secondly as members of a class they fear they may have betrayed by their own thoughtless stupidity. Then, snap! They are indifferent to the effect of such a situation on us.'

'Is that what you believe?'

'It's what I am told. People are always warning us. It is well known. Fortunately, unlike my father I have never felt the urge to make friends with any Englishman, or Englishwoman. But it is interesting to observe them. It is interesting to come across one of the friendly ones, like the elder Miss Layton. It is like being a student of chemistry, knowing a formula, waiting to see it proved in a laboratory test.'

'Your glass is empty. Help yourself.'

Ahmed got up to do so. Bronowsky held his own glass out as Ahmed was passing him. Ahmed took it, but for a moment the older man retained his own hold on it.

'Have you kept your promise to me and written to your father?'

'No.'

'Why not?'

'The same reason as always. I begin writing and stop, there isn't anything to say, and even if there were every word would be read by someone else before the letter reached him. It is very off-putting. I write to my mother. She tells him what I am doing.'

'It isn't the same.'

Ahmed, in possession of Bronowsky's glass, went to the drinks trolley and poured generous measures of White Horse: two fingers for himself, three for Bronowsky. He filled both glasses almost to the brim with soda-water and came back to the chair where Bronowsky sat looking up with his good eye half shut as if measuring an effect. Ahmed offered him the replenished glass, but Bronowsky did not take it immediately.

'It isn't the same,' he repeated. 'Is it?'

'No, but he's used to the idea that I'm a disappointing sort of son.'

Bronowsky now grasped the base of the tumbler and when Ahmed felt it held securely he let go.

'You are more used to it than he is,' Bronowsky said. 'I think the idea that you're a disappointment to him has become your basic security. You'd feel lost without it. You know, dear boy, the most disturbing thing that happened to me when I was about your age was discovering that my father approved a particular step I proposed to take.'

'What step was that?'

'Marriage. The girl was my cousin, we weren't in love, but she would probably have made me a good wife and we always got on well enough together. I decided on marriage because I thought my father particularly disliked her. I anticipated the most vigorous opposition. Instead he embraced me. He almost wept. Really very alarming. I cooled off the idea at once. I felt some regret, of course. Perhaps I loved her after all. But I felt better directly I told him I'd changed my mind. He turned away without a word, but with his old comforting look of utter disdain. I felt secure again and never again felt insecure until he died. Then I had to earn his posthumous disapproval in a variety of ways, doing things I felt he would despise me for. Making liberal gestures rather popular at the time among intellectual landowners. Not gestures I had my heart in, but then you don't need your heart in good to do it. I did the right thing for the wrong reasons, which is what you are doing, efficiently carrying out the job you are paid for, even earning the approbation of the ungracious Mrs Grace. But you are carrying it out well because you think your father disapproved of your taking it and would be ashamed to know that a woman like Mrs Grace described you as a potentially first-rate hotel manager. You want him to be ashamed because his being ashamed of you is what you understand. You feel exactly the same about it as another boy might feel about his father being proud of him. Determined to keep it up. But the question you should ask yourself is whether he is ashamed. Has he ever been? Isn't it truer to say you grew up in a household where clear views were held on a number of questions that concern India, that you expected to inherit this clarity as you might inherit a share of the household goods and chattels and were startled to find you didn't. Startled is the wrong word. It was obviously a much slower process. But the upshot of it all was compensation for feelings of inadequacy, transference of your disappointment. You imagined the disappointment was your father's. But perhaps the truth was that he observed your struggles to take an interest with affection and compassion but didn't know how to help you. You didn't make things easier by withdrawing from him although what you were really doing was withdrawing from yourself. It's because you are fond of him that you don't write to him in prison.'

Ahmed smiled.

'You shouldn't be afraid of your emotions,' Bronowsky continued. 'In any case to be afraid of them is un-Indian. Now there's a danger for you if you like. You young men ought to watch out for it — losing your Indian-ness. It's a land of extremes, after all, it needs men with extremes of temperament. All this Western sophistication, plus the non-Western cult of non-violence, is utterly unnatural. One without the other might do but the combination of the two strikes me as disastrous. After all the sophistication of the West is only a veneer. Underneath it we are a violent people. But you Indians see no deeper than our surface. Add to that the non-violence cult and the result is emasculation.'

Ahmed grinned. Bronowsky said, 'Fornication can be a refuge as well as an entertainment. Your visits to the Chandi Chowk are no proof of your masculinity, dear boy.'

'Oh well, what am I to do? Raise an army to release the prisoners in the Fort at Premanagar?'

'You could do worse. In fact I can think of nothing more splendid. It interests me that it's the first thing that occurs to you. Such a passionate idea. How could the world fail to respond to it? It's what sons are for, to lead armies to deliver their fathers from fortresses. The British would lock you up for ever. They would laugh as well, of course, because projects obviously doomed to failure have their comical side, but they would laugh un-maliciously. They would respect you. On the other hand if you announced your intention to fast unto death if they didn't release your father they'd let you get on with it. They'd feed you forcibly. They'd be furious with you for attempting moral blackmail. I must say I'd sympathize with them. Non-violence is ridiculous. I'm not in favour of it. Can you stay to dinner?'

'No, I had a sudden invitation from Professor Nair.'

'What is he up to?'

'Nothing he tells me about.'

'Perhaps you don't listen hard enough. He's always up to something. Nawab Sahib expects to be kept informed. He will be back on Friday, incidentally.'

'Did you enjoy your visit to Gopalakand?'

'It was amusing. I left Nawab Sahib to enjoy himself a few days longer. He will be pleased with poems of Gaffur. Which of them thought of it?'

'I don't know.'

'Have they been into the palace?'

'I took them over the public rooms this morning. Will Nawab Sahib be going to the reception?'

'He will if I say so. I think I shall say so. What is arranged for tomorrow?'

'They are going shopping again. But in the morning before breakfast Miss Layton wants to ride.'

'Which Miss Layton?'

'The inquisitive one. Miss Sarah.'

'Alone?'

'I'm expected to ride with her I think.' Ahmed sipped his whisky. 'I shall keep a respectful few paces behind, naturally.'

'Do you think she has her mother's permission, or that of this Captain Bingham?'

'I didn't ask. I exist to carry out orders.'

'Don't be upset if you find you've got up early and had horses saddled for nothing. Her mother or Captain Bingham might veto her little jaunt if she's arranged it without mentioning it and they find out about it.'

'Oh, I shan't be upset.'

'Who else is there in the wedding party?'

'A Major Grace is arriving on Friday. He is the bride's uncle.

Captain Bingham's friend sometimes visits – a Captain Merrick. He will be best man.'

'Merrick?'

'Yes. Do you know him?'

'I don't think so. Merrick. A vaguely familiar name. But in some other connexion —? Well, you'd better be off if you're dining with Nair.'

Ahmed drained his glass and returned it to the trolley. 'Thanks for the drink,' he said, and stood for a moment looking down at Bronowsky, who never shook hands or exchanged formal greetings or farewells with people he looked upon as intimates. For a man of nearly seventy, Ahmed thought, he had worn very well. His face was unlined, his complexion pink. In the early years of his administration as chief minister in Mirat the anti-Bronowsky faction – said to have been headed by the late Begum – had nearly succeeded in poisoning him. His rows with the Nawab were almost legendary. They still occurred. But his influence over the Nawab was now thought to be complete.

Ahmed himself owed his position at the court to Bronowsky although it had taken some time for this to become clear to him. Originally he had thought it was the Nawab who had the notion of taking under his wing the unsatisfactory younger son of a distant but distinguished kinsman, a boy who had failed abysmally at college and showed no aptitude for any career of the kind open to a Kasim of the Ranpur branch: law, politics, the civil service. True, it was Bronowsky who had written the letters and even visited Ranpur but he appeared to do so in the capacity of agent, not principal, and gave no impression of himself caring one way or the other about the outcome of the Nawab's invitation. To Ahmed that invitation looked like one founded on charity rather than on interest and he believed it looked like that to his father, with whom discussion had been brief. His father was then still head of the provincial ministry, a busy man, and a worried man, almost entirely wrapped in the business of protesting the Viceroy's declaration of war on Germany without prior consultation with Indian leaders. By the time Ahmed reached Mirat his father, following Congress instructions, had resigned.

But, 'Well, *you* are safe,' the Nawab had said to Ahmed when they had news of M A K's arrest in 1942. 'You are under our protection. For this you must thank Count Bronowsky.' Why

Bronowsky? Ahmed asked; and learned that it was the wazir's idea, not the Nawab's, that he should come to Mirat to learn something about the administration of a Native State. 'While you have been here,' the Nawab continued, 'you will have heard many adverse things about Bronowsky Sahib. It is not unknown for me to think and say adverse things about him myself. What you should know about him, however, is that his loyalty to the House of Kasim is without parallel even among Kasims, and that it is the future of the House he always thinks of.'

It was a loyalty Ahmed had not got the measure of, and he did not understand where he fitted in with whatever Bronowsky saw as the pattern of a scheme to promote the interests of Kasims. In the past year he had been aware of Bronowsky's appraisal; before that Bronowsky had scarcely taken any notice of him. His duties had been of an almost menial clerical kind, those of dogsbody to one official's secretary after another. The officials had grandiloquent titles. Ahmed had worked under the secretary to the Minister for Finance, under the secretary to the Minister for Education, under the secretary to the Minister for Public Works, under the secretary to the Minister for Health, under the chief clerk to the Attorney-General. Most of these ministers were related to the Nawab, two bore the name of Kasim. All were nominated by the Nawab and served as members of his Council of State.

The Council of State was Bronowsky's brain-child. In the twenty years of his administration he had transformed Mirat from a feudal autocracy where Ruler met ruled only at periodical durbars into a miniature semi-democratic state where the durbars still took place but where the machinery of government was brought out of the dark recesses of rooms and passages in the palace into, comparatively, the light of day.

He had separated the judiciary from the executive, reframed the criminal and civil legal codes, created the position of Chief Justice and during his chief ministership so far always succeeded in appointing to it a man from outside Mirat whose impartiality could be counted on – in one case an Englishman just retired from the bench of a provincial High Court of British India. Bronowsky had done all these things with the minimum of overt opposition because it was to do them that the Nawab brought him back from Monte Carlo in 1921. 'I must be a modern state,' the Nawab was reported saying. 'Make me modern.' What Bronowsky did by way of making the Nawab of Mirat modern was also the means by which he gradually cut the ground from under the feet of British officials of the Political Department who objected to the appointment of a 'bloody *émigré* Russian' as chief minister of a state with which, small as it was, they had always had what they felt to be a special relationship. For all they knew Bronowsky was a red, a spy, a man who would cause trouble and feather his nest at the same time.

The Resident at Gopalakand who advised the Nawab of Mirat as well as the Maharajah of Gopalakand had protested the appointment of Bronowsky and the sacking of the Nawab's brother to make room for him. Before the present Nawab succeeded as Ruler the British had thought badly of him, had favoured the brother who struck them as altogether more amiable, a more malleable, more temperate man – not given as the heir apparent was given to wild and extravagant behaviour with money and women. The ruler in those days, the present Nawab's father, was anxious for nothing so much as to live in peace with the representatives of the paramount power. He listened attentively to their stern warnings about his elder son's sowing of wild oats, reacted as they intended he should react to hints that if the boy didn't mend his ways he would never be thought fit to rule Mirat – whereas the old Nawab's second son was a model of a young prince. Such a model son, succeeding, would certainly be confirmed by the King-Emperor's agents. In his case there would be no danger of an interregnum, no danger of Mirat's affairs coming under the direct control of the political department. The old man began to manœuvre for a position from which he could effectively disinherit his elder son in favour of the younger. The elder got wind of the plot, but it was luck that came to his rescue, luck in the shape of a proposal for marriage with the daughter of the ruler of a less ancient but far more powerful state with whom the British had an even closer relationship. The old Nawab was flattered. He attempted to arrange the alliance, but through the marriage of the girl to his younger son. The girl would have none of it. She had seen the man she wanted, through the zenana screen at a wedding celebration. The marriage took place as she wished. The old Nawab – and the British too – hoped that perhaps the marriage would see the end of the elder son's extravagances. It did not. He had only married the girl to secure his inheritance. The British, he knew, would never dare depose him now because to do so would outrage and insult the powerful father-in-law he had so fortunately acquired. When his father died he was confirmed in the succession. His Begum, headstrong as an unmarried girl became intolerable as his wife. He hated her. He hated the brother who had tried to steal his inheritance and who now, following the tradition, had become his chief minister – and a lickspittle of the British. The Nawab took mistresses, eventually a white woman. The scandal had begun. Out of the scandal Bronowsky emerged.

'Well, good night,' Ahmed said. Bronowsky said nothing, until Ahmed was at the bottom of the veranda steps, putting on his bicycle clips.

'Give my felicitations to Professor Nair,' he called. 'And be sure to mention the fact that you are going riding alone tomorrow with one of the Miss Laytons.'

'Why?'

'He will advise you more satisfactorily than I how to comport yourself, how to interpret accurately and safely her many little gestures and inflexions of voice which you might be in danger of misinterpreting. He will speak of such things as he speaks of all things – from the vast fund of his experience.'

Ahmed smiled, took his bicycle from the rack and prepared to mount.

'Oh and one other thing,' Bronowsky said, lowering his voice but enunciating carefully. 'Find out what you can about his visitor.'

'Has he got a visitor, then?'

'Yes. Two. A woman not identified and an elderly scholar by name of Pandit Baba Sahib. He comes from Mayapore. The question is, for what purpose?'

'Must there be a special one?'

'Professor Nair's visitors usually have a purpose, or if they don't have one when they arrive they have one when they go home.'

'Considering you only returned from Gopalakand today you're well informed.'

'I pay to be. And Pandit Baba is not unknown to us in Mirat. Have you had enough whisky to see you through an evening of fruit juice?'

'I think I shall manage.'

'Have a good time then, dear boy. And take care if you are tempted to come home by way of the Chandi Chowk.'

Ahmed waved, mounted and rode down the gravel drive of

Bronowsky's bungalow to the gate which the watchman – already muffled in a shawl and armed with a stick – held open for him. Outside, he turned right, pedalled along the metalled road towards the city. To his left stretched the expanse of open ground which separated the City from the palace. Soft warm airs blew across it. The moon whose first appearance had ushered in the month of Ramadan was nearly full. It hung above the city, not giving much light, the shape and colour of an orange. It would wax and wane and become invisible. Its slender reappearance would announce the Íd. During this month more than 1,300 years ago it was said that the Koran had been revealed by Allah to his Prophet. A good Muslim was supposed to fast from sunrise to sunset. Ahmed, remembering the whisky, stopped pedalling, stood astride and felt in his pocket for the clove of garlic. He popped it into his mouth and crunched, resumed his journey. The road was unlit, his cycle lamp out of order, but the night was luminous and he liked cycling in the dark. It could be a risky business and he preferred activities that had an element of danger in them, so long as the activities themselves were of a commonplace kind and only dangerous by virtue of some extraneous circumstance. Riding a bicycle in the dark or a horse over rough country were one thing, deliberately courting danger was another. To Ahmed, the kind of danger that added spice to a situation was danger that came suddenly and unexpectedly; only so could it retain what he thought of as essential to it: spontaneity, or mystery, or both. He had once suggested to Professor Nair that his attitude to danger could be summed up by describing it as one that distinguished between the danger to a man who joined a riot and the danger to a man who found himself involved in one in the course of moving peaceably between point a and point b. Ahmed had experienced both kinds of danger as a student. It was the unexpected riot he enjoyed. 'One did not feel,' he told Nair, 'that one had to take sides, one merely hit out in one's own defence, and there wasn't any moral problem to puzzle out either before or after. I was knocked off my bicycle by one faction and subjected to rescue by the other. I dished out bloody noses indiscriminately and felt fine, and nobody noticed or thought to wonder whose side I was on, so when I'd finished having my fun I just rode away and left them all to it.'

Closer in to the city the road became overhung on one side by the trees in the grounds of the Hindu Boys' College, an institution

which like the Council of State owed its existence to Count Bronowsky. Numerically in a minority, a mere twenty per cent of the
population, the Muslims of Mirat had maintained a firm grip on the
administration since the days of the Moghuls. Until Bronowsky's
day few Hindus had held any public post of any importance. There
were more mosques than temples, not because the rich Hindus of
Mirat were unready to build temples but because permission to build
was more often refused than granted. The same restrictions had
been placed on the building and endowment of schools for Hindu
boys and girls, who were generally thought to be too clever by half.
For the Muslim children an Academy of Higher Education had been
established in the late nineteenth century, but its record was poor;
there was a saying that a boy left there with no qualifications except
for reciting passages from the Koran, but that this alone was
enough to pass him into the service of an official – particularly of a
tax-collector. Until the foundation of the Hindu Boys' College in
1924, non-Muslims whose parents wanted them educated above
middle-school standards had to compete for places in colleges outside Mirat, and having left Mirat the tendency was not to return
but to seek employment in the service of the Government of India.
Muslims, jealous guardians of their own entrenched position in the
administration of the State, saw no harm in this draining of potential talent among the Hindus whose job, in their opinion, was
trading and moneylending. But Bronowsky saw harm and persuaded the Nawab to see harm too, and to allocate a modest annual
sum from the State's revenue for a college that would be open to
the sons of rich or poor Hindus. The rest of the money was provided
by prominent Hindu businessmen. The building that was erected
reflected the combination of civic pride and sense of communal
and personal grandiosity with which the money was contributed:
red brick with white facings, Gothic windows and Gothic arches.
Coconut palms were planted in the forecourt. From the beginning
it had been a success.

•

'Is that you, Ahmed?' Professor Nair called as Ahmed – having
passed the watchman at the gate of the college and walked his
bicycle off the drive that led to the main building and on to a
narrow path – came in sight of the Principal's bungalow. Nair stood

at the head of the steps, silhouetted by the light from the open door. He was dressed in his white pyjamas.

'Yes, professor,' Ahmed called back. 'Am I late?'

'Oh no. At least only by a few minutes.'

'Count Sahib is back from Gopalakand. I had to call in. He sent his regards by the way.'

Ahmed put his cycle in the rack, climbed the steps and let his hands be taken in both of Nair's. The professor stood about a foot shorter than Ahmed.

'I have an important visitor,' he whispered. 'Do you mind taking off your shoes and socks? He's an awful stickler for orthodoxies. I'm afraid he won't eat with us.'

'Who is he?' Ahmed asked, bending to untie his shoe-laces.

'Pandit Baba Sahib of Mayapore. He is writing a commentary on the Bhagavad Gita. I don't mean right now. I mean it is his principal occupation. Please don't offer to shake hands, and don't sit where your shadow will fall on him. It's all rather nerve-racking. Frankly I came out to relax. I am longing for a cigarette but daren't smoke one in case he smells it. At times like this one's bad habits come home to roost. Had Count Sahib any interesting news?'

'None that he shared with me. May I keep my socks?'

'Oh by all means. The floors get so dirty. Come. Meet Panditji. Like me he is a great admirer of your father.'

The house smelt of incense, which was unusual. Pandit Baba Sahib had probably been in Mrs Nair's puja room. That was one of the rooms in Professor Nair's house that Ahmed had never entered. In fact he had only seen two rooms, the room where they sat and talked, which was entered from the right of the square hallway, and the room where they ate, which was entered from the left. An open door at the far end of the hall gave on to a courtyard, where Mrs Nair kept a tethered goat. Ahmed gathered that other rooms, such as the bedroom, bathroom and puja room were entered from this courtyard.

When he came into the living-room – Nair stepping aside and graciously waving him on – he saw that the chairs had been removed and cushions and rugs put down in their place. Pandit Baba Sahib was seated cross-legged on one cushion, resting his left elbow on a pile of three or four. He too was dressed in pyjamas. He had a grey beard and a grey turban. A pair of steel-rimmed spectacles with circular lenses were lodged half-way down his rather stubby nose.

98]

'This is our young visitor,' Nair said. 'Son of our illustrious MAK. A young gentleman of many talents but currently Social Secretary to the Nawab Sahib.'

Panditji stared at Ahmed above the rims of his glasses. The whites of his eyes were yellow. He did not smile, he made no gesture of greeting. He simply stared. There was a certain kind of Hindu who inspired in Ahmed involuntary little twitches of distaste, the relics no doubt of the racial and religious animosity his own forbears had felt towards the forbears of men like Pandit Baba Sahib. It was no hardship to him to keep his distance or to stand where even his shadow could not reach the figure on the cushions who had made no attempt to acknowledge Nair's introduction and continued to stare up with an expression Ahmed would have thought genuinely disapproving had he not guessed it was probably an expression that Pandit Baba assumed automatically when meeting strangers, especially if the stranger was young. Ahmed gazed back, with Nair at his side still holding him by the elbow.

Presently Pandit Baba spoke. He had a high light voice. He spoke in Hindi.

'You do not look like your father.'

'Oh, you know him,' Ahmed said, but in English. 'Most people would agree with you. They say I take after my mother. Personally I never see any resemblance in myself to any member of my family.'

Pandit Baba frowned.

'Why do you answer me, and at such length, in a foreign language?'

'Because I speak Hindi rather badly.'

'You wish us to converse in Urdu?' Panditji asked, switching to it.

'I should prefer English, Pandit Sahib. It's the language we always speak at home. My mother is a Punjabi you see, and English was the only language she had in common with my father. Even in Urdu I express myself poorly.'

'Do you not feel shame to speak always in the language of a foreign power, the language of your father's jailers?' Pandit Baba asked – reverting to Hindi. At any moment Ahmed expected a bit of Bengali, a sentence or two in Tamil, perhaps a passage in Sanskrit. The Pandit was obviously proud of his facility. His refusal so far to speak in English did not mean he spoke it badly or was not proud of understanding and being able to speak it; but it was fashionable among Hindus of Baba's kind to decry it, to declare that once the British had been got rid of their language must go with them; although what would be put in its place it was difficult to tell. Even Pandit Baba Sahib would fare badly if he went out into some of the villages around Mirat and tried to understand what was said to him. He would need an interpreter, as most officials did. And the odds were the interpreter would interpret the local dialect in the language and idiom of the British.

'No,' Ahmed said. 'I'm not ashamed.'

'*Baitho,*' Professor Nair interrupted, and squatted on a cushion, motioning Ahmed to follow suit, which he did. His trousers made it an uncomfortable operation. Pandit Baba scrutinized him, this time through the lenses of his spectacles. The Pandit – Ahmed now saw – was sitting on a double thickness of cushions. His was a commanding position.

'I do not know your father in person, only I am admiring him from the distance,' he said suddenly, in English, 'and familiarizing myself to his photographs. It is a face after all much known in newspapers.'

Ahmed nodded. Pandit Baba, having spoken, subjected Ahmed to further scrutiny. It was extraordinary, Ahmed thought, how men distinguished in one field – and he assumed that Pandit Baba Sahib was distinguished – seemed to claim for themselves wisdom in all spheres of human activity; wisdom and the right to make pronouncements which they expected you to listen to and learn from. The most amusing thing was to see a group of distinguished men together, with no one but each other to make pronouncements to. They were as suspicious of each other, then, as children. He had seen such gatherings in his father's house while – outside the compound walls – crowds waited in patient homage, or simple curiosity, for a sight of these extraordinary, benign and powerful faces, and he had observed the change that came over those faces when they parted company with each other and went out to meet the crowds. He thought that if Pandit Baba smiled now he would look like them, as they came from the house to the veranda, their games, sulks, quarrels temporarily suspended, and their suspicions making way for feelings of relief and pleasure at re-entering a familiar world whose plaudits reaffirmed the huge capacity they believed they had, individually and collectively, to solve its problems, its

100]

mysteries and its injustices. Perhaps (Ahmed thought, still meeting Pandit Baba's apparently unwinking gaze) it was his early experience of distinguished men that had led him to feel that there was distance between himself and other people and their ideas. Gandhi had once given him an orange, Pandit Nehru had patted his head, and Maulana Azad had taken him on to his knee; but oranges, head-pats and knee-rides – as he realized even at the time – were not the objects of those visitations, and the visitations themselves although promising excitement always left the excitement on the other side of the wall where the crowds waited. 'Why do they wait?' he had asked his elder brother Sayed. 'Because they know we are saving India,' came the steady reply. As a boy Sayed had been a bit of a bore. 'Saving India from what?' Ahmed asked. 'Well, from the British of course.' But in the morning, as he went to school, he noticed that the British were still there and looking quite unperturbed. When he got to school he found there weren't to be any lessons because the teachers and the older boys were on strike to protest the arrest the previous night of people who had been carried away with enthusiasm at the sight of the Mahatma visiting Ahmed's father, and – after seeing the Mahatma off at the station – had got out of hand and thrown brickbats at the police who were jostling them, hitting them with lathis and treading them under horse-hoof. Two days later his father was arrested too – for making the speech the Mahatma had asked him to make – and was in prison – that time – for six months.

'Speak what is in your mind,' Pandit Baba commanded. What insolence, Ahmed thought. There are two categories of things in my mind, he should say, the stuff people like you have fed into it and my own reactions to that stuff. The result is cancellation, so I have nothing in my mind.

'I was thinking of my father in prison,' he said. After a moment or two the miracle happened. The Pandit's lips lifted at the corners. He was bestowing a smile of sympathy and of elderly approval of a young man's filial regard. Ahmed considered its quality; it struck him as no less dishonest than the expression of disapproval. How could Pandit Baba be moved to feel either approval or disapproval when the person who was the object of it was a complete stranger to him? Well, it is this that puts me off (Ahmed told himself), this ease with which people feel emotions, or pretend to feel them.

[101

'I meant,' he continued, 'the first time, when I was quite young, a schoolboy still.'

The smile did not disappear. A man like Panditji could mesmerize you into submission, hypnotize you into regarding him as a source of spiritual comfort. It was undoubtedly his intention to try, and when you knew a man's intentions you were even more in danger of being subjected to them because to be aware of an intention somehow increased its force. I shall destroy you, one man might say to another; and at once he would have a confederate, the man himself. Ideas seemed to have a life, a power of their own. Men became slaves to them. To challenge an idea as an alternative to accepting it was to be no less a slave to it. Neither to accept nor challenge it was the most difficult thing of all; perhaps impossible. The idea of Pandit Baba as a personification of wisdom, a fount of knowledge and self-knowledge, which was presumably the idea the Pandit had of himself and worked hard at conveying, was not to be got rid of by privately or even publicly asserting that the man was probably a self-opinionated and pompous fool who relied on his venerable age and appearance to command what respect his behaviour and ideas in themselves could not.

'Do not think of it as prison,' Pandit Baba said, going back to Hindi. 'It is those who call themselves jailers who are in prison, and perhaps all of us who are outside the walls. For what is outside in one sense is inside in another. In time we must break the walls down. This duty to break them down is *our* sentence of imprisonment. To break them down will be to free ourselves *and* our jailers. And we cannot sit back and wait for the orders of release. We must write the orders ourselves.' In English he added, in case Ahmed had misunderstood, 'I speak metaphorically.'

Ahmed nodded. In India nearly everybody spoke metaphorically except the English who spoke bluntly and could make their most transparent lies look honest as a consequence; whereas any truth contained in these metaphorical rigmaroles was so deviously presented that it looked devious itself.

'You had a pleasant journey from Mayapore, Panditji?' he asked, to see how Pandit Baba would react to such a barefaced attempt to change the subject. The Pandit reacted, after a few seconds, with a vague gesture of the arm that rested on the cushions and then opened his mouth as if to continue his parable.

Ahmed said hastily, 'And is this your first visit to Mirat?'

102]

Professor Nair answered for Panditji. 'Oh no, not his first visit. Panditji was at one time living in Mirat.'

Ahmed glanced at Nair and noticed the miniscule gems of sweat encrusted on his bald domed head. It was quite cool in the room. A table-fan, set on the floor in one corner, moved its round whirring wire cage from side to side like a spectator at a slow-motion tennis match – more interested, Ahmed felt, in the conversation than he was.

'But for the last few years,' Nair was saying, but looking all the time at Pandit Baba as if the Pandit had become a museum-piece suddenly and Nair his curator, 'he has been in Mayapore.'

'Yes, I see,' Ahmed said, looking again at the Pandit – and the eyes, slightly enlarged by the spectacle lenses, that were still gazing at him. 'Then you were in Mayapore during the riots.'

'Which riots are you meaning?'

'The riots in August last year.'

Again Ahmed had to wait for a reply. Pandit Baba Sahib's sympathy had gone and his disapproval was undergoing a change. He now looked at Ahmed as if he felt he had been threatened with violence.

'You must be speaking of something that has escaped my notice,' he said at last. His heart had resumed the business of pumping cold blood. An old man like me, his expression now said, should not be put in danger of losing his temper. 'I am not remembering any riots in Mayapore in August last year.' He paused, continued. 'A riot – and since you are knowing English somewhat better than me, perhaps you will correct me or corroborate – a riot I believe according to English dictionary refers to the violent unlawful actions of unlawful assembly of people. In Mayapore and India in general only I remember spontaneous demonstrations of innocent and law-abiding people to protest against the unlawful imprisonment without trial of men such as your father, and in Mayapore, particularly, demonstrations against the unlawful arrest of innocent men accused of a crime none of them committed. If this is what you are mistakenly calling riots, then – yes – I was in Mayapore at this time, when many people suffered the consequence of resisting unlawful acts by those supposed to be in lawful authority.'

Ahmed inclined his head, a movement he had found useful in the last few years, a movement suggestive of submission without verbal acknowledgement of it. He had discovered that this combination often forced people to move from attack to defence. They felt compelled to justify the victory which had just been ambiguously conceded to them.

'It is necessary all the time to have the truth of things clearly in the mind, you see,' Pandit Baba said, 'and to speak of them in truthful terms. Loose speech leads to loose thinking. When you speak of riots you are speaking as the English speak. You must speak like an Indian, and think like an Indian.' The corners of his lips lifted again. 'I know it is not always easy. But to take only easy ways is often to end up with difficulties.'

Ahmed nodded and wondered what reason Nair had for asking him at short notice on an evening when there was another guest, a guest Nair had failed to mention in the note of invitation sent round that morning but whose presence had not escaped the notice of Bronowsky, that was to say – of Bronowsky's spies. He wondered whether he would catch a glimpse of the woman Baba had brought with him, but doubted it. It was an all-male evening. He wouldn't even see Mrs Nair.

'Professor Nair tells me you are writing a commentary on the Bhagavad Gita. Does the work go well, Panditji?'

Again the gesture of the arm that rested on the cushion. Interpreting this, now, as a cue for Professor Nair to interrupt, Ahmed looked at their host. The sweat still shone on Nair's head. He still gazed at Pandit Baba. His smile had become fixed. He said nothing. He smiled, stared and perspired. Ahmed had the feeling that if Panditji got up and left the room it would take Nair several minutes to regain his normal composure – or lack of composure: he was a restless man, usually. Surely Panditji's presence in itself wasn't as nerve-racking as Nair's almost catatonic reaction to it seemed to suggest? Ahmed looked back at Panditji and found himself still under scrutiny.

'Your father, I believe, is in the Fort at Premanagar,' Pandit Baba said.

'So people say.'

'You have no confirmation of this?'

'No.'

'You think he may be elsewhere?'

'Officially I have no information, Pandit Sahib. Unofficially it seems to be understood by people that he is, or was, in Premanagar.'

'But you are able to communicate. You write letters to him, and he writes back to you.'

'I usually communicate through my mother.'

'And the letters of course are directed through the prison authorities.'

'Of course.'

'And censored.'

'Naturally.'

'But occasionally you manage a more private kind of correspondence.'

For a while Ahmed did not answer. Eventually he said, 'I can't say whether my mother sometimes manages that. For myself the answer is no.'

'But before he went to jail, some kind of simple code was arranged, so that even a letter going through the authorities and the censor might contain some private or intimate information?'

Ahmed laughed, shook his head. Panditji raised his eyebrows.

'No such code was arranged?'

'No.'

'I am not an agent provocateur,' Panditji announced, and frowned. 'But let us talk of something else. Your father is in good health, I trust?'

'Yes, I believe so.'

'And your mother?'

'She is well, too.'

'Presumably she is not hopeful of being permitted to visit him.'

'No. She's resigned to everything. His being absent in prison is all a part of her experience of marriage.'

'You speak sadly or bitterly of that?'

Ahmed smiled. 'No. It is just the truth.'

Pandit Baba nodded. He said, 'It is perhaps more difficult for her – being of the Mohammedan faith – more difficult than for some other Congressmen's wives. Her family in the Punjab – they are perhaps more sympathetic to the policies of Mr Jinnah and the Muslim League than to those of the Congress?'

'That is correct,' Ahmed admitted.

'Since a long time, or since the political turncoating in the Punjab of Sir Sikander Hyat-Khan in 1937?'

'Perhaps, yes, since then.'

'This will no doubt be a sorrow to her, to have her husband

imprisoned, to have no family member to turn to without feeling disloyal to that husband.'

'Actually I think my mother is angry sooner than sad.'

'What makes her angry?'

'Oh, quite a lot of things. For instance she loses her temper when she hears people describe father as a show-case Muslim.'

'Show-case? What is this? I have not heard this expression.'

'It means Muslims whom the Congress chose for positions of power in order to prove to everybody that they're not a Hindu-riddled organization.'

'Ah. Yes. I see. Show-case. And so Muslims who follow Mr Jinnah and his Muslim League say that Mohammed Ali Kasim, a Congress man, is a show-case Muslim?'

'They do I suppose, but members of Congress say it as well. Members who are jealous and think such Muslims have unfair advantages because of their propaganda value.' Ahmed hesitated. 'There is of course some truth in that.'

'Truth is not divisible, Mr Kasim. There cannot be such a thing as some truth. You are meaning to say that in some cases it is true that a Muslim had unfair advantages over a Hindu in the Congress because the high command chose him for his propaganda value first and his talents second. This may or may not be true. But it cannot be a matter in which there is *some* truth.'

Ahmed again inclined his head.

'You are staying in Mirat for a week or two, Panditji?'

Pandit Baba smiled, the smile of a man willing to be sidetracked because for him all paths led eventually in the direction he intended to go. 'It will not be so long. I shall return quite soon to Mayapore, I believe.'

'Only a short holiday, then.'

'I am not taking holiday.'

'There are texts in the college library that Panditji wants to have a look at,' Professor Nair explained. He was still smiling, but in the last few seconds had wiped the sweat off his head with a folded handkerchief, had come out of the catatonic trance. 'It is to inspect these texts Panditji is honouring us with a stay,' he added, quite unnecessarily; and then, more informatively, 'but before he leaves I hope to persuade him to address our students.'

Pandit Baba closed his eyes, inclined his head modestly to the right and then to the left.

Ahmed said, 'If you live in Mayapore, Panditji, perhaps you knew that English girl, Miss Manners? One gathers her circle of friends in Mayapore wasn't exclusively English.'

'No, I did not know her personally.'

'She's dead now. She had a child. There was a notice in the newspapers.'

'It did not escape our attention, Mr Kasim.' Pandit Baba paused. 'You have some personal interest in this matter?'

'No, but it was talked about a lot at the time, and when anyone mentions Mayapore these days you automatically think of Miss Manners – and the rape in the Bibighar Gardens.'

'It is not established that there was rape. Only that there were arrests, and imprisonment without trial of suspects, imprisonment not for rape but for so-called political activities.'

'So-called?'

'So-called. How can one say definitely when nothing is made public, when there is such a convenient regulation as Defence of India Rule?'

'Do you mean that the whole affair was invented, never took place at all?'

'I did not mean this. Simply I was speaking of evidence. Clearly it was thought that rape had occurred.'

'I expect the girl thought so herself,' Ahmed could not resist saying.

'I agree that it is not an experience the victim could be in doubt about.'

'You think that perhaps *she* made it up?'

'I do not think anything, Mr Kasim. Only I am saying that to speak of the rape of Miss Manners in the Bibighar Gardens is to speak of an affair as if it had happened when it is not legally established as having happened. If you say there was rape I would not agree or disagree. Also I would not agree or disagree if you said no, there was no rape, the girl was hallucinated or lying and making up stories for one reason or another. Only I can agree if you state simply that it was generally accepted through reports and rumour that there was rape, that certain men were arrested as suspects, that presently the British attempted to hush everything up, that no case was ever brought to court, that it was said the girl herself refused to identify those arrested, that in the end there was officially no rape and no punishment for rape.'

'Did you know any of the men who were arrested, Panditji?'

'Yes. I knew. They were boys of some education.'

'Did you know the one who was friendly with Miss Manners?'

After a moment Pandit Baba said, 'You are speaking of Hari Kumar.'

'I think that was his name. Did you know Kumar?'

Again a slight pause. 'Once when he first returned from England his aunt sought my assistance to teach him Hindi. Of all these boys I knew him best. He also could only speak properly English. He was not at all a good student. He had no wish to speak his native language. He employed himself on a local newspaper that was published in English. Always he was attempting to forget that he was an Indian, because he had lived in England since earliest childhood. His father took him there when he was two years old only. He went to English public school and had English friends. He did not understand why he could not have such friends here. His father died, you see, and he had no relative but his aunt in Mayapore. She paid for his passage and gave him a roof and was kind to him, being a widow with no children. But to him she was a foreigner. All of us were foreigners to Hari Kumar. He knew only English people and English ways. Only he wanted these people and these ways. In Mayapore he could not have them. He was a most unfortunate young man. His case should be taken to heart.'

'But eventually he had one English friend, didn't he? I mean Miss Manners.'

'They were sometimes together. I do not know whether she was his friend.'

'People said they were friends and more.'

'I have no knowledge of this. I do not find it informative to take notice of idle gossip. They were sometimes together. This I can vouch for. People say she was unlike other English people. I do not know what they mean when they are saying that. English people are not mass-produced. They do not come off a factory line all looking, speaking, thinking, acting the same. Neither do we. But we are Indians and they are English. True intimacy is not possible. It is not even desirable. Only it is desirable that there should be peace between us, and this is not possible while the English retain possession of what belongs to us, because to get it back we must fight them. In fighting them we do not have to hate them. But also when we have got back from them what they have taken from us and are at peace with them this does not mean that we should love them. We can never be friends with the English, or they with us, but we need not be enemies. Men are not born equal, nor are they born brothers. The lion does not lie down with the tiger, or the crow nest with the swallow. The world is created in a diversity of phenomena and each phenomenon has its own diversity. Between mankind there may be common truth and justice and common wisdom to lead to amity. But between men there are divisions and love cannot be felt truly except by like and like. Between like and unlike there can only be tolerance, and absence of enmity – which is not at all the same thing as friendship. Perhaps the truth of this is most apparent to the Hindu who is born to understand and accept this concept of diversity.'

Ahmed waited a moment to make sure Pandit Baba had finished; then he said, 'A little while ago you said the people demonstrated against the arrest of Kumar and the others for a crime they hadn't committed, but how did they know they hadn't committed it?'

Pandit Baba smiled again.

'You are like your father in one way. You have perhaps some of his forensic skill. In a moment you plan to raise the question of riot again, you will say that it would be correct to describe the demonstrations as riots because the demonstrators had no means of knowing whether these boys were guilty or not at that time, and were only acting instinctively and therefore unlawfully, therefore riotously.'

'Isn't it a debatable point?'

'All points are debatable. But there are two things that must be taken into consideration. The first is that the demonstrations in Mayapore and the attacks on government installations were no different in main respect from similar demonstrations and attacks in other parts of the country, demonstrations against the arrest of Congress leaders – men such as your father. In Mayapore, however, there was additional weight and temper arising out of the arrests of these boys. But you see not out of the arrests as arrests but out of what quickly became known, that some of these boys were tortured and defiled by the police on the same night of their arrest in order to get them to confess. This knowledge came from the police headquarters itself, as did the knowledge that in spite of torture no confession was obtained. Some of these boys were whipped and they were forced to eat beef. They were Hindus, boys of some education.

One was Kumar. We did not think it possible that such boys could set upon and rape an English girl. Also it was believed that all they had been doing was drinking illicit liquor in a hut on the other side of the river from the Bibighar Gardens. It was in the hut that they were arrested. Kumar was not with them but they were known to the police to be acquaintances of Kumar. It was to find Kumar that the police went to the hut. The police went to find Kumar because of his association with the girl who was reported to have been raped. The head of the police in Mayapore, the English District Superintendent, he also was associated with the girl. It was the District Superintendent who personally conducted the interrogations, who ordered the boys to be beaten and forced to eat beef. All night he was there, in the police headquarters, asking them questions. Meanwhile, if there was rape, the real culprits, hooligans no doubt, made good their escape. But District Superintendent was not interested in them. Only he was interested in punishing these boys, especially Kumar, because of Kumar's association with the white girl. District Superintendent was an evil man, Mr Kasim. His cruelty and perversions were known to his men and consequently to some of us. It was one of his own Muslim constables who next morning whispered the truth to people outside, because he was ashamed of what had been done. He spoke too of a bicycle which the police found in the Bibighar Gardens when they searched there at night. It belonged to the girl. He said that District Superintendent ordered the bicycle to be put in the police truck. Later when they had arrested the boys in the hut they drove to the house where Kumar was living. District Superintendent told them to take the bicycle out of the truck and leave it in the ditch outside this house. Then they went into the house and arrested Kumar, pretended to search the area and so 'found' the bicycle and said that Kumar had stolen it from the white girl after raping her. Some of the police were thinking this was a great joke. But the man who told of these things did not think it was funny. Later, people were saying he became frightened and denied what he had secretly told. Perhaps if there had been a trial for rape he would have been persuaded to tell the truth of these things. But there was in any case no trial. District Superintendent had been too clever. Even people like Judge Menen and the Deputy Commissioner became suspicious that the wrong boys had been arrested, and Judge Menen heard the rumours of torture and defilement. He had the boys questioned but they were too frightened to say anything, we understand. Except Kumar who was not saying anything at all to anybody, and did not even seem to want to save himself. But chiefly there was no trial because Miss Manners herself was saying the men arrested could not have had anything to do with it. So now District Superintendent produced evidence that all these boys were engaged in subversive activities and no doubt the English thought it was not possible to set them free in any event. So they were imprisoned without trial under Defence of India Rule, as your father and many others are imprisoned.'

'Surely it would be difficult to produce evidence of subversive activities, Panditji, unless it was actually there?'

'Not so difficult, Mr Kasim. But no doubt in all but one case these boys had done and said things that patriotic young Indians say and do, boys of some education, and of certain temperaments. The police had files on them as they had files on many such boys. In the other case, in Kumar's case, also they had a file because once he was taken into custody for refusing to answer questions and for making difficulties about giving his proper name. Unfortunately the police officer whose questions he refused to answer was this same Englishman, the District Superintendent. If Kumar had answered District Superintendent properly, if he had said 'sir' and looked frightened and done some grovelling, District Superintendent would not have taken notice of him. But this was not Hari Kumar's way, who hated India, and wanted to be treated like an English boy, and spoke English and only English, and with what is called I understand Public School accent, and so was annoyed to be asked questions by District Superintendent who did not have such good education but expected to be treated all the time like a Sahib because of his white face. But to think of Hari Kumar engaged in subversive activities with other young Indians is to those of us who know him, Mr Kasim, only laughable. He did not like India. He did not like Indians. Only he liked England and his memories of being in England and having English friends. He was not a boy who would plot with other young Indians to get rid of the English.'

'Is he still in prison?'

'They are all still in prison, but I think not together. He is in the Kandipat jail in Ranpur, a long way from Mayapore. For many months his aunt did not know which prison they had sent him to.

Now at last she is permitted to write and to send him some food and some books. He thanks her for them but she cannot be sure that he is allowed to eat the food or read the books. I know these things because I am in her confidence. Poor lady. Her sufferings are most sad to see. She was very fond of her English nephew as she called him.'

Suddenly Pandit Baba looked at Professor Nair.

'You say nothing, my friend.'

'Oh, but I am listening with a great deal of interest. I did not know you were so closely concerned with this very interesting case.'

'Yes,' Pandit Baba said. 'It is interesting. You find this also? It is the kind of case – by which I mean the case of the arrest and punishment of six boys – the kind of case our young friend's father here would have loved to take charge of in the days when he was so illustriously practising the law and defending countrymen of his who were wrongfully accused.' He looked again at Ahmed. 'Unfortunately it is a case that can never be subjected to the searching eyes of the law. But this does not mean it should be forgotten. And it is not only in the courts that justice is done. You look hungry, Mr Kasim. Let me not keep you and Professor Nair any longer from your supper. I shall have retired before you finish, for I have some work to do, so allow me to say good night.'

Nair rose, and Ahmed – somewhat stiffly – followed suit, bowed to Panditji and followed Professor Nair out of the room and across the hall and into the dining-room. A servant who had been squatting in the doorway that led out to the compound got up, went out and shouted orders to the cook. Nair set the fan going and they sat at opposite ends of the table which was dressed Western-style.

'Do you mind vegetarian?' Professor Nair whispered. 'It's the smell of cooking you see. One has to think of everything.'

II

THE HORSES had been behaving badly. Sarah wondered whether young Mr Kasim had deliberately chosen them for their iron mouths and vicious natures or whether it had been a question of taking the best of a bad bunch from the palace stables. Her own mount, for instance, had shied twice at its early morning shadow, missed its footing on some shale and having reached the promising openness of the comparatively flat turf in the middle of the waste ground separating the palace from the city, resolutely come to a halt, stretched its neck and cropped grass. Mr Kasim, who seemed to be having difficulty restraining his own mount from surging forward in a gallop for the city gates, drew nearly level but some feet away and held it there by what looked like main force. She noted the ridged muscle on his bare forearms. The brim of his topee darkened his face and hid his expression.

'Are you a Sunni or a Shiah, Mr Kasim?' Because of the distance between them she had raised her voice. She thought she sounded like a games mistress.

'A Shiah,' Ahmed said, and wrenched his horse's head to the left to stop it closing in on Sarah's.

'Is there a great deal of difference?'

'I beg your pardon?'

'Much difference?'

Pandering to his horse to make it feel it had got its way he led it round in a tight circle and brought it to stand again in its original position.

'Not really. The Shiahs dispute the rights of the three Khalifs who succeeded Mohammed. You could say it's a political division.'

'Who are the Shiahs for?'

'What?'

'Who do they say should have succeeded Mohammed?'

'Oh. A man called Ali. He was Mohammed's son-in-law. We mourn his death at the beginning of Muharram. The Mohammedan new year. But then the Sunnis often join in the mourning too.'

'Is the Nawab a Shiah Muslim?'

'Yes.'

'Are there any Sunnis in Mirat?'

'Yes, a few.'

'I think if you rode on a bit this damned thing would stop eating grass and at least pretend to do what I want it to.'

For answer Ahmed set his horse towards her and when he was near enough reached over, took the reins from her and jerked. The horse brought its head up.

'Keep him like that,' Ahmed suggested, holding the reins in short, so that the horse's neck looked painfully arched. She slid her left hand along the reins until her fist touched Ahmed's. She could smell the garlic on his breath. Perhaps he meant her to because he had heard what her Aunt Fenny said.

'Thanks.'

She set the horse at a walk. It jerked its head continually, trying to force her to lengthen the rein. Ahmed resumed his position, a few paces behind her on her left. Obviously he had no intention of making conversation; but was it shyness, dislike or indifference? At least, she felt, you could rely on him. He'd made no bones about disciplining the horse for her and, no longer dressed in a lounge suit but instead in short-sleeved shirt and jodhpurs, he looked like a man her future brother-in-law Teddie Bingham would describe as being 'useful in a scrap', than which for Teddie there was probably no higher praise of his own sex. Muslim men, after all, did have this quality. Sarah corrected herself: not Muslim men, but Indians who were descended like Mr Kasim from Middle Eastern stock: Arabs, Persians and Turks. They had retained the sturdiness of races whom extremes of heat and cold (she was thinking of deserts) had toughened.

England's climate had also toughened her people. Years ago Sarah had written an essay with the rather grandiloquent title: The Effect of Climate and Topography upon the Human Character. The idea, she remembered, had first come to her in the summer holiday of the year great-grandpa died and she had walked across Mr Birtwhistle's field encouraging Aunt Mabel not to be put off by the cows and then stood by the brook thinking how much like Pankot in miniature her surroundings were; the year when she was struck by the difference between her Indian family and her English family. 'England,' she had written when she was a couple of years older, 'although temperate climatically speaking, combines within a very limited geographical area a diversity of weather and natural features. Such conditions react upon the inhabitants to make them strong, active, energetic and self-sufficient. It is these qualities which they take abroad with them into their tropical and subtropical colonies, lands whose native populations are inclined because of things like heat and humidity to be less strong, less active, less energetic and more willing to be led, a fact which has enabled European races in general but the English in particular to gain and keep control of such territories. Upon the return of our colonial exiles to the land of their birth they are struck by the smallness of everything and by the fact that the self-sufficiency of their race, thus re-

114]

encountered, is really the result of the self-satisfaction of a people who have had comparatively little to contend with in the human struggle against nature.' She remembered the opening paragraph almost word for word and also remembered the red-pencil comment of the headmistress in the margin, 'An interesting essay and well developed so far as the question of climatic influences is concerned. I do not fully understand your reference to topography as an influence, however, and perhaps you fail to understand it yourself, as witness your failure to develop that aspect of your argument.'

'But I do understand it,' Sarah had assured herself, 'and it's all there, she just hasn't read it.' Reading it again, though, she thought that perhaps a bit of clarification would do no harm, then that it would be a definite improvement; finally that the headmistress was right and that clarification was essential, but in her mind first and only then on paper; and in her mind the clarification obstinately refused to come. She was stuck with that single recollection of a notion that had reached her out of the blue, that the place near the brook in the spinney beyond Mr Birtwhistle's fields was like Pankot in miniature and that this somehow explained why her Indian family were not like her English family.

Over to the right of the waste ground there were a few trees and a road and facing the road a substantial bungalow behind grey stucco walls. 'Who lives there?' she asked Ahmed, holding the reins tight in one hand and pointing.

'That's Count Bronowsky's house.'

'Is he really a count?'

'Yes, I think so.'

'Dare we gallop?'

'If you'd like to.'

'Where to? To the city gates?'

'There's a nullah. We'll have to bear left and join the city gate road.'

'I don't mind nullahs.'

'It's too wide to jump.'

'Come on then.'

She dug in her heels. A moment she loved: the slight hesitation, the gathering of propulsive forces in the animal she sat astride, the first leap forward that always seemed to her like a leap into a world of unexplored delight which she could only cut a narrow channel through and which she would reach the farther end of too soon but

[115

not without experiencing on the way something of the light and mysterious pleasure that existed for creatures who broke free of their environment. Ahead she made out the broken line of the nullah and as the horse did not at once respond to movement of wrist and pressure of heel had a second or two of fear that had itself broken free into a curious region of stillness and excitement; and then the horse began veering left; a quick glance over her shoulder showed her Ahmed. She felt an extraordinary, exhilarating sense of the perfection of their common endeavour. Together they galloped along the line of the nullah and charged through the gap where the nullah petered out a few yards from the road. From here she could see the city gate, isolated relic of the city wall, and how the road led to it and had come diagonally across the waste ground from the palace. They passed through splashes of shade from the trees that lined the road, drew level with and passed a line of lumbering carts drawn by humped white oxen, and then a file of women with baskets on their heads. The air was saturated by the pale smell of centuries of dung-fire smoke. The city was close. Why, it looms, Sarah thought, I don't want it: and exerted pressure with her right heel and right wrist to bring the horse round in a fine galloping sweep. She sensed the animal's bloody-minded resistance. It seemed as if it would neither turn nor slow, but would charge mindlessly on and dash itself and her to pieces on the city of Mirat. But then she felt the slight change of rhythm and the neat little spasm of adjustment to the centre of gravity, and Mirat began to swing towards her left shoulder. She exerted pressure to slow the horse to a canter, and then to a trot. At this end of the waste ground there was a group of three banyan trees, two of them with a fine display of rooted branches. She reined in beneath the youngest of the trees and looked round. Mr Kasim had reined in too, and waited exactly as before, a few paces behind her, to her left. Such precision! She smiled at him, pleased for both of them. The smile she got in return, though, was as distant as ever. Obviously he had not shared her pleasure; instead, probably, shared her moments of dismay, wondering what blame would be put on him if she fell and was injured. In his position Teddie would have felt obliged to say, Are you all right? or, You'd better go easy on that brute. And have got himself ready to complain to the head syce when they returned to the palace; all of which – Sarah realized – would spoil the morning for her by introducing the all-too-familiar note of criticism that day in day out acted in you and on you as part of a general awareness of being in charge, of having to be prepared to throw your weight about, so that really there was nothing you could enjoy for its own sake, nothing you could give yourself over to entirely.

She looked towards the town and said, 'It's funny, Mr Kasim, but I've not once heard the muezzin since I've been here, and yet there are all those minarets.'

'The wind's been in the wrong direction, I expect.'

'They do call then?'

'Oh yes. They call.'

'Five times a day?'

'Yes.'

'Will the Id al-fitr prayers be said in the mosques or out here?'

'Out here. Why?'

'I read somewhere that they're supposed to be held in the open air if possible.'

'You must have seen such meetings before, in open places?'

'No. I don't think so. I suppose because I've only been in places where they make them stay in the mosques in case of trouble. Or perhaps I've seen them but not known what was going on.'

'Last year the Id fell during the wet season. The prayers were indoors then.'

'Why is it preferred for them to be in the open?'

Mr Kasim paused, as if considering; but he might have been reluctant to answer so many questions about his religion. She, after all, was an infidel. When the answer came, though, it suggested mockery; mockery of her and of the beliefs of his own people.

'Because of the crowds, I expect. The idea is wholly practical.'

'You mean you have to cater for all the people who never go into a mosque normally?'

'Yes,' Ahmed said. And added, 'But I'm no kind of authority. The Imam at the Abu-Q'rim mosque would probably have a different explanation.'

'When exactly will the Id fall?'

'When the new moon is seen.'

'Supposing it's cloudy?'

'Then you calculate and usually make it thirty days instead of twenty-nine or thirty after the beginning of Ramadan, to be on the safe side. But it won't be cloudy this year and of course the

[117

calculation is already made. In fact the Íd is due about a week after your sister's wedding.'

'Is it? But how nice. That means everybody will be happy.' She turned. It was uncomfortable having to sit askew in the saddle just to talk to him. She set the horse at a walk and then at a trot. Everybody will be happy. Everybody will be happy. Distantly she could see the roof of the palace. The sun was already hot and the short-lived freshness of early morning already staling. She noted the first phase of that curious phenomenon of the Indian plain, the gradual disappearance of the horizon, as if the land were expanding, stretching itself, destroying the illusion that the mind, hand and eye could stake a claim to any part that bore a real relation to the whole. It is always retreating, Sarah told herself, always making off, getting farther and farther away and leaving people and what people have built stranded. Behind her, she knew, Mr Kasim rode at a constant watchful distance, but as the land expanded it left them in relation to the horizon getting closer and closer together. She felt that a god looking down would observe this shortening of distance and wonder what it was about his lesser creations that made them huddle together when they might have emulated giants, become giant riders on giant horses. Why – Sarah cried to herself – that's how I used to feel! That's how I felt on the day of the wasp. And tried now to induce the feeling again, but failed. Well, I am full-grown, she thought, and those were growing pains. Full grown. Full grown. She persuaded the horse into a canter and thought of the men she might have married and the children she might have had since becoming full-grown, and wondered whether there was really such a thing as love and if there were what subtle influences it might have on the purely animal response, some men, but not Teddie, had wakened in her. She wondered if Teddie had awakened Susan in that way, and Susan Teddie; and envied her not for being woken but for apparently being endowed with a nature that was ready to take all the rest on trust. My trouble is, she thought, I question everything, every assumption. I'm not content to let things be, to let things happen. If I don't change that I shall never be happy.

Again they moved left to avoid the nullah which on this side did not peter out but passed under the road, through a culvert. It was shallow, though, and the banks were easy. Sarah urged her horse down into it. The clay bottom was cracked, so quickly had the post-monsoon sun dried out whatever water settled here during the

118]

rains, but there was mud still in the shadow of the culvert. The ground bore the imprint of cattle, goat and horses' hooves.

'Do you come this way, Mr Kasim, I mean when you ride alone?' she called.

She did not hear his reply clearly. It might have been 'Sometimes'. She took the rise back out of the nullah. They were now close to the house Mr Kasim said was Count Bronowsky's: newish-looking Anglo-Indian palladian, she noted; isolated in an extensive walled garden, probably built for him, by him. That sort of man knew how to feather his nest: a foreigner, a European, in the service of a native prince, a throw-back to the days of the nabobs of the old trading companies – French, English and Portuguese. She did not think she would like old Count Bronowsky, although it was said he had done fine things. Fine things for himself too, she imagined, judging by the house. She could not imagine her father retiring to live in such a place, rather to a gabled villa in Purley, or a timbered cottage in Pankot if he chose to live the rest of his days in India. People like Teddie and Susan closed their eyes to the fact that her father's generation must be the last generation of English people who would have such a choice. War or no war, it was all coming to an end, and the end could not come neatly. There would be people who had to be victims of the fact that it could not. She herself was surely one of them, and perhaps Mr Kasim too.

Suddenly she wheeled the horse round in the same kind of tight circle Mr Kasim had described before they set off on their gallop. She caught him before he had time to hang back, and so confronted him in the act of reining in, but having done so she could not find an acceptable way of explaining her impulsive action, either to him or to herself. Curiously, though, in the moment before being embarrassed at finding herself at a loss, she thought that the world might be a more interesting and useful place to live in if there were more such empty gestures as the one she had apparently made. They were only empty in the sense that there was room in them for meaning to be poured. That kind of meaning wasn't found easily. It was better, then, to leave the gesture unaccompanied. To make words up just for the sake of saying something would be incongruous. So she closed her mouth and smiled, turned her horse's head and continued on at a walk, listening to the sound that never seemed to stop between sun-up and sundown, was taken for granted and seldom heard consciously at all: the sore-throated calling of the crows.

When they returned to the guest house she saw her future brother-in-law and his best man waiting on the terrace.

'Hello,' she called. 'What a nice surprise. Are you here for breakfast?'

*

The officer Susan Layton was to marry, Teddie Bingham, was the kind of man Mrs Layton would have preferred her husband to be on hand to approve of. She had complained to Sarah that it was bad enough having to write to Colonel Layton and tell him that his youngest daughter was getting married to a man he had never heard of, could not meet and might not like, without the additional worry of searching for the right sort of phrases to convey to him the idea that in his absence she had done everything necessary to be reassured about Captain Bingham's background and found nothing amiss. She did not want to worry him. God knew he had worries of his own. Letters to a prisoner of war had to be cheerful and soothing.

'All you need tell him,' Sarah pointed out, 'is the name of Teddie's regiment and that Susan and he love each other. That's all he'll need to know. And that's all there is to tell. After all, nothing is amiss, is it?'

'There's the question of his parents. It's easier if a man has parents. All there seems to be is an uncle in Shropshire, a father in the Muzzafirabad Guides who broke his neck hunting and a mother who married again, had an unhappy time and died in Mandalay. Your Aunt Mabel says she knew some Muzzy Guides people but doesn't remember a Bingham, which is neither here nor there because she only remembers what she wants to. But it means all we've got to go on is Dick Rankin's word and Teddie himself.'

General Rankin was the Area Commander. Teddie had come to the Area Headquarters in Pankot from the staff college in Quetta. It was not a good posting for an officer who had commanded a company of the Muzzafirabad Guides in Burma, acted as second-in-command of the depleted battalion during the retreat. From Quetta he might have had a G2 appointment, or at least a posting to the

120]

staff of an active division. He admitted this himself. He hoped and believed the posting to Pankot was only temporary. The one good thing about it, he added, was that it had brought him and Susan together.

Before Susan it had brought him Sarah. She and Susan, both mustered into the Women's Auxiliary Corps, worked as clerks at Area Headquarters which had stationed itself permanently in Pankot for the duration to avoid the confusion and pressures of the yearly move from Ranpur to the hills and back again. Corporal Sarah Layton was the first of the two Layton girls he noticed, and for a time it seemed that he would prove to be the exception to the rule which, according to interested observers in Pankot, made it almost inevitable that any man first taking an interest in Sarah Layton would presently cool off her and start paying attention to Susan, who admittedly was prettier, livelier, always to be counted on to do what Pankot people described as making things go. The result was that one was never sure which group of men Susan would next be seen as the sparkling centre of, only certain that from time to time, in these groups, there would turn up a man who, briefly, had been conspicuous as a companion of her quieter, elder sister. Once he had succumbed to Susan's more obvious attractions he became one of a crowd; one ceased to notice him and, as a consequence, did not mark his disappearance. Susan, it was assumed, took none of her men seriously. They came, direct or via Sarah, danced attendance, and were replaced.

When Teddie Bingham showed signs of being Susan-proof it was to Sarah rather than to himself that he drew attention. The ladies of Pankot discussed this interesting situation over bridge, committee-teas, behind the counter of the canteen of the Regimental Institute for British soldiers of non-commissioned rank, and behind the scenes at rehearsals for their amateur theatricals. It was, they agreed, time that Sarah Layton settled down. She was all of twenty-two. She was very presentable, quite pretty, and well behaved. Her background was excellent, in fact impeccable within the context of Anglo-India in general and Pankot in particular. She was practically born in Flagstaff House (the senior ladies reminded those less well-endowed with detailed knowledge of Pankot history), her mother was a Muir, her maternal grandfather had been GOC Ranpur; her paternal grandfather had a distinguished career in the Civil, she was related by his second marriage to old Mabel

Layton, and her father – now a prisoner in Germany – had commanded the 1st Pankot Rifles in North Africa.

And, in herself, Sarah Layton was upright, honest, and, one imagined, a tower of strength to her mother. Mrs Layton, it had to be admitted, had not borne up under the strain of separation from her husband with the ease and cheerfulness one had the right to expect of a senior military wife. One found her vagueness and general air of distraction difficult to deal with. It had become an aggravating duty, where once it had been a pleasure, to partner her at bridge, for instance. She was not always meticulous about paying her losses, either. Fortunately, a hint to Sarah Layton was known to be effective. It was rumoured that native shopkeepers like Mohammed Hossain the tailor, and Jalal-ud-din, the general merchant, had taken to referring overdue accounts to Sarah as an insurance against painful accumulation. Honorary secretaries of ladies' committees on which Mrs Layton sat had become used to mentioning the dates and times of meetings to Sarah, because this seemed to be the best way of reducing the odds against Mrs Layton turning up. On top of all this, there was – how should one put it? – a tendency in Colonel Layton's lady towards over-indulgence with the bottle.

Sarah Layton, it was obvious, was the temporary rock on which the Layton household had come to rest, and it seemed unfair that her mother should be demonstrably more alert to the existence of her younger daughter. One could not exactly describe Mrs Layton's attitude to Susan as fond – one gave her credit for retaining, in public, a proper manner of emotional detachment from the affairs of her children – but if one assumed fondness behind the manner then Susan, clearly, was the favourite daughter – and seemed to know it. That she knew it was, perhaps, the one major flaw in the bright little crystal. The minor flaws – vanity and pertness – were probably marginal evidence of the existence of this major one. But one forgave her in any case. She could not help it if people were attracted to her. It would be unnatural of her to pretend this was not so and only a girl with a remarkable capacity for self-effacement would not take advantage of it.

All the same one was sorry for the comparatively – and it was only comparatively – less attractive sister. One had never doubted that eventually she would come across a man who, looking for more than a casual flirtation, would prefer the things she had to offer. What made the association between Teddie Bingham and Sarah

Layton so especially interesting to the ladies of Pankot was the fact that Teddie, in their majority opinion, was really rather good-looking; that is he was if sandy reddish hair and pale eyelashes weren't on one's personal list of things in a man one found disagreeable. The qualification was made and accepted because one lady, a Mrs Fosdick, said she was allergic to men with red hair and that she always counted pale eyelashes a sign of weakness and untrustworthiness. Another lady, a Mrs Paynton, said nonsense, pale eyelashes denoted an exceptionally amorous nature, and if that is what Mrs Fosdick meant by weakness and untrustworthiness she was all for it. The ladies smiled. Their interest in Teddie Bingham thus aroused in regard to a specific point, they turned to a reconsideration of Sarah Layton and agreed that in life it was the quiet and unassuming people who in the end surprised one most. One had to remember, too, that both the Layton girls had come back out with, as it were, the dew of maidenhood still fresh on their young faces. Parents in India, reunited with their daughters, were well aware of the attendant dangers. On any station there were never enough young girls to go round. Even the plainest poor creature might expect attention from young men fired by climate and scarcity. The girls were fired by the climate too, and the sensation of power over herds of – as it were – panting young men could easily go to their heads. The first year was the one to watch out for. A girl needed her parents then. Wise parents stood by and let a girl enjoy the illusion of having her head in the first six months. One might expect anything up to six announcements that she had met the one man in the world for her. In the second six months one had to shorten the rein because this was the period when having found and discarded six Prince Charmings she could be expected to select as a seventh a man who had shown no interest in her at all, probably because he was already spoken for and had dropped out of the game of romantic musical chairs.

When the year was up and a girl had been through a complete cycle of seasons, it was time for her parents to take a hand. It was remarkable how docile the girls became, how easily they could now be led into the right sort of match. The second year was the year of engagements and marriages; the third year was devoted to maternity. With the first grandson or grand-daughter one could sit back with a sigh of relief that one's duty had been properly done.

The war had disrupted this ideal pattern. The Layton girls, for instance, were among the last girls to come out as members of what old Anglo-Indian wags used to call the fishing-fleet. These days one only got people like nurses. On the other hand the supply of men had become a torrent of all sorts where once it had been a steady dependable flow mostly of one sort only – the right. (Pankot, for instance, was full of the most extraordinary people.) One felt, as it were, besieged. Through the smoke and confusion one tried to maintain contact. One sought the reassurance that the old nucleus was still established at the centre. It was heartening to know that the elder Layton girl seemed to have chosen a man one could describe as pukka. He was a Muzzy Guide. His father had been a Muzzy Guide. If his association with Sarah Layton developed as one hoped, one could then say that Colonel Layton's departure from the bosom of his family long before the end of that first traditionally difficult year when a girl stood in need of the steadying hand of a father as well as of the guiding hand of a mother, had not had any real ill-effect. One might congratulate Sarah Layton on her own good sense.

In this way the ladies of Pankot, at bridge, at tea, behind the counter of the canteen of the Regimental Institute and in rehearsal breaks in their production of *The Housemaster*, discussed the various ramifications of Sarah's friendship with Teddie. They seemed to have set their hearts on an engagement. One could – they said – always do with a really good wedding, and with a Layton girl involved one could expect a reception at Flagstaff House, perhaps count on the General to give the bride away. Life had become a shade drabber each successive year of the war. One was lucky if the Governor and his Lady spent more than May and June in the summer residence. Last year, 1942, when all that turmoil was going on down in the plain, there had hardly been even the shadow of a season. As for home comforts, those too were rapidly becoming a thing of the past. The influx of troops, the establishment of training camps, the departure of one's own menfolk, had driven one out of one's rightful bungalows to pig in at Smith's Hotel, the club annexe, or, if one was luckier than other grass widows, into (in Pankot idiom) grace and favour bungalows such as Mrs Layton and her daughters occupied in the vicinity of the old Pankot Rifles depot, although that meant one spent a fortune in tonga fares just to go to the club for morning coffee. By rights, the station felt,

124]

Mrs Layton and her daughters should have been living in Rose Cottage. As it was there was insufficient room there because old Mabel Layton, who had bought the cottage some time in the thirties, shared the place and expenses with Miss Batchelor, a retired missionary (and a born spinster if ever there was one) and both of them seemed destined to live for ever. On the whole, though, one envied the retired people who had their own places, although some of them had been reduced to taking in paying-guests, and as they died off the military requisitioned their bungalows for use as nurses' hostels and chummery messes.

Meanwhile, one coped and made what one could of any occasion that might briefly bring back memories of what life in India had been like before the war. In the heat generated by their expectations of the wedding, warmth was felt for the Laytons as a family and a symbol. One forgave Mrs Layton her vagueness, her forgetfulness, her understandable little indulgences. After all, she was still an attractive woman. Better a few too many chota pegs than the possible alternative.

The news that Teddie Bingham and Sarah Layton were no longer to be seen in each other's company came as a sad disappointment. Hopes that they had merely had a tiff and that a reconciliation would spur them on to a mutual declaration of affection were dashed when Teddie turned up at a club dance as a member of a trio of officers escorting Susan. It was calculated that he had more than his fair share of dances with her, including the last waltz. It was noticed that Sarah was not at the dance at all. Mrs Paynton reported an encounter with Sarah in Jalal-ud-din's shop the morning after and having received – in response to her friendly inquiry after Captain Bingham's health – an evasive reply that was barely polite. As Mrs Paynton said, Sarah Layton had always been punctilious in her observance of the rules laid down for the exchange of pleasantries – although (and perhaps the others would agree with her?) when one came to think of it she had never seemed entirely relaxed. In the present circumstances one had to make allowances. On the other hand perhaps one ought to consider more closely what it was about a girl who consistently lost men to her younger sister. Young men being what they were, nine times out of ten their desertion of Sarah in favour of Susan could be explained readily enough. But Teddie Bingham, surely, had been the one extra time, and ten out of ten suggested there was more to it than Susan's good looks and jolly temperament proving too strong as competition.

'If you ask me,' young Mrs Smalley said – and hesitated because she was never asked and had not been asked now. But she had searched for just such an occasion to make her mark with this group of her elders and betters. So, flushed but determined, she continued – 'the trouble is she doesn't really take it seriously . . .'

After an appreciable pause Mrs Paynton inquired, 'Take what seriously?'

'Any of it,' Mrs Smalley said. 'Us. India. What we're here for. I mean in spite of everything. In spite of her – well, what she was brought up to. I mean although men never talk about it they feel it, don't they? I mean in a more direct way than even we do. I think they're more sensitive than women are to, well, people – people like Sarah Layton. I believe that after a while they get a horrible feeling she's laughing at them. At all of us. Oh – I'm sorry. Perhaps I ought not to have said that . . .'

There was silence. The ladies looked at one another. Poor Mrs Smalley wished the ground would open and swallow her. She – a Smalley (for what that was worth) had criticized a Layton, in public. And had talked about – *it*. One never talked about *it*. At least not in so direct a way.

Suddenly Mrs Paynton spoke. Mrs Smalley stared at her. She thought she might have misheard. But she had not.

'My dear,' Mrs Paynton had said. 'How extremely interesting.' Now she turned to the others. 'I'm not at all sure Lucy hasn't put her finger bang on the spot.'

Trembling, Lucy Smalley accepted a cigarette from Mrs Fosdick.

'It was last year I first felt it,' she said, having been persuaded to explain in greater detail what she meant when she said Sarah Layton didn't take 'any of it' seriously. 'I mean whenever we talked about all those dreadful things that were going on in places like Mayapore.' When she said 'we' she was speaking figuratively. She had rarely ventured a word herself. Because she had not, she had had more time to watch and listen. Whenever Sarah had been present with Mrs Layton, Mrs Smalley had taken special note of her because Sarah was the one woman in the group Mrs Smalley could treat as junior to herself. 'I thought perhaps she was a bit shy, so I always made a point of talking to her. It was never anything she said, but gradually I couldn't help feeling she was thinking a lot.

I thought that sometimes she was bursting to come out with something, well, critical of us. Just as if she thought it was all our fault. And yet not, well, quite that. I mean I don't think she's a radical or anything. I think the best way I can describe it is to say that sometimes she looked at me as if I were, well, not a real person. I mean that's the reaction I had. She made me feel that everything we were saying was somehow a joke to her, the sort of joke she couldn't share.'

Again, the ladies exchanged glances. 'I think I know what you mean, Lucy,' Mrs Paynton said. 'And I think it's something like that, in the back of one's mind you know, that makes one feel even more strongly that it's time she settled down.'

The ladies agreed. Mrs Smalley was conscious that her moment of glory had passed its peak. The others, led by Mrs Paynton, now absorbed her suspicions of Sarah Layton, adapted them, and came to the conclusion that Miss Layton probably didn't mean to give people the impression of having unsound ideas and would be straightened out quickly enough if the right man came along. Perhaps Captain Bingham had been the wrong man. Things might be better for her when that little minx of a sister was married.

Three weeks later when Susan and Teddie took the station by surprise by announcing that they were to be married, Mrs Fosdick declared that a man who could woo one girl, switch his allegiance to her sister and end by marrying her was scarcely to be trusted to remain faithful for long, and that her opinion of the significance of pale·eyelashes had therefore been vindicated. The other ladies said that Captain Bingham's choice, wavering though it might seem, was proof of there being something in the Layton girls that appealed to his deepest sensibility and that his final choice as between the two of them showed up even more clearly that the elder girl, although perhaps outwardly possessed of whatever it was that appealed in this way, was inwardly unsatisfactory in this other way that men sensed more quickly than women but which had at last been pinned down as unsoundness, if only of the incipient kind; and when it was noticed that Sarah Layton smiled at Teddie and Susan the idea the ladies might have had that she bore no grudge and took it all like a good soldier was edged out of their minds by this other idea – the faintly disagreeable one that she was smiling at them instead of with them.

All the same, they looked forward to the wedding. When Captain

Bingham was posted quite suddenly as a G3 (Operations) to a new divisional headquarters stationed in Mirat, Mrs Fosdick said she wouldn't be in the least surprised if the whole thing now fell through and Susan, with so many other eligible men to choose from, decided she had made a mistake. The Laytons' departure for a late – last-fling-for-Susan – holiday in Srinagar strengthened her belief that Susan would soon find other fish to fry. The final surprise and disappointment came when the Laytons returned early from Kashmir and announced that the wedding, far from being either postponed or cancelled, had been hastened forward and would take place out of Pankot, in Mirat. One felt (the ladies said) that even taking into account the exigencies of war-time, and the fact that Captain Bingham was obviously soon returning to active service in the field, the Layton wedding had taken on a hole-in-the-corner air which it was somehow not easy to forgive.

'I'm not at all sure,' Mrs Paynton announced, 'that Mrs Layton should allow herself to be rushed like this. I get the impression she's really quite upset but is trying not to show it for the girl's sake. Apparently Susan is coming back to Pankot with them after the wedding because there'll only be a three-day honeymoon and after that Captain Bingham is off. You don't suppose . . .'

She did not say what was not supposed because she knew the other ladies must have supposed it already, as she had done, and rejected the supposition as too outlandish in relation to a Layton to be considered seriously for a moment – unless, perhaps, the Layton girl involved had happened to be Sarah. If Mrs Smalley was right and had put her finger on what was wrong with Sarah Layton, what was disturbing about her, then one could say that nothing was beyond the bounds of possibility.

*

Teddie Bingham's posting to Mirat and his discovery soon after arrival that if he wanted to get married his bride would have to come to him, be content with a seventy-two-hour honeymoon in the Nanoora Hills and prepared to kiss him goodbye as soon as it was over, were not the only events that threatened to disrupt the harmonious pattern of the wedding. Susan, somewhat to her family's surprise, shrugged these disappointments away and said that anyway being married in Mirat should be fun, especially if -- as was

128]

suggested – they stayed beforehand at the palace guest house. They could go to Ranpur (she said), meet Aunt Fenny and Uncle Arthur (who was to give her away), and travel to Mirat as a party. So, provisionally, it was arranged, but soon after the return from the Kashmir holiday Major Grace informed them he could not get down to Mirat earlier than the Friday before the wedding. He had to attend a series of conferences and there was no getting out of this disagreeable duty. Mrs Layton said she did not much care for the idea of travelling down and staying for nearly a week in the guest house without a man to look after them. Again Susan brushed the objection aside. The guest house would be perfectly safe. According to Teddie the Nawab of Mirat had handed it over to the station commander for the duration, to provide extra accommodation for military visitors (and their families) and although it wasn't in the cantonment it was in the grounds of the palace and was guarded. 'That still leaves the train journey,' Mrs Layton pointed out. 'You're forgetting Teddie's best man,' Susan reminded her. One of Teddie's friends in Pankot was a man called Tony Bishop, another old Muzzy Guide wounded in Burma and presently acting as ADC to General Rankin. Tony had already agreed to support him at the wedding. It would be the simplest thing in the world to get General Rankin to give him special leave so that he could go down to Mirat with them.

So Mrs Layton spoke to General Rankin and got his promise to allow Captain Bishop to escort them. But one week before the party was due to leave Tony Bishop went down with jaundice. Mrs Layton visited him in the military wing of the Pankot General Hospital.

'It's no good,' she said, 'he'll be there for three weeks, so now there's no best man. But it's a blow. Of all Teddie's friends Tony Bishop strikes me as the most sensible.'

'Best men are two a penny,' Susan retorted, and went up to Area Headquarters where she put a call through to Teddie at his divisional Headquarters and spoke to him personally. 'He'll get someone in Mirat, probably the man he shares quarters with,' she said when she came back. The remarkable thing, Sarah realized, was that for once Susan had done something herself instead of getting someone to do it for her. Her mother said no more about being unaccompanied on the train. It had never been a serious objection. There were bound to be plenty of officers on their way to Mirat and

Susan would only have to stand a few moments on the platform with her mother, Aunt Fenny and Sarah, before a gaggle of subalterns approached them and inquired if any help was needed. Which was precisely what happened.

*

There were two Mirats: the Mirat of palaces, mosques, minarets, and crowded bazaars, and the Mirat of open spaces, barracks, trees, and geometrically laid out roads with names like Wellesley, Gunnery and Mess. The two Mirats were separated by an expanse of water, random in shape, along one side of which ran the railway and the road connecting them. The water and the gardens south of it were the Izzat Bagh, so-called because the first Nawab declared that Kasims would rule in Mirat until the lake dried up: a fairly safe bet because it had never done so in living memory. But it was a boast, and boasts were always considered dangerous. Providence ought not to be tempted. A man could lose face simply as a result of tempting it. The inhabitants of the city anticipated the worst. Instead, so it was said, for two successive years after the Nawab's announcement the wet monsoon was abnormally heavy and prolonged. When, in the second year, the lake flooded its banks and destroyed the huts of the fishermen, drowning several, people took it as a sign of celestial approval of the reign of the house of Kasim whose honour – or izzat – had been so dramatically upheld. The lake was adopted as a symbol of the Nawab's power, of his fertility, of an assured succession reaching into the far distant future. The mullahs declared the lake blessed by Allah, and the Hindus – eighty per cent of the population – were prohibited from using it even during the festival of Divali. A mosque was erected on the southern shore and a new palace was built with gardens going down to the water. The court poet – Gaffur Mohammed – celebrated the establishment of the new palace and its garden in this verse:

> So you must accept, Gaffur,
> That your words are no more than the petals of a rose.
> They must fade, lose scent, and fall into obscurity.
> Only for a while can they perfume the garden
> Of the object of your praise. O, would they could grow,
> Lord of the Lake, eternally.

It was in these gardens that a guest house in the European Palladian style was built in the late nineteenth century, round about the time that a British military cantonment was established with the Nawab's approval in the area north of the lake.

•

There were two halts for Mirat: Mirat (City) and Mirat (Cantonment). The latter was the first arrived at if you travelled from Ranpur. The mail train was scheduled to reach Mirat (Cantonment) at 0750 hours but was usually anything between half an hour and one hour late. Having deposited its passengers at Mirat (Cantonment) it took a half-hour rest and then chugged out, at a rate never exceeding 10 mph, negotiating points, junctions and level-crossings, until it reached the long isolated embankment that separated the lake from the waste land that had once – before the coming of the cantonment – been characteristic of the northern environs of the city. The train crawled along the bleak strip of ground that raised the railway to one level and the trunk road to another, slightly lower, with a kind of reluctance, as if the engine-driver expected subsidence or, anyway, signals showing green that would flash red at the last moment, scarcely leaving him time to apply his brakes. Between the presiding power and the old glory there was, as it were, a sense of impending disaster.

Although the Laytons and Mrs Grace were to stay at the palace guest house it was at Mirat (Cantonment) they alighted, on Teddie Bingham's instructions. 'Make sure,' he had written to Mrs Layton, 'you don't get carried on into the city. Of course I'll be there to meet you, and even if I'm unable to I'll get someone to do so for me. But I thought it worth mentioning, just in case anything goes wrong, and remembering you're staying at the palace guest house you think you have to travel on into the city itself. No one ever does.'

'Things are looking up,' he said now above the din on the arrival platform. 'You're only twenty-five minutes behind schedule. I've got breakfast organized. I expect you're ready for it.' He pecked the cheek Mrs Layton offered, shook hands with Mrs Grace whom he had met only twice, held Sarah's hand for a prolonged few seconds as if the switch of his affections from her to her sister still needed some explanation, then turned and kissed and held on to pretty little Susan who had an air of being flushed and dishevelled in spite of the fact that not a hair was out of place and she had worked for half an hour on perfecting the pallor she had decided suited her as the wife-to-be of an officer who would soon be away to the war. It was on Teddie's cheeks a flush was actually visible, but he appeared brisk, fully in control of the problems posed by an arrival. The flush seemed to be one of pleasure combined with effort: the pleasure of seeing his future wife again and the effort he would always put into doing even the most ordinary things right, more especially when there were members of the opposite sex depending upon him for their comfort and safety. He had an Indian NCO in attendance whose khaki drill shirt and knee-length shorts stood out from his limbs and body in stiff, starched, knife-edged perfection. The man's pugree was an exotic affair of khaki cloth and diaphanous khaki muslin which gave his otherwise gravely held head a quirk of flirtatiousness and added a note of self-conscious gallantry to the way in which he stood by the open carriage and took charge of the mounds of luggage which the red-turbanned coolies were already fighting over.

'Don't worry about your things,' Teddie Bingham said. 'Noor Hussain's got the luggage *bando* taped,' and having thanked the officers in the adjacent compartment who had looked after Mrs Layton and her party on the journey from Ranpur and were now travelling on south, escorted the ladies through the crowd to the station restaurant, explaining that Noor Hussain would see the luggage safely stowed in a 15-cwt truck and taken to the guest house where they would find it waiting. For personal conveyance he had laid on a couple of taxis, and those too would be waiting directly breakfast was over.

Entering the restaurant behind her mother and Aunt Fenny, but ahead of Susan and Teddie who were obviously conscious of their duty as an engaged couple to stay close, Sarah concentrated on the smells coming from the kitchens. Whatever the day held in store breakfast was a meal she felt it was wise to give her undivided attention to. Once she was seated at the table, the orders given for cornflakes or porridge, egg and bacon, toast and marmalade, the first cup of tea or coffee drunk, and perhaps the first cigarette of the day lighted, she thought she would be able to view the sight of Susan and Teddie sitting together opposite her with more confidence in their future than she felt capable of drumming up at the moment.

There was (Sarah thought) something about Teddie Bingham that didn't wear well. He was not a man who grew on you. In this respect he was like the countless other young men to whom she had been mildly attracted and then lost interest in or lost to Susan with no hard feelings on either side. What was special about Teddie was the fact that Susan had agreed to marry him. Sarah could not understand why. She hoped, but did not believe, that they loved one another. She did not believe it because until they announced their engagement there seemed to have been nothing to distinguish him as a man apart, in the crowd of men round Susan.

'But then,' Sarah thought, 'we all have the same sort of history. Birth in India, of civil or military parents, school in England, holidays spent with aunts and uncles, then back to India.' It was a ritual. A dead hand lay on the whole enterprise. But still it continued: back and forth, the constant flow, girls like herself and Susan, and boys like Teddie Bingham: so many young white well-bred mares brought out to stud for the purpose of coupling with so many young white well-bred stallions, to ensure the inheritance and keep it pukka. At some date in the foreseeable future it would stop. At home you understood this, but something odd happened when you came back. You could not visualize it, then, ever stopping.

She looked across the table at Susan, at her mother, at Aunt Fenny, and remembered her Aunt Lydia saying that India was an unnatural place for a white woman. As a child she had not understood, but had understood since, and agreed with Aunt Lydia that it was. They did not transplant well. Temperate plants, in the hot-house they were brought on too quickly and faded fast, and the life they lived, when the heat had dried them out and left only the aggressive husk, was artificial. Among them, occasionally, you would find a freak in whom the sap still ran. She was thinking of her old Aunt Mabel in Pankot, and of the Manners girl's aunt in Srinagar who, in the midst of their conversation, had suddenly filled her with an alarming sense of her own inadequacy as a human being, so that on returning to her own houseboat she had sat in front of a mirror and stared at herself, wishing she were anything but what her outward appearance proved she was: an average girl whose ordinariness was like a sentence of life imprisonment.

[133

'You are not going to tell us, I hope,' Aunt Fenny said to Teddie when she had taken her place, fussed about a stain on the tablecloth, studied the bill of fare, ordered porridge and poached eggs and returned her spectacles to their red leather pouch, 'that the wedding has to be even earlier, tomorrow for instance, because if so there'll be no one to give Susan away. Arthur simply can't get down until Friday.'

'No, don't worry, Mrs Grace, Saturday it is.'

'What about your best man, Teddie?' Mrs Layton asked.

'It's all fixed. I asked the chap I share quarters with if he'd stand in and he said he'd be glad to. Since then he's been bustling around making sure everything's all right at the guest house. He'll be along after breakfast to help us get sorted out. His name's Merrick. I hope you'll like him.'

'Merrick?' Aunt Fenny repeated. 'It doesn't ring a bell. What is he?'

'A gee-three-eye,' Teddie said, who took so many things literally.

Aunt Fenny turned to Mrs Layton. 'Millie, wasn't there a Merrick on General Rollings's staff in Lahore in thirty-one? It could be the same family.'

'Oh, I don't remember, Fenny. It's all so long ago.'

'Of course you remember. He married one of those awful Selby girls. No. I'm wrong. . . .' Aunt Fenny paused. There was a family joke that Aunt Fenny kept the army List on her bedside table, and still referred to it whenever she gave a party and was in doubt about the seniority of one of her guests and consequently where to seat him and his wife. 'It wasn't Merrick. It was Mayrick. I don't know a Merrick. Is he an emergency officer?'

'He got an immediate commission, I gather,' Teddie explained. 'He was in the Indian Police.'

'Isn't that unusual?' Aunt Fenny wanted to know. 'Young Mr Creighton pulled every string there is to get out of the civil and into the army for the duration, but they wouldn't let him go. He told me he'd only heard of one instance of it being allowed and I think that was a case of the poor young man in question absolutely pining away at the prospect of not being in on the shooting and becoming quite useless at his work. Perhaps it was Mr Merrick. What is his first name?'

'Ronald.'

'Ronald Merrick. What rank?'

Teddie looked faintly surprised. 'Captain.'

'My dear boy, I gathered that when you said he was a G3 (I). I meant his rank in the police.'

'Oh, that. Superintendent or something, I think.'

'What district?'

'He did tell me. Now what was it? Is there a place called Sunder-something?'

'Sundernagar,' Aunt Fenny pronounced. 'A backward area. Relatively unimportant.' Captain Merrick thus disposed of she smiled blandly.

'Did you enjoy Kashmir?' Teddie asked.

'It was all right. The wrong end of the season and of course we had to cut it short.'

'I know. I'm sorry.'

'We had a vaguely unpleasant experience too. Millie wanted to move our boat up the lake to where she and John spent their honeymoon. There was only one other boat up there and it all seemed quite idyllic, if over-quiet and slightly inconvenient. Unfortunately our neighbour turned out to be someone on whom it was impossible to call. I'll give you three guesses.'

Teddie coloured up in anticipation of hearing something he'd rather not hear in front of Susan. Sarah glanced at her mother who was still reading the menu, apparently not listening. Only her mother knew about her visit to Lady Manners, and only for her mother's sake had Sarah said nothing to the others.

'I give up,' Teddie said.

'Old Lady Manners. And the child —'

'Oh, I see.' His blush deepened.

Mrs Layton put the menu down. 'What is the guest house like, Teddie?'

'I've only seen it from the outside, but the station commander says it's pretty comfortable. Ronald Merrick knows more about it than I do. He's been there a couple of times to check on the bando-bast. Incidentally, you'll have it all to yourselves. It's in the palace grounds and it's staffed by palace servants, but the Nawab's put it at the Station Commander's disposal for the duration, so it's really treated as cantonment territory and there's no need to stand on ceremony.'

'Shall we see the Nawab?' Susan asked.

Teddie assumed his playful expression. 'Why should you want to see the Nawab?'

'Because there was a scandal about him. He fell in love with a white woman and followed her all the way to the South of France.'

'Oh, did he? Who told you that?'

'I did, but I thought everybody knew,' Aunt Fenny said. 'The affair between the Nawab of Mirat and Madame X or whatever they called her, was quite a *cause célèbre* in the early twenties. She was Russian or Polish and pretended to be of good family, but was probably a lady's maid. I don't know what originally brought her to India but she got her hooks into the Nawab, played him for what he was worth, cried off when he wanted her to marry him as his second wife and scooted back to Europe with the Nawab after her. They ended up somewhere like Nice or Monte Carlo. I remember there was a story about some jewellery which she claimed he'd given her – presumably for services rendered. He threatened legal action and they say this Count Bronowsky acted as go-between – so successfully that the Nawab brought him back and made him his prime minister.'

'Oh yes,' Teddie said. 'I've heard of Bronowsky. He's still around.'

'If he was really a Russian count I'll eat my hat but the Nawab's been under his thumb ever since and he's even dazzled the Political Department, according to Arthur. But then of course he had to, otherwise they'd have made the Nawab get rid of him years ago.'

'You haven't answered my question, Teddie,' Susan reminded him, 'but of course once Aunt Fenny starts it's difficult to get a word in edgeways.'

She smiled at Mrs Grace, but Sarah recognized the hectic little flush spreading over her powdered cheeks as a sign of the temper her sister seemed to find it hard to control whenever she felt even fleetingly neglected. Content, often, to sit and listen and think her thoughts, her most casual remarks or gestures demanded and usually received immediate responses, from women as well as men. Sarah sometimes marvelled at the way Susan could suddenly divert a conversation by throwing into it a comment or a question, and at the way she could then just as suddenly retire from it and leave people disorientated. It was as if she periodically and deliberately sought to test the strength of the impact of her personality.

'I asked,' Susan said, turning back to Teddie, 'whether we shall see the Nawab.'

'I don't know. He's away at the moment but may be back at the weekend. Colonel and Mrs Hobhouse – that's the Station Commander and his wife – say we ought to invite him to the reception, but that it's not certain whether he'll come.'

'Why? Because the reception is to be at the club?'

'No. He's allowed in as a guest, you know. Because of Ramadan. I mean he'll be fasting between sun-up and sundown.'

'I'd like to have a Nawab at my wedding,' Susan said, 'especially one who used to be wicked. Besides, if we make a bit of a fuss of him he'll have to send a wedding present and it might turn out to be a tray of super rubies or a fabulous emerald, or a few spare ropes of pearls.'

Teddie smiled, and glanced affectionately down at her left hand, at the finger on which she wore his own modest cluster of engagement diamonds. She chose this moment to lean back in her chair, an indication that the others could again talk to each other.

Breakfast came to the table at last.

∗

There were twelve tables in the station restaurant. Sarah counted them. Ten were occupied. The floor was patterned by black and white tiles. The ceiling was high; three four-bladed fans, suspended from it, revolved at half speed. The windows on the platform side were frosted to shut out the sight of trains, travellers and coolies. On one wall there was a portrait of the King-Emperor, George VI, and on another a pre-war poster of invitation to Agra to admire the stale image of the Taj Mahal. The bearers were dressed in white and had cummerbunds of green and black, white gloves and bare feet. At one table two Indian officers, Sikhs, sat together. A nursing officer of the QAIMNS was breakfasting with a captain of Ordnance, an Anglo-Indian girl with a subaltern of the Service Corps. The rest of the customers were British officers. Some had arrived on the 07.50. Others would be waiting for a departure.

And presumably (Sarah told herself) with the exception of the two Sikhs and the little Anglo-Indian girl, we all represent something. And looked at her own family, considering them for the moment as strangers to her, like the rest of the people eating

English breakfasts in a flat and foreign landscape. There, she thought, watching Aunt Fenny, is a big-boned, well-fleshed woman. To look at her you'd say she has transplanted better than the thinner, sad-faced woman by her side, but her manner is a shade too self-assured, her voice a shade too loud, and when she stops speaking her mouth sets a shade too grimly, and the first impression that she has transplanted well is overridden by another, the impression that when she finds herself alone she will sit with a far-away look on her face, a look that would be gentle if it weren't for the mouth. However quietly or gently she moves or sits the mouth will stay fixed and grim so that all her thoughts and recollections will enter the room and surround her not with happiness but with regrets and accusations. Which means that even then you would not be able to feel sorry for her. The thinner, sad-faced woman is her sister. They have the same nose and a manner towards each other of intimacy that is neither casual nor closely affectionate and betrays a long but not necessarily deep experience of each other. Their real intimacy was over long ago. It ended with childhood, and was quite likely an intimacy only one of them felt, most likely the sad thin one who uses her hands with a curious vagueness, as if certain gestures which are habit are no longer appropriate because the person they were habitually made to, to express contentment, affection, to establish contact, to claim loyalty, to offer it, is no longer close to her.

Well, she was cheating, Sarah realized. No one looking at her mother would know that about her from her gestures. Would they know the other thing? Would they, by looking at her, be able to tell that the vagueness, the air of slight distraction, was proof — as Sarah knew it was — that Mrs Layton was already, at 8.30 in the morning, beginning to work out how long it would be before she could decently have a drink? You are still attractive, Sarah thought, and you are only forty-five. It is three years since you were with him. And India is full of men. So don't think I don't understand about the bottle in the wardrobe, the flask in your handbag.

She turned to Teddie and Susan. For her, the lightly but firmly sketched portrait of compatibility and pre-marital pleasure in each other's company which they presented in public, carried no conviction. In Teddie, Sarah was conscious of there seeming to be nothing behind his intentions — touchingly good on the surface — that gave them either depth or reality. In Susan she had become aware of a curious aptitude for deliberate performance. Susan was playing Susan and Sarah could no longer get near her. The distance between them had the feeling of permanence because the part of Susan called for a pretty, brown-haired, blue-eyed, flush-cheeked girl who entered, almost feverishly, into the fun and responsibilities of a life Sarah herself believed mirthless and irresponsible. It was mirthless because it was irresponsible, and irresponsible because its notion of responsibility was the notion of a vanished age. The trouble was, she thought, that in India, for them, there was no private life; not in the deepest sense; in spite of their attempts at one. There was only a public life. She looked again at the faces in the restaurant – ordinary private faces that seemed constantly to be aware of the need to express something remote, beyond their capacity to imagine – martyrdom in the cause of a power and a responsibility they had not sought individually but had collectively inherited, and the stiffness of a refusal to be intimidated; group expressions arising from group psychology. And yet they were the faces of people whose private consciousness of self was the principal source of their vitality.

Once out of our natural environment (she thought) something in us dies. What? Our belief in ourselves as people who each have something special to contribute? What we shall leave behind is what we have done as a group and not what we could have done as individuals which means that it will be second-rate.

She lit a cigarette and listened to Teddie and Aunt Fenny talking about Lord Wavell who was to be the new Viceroy and Lord Louis Mountbatten who was to be Supreme Commander of the new South-East Asia Command. Aunt Fenny was saying that it was a mistake to divest GHQ in India of its traditional military role. Teddie said Lord Wavell would make a good Viceroy because he was a soldier and people could trust him. New winds were blowing, but the dust they raised seemed to Sarah to be as stale as ever. Hot coffee was brought, the bearer sent with orders for morning papers: the *Times of India* for Mrs Layton, *The Civil and Military Gazette* for Aunt Fenny; nothing for Susan unless the new edition of *The Onlooker* was out; for Sarah the *Statesman* which Aunt Fenny disapproved of because although it was an English newspaper it was always criticizing Government or GHQ and was currently (she said) exaggerating the seriousness of the famine in Bengal, and blaming everybody for it except the Indian merchants who had hoarded tons of rice and were waiting for the market price to rise to an even more astronomic figure. 'Besides,' she said, 'the Bengalis won't eat anything but rice. There are tons of wheat going begging but they'd rather die than change their damned diet.'

Sarah tapped ash carefully into the glass ashtray and felt put off by the sight of the stub of her previous one, marked red by her lipstick, a sign of her personal private life, her none-too-hopeful message in a bottle cast back up by an indifferent tide on an island on which she sometimes felt herself the only one alive who still wanted to be rescued.

•

They were confronted by a forbidding openness, of water and unabsorbed light, a sort of milky translucence that deadened the nerves of the eyeballs and conveyed the impression that here one would live perpetually with a slight headache.

'There's the palace now,' Captain Merrick said. Sarah heard from her mother a low exclamation that could have been one of admiration or of disappointment. For the moment she herself was blinded by the vast area of sky and water.

'You're looking in the wrong direction, Miss Layton.' His voice was close. He was leaning forward. She had an impression that his fingers had touched her very lightly on the shoulder. The voice was resonant. There was something in its tone that acted as an irritant, although not an unpleasant one. 'I'm not looking in any direction,' she said. She raised her left hand to shade her eyes. 'There's so much glare.'

'I was afraid you'd find that, sitting up front. I'll tell the fellow to stop, then we can change places.'

Sarah shook her head. 'No. I can see the palace now —' Distantly, a dusty-rose-coloured structure with little towers, and a white-domed mosque with one slim minaret on the edge of the lake, reflected in the water – and – among the trees, at the end of the lakeside road they travelled on, a small palladian-style greystone mansion. The guest house.

The lake was on their left. Fishermen were casting nets from long low boats. The nets fell on the water, rippling its glassy surface as if sudden areas of chill were causing patches of gooseflesh.

Again the voice in her ear.

'You see where the reeds begin? That's the boundary of the fishing rights. They're not allowed to work closer to the palace. It's a traditional family occupation, the rights are handed down from father to son. They're quite a proud sect. Muslims, of course.'

Her mother spoke. When Captain Merrick replied his voice was no longer just behind her. He had sat back. But the voice was still resonant. It was a good voice, but not public school. Aunt Fenny had already commented on that fact, in the ladies' room at the station restaurant. 'Of course,' she said, 'you can get some peculiar people in the police. I don't suppose Captain Merrick's family would bear close inspection. But he's quite the little gentleman, isn't he, and terribly efficient over detail. That's a sign of a humble origin, too. Did you hear him tell Teddie the luggage has already arrived at the guest house? That means he called there to make sure, before coming to collect us. How shall we go? You, Susan and Teddie in one taxi, me, Sarah and Captain Merrick in the other?' But Mrs Layton said, 'No, I'll go with Sarah and Captain Merrick. Then I'll feel less like a mother-in-law.' She retired into a cubicle. Susan and Aunt Fenny went out. Sarah waited, gazing at her ordinary face in the mirror, combing her hair which was the same colour her mother's had been before it began to fade and she took to using bleach; a dark blonde, difficult to curl, badly in need of the permanent wave she would have to undergo before the wedding. She hated her hair. She hated her chin and cheekbones. They were too prominent. She repaired her make-up without interest. She envied Susan for having the kind of face that powder and lipstick could alter. Through these her own face always came back at her with a kind of dull incorruptibility, authentic bony Layton, quite unlike the rounder, more gently moulded Muir face. Well, she thought, it would wear better. There was a toughness in the Layton face that weathered storms. Her great-grandfather had had it, her father had it, and now she had it.

Mrs Layton came out of the cubicle. She had her handbag with her. Through the mirror Sarah saw her mother glance at her, then look away. Without speaking she came across to one of the handbasins, set her bag down, washed her hands, touched her hair and adjusted her hat. Silences between them were not unusual. They were strange silences which Sarah found difficult to break once they had set in. She sometimes thought of them as silences her mother used to establish between them a closeness that had never existed before and which she thought it too late to establish now except in this exchange of sentences unspoken and of gestures unoffered. There were occasions – and this was one of them – when Sarah felt a surge of almost hysterical – because pent-up – affection for this vague distracted woman who was her mother. The old forth-right manner with its edge of sharpness that demanded respect, loyalty, more than it demanded love, was gone. It seemed now that nothing at all was being demanded and nothing given, except whatever casual things they were that were asked and given by habit – and these silences, which seemed to express a need that went much deeper than mere reliance on Sarah to forget she had not been loved as much as Susan and to give the kind of help Susan never could have given.

*

Following her mother and Aunt Fenny out of the restaurant – but this time in the wake and not the van of Susan and Teddie because Teddie's best-man-to-be had gravitated as if by a force of nature to the role of escorting her, seeing that doors were kept open for her to pass through, that any remark she made would get a suitable response, and of making light and suitable conversation himself should she seem to be in need of cheering up – Sarah re-membered how within a few weeks of her arrival in Pankot in 1939 she had decided that India affected Englishmen in two ways: it made them thin and pale or beefy and red. Her father and – potentially – her new escort belonged to the former category, Uncle Arthur and (potentially) Teddie Bingham to the latter. The thin pale Englishmen were reserved and mostly polite to other people, including Indians even when they didn't like them; the red beefy ones acquired loud voices and were given to displays of bad temper in public. Between these two types of opposites there seemed to be no shades of colour or grades of behaviour worth noting. The young men fell potentially into one or the other of these categories directly they set foot in Bombay or went out to their first station. Their pinkness, you saw then, judging by its texture in each individual case, would fade or deepen; their flesh, depending upon built-in things like bone structure and muscle tone, would shrink or thicken; their good nature, according to the amount of self-control needed to sustain it, would become fixed

142]

and frozen, or would explode dramatically under the pressure of the climate and their growing inability – Uncle Arthur was a case in point – to take any real pleasure in the company kept.

But one thing was shared in common by these two broadly distinguishable types of men: their attitude to English women. After a time Sarah had been able to analyse it. They approached you first (she decided) as if you were a member of a species that had to be protected, although from what was not exactly clear if you ruled out extinction: it seemed to be enough that the idea of collective responsibility for you should be demonstrated, without regard to any actual or likely threat to your welfare. In circumstances where no threat seemed to exist the behaviour of the men aroused your suspicion that perhaps it did after all but in a way men alone had the talent for understanding; and so you became aware of the need to be grateful to them for the constant proof they offered of being ready to defend you, if only from yourself.

This collective public approach also affected their personal, private approaches. When young men talked to her, danced or played tennis with her, invited her to go riding, to watch them play men's games, to go with them to a show, became amorous or fumbled with her unromantically in the dark of a veranda or a motor-car, she had the impression that they did so in a representative frame of mind. 'Well here I am, white, male and pure-bred English, and here you are pure-bred English, white and female, we ought to be doing something about it.' The potential red beefy types were usually more enthusiastic for doing something about it than the potential thin pale types, but however hot or cold the degree of enthusiasm was Sarah could never feel it as an enthusiasm for her, but instead as an enthusiasm for an ideal she was supposed to share and which the young man in question apparently assumed was a ready-made link, a reliable primary connexion between them that might or might not be more intimately strengthened according to taste. The ideal was difficult to define and Sarah had thought she ought to define it before deciding whether she should reject it or uphold it. She certainly had no intention of casually accepting it and becoming thoughtlessly implicated in it, which is what she believed Susan had done.

In the station concourse Sarah said to Captain Merrick, 'Mother would like you to come with us. Teddie can take Susan and Aunt Fenny,' and got her mother into the back of the first taxi. She saw

[143

Teddie approaching and wondered whether her mother's objections were not so much to being made to feel like a mother-in-law as to Teddie himself. She said, 'I want to ride in front, Captain Merrick. You go in with Mother.'

The driver was an Indian civilian. He would probably smell. Captain Merrick hesitated, but both doors were open and she got in. Teddie joined them. 'Are you all right?' he asked Mrs Layton. She said she was and told him to look after Susan. A few moments later they were settled and the taxi moved away, out of the shade. The heat coming from the engine and the hot air blowing through the open window combined with the glare and the baked musty stench of the taxi-driver to smother Sarah in that blanketing numbness which, in India, was a defence against the transformation of the illusion of exhaustion into its reality. She half-closed her eyes. They were going down a wide street of arcaded shops – the cantonment bazaar. The jingling harness of horse-drawn tongas, bicycle bells, the sudden blare of Indian music from a radio as they passed a coffee-house were sounds which this morning rubbed the edge of a nerve already raw from the irritation of feeling that everything was going inexorably forward and leaving her behind, that she could not catch up, could not cope. The taxi turned from the bazaar into a wide avenue. Ahead, the centrepiece of a roundabout, was the inevitable statue of the great white queen, Victoria, in profile to them on the line of their approach to it, the head slightly bowed under the weight of the dumpling crown and an unspecified sorrow.

The road was now shaded by trees, lined by the grey-white walls of compounds behind which gardens and old bungalows of military family occupation were occasionally revealed in glimpses of deep shadowy verandas, patches of sun-struck lawns, beds of the ubiquitous crimson canna lilies. A scent of dew and strange blossom entered on the artificially created breeze and Sarah inclined her head, as if to a narcotic that might lift her spirits.

'We're coming to the church,' Captain Merrick said, and told the driver to slow down when they got to it so that the Memsahibs could see it better. His Urdu was fluent.

A greystone spire, Victorian Gothic; a churchyard, and leaning palm trees which always reminded Sarah of the India of old engravings. Behind their taxi the other taxi carrying Susan, Teddie and Aunt Fenny, also slowed. Mrs Layton did not remark on the church. Presently they regained their former speed.

'The chaplain's name is Fox, by the way,' Captain Merrick said, and then began to rehearse the next few days' programme. A small party at the club tonight to introduce them to the General who would be out of station for the wedding itself, and to the Station Commander and his wife. Dinner at the Station Commander's the following evening which the Chaplain would certainly attend. The G 1 and his wife, the Station Commander and his wife, would have to be invited to the wedding. Teddie and Mrs Layton could work out between them who else among Teddie's fellow-officers and who else on the station should be invited. The club contractor was working on the basis of a small reception catering for between twenty and thirty people. Had Mrs Layton managed to get the cards printed in Ranpur? If not the printer Lal Chand who printed and published the *Mirat Courier* could produce them in twenty-four hours. The tailor Mrs Layton had mentioned in a letter to Teddie had been told to be at the guest house at midday to receive preliminary instructions. The steward in the guest house was under the control of the station staff officer, and would present the bill for meals and drinks at the end of their stay. Captain Merrick understood that these would be approximately at club prices. The rest of the guest house staff was supplied by the palace and there was no charge for accommodation, services or laundry other than personal laundry, all of which were to be accepted as part of the hospitality of the Nawab of Mirat to members of the services visiting the cantonment and unable to get accommodation in the club or the Swiss Hotel. The guest house was in the grounds of the palace, but there was a private way in and a separate compound. The private entrance, like the main entrance, was under armed guard, and there was a chaukidar. A palace motor-car would, Captain Merrick believed, be put at their disposal to help with things like shopping trips, and other motors from the palace garage would be lent for the wedding itself.

'I think that's about all, Mrs Layton, except that there's a young fellow who's distantly related to the Nawab and whose job it is to see that you have everything you need. He's an Indian, of course, a Muslim, and I think you'll like him. His name is Ahmed Kasim and he's a son of Mohammed Ali Kasim, the Chief Minister in the provincial government of thirty-seven to thirty-nine.'

'MAK? But isn't he locked up?' Mrs Layton asked.

'Exactly, that's the point. I mean it's something I think necessary to remember when dealing with young Kasim. He's an attractive young fellow, well-educated, speaks first-rate English, not in the least the usual surly type of Westernized Indian who thinks he's a cut above everybody – and believe me I've had some experience with that sort —'

Mrs Layton said, 'Yes, I'm sure you have. Teddie tells us you were in the police. My sister is dying to hear how you managed to get out of that uniform into this. She knows a young man in the Civil who's tried everything but still hasn't managed to swing it. Were you ever in Ranpur?'

'Yes, some years ago, in a very junior capacity.'

'And before your army commission?'

'I was DSP Sundernagar.'

'Ah yes. We lived there once. Rather a remote district. Was there much trouble there last year?'

'No, very little. Fortunately. It helped me persuade the powers that be that I could be more usefully employed.'

Presently Mrs Layton said, 'You were telling us about Mr Kasim's son.'

'Yes, I was.' A further hesitation. 'I don't quite know how to put this. In Ranpur he'd present no problem, but this is native sovereign territory and as a representative of the palace young Kasim is entitled to – well, certain consideration. One can't just treat him as a sort of errand-boy. The State's barely more than the size of a pocket-handkerchief but it's run on very democratic lines and has a tradition of loyalty to the crown. One of the Nawab's sons is an officer in the Indian airforce and of course the Nawab handed his private army over to GHQ on the first day of the war. It was mustered into the Indian Army as the Mirat Artillery, and got captured by the Japs in Malaya. In other words, officially the military in Mirat take an extremely good view of the Nawab.'

'And of all his entourage, including Mr Kasim. Oh, we promise to be well behaved.'

Presently Captain Merrick said, 'I beg your pardon, Mrs Layton. I've put everything very clumsily. The point I intended to make was that friendly and co-operative though Kasim is on the surface, it's as well to treat him cautiously as well as considerately because it would be unnatural if he didn't resent us a bit.'

'We probably shan't have time to let it worry us, Captain Merrick.'

146]

'No.'

And then, suddenly, they had left the avenue of trees behind and were driving alongside the lake. Dazzled, Sarah heard his voice: 'There's the palace now,' her mother's low exclamation and then his voice again, close to her ear. 'You're looking in the wrong direction, Miss Layton.'

*

Beyond the reeds the lake curved away and the road became splashed again by shade from old banyan trees. A high brick wall, topped by jagged bits of broken glass, had come in from the left. The taxi was slowing. Ahead, a culvert marked the private entrance to the guest house. There was nothing to be seen of it, nothing to see at all apart from the long straight road which eventually led – Captain Merrick said – through the waste ground into the old city of Mirat. There were walls on both sides of the road now. They turned in through an open gateway. A grey-bearded sepoy with a red turban and red sash round the waist of his khaki jacket came to attention. The taxi continued along a gravel drive that was flanked on either side by bushes of bougainvillaea and curved towards the left. The bushes thinned, there were patches of grass, and through trees a glimpse of rose-coloured stone.

'Do you know,' Mrs Layton said, 'it reminds me of the drive up to grandfather's old place.'

'But that was all laurel and rhododendrons,' Sarah pointed out, remembering – none too clearly – her great-grandfather's house which she had last seen the year of his death, as a child of twelve.

'The effect is the same.'

Sarah did not agree but did not say so, content anyway that her mother had settled momentarily into the kind of nostalgic mood that suggested the actual arrival would go well, although later that night there might be a hint of tearfulness at lonely bed-going – a whiteness under the rouge unfashionably applied low instead of high on the cheeks, an inner disintegration betrayed by a marginal relaxation of the muscles of the jaw and neck that produced a soft little pad of tender aging flesh under the courageous chin. Presently held high (as Sarah saw, looking over her shoulder) to receive a dab or two from the puff of a compact, there were, in its structure, the presentation to the world, signs of effort-in-achievement. Almost unconsciously bringing her hand up to stroke her own chin and neck in a gesture partly nervous and partly investigatory she marvelled at the havoc a few years would wreak on flesh so firm. There came a time when the face changed for ever, into its final mould. Hers had not done so, but her mother's had. Some faces then went all to bone, others went to slack, fallen, unoccupied folds and creases of skin. Her mother's would do that, and perhaps Susan's too, years hence. Her own would tauten. As an old woman she would probably have a disapproving but predatory look. Her mother would go on softening whereas she herself would harden exteriorly, become brittle interiorly. She would break into a thousand pieces, given the right blow. To kill her mother in old age would be a bloodier, more fleshy, less splintery affair. Her mother was protected already by incipient layers of blubber (like Aunt Fenny, but unlike Aunt Lydia). All the more credit to her therefore, Sarah thought, that she managed to convey a certain steeliness from within the softness.

Even at the most exasperating moments Sarah could feel, for her mother, a surge of love and deep affection that sprang goodness knew not from a long uninterrupted experience of her as a mother – the separation had been too long for that – but rather from a sensation of being able to treat her as if she were a human being towards whom she had a duty that was scarcely filial at all: almost as if she were a stranger of a kind suddenly encountered. She felt such a surge now, but as usual was unable to express it because her mother was not even looking at her, but putting the compact away. Well, so it goes, Sarah thought. And so it went: the taxi moving slowly through a tunnel of alternating bars of sunlight and strips of shadow and then coming out abruptly into the gravelled forecourt where the NCO with the diaphanous pugree stood by the side of the parked fifteen hundredweight that had brought their luggage. They drove in under a shadowy porticoed entrance and drew up at the bottom of a shallow flight of steps. At the head of the steps two men were waiting. As Captain Merrick spoke they were joined by a third.

'The chap in the scarlet turban is Abdur Rahman. He's head bearer and belongs to the Nawab. The little fellow holding his topee is the steward, his name's Abraham – an Indian Christian. He's the SSO's chap. And yes – there's Mr Kasim.'

148]

Sarah, looking up, saw Ahmed emerge from the dark interior.

*

'Was it wise?' she heard her Aunt Fenny asking, and recognized her mother's first-drink-of-the-day voice: 'Was what wise?'

'Letting her go riding alone with Mr Kasim.'

'I didn't let her as you call it. I didn't know.'

'Didn't know? You mean she just sneaked off?'

'Oh, Fenny, what's wrong with you? My daughters don't sneak off. They go. They don't have to ask permission. They're of age. They do what they like. One gets married. The other goes riding. How am I supposed to stop them? Why should I try?'

'You're becoming impossible to talk to sensibly. You know perfectly well why it's unwise for Sarah to ride alone with an Indian of that kind.'

'What kind?'

'Any kind, but especially Mr Kasim's kind.'

Sarah said, 'What of Mr Kasim's kind, Aunt Fenny?' and shaded her eyes from the glare of the lake that at midday always seemed to penetrate the shade of the deep porticoed terrace on which her mother and aunt were sitting, on chairs set back close to one of the open french windows which gave access to the terrace from the darkened sitting-room, and through which she had now stepped. She could not see the expressions on her aunt's or mother's face, and did not join them. She stood near them, gazing at the lake, letting that milky translucence work its illusion of detaching her from her familiar mooring in a world of shadow and floating her off into a sea of dangerous white-hot substance that was neither air nor water.

'I'm sorry,' Aunt Fenny said. 'I didn't know you were listening. I was saying I thought it unwise for you to ride alone with Mr Kasim.'

From the midst of that buoyant, dazzling opacity she said, 'Yes, I agree – it was unwise.' When they returned the syce had been waiting. He followed them round to the gravel forecourt below the terrace on which she presently stood and held her horse's head while she dismounted. Mr Kasim dismounted too. 'Come in and have some breakfast,' she suggested. He thanked her and said, 'Some other time perhaps,' asked her if there was anything special that

[149

either she or her family wanted to do, to see, or to have him bring or make arrangements for. 'No, I don't think so,' she said, 'thank you for taking me riding.' She wondered whether for some reason or other they should shake hands. He remounted, touched his topee with the tip of his crop and brought the horse's head round – all, as it were, in the same capable movement. As she came on to the terrace she listened to the sound of the hooves on the gravel.

'We shan't go riding again,' she said and lowered her head, turned, looked at Aunt Fenny and found the older woman's face set in that extraordinary mould that was the answer to the need to express something beyond the private emotional capacity to understand.

Sometimes she hated Aunt Fenny, mostly she was irritated by her. For the moment she felt inexplicably close to her and to her mother who had her eyes closed, one hand at rest on the arm of the wicker chair, the other clasping a half-empty glass of gin and lemon, apparently waiting for the day to come into its familiar focus as one totally indistinguishable from any other.

Well, they are my family, Sarah told herself. I love them. They are part of my safety and I suppose I'm part of theirs.

'What happened?' Aunt Fenny asked. Her voice, normally rich and well-risen, sounded flat and dry.

'Nothing happened. I meant it was unwise because it made us both self-conscious. It never occurred to me that it might. It wasn't until we actually set out that I realized it was the first time I'd been alone with an Indian who wasn't a servant. And there seemed to be nothing to talk about. He only spoke when spoken to and kept almost exactly the same number of paces behind me from start to finish.'

The stiffness had left Aunt Fenny's face but this softening only emphasized the lines that years of stiffening had left permanently on her, the private marks of public disapproval.

And what I remembered on the way back (Sarah thought, half-considering this face that was Aunt Fenny's but also that of an English woman in India) was the luggage in the little cabin, with that girl's name on it. She was never real to me until I saw the luggage. She was a name in a newspaper, someone they talked about in Pankot. She began to be real when I saw the luggage in the houseboat in Srinagar. The child must belong to the Indian they said she was in love with, otherwise why should that old lady keep it? But it might have been any half-caste baby. The luggage was different. It was inert. It belonged only to her. She was no longer alive to claim it, but this is what brought her to life for me. And this morning as I rode home, a few paces ahead of Mr Kasim, she was alive for me completely. She flared up out of my darkness as a white girl in love with an Indian. And then went out because – in that disguise – she is not part of what I comprehend.

'He is a perfectly pleasant young man,' Aunt Fenny said, 'and I understand his brother is an officer. But these days one simply can't tell what these young Indians are up to, let alone what they're thinking.'

'Perhaps they find the same difficulty in regard to us.'

'Yes, perhaps they do. But on the whole, my dear, we ought not to let that concern us. We have responsibilities that let us out of trying to see ourselves as they see us. In any case it would be a waste of time. To establish a relationship with Indians you can only afford to be yourself and let them like it or lump it.'

'Yes,' Sarah said. 'I suppose you're right. But out here are we ever really ourselves?'

III

THERE WAS, to begin with, the incident of the stone.

Apart from the black limousine travelling some seventy-five or hundred yards behind a wobbling bicycle ridden by an Indian carrying a raised umbrella as a protection against glare, there was no traffic on Gunnery Road; neither were there any visible pedestrians at the place where the incident occurred – the Victoria roundabout where a car coming down Gunnery Road and wishing to turn into Church Road had to slow down and describe a three-quarter circle round the monument. The driver of the limousine, an elderly man with a grey beard and wearing palace livery, having passed a file of peasant women with baskets on their heads going in the opposite direction, then began to concentrate on the cyclist and the possible obstacle he represented. He began to decelerate. Gunnery Road and the three other roads meeting at the roundabout were well shaded by big-branched thick-boled trees. The wobbling cyclist turned left. The way now seemed clear for the driver of the limousine to negotiate the roundabout, but encroaching age and several minor accidents had made him cautious, distrustful of what an apparently empty street might suddenly conjure in the shape of fast-driven vehicles.

The sound, when it came, did not immediately register. He allowed the limousine to continue to glide towards a point on the roundabout where he would be able to see what threatened from the left and how clear it was to the right. When the sound did register he braked, stared at the bonnet and the windscreen, then twisted round to confront the pane of glass dividing him from his passengers and, finding it unblemished, only then looked through it.

The passengers, both British officers, were thrust back hard, each into his separate corner. Their arms were still held in half-defensive attitudes. They were looking from floor to window to floor and to the space between them on the seat: as one might look for some suspected poisonous presence – a snake for instance. The last thing the driver noticed was the shattered window on the nearside of the car – not the window in the door, which was lowered, but the fixed window that gave the passenger a clear view. It took the driver several seconds to realize that neither officer could have broken it, that something had been thrown. At this point both officers came to life, shouted something at him, each opened a door and jumped out. One word, one idea – half formed into the shape of an image actually seen – came into the driver's head. Bomb. He had heard of such things happening, but had no experience of them. He opened his own door, stumbled out and found himself climbing marble steps. He missed his footing, fell and lay motionless with his hands covering his head, waiting for the explosion.

After a while he sat up. Above him loomed the plinth on which the White Queen sat, hardened and insensitive, gazing up the length of Gunnery Road, which was still empty of traffic. The file of village women, now some four hundred yards away, continued their journey uninterruptedly. Turning he found both officers standing in the road a few feet from the car. They were looking towards and making gestures at the low grey stucco wall that marked the boundary of a compound. One of them had a handkerchief held to the left side of his face. They stopped looking at the wall and looked at him.

'Sahib,' he said to the one without the handkerchief, after he had picked himself up, walked down the steps and approached them, 'I thought you jumped out because a bomb had been thrown.'

The officer did not smile. He had blue eyes. The driver was always fascinated by Sahibs with blue eyes. The eyes of the other Sahib were not so blue, hardly blue at all, but he had very pale eyelashes. There was blood on the handkerchief.

He followed the Sahibs back to the car and watched while they looked at the shattered window and into the back. He went round to the offside door and helped them to look. He did not know what he was looking for. An object of some kind. He found the object wedged in a corner under one of the tip-up seats. He picked it up. A stone. He said, 'Sahib, this is it.' He handed it to the Sahib with the blue eyes. The Sahib took it and showed it to the other Sahib.

Presently the unwounded Sahib looked across at him and said, 'Did you see who threw this?'

'I saw no one, Sahib. Only the women with the baskets but we had gone many yards past them before it was thrown. The person who threw it must have hidden behind that tree, Sahib. There may have been such a man. I do not know. My mind was not on this kind of matter. There was a man on a bicycle in front of the car. He was not making signals. My mind was on this man on the bicycle. He is gone. He went to the left. I did not see any other man. I am sorry, Sahib. It is not an auspicious beginning.'

'You're damned right it isn't,' Teddie Bingham said. 'For God's sake, Ronnie, is there any blood on my uniform?'

'It'll sponge out. Let me have a look at that cut.'

Teddie took the handkerchief from his cheek. Blood oozed out of a jagged cut below the cheekbone. Captain Merrick clapped the handkerchief back on.

'It may need a stitch and there may be glass in it.'

'But, Christ, there isn't time.'

'You can't get married bleeding like a stuck pig. Come on. Get back in and mind you don't sit on a splinter or you'll really be in trouble. When we get to the church I'll root out the chaplain and use his phone to get a doctor. There may be time to ring through and warn Susan and Major Grace. It'll mean putting the ceremony back a few minutes.'

Before sitting Merrick inspected his own and Teddie's side of the seat for splinters, then told the driver to get on quickly to the church.

'The bloody bastard,' Teddie said. 'Whoever it was. Bugger him and bugger the Nawab. And bugger his bloody limousine.'

[153

'Why?'

'Well, it's obvious, isn't it? A crest on the door as big as your arse. A bloody open invitation for some bolshie Nawab-hating blighter to heave a bloody great rock through the window.'

Merrick smiled; and was silent, contemplating the stone which he held balanced on the palm of his right hand.

*

Nawab Sahib was having the frayed end of his coat sleeve trimmed when Count Bronowsky told him there had been an incident involving one of the motor-cars on loan to the wedding party. The car, a 1926 Daimler, once the property of the late Begum, had been struck by a stone as it turned into Church Road at the Victoria roundabout. A window had been shattered and Captain Bingham cut on the cheek. The other occupant of the car, a Captain Merrick, was unhurt. He had telephoned the information through to Ahmed Kasim from the chaplain's house where Captain Bingham was receiving attention from a medical officer. The ceremony had been delayed for half an hour and the reception at the Gymkhana Club would now begin at 11.15 instead of at 10.45. There was therefore nò need to hurry.

Nawab Sahib, who was standing patiently in the middle of the room – his left arm held out while his personal body-servant snipped stray bits of thread from his cuff – glanced at Bronowsky. The Count was dressed in a starched cream linen suit, cream silk shirt and dove-grey silk tie. He had his best ebony gold-topped cane to lean on. The Nawab then looked at young Ahmed who wore a grey linen jacket and trousers, noticeably less expensive but quite well cut and properly pressed.

The silent inspection over, the Nawab returned his attention to the make-and-mend operation on his own coat, and said,

'Has a substitute car been sent?'

'It was offered but declined. Captain Merrick insists the damaged one is perfectly serviceable.'

'Has the chief of police been informed?'

'Ahmed has telephoned him, your Highness.'

'Will he think to make contact with the military police in the cantonment? Or will he rush about in the city arresting every likely culprit?'

154]

The questions, recognized by the Count as rhetorical, were left unanswered. Ali Baksh, the chief of police in Mirat, was currently under the cloud of the Nawab's unpredictable but cautious displeasure. Another reason for Bronowsky saying nothing was his understanding that the Nawab's composure was deceptive and so best left untampered with. Bronowsky had trained the Nawab to think of himself as a man who had to deny himself the luxury of violent criticism, even of expressing an opinion about anything except strictly personal matters, and who had a duty to the one million people he ruled never to leap to a conclusion or take any unconsidered action. But Bronowsky knew that although the Nawab had so far made no comment on the incident of the car his sense of outrage had been disturbed and fired.

Bronowsky smiled. Within sight of the end of his own reign he allowed himself the full pleasure of self-congratulation. Nawab Sahib had been transformed, step by painful step, from a tin-pot autocratic native prince of extravagant tastes and emotions into the kind of ruler-statesman whose air of informed detachment and benign loftiness was capable of leaving even the wiliest mind guessing and the coldest heart warmed briefly by curiosity; and wily minds and cold hearts were the combination Bronowsky found most common in English administrators. Nawab Sahib was Bronowsky's one and only creation, his lifetime's invention. He had fallen possessively in love with him and watched with compassion the struggle Nawab Sahib sometimes had to discipline himself to act and move – and think – in the ways Bronowsky had taught him.

Nawab Sahib removed his arm from the gentle support of the servant with the scissors and inspected the cuff. His private austerities were the last remarkable flowering of Bronowsky's design for a prince; remarkable because Bronowsky had not planned them. For Bronowsky, the austerities were to his design what the unexpected, seemingly inspired and unaccountable stroke of the brush could sometimes be to a painting, the stroke that seemed to have created the need for itself out of the combined resources of the canvas and the man who worked on it, and so was definitive of the process of creation itself and of the final element of mystery in any work of art.

The frayed cuff coats were not worn with the bombast of a rich miser, and it was difficult to say what emotion it was, precisely, that a man felt when he first noticed the spotless but threadbare cloth of the long-skirted high-necked coats, the clean but cheap and floppy trousers, the clean bare feet in old patched sandals or polished down-at-heel shoes; but Bronowsky believed that a major part of that response was made up of respectful wariness, much the same – possibly – as one's response would normally be to the sight of a gentleman down on his luck, but without the measure of pity and contempt such a condition evoked. The Nawab was rich enough for any but the most exaggerated taste. He was surrounded by proofs of his public comfort and of his private generosity. His austerities were reserved wholly for himself. They appeared at once as the badge of his right to lead a personal, private life and as evidence of how spare such a life had to be when so much of his interest and energy was expended for the benefit of the people it was his inherited duty to protect and privilege to rule. And it was this – the duality of meaning to be read into the Nawab's appearance – and the fact that the appearance was not deliberately assumed, that excited in Bronowsky the special tenderness of the artist for his creation. The austerities had been gradual, so that neither Nawab Sahib nor Bronowsky had ever commented on them. Equally gradual, Bronowsky supposed, had been the growth of dandyism in himself. It was as though the love that existed between him and the Nawab had exerted an influence to make them opposites, but what pleased him more was the realization that when they were together the comparative splendour of his own plumage looked like that of a slightly more common species. People, observing them, would be less inclined to believe what they heard – that Bronowsky was the power behind the throne. In Bronowsky, pride in what he had made was stronger than personal vanity. It was part of his pride that Nawab Sahib alone should be credited with the talents and capabilities Bronowsky had worked hard to train him to acquire and exercise.

He believed that Nawab Sahib was quite unconscious of there being any particular meaning to read into his habit of wearing old and inexpensive clothes. The Nawab had said once as they were preparing to go out on a public occasion for which Bronowsky had arrived dressed in his uniform of Honorary Colonel, Mirat Artillery (a uniform he had designed himself and which incorporated certain decorative flourishes reminiscent of the uniform of the old Imperial Guard to which Bronowsky had never belonged): 'Sit low in the carriage, Dmitri. Otherwise how will they tell that it is not you who is Nawab?'

'Should I sit higher than a man can sit, your Highness,'

Bronowsky said, 'they would still know I was but Bronowsky. A wazir must dress to the honour to the State and the Nawab Sahib is the State. His raiment is Mirat.'

The Nawab smiled: the same slow, grave smile that had been one of the persuasions the Russian felt to follow the small, lost, dark-skinned man of passion, sorrows and absurdities to his curious little kingdom in an alien land. And since the occasion of this particular courtly exchange Bronowsky had noticed how whenever he entered a room where the Nawab stood the Nawab said nothing until he had taken in at one short or prolonged glance – depending on the amount there was to scrutinize – the details of his wazir's dress and accessories. The ritual had become one he felt the Nawab depended on for reassurance. For some time Bronowsky had encouraged Ahmed also to take an interest in his clothes (or, anyway, to submit to directions and suggestions because interest in anything seemed to be something Ahmed was incapable of taking, unless visits to the Chandi Chowk could be counted as an interest as distinct from a compulsion).

That Ahmed should find increasing favour in the eyes of the Nawab was a continuing concern of Bronowsky's present policy, one of whose objects was the marriage of Ahmed to the Nawab's only daughter, Shiraz, whom the late Begum had brought up, out of spite, in a rigidly traditional manner, with the result that Shiraz, after her mother's death, would not come out of the seclusion she had been taught to regard as obligatory for a woman. Her mother had died just before Shiraz reached the age of puberty, and so she had never gone officially into purdah. The Nawab, urged by Bronowsky, had withheld his permission for that step to be taken; but the girl was so timid her father did not have the heart to follow Bronowsky's advice further and insist on her adopting the modern ways of the palace. She was now sixteen, virtually untutored, and proved to be tongue-tied in the presence of strangers on the few occasions Bronowsky had succeeded in persuading the Nawab to command her out of her self-made zenana to pay her respects to visitors Bronowsky considered important. She had been taught by her mother to regard the wazir as an ogre, a man who had her father in thrall and whose private life was so wicked as to be unspeakable; and it was only with patience that he had gradually succeeded in removing from her mind the idea that simply to look him in the eye was tantamount to gazing at the Devil. Mostly, denied the privacy

[157

of the veil, she kept her eyes downcast and fled to the security of her rooms at the first hint that she had done her duty.

The sad thing, Bronowsky thought, was that she was ravishingly pretty. He assumed – because neither the Nawab nor either of his two sons was handsome – that this prettiness, like the perverted desire to hide it, was a legacy from her mother. Bronowsky had never been permitted to see the Begum. She submitted him to long and unkind interrogations from behind a purdah-screen which left him no notion of her except what could be gathered from strong whiffs of expensive imported perfumes, the glint of rich silks and brocades through the tiny carved apertures, and the harshness of a high-pitched voice in which passion, cruelty and bitchiness were in roughly equal proportions. From such one-sided interviews Bronowsky would retreat confirmed in his hatred of women, raging impotently against the enormity of their abuse of the moral weapons God had mistakenly given them as armour against the poor savage male and his ridiculous codes of honour. Sometimes, looking at Shiraz – a dark red blush under the pale brown skin of her cheeks, her eyes downcast, the fabric of her saree shimmering not from reflections but from the trembling underneath – Bronowsky wondered how much of her mother's temperament was concealed there and what it would take to release it and make some man's life – Ahmed's for instance -- a misery. He comforted himself with the belief that the Begum, from all accounts, had always been a strong-willed woman and that what she had taught her daughter, once untaught, would release a temperament no more like the Begum's than the two sons' temperaments were like their father's.

Bronowsky thought little of either son. Both had eluded his influence. Mohsin, the elder, the future Nawab, product of the English tutors and public-school style college Bronowsky had agreed to early on as a sop to the Political Department, had acquired the pompousness of the English without the saving grace of their energy and without that curious tendency to iconoclasm which they called their sense of humour. He spent most of his time in Delhi, worthily and dully engaged in what he called his business interests, and as little as possible in Mirat, a place which his Westernized wife despised as socially backward. The younger, Abdur, similarly schooled, had acquired different English characteristics. He was a harmless young man who had graduated from an absorbing interest in cricket which he played badly to an equally absorbing interest in aeroplanes which he had not yet succeeded in learning to fly to the satisfaction of the Air Force.

Bronowsky admitted to himself that part of the reason for his letting the education and shaping of Mohsin and Abdur become the concern of others was to be found in the fact that neither of them had ever been well-favoured in appearance or manner. He thought, though, that it had been just as well. Their plainness and physical awkwardness had enabled him to concentrate the whole of his emotional impulse on the task of making a Nawab. A couple of handsome, active youths on hand could have caused his mind and will to wander in the bitter-sweet region mapped by his inclinations, explored by his imagination, but never – for many years – entered into. The discipline and self-denial involved in voluntary withdrawal from direct physical satisfaction of his needs had not been undergone only in order that he should never be guilty of corrupting another. He had come to recognize that the type of youth who attracted him was one whose attributes were wholly masculine and who therefore was attracted exclusively to women. The first sign that this was not necessarily so destroyed, for Bronowsky, the romantic fervour and loving admiration a young man could inspire in him, and left behind it only what he found grotesque. The man he could embrace was not the man for him. It had been as simple as that. The cessation of sexual activity had not been onerous. His affairs with men had been few: three in the twenty-one years between his nineteenth and fortieth birthdays. Physically there had been no women in his life.

Now, approaching seventy, he did not regret chances missed or opportunities wasted. He believed that if he had been born a woman he would have loved one man long, devotedly and faithfully. But having been born a man he did not now crave to have been blessed with normal appetites. He thought that anyway he had experienced to an extent few could claim the joy as well as the pain of loving unselfishly, from afar. He did not delude himself into supposing that his affection for Ahmed was the sentimental longing of an old bachelor for a son. He faced the truth. Ahmed was the latest manifestation of the unattainable, unattempted golden youth who came, sweetened the hour with his presence, and went unmolested into the arms of a deserving Diana, so that the whole world sang and the day was properly divided from the night. It amused him that this golden youth was brown, and touched him that in his old age the object of his undeclared and regulated passion should be someone his professional interest allowed a close connexion with. It was as though the old Gods of the forest had rewarded him for his abstentions. He treated the reward with almost excessive care, conscious of the need to balance his emotional with his worldly judgement. Ahmed had become a feature of the policy he was formulating. It was a bonus that he filled so well Bronowsky's personal need: a bonus and a snare. It would never do to confuse the policy with the need or the need with the policy. And Bronowsky knew that if the interests of the need and the policy came into conflict for any reason, it was Ahmed who would be sacrificed because the policy, through all its shifts and changes to adapt to circumstances, was pre-determined by one thing that never altered: Bronowsky's devotion to his Prince.

*

'It is not auspicious,' the Nawab said. And sat down. 'A stone?'
'A stone, Sahib.'
'At one of the motor-cars?'
Bronowsky inclined his head. He motioned Ahmed to leave them. When Ahmed had gone the Nawab indicated a chair and said in the low voice Bronowsky automatically registered as a sign of special self-control, 'Please sit.' Bronowsky did so. He rested both hands on the gold knob of his cane. His white panama was on his lap. The Nawab sat with folded hands and crossed ankles, leaning his weight on his left elbow. The arms of the chair were carved with diminutive lion heads at the protruding tips. The room was dark from the closed shutters. A slanting column of sunlight, admitted by the gap between one set of shutters left partly open, fell just short of the Nawab's chair. The room was overfurnished. There was a preponderance of potted palms. Strangers coming to the palace were sometimes disturbed by a resemblance they could not quite give a name to. Only the elderly and well-travelled hit easily upon the explanation. The public rooms were furnished in the manner of a plush and gilt hotel of pre-Great War vintage on the Côte d'Azur. Only the dimensions of the rooms, the arched windows, the fretted stone screens, some of the mosaics and the formal courtyard around which the main part of the palace was built remained Moghul in spirit and appearance.

160]

'I'm afraid I do not understand this incident of the stone, Dmitri.'

'No,' Bronowsky agreed. 'It is a puzzle.'

'It is ten years since a stone was thrown.'

Bronowsky nodded.

The Nawab looked towards the window.

'It was thrown at the Begum.'

Bronowsky nodded. He remembered the occasion well. It had enlivened his convalescence from a bout of gastro-enteritis that laid him low for a week, an illness which his servants attributed to his having been given coffee and cakes during an interview in the Begum's apartment.

'From what young Kasim tells me,' the Count said, 'I believe it is one of the late Begum's motor-cars the stone was thrown at this morning.'

'Is that significant?'

'I should not think so – unless the culprit is a madman.'

'Do we understand correctly that he wasn't apprehended, and that there is no information about him at all?'

'That seems to be correct, Nawab Sahib.'

'Then it is unlikely that he will be caught.'

'Very unlikely.'

'One man alone is not usually responsible for such an incident. It is the kind of activity several people decide. Several decide. One acts. But this is relatively unimportant. What is important is to know why the stone was thrown.'

'May I suggest we put it another way, Sahib, and ask ourselves at whom, or even at what, the stone was thrown? If we can answer that the answer to the question why it was thrown probably follows.'

'Very well. At whom or at what was the stone thrown?'

'We know it was thrown at the car, but whether at the car or the occupants is the beginning of the puzzle. Let us assume it was thrown at the car. The car bears your Highness's crest. The symbolism would then be inescapable. Ergo – the stone was thrown at your Highness. The thrower may even have thought your Highness was riding in the car. But as you say, a stone has not been thrown for ten years and when it was thrown it was thrown at the Begum. Your Highness has never been subjected to any kind of personal or even symbolic attack. And it is Ramadan. A Muslim subject would not throw a stone during Ramadan. Your Highness's Hindu subjects are content. Those areas of the State of Mirat which suffered a poor crop are being assisted effectively by the Famine Relief Commission. Your Highness and I spent a week together in Gopalakand meeting the new Resident. I returned ahead, nothing untoward was reported to me when I returned. Your Highness was greeted on your own return last night at the station with the usual loyal address and popular demonstration. Ergo – let us assume from all this evidence that the stone was not thrown at the car but at the occupants.'

'Who are —?'

'Captain Bingham and Captain Merrick, both – so Ahmed tells me – staff officers in the divisional headquarters recently formed, temporarily stationed in Mirat, and due to leave in the middle of next week for special training prior to active duty in the field. In other words, officers without any military or administrative employment in the cantonment as such, detached from local affairs, virtually strangers to the population.'

'But British officers all the same, Count Sahib.'

'Quite so.'

'An anti-British demonstration —' The Nawab frowned. 'In which case, also an anti-palace demonstration. The wedding party are our guests.'

'We can't assume that the man who threw the stone at British officers riding in a limousine knew that they were on their way to a wedding, Sahib. Nor that the ladies in the wedding party have been staying at the guest house.'

'This nevertheless is the situation. The stone was thrown at our guests.'

'Beg pardon, Sahib. Captain Bingham is not a guest. He is the groom.'

'That is worse. It is a great mischief. They have given me a beautiful gift. We reply with a stone.'

'It happened in the cantonment, Sahib.'

'They are our guests wherever it happens. What am I to say to them when I meet them? That they have Mirat's hospitality but not Mirat's protection? I shall want a full report.'

'It will be as full as possible. Meanwhile your Highness can only express your regret. Your Highness might add that you are astonished and pained that such a thing should happen in Mirat, either in the cantonment or out of the cantonment.' Bronowsky paused. 'Even last August there were no anti-British demonstrations in Mirat. The prohibition of political demonstrations and meetings the previous July was extremely effective. Known agitators were made *persona non grata.* The police have been active in smelling out refugee-agitators from British India, and sending them back where they came from. The incident of the stone this morning is therefore a mystery.' Bronowsky glanced at his watch. 'If you are ready, Sahib, I think we should go. In the circumstances it would be a proper gesture to be at the reception early rather than late.'

*

A stone: such a little thing. But look at us – Sarah thought – it has transformed us. We have acquired dignity. At no other time do we move with such grace as we do now when we feel threatened by violence but untouched by its vulgarity. A stone thrown by an unknown Indian shatters the window of a car, a piece of flying glass cuts an Englishman on the cheek and at once we sense the sharing of a secret that sustains and extends us, and Teddie instead of looking slightly absurd getting married with lint and sticking plaster on his face looks pale and composed. The end of Teddie is not reached so easily after all. I was wrong when I thought he had nothing more to offer that he hadn't already given. He will always be ready to offer and willing to give himself in the cause of our solidarity.

And it was a special kind of solidarity, Sarah realized. It transcended mere clannishness because its whole was greater than all its parts together. It uplifted, it magnified. It added a rare gift to a life which sometimes seemed niggardly in its rewards, and left one inspired to attack the problems of that life with the grave simplicity proper to their fair and just solution. The hot-tempered words and extravagant actions that might have greeted the incident of the stone were sublimated in this surrender to collective moral force.

From her position behind Susan at the altar steps she observed the way Teddie stood, at attention, with a military rather than a religious deference to God. To her left, and a pace or two in front, stood Uncle Arthur who had just made the gesture of confirmation that it was he who gave Susan to Teddie. He was also at attention.

He seemed to be staring up at the stained-glass window above the altar as if it might be through there that some light would fall to disperse the perpetual shadow of professional neglect it was understood by the family he suffered from and gamely plodded on in spite of. Glancing from Teddie to Uncle Arthur and back again Sarah thought: Why, what a curious thing a human being is; and was not surprised to hear Aunt Fenny sniff and to see that Susan was trembling as she put out her hand for Teddie to fit the ring on her finger. It is all over in such a short time, Sarah told herself, but in that short tiime everything about our lives changes for ever. We become something else, without necessarily having understood what we were before.

Teddie kissed his bride. Mercifully the cut had not been deep enough to need a stitch and the doctor had pronounced it free of splinters. Presumably it was not over-painful, but he cocked his head at an awkward angle, perhaps so as not to tickle Susan with any stray end of lint or sticking plaster. The kiss, Sarah noticed, was a firm one in spite of the angle at which contact was made. He did not wince; but breaking free smiled and touched the wound gingerly as if in a dumb show of apology for the inconvenience of it. It was the innocent gesture of a boy and the contrived one of a man with a sense of theatre who guessed that people were bound to wonder to what extent delayed shock or plain discomfort might impair the ardour of his performance, later, of private and more intimate duties.

Sarah stooped and gathered the folds of the bride's veil, followed the family into the vestry. The organist was playing a tune she thought was probably 'Perfect Love'. 'Hello, Mrs Bingham,' she said, and kissed Susan on one flushed happy cheek. 'I wanted to say it first.'

'I couldn't stop shivering,' Susan said. 'Did it show? I felt everybody could see.' She kissed her mother, and Aunt Fenny, and Uncle Arthur. 'It sounds funny,' she said at one point. 'Susan Bingham.'

'Oh, you'll get used to it,' Teddie said. 'Anyway you'd better.'

They signed the register.

*

Within half an hour of the incident of the stone two NCOs of the British Military Police had arrived on duty outside the church. Mounted on motor-cycles they led the bride and groom from the ceremony to the reception at the Gymkhana Club where they were to remain until the time came for them to escort the bridal car to the station. Their instructions were to keep an eye open for any further attempted act or demonstration of an anti-British nature – for as such for the moment, it was thought, the incident of the stone had to be treated.

The roar of the motor-bikes and the stand-no-nonsense demeanour of the men astride them seemed to release in the people who had attended the ceremony and now watched the departure of Teddie and Susan and presently made their way to their own waiting cars and taxis (and in one case a military truck, logged out as on civil duties), an animus of a subtly different nature from the one which had made them feel calm, remote and dignified. It entered and stirred them like the divine breath of a God who had bent his brow to call forth sterner angels.

The affair of the stone, first reacted to with a sense of shock, then treated as lamentable, regrettable, a challenge of the kind to which the only answer was to rally round and make the young couple feel that after all their day had not been ruined, was now seen as contemptible; mean, despicable, cowardly. Typical.

The scene of the crime, the Victoria roundabout, significantly marked by the presence of a police truck and three armed MPs, caused among the occupants of the cars as they passed by it on their way to the club some speculation about the exact spot from which the stone had been thrown and the likely escape-route of the demonstrator. Neither young Bingham nor his best man had apparently seen a thing. They had been looking at the memorial or intent on what they were saying to one another. The shock of the stone coming through the window, the fact that young Bingham was hurt and that the car took some time to pull up – according to the best man who had to explain things to the guests as they arrived as well as get the doctor, ring the police, and warn the bride and her uncle to hang on at the guest house for an extra half-hour; all of which he had done with an admirably cool head – were contributing factors to the ruffian having got away unseen.

It was probably the work of some fellow with a grudge, someone who had been dismissed for stealing from his master as likely as not – and who had heard about the wedding from a friend still employed in the cantonment and had hung about hoping for a chance to get his own back, not caring who it was he actually threw a stone at. If the culprit wasn't a fellow of that sort he was some clerk or student whose head was crammed with a lot of hot air about the iniquities of the *raj*: the kind who needed a kick up the backside or shipping out to Tokyo as a present to Hirohito or Subhas Chandras Bose. If he was that kind of fellow he was probably a member of a group at work outside the cantonment, in Mirat City, where the cantonment police had no jurisdiction.

Some of the princely states were jam-packed with political agitators who fled from the British provinces at the time of the mass Congress arrests, over a year ago, and even a small place like Mirat was known to have had its share. There was probably still a nucleus that had escaped the Mirat city police net. In any case the city police were probably corrupt. The princes were loyal to the crown because the crown protected their rights and privileges. A prince's subjects were often only loyal to him because they were terrified of the consequences of not being. At heart a lot of them shared the same aspirations as the Indian nationalists of British India, or had been persuaded by propaganda to believe they did. Perhaps the incident of the stone was a warning shot, a sign that dear old Mirat was suddenly going to explode. On the whole that might not be a bad thing. The Nawab would come running to the cantonment authorities for help and that would give the police the opportunity to root out the hidden subversive elements.

The danger of such elements lay in the contact they might have with Indian troops. That had always been the nightmare. It was the finest army in the world. Subvert it and it could turn and destroy its creators like a man swatting flies. With the war the dangers of subversion had increased. The army's ranks had been swelled with recruits whose loyalty to the salt they ate could not be counted on as part of the martial tradition of tribe or caste. And yet its loyalty seemed as sure as ever, which seemed in turn to prove that pride of service could inspire men of any race and any colour, given the opportunity. Such thoughts, spoken or left unspoken, led to the third and final change of mood. This was a mood in which it was felt that the stone had not found its mark but had rebounded from its impact with the impenetrable and unbreakable defences that always surrounded any inviolable truth. The stone changed nothing. Someone ought to pay for it but in the meantime it had to be treated as a joke; a joke in bad taste, certainly, but what else could be expected?

The two MPs who had escorted the bridal car greeted the guests on their arrival in the forecourt of the old Gymkhana Club by stopping each car and indicating where it should be parked. The MPs were brisk, cheerful and efficient, and the guests accepted their polite but firm directives with the friendly nods of people who, used to giving orders, enjoyed obeying them in circumstances they knew called for attention to the small details of security and discipline. From their cars they entered the club by steps unfamiliarly but pleasantly got up in red carpet. They went in twos and threes into the dim fan-cooled entrance hall of busts, mounted trophies and padding barefoot servants; through the ante-room, a lounge, and out through one of the open french windows on to the terrace with its view on to an emerald-green lawn where a sprinkler was still at work.

*

Just as Captain Merrick returned to Sarah with a replenished glass of fruit-cup, the club secretary pressed through the adjacent group of people and said, 'Excuse me, Miss Layton. Have you seen your mother and uncle?'

'Mother was here a few minutes ago. I don't know where Uncle Arthur has got to.'

'I think they'd better be found.' He showed Sarah a card which she recognized as one of the wedding invitations. 'A servant just brought me this. One of the MPs sent it through. I'm afraid he's stopped the Nawab from coming in.'

'Stopped him? But why?'

'I suppose because he wasn't expecting an Indian to show up. I'll have to go out and start putting it right, but if your mother and uncle could be found and asked to come through I'd be grateful.'

'What's up?' a guest asked.

'The MPs have got the Nawab and his party stopped at the front door.'

'Good grief!' the guest said, laughed, and turned to pass the news on.

'I think I can probably find Major Grace,' Merrick said, '– if you'd scout round for your mother.'

'I'll try and keep him happy in the ante-room,' the secretary called.

Sarah made her way through the guests to the far end of the terrace. She found her mother listening to Mrs Hobhouse.

'Mother, the Nawab's arrived,' she said, interrupting a flow of reminiscences about the 1935 earthquake in Quetta.

'Oh, my dear,' Mrs Hobhouse said. 'Down tools. Fly. We *are* honoured. He only got back from Gopalakand last night. I'd better come with you. He's an old dear, but terribly hard going. Thank God for the red carpet. He'll probably think it's for him.'

'I'm afraid he won't,' Sarah said – taking the glass her mother seemed not to know she had in her hand and putting it on a near-by table. 'He's been refused entry.'

'Refused entry?' Mrs Layton repeated. 'I don't understand.'

Mrs Hobhouse grasped Sarah's elbow. 'My dear, whatever do you mean?'

'The MPs stopped him coming in. Captain Merrick's gone to find Uncle Arthur and the secretary wants us in the ante-room.'

She began to guide her mother back along the terrace. Mrs Hobhouse followed. 'But they can't have,' she said. 'I mean surely they were warned.' Suddenly she took Mrs Layton's other arm. 'Hold on. This is our job. Stay here with Sarah, and my husband and I will bring the old boy out. It's not right that either you or your brother-in-law should be placed in a position of having to apologize. If it really has happened it's club business or station business. Nothing to do with the wedding. Just stand here close to the door. Or better still go down on the lawn. I see Teddie and Susan are there. We'll bring the Nawab straight through and down. He'll feel it's a more conspicuous place anyway, better than hobnobbing in this crush.'

'I think Mrs Hobhouse is right, Mother. Come on.'

She led her mother down the stone steps into the glare. It was not unbearably hot. A light breeze had sprung up, was tangling Susan's veil. She stood in the middle of a group of Teddie's fellow officers, laughing. Sarah, catching sight of Captain Merrick leading Uncle Arthur along the terrace, called out and beckoned them down.

'I must say,' Uncle Arthur said when reaching them, 'this is turning out to be the most jinx-ridden affair I've ever been mixed up with, and that's saying something. Where's Fenny?'

'Shall I find her?' Captain Merrick asked.

'Well, that's easier said than done in this crush. I have a feeling there are more people drinking our drink and getting up their appetites for our food than were ever invited. Why couldn't they have set up a marquee or something? Separate the sheep from the goats. I'd swear half that gang on the terrace are just ordinary members of the club muscling in on the festivities. I've been having a word with the contractor's chap and warned him we're not going to pay a penny over the quotation. He's making a packet as it is. I say, cheer up, Mildred.'

'What?'

'You look half asleep.'

Mrs Layton stared at him, then said to Sarah, 'I'd better tell Susan and Teddie what's happened.'

'Aren't we going to the ante-room?' Captain Merrick asked Sarah, as her mother left her side and went over to the group of men clustered round the bride.

'Mrs Hobhouse thought it better if we stayed here and she and Colonel Hobhouse brought the Nawab down.'

'Good idea,' Major Grace said. 'Then we can pretend we know nothing about this snarl-up or whatever it is. I say, is this him now? Must be. How extraordinary. He looks like some downtrodden munshi.'

The chattering and laughter on the terrace did not lessen, but Sarah thought that abruptly it changed key. The Station Commander was walking slowly across the width of the terrace with a short little Indian, the top of whose truncated cone of a hat came level with Colonel Hobhouse's left epaulette – which in any case was lower than the right because the Colonel was bending slightly. The impression given by this sideways and downward inclination was one of deafness more than deference. Behind Colonel Hobhouse and the Nawab Mrs Hobhouse was similarly dwarfed by a tall thin man with an eye-patch.

'That must be Count Bronowsky,' Captain Merrick told Sarah, keeping his voice low. 'He's supposed to have been blown up by a bomb in St Petersburg but some unkind people say it's the result of peeping through keyholes. I'm told he's about seventy. He doesn't look it, does he?'

Behind Bronowsky and Mrs Hobhouse, the secretary walked with young Kasim.

At the head of the steps the Nawab paused, half turned with his left hand held in a gesture of command and invitation, and Ahmed detached himself from his position at the rear, came to the Nawab's side, made a firm elbow upon which the Nawab now placed his hand. Slowly they descended the steps. Sarah saw the thin face of the old man with the eye-patch twitch, as if something had both pleased and amused him.

When they reached lawn level the Nawab removed his hand and Ahmed stood back to enable Mrs Hobhouse and the Count to precede him.

'Mrs Layton,' Colonel Hobhouse said, 'his Highness, Nawab Sir Ahmed Ali Guffur Kasim Bahadur.'

Mrs Layton nodded her head and murmured, 'How do you do. I'm so glad you were able to come.'

The Nawab returned the nod and waited.

'Nawab Sahib,' Colonel Hobhouse said, 'Mrs Layton wishes me to say on her behalf and on behalf of her family how deeply she has appreciated your many kindnesses in regard to the arrangements at the guest house.'

'Indeed, yes,' Mrs Layton murmured again.

The Nawab raised one hand, palm outwards. The lids fell over his eyes. The head jerked fractionally to one side.

The Station Commander hesitated, as if he had not been fed with a line and felt he could not now say what he had rehearsed and make sense. Sarah guessed his predicament. He had expected the Nawab or himself to make some reference to the incident of the stone, to express regret or make light of it. But the stone and the insult just given at the door cancelled each other out. Thanks had been offered for hospitality, been autocratically dismissed as quite unnecessary and without the formal expression of regret and reassurance that might have followed in regard to the stone there had emerged a silence which although short-lived was profound. Sarah, narrowing her eyes against the sunlight, was moved to a special intensity of feeling for the texture of the clothes she wore. The breeze was pressing the ankle-length skirt of her bridesmaid's gown against her legs. She had a fleeting image of them all as dolls dressed and positioned for a play that moved mechanically but uncertainly again and again to a point of climax, but then shifted its ground, avoiding a direct confrontation. Each shift was marked by just such a pause and the wonder perhaps was that the

170]

play continued. But the wind blew, nudging her through the creamy thinness of peach-coloured slipper satin and she and they were reanimated, prodded into speech and new positions. The Count Bronowsky, Chief Minister in Mirat. My daughter, Sarah. My brother-in-law, Major Grace. Captain Merrick. And this is my younger daughter, Susan, now Mrs Bingham.

Almost imperceptibly they had moved closer to the group that had surrounded Susan and which had now opened out leaving her exposed, vulnerable, tiny and tender in the ethereal whiteness of stiffened, wafting net and white brocade, several paces away from the spot where the Nawab's slow progress had finally come to a halt. For an instant Sarah thought that her mother would allow the presentation to end there – as if her duty were to show the Nawab no more than an image of the bride, an effigy set up to demonstrate the meaning and purpose of an alien rite. Her mother made a gesture, vague, evasive, but it – or some instinct of Susan's own – prompted the bride into motion, the totally unexpected motion – charming, unprecedented – of a curtsy. She sank into the billowy whiteness, bringing the effigy to life, and causing a hush among the watchers on the terrace. An Englishwoman did not curtsy to an Indian prince. But the hush was only one of astonishment and disapproval for the time it took for the watchers to feel what those closer to her felt almost instantaneously: a little shock-wave of enchantment: and when the Nawab was seen to take a hesitant step forward and then a firm one, and offer his hand, keeping it there until, rising, she put her own into it, the prettiness of the picture she made was enhanced by recognition of the fact that her impulsive action – so delightfully performed – had achieved what words and formal gestures could not – the re-establishment without loss of face of the essential *status quo*.

'Thank you for coming to my wedding,' Susan said, and Sarah – losing the drift of the Nawab's response, his involved but courteous good wishes for the health and happiness of bride and groom – considering still what Susan had just said, sensing something odd about it, turned her head and let her gaze come to rest on Count Bronowsky. By his side Mrs Hobhouse stood, silently watching – with a contented smile – the exchange of pleasantries between the Nawab and Susan and Teddie who by now had also been introduced. Bronowsky had a panama hat in the hand unencumbered by the ebony, gold-topped cane. She imagined what he would look like with it on and wondered whether he had worn it in the motor-car. Perhaps, under the hat, the pale pink skin would look like that of a high-caste Hindu. If he wore a cap such as the Nawab had on he might look very like a wealthy Muslim from the north – so subtle sometimes was the distinction between that kind of Indian and thin gaunt Europeans who had lived for years out East. Additionally shaded by the brim of a hat, travelling in a car with two Indians, the MPs could have assumed there was no white man in the small party arriving and expecting admittance.

She tried to assess the degree of humiliation Bronowsky would be capable of feeling. If he was really a count, the white Russian *émigré* who had been found by the Nawab in Monte Carlo and made use of as a go-between in the affair the Nawab was having, or had had and was trying to continue, with a European woman, and considering the fact that he had served for twenty years in a position that must have been even more testing than that of a British political adviser to an Indian ruler, then he had probably acquired a degree of immunity from attacks on his prestige and self-esteem.

But then, Sarah reminded herself, it was impossible to assume anything when it came to such matters. And often it was the thoughtless action, the unintentional insult, the casual attack which, catching you off guard, hurt most. Remembering the twitch of amusement when the Nawab made his imperious but frail, attractive gesture of command to be helped down the steps, Sarah was struck by the idea that perhaps the crooked fleeting smile was one of amusement at the Nawab's expense, an involuntary sign of underlying resentment of the fact that he, Bronowsky, should be subjected to the same humiliation as the Nawab, his master, but be denied the opportunity to get his own back so swiftly. 'One never knows,' Mr Hobhouse had said recently, 'what to make of the Count, but of course it's probably important to remember he's a dispossessed Russian and that the Nawab is not, after all, a little Tsarevich saved from a cellar in Ekaterinberg.'

Sarah wished she had seen how he reacted to the sight of Susan curtsying to the man who was not a little Tsarevich, or could see his expression now, as he waited his turn to be introduced. He stood, slightly stooped, his head inclined to catch whatever Mrs Hobhouse next said to him, but looking away half right, so that Sarah saw only his eye-patch profile. Was a black patch, on its own, expressive? Sarah thought that it was. Seen by itself, thus, it looked like the round bulging eye of a nocturnal creature abroad in sunlight, staring myopically, alerted by some unexpected but familiar sound of which it awaited a repetition in order to be certain of the accuracy of its judgement of the source: and Sarah, glancing in the direction indicated by the fixed intensity of the imaginarily luminous black patch, found that the source appeared to be Captain Merrick who, for the moment, stood alone, hands behind his back, unaware of the scrutiny he was under, taking a breather from the cumulatively exhausting duties of best man. Hatless, in full unflattering sunlight – the first time she was conscious of seeing Captain Merrick so – the years he could give Teddie showed. He was probably nearing thirty. In the company of Teddie and the young officers who surrounded Susan, he looked hardened, burnt by experiences distant from their own and placing him at distance now. He was not really Teddie's type. Chance alone – the sharing of quarters with Teddie and Captain Bishop's jaundice – had led to his presence at the wedding.

But the same could be said of all the other guests. And realizing that, Sarah understood what was odd about the thing Susan had said. The oddness was in that possessive phrase, 'my wedding'. She should have said 'our wedding' if the wedding had to be mentioned at all. She should not have said 'my wedding'. She should not have curtsied. She should not have been so composed, earlier, when she arrived promptly at the church at the postponed hour, and made no comment on the cause of the delay, walked slowly up the aisle on Uncle Arthur's arm and appeared not to see the damage to Teddie's cheek. Even in the vestry afterwards she had said nothing about the stone. She had said little about anything except to express concern that her shivering at the altar might have been too obvious and uncertainty about the suitability of the new name given her in exchange for the old one.

But she was guilty of all these acts and omissions, and 'my wedding' was – to Sarah – suddenly and touchingly significant, revealing as it did the extent to which Susan was conscious of the fact that no one else except Teddie seemed much concerned about it. Being married to Teddie was something she had set her heart on, presumably because in her mysterious self-sufficient way she was prepared to love him and be loved by him, but whatever the reason for the marriage the wedding was the one conclusive step she had to take to demonstrate in public the importance of what was happening to her. It was, on a much larger scale, like the gesture she made or sudden word she spoke which interrupted the flow of other people's thoughts and drew attention back to her existence. But the wedding, among strangers, in unfamiliar surroundings, already marred by the incident of the stone and the insult to the Nawab, was an affair that threatened to overwhelm her. She was fighting the threat with a single-minded determination, a tense, febrile assertion of her rights to her own illusion which Sarah, now that she understood, admired her for, loved her for, because she judged the amount of courage it took to close the eyes to the destructive counter-element of reality that entered any state of intended happiness.

She thought: That sort of courage is what distinguishes Susan from me, apart from her prettiness, and why men like Teddie have always finally preferred her company to mine. She creates an illusion of herself as the centre of a world without sadness and allows them entry. It is like when we are children. She is the little girl with the gift for making let's-pretend seem real; although when she was young it was the last talent I suspected in her. If she had it then she kept it secret, closely guarded. Now it has blossomed. One senses it in her as something tough and enduring but delicately poised, in constant need of fine adjustments so that it can contain or be contained, be shared, withheld, never diminished by exposure to ridicule.

The old protective instinct which she had thought atrophied by long disuse quickened and then lay still. All the outlets for it were overgrown and it understood it had woken to no purpose and must sleep again, become oblivious of its awakened hunger. Abruptly she moved away – taking the opportunity given by a general movement as the Count went forward to meet the bride and groom – and found herself facing Ahmed: a re-enactment in different dress and circumstances of the occasion on the waste ground when she rode at him, smiling and speechless, and he stared back, smiling less but just as silent: a meaningless situation then, equally meaningless now. They might have come from different planets. It was impossible to establish common ground; neither sense of duty nor personal compulsion would ever bridge the distance or shatter the glass from behind which they smiled and stared vacantly at one another like specimen products of alien cultures in display cabinets

174]

in a museum placed close together through an administrative over-sight, or odd stroke of chance.

'He is very pleased with the book,' Ahmed announced suddenly.

'Oh yes. Gaffur. I'm glad.' She turned her head slightly, because of the garlic. It really was a revolting smell. The poems of Gaffur and the smell of garlic: a dark vision of an old lady under an awn-ing on the sun-deck of a houseboat, and of trunks, musty, unclaimed, containing what was left of that girl: passed over Sarah's conscious-ness of her presence on a sunlit scene – inconsequential but positive – like vapours casting actual shadows.

'It was a bit of luck,' she said. The old lady knew so much: more than facts – the shape and substance and significance of an accumu-lation of detail that so often, in the mind, passed by, as a procession of irrelevancies.

'What was a bit of luck?'

The voice was not Ahmed's but that of Captain Merrick who had arrived at her side.

'The poems of Gaffur,' she replied, glancing up at Merrick. 'Just something we brought for the Nawab. Someone we met in Kashmir told us that Gaffur was a Kasim too, so we had a copy bound up, we wouldn't have known otherwise.'

'I don't even know about Gaffur. Is he famous?'

'Oh, not is, was.' She turned to Ahmed again. 'I mean in the sense of "was, not is" because he's dead. But he's still famous as a classic, isn't he?'

Ahmed put his head on one side, letting the eyes close. He rarely made a typical Indian gesture. He held and used himself with the stiff composure of an Englishman. She had absorbed that fact un-consciously, was only conscious of it now when he responded with the gesture of the head, like any other Indian deflecting a compli-ment to himself or his country from its target.

'But something tells me,' she went on, 'you don't go in much for poetry. What did Gaffur write about? Deserts and roses, and moon-lit gardens? Jugs of wine?'

Merrick laughed. 'That's Omar Khayyam.'

'Oh, no, just Persian,' she said. 'I mean they all wrote like that surely, Persian poets, Urdu poets. Was Gaffur an exception?'

'No, I think he wasn't,' Ahmed said. 'Roses and deserts and moonlit gardens pretty well fill the bill from what I remember.'

'Did you have to learn him as a boy?'

[175

'Read is a more accurate word.' Ahmed hesitated, then added, 'I never learned anything my teachers thought important. In the end they gave me up.'

'I know what you mean,' Sarah said. 'It's how I feel about me, more or less, except that I think I'd say I never saw the importance of what I was taught and always felt I wanted to be taught quite different things – the sort of things no one thought of teaching. I was the kind of child who automatically asked why when I was told the cat sat on the mat. My teachers said I ought to curb a tendency to squander curiosity on the self-evident.'

'Then from their point of view, you're in the right place, Miss Layton. In India nothing is self-evident.'

She looked at him, puzzled. Ask him a question and he would answer, usually with that brevity which made asking a further question a grindingly self-conscious business. She did not remember him making comments – of the kind that could remove verbal exchange from the level of an interrogation to that of a conversation – but in the last few moments he had made two, although the second had the familiar characteristic of those answers of his which seemed to kill a subject stone-dead, and left her suspended (she felt) like a vulture hovering over a carcass with no meat left on. She smiled, found herself tongue-tied, but hoped her silence would be interpreted as politeness and interest and would encourage him – if for once he was in the mood to talk – to continue. But it did not. He was not even looking at her now: instead at Captain Merrick, holding his head at an angle that disclosed an aggressive set of chin and jaw. He did not look angry but she wondered whether he was. He had been stopped at the door too, and had even less opportunity than Count Bronowsky to even up the score.

'Actually,' Captain Merrick said, 'that's something I feel bound to disagree with. I'd say things that are self-evident are common to all countries.' He was smiling and so now was Mr Kasim, but glancing from one to the other Sarah thought: No, you mustn't tangle with each other. She felt powerless to stop them. She saw Aunt Fenny hastening down the steps and moved to intercept her; but that was unnecessary. She was coming to them in any case.

'What's been going on?' she asked before she had quite reached them.

'Nothing's been going on, Aunt Fenny. The Nawab has arrived.'

'Well I know that. People up there are saying he had difficulty

176]

getting in.' She did not trouble to lower her voice. Aunt Fenny never did. She seemed not to have seen Mr Kasim standing almost next to her, but turned on him abruptly, thereby proving she had, and said, 'What a chapter of accidents!' and came back to Sarah, leaving her exclamation as it were – bouncing, to work its own way to a position of rest. 'I've been putting out Susan's going away things. I can't find the hat-box.'

A room in the annexe had been set aside for the bride's use. Sarah and Aunt Fenny had brought Susan's luggage with them. 'It must still be in the car,' Sarah said. 'I'll go and see.'

'No, I'm sure Captain Merrick won't mind —'

Seeing he was wanted he came closer.

'A hat-box. We think it's still in the car. The one Sarah and I came in.'

'I know where it's parked. I'll check. What should I do with the box, bring it to you or take it to the annexe?'

'If you'd bring it to me? Well, whatever you think. So long as it's found. God knows what we'll do if it's not there or been stolen. There wasn't a servant in sight at the annexe just now. Anyone could have walked in. I've nabbed a spare body and made him stand guard on peril of his life.'

Captain Merrick nodded and went. 'Come,' Aunt Fenny said. 'I must meet the Nawab.'

As Sarah followed Mrs Grace she carried with her an impression of Ahmed alone, disengaged; standing restricted in the centre of a world she would never enter, did not know and could not miss. How lucky we are, she thought. How very, very lucky.

*

'Nobody told us you was expecting any Indian gentleman, sir,' the MP explained as he accompanied Captain Merrick to the place where the bridal cars were parked.

'I realize that. It was very remiss of us.'

'We didn't think you allowed Indian gentlemen into the club, so the corporal and me, sir, we thought those three gentlemen was havin' a lark. I mean anyone could've got hold of one of those cards, sir, and written a fancy name on it.'

'You did your duty as you saw it, Sergeant, no one is blaming you.'

'All the same we dropped a right clanger, didn't we, sir? Especially seeing one of 'em was a white gentleman after all and another was his nibs.' The sergeant grinned. 'Captain Bates'll have my guts for garters.'

'Is he your officer?'

'That's right, sir. But no sweat. We live and learn. And I'll know the nabob next time, won't I?'

They stopped at the line of limousines. One of the drivers left the circle of men squatting under one of the old trees shading the lawn, but the sergeant ignored him, opened the doors and presently found the box on the floor under one of the tip-up seats. 'Here you are, sir, one hat-box, brides for the use of.'

'Thank you, Sergeant. Are you staying with us or expecting a relief?'

'Orders are to wait and escort the cars to the station, sir.'

'In that case there'll be something for you and the corporal to toast the bride and groom in. I'll lay it on and send one of the stewards out to take you round and show you where. But you'd better go one at a time.'

'Thank you, sir. That'll be very much appreciated.'

'Well even a copper has to eat.'

The sergeant grinned again, came to attention and saluted. Merrick, encumbered by the hat-box, and capless, sketched the idea of a salute in reply and made back towards the club entrance. As he reached the steps he paused, looked at the hat-box, and then instead of entering continued along the front until he reached the corner of the building where a path led off through a shrubbery marked by a directional finger on which the word Annexe was painted black on white. He returned a few minutes later, without the box, and walked along the side of the clubhouse, between a flower-bed and the tennis courts where an old man in shirt and dhoti and a youth in a ragged pair of khaki shorts were restoring the lime-wash markings. Merrick stopped, reached into his pocket for his cigarette case, selected one, lit it and began leisurely to smoke and watch, as if concerned about the straightness of the lines that were reappearing, brightly, on their faded predecessors. The youth was doing all the work. It was not arduous but the sun was hot and the gleam on his shoulders showed that he was sweating. He became conscious of the spectator, made a mistake in the marking. The old man spoke to him sharply. Merrick did not

178]

move. He inhaled smoke slowly, deeply, continuing to watch until, growing tired of the scene, he threw the cigarette half-smoked into the flower-bed and continued along the path.

The lawn was now deserted. A single voice, a woman's raised in laughter, came from the almost equally deserted terrace. The wedding party had gone inside for the cold fork-lunch wedding breakfast and the ceremony of the cutting of the cake. Merrick looked at his watch. Ten minutes short of midday. He walked on the lawn, making for the steps, paused near them, stooped and picked up shreds of pink and white paper where someone had stood and brushed confetti from a dress or uniform. Straightening he saw himself watched by Count Bronowsky who had appeared at the head of the steps alone.

As Merrick joined him Bronowsky said: 'Ah, there you are, Captain Merrick. I suppose you have been undertaking yet another of the onerous duties of best man.'

'Just a small errand to recover a hat-box.'

'Well, you are a man for detail. I can see that. For instance, you share my compulsive instinct for tidiness. What was it, confetti?'

Merrick opened his hand.

'They say it's significant,' Bronowsky said, picking the scraps of paper from Merrick's palm and dropping them into the empty glass a guest had left on the balustrade. He picked the glass up too and placed it on a near-by table, for greater safety. While he did these things he continued to talk. 'I mean significant psychologically. Compulsively tidy people, one is told, are always wiping the slate clean, trying to give themselves what life denies all of us, a fresh start.' Having finished with the confetti and the glass he now looked at Merrick and, putting a hand on his shoulder, began to lead the way along the terrace towards the distant hum of conversation in the inner room where the bride and groom and guests had re-assembled. 'You are married?' he asked casually.

'No —'

'Neither am I. Far better not. We'd drive our poor wives crazy, wouldn't we? Besides which, of course, there is this other thing about us – I mean about our tidiness. They say it's characteristic of someone who wishes to be the organizing centre of his own life and who has no gift for sharing.'

Bronowsky had stopped walking, but he retained his hold on Merrick's shoulder. The two men were of equal height.

'I am sorry,' Bronowsky went on. 'I am sorry about the incident this morning. You were not hit yourself?' He removed his hand but stood his ground, keeping Merrick waiting.

'No, apart from Captain Bingham's scratch the only damage was to the car.'

The Chief Minister remained where he was and did not answer. Merrick also kept still. Presently he said, 'Is there something you want, Count Bronowsky?'

'Yes. The answer to a question. But the question is impertinent. I hesitate, naturally —'

'Please don't.'

'Well. I have been wondering if you thought that perhaps the stone was thrown at you.'

'Oh? Why should you wonder that?'

'Mrs Grace tells me you were in the Indian Police.'

'That's quite true.' Merrick took out his cigarette case, opened and offered it to Bronowsky.

'No, thank you. I never smoke until evening.'

He watched while Merrick lit a cigarette then said, 'We shan't be missed for a bit, so let me tell you a little story. Years ago, when I was overhauling the administration in Mirat, I brought in a man who rather later in life than he felt he deserved had risen to be a judge of the High Court in Ranpur. I made him the State's Chief Justice, a grandiloquent title but with a salary to match. He retired in far greater comfort than would have been the case if he'd stayed in the ICS. He died peacefully in bed, but was once the victim of what the newspapers of my youth would have described as a murderous attack by a couple of ruffians who set on him in the dark as he walked from my house to his. I often warned him of the danger for a man in his position of walking alone, at night, in a usually deserted road. In fact for a time I made sure he was followed by a couple of my own stout lads. But he caught on to it and told me he would never visit me again if I treated him like that. So I withdrew the guards and then this thing happened. Two men whom he never got a proper look at jumped out at him. He was badly beaten.'

Merrick blew out smoke, and nodded his head.

'For a time,' Bronowsky continued, 'our police were completely at a loss because none of our own known malcontents continued for long to be real suspects. The most likely ones had been arrested on suspicion of course, but protested their innocence vehemently – indeed with fortitude. In those days I had not yet succeeded in persuading the Mirat police to dispense with certain old-fashioned interrogatory methods. Anyway, for a time it looked as if the mystery of the attack on my highly prized Chief Justice would go unsolved, but then we had a stroke of luck. I was discussing the case with the poor fellow – who was still laid up and only just regaining his faculties – and he said, "You know, Bronowsky, I think I had a premonition about it." I asked him when and how. He thought for a bit and said he believed the premonition dated from a day about a week before the attack, when he was presiding over his court. It was a hot afternoon and the case before him was extremely complex. The people who had been admitted to the public seats were restless – fanning themselves with papers, whispering, that sort of thing, very distracting. He kept thinking, "In a minute I shall call them to order. In a minute I shall clear the court." But he somehow couldn't summon the necessary determination. He said, "I had an extraordinary sensation that something else" – and he didn't mean the case being heard – "– that something else had to be done first, done, or seen through, attended to. I felt I was being not watched exactly but waited for." After a while he stopped examining the faces of the pleaders and witnesses and the face of the accused and looked across at the public benches.'

Bronowsky had been holding his panama hat in the same hand that held the ebony cane. Now he took the hat in his free hand, hesitated, then gestured with hat and cane, raising his arms slightly as though conjuring an image of the courtroom and the judge's perplexity.

'Nothing extraordinary there, but after a while he noticed a young man who was not fanning himself, was not whispering to his neighbours, but leaning forward apparently absorbed. He found himself returning to meet this man's gaze many times. I asked him if the face of the young man had been familiar. Could it have been a man he had once sent to prison? He said no, not familiar, not exactly familiar. He never forgot a face, especially the face of a man he had sentenced. I asked him to think back carefully during the next day or two, particularly about the more sensational cases he had tried since coming to Mirat, because the young man might have been a relative of someone he had sentenced to hang or to prison for life. When I next saw him he said, "I've been thinking, as you told me, but not about sensational cases, nor about cases I've dealt with in Mirat. I've been considering the two cases I've never been able to shelve satisfactorily as over and done with because of the element of doubt. They were cases which *seemed* clear cut enough, but left me vaguely troubled. Both took place a long time ago, one when I was a District and Sessions judge and the other when I first became a judge of the High Court in Ranpur. In the Ranpur case I had to send a man to the gallows. The young man who watched me in court two weeks ago could easily have been his son. When you sentence a man to death you never forget the expression on his face while he listens to you. This was the same expression." I asked him to tell me the dead man's name, and suggested we got the co-operation of the police in Ranpur to find out whether the son or some other close relative had been in Mirat two weeks ago.'

Bronowsky stopped, again made the gesture of half-raising his arms.

Merrick said, 'And so you caught the chap.'

'Oh, no. The Chief Justice wouldn't hear of it. Because of the element of doubt that had stayed in his mind all those years. All the same I conducted private inquiries and established to my own satisfaction that the hanged man's son was in Mirat at the time of the attack. You see I was after the accomplice. The result of my inquiries in that direction pointed to the guilt of a young gentleman of Mirat of hitherto unblemished character, but on whom the police were now able to keep an eye. Their vigilance was rewarded later. You of course will understand the necessity of such precautions. Professional criminals and openly organized political agitators are one thing. One can always cope with them. It is these others – the dark young men of random destiny and private passions who present the greater difficulty. For instance, the stone this morning – ostensibly thrown at the Nawab Sahib's car. If it had happened in the city it could have sparked off a communal riot. The Muslims might have blamed the Hindus and set fire to a Hindu shop. The Hindus might then have retaliated by slaughtering a pig outside the Abu-Q'rim mosque. The police would then have had to break up the fracas with lathi charges and hooligan elements would then have attacked the police station. All this for a stone, thrown at you perhaps, by one of these young men because in the past you carried out some duty with a vigour he thought cruelly unjust.'

Merrick laughed. 'I'll shoulder the responsibility if that helps to explain the damage to the Nawab's car to everyone's satisfaction. When I was a police officer I had enough brickbats chucked at me during riots and demonstrations to learn you can't dodge them all.'

'My dear Captain Merrick. You totally misunderstand the reason for my waylaying you like this —'

'Yes, well, I realize it isn't a chance meeting.'

'Quite so. I came to look for you. But not to ask you to shoulder responsibility. To seek your help in placing it.'

'What does that mean?'

'It means that directly Mrs Grace told me you had been in the Indian Police a number of apparently unrelated things fell into a pattern for me and even pointed to a likely source of inquiry. My interest isn't in you or the stone or the damage to Nawab Sahib's car. My interest is in Mirat.'

Merrick shrugged slightly and smiled. 'Well, don't worry. If I was the target you can rest assured that by this time next week the target will be in quite a different place, a long way from here.'

'But can you say the same of the man or youth who threw the stone, or of the people who put him up to it, of the people he discussed it with, whose help he had in plotting the time and place and day? I hardly have to tell you that such an incident was almost certainly planned, and planned in concert.'

'Perhaps, but it seems a lot of trouble to go to, I mean just to get a crack at an unimportant, comparatively junior police officer who's no longer even in the force.'

Bronowsky said nothing for a while. He transferred the hat back to the hand that rested on the ebony stick, then looked up.

'But you are not unimportant. Surely you are the Merrick who was district superintendent of police in Mayapore last year, at the time of the August riots and of the rape of the English girl, Daphne Manners, in the Bibighar Gardens?'

Merrick, arrested in the act of carrying the cigarette to his lips, now completed the movement. He inhaled and expelled then held the cigarette in a position suggestive of stubbing. Bronowsky pushed forward the ashtray on the table they stood next to and waited while Merrick, accepting the cue, carefully extinguished the tip, tapping and then pressing, then letting go and rubbing thumb and finger-tips to clear them of clinging particles.

He said, 'How do you arrive at that conclusion?'

'I deduce it. My deduction is correct? You are that officer?'

'I've no reason to deny it.'

'Nor to advertise it? Mrs Grace says you were DSP in Sundernagar, which I take it is the district you were transferred to after the Mayapore affair, and which you mention when anyone asks where you were before getting your commission. I imagine you are ready to talk about Sundernagar and other places, but prefer for personal reasons to gloss over Mayapore. If so I'm afraid I inadvertently let the cat out of the bag. I was telling Mrs Grace how much we appreciated your thoughtful action in ringing through to Ahmed and she said you were an excellent man for detail, probably as a result of your experience as a police officer. Well directly she mentioned that, certain bells – which for reasons I'll explain were very ready to ring – rang loud and clear, and I'm afraid I said almost at once, Merrick? Police? Surely that's the fellow who was DSP in Mayapore at the time of the Bibighar Gardens affair? I was so positive that it took me aback when she looked surprised and said she only knew about a place called Sundernagar. I'm afraid I insisted I was right, and she was obviously so intrigued I thought it fair to try and have a word with you before you go in.'

'Well, it's a bit of a nuisance, but it can't be helped. You'd better tell me about the little bells.'

'To begin with there was just the name, Merrick. It was vaguely familiar when Mr Kasim first mentioned it to me on Wednesday evening. But a young army officer called Merrick meant nothing to me. In fact I doubt whether the same young officer described by Mrs Grace as late of the Indian Police a moment ago would have meant anything either but for two other things that I was thinking about on the way here, wondering whether there could possibly be a connexion between them. The incident of the stone, and a report I had from Mr Kasim on Thursday morning. Tell me, Captain Merrick, does the name Pandit Baba mean anything to you?'

Merrick did not answer immediately, but his expression was that of a man sorting out a number of images conjured by the name rather than that of someone taking time to search the dim reaches of an uncertain memory.

'As a matter of fact, it does.'

'Please tell me what.'

'He's one of those so-called venerable Hindu scholars who

manages never to get caught inciting his eager young disciples to commit acts of violence against the Muslims, against the British, against anything the Pandit currently disapproves of.'

'But he does incite them?'

'I'm sure of it. In Mayapore I could never lay a finger on him though. Anything he did in public, like making a speech to college students, was all sweet reason and high-mindedness. He was quite capable of criticizing the Congress Party, too. I think the line he took was that they were poisoning Hinduism with politics, but he shunned publicity and discouraged any attempt to turn him into a renowned local figure. He was the perfect dedicated scholar. As far as I was concerned he was too good to be true. I also think he was a snake. A lot of the educated young Indians who got into trouble in Mayapore were under his influence at one time or another. We once arrested a chap for handing out seditious leaflets among workers in the British-Indian Electric factory. He said his pamphlet only repeated things Pandit Baba had discussed with a group of young men about ten days before. I thought I'd got him at last. We picked up some of the other boys, and then hauled in Baba Sahib. Within ten minutes the Pandit had them all grovelling and weeping and begging his forgiveness for misinterpreting his teaching. The one we'd arrested actually said he deserved to go to prison for his stupidity and unworthiness and the Pandit made a great show of being willing to go to prison in his stead as a penance for being such a poor *guru* that his innocent words could lead boys into trouble. Of course he knew he was as safe as houses. All the same he was more cautious afterwards.'

'Good. Thank you, Captain Merrick. Then you'll be interested to know that Pandit Baba is in Mirat at the moment. Mr Kasim was asked to meet him the other evening, ostensibly to enable Pandit Baba to be introduced to a son of M. A. Kasim, whom he professed to admire, which I doubt. But according to Mr Kasim, the Pandit spent most of the time talking about the Bibighar Gardens affair, with particular reference to the activities of the District Superintendent of Police, whom he can't have named, otherwise Ahmed would have hit on the connexion at once. No doubt the omission was intentional. He knew Ahmed had already met you. I find Ahmed a useful extra pair of eyes and ears because of his objectivity. He tells me what happens more or less exactly as it happens and I then consider the implications. In this case I wasn't very sure what the implications were. To involve Ahmed in something? To pump him about something? Something to do with Ahmed's father? Perhaps, perhaps. But it made little sense. Neither did the stone-throwing. However, it all makes very good sense when the police officer whose reputation Pandit Baba was carefully tearing to shreds the other evening turns out to be one of the officers riding in a car that has a stone thrown at it. The venerable gentleman used to live in Mirat, incidentally. We felt very much the same about him as you did when you were in Mayapore. By we I mean the then chief of police and myself. He never actually became *persona non grata*, but things were going that way. I was glad when he made the decision for us, and went off to Mayapore.'

'And you believe he was behind the incident this morning?'

'Oh, I think so, don't you?'

Merrick turned, placed his hands on the balustrade and looked out across the dazzling garden. Bronowsky came to the balustrade as well but continued to support himself on the cane.

'Not that we should be able to prove it,' Bronowsky continued. 'I don't intend to try. The Pandit is playing a little game with me, I think. The opening move was his invitation to Ahmed. He knew every word would be reported back to me. He also knew that directly I realized he was back in Mirat I would set my spies on him. My spies tell me he didn't come to Mirat alone but with a woman, who keeps in seclusion in the private rooms of Mrs Nair, who is the wife of the principal of the Hindu College, in whose bungalow Pandit Baba is staying. My spies also tell me that this morning between nine-forty-five and ten-forty-five, Pandit Sahib was scheduled to speak to the students of the college on the subject of his new study of the Bhagavad Gita. No doubt he did so, in full view of several hundred youths, standing on a dais, splendidly detached from anything so violent and vulgar as stone-throwing. Where my spies have been less successful is in getting the names of any of the young men with whom he has had private conversations. Perhaps he has had none. Perhaps it was all done before he actually reached Mirat. He is almost certainly in touch with very many people, throughout India.'

'Aren't you exaggerating a bit?'

'Oh, am I? Was the stone this morning then the first evidence you've had that you've been carefully tracked since leaving Mayapore?'

Bronowsky waited. Presently, as if reluctantly, Merrick said, 'Go on.'

'There was an incident in Sundernagar, perhaps? An anonymous letter referring to the fate of what, if I remember correctly, were called the innocent victims of the Bibighar Gardens? And in your first military establishment – another letter, or something even more direct to suggest there was some ill-wisher close at hand. For instance an inauspicious design drawn in chalk on the threshold of your quarters? Wherever you have been? Didn't it begin in Mayapore itself, and hasn't it continued, at intervals nicely calculated to make you believe that your last posting shook off whoever was intent on your discomfiture?'

Merrick allowed several seconds to elapse before replying.

'It's been much as you say. But it hasn't bothered me, and Mirat is their last opportunity. They can hardly go on persecuting me where I'm going unless some sepoy has been bribed to put a bullet through my head when nobody's looking.'

Bronowsky smiled. 'I don't think killing you is the idea, although I'm surprised they haven't thought of a more dramatic way of embarrassing you than throwing a stone. As you say, Mirat is their last opportunity for some time to come. The wedding would have been an excellent background for something colourful. I understand, incidentally, that you're not a close friend of the groom. Did it pass through your mind that taking part in the wedding might bring your persecutors out into the open?'

Merrick said, 'No, it was the other way round. I agreed to be best man and then realized I was probably the worst possible choice. But it was too late to withdraw and I wouldn't have known how. All that business is something I prefer to forget. I'm sorry you've identified me.'

'My dear fellow, why? All I can say is that if I've correctly judged Mrs Grace's reactions to my quite unintentional disclosure, you are now an object not only of interest but of admiring curiosity. They will remember how at the time the DSP Mayapore was singled out by the English press for praise and congratulation. One recalls it all well enough, the newspaper reports and the gossip here in the club, on this very terrace. Well you can imagine. An English girl criminally assaulted by Indians, not just any English girl – if there could possibly be such a thing in India – but a connexion of a one-time Governor in Ranpur who stayed at the palace in the thirties. Within – what was it, an hour or two – the police in Mayapore under their DSP had arrested the six culprits. Technically they were only suspects and not proven culprits but that hardly diminished the blaze of satisfaction at thoughts of revenge already afoot. It's all people talked about for days. Mirat has always had a floating population and we had people in from Mayapore who naturally enjoyed their reputations as experts on the rape and the riots, although these weren't really connected, were they? The rape was a local affair and the riots were on a national scale. Being a military and not a civil station, of course, the major focus of interest here was on that brigadier you had in Mayapore who took charge when the civil authorities decided they couldn't cope.'

'Brigadier Reid.'

'That's him. Reid. Most of the talk was of Reid but what it came down to in the majority view was that both the army and the police in Mayapore had acted with commendable vigour, whereas the civil had shilly-shallied. Well you know how people think these days – they say the civil has become so riddled with Indians that the old dependable type of English civilian has more or less died out and it's only the English army and police officer who can really handle an explosive situation. I remember a fellow sitting somewhere along there' – Bronowsky pointed to the far end of the terrace – 'one evening when I was having a drink with the Station Commander, not Hobhouse, his predecessor. There'd been a paragraph in the *Courier* about a farewell party in the Artillery Mess in Mayapore for Brigadier Reid, and, of course, the implication was that he'd got the sack. This fellow leaned across, pointed at the paragraph and said, "There you are. Reid saves the situation and then gets kicked out because he saved it his way, which probably means he killed twelve Indians where the Government thinks ten would have been enough. But the deputy commissioner who sat on his backside will probably get a plummy job in the Secretariat and a CIE." '

Merrick said, 'The Deputy Commissioner was a good enough man. And Reid didn't get the sack. He was given another brigade. It was a better job really. The brigade he had in Mayapore was only half-trained. The one he got was ready to go into the field. He's back at a desk now, though, so I've heard. Perhaps he didn't measure up. Perhaps he was a bit too old. His wife was dying when all that business was going on. We didn't know about that until afterwards.'

'Ah well, the truth is always one thing, but in a way it's the other thing, the gossip, that counts. It shows where people's hearts lie. Reid saving the situation and getting the sack is what they wanted to believe. Just as they wanted to believe that the fellow in charge of the police in Mayapore had arrested the right men in the Bibighar rape business. They blamed the civil for any excessive use of force the Brigadier was guilty of and they blamed the civil when it was gradually realized that the rape case was coming to nothing. Not even coming to court. They never thought of blaming the District Superintendent for arresting the wrong men because they were convinced they must have been the right men. And the people we got here from Mayapore during those few weeks following the rape took the line that it would have served the six suspects right if the rumours going round were true.'

'What rumours?'

'That the six boys were whipped and forced to eat beef to make them confess.'

'I see. That tale even reached Mirat, then?'

'Indeed it did.' Bronowsky paused. 'Was there any truth in it?'

'The beef business was a result of some minor confusion, I believe.'

'Confusion?'

'The jailers were Muslims and some food sent in for them was mistaken by an orderly for food sent in for the prisoners, who were all Hindus.'

'Ah, yes. A very reasonable explanation. And the whipping?'

'Judge Menen satisfied himself on that score by having the men examined.'

'Physically? Or merely by questioning?'

'I gathered questioning was all that was necessary. They all denied the rumour and swore they'd not been ill-treated.'

'You didn't examine them yourself?'

Merrick, who had answered most of Bronowsky's questions without facing him now did so. 'Why should I have? I'm the chap who was being accused of defiling and beating the prisoners.'

'Not actually accused, though? It was merely gossip, surely. Enough of it to cause the District Judge uneasiness?'

'Yes.'

'But not you?'

'No.'

'You ruled out the possibility of your subordinates having beaten the suspects?'

'I took personal charge of the interrogations. I knew everything that went on.'

'Except about the beef. You said there may have been confusion over the beef but you weren't present when the confusion arose?'

'I'm not in the witness-box.'

'Captain Merrick, I'm sorry. I don't mean to cross-examine you. But I have a natural curiosity. Would you satisfy it on one point? Were those men you arrested guilty of the rape?'

Merrick again looked across the balustrade, fixing his eyes, it seemed, on some intense but distant vision of incontrovertible truth.

'I think,' he said at last, 'that I shall believe they were until my dying day.'

After a while Bronowsky said, 'Our venerable pandit told Mr Kasim that he is acquainted with the aunt of one of your principal suspects, and was once engaged to try to teach him Hindi, the young man in question having lived most of his life in England.'

'Hari Kumar. That's quite correct. The aunt was a Mrs Gupta Sen.' He looked round at Bronowsky. 'Kumar wasn't just one of the principal suspects. He was *the* principal suspect. I believed then and believe now that he planned the whole thing. He'd been going out with Miss Manners for weeks, quite publicly. People were talking. In the end I warned her against that kind of association.'

'Oh, you knew her personally then?'

Merrick flushed. He took a fresh grip on the balustrade. 'Yes, I knew her very well.' He hesitated before continuing. 'Sometimes I blame myself for what happened to her because I think she partly took heed of my warning. She seemed to stop seeing him. She came more often to the club. She did voluntary work at the local hospital, and was living with an Indian woman. But that was all right, in its way. Lady Chatterjee was a very old friend of Miss Manners's aunt, Lady Manners. All the same, living with an Indian woman like that meant she came in contact with Indians socially. That was part of the trouble. But Kumar didn't run in those circles at all. He was nothing but a tin-pot reporter on the local gazette and gave himself airs because he'd been brought up expensively in England. I don't really know how she first met up with him, but I saw her go up to him once at one of those war week exhibitions that were all the

190]

rage last year, and it was obvious they already knew each other. I
think he'd been once to the MacGregor House where she lived. But
I knew him from the time I had to haul him in for questioning.
We'd been making a search of a place called The Sanctuary where
a mad old white woman used to take in the dying and starving. We
were looking for a chap who'd escaped from prison, a fellow called
Moti Lal who specialized in organizing subversive activities among
well-educated youths. Needless to say he was an acquaintance of our
venerable pandit. So was Kumar. Kumar was at The Sanctuary
because that mad woman had found him drunk the night before. He
needn't have been in any trouble the morning we found him but
he chose to make a mystery out of his name. In England he'd been
known as Harry Coomer. He thought he was too good to answer
the questions of a mere district superintendent of police. I let him
go because there was nothing to pin on him, but he went down on
my list all right, and before long I'd connected him with most of
our other suspected trouble-makers, including of course our venerable pandit. I didn't like the idea of a girl of Miss Manners's kind –
well, any kind of decent English girl I suppose – getting mixed up
with Master Kumar. In the end I warned her. And although she
said it was really none of my business who she chose to be friends
with I think she realized she wasn't doing herself any good. And
I think she tried to end the association. Kumar wasn't going to
stand for that. And she must still have been infatuated. The way
I see it is that he bided his time, then sent her a message begging
her to meet him again at the place they apparently often met, the
Bibighar, and waited for her there with those friends of his. She
denied having gone there to meet Kumar and made up a cock and
bull story about passing the gardens that night and being curious to
see if there really were ghosts there, as the Indians said. She and
Kumar both swore they'd not seen each other for several weeks.
She said she never saw the men who attacked her. Well, perhaps
that was true. She said they came at her from behind, in the dark,
and covered her head. Perhaps she simply wasn't prepared to believe Kumar could plan such a thing or be mixed up in it at all. In
the end that infatuation of hers led to the whole damned thing
going unpunished. When she found out we'd arrested Kumar she
refused even to attempt to identify the other boys and started load-
ing her evidence or threatening to load it, and if the thing had gone
to trial she'd have turned it into a complete farce. I'd have been

prepared to let her try but others weren't. She changed her story, only slightly, but just enough to turn the scales. She said she'd not seen the men because of the darkness and because they'd come upon her suddenly, but she had a clear impression of them as dirty, smelly hooligans of the kind who might have come in from one of the villages because of the news of the riots and disturbances that were just breaking out all over the province. She knew that the boys we had in custody were the last type you could describe as dirty and smelly. You can appreciate the visual impression there'd have been in court, with these six Indian youths in the dock in Western-style dress, most of them ex-students, and Miss Manners in the witness stand describing a gang of stinking whooping bad-mashes. She might have changed her tune if she'd seen them all as I did the night I arrested them. Five of them half pissed in a dere-lict hut where they'd gone to celebrate on home-made hooch, and Kumar back home, actually bathing his face to try and clean up the marks she made on it, hitting out at her first attacker.'

'How did Kumar explain the marks?'

'Explain? Oh, Master Kumar never explained anything. He was above explanations. His speciality was dumb insolence. He refused to explain the marks. He refused to answer any question until he was back at my headquarters and was told what he was being charged with. His answer to that was that he hadn't seen Miss Manners since a night two or three weeks before when he'd gone to a local temple with her. What struck me as extraordinary really was that she said exactly the same thing. They were both so specific about their last meeting having been the visit to the temple it was as if they'd rehearsed it, or rather as if he'd terrified her or hypnotized her somehow into using just those words: I've not seen Hari Kumar since the night we visited the temple: while he for his part said: I've not seen Miss Manners since the night we visited the temple. I thought it didn't ring true, but everyone else thought it would sound pretty conclusive in court. I always hoped we could get it into court because on oath and in those sort of surroundings the terror and shame I think she was suffering might have been lifted. I'm sure she was under a kind of spell. I'll never understand it. I can never get it out of my head either. The picture of her running home as she did, all alone along those badly lit streets. I expect you know she died nine months later, in child-birth?'

192]

'Yes. As I recall it, her aunt inserted notices.'

'That was extraordinary too, wasn't it? Inserting notices. The death, yes. But the birth of an illegitimate half-caste kid whose father couldn't be identified?' Merrick raised his hands and let them fall again on to the balustrade.

'It shocks you?'

'Yes.' Merrick paused, as if considering the nature and depth of his reaction. 'It's like a direct challenge to everything sane and decent that we try to do out here.'

'It was a human life lost, and a human life beginning. Why not mark the occasion?'

'I'm sorry. I can't see it that way.'

'Most of your countrymen would agree with you,' Bronowsky said. 'I find it sad that in the end Miss Manners inspires more contempt than she does compassion, but I recognize that this is the way it has to be. You English all felt that she didn't want you, want any of you, and of course among exiles that is a serious breach of faith. It amounts to treachery, really. Poor lady. The Indians didn't want her either. There were those things that happened to Indian boys because of her. Happened or didn't happen. In any case they went to prison, and no one seriously believed their political affiliations or crimes or whatever it was that was used as an excuse to keep them under lock and key were of a kind to warrant detention. Even the English thought it a pretty transparent ruse to hold the suspects, a handy alternative to punishing the culprits. It was the kind of ruse that wouldn't have worked in more settled times. One forgets how highly charged the whole emotional and political atmosphere was. There were English here who talked as if a new Mutiny had broken out. Later, I remember, some of your more liberal-minded people had prickings of conscience. There was an article in the *Statesman*. I expect you saw it. It interested me but I looked in vain for any further developments. I thought, well that police officer was sticking his neck out but no one is going to cut it off. He's weathered the storm. I'm sorry to realize you didn't. Sundernagar was something of a backwater, wasn't it? Tell me, if you'd had a chance to serve in the police force of an Indian state such as Mirat, would you have been interested? Or would the army have exerted a stronger fascination? I know how much many of you young Englishmen in the civil and the police dislike the general policy of treating these as reserved occupations.'

[193

'Would *you* have given me such a chance?'

'I don't know. Perhaps not. But I've never been inhibited, by any reservations I might have about the consequences, in taking controversial action and making unpopular appointments, if that action or appointment attracts me strongly enough. My own appointment, after all, was monumentally controversial. Let me put it this way, rather. Were you not presently committed in quite a different direction, I should be interested to discuss such a possibility with you.'

'May I ask why?'

Bronowsky smiled. 'Because my instinct tells me you are something of an anachronism in this modern world of files, second-hand policies and disciplinary virtues. The Indian states are an anachronism too. The rubber-stamp administrator or executive is too advanced an animal for *us*, although ideally that is the likeness one looks for in the outward appearance. Detachment. Objectivity. Absolute incorruptibility – I don't mean in the venal sense of the word, or the word's opposite I suppose I should say. But a man can be – swerved – by his own passions, and to me incorruptibility always suggests a certain lack of concern. The concept of justice as a lady with a blindfold and a pair of scales someone else may lay a decisive finger on without her noticing has often struck me as questionable. It presupposes a readiness in those among whom she dispenses her gifts to keep their hands to themselves. You must agree that would be a perfect world and in such a world she would be a redundant figure. But we are dealing in imperfection. Keep the figure by all means, as a symbol of what might be achieved. Keep the illusion of detachment. Cultivate its manner. But admit it cannot be a controlling force without compromising itself. What is detachment, if it's without the power to make itself felt? Ah, that's the common factor – power! To exercise power in Mirat you need eyes in the back of your head as well as an unblinkered pair in front. And you need men around you who do not lack concern, who have enough concern to be in danger of it getting the better of them and leading them into error. God save us anyway from a world where there's no room for passionate mistakes.'

'You think I made one?'

'I think it's possible. For instance you haven't said what led you to the hut where the boys were celebrating, or to Kumar's house where you found him bathing his face. It strikes me as a significant omission. It suggests that your only reason for visiting Kumar so soon after you heard Miss Manners had been raped by a gang of unknown Indians was that Kumar had been associated with her in the past.'

'You think that reason insufficient?'

Bronowsky shook his head and looked down at his shoes, considering. 'This hut,' he said, 'where the other boys were found half-drunk. It was close to the Bibighar?'

'Just the other side of the river, in some waste ground.'

'And Kumar's house?'

'That was also on the other side of the river.'

'In roughly the same area as the hut?'

'No. But not far.'

'How soon after the rape, approximately, would you say you found the boys in the hut?'

'At the time I estimated it at approximately three-quarters of an hour.'

'Time enough for the five boys to get across the river to the hut and open a bottle.'

'Of course.'

'And get half drunk.'

Merrick paused. 'I used the expression loosely.'

'All the same it was the impression you had. That they were in liquor.'

'Yes.'

'And I suppose about ten minutes later you got to Kumar's house?'

'Yes.'

'So he had had at least three-quarters of an hour to get away from the Bibighar?'

'Yes.'

'And yet he was still bathing his face?'

'Yes.'

'Perhaps he hadn't gone straight home.'

'Perhaps.'

'He could have gone to the hut with the others and had a drink. Then one of them might have noticed the tell-tale marks in the light of whatever lamp they lit, and he thought it wiser to go home and clean up.'

'Very possibly.'

'There was a lamp?'

'Yes.'

'Did they say they'd seen Kumar that night?'

'They said they hadn't. Only two or three of them were friends of his so far as I knew. They insisted they'd spent the whole evening in the hut, alone.'

'Where might Kumar have gone if he hadn't gone straight home?'

'Anywhere. He might have waited in his own garden until he thought it safe to go in and upstairs.'

'Without being seen by his aunt, you mean?'

'His aunt, or a servant.'

'If he'd gone straight home how long would it have taken him?'

'About fifteen minutes. Twenty at most.'

'Walking?'

'Yes – walking.'

'Say ten or less if he'd had a bicycle?'

Again Merrick hesitated.

'Naturally.'

'I wonder about the business of bathing his face, you see. Working from the basis of the earliest moment he could have got home and into his room and started to clean himself up he would then have had a good half-hour before you arrived.'

'If he did go straight home then half an hour wasn't enough, was it? He was bathing his face. Do you really think I had insufficient reason for going to his home? The boys in the hut first, boys of Kumar's kind, two or three of them Kumar's friends, swilling hooch, laughing and joking. What more natural than that having started combing the area of the Bibighar and found them I should go straight to look for Kumar?'

'Well forgive me. That wasn't clear to me, the order and circumstances of arrest. All this is impertinent, I know, but perhaps not without interest to yourself, to talk about it again, with a stranger. And I am trying to get a picture. For instance, presumably you went immediately to the scene of the crime, the Bibighar, in case some of those fellows were still there and in any case to examine it. Now, if you stood in the Bibighar and said Yes, this is Kumar's work, would the route you then took to Kumar's house, presumably in a truck or jeep with some constables, would it have led you over the bridge and past the waste ground?'

'Yes.'

'So you saw the hut. I think earlier you used the word derelict. And perhaps we have established that there was a light showing *from* it?'

'Yes.'

'Well, is that the picture? That you saw the light, stopped the vehicle and rushed across the waste ground to the hut and found those boys?'

'Yes.'

'Well, wasn't there something strange about that? Didn't it strike you as odd? There you had a group of young men supposedly guilty of the most heinous crime of all, the rape of a white girl, getting on for perhaps an hour after they'd left her, but barely a few minutes away from the scene of the crime, in what sounds like a rather conspicuous place, a derelict hut in the middle of some waste ground, showing a light, laughing and joking and getting sozzled.'

'You find that inconsistent?'

'I do rather. It sounds to me more like the behaviour of boys who'd done what they insisted they'd done, and no more. Spent the whole evening in the hut, drinking illicit liquor, lighting a lamp when it got dark, just intoxicated enough to be careless about who saw it. The distillation and drinking of illegal hooch is not a very serious misdemeanour.'

Merrick smiled. 'You've drawn your picture out of context. You're forgetting what day it was and what had happened during the day. It was the ninth of August. On the eighth the Congress passed their Quit India resolution. On the morning of the ninth we arrested not only leading Congressmen but Congress members of sub-committees throughout India. Everything had come to the boil. In the afternoon in a place called Tanpur some police were abducted and an English mission teacher called Miss Crane was attacked by hoodlums. The fellow with her, an Indian, was murdered. We got Miss Crane back into the Mayapore hospital at about five o'clock. Nobody knew what would happen next. Shopkeepers put up their shutters and people stayed in their homes. I know the Congress has denied that there was any underground plan for rebellion. But I'd say later developments provided sufficient evidence of organized rebellion to make their denial look silly. Boys like the ones we arrested for the rape may not have been directly involved in that kind of organization, but that's what they wanted, that's what they had their hearts in, that's the kind of activity that appealed to them. They laugh at Gandhi, you know, all that crowd. All that passive resistance and non-violence nonsense is just a joke to them, just as it's a joke to the militant Hindu wing of the Congress and organizations like the Mahasabha and the RSSS. When you get down to the level of the educated fellow who thinks the world owes him a living in exchange for his matric or BA failed, the kind of chap who loathes the English who gave him the chance to rise above the gutters of the bazaar but is very happy to ape English manners and dress English style, then you're down at a level where nothing but anarchy reigns. When trouble comes decent people in the towns put up their shutters and close their doors. In the villages they harbour their cattle and guard their property and their lives. And out come the badmashes in the countryside, and the hooligans in the cities. But in the cities a lot of the hooligans can quote Shakespeare at you. When I went across the river that night I wasn't looking for people hiding in their homes, but foot-loose fellows like those in the hut. You see my interpretation of your picture of the fellows in the hut is quite different. What made them careless, showing a light, lounging around only a few minutes away from the Bibighar was an intoxication that only had a bit to do with the liquor. The rest was cockiness. They'd had a white woman. They thought the country was rising. Their day was dawning. They could see it quite clearly. The *raj* was on the run. The long knives were out. In a day or two the white men would be crawling, licking their shoes, and there'd be as many white women to rape or murder as they wanted.'

'And Kumar?'

'Kumar? Oh, Kumar! He was the worst of the lot. Have you heard of Chillingborough?'

'Chillingborough . . . yes. One of your big public schools at home?'

'Exactly. Well that's where Kumar was educated. To hear him speak, I mean if you looked away while he spoke, he sounded just like an English boy of that type. His mother died very early and his father took him to England when he was about two with the express intention of bringing him up not only to act and sound like the English, but to *be* English. The father was rich, but got involved in some sort of financial trouble, lost all his money and

198]

died leaving Kumar penniless. This aunt of his in Mayapore, a decent enough woman she was too, paid his passage back to India and tried to look after him. But nothing was good enough for him. He couldn't take what it involved, to be just another Westernized Indian boy in a place like Mayapore.'

'Poor Mr Kumar. It can't have been a happy experience.'

'Good Lord, you'd think a boy who'd had those advantages would have been man enough to face up to a set-back like that. I can't share your sympathy for him. But then I met him face to face. Kumar wasn't just a theory to me. I knew his type too well, and he was the type multiplied. To me it was quite clear what he was up to. He was out for revenge. Out to get his own back on us because back in India he couldn't pretend to be English any longer. One of the executives in the British-Indian Electric factory told me he could have had a decent job there as a sort of apprentice or trainee. But Mr Kumar refused to call the managing director sir, and was insolent to the man he'd have been working under. His aunt's brother-in-law was a merchant and contractor and for a time Kumar did some clerical work in the warehouse. That didn't suit him, but that's where he would have been first in contact with this chap I was telling you about who escaped from prison. Moti Lal. Moti Lal was a clerk in the same business.' Merrick suddenly slapped the balustrade. 'It's so damned obvious. Moti Lal. Pandit Baba. Going around with those boys who were drinking in the hut. Working as a journalist. And we found a letter in his room when we searched it. A letter from an English boy warning Kumar not to write bolshie things, because the boy's father had opened some of Kumar's letters and objected to his son getting such letters while he was still recovering from wounds got at Dunkirk. And he had a photograph in his room too. A photo of Miss Manners. Having a white woman running after him was the final perfect touch, from his point of view.'

Suddenly Merrick looked round at Bronowsky. He said, 'I didn't have to stand in the Bibighar and tell myself, yes, this is Kumar's work. I knew it was Kumar's work the moment I got to the Mac-Gregor House and Lady Chatterjee told me Miss Manners had come back, in that state. I'd been at the house before. It wasn't the kind of night you allowed a white girl to be missing, and that's what it looked as if she was, missing. Sometimes I used to give her a lift home from the hospital. I was at the hospital that evening because of Miss Crane and when I left I looked for Miss Manners. They told me she'd gone to the club. Later I was at the club myself and inquired after her. I was told she'd not been in the club. I thought, so that's it, she's gone back to meeting Kumar. There was nothing I felt I could do about it, and with everything that was going on I had my hands full. But later I went round to the MacGregor House, which was a pretty isolated place. I thought I'd make sure they were all right. I found Lady Chatterjee alone, Miss Manners hadn't been back, and she was worried. At least, she was worried when I told her Miss Manners hadn't been at the club. I had to go back to my headquarters. It must have been getting on for nine o'clock. On my way back to headquarters I remembered Miss Manners sometimes went over the river to that place called The Sanctuary. She helped Sister Ludmila with the clinic. So I went to The Sanctuary and found she had been there, but had left before dusk. It's not far from The Sanctuary to the house Kumar lived in. I thought the situation was serious enough to go and see if she'd arrived at Kumar's. She hadn't. And Kumar's aunt said Kumar wasn't at home either. Well that made it obvious to me. They were off somewhere together. I thought, well, God, she's welcome to him if that's what she wants, and drove back to the kotwali at the Mandir Gate. If I'd gone the other way, over the Bibighar bridge, I'd have come across her, running home along those dark streets. I'd probably have come across Kumar as well, and those others. But I went to the kotwali. It was chance that made me decide to detour to the MacGregor House when I finally set off back for my headquarters. I got there ten or fifteen minutes after she'd returned, exhausted, in that awful condition. Lady Chatterjee had sent for the doctor, but not the police because Miss Manners hadn't explained her condition. But Lady Chatterjee suspected and I made her go up and get confirmation. The message I got back wasn't clear, but it was enough. Attack, criminal assault, five or six men, in the Bibighar Gardens. I had to drive back to get a police patrol, and order a comb. A good thirty minutes or more must have passed between her leaving the Bibighar and my arriving there. We were probably ten minutes beating through the gardens, and another five at the level-crossing hut, interrogating the keeper and searching the area. And all the time I knew I was wasting time. I knew where I ought to be looking. When I finally set off for Kumar's house I very nearly ignored that hut, in spite of the light showing that someone was there. I think what made me stop was partly a sort of automatic professional response, a realization that nothing could be overlooked, and partly a twinge of conscience, a recognition of the unfairness of leaping to a conclusion. But the sight of those boys, the revelation of what they were, who they were – well I had them out of there and into a truck and on the way back to my headquarters before they knew what had hit them. And I went on in my own truck, with three or four constables, to get Kumar. The aunt tried to stop us going upstairs. She was scared stiff. I knew I was right, then.' Merrick laughed. 'And do you know what he said, when we went into his room? Well, there he was, stripped to the waist, bending over a bowl, holding a flannel to his face. He looked up and said – "Who gave you permission to burst into my room, Merrick?" '

Bronowsky laughed, and presently Merrick replied with a sour grin, looked at his watch and moved from the balustrade.

'I shall have to go in I'm afraid.'

'We both must,' Bronowsky said. 'I'm sorry to have kept you so long, but sorrier that all we had to discuss needed to be compressed into what amounts to no more than a brief encounter. Perhaps in the not wholly unforeseeable future we may have the opportunity to resume. Anyway, if you are ever in Mirat again, or disposed to contemplate coming back, I hope you will let me know.'

They began to walk down the terrace. The sound of talk and laughter from the inner room had become louder in the last ten minutes or so. 'You could do with a drink, I expect,' Merrick said. 'I know I could.'

'I could but I must not. You'll find Nawab Sahib holding a glass of orange or lemon for politeness's sake, so I follow suit to keep him company. He takes Ramadan very seriously and as a matter of fact I think he enjoys the discipline of holding a glass and not so much as moistening his lips. Tonight he begins a special period of fast and prayer and cuts his intake almost to nothing, even after sundown. The Íd is in ten days' time. I'm sorry you won't be here for it and that the charming Layton ladies will be gone too. Nawab Sahib would have liked to have you as guests to a meal in the palace.'

'He has been more than generous as it is —'

They turned in at the french windows. Several guests stood in the room they entered, presumably having come in there to avoid the crush in the room beyond, through whose open door the wedding party could now be seen.

Bronowsky paused and made Merrick do so too by holding his arm in a way which a stranger, had he been watching, might have interpreted as proof of intimacy and of knowledge and interests shared.

'Tell me,' the count said in a low voice so that Merrick automatically bent his head closer. 'Who is the outstandingly handsome young officer with the dark hair, talking to the girl in blue?'

Merrick glanced quickly round the room.

Oh that, he seemed about to say, *that is —*

But as if suddenly unsure of something – the name of a man, the colour of a dress, his questioner's intention, he looked back at Bronowsky and for a moment the question itself seemed to hang in the balance; and Bronowsky, observing the way the colour came and went on the ex-District Superintendent's cheeks, released his hold on his companion's arm and murmured:

'Well, it doesn't matter. Come, let's go in,' and led the way.

*

'He was in love with her,' Aunt Fenny said, beginning the job of unbuttoning Susan out of her wedding-gown while Mrs Layton folded the veil and Sarah laid out the going-away clothes on the bed in the little room in the annexe. 'A woman I met who'd been in Mayapore told me. She said it was well known at the time. The DSP definitely set his cap at Miss Manners, and everyone was surprised because they'd thought of him as a confirmed bachelor and all the unmarried girls who'd been trying to hook him wondered what he saw in her. I expect her background had a bit to do with it, but when a man like that decides to take the plunge he takes it terribly seriously. It must have been awful for him when she became infatuated with one of those dreadful Indian boys. I remember this woman saying he looked positively ill after Miss Manners had been assaulted and they were trying to make the charges stick. He must have been nearly out of his mind at the thought of those men getting away with it. No wonder he wangled his way out of the police and into the army and never mentions anything about having been in Mayapore. Count Bronowsky must have an extraordinary memory for names. Captain Merrick was obviously upset having it all come out like that. Did you see his face when he got back from fetching the hat box?'

'Stop it, Aunt Fenny!' Susan shouted. 'Stop it! I'm trying, trying, *trying* to pretend that it's a nice day. I'm trying, *trying* to remember that I'm being married to Teddie —' She jerked at the dress – not yet completely unbuttoned down the back – and pulled it away from her body, wrenched her arms out of the sleeves and pushed the unwieldy billowing damask down over her hips, breaking the thread of one of the buttons. Clothed now in only her brassiere, pants and suspender belt, she twisted round and kicked the discarded dress away from her feet. 'My dear child,' Aunt Fenny began – but Susan, flushed of face and white of body, snatched a sponge bag from the bed, said 'We've got fifteen minutes, Mummy,' and grabbing the neat little pile of fresh underclothes made for the bathroom.

'What have I done?' Aunt Fenny asked her sister.

'Nothing, Fenny. It's what you were saying, not what you were doing. The subject was hardly a suitable one in the circumstances, was it?'

'Oh dear. Yes, I do see. I am sorry. Poor pet. What are you looking for, Sarah?'

'One of the buttons came off.'

'I'll find it. Millie, you pack the dress away, and let Sarah get on with her own changing.' Fenny went down on her knees. 'I told him about our being moored close to Lady Manners's boat in Srinagar, but he never knew her. It was a bit of a relief because it slipped out, I mean about the houseboat business, and if he'd been a friend of old Lady M's it would have been rather embarrassing having to admit we'd not actually met her, he mightn't have understood how difficult it was for everybody. I was dying to hear something straight from the horse's mouth, but he was positively evasive when I suggested he come over to the guest house tomorrow or Monday and spend an evening with us. He said he might have to go to Calcutta, I mean go for good before Teddie and the rest of them leave next week. What a shame. He's been quite attentive to you, hasn't he, Sarah, pet?'

'Aunt Fenny, I just don't understand you.'

'Ah here it is. Millie, put it in your handbag for safety. Help me up, Sarah. What don't you understand?'

'You're still talking about that Manners business —'

'But Susan can't hear —'

'That's not what I mean. I mean you're quite prepared to gloat over the details, you're willing to sit Captain Merrick down, stick a glass in his hand and prise every last juicy bit of the story out of him, without any thought for his feelings at all. But when we had an opportunity to show friendly to the poor girl's aunt it was you who found the perfect excuse for keeping our distance. You said a visit would embarrass her.'

'Well, so it would,' Fenny said, turning to help Mrs Layton fold the dress into the suitcase. 'And if it hadn't embarrassed her it would certainly have embarrassed me. Everyone agrees that that woman's behaviour has been quite extraordinary.'

Sarah began to undress, contorting herself to get at the row of satin-covered buttons. She felt a tide of anger and frustration spread through her body.

'You could actually hear that revolting crying,' Fenny added. 'It was like being next door to some awful Indian slum. It made one feel quite sick, the thought of an English woman living in it.'

'I was in it too,' Sarah said, and as she did so seemed to discover, through her finger-tips, the secret of undoing the dress, and to touch, as well, the spring of some deeper secret that had to do with the unlocking of her own precious individuality. She let the slipper-satin gown fall to her feet where it lay like an unwanted skin. 'I spent a whole hour in the slum, talking to the extraordinary woman and looking at the revolting baby. Of course it wasn't a slum and the baby wasn't revolting. But I'd agree about Lady Manners. She wasn't ordinary.'

'You went to see her?'

'Yes.'

'What for?'

'To apologize for us. Perhaps the rest was just curiosity, like yours, Aunt Fenny.'

She picked up the sloughed dress. It was a garment she would never wear again. Suddenly, the waste no longer offended her; she was glad – glad Susan had insisted on peach slipper-satin, had re-sisted her own puritan preference for a material that, with adapta-tions, could have served secondary long-term purposes.

'Did you know about this, Milly?' Aunt Fenny asked.

'Yes, I knew.'

'And approved?'

'I find it difficult to approve or disapprove of what I don't under-stand. Let's just say I knew you and Arthur would understand it even less. I told her not to mention it. But it doesn't matter now. May we forget it, please? May we just concentrate on getting Susan safely to the train?'

'You're absolutely right. I don't understand. Apologized for *us*? My dear child, sometimes you worry me. You worry us all. You worry us very much.'

'Yes, I know,' Sarah said, packing the bridesmaid's dress and satin shoes into tissue. 'I worry me too. Shall I put Susan's veil in my case? There's more room.'

Automatically Aunt Fenny handed the folded veil and tissue over. Fragile, even insubstantial, its packed bulk yet called for two hands to support it. Carefully, Sarah placed it in the suitcase on top of the other things: the veil, the most important of all the trappings of Susan's determined illusion, now done with, put away. She re-membered the day spent in Aunt Lydia's glory-hole, the armfuls of stuff taken down into the Bayswater garden and burnt in the in-cinerator from whose heat she had stood back, shielding her face with a grubby hand and thinking of the perpetual light that seemed to shine upon the members of her family.

Perhaps, she thought, I am no longer in darkness, perhaps there is light and I have entered it. But she did not know what light exactly, nor what entering it would already have laid on her by way of obligations. But if it was light she wanted to share it. She looked at Aunt Fenny and at her mother, snapped the locks of the case shut as if completing, with a happy flourish, some special con-juring trick.

'But don't let's worry just now,' she said. 'It's not only Susan's day, it's ours too.'

*

And to end it, adding a third link to the chain forged by the throwing of the stone and the barring of the club doors to the Nawab, there was the curious incident of the woman in the white saree who appeared from out of the crowd on the platform of the cantonment station where the train for Nanoora was drawn up, and who seemed intent on joining the group seeing Teddie and Susan off, although she stayed a few paces behind them.

At first only the officers on the fringe of the group noticed her, and they thought nothing of her presence. But now from farther down the platform a warning whistle blew and as Captain Merrick came down from the compartment, leaving Mrs Layton and Sarah and Major and Mrs Grace to make their private family farewells to the departing couple, the group moved to give him room, spreading out, leaving a clear space, so that Merrick, turning, found the woman a few feet away, and coming closer.

The saree was only of cotton, but being white, suggestive of widowhood and mourning, the cheapness of the material could not be counted a sign of poverty. The thought that she might be a beggar did not enter the heads of any of the officers near by. She was not very dark skinned, and she looked clean, respectable. In fact the immediate impression everyone had, including Mrs Grace who now also left the compartment with her husband and Sarah, was that an unpleasant scene was about to take place, with the Indian woman claiming a seat in the first class.

But she seemed to be a beggar after all. She had begun to speak, in Hindi, which the nearest of the officers got the drift of, and it was clear to others that Captain Merrick understood too because he answered her, also in Hindi. Help me, she had said, your Honour alone can help now. I beg you. Be merciful. To which Merrick replied: Please go away. There is nothing I can do for you.

She cried out, and fell to her knees – an alarming spectacle which, moving as it might have been on a stage to an audience already translated to a state of suspended disbelief, could only be a cause of embarrassment on a public platform. And the cry, the act of abasement, were not all. She pulled the saree from her head, revealing greying hair, reached out and grabbed poor Captain Merrick's feet and placed her forehead on the dirty ground, moaning and keening. It was impossible to touch her. One of the officers said, 'Jao! Jao!' and tried to help Merrick urge her away by pressing on her shoulder with his shin. She let go, but held her ground, scrabbled in the dirt and dust of the platform and symbolically smarmed her head with ash. She rocked and swayed, crying out the while inarticulately.

The extraordinary scene came to an abrupt end. An Indian railway official, the man who was checking reservations, emerged from a near-by compartment, saw what was happening and came at a run. He grabbed the woman roughly, pulled her to her feet, pushed her away, once, twice, as often as was necessary to press her back into the crowd of watching Indians, shouting angrily, theatening her with the police. Back among her own people she fell to her knees again, resumed her crying and gesturing, crazed by some grief that the bystanders could not understand or share, and which therefore seemed absurd to them. They watched her curiously, then parted as an elderly Indian with a grey beard and wearing steel-rimmed spectacles pushed his way through, approached her, spoke, raised her to her feet and led her away out of sight, down the platform.

'A madwoman,' the man in charge of reservations said. 'Please, no one is badly molested?'

That she was a madwoman seemed unquestionable, but to hear her so described by this particular man was like having official confirmation of the fact. It could be assumed that the woman was known: a poor, mad, harmless creature who pestered sahibs on railway platforms.

Teddie had his head thrust through an open window. A clean piece of sticking plaster adorned his cheek. 'What was all that?' he asked cheerfully. But he was not looking for an answer. There was another blast on the whistle. He turned back into the compartment.

'You'd better go, Mummy,' Susan said, and Mrs Layton broke away, pecked Teddie on the undamaged side of his face and allowed him to escort her to the doorway where Major Grace completed the task of handing her down. Teddie shut the door and Susan joined him at the open window.

'Somebody catch,' she shouted, and flung the tired little bouquet she had carried all morning into the air, but in Sarah's direction. Sarah caught it and instinctively raised it to her nose to sniff the still sweet-smelling blooms. She looked up and found Susan watching her, waiting perhaps for some particular word or gesture but there was no word or gesture to find beyond a mouthing of the word 'Thanks'. All I can do as well, Sarah said silently, is wish you happiness.

And that seemed to be enough.

IV

CAPTAIN MERRICK came to the guest house at the beginning of the short twilight. Sarah was alone on the terrace waiting, she explained, for the darkness to fall and the fireflies to come out. The rest of her family were still in their rooms.

'Haven't you slept this afternoon?' Merrick asked. She still wore the dress she'd changed into for the farewells at the station.

'Oh, I meant to rest but the place was too quiet. It's been such a hive of activity all week. So I wrote letters, well – one letter, to Father, about the wedding.' She looked at her watch. 'They'll be in Nanoora soon. Won't you ring for a drink?'

'If you'll have one too.'

'I may as well.'

Merrick went to the bell-push set in the wall near the french windows. He had changed out of best KD into a cotton bush shirt and slacks. After he'd rung he stood by the balustrade.

'The last place the light goes from is the lake,' Sarah said. 'But when it's really dark the lake's much darker than anything.'

'Water reflects the sky,' Merrick said, prosaicly. He took out his cigarette case, came towards her. She shook her head.

'No, thanks. Not just now. But you do. It's part of the pleasure of this particular time of day. Smelling someone else's tobacco smoke.'

'You're very sensitive to atmosphere.'

'I suppose I am.' She thought for a moment. 'But not more than anyone else. Perhaps I think about it more.'

Abdur Rahman came out.

'What will you have, Ronald?' she asked, using his given name because for the first time it seemed natural to do so.

'Whisky if I may.'

'Whisky soda, Sahib *ke waste*, Abdur. *Burra peg hona chahie. Aur* Tom Collins *meri lie.*'

'Memsahib.'

When Abdur Rahman had gone Merrick said, 'You think I need a *burra peg* then?'

'I don't know about need. Deserve.'

'I used hardly to drink at all.'

He sat opposite her, lit his cigarette, then said, 'I'm off to

Calcutta first thing in the morning, so I've really come to say good-bye to everybody.'

'Oh, I'm sorry.'

'The signal was in when we got back from the station. Three of us have to go, but it wasn't unexpected. The General warned us before he went himself. I think it means some change of location for the training and forming-up area. Perhaps things are on the move.'

Sarah said nothing for a while. The light, fading fast, perceptibly, had begun its tag-end of the day business of investing people you sat close to – Ronald Merrick in this case – with a curious extra density, a thickness and solidity that compensated for the darkening and fading of features, hands and clothes so that the person on whom darkness fell was not diminished but intensified. She thought of what he meant when he referred to things being on the move. Those things seemed to be so far away that they were almost unimaginable, and yet within a day or two he could be close to them and she could reach out and touch him now and he could carry the impression of her touch into areas of danger.

'Does it ever strike you,' she asked, 'how odd it is about war, I mean about the way it's concentrated in special places? And in between the places huge stretches of country, whole continents where life just goes on as usual?'

'Like here?'

She nodded. 'Like here.'

He said, after a while, 'I suppose the other curious thing is wanting to go to it. I needn't have.' He glanced at her. 'Will you write to me sometimes?'

She glanced back, ready to smile, taking it as a light hearted, vaguely sentimental suggestion of the kind she could forgive him because he was, all said and done, a soldier; but she was aware, meeting his glance, of the request perhaps being as serious as it was unexpected.

'Yes, of course.'

'Thank you.'

He might have intended to add something but Abdur Rahman came out with the tray of drinks. Sarah took the tall cold glass, waited until Merrick had said '*bus*' to the pouring soda water, then called 'Cheers'. The ice burned her lips, numbing them. This first moment of drinking chilled liquid always reminded her of the

[209

feeling in the lips as injections in the mouth wore off. She swallowed, closed her eyes and put her head back, making a faint exclamation of satisfaction she only partly felt.

Merrick said, 'I've enjoyed meeting you all, you know. It's been a long time since I was – with a family.' He sipped his whisky. 'I came to say goodbye but also with the hope of being able to apologize. I think I can to you. If you weren't alone I probably wouldn't think it opportune. It's not the sort of thing one can say to several people.'

Sarah had opened her eyes and turned her head, but he was looking doggedly in the direction of the lake.

'That stone someone chucked this morning was really thrown at me. I know it sounds childish and melodramatic but persecution of that kind has been going on ever since I left Mayapore. It's never bothered me but today all of you were involved. And that's what I want to apologize for, for two of the things that spoilt the day for Teddie and Susan, and all of you. The stone, and that unpleasant scene on the platform. I'm not sure I oughtn't to apologize for the insult to the Nawab too. I ought to have made sure those lads from the military police knew there were to be Indian guests. In any case they wouldn't have been on duty if the stone hadn't been thrown. I'm sorry. I was the worst best man Teddie could have chosen.'

'Oh, no! —'

'It's all to do with that Mayapore business.' He was looking at her now. 'You know about my connexion with that?'

'Yes, I know.'

'I'm sorry – I mean for not saying who I really was and then being, well, faced with having to deny it and tell a lie or admit it and look as if I'd been telling one. It made me feel and look ridiculous, made it seem I'd something to hide or be ashamed of, but all I've wanted is to forget it, not have to answer questions about it in every new place I go to. I hope your mother in particular understands that. She's had me under her roof. I'm not unconscious of the obligation that has put me under.'

Sarah resumed her watch on the lake. She felt vaguely ill-at-ease, conscious of those things about Ronald Merrick that Aunt Fenny put down as signs of a humble origin. Phrases like 'under her roof' and 'not unconscious of the obligation' had a stilted, self-advertising ring that she didn't altogether care for. It alarmed her to realize

210]

that she could respond, as automatically as Aunt Fenny, to the subtler promptings of the class-instinct. Why should I question his sincerity? she asked herself; realizing that this was what she was doing.

'We all understood,' she told him. 'I'd say it was the natural thing to do.'

'Thank you.'

'But I don't really understand about the stone and the woman on the station. Was she the mother of one of the boys that got arrested?'

Merrick smiled, took another drink.

'Well, you do understand, you see. It's all quite simple once you know who I am. But she wasn't the mother of one of the boys, she was his aunt. Although pretty much like a mother to him. It wasn't pleasant seeing her like that this morning. I remember her as respectable and dignified.' He drank again. 'I shan't forget it in a hurry. But of course I'm not supposed to. They want it to prey on my mind until I'm as convinced as they are that I made a terrible mistake, the kind of mistake I shan't be able to live with because it'll be impossible to correct it. But it's impossible now. They must know that. That poor woman was being used. She probably thought there's a chance I could work a miracle for her.'

Dim as the picture was Sarah comprehended vividly enough the essence of what it would convey if a whole light shone on it. She understood that he had carried a burden a long way, for a long time, had suddenly put it down and was intent on showing her – and himself – what it was before he shouldered it again and took it with him wherever he was going. Perhaps he hoped that showing it would lighten it, although – in the swiftly encroaching dark through which he was beginning to loom he looked capable of rejecting any claim that showing it might give a would-be sharer.

'Did you see that man who took her?' he asked. 'He's behind it. I heard he was in Mirat, and had a woman with him. He put her up to it, brought her all the way here from Mayapore, getting her hopes up that I could be moved by that kind of appeal, that I could do something. It's pretty cruel. He probably doesn't care a fig for her, or the boy, any of them. It's sheer pretence. The case is useful to him, that's all. It serves his purpose. But that's India for you. They're quite indifferent to one another's sufferings when it comes down to it, and we've become so lofty and detached, so starry-eyed about our own civilized values and about our own common-sense view prevailing that our policy has become one of indifference too. We don't rule this country any more. We preside over it, in accordance with a book of rules written by the people back home.'

'Yes,' Sarah said. 'Yes, I think that's true.'

Merrick drained his glass.

'When I was a youngster one of the first questions I asked the District Superintendent I worked my probationary period with was how much longer he thought we'd rule India. I was thinking of my future which was something I'd somehow never thought of as necessary when deciding to try for the Indian Police. But when I got out here it all seemed so unreal, like a play. I suddenly couldn't picture it as a thing I'd work at all my life. So I asked this extra-ordinary question, extraordinary I mean because it was absurd to be wondering about much more than learning the job I'd chosen and worked hard to get. He didn't think it extraordinary, though, and I've always remembered his reply. He said: "Don't bother your head about that, Merrick, because there's not a thing you can do. India will be ours until one day between questions and other busi-ness in the House of Commons the British people through their elected representatives will vote to get rid of it. The majority won't have the least idea what they're doing. Getting rid of India will be just one clause in a policy of reform dreamed up by intellectuals and implemented by the votes of mill-hands and post-office clerks, and if you think there's any connexion between *their* India and the one you're going to help police you might as well go home now." '

He set his empty glass down.

'I've never accepted that,' he said. 'The fact, yes. But not the mentality that so often goes with it. Well, you know the sort of thing, I expect, although you don't really get it in the army be-cause it's a tradition that you have your own self-contained com-munity and a job to do that nobody outside thinks worth a button until the shooting begins. While there isn't any shooting you take it as all part of the game to be mucked about. You accept it philo-sophically. But in the civil and the police, in the business of daily administration of the country, there's the constant irritation of being strait-jacketed by policy from above. At the top the Government of India tries to fight the Secretary of State in Whitehall and at the bottom the district officer tries to fight the Government. But it's

212]

always a losing battle. You find yourself automatically implementing a policy you feel passionately is wrong and the only thing you can do short of resigning is detach yourself from the reality of the problem, from the human issues if you like. You become – a rubber stamp. That's the mentality I mean. It's something my first superintendent encouraged me to resist. Perhaps he was wrong. He was an officer of the old school. He'd seen what he called better times, times – he said – when you were master in your own bailiwick. I suppose I should have recognized that it was an older school, not mine, and that I live in a rubber-stamp age. And don't get the wrong impression, Miss Layton. I haven't been kicked out of the police. I applied for permission to transfer to the army at the beginning of the war. I pulled every string I knew, just like Mrs Grace's friend. It needed the Mayapore business, needed me to become what's known as a locally controversial figure, to persuade them to release me for the duration, but I had to plead pretty hard even then. I sometimes think that if I'd done something terribly wrong the rubber stamp would have endorsed it. That's its danger. It's a controlling force without the ability to judge. Once you're part of the rubber-stamp process yourself you could almost get away with murder. And that's wrong. Must be. You ought to be answerable for your actions, but you ought to be able to act, you ought to be involved. As an individual. As a person. As a fallible human being.'

'There are times,' Sarah said, 'when I think I don't know what a human being is.' Times – she told herself – when I look up and see that heaven is empty and that this is an age when all of us share the knowledge that it is and that there has never been a god nor any man made in that image. It is an intensely bleak discovery because it calls our bluff on everything. 'But I know what you mean,' she continued. 'It's easier for men. Being involved. No. That's a facile remark. It's not easy for any of us.' She looked at him. 'What was *she* like? the girl. The girl in the Mayapore business.'

'Rather like you,' he said, without hesitation, as if he had expected the question and knew in advance what his reply would be. 'Not physically. Well, she was taller.' He fingerd the empty glass, slithered it to and fro, a few inches, on the table. 'I suppose a bit clumsy. She knocked things over. She made a joke of it. But she was very sensitive. She said she'd been gawky as a child. She still felt like that. Unco-ordinated. But I only saw her as – peculiarly graceful. Grave. Slow. Beautiful almost, because of that. The kind of girl you could talk to. Really talk to. Or just sit with. Our tastes were – much the same. In music. Pictures. That sort of thing. Our backgrounds were quite different, because mine is very ordinary, but Daphne didn't give a damn who your parents were or what school you went to.'

Sarah felt compelled to say it.

'Were you in love with her?'

He played with the glass a few seconds longer, then gave it up, stubbed his cigarette, studied the hand that had moved the glass, holding it stiffly with the fingers splayed, rubbing the back and the palm with the thumb and finger of his other hand.

'I don't know. I thought I was for a while. But if I was it wasn't at first sight. I'd met her several times and not thought of her that way. In fact my first impression of her was a bit unfavourable. I thought, Here we are, another of those English girls who come out here with bees in their bonnets about the rotten way we treat Indians. Give her time to find they're taking advantage of her and she'll get over it, she'll go the other way, be worse than any of us. In a year she won't have a good word to say for them. She was living with an Indian woman. You had to take that into account. Lady Chatterjee was one of those Westernized aristocratic Rajputs, an old friend of Daphne's aunt, and Daphne had come down with her from Pindi to see what she called something of the real India. I can't say I cottoned much to Lili Chatterjee. She belonged to that top layer of Indian society that mixes with our own top layer, but that's not real intimacy. More like necessary mutual recognition of privilege and power. A banquet at Government House, a garden party at Viceregal Lodge. You'd find a lot of Lili Chatterjees there. You'd also find this particular one playing bridge in Mayapore with the Deputy Commissioner's wife. But not at the Mayapore club, not among ordinary English men and women when they were off duty. They pretend they don't care, the Lili Chatterjees I mean. Pretend they don't need to rub shoulders with the English middle-class in their cosy middle-class clubs and homes. But they resent it. Daphne resented it too. She wasn't able to draw the distinction. She didn't see why a line had to be drawn – has to be drawn. But it's essential, isn't it? You have to draw a line. Well, it's arbitrary. Nine times out of ten perhaps you draw it in the wrong place. But you need it there, you need to be able to say: There's the line. This

214]

side of it is right. That side is wrong. Then you have your moral term of reference. Then you can act. You can feel committed. You can be involved. Your life takes on something like a shape. It has form. Purpose as well, maybe. You know who you are when you wake up in the morning. Well sometimes you can rub the line out and draw it in a different place, bring it closer or push it farther out. But you need it there. It's like a blind man with a white stick needing the edge of the pavement. Poor Daphne tried to do without all that. I attempted to stop her – well, crossing the road. She didn't seem to know she was crossing it. I suppose that's when I first really looked at her, first considered her. And found out she wasn't just another of those English girls with bees in their bonnets. She was *this* girl. And it wasn't a bee. I don't know what it was. It was quite beyond me. But whatever it was it destroyed her.'

He cocked his head, considering her.

'I'm sorry, I said she was rather like you, didn't I, but I've mostly been describing the things that made her different. I'm not sure I can put my finger on what it was about you that reminded me of her.'

'Does that mean I don't any longer?' Self-conscious under his scrutiny she defended herself from it with the thought that he was an appalling man whom she didn't trust. He had a lively intelligence, perhaps less lively than its activity within the confines of a narrow mind made it seem; but she did not have to pay for the pleasure, of listening to a man – an Englishman in India – talking seriously, by liking him. She was interested in finding out why she reminded him of Miss Manners, but did not care whether the reason was flattering or the opposite of that.

'What I'm going to say,' he said, 'may sound impertinent.'

'No – I'm sure it won't.'

'Well – that first morning. When I'd joined you all in the station restaurant and you sat in front of the taxi next to the driver. I felt from your manner you were making the same sort of judgements of us that she did. And I thought – please forgive me – here's another one who doesn't see why a line must be drawn. But it was none of my business. And I was wrong anyway.'

'Why do you say that?'

'Because I can see the line's been drawn for you. You accept it. Do you remember in the taxi how I made rather heavy weather of young Kasim's position, and your mother very understandably thought I was speaking out of turn?'

'Yes, I remember that.'

'Talking about Kasim. It was a sort of Pavlovian response on my part. I'd met him and I think subconsciously he'd impressed me as a man of Hari Kumar's type.'

'Who is Hari Kumar?'

'The chief suspect in the Bibighar Gardens case. The man she was friendly with.'

'Yes, I see.'

'And yet not Kumar's type. Physically, yes, but finally Kasim bears no more resemblance to Kumar than you do to Miss Manners. But in the taxi I think there was a sort of fantasy in my mind of Hari and Daphne being about to come together again. I'm sorry – it sounds awful, but there it was. You sat there in the front seat, shading your eyes – and that was like her. She had a way of standing, peering at things a long way off, with just that gesture. And at the end of the journey, the guest house, and Ahmed there, well – waiting. On the other side of the line.'

For an instant Sarah held in her mind's eye an exact image of Ahmed as she had first seen him at the entrance to the guest house, emerging from the dim interior, and of herself still dazzled by the lake whose glare had become trapped inside her head, making it ache; and then this vision dissolved into another, of herself and Ahmed riding across the waste ground with constant distance between them except at those two moments, Ahmed's seizing of the reins, herself wheeling round suddenly to face him.

'That morning you went riding with him,' Ronald Merrick was saying, 'and Teddie and I turned up unexpectedly for breakfast. When we saw you coming back I thought, Well, that's it, I was right, it's all happening again. But then when you both got off your horses I realized it wasn't happening at all. You were friendly enough, but the barriers were up. The way you stood I could see you weren't sure how to leave him, I could see it crossing your mind: What do I do now, how do I get rid of him politely? You invited him in to breakfast, didn't you? Now if it had been Kumar he'd have accepted. But Mr Kasim knows where the line has to be drawn too. It was a relief to you both when he got back on and rode off. Am I right?'

Sarah felt he was right for the wrong reasons. She did not answer him immediately. He aggravated a grinding impatience in her which she knew she must discipline.

'I can't speak for Mr Kasim,' she began.

'Then for yourself,' he urged. 'It was a relief.'

'I wasn't under pressure.'

'We're always under that. Resisting it or pretending it's not there only adds to it.'

'What are we talking about, Ronald?' – she used his name again deliberately, as a little punishment for calling her Miss Layton after she had herself dispensed with that formality. 'The social pressure that keeps the ruled at arm's length from the rulers, or the biological pressure that makes a white girl think she mightn't like being touched by an Indian?'

Did he blush? She was not sure. The light was too far gone, absorbed, drained into the lake. He put up a hand and rubbed his forehead: a gentle action – a reflex, it seemed, of his mental registration of the need, now, to tread decisively but delicately on ground set with traps for the unwary.

'They are connected,' he said. 'If you visualize such a union, or if you consider its counterpart, the connexion is quite clear. A white man, well, supposing I – or Teddie – I mean if one's tastes ran that way, to marry an Indian woman, or live with her. He would not be – what is the right word? Diminished? He wouldn't feel that. People would not really feel it of him, either. He has the dominant role, whatever the colour of his partner's skin. The Indians themselves have this prejudice about paleness. To them a fair skin denotes descent from the civilized Aryan invaders from the north, a black skin descent from the primitive aboriginals who were pushed into the jungles and hills, or fled south. There is this connotation paleness has of something more finely, more delicately adjusted. Well – superior. Capable of leading. Equipped mentally and physically to dominate. A dark-skinned man touching a white-skinned woman will always be conscious of the fact that he is – diminishing her. She would be conscious of it too.'

He relapsed into silence. Presently he said, 'I've said it all very badly. And I've broken one of the sacred rules, haven't I? One isn't supposed to talk about this kind of thing. One isn't supposed to talk about anything much.'

'I know,' she said. 'It's how we hide our prejudices and continue to live with them. Will you have the other half?'

'No, thank you. I ought to be going. I'm only half packed. Will you say goodbye and make my apologies to your family?'

Sarah glanced to her left. A light fell on the terrace from Aunt Fenny's and Uncle Arthur's room. A servant had wakened them. Her mother's room was dark.

'I expect Aunt Fenny will be out in a while.'

'I mustn't stay.'

He sat on for perhaps as long as half a minute, then rose.

'There's one,' he said. 'A firefly. The end of your vigil.'

But she did not see it. Standing, she thought of Teddie and Susan arrived already at the Nanoora Hills Hotel, observing the scene spread out below the balcony of their bridal room.

'The end of your vigil,' Merrick repeated, 'and the signal for me to depart.'

She smiled, went to the light-switch on the wall near the bell-push and flicked it on. Merrick, bathed in yellow light, lost that faded density. The sleeves of his bush shirt were still rolled up to the elbows. His arms were covered in fine blond hairs. Beneath the flesh on his cheeks the bone structure was emphasized by down-ward-pointing shadows. His eyes, his whole physical presence, struck her as those of a man chilled by an implacable desire to be approached, accepted. She felt reluctant to take the hand he slowly, consideringly held out as if uncertain that anyone would welcome contact.

'Well, goodbye,' she said, letting their hands meet. His felt warm and moist. The light had already attracted insects. They encircled the shade, distracting her. For politeness's sake she began to accompany him down the terrace but he said, 'No, please don't bother. Besides, you'll miss the next firefly.'

She watched him go – puzzled that by going he made her feel lonely. He did not look back. She returned her attention to the garden. After a while she heard the sound of the truck engine.

＊

She paused in her walk below the terrace. The night air was India's only caress. She was among the fireflies now. One passed within a few feet, winking on and off. Since Ronald Merrick left she had bathed and changed, but still was the first out to begin the ritual of the evening at home – home being anywhere, any place there was – say – a veranda, a bit of a view and the padding slap of a barefoot servant answering a summons. Home, such as it was,

218]

was the passing of the hours themselves and only in sleep might one wander into the dangerous areas of one's exile (and perhaps, in one's thoughts, between one remark and another, one gesture and another). One carried the lares and penates, the family iconography, in one's head and in that sequestered region of the heart. Why we are like fireflies too, she told herself, travelling with our own built-in illumination; a myriad portable candles lighting windows against some lost wanderer's return.

She laughed, chasing one of the luminous pulsating bugs and then stopped, having remembered her father. 'I hope you are not lonely,' she said aloud. 'I hope you are well, I hope you are happy, I hope you will come back soon.' And turned back towards the terrace and was in time to see Aunt Fenny and Uncle Arthur come out and stand for a moment arrested by some unexpected thought, consideration, recollection. From this distance their exchange was all dumb show, and not much of it either. Two or more English together were very uninteresting to watch. Fenny left Uncle Arthur's side and went to her sister's room from which light showed behind the louvres of closed shutters. Fenny must have tapped. A vertical band of light appeared, widened, and Fenny went inside.

Alone, Uncle Arthur now sat in a wicker chair. Alone he relaxed. Alone he became almost communicative with himself. He shouted for the bearer, crossed his legs, jerked one rhythmically up and down, smoothed his balding head, scrubbed his moustache with the first joint of his left index finger, shifted his weight in the chair, drummed on the adjacent table with his right hand. Yawned. Eased his tie. Scratched his crotch. And hearing Abdur Rahman approach, stretched his neck back to speak to him. Perhaps he asked where she was because Abdur seemed to invite his glance to fall upon, to attempt to penetrate, the darkness of the garden beyond the geometrical patterns of light falling upon gravel and grass.

Just then the vertical strip of light appeared again and widened and Aunt Fenny came out with Mrs Layton who brought her glass with her, and at once, so it seemed, a different pattern of the play was established and Uncle Arthur was on scene again, erect, sparing of movement. With the two women an element of grace entered. They sat, one on either side of Uncle Arthur who sank to his chair again, crossed his legs but kept the restless one still. Aunt Fenny was talking. The lone sound, the steady vibration of her voice reached Sarah, but not the words.

She began to walk towards them, conscious of coming at them from a great, a lonely distance away. She shivered a bit and the thought occurred that it was foolhardly to walk at night alone. She did not want to be alone. She remembered the sense she had had of being left behind when she saw that only one of the beds in her and Susan's room had been prepared for the night, mosquito net unrolled and draped, it's counterpart left stiff and bunched above a smooth virgin counterpane.

'My family,' she told herself as she entered the geometrical pattern of light and the circle of safety. 'My family. My family. My family.'

Book Two

Orders of Release

Part One ❧ The Situation

I

May 1944

THE CAR took what she and her husband had called the Household
Gate out of the grounds of Government House. Had it been called
the Household Gate before her husband's term of office? She could
not remember. She brought her hand up, seeking the reassurance
of the pleated front of her blouse and the mother-of-pearl buttons.

The car was headed towards the city, but at the complex of
roads that met at the Elphinstone Fountain the driver bore right,
north, taking the road through the noisy, heavily trafficked commercial quarter. Behind the grandiose stone buildings of the offices
and banks lay the labyrinth of the Koti Bazaar where she had
shopped accompanied only by Suleiman, to the despair of Henry's
aides. She glanced at the *aide* who accompanied her now and
realized that she had already forgotten his name.

'You have a question, Lady Manners?'

How well trained he was. She nodded. 'I'm afraid I suddenly
can't remember your name.'

'Rowan,' he said, without fuss.

'Rowan. It is a curious thing, memory. My husband had an
astonishing one. Mine was only so-so. I used to try and bluff my
way out of the awkward situations it seemed to lead me into, until
I realized the situations weren't awkward at all, but the bluff was.
The gate we left by, is it still called the Household Gate?'

'I've not heard it called that. H.E. calls it the side way. I think
the official description is Curzon Gate because of the statue opposite.'

'But Government House was built before Curzon.'

'That's true. How about Little West?'

'It will do. But so will sideway. The next Governor will call it
something else. It's a way of making ourselves feel at home in an
institution. Shall you return to active duty, Captain Rowan?' Today
he was wearing mufti but she recollected from their brief meeting

the day before in the Governor's private office the ribbon of the Military Cross.

'No, I'm told not. But that's probably a good thing because I wasn't made in the mould of a good regimental officer.'

'Were you wounded?'

'Nothing so distinguished, I'm afraid. But I managed to contract a number of tropical things, one after the other.'

'What do you intend? A regular staff appointment?'

'No. I've applied to get back into the political department, which is what I always wanted. I was seconded before the war and served a probationary period, but then of course the army reclaimed me.'

'And you were in Burma?'

'Yes.'

They were through the commercial quarter, travelling along a tree-lined section of the Kandipat road with the railings of the Sir Ahmed Kasim Memorial Gardens on their right and on their left the houses of rich Indians, in spacious compounds. Most of the iron gates were padlocked, the occupants having retreated into the hills. An exception was number 8. She found herself uncertain which of the houses along this stretch of the Kandipat belonged to M.A.K. And another name was troubling her – the name of the girl with the look of envy who had sent a parting gift of flowers – a Pankot name.

She turned and said, 'Do you have the photograph, Captain Rowan?'

'H.E. gave me an envelope which he said you might ask for.'

'I'll have it now, if I may.'

He zipped open the leather document case on his knee, reached in and brought out a square buff envelope.

'Would you unseal it for me?'

She watched while he sought for an ungummed section of the flap. Having widened it he made a neat break with his finger. He handed the envelope to her. She had taken her reading-spectacles case from her handbag in readiness and now put the glasses on. From the envelope she withdrew a rectangular matt-surface print. There were two pictures on it, side by side; profile and full-face.

For a time she avoided the flat stare of the full-face, considered instead the side-view of it, the whorls of the neat, masculine ear, the black, apparently oily, neatly-cut hair. In the processing the skin had retained the two-level density of a dark face under artificial lighting, the impression that negative and positive were aligned, one on top of the other. So that is what he looked like, she thought, and stared at the full-face, at the oddly expressionless eyes whose whites conveyed an idea that they might be bloodshot. She closed her own eyes to consider, uninfluenced, a different but familiar image and, having conjured it exactly, reopened her eyes and felt a stab of recognition which in the next moment she did not trust. She replaced the photograph in the envelope, took off her spectacles. They had entered a semi-rural area of hovels. There was a smell of human and animal excrement. A naked ash-smeared Sadhu leaned against a parapet and watched them go past, his arms folded, his head tilted. She saw his mouth open and his neck muscles swell, but could not distinguish his shout above the shouting of little boys who ran alongside the car calling for baksheesh; keeping up with it because it was slowed by a farmer's cart ahead and a string of cyclists coming in the opposite direction. The light was opaque: one particle of dust to one particle of air. The temperature was in the hundreds.

She returned her spectacles case to her handbag. The envelope was too big to go in too. She gave it back to Captain Rowan.

'I shan't want it again.'

Rowan put the envelope back into his briefcase. He looked at his wrist-watch and then at her. Their glances met. 'We have about ten minutes, Lady Manners. Would you like me to go through the arrangements so that you know what to expect?'

Again she sought the reassurance of the pleats and buttons. She looked through the double thickness of glass at the necks of the driver and his companion.

'I've no doubt H.E. has arranged everything as I would wish.'

'Not without a certain element of awkwardness being involved. Awkwardness for you.'

'I couldn't expect otherwise.'

'Before we reach the Kandipat I shall pull the blinds down over the windows. The man sitting next to the driver has all the necessary documents to pass us through the gates. The car will stop twice. When it stops the second time we shall be inside the prison. We should be immediately next to a doorway that leads into a corridor and eventually to the jail superintendent's private quarters. We shall go to the end of the corridor and into a room marked "O". I shall leave you alone in room "O". There are a few details about room "O" but I can explain those at the time. There is only the one door. The man sitting next to the driver will be on duty in the corridor.'

'And I shall be alone in the room – throughout?'

'Yes.'

'I understand. I shall see and hear but not be seen or heard?'

'Yes. Afterwards it will take me about five minutes to rejoin you.'

'And I should wait in the room until you come for me?'

'If you would, Lady Manners.'

'Shall I be required to meet anyone at all?'

'No one.'

'Thank you.'

'When we leave, the car will have been reversed in the courtyard and will be parked ready. We shall then drive straight out and back to Government House.'

Again Rowan checked his watch. He leaned far back in his seat, canting his head to get a glimpse of the area they were approaching. He said, 'I think perhaps we should lower the blinds now. We're coming into Kandipat.'

He reached forward, pulled down one of the tip-up seats and transferred himself to it, stretched across to the little roller-blinds on her side of the car. Gradually the back of the car was filled with sub-aqueous light. She lost the sensation of forward movement. When he had completed the operation he resumed his seat next to her, resettled the document case on his lap. She raised her hands, feeling for the veil, groped round its prickly edge until she felt the smooth round knob of the hatpin. She pulled the hatpin out, jabbed it gently into the buff cord upholstery and coaxed the veil out of its folds, until it hung loose, shading the whole of her face and neck. Retrieving the pin she replaced it in the back of her hat.

'In case I forget – afterwards – Captain Rowan, thank you for what you have done, are doing, and have undertaken to do. Can I rely utterly on your discretion?'

'Of course.'

'I understood from H.E. that he chose you for a reason that would become clear to me. If he meant your courtesy and efficiency it has already done so. But whatever the reason he had in mind, I'm grateful. Forgive me for raising the question of discretion.' She

226]

smiled, then wondered whether he would see that she did, through the veil, in the dim museum-like light. He was not smiling. But her compliments had not embarrassed him. Well, she thought, you are a man who knows his worth, accepts its obligations with interest and its rewards with dignity, and I particularly thank God for you today.

*

She thanked God too for Captain Rowan not talking, for not attempting to disrupt her contemplation of the mystery of the inhumanity of man towards man that a prison was the repository of and which was entered consciously even when the actual entry was made blindly, so: stop and pause, start and move and stop finally. At some point, when the back of the car was overtaken by a violently sudden darkness the line dividing contemplation of the mystery from experience of it was crossed. A chill smell of masonry conjured the sensation of enclosure within walls sweating from a low but insistent fever – the fever of defeat and apprehension. The door on Captain Rowan's side of the car was opened. The cold damp smell of stone strengthened, came on a shaft of funnelled air with the implacable impact of an actual touching, so that Captain Rowan's hand, offering itself to hers, was a momentary shock, the flesh-touch of someone who had accompanied her into an area of distress. There were on either side of her glimmers of filtered light and, in front, steps and a narrow doorway that was open. She mounted the steps, grateful for his cupped hand at her elbow. The corridor was stone-flagged, stone-walled, lit by one naked bulb at its farther end where already she could make out the letter 'O' painted in white on a closed brown door. Reaching it she saw that the corridor turned at a right-angle towards flights of wooden stairs – up and down. After he had left her alone in Room O he would ascend or descend by one of those flights: descend, more likely.

He opened the door of Room O. A cold dry draught and a faint humming in the darkness, a subtle lethal scent as of chilled milk in frosted zinc containers – a scent that always caught her high up in the nostrils and made her conscious of the space between her eyes – distinguished the room at once as one whose atmosphere was regulated by an air conditioner. She thought: I shall catch a cold. Captain Rowan entered the room ahead of her and switched on the light – an act which registered in her mind as a consequence of particular rehearsal rather than of general familiarity.

The room was a square of bare whitewashed walls. It contained a table and a chair. On the table, which was covered by a piece of green baize, were a carafe of water with an inverted tumbler over its neck, an ashtray, a pad, two pencils, a table-lamp and a telephone. The chair had its back to the door. It stood close to and facing the farther wall. Into that part of the wall a grille was let in at eye-level for someone sitting in the chair. Above the grille was a smaller grille with a fine steel mesh. The table was set against the wall to the right of the chair.

Captain Rowan went to the table and switched on the lamp. It threw a small pool of light on to the white notepad.

'If you would sit, Lady Manners, I'll turn off the overhead light.'

She sat, lifted her veil. She could see nothing through the grille, but when the overhead light went off the grille was transformed into a faintly luminous rectangle. She felt Captain Rowan come close. He reached in front of her, manipulated a catch on the grille and opened it. Behind it was a pane of glass and behind the pane wide-spaced, downward-directed louvres of wood or metal. She found herself looking through the louvres into a room on a slightly lower level. There were a table, several chairs and a door in each of the three walls she could see. The table was covered in green baize. There were pads, pencils, two water carafes and – placed centrally – a telephone. Suspended above the table was a light. It was on and seemed to be powerful. There was no one in the room.

'Actually there's not much to explain,' Captain Rowan said. 'You can keep the table-lamp on without any light on this side of the window attracting attention from below. The light over the table down there is rather strong and the shade is adjusted so that the man sitting in the chair facing you tends to be a bit dazzled by it. I've tried it myself and I assure you that if you look up you simply can't see this grille let alone see anyone watching through it. But if the table-lamp here distracts you, just switch it off.'

'I think I should prefer it switched off.'

He pressed the button on the base of the lamp.

'Yes,' she said, 'now I feel less vulnerable.'

'Good. The microphone is in the telephone down there.' He switched the lamp on again. 'This is the speaker, above the grille.

When I get down I shall ask whether you can hear. If you can, press the button that you'll find under the arm of the chair.'

She felt for it.

'Yes, I have it.'

'Would you press it now and watch the telephone downstairs?'

She did so. A green light on the instrument in the room on the other side of the grille came on in response to the pressure.

'That is also your line of communication. If the relay system breaks down all you need do is press the button. I will then pick up the telephone and say "Hello". Once the telephone is picked up there's a direct private connexion between this room and that. All you need do is pick your own telephone up and tell me what's wrong. My reply may not seem relevant, naturally. But please don't hesitate to communicate if you think it necessary. The business can always be adjourned if you want to discuss any points with me.'

'Thank you, Captain Rowan.'

'Are you close enough to the grille?'

'Yes, and I shall put on my distance glasses.'

'Shall I turn the light off again?'

'If you would.'

Again the room darkened and the picture of the room below became brighter, clearer. She leaned forward.

'Then if everything is satisfactory, Lady Manners, I'll leave you.'

She nodded and said, 'Yes, please carry on with your own side of things.'

Presently she heard the door open. Light from the corridor came and went across the wall she faced. She fumbled for the clasp of her handbag, found it and opened a way for her hand into the familiar homely clutter. Without removing the case she opened it and took out her distance spectacles, put them on. Now she could appreciate the fuzzy quality of the baize, the contradictions of texture between the baize and the wood of the chair that would be the focus for her attention. There was a clock on the wall above the door behind the chair. It showed twenty minutes after ten.

Just before it showed twenty-five past the door below it opened and Captain Rowan entered. He put his briefcase on the table and sat in the chair the prisoner was to sit in and gazed at a point directly in front of him. His voice reached her rather metallically from the wall just above her head.

'The table is on a low dais and someone seated opposite sits

[229

slightly higher than the person in this chair. The head of the person in this chair is therefore raised a bit when he looks the other person in the eye. So.' Captain Rowan raised his head fractionally. 'You should now have a fuller face view. More chin and less forehead. If you have heard and understood please press the button twice.'

She did so. The green light on the telephone pulsed on and off, on and off.

'Good. Perhaps we should test the telephone connexion.' He stood, leaned over and picked the receiver off the rest. She turned to her right, groped for her own instrument, found it, lifted the receiver and placed it against her ear. His voice was now in the instrument.

'Can you hear me?'

'Yes, thank you. It's working perfectly.'

'Shall we begin, then?'

'Please.'

'I'll wait until I hear you put your phone back.'

She replaced the receiver.

He looked up, narrowing his eyes against the bright light, put his own receiver down and said – his voice coming again through the speaker – 'I assure you no one can see the little window. I'm going outside for a moment. A clerk will come in. When I return I shall have an official from the Home and Law department of the Secretariat with me. The clerk and the official are both Indians. The clerk's duty is to make a shorthand transcript of the proceedings. The official from the Home and Law department is here because of the nature of the business which H.E. felt shouldn't be left entirely in the hands of someone on his private and personal staff.'

Rowan, while talking, had come round to the other side of the table and stood with his back to her. He took some papers from the briefcase. She saw him hesitate over the buff envelope which she had returned to his care.

He said, 'Although H.E. handed this envelope to me without explaining what was in it I gather it's a photograph of the man in question. I feel I ought to warn you that if so it was probably taken the year before last, sometime in August 1942. There are bound to be changes.' He put the envelope back in the briefcase. He looked round the table, then walked across to the door under the clock, opened it and went out.

She glanced at the clock. It showed about a quarter of a minute

230]

short of ten-thirty. The door on the left of the room opened. The clerk came in a middle aged Indian with a balding head and gold-rimmed spectacles. He wore a homespun cotton shirt and dhoti. His feet, sockless, were tucked into black leather shoes. He came down to a chair placed several feet to the left-rear of the table almost out of her sight, and sat. The sounds he made were clearly relayed. She could just make out his crossed legs and the shorthand notebook which he held ready on his knee. He made a few marks on it with his fountain pen, testing the nib and the flow of ink. Satisfied, he put the cap back on the pen and began to adjust the folds of his dhoti. It seemed an act of vanity, like that of a woman wearing a long-skirted dress making sure it hung grace-fully. She particularly noted the action. The clerk was unaware of the presence of an invisible audience. He coughed, cleared his throat, began to tap the pen on the notebook; puk, puk, puk. She found herself fighting a tickle in her own throat and then remem-bered that no one could hear her if she coughed to clear it. She did so. The tapping continued uninterrupted: puk, puk, puk, puk.

Abruptly the door under the clock opened again – the tapping stopped and the clerk stood – and Captain Rowan entered followed by the official from the Secretariat – a lean elderly Indian wearing a grey chalk stripe suit and a pink tie. He carried a black document case. He cast an upward glance in the direction of the grille, then came and sat with Captain Rowan. Their backs were towards her. They sat with plenty of space between them. Midway, on the other side of the table, the empty chair faced her directly and her view of it was not obscured. The crackling of the papers the two men were leafing through was now the only sound.

'Shall we begin?' Captain Rowan asked suddenly.

The lean Indian's voice was soft and low-pitched.

'Oh yes. I am quite ready if you are.'

'Tell them we are ready, Babuji.'

The clerk went to the door in the right-hand wall, opened it and spoke to someone in Hindi, then closed the door again and went back to his chair.

For an instant Lady Manners closed her eyes. When she opened them the room still contained only the three men. Her hand tugged at the pleats and mother-of-pearl buttons and then lay inert. She breathed in and out slowly in an attempt to slow her heart-beat. The door opened again. She could not see who opened it because it opened on a side that would hide whoever entered until he was inside the room out of range of the door's arc. For a moment or so the door remained as it was at an angle of ninety degrees to the wall and no one came from behind it.

When he did he came hesitantly – a dark-skinned man dressed in loose-fitting grey trousers and a loose-fitting collarless grey jacket buttoned down the front. He wore chappals without socks. Having emerged beyond the range of the door he stopped and glanced at the occupants of the table and then at a man who was holding him by the right arm – to guide or restrain, or both; it wasn't easy to tell. The other man was in uniform – khaki shirt and shorts. He wore a pugree and carried a short baton. The hand on the arm suggested authority but also aid or comfort such as might be given in an unfamiliar situation to a man who normally gave no trouble, whose mind and body were disciplined to routine and were slow to respond to unusual demands.

The hand was on the arm for no longer than a few seconds. The guard let go, came to attention and dismissed, closing the door behind him. The man in the floppy collarless jacket and trousers stood alone.

'Sit down, please,' Captain Rowan said. He indicated the chair.

It was the same profile as in the photograph: the same neat, masculine ear. But not the same. The face of the man in the photograph had been held erect, was well fleshed; a dark, handsome face with hair that curled – a bit unruly on the forehead. This man's hair looked as though it had been cropped some months ago and had not grown out in its former fashion. Under the brown pigment of the face there was a pallor. The cheek was hollow. The head looked heavy, as if long stretches of time had been spent by the man, seated, legs apart, hands clasped between them, eyes cast down, considering the floor, the configuration of the stone. He moved towards the table, stood by the chair, still in profile.

'Baitho,' the official from the Home and Law department repeated.

The man extended his right hand, clutched the back of the chair and then with an awkward movement twisted round and sat, holding the back until the weight and position of his body forced him to release it. He gazed down at the table. His shoulders were hunched. It looked as if he might have his hands between his knees.

232]

'*Kya, ham Hindi yah Angrezi men bolna karenge?*' Captain Rowan asked.

Briefly she had an impression from the man's glance at Rowan of eyes startlingly alert, in sockets which compared to those she recalled from the photograph were large and deeply shadowed. The man looked down again.

He said, '*Angrezi.*' The voice was notably clear.

'Very well. In English, then.'

Rowan opened a file.

'Your name is Kumar, your given name – Hari.'

'*Han.*'

'Son of the late Duleep Kumar of Didbury in the county of Berkshire, England.'

'*Han.*'

'At the time of your detention you were living at number 12 Chillianwallah Bagh in Mayapore, a district of this province.'

'*Han.*'

'The occupier of the house in Chillianwallah Bagh being your aunt, Shalini Gupta Sen, *née* Kumar, widow of Prakash Gupta Sen.'

'*Han.*'

'You were taken into custody on August the ninth, nineteen forty-two by order of the District Superintendent of Police, in Mayapore, and detained for examination. On August the twenty-fourth as a result of that and subsequent examinations an order for your detention under Rule 26 of the Defence of India Rules was made and you were thereupon transferred in custody to the Kandipat jail, Kandipat, Ranpur, where you have remained in accordance with the terms of the order.'

'*Han.*'

'I understood you elected to speak in English. So far you have answered in Hindi. Do you therefore wish to have these proceedings conducted in Hindi and not English?'

Again Kumar looked up from the table, but this time his glance was not brief and only now was she convinced that the man in the room was the man in the photograph and the conviction did not come from the speaking of his name or his acknowledgement of it but from the sudden resemblance to the photograph that had become superimposed on his prison face, the prison structure of bone. The resemblance, she thought, must lie in the expression. He gazed at Captain Rowan in the way that he had gazed to order into

[233

the lens of a camera – as into a precision instrument that could do no more than the job it was designed for and could not penetrate beyond whatever line it was he had drawn and chosen to make his stand behind, the demarcation line between the public acceptance of humiliation and the defence of whatever sense he had of a private dignity.

'I beg your pardon,' he said – and she shut her eyes, to listen only to the voice – 'it was a slip. I seldom have the opportunity of speaking English to anyone except myself.'

A pause.

'I understand,' another voice said above her head. She kept her eyes shut. The voices were those of two Englishmen talking. 'These proceedings,' the second of the two voices went on, 'are authorized by an order of the Governor in Council dated the fifteenth of May, nineteen hundred and forty-four and the purpose of the proceedings is to examine any facts relevant in your case to the detention order under the Defence of India Rule. You may if you wish decline to submit to the examination, in which case the proceedings will be terminated immediately. I am also instructed to advise you that the purpose of the proceedings is to examine and not to make a recommendation in regard to your detention. You should not assume that refusal or acceptance of the examination or the examination itself will have any bearing on the order for your detention or upon its eventual termination. On that understanding I now ask you whether you decline or submit to the examination.'

A pause.

'I submit to the examination on that understanding.'

'Your submission is recorded. In the case of Kumar, Hari, son of the late Duleep Kumar, at present lodged in the Kandipat jail, Kandipat, Ranpur, under warrant dated August twenty-four, nineteen hundred and forty-two, Rule 26, Defence of India Rules, and in accordance with order dated fifteen May nineteen forty-four, of the Governor in Council, Government House, Ranpur, Captain Nigel Robert Alexander Rowan and Mr Vallabhai Ramaswamy Gopal examining. Examinee not under oath. Transcript of proceedings for submission on confidential file to His Excellency the Governor, copy on the confidential file to the Member for Home and Law, Executive Council.'

Again a pause. She opened her eyes. Kumar still sat with his shoulders hunched. He had returned to his contemplation of the table, as if in deference to a formal rigmarole that was no particular concern of his, but as the silence lengthened, was filled by nothing more enlivening to the ears than the sound of Captain Rowan adjusting and checking the papers in front of him, Kumar glanced up again to stare at his chief examiner and again she was struck by the alertness his eyes – and the clarity of his voice – were evidence of. She could not interpret it beyond that. Impossible to say whether he sensed danger or saw the examination as a source of hope. It could be either. It could be both. But whichever it was the alertness and the clarity betrayed the presence of the man inside the hunched submissive figure of the prisoner.

'Since a detention order under the Defence of India Rules is made without recourse to trial in the criminal courts,' Captain Rowan began, 'the documentary evidence in front of this examining board consists of summaries of evidence, statements and submissions by the civil authorities of the district in which you resided. In this instance, which involved five other men as well as yourself, the documents were submitted to the office of the Divisional Commissioner before the order for detention was made on you and these five other men. We are however only concerned with these documents as they relate to you. It is not within the terms of reference of this board to disclose the details of these documents to you, but it is upon them that we shall base our questions. I shall begin by reading to you a list of names. The question I ask in each case is – were you at the time of your detention personally acquainted with the man whose name I read out. I invite you to answer yes or no as the case may be, after each name. With the name I shall give a brief description – for example occupation – to reduce the risk of confusion. Is that understood?'

'Yes.'

'The first name is S. V. Vidyasagar, sub-editor employed on the *Mayapore Hindu*, originally employed as a reporter on the *Mayapore Gazette*. Were you acquainted with this man?'

'Yes.'

'Narayan Lal, employed as a clerk in the Mayapore Book Depot.'

'Yes.'

'Nirmal Bannerjee, unemployed, graduate in electrical engineering of the Mayapore Technical College, son of B. N. Bannerjee, a clerk in the offices of Dewas Chand Lal, Contractor.'

'Yes.'

'Bapu Ram, trainee at the British-Indian Electrical Company's factory, Mayapore.'

'Yes.'

'Moti Lal, last employed as a clerk at the warehouse of Romesh Chand Gupta Sen, contractor of Mayapore, sentenced to six months imprisonment in 1941 under section 188 of the Penal Code. Escaped from custody during February 1942, and according to this document not apprehended at the date of the document's origin.'

'Yes.'

'Puranmal Mehta, stenographer employed in the office of the Imperial Bank of India, Mayapore.'

'Yes.'

'Gopi Lal, unemployed, son of one Shankar Lal described as a hotel-keeper.'

'Yes.'

'Pandit B. N. V. Baba, of B-1, Chillianwallah Bazaar road, Mayapore, described as a teacher.'

'Yes.'

'I shall now divide those names into two groups. In the first we have two names – S. V. Vidyasagar and Pandit Baba. The questions I shall ask relate to the kind of acquaintanceship you had with these men. In the case of Pandit Baba the records at my disposal, those on your case file, give me no idea why at the time of your arrest you were asked what you knew of him. Perhaps that would be clear after a study of the case files of the other men arrested at the same time as yourself, but those case files are not available to this examining board because they aren't pertinent to this examination. I would stress the latter point to you. This board examines you wholly on the basis of the file pertaining to your own arrest and subsequent detention. In other words, you are examined by a board unprejudiced by anything that is recorded in the cases of the other men arrested. My first question, with regard to Pandit Baba, is therefore this: Would you tell the board why – in your opinion – you were asked what your relationship with him was? I would remind you that your reply to this question as recorded in the file was to the effect that you had nothing to say. In fact ninety-nine per cent of your recorded replies to questions were to that same effect. I hope the same situation isn't going to arise this morning. Will you then answer the question? Why should you have been asked if you knew this Pandit Baba? Have you any idea?'

There was an appreciable pause but when Kumar spoke any initial hesitancy he might have felt to answer questions was quite absent from the tone of voice.

'I believe he was thought to have a lot of influence over young Indians of the educated class.'

'Who thought this?'

'The civil authorities in Mayapore.'

'Including the police?'

'Yes. The police once had him in for questioning because one of his disciples got into trouble.'

'Disciples?'

'Young men who gathered round him to listen to him talk.'

'What sort of trouble had this particular follower got into?'

'I believe he'd published or distributed a political pamphlet, or made a speech. I forget which.'

'Were you one of Pandit Baba's followers?'

'No.'

'Did you know the man who got into trouble?'

'No.'

'Then who told you about this affair?'

'I heard it as a matter of course. I was employed on the *Mayapore Gazette*. In a newspaper office you hear quite a lot that never becomes common knowledge.'

'What happened to the man who published this pamphlet or made this speech?'

'He was sent to prison.'

'What was his name?'

'I forget.'

'What happened to the Pandit?'

'Nothing.'

'How well did you know Pandit Baba?'

'I knew him as a man my aunt hired to try to teach me an Indian language.' A pause. 'He smelt strongly of garlic.' A pause. 'He was very unpunctual.' A pause. 'The lessons weren't a success.'

'When was this?'

'In 1938.'

'He tried to teach you Hindustani?'

'Yes.'

'Until then you knew no Indian language at all?'

'None.'

A rustle of paper. Then Gopal's voice: 'I have several points in regard to the detenu's early background and I should like to raise them at this juncture.'

Rowan nodded. Gopal addressed Kumar direct:

'Your father took you to England when you were aged two, according to this document. You were born in the United Provinces. Your father was a landowner there. Have you an inheritance in the United Provinces?'

'No. My father sold his interest to his brothers before leaving for England.'

'Your father never taught you your native tongue?'

A pause.

'He was at pains to try to teach me nothing.'

'Why?'

'He wanted me brought up in an entirely English environment so far as that was possible. I had a governess, then a tutor. Then I went to a private school and on to Chillingborough. I didn't see much of him.'

'Why was he wanting this – did he tell you?'

'He wanted me to enter the Indian Civil Service, as an Indian, but with all the advantages of an Englishman.'

'What were those advantages, was he saying?'

'I think he thought of them as advantages of character, manner and attitude. And language.'

'Because he thought the English character, manner, attitude and language were superior to the Indian?'

'No. More viable in relation to the operation of the administration.'

'I am not fully understanding that reply.'

'It is an English administration, based on English ideas of government. He thought an Indian at a disadvantage unless he had been trained to identify himself completely with these ideas. He admired the administration as such. He thought it would be best continued by fully Anglicized Indians.'

'Did you share his ambition for you?'

'Yes.'

'Why?'

'I knew no other.'

'You wished to enter the Indian Civil Service and serve the administration?'

238]

'Wish is the wrong word. It suggests the existence of an alternative choice and a preference for one of them. In my case I was never aware of an alternative.'

'From this document,' Gopal went on, 'I see that your mother died soon after you were born. Did the loss of your mother contribute to your father's decision to leave India and establish himself as a businessman in England?'

'It made it easier for him to put his plan into practice.'

'It was some two years after your mother's death that he took you to England. Presumably it took a little time for him to make the necessary arrangements?'

'He had to wait until his own mother died.'

'She was ill?'

'No. He had promised his father to look after her.'

'Your grandfather was dead?'

'He'd left home.' A pause. 'He renounced his worldly goods and left home wearing a loin-cloth and carrying a begging bowl. He intended to become what is called *sannyasi.*' A pause. 'The family never saw him again, but my father kept his promise and stayed until his mother died.'

'I see. Had he always hoped to leave India and go to England?'

'If he had a son.'

'He had been in England before?'

'He studied law there before the First World War but failed the examinations. He had a business sense but no academic sense.'

'He was what we are calling Anglophile? He admired the English way of life?'

'He thought an intimate understanding of and a familiarity with it essential for anyone serving the administration.'

'What were his political views in regard to India?'

'We never discussed politics as such.'

'Was he in favour of constitutional development leading eventually to a form of independence or of more hasty means to that end?'

'The former I imagine. He said India would remain under British rule well beyond his lifetime and probably far into mine.'

'Would you then say that he was anxious that you should become the kind of Indian whom the British would be happy to see as one of their administrative successors?'

'Yes. In later years he talked much along those lines, whenever I saw him.'

'Was that also your ambition? To become that kind of Indian?'

'I had no recollection of India whatsoever. I didn't know what different kinds of Indian there might be. My upbringing was entirely English. There was probably little difference in my attitude to the prospect of coming to India when I was older and the attitude of the average English boy whose family intended he should have a career out here.'

'You had, then, no sense of coming home when eventually you came to India?'

'The sense I had was the exact opposite.'

'Were you perturbed by what you found?'

'Yes.'

'Perturbed by the condition of the people?'

'I was perturbed by my own condition.'

'You did not look around you and think – these are my people, this is my country, I must work to free them of the foreign yoke that weighs them down?'

'I wanted nothing more than to go home.'

'Home – to England?'

'Yes.'

'But later, perhaps, you were ashamed of this selfish attitude and began to listen to young men of your own age and kind, to be affected somewhat by their hot-headed but understandable talk and ambitions?'

'They might have been of my age. They weren't of my kind. I was a unique specimen.'

'Unique? Just because you had been brought up in England?'

'No. Because I came back to a family my father had cut himself off from – a middle-class, orthodox Hindu family.' A pause. 'My uncle-by-marriage tried to make me undergo a ritual purification to get rid of the stain of living abroad. The ritual included drinking cow-urine. It was a family that didn't believe in education, let alone Western-style education. Not a single member of the Kumar family or of the Gupta Sen family my aunt married into had ever entered the administration. They were middle-class Hindus of the merchant and petty landowning class. Against this background – yes, I was unique.'

Gopal said, 'Thank you, Mr Kumar. I have no further questions on this subject.'

Rowan nodded, glanced at his open file, then looked up at

Kumar who slowly transferred his attention from Gopal. For a while the two men – whose voices sounded so alike – stared at each other.

'In England, you say, there was little difference between you and the average English boy who was being trained for a career out here. Why, then, were you so shocked by what you found? The average Englishman arriving in India isn't shocked at all. In fact, he's rather excited. How do you explain this difference?'

She saw Gopal look at Rowan, as if astounded that he should bother to ask such a question. She too wondered why he had. If Kumar's face had been capable of changing expression she imagined it would now reflect an astonishment the equal of Gopal's. Perhaps the time he took to reply reflected it. Eventually he said:

'The India I came to wasn't the one the Englishman comes to. Our paths began to diverge in the region of the Suez Canal. In the Red Sea my skin turned brown. In Bombay my white friends noticed it. In Mayapore I had no white friends because I had become invisible to them.'

'Invisible?'

'Invisible.'

Rowan looked down at his file.

'I see that your father died in Scotland early in 1938 and that you came out in May of that year and went to live with your father's sister, Mrs Shalini Gupta Sen, in Mayapore. Was she your only surviving relative?'

'She was the only relative my father kept in touch with.'

'Why?'

'He had personally supervised her education when she was a young girl. The Kumar women were all illiterate but he taught her to read and write English, and speak it. They remained very fond of each other. When she was about fifteen she was married to a man of more than thirty – Prakash Gupta Sen of Mayapore. He died before they had any children. She was always interested in her English nephew – which was the way she referred to me in letters to my father.'

'Your father's solicitors communicated with her and she agreed that you should live with her?'

'Yes. She borrowed the passage money from her brother-in-law.'

'The contractor, Romesh Chand Gupta Sen of Mayapore, whose office you worked in for a time?'

'For a time.'

'Was there no possible means of maintaining you in England to finish at your public school and then study for the ICS examinations as your father had wished?'

'The means perhaps, but they weren't offered. My father committed suicide. He'd had business failures. He tried to recoup but lost everything. That's why he killed himself. His English-style son existed only as long as the money lasted. He probably couldn't face telling me my English life had ended and my Indian life was beginning several years too soon.'

'Did you ever ask your relatives in Mayapore if they'd maintain you in England until you'd qualified?'

'The solicitor wrote to my Aunt Shalini, suggesting that.'

'I presume you had some friends in England whom you could have lived with?'

'It seemed like it – for a time.'

'The family of one of your friends at school perhaps?'

'Yes.'

Again the rustle of paper.

'In one of the reports on this file there's a reference to a letter which the police found in your room and took charge of. It was signed Colin and had a Berkshire address. Was Colin the boy whose family might have looked after you?'

'Yes.'

'But your aunt was unable to raise the money to keep you in England, until you'd qualified?'

'She had no money of her own. She was a childless widow whose husband died in debt to his brother. She depended on this brother of his for practically every penny.'

'We're speaking of Romesh Chand Gupta Sen, I take it?'

'Yes. He offered passage money, and offered her an allowance for taking me in. The solicitor said it was very generous. According to him I was probably only losing my last term at school. He said I could study for the ICS in India.'

'You still intended to enter the ICS then? You came out with that ambition unimpaired?'

'Yes.'

'You discussed it with your aunt, and her brother-in-law?'

'Yes. But it was made plain by Mr Gupta Sen that there was no money for any kind of further education. I was expected to start earning my living.'

'Which is when you started working in your uncle's warehouse?'

'Yes. In the office of his Chillianwallah Bazaar warehouse. I remember the leper.'

'The leper?'

'He stood at the gate of the bazaar.'

'Why do you remember this?'

'When I saw the leper I thought of my grandfather. I wondered whether he had become a leper too.'

'And it was during this period that you had Hindustani lessons from Pandit Baba?'

'Yes.'

'It must all have seemed very strange to you.'

'Very strange. Yes.'

'The next note on your file is that during the summer of 1939 you applied to be taken on as a trainee at the British–Indian Electrical factory. A trainee in what?'

'They had a scheme for training suitable young Indians for junior executive positions.'

'You failed to get taken on, I see. In fact the note says: "The applicant was turned down chiefly as a result of his sullen and unco-operative manner." Would that be a reasonable description of your attitude?'

'It would depend on who was describing it.'

'I infer from the note that the man who found you sullen and unco-operative was the manager in charge of technical training. An Englishman. What happened?'

'I'd already passed two interviews, with one of the directors and with the managing director. The interview with the technical training manager was supposed to be a formality but he insisted on asking me technical questions which I told him at the outset I wouldn't be able to answer. When he'd finished he insulted me.'

'How?'

'By suggesting that I was an ignorant savage.'

'Are those the words he used?'

'No. He said: Where are you from, laddie? Straight down off the tree?'

'What did you say to that?'

'Nothing.'

'And so the interview ended —'

'Not then. He said something else.'

[243

'Well?'

'He said he didn't like bolshie black laddies on his side of the business.'

'How did you respond?'

'I got up and walked out.'

'Yes, I see.' Rowan turned a page of the file. 'The next note shows you as having taken employment as a sub-editor and reporter on an Indian-owned newspaper published locally in Mayapore in the English language. The *Mayapore Gazette.* I presume this went well because you were still employed there at the date of your arrest in 1942, some three years later. What led you to choose journalism as a profession?'

'I didn't think of it as journalism or of myself as a journalist. A few months living in Mayapore showed me I'd only one qualification to put to practical use. My native language. English. The *Gazette* was owned, edited and written entirely by Indians. The English it was printed in was often very funny. So far as I was concerned I worked on the *Gazette* as a corrector. I became an occasional reporter because I could earn four annas a line for anything I wrote which they published. In addition to my salary of sixty rupees a month.'

'Did your aunt and uncle-by-marriage approve of this job?'

'My aunt did. She used to buy the *Gazette* for me so that I could read about local affairs. She liked reading it too. She liked being able to talk English again. She was always very good to me. She did her best to make me comfortable and happy. It wasn't her fault that I was neither.'

'Your aunt approved but her brother-in-law didn't?'

'When I got the job at the *Gazette* he reduced my aunt's allowance.'

'Why?'

'He said I could contribute to my upkeep out of my salary. He gave me nothing when I worked in his office.'

'I now go back,' Rowan said, 'to the first group of names, which consists of two: Pandit Baba and S. V. Vidyasagar. It was in the *Mayapore Gazette* office that you met the second man, Vidyasagar?'

'Yes. It was Vidyasagar who showed me the ropes.'

'What kind of ropes?'

'Finding my way round the Civil lines. Where the District and Sessions court was, who the deputy commissioner was and where he lived. Which was police headquarters. Who to apply to for permission to attend and report on some social function on the *maidan*. Before I joined the *Gazette* there'd been no occasion for me to cross the river and enter the Civil lines and cantonment.'

'Your job on the *Gazette*, then, took you into what from your point of view were more pleasant surroundings, a happier environment altogether?'

'It was interesting to observe that environment.'

'You felt yourself no more than observer?'

'I was no more than an observer. Perhaps I was even less than that. But it was interesting. Observing all the things English people did to prove to themselves they were still English. Interesting and instructive. It taught me to see the ridiculous side of my father's ambition. I realized he'd left an important factor out of his calculations about my future.'

'And what was that?'

'The fact that in India the English stop being unconsciously English and become consciously English. I had been unconsciously English too. But in India I could never become consciously English; only consciously Indian. Conscious of being something I'd no idea how to be.'

Again Rowan looked down and referred to his file.

'Vidyasagar is also described as a sub-editor on another Mayapore newspaper, the *Mayapore Hindu*. How long were you working together at the *Gazette*?'

'About three weeks.'

'Vidyasagar then left and joined the *Mayapore Hindu*?'

'He was sacked.'

'Do you know why?'

'When the editor of the *Gazette* took me on he did so with the intention of sacking Vidyasagar.'

'Did you know that?'

'No. But Vidyasagar did.'

Rowan hesitated. 'So there was cause there for some friction between you and Vidyasagar? Did he harbour any kind of grudge?'

'If he did he never showed it. When he was sacked he said he'd expected it and that it wasn't to worry me because he could easily get a job on the *Mayapore Hindu*. He always remained friendly.'

'Why did the editor of the *Mayapore Gazette* prefer you to Vidyasagar?'

'I wrote correct English. Vidyasagar had only been at the Govern-ment Higher School.'

'The editorial policy of the *Gazette* has always been pro-British, wouldn't you say? I mean in comparison with the *Mayapore Hindu* where Vidyasagar was subsequently employed. A note here men-tions that the *Mayapore Hindu* had a history of closure by the civil authorities. In fact it was closed down for a time during the riots in August 1942. The *Mayapore Gazette* on the other hand has never been proscribed.'

'The *Gazette*'s policy was to print nothing that caused the authorities any misgivings. I don't know if that amounts to pro-Britishness.'

'I ask the question to find out if you think there'd be any-thing to be said for a view that as a young reporter and sub-editor your attitude to affairs in general was more in keeping with the paper's editorial policy than was the attitude of Vidyasagar, for example.'

'I had no comparable attitude. Vidyasagar was an ardent national-ist, like ninety-nine per cent of other young Indians of his age and class and education.'

'That's what I mean. The editor of the *Gazette* might have found such a young man an embarrassment. With you he felt on safer ground?'

'The editor never asked me if I had any political views or affilia-tions. He hired me because of my ability to transcribe copy into correct English.'

'Did you have any political views and affiliations when you joined the paper?'

'No.'

'I believe a great deal of the *Gazette* was taken up with reports of social and sporting functions organized by the English com-munity in Mayapore.'

'Yes.'

'And you sometimes attended such functions in your capacity as a reporter?'

'In that capacity, yes.'

'You would be a more suitable representative of the *Gazette* at such a function than Vidyasagar –? I mean from the editor's point of view.'

'Perhaps.'

'And from the point of view of the people attending the function?'

'From their point of view I would be no different from Vidyasagar.'

'Why?'

'We both had black faces.'

A pause.

'But as time went by you were able better than Vidyasagar to break down this rather artificial barrier. You got to know a few English people.'

'I got to know one.'

'You're referring to Miss Manners?'

'Yes.'

'During your interrogation, whenever you were asked to describe the circumstances in which you became acquainted with Miss Manners you always replied: I have nothing to say. The question was simple enough, surely?'

'It was also unnecessary. The person asking it knew those circumstances as well as I did.'

'This board does not. So I ask the same question. What were the circumstances in which you got to know Miss Manners?'

'I was invited to the house where she was staying.'

'Can you remember the date?'

'Either the end of February or the beginning of March, nineteen forty-two.'

'I see. Then that would have been soon after an occasion in February 1942 when you were taken to the police station at the Mandir Gate bridge and asked questions about your identity and occupation?'

'The invitation was a consequence of that.'

'You mean you were invited to the house where Miss Manners was staying because you'd been questioned by the police?'

'My being questioned by the police made certain people in Mayapore aware of my existence, yes.'

'Please elucidate.'

'I was arrested in a place called The Sanctuary —'

'Arrested?'

'I was dragged into a police truck, taken to the police station, held, questioned and then released. It seemed to me like being arrested.'

'Very well. Continue —'

'The Sanctuary was run as a private charity for the sick and dying by a woman known as Sister Ludmila. After I was arrested – taken away – she got word to Romesh Chand Gupta Sen. He sent for his lawyer, a man called Srinivasan. Srinivasan was a friend of Lady Chatterjee who lived in the MacGregor House. Miss Manners was staying with her there. Sister Ludmila also mentioned my arrest to a German woman who was in charge of the Purdah Hospital. Doctor Klaus. Doctor Klaus was also a friend of Lady Chatterjee. By the time Mr Srinivasan got to the police station to ask why I had been taken there I'd been released. But Lady Chatterjee heard of the incident from Dr Klaus and asked Mr Srinivasan about me. So she became interested in my case.'

'Your case?'

'My personal history.'

'You mean she thought you sounded like a young man in need of some help?'

'I don't know. I assumed she was interested in what she was told about me by Srinivasan, otherwise she wouldn't have invited me to the MacGregor House to one of her mixed parties of British and Indian guests.'

'Lady Chatterjee has some influence in Mayapore?'

'She was the widow of the man who founded and endowed the Mayapore Technical College. That's what he was knighted for. She was a friend of Miss Manners's aunt, Lady Manners, the widow of an ex-Governor of this province. In Mayapore the British always accorded her respect.'

'To have her interested in you was an asset, would you say?'

'I imagine it could be.'

'When you accepted her invitation was it in your mind that Lady Chatterjee might help you?'

'I don't know.'

'It was an opportunity for you, surely, to meet influential Indians and English people socially?'

'It was an opportunity I was in two minds about grasping.'

'Why?'

'I'd been in Mayapore for nearly four years. It struck me as significant that it needed my arrest to open the door to that kind of opportunity.'

'Significant of what?'

'I wasn't sure. Perhaps it was to find the significance that I accepted and went along.'

'And did you find this significance?'

'Influential people are always anxious to exercise their influence. They enjoy helping lame dogs of the right kind. But they're also always very busy. Only lame dogs who have tripped up ever come much to their notice. By then, from the lame dog's point of view, it's usually too late. Lady Chatterjee was about three years too late. I'm not criticizing. It was simply so. Having me at the party wasn't a success.'

'Any particular reason?'

'Influential people like to be thanked. I didn't thank her. And it worried her when Miss Manners was so friendly to me.'

'There are two points there. What did you have to thank Lady Chatterjee for?'

'Nothing.'

'You mean nothing in your opinion. What in hers?'

'She asked Judge Menen to inquire why a fellow called Hari Kumar had been dragged into a police truck and carted off to answer stupid questions. I don't suppose it did me any good in Merrick's book.'

'District Superintendent Merrick of the Indian Police?'

'Yes. That Merrick.'

'And Miss Manners's friendliness towards you. You think it worried Lady Chatterjee. Why?'

'Miss Manners was in her care. She felt responsible for her to Lady Manners.'

'I quite understand that. I don't understand why Miss Manners's friendliness to you should worry her. Surely it was to make you feel that you had friends that she invited you to the party?'

'Miss Manners was a white girl. Her friendliness towards me was of a kind that embarrassed people to watch.'

Rowan hesitated. From her air-conditioned place of observation she thought she detected, in Rowan, a certain stiffening of the neck and shoulders. She felt it in her own.

'I'm not sure I understand,' he said. 'What are you suggesting?' He hesitated, then abruptly, coldly said, 'That Miss Manners threw herself at you?'

Kumar stared at Rowan. There was a muscular spasm low on one cheek.

'I'm suggesting that even someone like Lady Chatterjee was incapable of accepting immediately that a white girl could treat an Indian like a man. I found it difficult to accept it myself. For a time I thought she was making fun of me. She talked so readily. Without any kind of artificiality – or so it seemed. Just as if we'd been back home. Lady Chatterjee very naturally treated me with caution after that.'

'Why "very naturally"?'

'She probably thought I might take advantage of Miss Manners. That's the popular assumption, isn't it? That an Indian will always take advantage of an English person who is friendly.'

'It may be an assumption generally held among certain types of English who come into contact with certain types of Indian. I can't think why Lady Chatterjee should think you'd take advantage of Miss Manners unless you gave her cause.'

Kumar seemed lost momentarily in thought. He said, 'I may have done for all I know. My behaviour at that time left a lot to be desired.'

'In what direction?'

'I'd forgotten how to act in that kind of company. Or if I'd not forgotten, trying to act as I remembered I should act seemed – artificial. I said very little. I was socially ill-at-ease. Miss Manners told me later that I stood and stared at her. I wanted to say things but the right words wouldn't come. I was a bit suspicious. I wasn't shy. Suspicious, and then astonished – to be treated as an equal by a white person. The comparison between this and what I'd just experienced was so extraordinary.'

For a while none of the three men at the table spoke. Gopal suddenly opened his file again and said, 'With regard to that recent experience I have a question —'

'Is it in regard to what he calls his arrest?' Rowan asked.

'Yes —'

'I should like to go back a bit further and come to that in its turn.'

'By all means.'

Gopal rested again.

'You mentioned The Sanctuary,' Rowan began. 'You called it a place run as a private charity for the sick and the dying. I have a record here of the occasion when you were asked to go with the police to the kotwali after you'd refused to answer questions put to you by police officers who visited The Sanctuary and found you there. The record has a note to the effect that according to the person in charge of The Sanctuary – here called Mrs Ludmila Smith, not Sister Ludmila – you had been found the night before by her stretcher party, lying unconscious in some waste ground near the river. Imagining that you were ill or hurt they took you back to The Sanctuary – as was their habit whenever they found someone ill, starving or dying in the street. It turned out, however, that you were merely dead drunk. Is that correct?'

'Yes.'

'It was your habit to drink excessively?'

'I had never been drunk before. I was never drunk again.'

'When you were questioned by the police at the kotwali you were not at all co-operative. But you admitted you'd been drunk and that your main drinking companion of the night before had been Vidyasagar, and that the names of the others were Narayan Lal, Nirmal Bannerjee, Bapu Ram. You were uncertain about Puranmal Mehta – but said there was a fifth man there who might have been called Puranmal Mehta. Therefore three if not four of the men you got drunk with on that night in February were among the five other men who were arrested under suspicion of being implicated in the criminal assault on Miss Manners. The question I must ask you is – for what purpose had you and these other men, including Vidyasagar, gathered together on the occasion you got drunk?'

'There was no purpose behind the gathering together.'

'It was simply your habit every so often to foregather with these men?'

'No. It was the first time – and the last.'

'But you said some while ago that you always remained friendly with Vidyasagar.'

'I said he remained friendly with me.'

'You met quite often.'

'Our occupation brought us into frequent contact.'

'You would meet – as reporters – at some function or, say, in the law courts. Then perhaps, when you'd done your jobs, you'd go off together – as acquaintances?'

'No. We would meet as reporters. Once or twice he invited me to have coffee. I always refused.'

'Why?'

'I didn't want to become involved.'

'Involved how? Politically?'

'Not politically. Socially.' A pause. 'In those days I was at pains to preserve everything about me that was English.' A pause. 'I lived a ridiculous life, really. But I didn't see that. I thought of their life as ridiculous.'

'Vidyasagar's and his friends'?'

'Yes.'

'You despised them? Because they hadn't had your advantages?'

'No. I didn't despise them. But I thought them ludicrous, through no fault of their own.'

Gopal interrupted. 'In what way, ludicrous?'

'They were always laughing at the English. They pretended to hate them. But everything about their way of life was an aping of the English manner. The way they dressed, the style of slang, the things they'd learned.' A pause. ' "I say, Kumar old man, let's dash in for a cup of coffee." Perhaps it was exaggerated for my benefit. I was a bit of a joke to them. But it seemed ridiculous.'

'You say "they". You were – if only in a limited sense – acquainted with these other men as well as Vidyasagar?'

'I came to Mayapore in 1938. I met Vidyasagar in 1939. Obviously I saw something of them between then and August 1942. I knew them by sight, whether they were with Vidyasagar or alone. After the night I got drunk I knew most of them by name.'

'The night you got drunk was the beginning of a closer relationship?'

'You don't get drunk with men without establishing something more intimate in the way of relationship. But it was still distant. And shortly afterwards of course my life changed completely.'

'How?'

'I became friendly with Miss Manners.'

'What hasn't been dealt with yet is the reason for your sudden switch in attitude to Vidyasagar and his friends. Until a night in February 1942 you say you found them ridiculous – to the extent that you would even refuse to have a cup of coffee with them if one of them asked you when he met you in the street, or at some official function. But that night you join Vidyasagar and his friends not just for a cup of coffee but for a hard bout of drinking – which ended so far as you were concerned in waste ground near the river in a state of complete intoxication. What led to this sudden reversal of what we might call your policy in regard to men like Vidyasagar?'

'The realization that after all it was I who was ridiculous.'

'Please elucidate.'

'It is a private matter.'

'You could say that practically everything we are discussing is a private matter. I suggest that this is no more, no less private. If you find it difficult to talk about, to know where to begin for instance, suppose we begin by discussing the events of that night. How, for example, did you find yourself in the company of Vidyasagar?'

'We were both on the *maidan*.'

'As reporters?'

'Yes.'

'What was taking place on the *maidan*?'

'A cricket match.'

'Between which teams?'

'Teams from regiments stationed in the cantonment.'

'You were watching cricket with Vidyasagar?'

'No. We met as we were coming away.'

'He invited you to come and have a coffee?'

'He invited me to his home.'

'And you accepted?'

'Yes. I accepted.'

'Why?'

'There no longer seemed to be any point in refusing.'

Rowan said nothing for a while. 'Because your resistance was worn down at last or because something had happened to upset you?'

'I suppose it was a combination of the two.'

'Then what exactly was it that had happened to upset you?'

Kumar stared at the table.

'He was there.'

'Who was there?'

'Someone I used to know.'

'Someone you had known in England?'

Kumar nodded.

'Colin?'

Kumar nodded.

'Your old school friend? The boy whose parents might have given you a home after your father died?'

'Yes.'

'Why was this upsetting?'

No answer.

'You met and talked, and thought that he was less friendly than you remembered? Or did you only see him from a distance?'

'He was as close to me as I am to you.'

'Are you saying that he was close to you but didn't talk to you?'

'We neither of us spoke.'

'Are you sure it was this man, Colin?'

'Yes.'

'You knew he was in India?'

'He wrote to me when he first came out, in 1941. He wrote several times, from different places. He talked about coming to Mayapore. Later he talked about how unlikely it would be that he could travel so far. Later he didn't write at all.'

Gopal said, 'And what construction did you put on that?'

'I thought that he had gone on active service. I thought he was having a bad war. First Dunkirk, now perhaps the Middle East. But he came to Mayapore. I guessed he had come to Mayapore when I saw soldiers in the cantonment wearing the regimental flash.'

'The flash of the regiment you knew Colin was serving in?'

'Yes. When I started seeing the soldiers with the flashes I began to expect him any day. I mean expecting him to turn up at my house. Then I realized that probably wasn't possible, because my side of the river was out of bounds to soldiers stationed in the cantonment. So then I began expecting a letter asking where we could meet. There was never such a letter. So then I thought Colin hadn't come to Mayapore with his regiment.'

'Are you still sure that he did?'

'He was there, on the *maidan*, watching the cricket. I went up to him, to make sure. It was Colin. You don't forget the face of a man you grew up with.'

'Why didn't you speak to him?'

'He turned and looked at me.'

'Yes?'

'He didn't seem to recognize me. In India, you see, all Indians look alike to English people. It was the kindest construction I could put on it. Either that, or that he had been in India long

254]

enough now to understand that it would be hopeless for a British officer to have an Indian friend who lived on the wrong side of the river and had no official standing. But whichever it was the effect was the same. To Colin I was invisible.'

'I see. And that is why when you met Vidyasagar and he invited you home you accepted?'

'Yes. For all his faults – what I thought of as his faults – I realized he had a gift.'

'What sort of gift?'

'A gift for forgiveness.' Kumar looked up at Rowan. 'They still all laughed at my ridiculous English manner – at the absurdity of it in someone born an Indian, and still an Indian, incapable of being anything in India except an Indian – but their laughing at me was meant with kindness. That's why I got drunk. They used to get hold of home-made hooch. One of them sometimes distilled it himself. That's the sort of stuff we drank that night. They were used to it, but I wasn't. I don't remember much after they'd helped me burn my topee —'

'Burn your topee?'

'The topee was a joke to them too. They said only Anglo-Indians and Government toadies and old-fashioned sahibs wore topees. So we burned mine. Then I suppose I passed out. When I met Vidyasagar later he told me they'd taken me all the way home to my house in Chillianwallah Bagh, so that I wouldn't get picked up by the police. But after they'd left me in the compound I must have wandered out again, on to that waste ground where Sister Ludmila found me.'

Rowan nodded. He now turned to Gopal.

'You have a point or two about Kumar's questioning by the police after he was found at The Sanctuary.'

'I think perhaps it has been taken care of. I had intended to question the examinee about his apparent reluctance to answer questions when he was taken to the kotwali. The reason for that reluctance now seems quite clear. Please continue the examination along whatever lines you decide.'

'Well, let's deal with that reluctance, nevertheless. When you were questioned at the kotwali you were not at all co-operative, according to the report on this file. You admitted that your main drinking companion of the night before had been Vidyasagar, though. Is that correct?'

'Admit is the wrong word. It suggests I'd felt I had something to hide and then changed my mind.'

'How would you describe your attitude to the police at the kotwali, then?'

'As that of someone responding quite naturally to a situation that involved him in unpleasantness without any explanation.'

'It was not clear to you why you were asked to accompany the police to the kotwali?'

'It wasn't clear to me why the District Superintendent had me forcibly taken from The Sanctuary, thrown into a truck, driven to the kotwali and then pushed into a room there.'

'Was he aware that force was used?'

'He watched it.'

'Isn't it true to say, though, that you brought it on yourself by being truculent when asked to identify yourself in The Sanctuary?'

'Perhaps. It wasn't easy that morning for me to identify myself.'

'What were you doing when first approached by the police officers who visited The Sanctuary?'

'Washing.'

'Where?'

'In the compound. Under a tap.'

'Getting rid of a thick head?'

'Yes.'

'Let me read from the report: "On being asked in Urdu what his name was Kumar affected not to understand any Indian language. Mrs Ludmila Smith then said – 'Mr Kumar, these are the police. They are looking for someone. It is their duty to question anyone they find here for whom I cannot personally vouch. I cannot personally vouch for you because all I know of you is that you were found by us last night unconscious from drink.' Kumar then made a gesture of defiance. The DSP addressed him directly as follows: 'Is that your name, then – Kumar?' To which Kumar replied, 'No, but it will do.' DSP then directed his sub-inspector to escort Kumar to the police truck. No evidence being found at The Sanctuary in regard to the escaped prisoner Moti Lal, DSP proceeded to the kotwali at the Mandir Gate bridge and formally questioned the man Kumar." Is that an accurate record of the events as you remember them?'

'Broadly. I don't remember a gesture of defiance unless I shrugged. And the report omits to mention that the sub-inspector

256]

raised his hand to hit me and would have done so if Sister Ludmila hadn't objected in the strongest terms to any violence being shown by anyone in her presence, on her private property.'

'Why did you say "No, but it will do" when DSP asked if your name was Kumar?'

'He pronounced it incorrectly. There was too much stress on the last syllable. And I was still in the habit of thinking of myself as Coomer, which is how we spelt the name at home. I mean, how we spelt it in England.'

'Weren't you being unnecessarily obtuse?'

'Not unnecessarily. Merrick spoke to me as if I were a lump of dirt. I wasn't in the mood for that. I had a hangover, to begin with.'

'At The Sanctuary, then, you admit you weren't in the mood – as you put it – to answer fairly and squarely questions put to you by the police in the course of their duty?'

'The course of their duty didn't automatically give them permission to treat me like a lump of dirt. In my view.'

'When you got to the kotwali, however, you became more co-operative?'

'I answered questions as soon as Merrick explained why he'd brought me in.'

'You mean the District Superintendent.'

'To me he was always Merrick. We came to have a special personal association.'

'What do you mean?'

'It will become clear if you ask enough questions about my various interrogations.'

'At the kotwali it was explained that the police were looking for an escaped prisoner – one Moti Lal – who had lived in Mayapore and was thought possibly to have come back and gone into hiding there. It so happened that although the DSP didn't know when he took you in for questioning that you knew this man, Moti Lal, you in fact did know him, and had to admit it when questioned.'

'Again admit seems to me to be the wrong word. I'd met Moti Lal because he was once employed by Romesh Chand Gupta Sen in the office of the warehouse in the railway sidings. I also knew Moti Lal had been sacked. Romesh Chand disliked his employees being politically active. He thought all their energies should be devoted to their work. I knew that sometime after he was sacked Moti Lal was sent to prison for subversive activities. I was in the District and Sessions court when he was brought up for his appeal. I didn't know he had escaped. And I didn't know the man at all – apart from what I've just told you.'

'Didn't you know that Moti Lal had been a very popular figure among young men like Vidyasagar?'

'One couldn't help knowing. One knew of Moti Lal's popularity just as one knew of Pandit Baba's.'

'We now come to more detailed consideration of the names in group two. In group one there were Pandit Baba and Vidyasagar. In group two there are six names. The first is Moti Lal, who at the time of your arrest under suspicion of criminal assault was still apparently unapprehended as an escaped prisoner. The five other men are Narayan Lal, Nirmal Bannerjee, Bapu Ram, Puranmal Mehta and Gopi Lal. According to police records these men were all intimates of Vidyasagar's. And according to your testimony at least three of them were your drinking companions with Vidyasagar on the occasion in February after the cricket match on the *maidan*. You would in fact agree that you had some kind of relationship with all the men in the two groups – however passing a relationship you may judge it to have been?'

'Yes.'

'With the exception of Pandit Baba, these were all young men whom you would describe, more or less, as ardent nationalists who looked forward to an early end to a British controlled administration?'

'They were all young men – Indians – therefore they would almost inevitably look forward to that.'

'After the night you drank with a certain number of them, would you say that you became more directly aware of their political desires and affiliations?'

'No.'

'Did you not in fact become privy to their political activities?'

'I never assumed that they ever did more than talk politics.'

'For what purpose then would you imagine they got together?'

'To drink bad liquor and exist for a while in a state of euphoria.'

'Are you aware that a couple of days after your arrest in August nineteen forty-two Vidyasagar was arrested in the act of distributing seditious pamphlets?'

'Yes. Merrick told me. He said Vidyasagar had confessed to acts of sedition and had implicated me as the leader of a plot to attack Miss Manners.'

'What was your reaction to that?'

'I didn't believe he had implicated me.'

'But you believed he had confessed to acts of sedition?'

'It didn't surprise me. The whole of Mayapore was by then engaged in such acts – or so one gathered.'

'You insist that neither before nor after the occasion when you drank home-made hooch with Vidyasagar and his friends were you involved in any way with their political activities.'

'Yes, I insist that.'

'But you saw quite a bit of them? I mean after the night you got drunk?'

'If anything I saw less.'

'How was that?'

'I've already said. I had become friendly with Miss Manners.'

'From a time towards the end of February or the beginning of March, until August, in nineteen forty-two, your social life became more or less exclusively involved with your friendship with Miss Manners.'

'It was the first time I'd had a social life. So it did not *become* exclusively involved with that.' A pause. 'And the date is wrong. It was from February or March until towards the end of July. At the time of my arrest on August 9th I had not seen Miss Manners since the night we went to the temple. About three weeks previously.'

'So you always insisted. But let us concentrate on these men, other than Moti Lal and Vidyasagar. And of course other than Pandit Baba. That leaves us with Narayan Lal, Nirmal Bannerjee, Bapu Ram, Puranmal Mehta and Gopi Lal. You say that you knew them as among Vidyasagar's friends but that if anything you saw less of them after the night you got drunk. I want you now to tell me about the last occasion you saw them. When was that?'

'I saw them last on the night of my arrest as a suspect in the criminal assault on Miss Manners.'

'In what circumstances?'

'They had also been arrested. I was taken through the room in which they were held.'

'Taken through a room at police headquarters?'

'Yes.'

'You were taken through the room as distinct from lodged in it?'

'I was in the room for about half a minute.'

'Did you speak to them?'

'No.'

'Did they speak to you?'

'One of them said, Hello, Hari.'

'You didn't reply?'

'No.'

'Why?'

'They were behind the bars of a cell in the room.'

'What was their demeanour?'

'They were laughing and joking.'

'And you were not?'

'No. I was not.'

'What happened then?'

'I was handed over by the two policemen who held me to two other policemen and taken to a room downstairs.'

'So you saw those five men in a cell on the night of August the ninth and recognized them all?'

'I recognized about three of them in the sense of being able to put a name to the face.'

'All the faces were familiar as men you knew but you didn't immediately recall all their names.'

'That is right.'

'You remembered all the names later?'

'No.'

'Please elucidate.'

'I was told the names.'

'By whom?'

'By District Superintendent Merrick.'

'Your memory is clear on that point, that District Superintendent Merrick told you the names of the men in the cell?'

'Yes.'

'He read out a list of names?'

'Yes.'

'And asked you whether you were acquainted with the men?'

'No.'

'No? What then?'

'He read out the list of names. Then he made a statement.'

'What was the statement?'

'He said: These men are all friends of yours and as you saw we have them under lock and key.'

'What did you say?'

'I said nothing.'

'Why?'

'It wasn't a question.'

'On reconsideration would you not agree with a statement to the effect that "when asked whether he knew the five other men in custody and with whom he had been confronted the prisoner refused to answer"?'

'No.'

'Would you not agree with the following statement? Upon being told dates and times and circumstances when he had been seen in the company of one or several of the other prisoners the prisoner Kumar refused any comment beyond the words: I have nothing to say.'

'Yes. I would agree with that.'

'Why did you have nothing to say?'

'I refused to comment on any statement because I didn't know what I was being charged with.'

'When did you ask what you were being charged with?'

'When I was taken into custody.'

'At number 12 Chillianwallah Bagh?'

'Yes.'

'Not at police headquarters?'

'I asked first in my room at 12 Chillianwallah Bagh. I asked again at police headquarters. I asked several times.'

'When were you first told?'

'After I'd been in custody for about an hour.'

Gopal suddenly interrupted. 'Please recollect carefully. Would it not be more accurate to say something to this effect': He glanced at his file and read out: 'At 22.45 hours the prisoner Kumar, having continually refused to answer questions relating to his activities that evening asked for what reason he had been taken into custody. Upon being told it was believed he could help the police with inquiries they were making into the criminal assault on an English-woman in the Bibighar Gardens earlier that evening he said: I have not seen Miss Manners since the night we visited the temple. On being asked why he named Miss Manners he refused to answer and showed signs of distress.'

'No,' Kumar said, 'it would not be more accurate.'

[261

'In what way is that statement inaccurate in your view?' Gopal asked.

'I may have asked at 22.45 hours why I was taken into custody but it wouldn't have been for the first time. I asked several times. It was probably at 22.45 hours when the District Superintendent finally told me. But it didn't happen in the way it's written down there. He said he was making inquiries about an Englishwoman who was missing. His words were: "An Englishwoman, you know which one." He then made an obscene remark.'

'Let us be quite clear,' Gopal continued. 'According to you the investigating officer did not say "We believe you can help us with inquiries we're making into the criminal assault on an English-woman in the Bibighar Gardens" – to which you replied "I haven't seen Miss Manners since the night we visited the temple".'

'No. It wasn't like that. He made the obscene remark and followed it with another.'

'Are you saying it was from these remarks that you gathered who the Englishwoman was and what had happened to her?'

'I'm not saying what I gathered, only what was said to me.'

'Are you saying that what was said to you accounted for what is described as your distress?'

'I don't know what he meant by distress.'

Gopal said: 'Then how would *you* describe your demeanour at this stage of your interview at police headquarters?'

Kumar looked down at the table. Presently he said, 'I was shivering. It would have been noticeable.'

'Shivering?'

'The interview was in a private room in the basement. It was air-conditioned.'

'This room is air-conditioned. You are not shivering now, are you?'

'No.'

'Why were you shivering on that occasion?'

'I had no clothes on. I had had no clothes on for nearly an hour.'

'No clothes?' Gopal asked. 'You were asked questions by a police officer in a state of undress?'

She was observing the hollow-cheeked face intently. A tremor passed over it. It might have been a smile.

'The police officer who asked the questions was fully dressed,' Kumar said. 'But I was naked.'

262]

'That is what I said,' Gopal snapped. 'Why were you naked?'

'I had been stripped. My clothes were piled on the table.'

'I meant for what purpose were you stripped?'

'Originally for inspection I believe.'

'A physical examination?'

'Inspection would be more accurate. There was no doctor present.'

Gopal said, 'No doctor? Then who carried out the examination?'

'The District Superintendent.'

Gopal hesitated, then said, 'What kind of examination was it?'

'An inspection of my genitals. Doesn't it say so in the reports? He inspected my genitals for signs of blood.'

'Did he tell you that?'

'No. But it became obvious.'

'How?'

'When he'd finished he said: "So you've been intelligent enough to wash, we almost caught you at it, didn't we?" Later he said: "Well, she wasn't a virgin, was she, and you were the first to ram her?" So it was obvious the inquiry was about a woman who'd been assaulted.'

Captain Rowan interrupted: 'All this is, in a sense, irrelevant to the purpose of the inquiry. I should like to return to the main line of questioning,' but Gopal shook his head, and said:

'All this is most important. It has a direct bearing on the detenu's statement that he was not immediately informed of the reason for being in custody and a direct bearing on the question of his distress as recorded. The impression I am getting here is that the physical examination and the references to other physical matters occurred before 22.45 hours. Hitherto the official suggestion has been that until then questions were asked in an ordinary line of interrogation and not answered and then at 22.45 hours the detenu was told the reason for the inquiries, appeared to incriminate himself by naming the woman and then showed signs of distress.'

'Perhaps,' Captain Rowan began, but she had pressed the button under the chair arm. The green light flicked on. Captain Rowan lifted his receiver as she lifted hers.

'Hello: Rowan here —'

'I have a question to ask – and something to say —'

'Oh, yes.'

'Does Mr Gopal know I'm listening? He glanced up at the grille when he came into the room.'

Rowan waited before replying, as if his caller had asked a longer question.

'The answer to that – the official answer – is no. But in that particular case I'm not sure. I'm in the middle of an examination. Is it urgent?'

'What I wanted to say is forget that I am here. You have your job to do. I don't want you to worry about trying to spare me from hearing unpleasant things.'

'Very well. I'll attend to it.'

'One other thing —'

'Yes?'

'Does Mr Kumar know that my niece is dead?'

'I'm not sure.'

'I should like to be sure.'

'Very well, and thank you. Goodbye.'

For a while after he put the telephone back on its rest no sound came through the speaker other than the slight rustle of paper. Then he spoke.

'Since we've had an interruption I think this is a suitable moment to break the examination off for five minutes.' He slapped the file shut. 'Babuji – tell the guard to hold the prisoner outside.'

The clerk got up and went to the door through which Kumar had entered, opened it and spoke to the guard. Kumar glanced round. His movements suggested that he had not clearly understood what Rowan said.

'We shall call you back,' Rowan told him. Kumar stood up.

'In about five minutes we shall continue the examination.'

It was extraordinary, she thought. When he stood he gave the appearance of a shambling man – one who might not be expected to think clearly or speak precisely. He ducked his head, then turned. The guard had appeared and now accompanied him out. The clerk also went out – closing the door behind him, leaving Rowan and Gopal alone.

Rowan said, 'Let's use these few minutes to consider really what our terms of reference are. If I may say so these questions about his interrogation by District Superintendent Merrick in regard to the criminal assault tend to lead away from the main point about his association with a group of fellows who were clearly politically committed and politically involved —'

'I'm sorry to disagree with you, Captain Rowan. Perhaps I have

264]

had less time than you to study the files of this curious case, and it is most unusual for a detenu to be examined, in fact I have never come across it before, neither has my superior. I have assumed that since His Excellency personally ordered the examination some serious doubt has arisen about the order for detention. From my reading of the files – coupled with my recollections of the actual circumstances – I feel that the order rested entirely on the original suspicion this young man was under in regard to the criminal assault. For that reason I feel that the criminal assault aspect should now become the focus for our questions. It would have been useful if you had agreed to a previous consultation, but my clerk told me you were unable to find the time.'

'Well let me put it to you that the man was never charged with criminal assault although I agree the assault was the original cause of his arrest. He seems on the other hand to have been known to the police as a man to keep an eye on over anti-government activities of a seditious nature —'

'– on the frailest evidence, in my opinion —'

'Well, that's really what we're out to examine. I think the situation here is that at the *time* of his detention the circumstantial evidence of his implication in the assault was so strong that neither the Deputy Commissioner nor the Commissioner felt it reasonable to set him free —'

'– and used this ridiculous evidence of a connexion with subversive elements as an excuse to imprison him without trial.'

'One has to consider the affair in the context of the time and circumstances. If the detention order was unjustly made we have the opportunity of seeing that now in clearer perspective. What we're not out to do is apportion blame among the several authorities who had the difficult job of investigating at the time. I am strongly against a line of questioning that can help the man to level accusations against particular officials. It will only confuse the issue from H.E.'s point of view. Kumar isn't under oath and the officials aren't here to answer. The man himself has never petitioned against the order and there's some cause to think he may have counted himself extremely lucky to get away with simple political detention.'

'Who has petitioned, then?'

'No one. No one can except the man in question.'

'Then why has H.E. suddenly ordered an examination?'

'I think chiefly as a result of private pleas – for instance by his relative – his aunt, Shalini Gupta Sen.'

'And perhaps by the late Miss Manners's aunt – Lady Manners? She, surely, must eventually have learned the truth?'

'That I wouldn't know,' Rowan said.

'I thought perhaps new evidence had come up and that the examination might be a preliminary to other proceedings.'

'Not to my knowledge.'

'Are the other five men to be examined?'

'I have no instructions. And their cases were different. They denied the criminal assault but never denied subversive political activity, even if they denied being engaged in such activities on the night in question which they said they'd spent drinking in a hut on some waste ground close to the Bibighar.'

'But Kumar did deny subversive activity —'

'According to the file his answer to every question was: "I have nothing to say".'

'It is somewhat different this morning, isn't it?'

'This morning he is not under suspicion of criminal assault. Which brings me back to the point. In my opinion the line of questioning should be confined as nearly as possible to facts bearing on the ostensible reasons for his *detention* – detention as distinct from arrest. The criminal assault is a dead file. The girl herself is dead. If she was intent on protecting him – for emotional reasons, as was thought at the time – we shall never know. A line of questioning that concentrates on facts relating to the assault and on the details of his arrest on suspicion of being guilty of rape can only be abortive, I believe.'

'I disagree. If there had been no rape he would never have been arrested. It is clear he was arrested only because he was known to consort with her. It has always been clear, Captain Rowan, if you will forgive my saying so, that Kumar was victimized by the British authorities in Mayapore for his association with a white girl. It is common knowledge.'

'Common knowledge isn't evidence. We must base our inquiries on the evidence in this file.'

'The evidence is worthless to a large extent, Captain Rowan. You have only to read it to see it is all too – what is the word you use?'

'Pat?'

'All too pat. Rigged. The girl knew what would happen. The

266]

record of her private examination before the District Judge and the Assistant Commissioner makes it perfectly clear that the case could never have come to trial with the six men who'd been arrested because one minute of her evidence in the witness-box would have killed the case for the prosecution stone dead. She remembered her attackers as men of the badmash-type – men who'd probably come in from the villages because of the rumours of riot and the prospect of loot.'

'Perhaps, but I think the prosecution might have built a lot on her *first* statement to the Assistant Commissioner, that it had been too dark to see who they were. It's clear to me that the case never came to trial for two reasons – firstly that the evidence against the arrested men was wholly circumstantial and secondly that the girl – presumably for emotional reasons – was obviously prepared – even to the extent of perjury – to explode the case in everyone's face if they attemped to bring it into court. As you will have read in the file, she even threatened to suggest her attackers could have been British soldiers with their faces blacked. It was never a serious suggestion but you can imagine what effect her making it, even as a joke, would have had on a jury. She could never have killed the case for the prosecution but with the chief witness working against the prosecution it's most unlikely that their case could have been proved.'

'And so the men would have gone free, Captain Rowan. The detention orders were made to ensure that never happened. The whole thing stank, Captain Rowan. You know it, I know it. H.E. knows it. That young man was as much a threat to the defence of India as I am. His only crime was to have been the friend of a white girl who got raped by a gang of hooligans or looters. What can we possibly turn up now that will shed any positive light at all on his political ideas and activities? The evidence on this file that attempts to point to political affiliations is laughable. I hardly see how one can even begin to frame viable questions from it. I will say frankly, Captain Rowan, that if we are to put this poor fellow through this examination we must give him every chance to tell us exactly what happened and not bother our heads about what it will look like on paper or what muck might be raked. I did not ask to be appointed one of his examiners, but since I am one I intend to examine and not be blinkered by any narrow interpretations of terms of reference that leave the record not worth the paper it's written on.

[267

Frankly I do not care anything about confusing H.E. with details about the assault. Once the examination is over we are both personally powerless to take any step or press for any step we think is justified. I shan't be surprised if the record simply goes on file and is conveniently forgotten and that poor fellow who may be having his hopes raised has them dashed again. But we are not powerless to pave the way for a justified step to be taken. Forgive me. I am perhaps overheated.'

As if by an association of ideas Gopal lifted the tumbler from one of the carafes and poured himself a glass of water. He sipped it delicately, then patted his lips with a folded handkerchief from his breast pocket.

'Very well, but if it's H.E.'s intention to review the detention order an examination that weighs heavily on the side of questions relating to the criminal assault may have a contrary effect. He may throw the record out as irrelevant. And of course you do realize that the examination might give grounds for renewed suspicion that the assault was an aspect of subversive activities plotted and executed by Kumar and others? You speak as if there was no evidence implicating Kumar in the rape. He was absent from home at the relevant time, never accounted for his movements and was bathing cuts and abrasions on his face when the police arrested him.'

'So the police record states. The first police report – the one signed by a sub-inspector – also mentioned that the girl's bicycle was found in the ditch outside Kumar's home. The second report, by the District Superintendent, dated one or two days later, states that this was an error and that the bicycle was found at the scene of the rape, in the Bibighar Gardens, and put in the back of the truck before the visit to Kumar's home. Which smells to me like an abortive attempt to plant evidence which the District Superintendent later realized wasn't going to wash. I personally have no faith whatsoever in the statements to the effect that Kumar was bathing his face when arrested. If Kumar's face was cut and bruised it was just as likely because the police hit him.'

'Then why didn't he say so? He was examined by the Assistant Commissioner, and by a magistrate appointed by Judge Menen, as well as by the District Superintendent.'

'Who would have believed him? He had listened to innumerable criminal cases in the courts as a reporter for the *Mayapore Gazette* and knew what he was up against. He is an intelligent man – a product of your own English public schools.'

'I know. I went to the same one.'

Gopal stared at Rowan – as if suddenly suspicious.

'Oh? Does he recognize you then?'

'No. I was in my last term when he was in his first. But I remember him. He was the first Indian Chillingborough ever took, a bit of a showpiece. A few years later I watched him play cricket for the school against the old boys. He was very popular. I have a vague recollection of his friend Colin, too.' Rowan poured a glass of water also. 'It's one of the reasons H.E. chose me to make the examination. Until the other day I'd no idea the chief suspect in the Bibighar case was the fellow I knew as Harry Coomer. I wish I'd known years ago what he was having to face. There must have been several old Chillingburians out here who'd have been willing to help him.'

After a while Mr Gopal said, 'Do you think so, Captain Rowan? Willing, perhaps. Able – no. He is an English boy with a dark brown skin. The combination is hopeless.'

'Yes,' Rowan said after a while. 'Perhaps it is.'

II

'THE EXAMINEE'S last statement, please.'

The clerk flicked back one page of his notebook.

' "So it was obvious the inquiry was about a woman who'd been assaulted." '

'No – the whole of it.'

The clerk cleared his throat and recited in a monotone, ' "When he'd finished he said – So you've been intelligent enough to wash, we almost caught you at it, didn't we? Later he said: Well, she wasn't a virgin, was she, and you were the first to ram her? So it was obvious the inquiry was about a woman who'd been assaulted." '

'Thank you. Mr Gopal – you were making a point.'

'Yes. It is really a question of the order and time at which the detenu alleges certain things were done and certain things said.' Gopal now spoke directly to Kumar. 'I should like to go back to the moment when the police came to your house and took you into

[269

custody. According to the police report this was at approximately 21.40 hours. Is that correct?'

'I expect so.'

'I see — also from the report — that some three-quarters of an hour earlier the DSP called at your home to see if Miss Manners happened to be there. He spoke to your aunt. She said she had not seen Miss Manners for several weeks. She said you had not yet returned from the newspaper office. Is that correct?'

'Yes.'

'Later when you came in she told you of DSP's visit and inquiry?'

'Yes.'

'At what time did you get home?'

'I didn't think to look.'

'Did your aunt not say something like, The DSP came here asking if Miss Manners was with us, because Lady Chatterjee has reported her missing?'

'She said the DSP had called wanting to speak to Miss Manners.'

'And you then asked how long ago?'

'Yes — I did. But she didn't reply.'

'Oh? Why was that?'

'Her attention was taken.'

'Taken by what?'

'She had noticed the state I was in.'

She sensed the little wave of Gopal's shock. Rowan's voice cut in, 'According to the police report that state was as follows: "An abrasion on his right cheek and a contusion on his left cheek, stains on shirt and trousers from contact with muddy ground or dirty floor." Is that an accurate report?'

'Yes.'

'Is it also correct,' Rowan continued, 'that when the police, led by District Superintendent Merrick, entered a room on the first floor of number 12 Chillianwallah Bagh, the shirt and trousers in which you'd come home were found discarded, that you were wearing a clean pair of trousers, no other garment, and were bathing your face in a bowl of water?'

'Yes.'

'After reaching home and speaking briefly to your aunt who told you DSP had called looking for Miss Manners you went upstairs, changed and began to wash.'

270]

'Yes.'

'You were still washing when the police arrived, so you can't have been back home for longer than, say, ten minutes?'

'It would have been about that.'

'So if the police arrived at 21.40 you reached home about 21.30?'

'Yes.'

'According to the statement of Mr Laxminarayan, the editor of the *Mayapore Gazette*, you left the office of the *Gazette*, which was in the Victoria Road in the Civil lines, at approximately six-fifteen that evening.'

'Yes.'

'During interrogation, whenever you were asked to account for your movements between 6.15 and 9.40 p.m. your invariable reply was: "I have nothing to say." Do you have anything to say now?'

Kumar glanced down at the table. Gopal suddenly came to life. 'I have a point here,' he said. Rowan nodded. 'This contusion on the detenu's left cheek. There is a copy on this file of the medical report made out when the detenu was admitted to this prison. It was dated August 25th. It referred to traces of contusion still being visible on the face. Still visible, that is to say, after sixteen days. Unless further bruising was inflicted one might assume that the original blow or blows were therefore of considerable strength. Of course, it was never established what caused the contusion, but in the absence of any explanation by the detenu the impression the police reports seemed to leave was never counteracted. That impression was that the bruising was the result of blows by a woman defending herself from attack.' Gopal took out his handkerchief again, dabbed his lips. 'It is a point which a court of law might well have subjected to deeper consideration – the extent to which the contusion suffered could have been caused by a member of the female sex. I make the point in case it encourages the detenu to say what he was doing that led to his return home in the state described.'

'You have heard Mr Gopal's point. Are you prepared to comment on it?'

'I'm prepared to comment on it.'

Gopal nodded. 'Please do so.'

'It is a good point. I appreciate it being raised. I don't think it would have helped me in a court of law, if things had come to that.'

'Why?' Gopal wanted to know.

'Expert medical evidence would probably have held that a frightened woman can hit as hard as a man. But even if that had been expertly refuted the prosecution could have turned the point to my disadvantage.'

'How?'

'By suggesting that the men who assaulted Miss Manners fought among themselves.'

'Is that what happened?' Rowan asked, casually.

Kumar stared at him. 'I have no idea.'

'Are you prepared to say where you were between 6.15 and 9.30 p.m. on the night in question?'

Kumar glanced at the table, then back at Rowan.

'No. I'm sorry. But I'm not.'

Rowan leaned back in his chair. Watching, she became aware – as though she sat at it herself – of the expanse of table-top that separated the interrogators from the interrogated. It was an area of suspicion that none of them apparently had the capacity to diminish – although Rowan was now attempting to do so.

'I find it difficult to understand,' he had begun. 'So far this morning you have been extremely co-operative. The impression you have made is of frankness and candour. Now suddenly you revert to that unhelpful attitude of "I have nothing to say" which nullified every attempt made at the time to allow you to state a case. I use the word unhelpful advisedly. It does not help us and it certainly doesn't help you. The purpose of this examination is to go over evidence which at the time seemed strong enough to warrant your detention. It may or may not be so that at the time other considerations – well let us call them suspicions – coloured the views of those whose responsibility it was, at a moment of acute crisis resulting from civil disorder, to weigh the evidence in regard to that detention. Such suspicions do not enter into what is being considered this morning. I hope that has become clear as the examination has gone forward. These suspicions do not enter into the question of what is being considered, but if the record suddenly disclosed a lack of candour that today might be called uncharacteristic you must see how that would allow room for suspicion once again to enter into the weighing of all the various considerations.'

'Yes,' Kumar said. 'I see that. But the suspicion is unavoidable. However hard you try to avoid questioning me about the criminal assault you'll find everything leads to it. And every time the question of the assault comes up the suspicion comes up too.'

'Well, need it? It's come up now, certainly. Perhaps it could be eradicated by your answering the question. I wonder if you realize how foolish your original refusal to answer was? I wonder if you realize how very close you were to being charged? Or if you realize the extent to which that charge – rather, I should say, the failure of the charge to be made – depended almost exclusively on Miss Manners's vigorous rebuttal of any suggestion that you were involved in any way whatever? If she had shown the slightest uncertainty, if she had – however reluctantly – admitted that in all fairness she could not actually swear you weren't among those who attacked her, in the dark, suddenly, then you would have been charged and tried. I put it to you, if you had been charged and tried, in court, been put on oath, would you in those circumstances have refused to answer this question?'

'I should have refused.'

'In court that refusal could have been fatal.'

'I know.'

'Have you truly and deeply considered the reasonableness of this attitude?'

'I have truly and deeply considered the attitude. I have considered it daily, since the night of August the ninth, nineteen forty-two. For one year, nine months and twelve days.'

'And you still find it reasonable?'

'I have never said it was reasonable. It has never been a question of reason. It isn't now.'

'A question of loyalty, perhaps?'

'It's not a word I much care for.'

'Care for it or not, it gets us a bit further? Can we go a bit further still and establish to what or to whom you felt you were being loyal by maintaining what looked to everyone else like an unreasonable silence?'

'I'm afraid we can't go further. At least, not in the same direction.'

Rowan leaned forward again, and referred to his file. Eventually he spoke. 'Only two things of interest to the police seem to have been found in your room. A photograph of Miss Manners and the letter from Colin. The photograph was self-explanatory. She had given it to you. The letter from Colin is interesting though because

[273

– by your own evidence today – you had other letters from him. In fact I imagine that you heard quite often from him – at least until he came to India.'

'Yes.'

'I wondered why of all those letters you kept this particular one. It was an unfortunate choice because it was the one in which Colin told you two of your letters were opened by his father and not forwarded because his father thought them unsuitable reading for a young officer away on active service. The phrase "a lot of hot-headed political stuff" was the way he said his father described those letters. Why did you keep this particular letter from Colin?'

'It was the only one I ever had from him that really struck an authentic note. He went through various phases after he left school. But that one was from the man I remembered.'

'What sort of man was that?'

'The sort that found the liberal atmosphere of Chillingborough the right kind of atmosphere.'

'You would call Chillingborough a liberal institution?'

'It wasn't a flag-wagging place. It turned out more administrators than it did soldiers.'

She smiled and wondered if Rowan smiled too to be reminded so unexpectedly of his own words – 'I wasn't cast in the mould of a good regimental officer.'

'But for a time after leaving school,' Rowan said, 'your friend Colin became what you call a flag-wagger?'

'He was infected by the atmosphere of 1939, I think. He joined the Territorial Army, and wrote of nothing else.'

'The letter which you kept was one he wrote after he'd been wounded at Dunkirk, I gather?'

'Yes.'

'His baptism of fire had an effect on him which you approved of?'

'The effect of making him sound like the friend I knew.'

'And what was the hot-headed political stuff his father objected to in your letters?'

'It must have been mainly what I wrote about the pros and cons of Congress's resistance to the declaration of war, and their resignations from the provincial ministries.'

'And what were your views on that?'

'I think it was to find out if I had any that I wrote to Colin about the pros and cons.'

274]

'You would write that kind of thing to Colin. Would you discuss it with Vidyasagar?'

'No.'

'In spite of the distance between you, Colin remained your closest friend, your confidant?'

'In my mind he did.'

'It was a way of maintaining contact with – what shall we call it – your inner sense of being English?'

'Yes.'

Rowan sat for a while without speaking. Then abruptly he said: 'Have we been discussing in any way the question you said we couldn't explore further in the same direction?'

'We've been discussing it.'

'But not exploring it further?'

'But not exploring it.'

'So we are back to the moment when you were found by the police bathing your face?'

'Yes.'

'With this vital period between 6.15 and 9.30 p.m. unaccounted for?'

'Yes.'

'If you had been with Miss Manners that evening, where would you have been likely to meet?'

'The most likely place would have been The Sanctuary.'

'Why?'

'Apart from caring for the sick and dying, Sister Ludmila ran a free evening clinic. Miss Manners helped fairly regularly in the clinic in her spare time from the Mayapore General Hospital.'

'You both found The Sanctuary a suitable place to meet?'

'We were both interested in the work Sister Ludmila did.'

'Is that the frankest reply you can give me?'

'No. Let's say that The Sanctuary was one of the few places in the whole of Mayapore where we could meet and talk and not attract abusive attention.'

'Abusive attention?'

'The attention paid by Europeans to the sight of a white girl in an Indian's company.'

'Apart from these meetings at The Sanctuary you also visited one another's houses?'

'Occasionally.'

'Where else did you spend time together?'

A pause.

'Sometimes, on a Sunday for instance, we went to the Bibighar Gardens.'

'I gather from the descriptions in the file that these Gardens consist of a comparatively small, wild, overgrown area – the site of the old garden surrounding a building once known as the Bibighar – a building no longer in existence but where an open-sided pavilion or shelter has been erected on part of the old foundations.'

'Yes. It was a quiet and pleasant place to talk.'

'During the daytime —'

'During daylight.'

'You never went there together except in daylight?'

'Never.'

'Because of the old stories about it being haunted?'

'Because it was hardly a suitable place to go to at night.'

'How many people knew that you used to go to the Bibighar?'

'No one, so far as I know.'

'You were always alone there?'

'We once frightened some children playing there. Indian children.'

'How?'

'They thought we were ghosts I expect.'

'Daylight ghosts?'

'Yes.'

'It was usually quite deserted even in daylight?'

'It was the place only Indians went to – but it was on the civil lines side of the river. I think Indians went there for picnics in the dry, cooler weather.'

'How many people other than Sister Ludmila and her staff knew you and Miss Manners used to meet at The Sanctuary?'

'Not many I think.'

'She mentioned The Sanctuary and her interest in it to District Superintendent Merrick, though?'

'She must have done.'

'Why must have done?'

'On the night she was missing he called there.'

'How do you know that?'

'He told me so himself – during my interrogation. He said he called at The Sanctuary because he remembered Miss Manners say-

276]

ing something about the place. I expect he made particular note of it because it was the same place he'd found me the previous February.'

'Did he tell you what he discovered when he called at The Sanctuary looking for Miss Manners?'

'He said Sister Ludmila admitted Miss Manners had been there but had left just as it got dark. So then he called at my house and spoke to my aunt.'

'Because Sister Ludmila told him that you and Miss Manners had often been at The Sanctuary together?'

'Perhaps. He would have called at my house anyway.'

'He was well acquainted with the fact that you and Miss Manners were friends?'

'Of course.'

'You have said that occasionally you visited Miss Manners at the MacGregor House. Did you ever meet Mr Merrick there?'

'No. She kept us well apart.'

'Kept you apart? Because of what had happened between you and Mr Merrick when he took you in for questioning that first time?'

'She didn't know until much later that Merrick had been personally involved in that. She kept us apart because she assumed in any case Mr Merrick wouldn't approve of our friendship.'

'I'm not sure why you use this expression – keeping apart.'

'He became a personal friend of Miss Manners too.'

'I see. You say became. You mean he became friendly with her after you and she had already established a friendly association.'

'Yes. He was on the *maidan* during the War Week Exhibition and saw her leave her English friends and come up and speak to me. Until then, so far as I know, he'd never taken any notice of her. After that he started inviting her out.'

'If his interview with you after your drinking bout left him under the strong impression that you were a man on whom the police should keep an eye – as seems to have been the case – it would follow, I think, that directly he saw you and Miss Manners were on friendly terms he would feel it his duty to try to protect her from what in his view was an undesirable association?'

'Yes, that could follow. It's a very reasonable explanation.'

'Did he in fact ever say anything to her about her association with you?'

[277

'Yes.'

'She told you this?'

'Yes. It came up when I took her home after we'd visited the Tirupati temple.'

'She told you Mr Merrick disapproved of her going out with you?'

'She said Merrick's view was that I was a bad bet.'

'What was your reaction to that?'

'I said that Merrick should know if I was a bad bet or not.'

'Were you quarrelling?'

'Yes.'

'Why? Over something that happened at the temple?'

'Why do people who have grown fond of each other quarrel? I was in an over-sensitive mood. We both were. I realized what a ridiculous figure I made and what a lot of time she was wasting on me. She accused me of acting in a way calculated to put her off, which was true. That's when she told me Merrick said I was a bad bet. I told her he should know. I thought she always understood that Merrick was personally involved in that trouble I'd been in. It turned out she didn't. It made her feel she'd been made a fool of — unwittingly going out with Merrick as well as me. We parted on not very good terms.'

'But later you made it up?'

A pause.

'You're forgetting. We'd just come from the temple. I haven't seen Miss Manners since the night we visited the temple.'

'What night was that?'

'A Saturday. Three weeks before the night I was arrested under suspicion of assaulting her with five other men.'

Rowan leaned back again and turned to Gopal. 'I think we're now back to the question of the order and time at which he alleged certain things were done and certain things said. You were anxious to clarify that. Perhaps you would like to ask the questions.'

'Thank you.'

Gopal sipped water while reading a note on his file. Then he put the glass down, again dabbed his lips with the folded handkerchief. 'You were taken from 12 Chillianwallah Bagh at approximately 21.45, by truck to police headquarters in the Civil lines. You were held for perhaps a minute or less in a room where you saw five men whose faces you recognized even if you couldn't immediately recall

all their names. You were then taken to a room downstairs. Up until this time, you allege, you were not told the reason for your removal from your home to police headquarters?'

'I wasn't told.'

'At 12 Chillianwallah Bagh the police entered the room and apprehended you without saying anything?'

'Things were said, but not about the reason for the arrest.'

'What sort of things were said? Can you recall, for instance, the police officer's first words to you?'

'He didn't speak for a while.'

'What then did he do?'

'He stood and smiled at me.'

'Smiled?'

'I also noticed a nervous tic develop on his right cheek.'

'A smile and a nervous tic.'

'Then he pointed at the clothes lying on the floor and asked me if I'd just taken them off. I told him I had. He told me to put them on again. I asked him why. He said – Because you're coming with me. We're going to have another of our chats.'

'Did you obey immediately?'

'Not immediately. I asked him what we were going to have a chat about. He said I would find out. Then he asked if I would dress myself or prefer to be dressed forcibly. There were several constables with him, so I changed back into the clothes I'd taken off. Then I went downstairs with two constables holding my wrists behind my back. My aunt was being held in the living-room. I could hear her calling out to me. I wasn't allowed to see or speak to her. I was put into the back of a truck and driven to police headquarters.'

'Where you saw the five other men who had been arrested, one of whom said, "Hello, Hari" – a greeting which you did not return because unlike these other five you were not feeling like laughing and joking. When you saw these men, saw them behind bars – what conclusion did you reach?'

'Conclusion?'

'You saw they had been arrested, as you had been. What did you think they'd been arrested for?'

'I assumed they'd been caught drinking their home-made liquor.'

'Their demeanour was commensurate with that of boys who had broken a minor law and were still under the influence of liquor?'

[279

'Yes.'

'And what was going through your mind about the possible causes of your own arrest?'

'I felt it could only have something to do with Miss Manners.'

'Why?'

'Because Merrick had been at my house earlier asking for her. People were very edgy that night. A European woman had been attacked out in a place called Tanpur while trying to protect an Indian teacher from her mission. The man had been murdered and she had been knocked about. Some of the country police had been locked in their own stations by roving mobs. Telegraph wires were down and people were talking about a new Mutiny. As you know, there'd been a lot of arrests early that morning from Gandhi all down the line. For instance Mr Srinivasan had been arrested – as a leading member of the Local Congress Party sub-committee. I knew I couldn't be arrested for any political reason, but it seemed likely I'd be the first to get arrested if the police thought something had happened to Miss Manners.'

'So really your arrest was not such a puzzle to you, you are saying?'

'I'm merely telling you what was passing through my mind. I'm answering the question. I'm telling you that and stating again that I was in custody for a long time before the District Superintendent actually accused me of criminal assault. Once he'd done that I realized from other things he'd said and asked me that the five men upstairs were supposed to have been my accomplices in that assault.'

'Very well. Let us come to the moment when you were taken downstairs. What was the first thing that happened?'

'I was ordered to strip.'

'Who gave the order?'

'The District Superintendent.'

'In this room there were yourself, the District Superintendent and two constables?'

'At this stage, yes.'

'When you were stripped the DSP then inspected you as you have previously described?'

'When I was stripped the two constables held me with my arms behind my back, in front of Merrick's desk. Merrick sat on the desk and poured himself a glass of whisky. Then he just sat and smiled at me until he'd drunk it. He took about five minutes to drink it. After that he stood up, carried out the inspection and said, "So you've been clever enough to wash, we nearly caught you at it, didn't we?" I asked him why I'd been brought in. He said I'd find out. He said we had plenty of time. He told me to relax because we had a lot to talk about. He then ordered the constables to manacle my wrists behind me. When they'd done that he sent them out of the room.' Kumar paused. 'Then he began to talk to me.'

'You mean, to question you?'

'No. It was talking mostly. Every so often he put in a question.'

'What you describe as talking mostly' – Gopal said – 'what kind of talking?'

'He talked about the history of the British in India. And about his own history. About his ideas. About his views of India's future and England's future. And his future. And mine.'

Gopal appeared to be nonplussed. He hesitated before saying, 'Why should he talk about such things? You are remembering accurately? The impression one has been getting is that District Superintendent exerted himself a great deal first to find Miss Manners and then to bring her attackers to book. Now you are saying he sat and talked to you about such irrelevancies.'

'They weren't irrelevancies to him.'

'You are saying that to talk to you about the history of the British in India was just as important at that moment to District Superintendent as to question you about your movements that evening?'

'Neither talking nor questioning was of paramount importance to him.'

'Not of paramount importance? What are you suggesting was?'

'The situation.'

Gopal looked at Rowan and asked, 'What is he talking about? I don't undertsand him.'

Kumar answered before Rowan had a chance to speak.

'It was a question of extracting everything possible from the situation while it lasted.'

'The situation?'

'Yes.'

'But *what* situation?'

'The situation of our being face to face, with everything finally in his favour.'

'Finally? You are suggesting he anticipated this face-to-face situation?'

'Yes. That almost goes without saying.'

'Are you claiming -- are you claiming that he was a rival for the friendly attention of Miss Manners and had therefore looked forward to a situation which would place you – at disadvantage? Is this what you allege? You claim that an aspect to be considered is that of jealousy?'

Kumar hesitated. 'That would be an over-simplification. And there'd then be the question, jealousy of what kind, and jealousy of whom?'

'I cannot follow these arguments. Let us leave the matter of what you allege he talked about and consider the questions you allege he occasionally put in. Perhaps those will be easier to understand. Can you remember any of those questions?'

'Broadly.'

'Then say what you remember broadly.'

'They were such questions as: Those fellows up there admire you a lot, don't they? They'd do anything you say. Who marked your face? Why didn't you go to The Sanctuary tonight? Who's Colin? She wasn't a virgin, was she, and you were the first to ram her, weren't you?'

'Did you reply to any of those questions?'

'I told him if he wanted answers he first had to tell me why I'd been brought in.'

'And these questions were interpolated, you are saying, into his talk on other matters?'

'Yes.'

'For instance he would be talking about the future of the British in India and would suddenly say, Who is Colin?'

'Yes.'

'And always you replied as you have described?'

'Not always. Some of the questions I treated as rhetorical.'

'But you said, more than once, that you would only answer questions if he told you why you were in custody?'

'Yes.'

'Gradually, however, you suggest, you got a clear impression that you and the others upstairs were suspected of criminal assault on a lady?'

'Yes.'

282]

'And did you at the same time suspect that this lady was Miss Manners?'

'Yes.'

'Did you not ask?'

'No.'

'You were a close friend of Miss Manners. You knew the police had been looking for her, you knew of the troubles in the district, you guessed a woman had been assaulted and realized that this woman might be your friend Miss Manners, but you did not say, "Has something happened to Miss Manners?" '

'No.'

'Why?'

'I realized that's what he was waiting for me to do. I think it was a basic aspect of the situation.'

'Let us forget what you call the situation.'

'It's impossible for me to forget the situation. It had a very special intensity.'

Rowan spoke, taking advantage of Gopal's hesitation.

'I think we should do better to leave any inner significance the situation may have had for both DSP and the prisoner and concentrate on the form and order of the interrogation. If there was an inner significance it might even become clear to us what it was if we confine ourselves rigorously to the outer forms.'

'It is what I have been trying to do,' Gopal said. He rustled his papers; eventually spoke again to Kumar.

'There came a point when according to your previous testimony DSP said that he was making inquiries about an Englishwoman who was missing, and added "You know which one", and followed this with what you call an obscene remark. What was that remark?'

'I prefer not to say.'

'What did you understand from it?'

'That he was definitely referring to Miss Manners and to the fact that she'd been assaulted by more than one man, all Indians.'

'And it was at this point that you said you hadn't seen Miss Manners since the time you visited the temple?'

'Yes.'

'In that case I'm afraid I must press you to repeat the obscene remark. I must press you because without it your refutation of the official statement – that you yourself were the first to mention Miss Manners – is incomplete.'

'I'm sorry. I still prefer not to say.'

'Why?'

'It was slanderous as well as obscene.'

Rowan said, 'I think we needn't press this —'

'Oh, but I think we must,' Gopal said. 'I do not understand what detenu is getting at when he talks of a situation, but there is here a situation of which we are getting a picture and it is important that the picture should be as complete in every detail as possible. The situation I speak of is one in which the detenu, under suspicion of rape, is kept standing naked for a very long time by the senior police officer of the district, who sits on his desk drinking whisky and conducting an interrogation with, if detenu is to be believed, a total disregard for detenu's dignity as a human being, and asking questions in a manner calculated to insult, outrage, and to provoke to make comments which are then recorded as incriminating evidence of detenu's knowledge of events he could not have known about if he was innocent only. And the picture of this situation is not easy to believe. It is necessary that detenu should be examined closely on it because it arises only out of what he has been saying. He cannot suddenly stop saying because it suits him.'

Again she sought the reassurance of the pleats and buttons of her blouse. Gopal was making statements which on the record would convey an impression of doubting Kumar, of disbelieving that a police officer would act as Kumar had said. But Gopal did not want to doubt or disbelieve. Underneath that apolitical, civil service, collaborative exterior pumped the old Anti-British fears, prejudices and superstitions. It came to her that Gopal disliked Kumar for the type of Indian Kumar was – which in every important way from Gopal's point of view was not an Indian way at all. It was not without pleasure that he assumed the hectoring tone, emerged suddenly, almost unexpectedly, as animated by a passion the record would show as one for a clinical sense of justice, the opposite of the real animus – a fastidious dislike of the white usurper on whose bandwagon he had a seat. Below her, yet another situation was in process. It fascinated, disturbed her, to have, suddenly, an insight into it. 'So I must press detenu,' Gopal was saying. It was the white man in Kumar he enjoyed attacking. But the objective was the revelation of the full outrage and unjust pressure Kumar the Indian had suffered.

'I am sorry,' Kumar said.

284]

Gopal made an impatient gesture. How thin his fingers were, disapproving, permissive. They inspired her with dislike and pity: the twin responses to the odd combination of triumph and defeat the gesture implied.

Rowan took over.

'When – as you suggest – you understood from whatever it was you imply District Superintendent conveyed to you – that Miss Manners had been criminally assaulted and that you and the other men were under suspicion for that, you presumably made the statement as it appears in DSP's report. "I have not seen Miss Manners since the night we visited the temple." '

'Yes.'

'So the report is correct in that detail?'

'In that detail, yes.'

'And you are not inclined to dispute that this was at 22.45 hours?'

'No.'

'So a second detail of the report is correct.'

'Yes.'

'And you showed signs of distress, at this point, in that you were shivering, which makes the report accurate on three counts. I imagine, too, that you would not dispute the statement the report goes on to make that from that moment you reverted to the invariable reply to any question: "I have nothing to say." '

'I would not dispute that.'

'How long did your interrogation continue? How long were you in fact making this statement that you had nothing further to say?'

'I don't know.'

'Why not?'

'I lost track of things like time.'

'As long as an hour, two hours?'

'Perhaps.'

'Longer?'

'It could have been.'

'You were alone with the examining officer for two hours or more?'

'No. Other people came in after a bit.'

'The two constables?'

'Yes.'

'Anyone else?'

'One certainly. There may have been others.'

'Can't you remember?'

'I thought so. It seemed like it.'

'Are you saying you were confused? A bit giddy perhaps? And cold? Standing naked a long time in a cooled room?'

'I wasn't standing all the time.'

'You were allowed to sit?'

'No.'

Gopal re-entered the arena. 'I don't understand,' he said. 'You were not standing all the time but also you were not sitting. What were you doing? Lying down?'

'I was bent over a trestle.'

'Bent over a trestle?'

'Tied to it.' He hesitated, then added, 'For the persuasive phase of the interrogation.'

A pause.

Gopal said, 'Are you stating that you were physically ill-treated?'

'A cane was used.'

A rustle of paper. Captain Rowan's voice:

'Among the documents there is a copy of a report by a magistrate, Mr Iyenagar, who interviewed you at police headquarters on August 16th at the direction of the civil authorities. Do you recall that interview?'

'There were many interviews.'

'The one on August 16th was ordered by the civil authorities to inquire into rumours circulating in the bazaar of whipping and defilement of the prisoners held under suspicion of rape. Do you recall that now?'

'Yes, I recall it.'

'The report reads: *Iyenagar:* Have you any complaints to make about your treatment while in custody? *Kumar:* No. *Iyenagar:* If it were suggested that you had been subjected to physical violence of any kind, would there be any truth in that? *Kumar:* I have nothing to add to my first answer. *Iyenagar:* If it were suggested that you had been forced to eat any food which your religion made distasteful to you, would there be any truth in that suggestion? *Kumar:* I have no religious prejudices about food. *Iyenagar:* You understand that you have the opportunity here of making a complaint, if one is justified, which you need not fear making? *Kumar:* I have nothing more to say. *Iyenagar:* You have no complaint about your treatment from the moment of your arrest until now? *Kumar:* I have no complaint.'

Rowan looked up from his reading.

'Is that an accurate record of your interview with the magistrate?'

'Yes.'

'It is an accurate record, but you weren't telling the truth?'

'I was telling the truth.'

'You have just alleged that you were tied to a trestle and beaten with a cane.'

'Yes. I was.'

'Then why did you deny it when the magistrate asked you?'

'He asked if I had any complaint. I said I hadn't. I spoke the truth.'

'You had no complaint about being caned?'

'No.'

'Why?'

No answer.

Gopal said, 'Are you suggesting you were afraid of the consequences of complaining?'

'No.'

'What then?'

'It's difficult to explain now.'

'You did not complain, for reasons that now strike you as questionable?' Rowan asked.

'Not questionable.'

'What then?'

No answer.

'You are not on oath. The people you now complain about are not here to answer your accusations. Are you taking advantage of that?'

'No, and I am not complaining.'

Rowan's voice took on an edge. 'I see. You're merely stating facts. A bit late in the day, isn't it?'

'I don't know about late in the day —'

'Facts which you failed to state at the time for a reason you now find it difficult to give us.'

No answer.

'You say you were caned. How many times were you hit with this cane?'

'I don't know.'

'Six times? Twelve times?'

[287

No answer.

'More than twelve times?'

'I didn't count.'

'On what part of the body were you hit?'

'On the usual place for someone bent over.'

'The buttocks.'

'Yes.'

A rustle of paper.

'On your arrival in Kandipat you underwent the routine physical check. The documents are here. The examining doctor found you physically A1. Judging by this document it seems no marks were found that would have pointed to your having received a number of strokes with a cane on your buttocks. There is a note about traces of bruising on your face. The examination was made sixteen days after your arrest and first interrogation. The caning perhaps was not so severe as to cut the skin? Sixteen days is not a long time. Wouldn't you say that if your skin had been cut the marks would still have been visible?'

'They were visible.'

'The doctor saw them?'

'I don't know.'

'You must answer more fully than that.'

'If he saw them he made no comment.'

'Nor any record. It is usual before the examination for a prisoner to be bathed. Were you so bathed?'

'Yes.'

'I understand such bathing is conducted under the eye of a prison officer. Was it so conducted?'

'Yes.'

'Did the prison officer comment on any marks there may have been on your buttocks?'

'No.'

'The marks were invisible to him too?'

'Indians of the lower class keep a pair of drawers on while bathing. I suppose it's because they're used to bathing in public. That's what happened when I was told to take a bath that day. I was told to keep my drawers on.'

Gopal said, 'It's a point I was about to make, Captain Rowan. And in the case of the physical examination it is doubtful that the doctor – who I see from the medical report was an Indian – would

288]

have asked for the drawers to be removed for longer than was necessary to examine the pubic region. Was that the case, Kumar?'

'There was also an examination of the anal passage.'

A pause.

Rowan said, 'What you're suggesting then is that the doctor was either incompetent and failed to see what was under his nose, or saw the marks and ignored them in his report.'

'I'm not making a suggestion.'

'Are these marks you say you had still visible to any degree?'

'No.'

'You were not hit severely enough for the marks to be permanent.'

'I was hit severely.'

'To the point where blood was drawn?'

'I think it was when they started to draw blood that they covered me with a wet cloth. Then they carried on.'

A pause.

Gopal said, 'Who were "they"?'

'I couldn't see. It must have been the constables. They tied me to the trestle anyway. They started when Merrick gave the order and stopped when he said so. When they stopped Merrick talked to me. When he stopped talking he gave the order and they started again. It went on like that.'

Gopal said, 'Until you lost consciousness?'

'I didn't lose consciousness.'

Rowan said, 'But you have no idea how many times you were hit?'

'It's difficult to breathe in that position. It's all you think of in the end.'

Rowan continued: 'You allege that when the investigating officer told the constables to stop he talked to you. You mean he questioned you?'

'It was more like talking.'

'What was he talking about this time?' Gopal asked acidly. 'Not surely about the history of the British in India?'

'He was talking to encourage me.'

'Encourage you? To confess?'

'That was part of it. Perhaps not the most important.'

'But important enough for us to concentrate on,' Gopal said. 'What did he say to encourage a confession?'

'He said Miss Manners had named me as one of the men, that she said she'd been stopped by me outside the Bibighar and attacked while I held her in conversation, then that she'd been dragged into the gardens and raped, first by me and then by my friends. He said he didn't believe her. He suggested I should tell him the real truth. He told me he knew the truth but wanted to hear it from me first.' A pause. 'I'm sorry. I've got confused. He said that before he had me tied to the trestle. But after they tied me to the trestle he said it again, only this time he left out the bit about wanting to hear the truth from me. He said he'd tell me what he knew to be the truth and all I had to do to stop being beaten was confirm it.'

'And what do you allege he told you?'

'He said she'd obviously asked us to meet her, egged us on, that then we'd given her more than she'd quite bargained for, and that she was now trying to have us punished for something we'd only been technically guilty of.' A pause. 'He made it sound very plausible. He left me to think about it. He seemed to be away for quite a long time. When he came back he had one of the other men with him. He told me one of my friends had come down to hear me confess. I don't know which of the men it was. I heard this man trying to tell me he knew nothing and had said nothing. They started hitting me again.' A pause. 'After that I think Merrick sent everyone out. I think we were alone. He spoke and acted even more obscenely.'

Rowan said, 'The word obscene is open to different interpretations. Your allegation of obscenity – the second you have made – is against an officer of the Indian Police and is damaging to the reputation of that officer. You must give examples of obscenity so that anyone reading the record of this examination may form his own conclusion whether the word is justified in the context of the allegation.'

Kumar had slowly transferred his gaze from Gopal to Rowan. He said, 'He asked me if I was enjoying it.'

'Enjoying it?'

'He said, "Aren't you enjoying it? Surely a randy fellow like you can do better than this?" '

'Is that all?'

'He said, "Aren't you enjoying it? Surely a randy fellow like you can do better than this? Surely a healthy fellow like you doesn't

290]

exhaust himself just by having it once?" ' A pause. 'He had his hand between my legs at the time.'

Gopal seemed to recoil. Rowan spoke sharply to the clerk. 'Strike that from the record. Delete everything that followed the detenu's statement "I think we were alone". When you've done that leave your notebook on this desk and wait outside until I recall you.'

When the clerk had obeyed and closed the door behind him Gopal moved as if to protest, but Rowan said to Kumar:

'Why are you making allegations of this kind?'

'I'm answering your questions.'

'Are you? Or are you lying?'

'I'm not lying.'

'I put it to you that you are, that you are telling a pack of lies, very carefully rehearsed over the past year or so for just such an occasion as this, or to cause trouble on your release. If such out-rageous things were done to you – really done to you – you would have said so when examined by the magistrate specially appointed to question you on just this kind of point. I put it to you that you did not say so because they had not happened. I put it to you that you are basing this story on tales and rumours you've heard since being imprisoned, rumours that were investigated at the time and totally unsubstantiated. I put it to you that you have made these things up in the belief that they may protect you from the danger you'd still be in if the charge of rape were made even at this late stage. I put it to you that your entire testimony this morning has been compounded of omission, exaggeration and downright false-hood and that your detention is no more than you richly deserve. You have now an opportunity to retract. I advise you to think most carefully whether you should or should not take that opportunity.'

'I've nothing I wish to retract. I'm sorry. I seem to have mis-understood.'

'What do you mean, misunderstood? Misunderstood the ques-tions?'

'Not the questions. The reason for asking them.'

'The reason was made clear at the beginning.'

'No, the form the questions would take was made clear. The reason for asking them was left for me to guess at. I made the wrong guess. Something has happened to her, hasn't it?'

'Do you mean to Miss Manners?'

'Yes.'

'Why do you ask that?'

'Because the guess I made was that perhaps she'd finally managed to persuade someone I'd done nothing to deserve being kept locked up. But this examination increasingly smells of uneasy consciences. Something's happened to her and I'm the loose end someone thought it would be a relief to tie neatly off. I'm sorry. When we began you were so fair-minded it would have hurt if I'd still been capable of feeling hurt. And it would have been nice if I'd been able to answer your questions truthfully without it becoming clear that I can't be neatly tied off and that nobody's conscience can be soothed down. But I answer them truthfully, as truthfully as I can, and you begin to see that I'm the least important factor and that without intending to you're asking questions about what I call the situation. That's why you're annoyed and accuse me of lying, because the situation threatens to be more than any conscience can cope with. What's happened to her? Is she dead?' A pause. 'I've sometimes felt it but never let myself think it. If she is, you should have said so. You should have said —'

'We assumed that you knew. You're not cut off completely from the outside world. You exchange letters with your aunt. You have newspapers, surely? You talk to fellow-prisoners – new arrivals, for instance.'

'My aunt's letters are heavily censored. In any case she would never refer to Miss Manners. She's never forgiven her. I think she found it easier to blame Miss Manners than anything or anyone else for what happened to me. And I'm in the special security block here. We're allowed books, but not newspapers. Once a week they circulate a foolscap page of war news, full of victories and pious platitudes. How and when did she die?'

'She died of peritonitis. About a year ago.'

'A year ago? Peritonitis?' A pause. ' – That's blood-poisoning, isn't it? Burst appendix, that sort of thing?'

'I gather the peritonitis was the result of a Caesarean operation undergone in far from ideal conditions.'

'A Caesarean? Yes. I see.' A pause. 'She married?'

'No. She didn't marry.'

'I see.'

'Do you still have nothing to retract?'

'Nothing.' A pause. 'Nothing.'

For a while after that he did not speak. He sat staring at Rowan.

At first she did not detect it – there was no sound of it, no sign of it except (and now she saw it) this curious unemotional ex-pulsion from the deep-set eyes of rivulets that coursed down his cheeks: opaque in the glaring light like phosphorescent trails, a substance that released itself without disturbing the other mechanisms of his body. She shut her own eyes. She had had a sudden, astonishingly strong compulsion to touch him. No one had ever cried for Daphne, except herself; and this one person beside herself she could not reach. Between them there were a panel of thick glass and downwardly directed slats of wood or metal. The barrier that separated them was impenetrable. It was as if Hari Kumar were buried alive in a grave she could see down into but could not reach into or even speak to, establish a connexion with of any kind.

She opened her eyes again. The twin rivulets gleamed on his prison cheeks, and then the image became blurred and she felt a corresponding wetness on her own – tears for Daphne that were also tears for him; for lovers who could never be described as star-crossed because they had had no stars. For them heaven had drawn an implacable band of dark across its constellations and the dark was lit by nothing except the trust they had had in each other not to tell the truth because the truth had seemed too dangerous to tell.

In her mind was the image of Suleiman with the box held to his breast in the manner of someone holding a reliquary. The truth was in the reliquary and in the mind that held the image of Suleiman and in the mind of the man in the room behind the glass panel: the truth and memory of their having been in the Bibighar that night, as lovers, moving to the motion of the joy of union; and of the terror of their separation and of how, afterwards, she had crawled on hands and knees across the floor of the pavilion and untied the strips of cotton cloth the spoilers had torn from their own ragged clothing and bound him with. For a while they held each other like children afraid of the dark, and then he picked her up and began to carry her away from the pavilion.

I look for similes (she had written – secretly, in the last stages of her pregnancy, her insurance against permanent silence) for something that explains it more clearly, but find nothing, because there is nothing. It is itself; an Indian carrying an English girl he has made love to and been forced to watch being assaulted – carrying her back to where *she* would be safe. It is its own simile. It says all that needs to be said, doesn't it? If you extend it – if you think

[293

of him carrying me all the way to the MacGregor House, giving me into Aunt Lili's care, ringing for the doctor, ringing for the police, answering questions, and being treated as a man who'd rescued me, the absurdity, the implausibility become almost unbearable. Directly you get to the point where Hari, taken on one side by Ronald Merrick for instance, has to say, 'Yes, we were making love,' the nod of understanding that *must* come from Ronald *won't*, unless you blanch Hari's skin, blanch it until it looks not just like that of a white man but like that of a white man too shaken for another white man not to feel sorry for, however much he may reproach him.

The image sharpened. She understood it in an exact depth and dimension as if she were Daphne and the man sitting in the chair down there were actually standing, waiting to pick her up again after a brief rest. He tried to take hold of my arm. I moved away from him. I said, 'No. Let me go. You've not been near me. You don't know anything. You know nothing. Say nothing.' He wouldn't listen to me. He caught me, tried to hold me close, but I struggled. I was in a panic, thinking of what they'd do to him. No one would believe me. He said, 'I've got to be with you. I love you. Please let me be with you.' I beat at him, not to escape myself but to make *him* escape. I was trying to beat sense and reason and cunning into him. I kept saying, 'We've not seen each other. You've been at home. You say nothing. You know nothing. Promise me.' I was free and began to run without waiting to hear him promise. At the gate he caught me and tried to hold me back. Again I asked him to let me go, please to let me go, to say nothing, to know nothing for my sake if that was the only way he could say nothing and know nothing for his own. For an instant I held him close – it was the last time I touched him – and then I broke free again and was out of the gateway, and running; running into and out of the light of the street lamp opposite, running into the dark and grateful for the dark, going without any understanding of direction. I stopped and leaned against a wall. I wanted to turn back. I wanted to admit that I couldn't face it alone. And I wanted him to know that I thought I'd done it all wrong. He wouldn't know what I felt, what I meant. I was in pain. I was exhausted. And frightened. Too frightened to turn back. I said, 'There's nothing I can do, nothing, nothing,' and wondered where I'd heard those words before, and began to run again, through those awful ill-lit deserted roads that

should have been leading me home but were leading me nowhere
I recognised; into safety that wasn't safety because beyond it there
were the plains and the openness that made it seem that if I ran
long enough I would run clear off the rim of the world.

Well – she had gone. Yes, eventually, she had gone clear off the
rim of the world – then or later; keeping faith with a promise that
was as well an imprisonment. For him it would have been then
that she had gone. He must have watched her, perhaps he followed,
perhaps followed her nearly all the way to the house and then felt
for himself something of the terror she had felt for him, so that he
too ran home and in the privacy of his room began to bathe his face
because it was cut and bruised by the men who had come at them
out of the dark; the unknown watchers, the unknown spoilers, the
men for whom a taboo had been broken by watching Hari love her.
He had said nothing, explained nothing. 'Say nothing,' she had
begged. He had kept faith with that. They had both kept faith. She
wondered whether he would see her death as releasing him from
a promise made and almost absurdly kept. The promise had betrayed and imprisoned them both. Considering this she felt soiled
as from an invasion of territory she had no title to.

'Do you want a few moments to compose yourself?' Rowan
asked.

'I am composed. But you should have told me. You should have
made it clear.'

'Are you saying that if you'd known Miss Manners was no longer
alive your answers to some of our questions might have been
different?'

'I answered the questions because I thought the examination was
the result of some effort of hers. I answered the questions because
I thought she wanted you to ask them. If I'd known she had nothing
to do with it, and that it was only a case of bad consciences I
wouldn't have answered the questions at all.'

'There was one important question you didn't answer.'

'I shall never answer it.'

'Did it strike you at the time that your refusal to answer questions
was unhelpful not only to you but to those five other men who
were suspected?'

'Yes, I had to consider that. It was part of the situation.'

'Do you know what happened to them?'

'I was told they were sent to detention.'

'Did you think that justified?'

'No.'

'You believed them innocent of anything, except perhaps illicit distilling and drinking?'

'On that night I'm sure they were innocent of anything else. I don't know how or why they were arrested but I know none of us would have been arrested if it hadn't been for the assault. We were all punished for the assault, when it came to it. There was nothing I could do about that. Whether they deserved detention for political crimes, more or less than I do, I can't say. I wasn't able to let that enter into it.'

'Would it be in your power at all to remove the last shred of suspicion that they were implicated in the assault? It is accepted by this board that those suspicions were unavoidably part of the atmosphere in which your cases had to be examined when the question of detention under the Defence of India Rules came up. If you were being absolutely frank with us – for instance about your activities and movements on the night of the assault – would that frankness be helpful to those five men?'

'Are they still in prison?'

'Yes.'

'Are their cases also being reviewed?'

'That might depend a great deal on the result of the review of yours.'

'No,' Kumar said. 'You can't get rid of responsibility so easily. I think that is part of the situation too.'

The notion that Kumar could help five men who had never enjoyed Kumar's advantages seemed to interest Gopal.

'You are trying to cover everything with all this clever talk of a situation, but you are saying nothing about this situation. Time and again you leave an answer apparently complete but in fact it is only half-finished because of this so-called situation to which you relate it, and which you seem to want to mystify us with. What in fact was this situation?'

The rivulets were still visible. He did not seem to be aware of them and they now appeared to be motionless. She had an impression that they had ossified, that Rowan could have reached over and picked them away from Kumar's cheeks with his finger-nails, a piece at a time, and that each piece would fall with the light gyrating motion of something fragile, like an insect's wing.

296]

'It was a situation of enactment.'

Gopal was impatient. 'Most situations are.'

'According to Merrick most situations are the consequence of one set of actions and the prelude to the next but negative in themselves.'

'These ideas of what you call the situation were DSP's not your own?'

'Yes. He wanted them to be clear to me. In fact from his point of view it was essential that they should be. Otherwise the enactment was incomplete.'

'And he made them clear?'

'Yes.'

'Perhaps,' Gopal suggested, 'you would be good enough to make them clear also to this board.'

'In a way that's impossible. The ideas, without the enactment, lose their significance. He said that if people would enact a situation they would understand its significance. He said history was a sum of situations whose significance was never seen until long afterwards because people had been afraid to act them out. They couldn't face up to their responsibility for them. They preferred to think of the situations they found themselves in as part of a general drift of events they had no control over, which meant that they never really understood those situations, and so in a curious way the situations did become part of a general drift of events. He didn't think he could go so far as to say you could change the course of events by acting out situations you found yourself in, but that at least you'd understand better what that situation was and take what steps you could to stop things drifting in the wrong direction, or an unreal direction.'

'An interesting theory,' Rowan said. 'But is it relevant to the events you've been alleging took place?'

'You ask the question the wrong way round. You should ask how relevant the events were to the theory. The theory was exemplified in the enactment of the situation. The rape, the interrogation about the rape, were side issues. The real issue was the relationship between us.'

'What exactly does that mean?' Rowan asked.

'He said that up until then our relationship had only been symbolic. It had to become real.'

'What in fact did he mean by symbolic?'

'It was how he described it. He said for the moment we were mere symbols. He said we'd never understand each other if we were going to be content with that. It wasn't enough to say he was English and I was Indian, that he was a ruler and I was one of the ruled. We had to find out what that meant. He said people talked of an ideal relationship between his kind and my kind. They called it comradeship. But they never said anything about the contempt on his side and the fear on mine that was basic, and came before any comradely feeling. He said we had to find out about that too, we had to enact the situation as it really was, and in a way that would mean neither of us ever forgetting it or being tempted to pretend it didn't exist, or was something else.' A pause. 'All this was part of what he talked about before he put me through what he called the second phase of my degradation. Before he had me strapped to the trestle. The first phase was being kept standing without any clothes on. The third phase was his offer of charity. He gave me water. He bathed the lacerations. I couldn't refuse the water. I was grateful to him when he gave me the water. I remember thinking what a relief it was, having him treat me kindly, how nice it would be if I could earn his approval. It would have been nice to confess. I nearly did, because the confession he wanted was a confession of my dependence on him, my inferiority to him. He said the true corruption of the English is their pretence that they have no contempt for us, and our real degradation is our pretence of equality. He said if we could understand the truth there might be a chance for us. There might be some sense then in talking about his kind's obligations to my kind. The last phase could show the possibilities. He said I could forget the girl. What had happened to her was unimportant. So long as I understood how responsible I was for it. "That's what you've got to admit," he kept saying, "your responsibility for that girl getting rammed. If you were a hundred miles away you'd still be responsible." What happened in the Bibighar Gardens he saw as symbolic too, symptomatic of what he called the liberal corruption of both his kind and my kind. He accepted a share of responsibility for what happened, even though there was no common ground between himself and the kind of Englishman really responsible. The kind really responsible was the one who sat at home and kidded himself there was such a thing as the brotherhood of man or came out here and went on pretending there was. The permutations of English corruption in India were

298]

endless – affection for servants, for peasants, for soldiers, pretence at understanding the Indian intellectual or at sympathizing with nationalist aspirations, but all this affection and understanding was a corruption of what he called the calm purity of their contempt. It was a striking phrase, wasn't it? He accepted a share of responsibility for the rape in the Bibighar because even the English people who admitted to themselves that they had this contempt pretended among themselves that they didn't. They would always find some little niche to fit themselves into to prove they were part of the great liberal Christian display, even if it was only by repeating *ad nauseam* to each other that there wasn't a better fellow in the world than the blue-eyed Pathan, or the Punjabi farmer, or the fellow who blacks your boots. He called the English admiration for the martial and faithful servant class a mixture of perverted sexuality and feudal arrogance. What they were stirred or flattered by was an idea, an idea of bravery or loyalty exercised on their behalf. The man exercising bravery and loyalty was an inferior being and even when you congratulated him you had contempt for him. And at the other end of the scale when you thought about the kind of Englishmen who pretended to admire Indian intellectuals, pretended to sympathize with their national aspirations, if you were honest you had to admit that all they were admiring or sympathizing with was the black reflection of their own white ideals. Underneath the admiration and sympathy there was the contempt a people feel for a people who have learned things from them. The liberal intellectual Englishman was just as contemptuous of the Westernized educated Indian as the arrogant upper-class reactionary Englishman was of the fellow who blacks his boots and earns his praise.'

A pause.

'He said he was personally in a good position to see through all this pretence because his origins were humble. If he hadn't had brains he'd have ended up as a clerk in an office, working from nine to six. But he had brains. He'd got on. In India he'd got on far better than he could have done at home. In India he automatically became a Sahib. He hobnobbed on equal terms with people who would snub him at home and knew they would snub him. When he considered all the things that made him one of them in India – colonial solidarity, equality of position, the wearing of a uniform, service to king and country – he knew that these were fake. They didn't fool either him or the middle and upper class people he hobnobbed with. What they had in common was the contempt they all felt for the native race of the country they ruled. He could be in a room with a senior English official and a senior Indian official and he could catch the eye of the English official who at home would never give him a second thought, and between them there'd be a flash of compulsive understanding that the Indian was inferior to both of them, as a man. And then if the Indian left the room the understanding would subtly change. He was then the inferior man. He said you couldn't buck this issue, that relationships between people were based on contempt, not love, and that contempt was the prime human emotion because no human being was ever going to believe all human beings were born equal. If there was an emotion almost as strong as contempt it was envy. He said a man's personality existed at the point of equilibrium between the degree of his envy and the degree of his contempt. What would happen, he said, if he pretended that the situation was simply that of a just English police officer investigating a crime that had taken place and I pretended that I had no responsibility for it, and that there was such a thing as pure justice that would see me through, and if both of us recognized each other's claims to equal rights as human beings? Nothing would happen. Neither of us would learn a thing about our true selves. He said that the very existence of laws proved the contempt people had for each other.'

A pause.

'At one point he smeared his hand over my buttocks and showed me the blood on his palm. He said, "Look, it's the same colour as mine. Don't be fooled by that. People are. But prick an imbecile and he'll bleed crimson. So will a dog." Then he smeared his hand on my genitals. I was still on the trestle. After he'd had me taken from the trestle I was put in a small cell next door. It had a charpoy with a straw mattress. I heard them caning one of the others. Afterwards he came in alone with a bowl of water and a towel. My wrists and ankles were manacled to the legs of the charpoy. This was the third phase. I was still naked. He bathed the lacerations. Then he poured some water in a tin cup, pulled my head up by the hair and let the water come near my mouth.' A pause. 'I drank.' A pause. 'After I drank he told me I must say thank you, because he knew that if I were honest I'd admit I was grateful for the water. He said he knew it would be difficult to swallow my pride, but it had

300]

to be done. He would give me another drink of water. He would give it to me on the understanding that I was grateful for it, and would admit it. He pulled my head back again and put the cup close to my lips. Even while I was telling myself I'd never drink it and never say thank you I felt the water in my mouth. I heard myself swallow. He put the cup down and used both hands to turn my head to face him. He put his own head very close. We stared at each other.' A pause. 'After a bit I heard myself say it.'

A pause.

'That was one of the reasons why when they asked me if I had anything to complain about I said I hadn't. It was a way of making up to myself for thanking him for the water. After I'd said thank you he let go of my head. He smoothed my hair and patted my back. He said we both knew where things stood now. I could sleep now. There'd be no more questions for the present. I didn't have to confess tonight. The girl had incriminated me but it didn't matter. Tomorrow there would be questions. Tomorrow I could confess. When I woke up I'd be anxious to confess. My confession would show the girl up for a liar. I would be punished, but not for rape, because surely I could prove she'd agreed to the meeting, wanted the meeting? He would help me if I would confess to the truth. When I woke up I'd realize he was my one hope. I'd be grateful. I'd already thanked him for the water. That was enough for tonight. Now I could go to sleep. He rinsed the towel out and put it over my buttocks. Then he covered me with a blanket. I don't know how long I slept. I remember waking in the dark. My wrists and ankles felt as if they were still manacled to the charpoy. It was a shock to find they weren't. I had an impression of falling through space. I called out for help. The name I called was Merrick.'

A pause.

'Nobody answered. That gave me time to reason. The most humiliating discovery I made was that I'd believed what he said about Miss Manners incriminating me. I say had believed, but I was still believing it for minutes at a time, and then for another few minutes believing he was lying, then that he wasn't. Like that. Alternately. There can come a point, can't there, when the only attractive course of action for a man completely surrounded by others bent on his destruction is to help them destroy him, or do the job for them before they've quite mustered force for the final blow. It's attractive because it seems like the only way left to exercise his own free will. I made up my mind to confess to whatever he wanted. I thought, well anyway what's going to be destroyed? Nothing. An illusion of a human being, a ridiculous amalgam of my father's stupid ambition and my own equally stupid preferences and prejudices. A nonentity masquerading as a person of secret consequence, who thinks himself a bit too good for the world he's got to live in. He might as well be got rid of or, better still, get rid of himself, and who would feel there was any loss in that, except perhaps Aunt Shalini?'

A pause. She leaned back, closed her eyes, so that her understanding should come to her through only the unidentifying voice.

'But then, you see,' the voice said, 'the question arose – What did nonentity mean? And the answer was quite clear. It meant nothing because it was only a comparative – a way of comparing one person with another, and I wasn't to be compared, I was myself, and no one had any rights in regard to me. I was the only one with rights. I wasn't to be classified, compared, directed, dealt with. Nothing except people's laws had any claim on me and I hadn't broken any laws. If I had broken any it was the laws and not the people who operated them I had to answer to. There wasn't a single other person except myself I was answerable to for anything I did or said or thought. I wasn't to be categorized or defined by type, colour, race, capacity, intellect, condition, beliefs, instincts, manner or behaviour. Whatever kind of poor job I was in my own eyes I was Hari Kumar – and the situation about Hari Kumar was that there was no one anywhere exactly like him. So who had the right to destroy me? *Who had the right as well as the means?* The answer was nobody. I wasn't sure that they even had the means. I decided that Merrick had lied and that far from incriminating me she probably didn't even know yet I'd been arrested. That's the moment when I knew I was sick of lying passively there in the dark. I managed to crawl out of bed and grope round the wall until I found the light-switch. It was pitch black and it took me quite a long time just to stand upright. When I had the light on I noticed he'd left the tin mug near my bed. There was still some water in it. I put the towel round my middle and walked up and down so as not to stiffen up again. The water was warm, the room was probably stifling, there wasn't a window, only a ventilator high up, but I was shivering. Even after I'd drunk the water I went on walking up and down, holding the tin mug. What I was doing reminded me of something but for a while I couldn't think what. Then I got it. Like my grandfather, going off to acquire merit. The loin-cloth and the begging-bowl. It was funny. Aunt Shalini's in-laws were always on at me about becoming a good Indian. This wasn't what they meant but I thought, well, here I am, a good Indian at last. Up until then whenever I thought of that story my father told me about his father leaving home, shrugging off his responsibilities it hadn't seemed possible that I was connected with a family where such a thing could happen. But walking up and down as I was, dressed in that towel, holding that cup, I understood the connexion between his idea, and my idea that no one had any rights over me, that there wasn't anyone I was answerable to except myself. And I saw something else, something Merrick had overlooked. That the situation only existed on Merrick's terms if we both took part in it. The situation would cease to exist if I detached myself from it. He could ask his questions but there was no power on earth that said I had to answer them. He could try and probably succeed in making me answer them by using force, but it would be my weakness and not his strength that made me speak. So I came to a decision to go on saying nothing. I wouldn't answer his or anyone's questions except as it pleased me. I would never thank him again for a cup of water. I'd rely on no one, no one, for help of any kind. I don't know whether that made me a good Indian. But it seemed like a way of proving the existence of Hari Kumar, and standing by what he was.'

She opened her eyes and stared down into the room, was struck again by that extraordinary incongruity: the hunched submissiveness of the man's body, the alert and responsible intelligence of the man himself.

'Walking up and down with the tin mug – that's how Merrick found me when he came in. He looked as if he'd been home to bathe and change but not to sleep. He was very pale. I thought I saw the tic start up again on his cheek, but it was only for a second or two. I asked him what the time was. His response was automatic. He said it was six o'clock. Answering automatically like that showed him that our relationship had changed. He began to look puzzled. I walked up and down and every time I turned to face him I saw this expression on his face, a sort of dawning mystification, and I thought, my God, the risks he's taken, he must have been very sure, he must have been absolutely convinced of my guilt. And

[303

he was still sure, still absolutely convinced, but he guessed or knew it had all begun to go wrong, and he couldn't work out why. I had a flash of admiration for him. He was totally unconcerned about what I could say or do that could get him into trouble. He said the constables would bring me something to eat and some fresh clothes to put on that had been collected from my home. They brought the food and clothes. Then they took me to a new cell, the one that turned out to be my home for a couple of weeks. I never saw anyone all that time except the two constables and Merrick, unless I was taken upstairs and examined by people like Iyenagar and the Assistant Commissioner. When Merrick examined me it was always in the room where the trestle was but there was never any physical violence. He questioned me every day, sometimes twice or three times, and I could tell that the conviction never left him. I was guilty. The day he told me Vidyasagar had been arrested he tried lying again, tried to make me believe Vidya had incriminated me by accusing me of trying to get him to take part in a plot to attack Miss Manners, but I had the impression that making me confess didn't interest him any more. Our last full session was the day after I'd been examined by Iyenagar. Merrick said he understood what I was doing. He called it pretending nothing had happened, wasn't happening and wouldn't happen. He said I was wrong, it had happened, was still happening and would go on happening and that he had more contempt for me than ever before. It wouldn't have done me any good to complain to the lawyer, but it disappointed him I hadn't had the guts to accuse him when I had the opportunity. He wouldn't bother to question me again. He admitted he'd lied about Miss Manners accusing me. He said she'd told a cock and bull story about going into the Bibighar Gardens because as she rode past she had a sudden idea that she might see the Bibighar ghosts if she went in. So she'd gone and sat in the pavilion and then been attacked by five or six men she hadn't got a proper look at. Then he said, "But it's not true. You were together in the Bibighar. You rammed her. You know it, she knows it, I know it. She's lying and you're lying. She's lying because she's ashamed and you're lying because you're afraid. You're so scared you're trying to convince yourself the whole business is an illusion, like some naked Hindu fakir pretending the world doesn't exist. What price Chillingborough now?" Then he got up and stood very close to me and reminded me step by step of all the things he'd done to me. He invited me to hit him. I think he really wanted me to.'

Kumar slowly looked down, as if to indicate that he had finished. After a while Rowan said, 'I shall call the clerk back in. Do you wish to make a statement to this effect?'

He shook his head, then raised it. For the first time a smile was fully recognizable. 'I've said it all. The clerk wasn't here to record it. That's part of the situation too, isn't it?'

She felt the first wave – scarcely more than a milky ripple – of an extraordinary tranquillity the nature of which she had no energy to determine; instead only the temptation to surrender to as a runner tired of the race would give in to the temptation to fall out of it. It will end, she told herself, in total and unforgivable disaster; *that* is the situation. As she continued to look down upon the tableau of Rowan, Gopal and Kumar – and the clerk who now re-entered, presumably as a result of the ring of a bell that Rowan had pressed – she felt that she was being vouchsafed a vision of the future they were all headed for. At its heart was the rumbling sound of martial music. It was a vision because the likeness of it would happen. In her own time it would happen. She would live to see what she had been committed to enshrined in the glittering reality of an actual deed, and the deed itself would be a vindication of a sort. But it would never happen in her heart where it had been enshrined this many a year. The tranquillity she felt was the first tranquillity of death. For her the race had ended in the Kandipat in this room with its secret sordid view on to another. The reality of the actual deed would be a monument to all that had been thought for the best. 'But it isn't the best we should remember,' she said, and shocked herself by speaking aloud, and clutched the folds and mother-of-pearl buttons in that habitual gesture. We must remember the worst because the worst is the lives we lead, the best is only our history, and between our history and our lives there is this vast dark plain where the rapt and patient shepherds drive their invisible flocks in expectation of God's forgiveness.

*

The room was empty. Only the light remained, the dim light, and the glaring light that shone on the empty chair. Kumar had gone with the rest. A hand had touched her shoulder. Looking round she was aware of Captain Rowan and of his voice repeating a question, 'Are you all right, Lady Manners?'

'Yes,' she said, and let him help her out of the chair. Standing she put her handbag on the table, took off her distance spectacles and returned them to the case. She thought how odd such human preparations for departure were. In the passage the weight of un-conditioned air threatened to extinguish her. Her legs were shaky from the long inactivity of sitting. They went by stages through degrees of cold and heat: from the cool room to the close, warm corridor, out into the oven-scorched air and the furnace of the waiting motor-car. She sat with her eyes closed, felt the subsidence of the cushion as he lowered himself into the seat's opposite corner. Then the movement: the villainous shadow of the prison gateway. No pause this time. Sun-fish swam across her lowered lids. She raised them and was blinded by a spike of light that pierced the blinds as the motor-car turned at an angle into the sunlight and smell of Kandipat.

'He told the truth,' she announced with a suddenness that caused him to glance at her sharply.

'I'm glad you felt that,' he said. 'Sitting so close to him it was painfully apparent to me that he did.'

'You never mentioned to him that you remembered him at Chillingborough.'

'It seemed unnecessary. It could have struck a false note, too.'

She stayed silent for a moment or two then said, 'I expect you've realized *why* H.E. asked you to look into the files.'

'I've imagined he did so because you asked him to.'

'Then you're probably wondering two things. You're wondering why I should ask him and why I should wait a year after my niece's death before asking him. Is it safe now?'

'Safe?'

'To have the blinds raised. I feel I'm driving to my grave.'

Why, and so you are, a voice told her. She recognized it from other occasions. Old people talked to themselves. From a certain age. No. Always. Throughout life. But in old age the voice took on a detached ironical tone. Passion had this determination to out-live its prison of flesh and brittle bone. As it made arrangements to survive it grew away, like a child from its favourite parent, impatient for the moment of total severance and the long dark voyage of intimate self-discovery. And so you are, her voice said.

Driving to your grave. The parting of our ways. A release for both of us. One to oblivion, one to eternal life so unintelligible to either of us it ranks as oblivion too. And already our commitment to each other is worked out and nearly over. Momentum will carry you through what motions are left to you to show your grasp of situations and responsibilities.

'The child,' she said. 'But even now I can't be sure. Only surer. She was so sure. To look at her towards the end you'd think, how astonishing! That combination of ungainly ordinariness and state of grace. One has to make do with approximations. Lies and approximations. When we say he spoke the truth we mean this. Everything becomes distorted. When the child cries its needs are so simple. When he cried he scarcely seemed to know it. Who will read the record?'

'H.E.'

'And the member for home and law?'

'He's an Englishman.'

'Why do you mention that?'

'Because it's pertinent. But Kumar will be released.'

'To what? In any case I don't want to know. I've had my amusement.'

'Amusement?'

'Isn't it all a charade? Over now. We go back into our corners and try to guess the word. Hari Kumar will have to guess it too. And Mr Merrick. Nothing can happen to Mr Merrick, can it? – everything in the file is the uncorroborated evidence of a prisoner. Nothing will touch him. That is part of the charade too.'

'It's safe now,' Rowan said. And began, one by one, to raise the blinds.

Part Two ❧ A Christening

I

March–June 1944

THE YEAR had begun quietly, but the death in captivity of Mrs Gandhi and her husband's own illness and release, ostensibly on compassionate grounds, marked a time which seemed, in retrospect, to be one of dreams and auguries.

Early in March, when he came in from a tour of his subdivision, young Morland, an officer on the staff of the Deputy Commissioner for the Pankot district, reported a curious tale that was being circulated in the hills; the rumour of the birth to a woman whose husband had abandoned her of a child with two heads. The mother had not survived an hour and the child – a boy – died before the sun set on the first and only day of its life. Morland, suspecting that the death of a child with any considerable deformity might well have been assisted (although two heads had to be taken with a pinch of salt), had spent two weeks attempting to trace the rumour to its source, but had no luck. Everyone knew it had happened, but nobody was sure of the exact locality. Places were suggested, but going to them Morland was told: Not here, not here: and another village would be named, usually the one he had come from. The closer he tried to get to it the farther away the scene of the event became. But the effect on the people who discussed it with him was clear enough. Such things did not happen without a reason. It was a forewarning. But of what? Heads were shaken. Who could tell? On the journey home Morland noticed the constant freshness of the flowers placed on the little wayside shrines of the old tribal gods.

Having rid himself of the accumulated stains and strains of his tour, and taking his ease at the club, manipulating with excessive, youthful care that symbol of mature and contemplative manhood – a stubby briar – brick-red of face and bleached of head, Morland admitted he himself had come rather under the spell of the superstitious anxiety of the people of the hills and found his sleep disturbed by an odd sort of dream which, when he woke up, he never

could remember anything of except that it seemed to have something to do with death by drowning. Morland always paused before
he added, 'I don't know whether you know, but actually I swim
like a fish.'

Within a week Morland was posted to the secretariat in Ranpur,
his dream of death by drowning and the tale of the two-headed
infant monster were all but forgotten, and Morland himself passed
out of sight and mind (as he passes now into the limbo of only
marginal images). But on March 18th, when the people of Pankot
were startled by the news that the Japanese had crossed the Chindwin in force the day before, there were some who at once recollected
the expectations of disaster Morland had brought with him from
the remoter areas of the region. Five days later the Japanese crossed
the frontier between Burma and Assam and stood on Indian soil,
poised for the march on Delhi.

By the end of the month Imphal and Kohima and the whole of
the British force in Manipur were isolated. Rumour ran that Imphal
had fallen. In Delhi, the Member for Defence, Claude Auchinleck,
assured the Assembly that it had not, that his information from the
supreme commander, Mountbatten, was to the effect that it was still
strongly held. In the Pankot club a wag said that Morland's tale of
the monster with two heads was probably set going by natives who
had heard about the separation of GHQ, Delhi, from its old responsibilities in the field; that all this streamlining and moderniza-
tion was a lot of poppycock; and that the Japs would never have
invaded India if the army in India hadn't been put in the way of
its right hand not knowing what its left hand was doing. The joke
was ill-received, not because the joker was necessarily thought to be
talking nonsense but because, pretty clearly, it was no time for
laughter. At Area Headquarters a picture was emerging on the
map in General Rankin's office of total encirclement of the forces
in Assam, and of the movements of formations from other parts
of the front and from training areas in India in reinforcement.
Rankin was heard to say, 'Well, this is it.'

Morland's dream was not the only one Pankot heard of. In
Rose Cottage for instance, Miss Batchelor, the retired missionary
teacher who lived with old Mabel Layton, also dreamed; and, unlike Morland who had been reticent, told everyone who cared to
listen all the details that she could remember. She dreamed she woke
and found Pankot empty. She walked down the hill from Rose

Cottage and saw not a soul until she got to the club where one solitary tonga waited. Between the shafts there was a lame horse. Well, not really a horse. The more you looked at it the more obvious became its resemblance to an ass, a creature such as Our Lord sat astride of for the entry into Jerusalem.

'You'd better jump in,' the tonga wallah said, 'they're coming and everyone's gone on ahead to catch the train.' She hesitated to accept the invitation because this particular tonga wallah was a stranger to her and she didn't trust him. 'What are you waiting for, Barbie?' he said, and she saw that it was really Mr Maybrick – the retired tea planter who played the organ in the protestant church – but with his face stained and wearing native costume. So she jumped in and made room for herself among the piles of organ music, and off they bowled at a smart and pretty pace down the hill, past the golf course, where there were people playing, carrying coloured umbrellas. 'Those are the fifth-columnists,' Mr Maybrick shouted at her. 'The golf course is the rendezvous.' It was known that the Japanese had stealthily surrounded Pankot during the night. 'We must take refuge, there's no time to catch the train,' she cried, trying to shout above the noise and rushing of air caused by the tonga's swift passage. Mr Maybrick was now driving four-in-hand. His whip whistled and cracked in the air above the wild-maned heads of a team of galloping black horses. 'To St John's! To St John's!' she shouted and was then at the reins herself and it was her own short-cropped grey hair that was wild and flying. 'Alleluia!' she called, 'Alleluia!' But the church had gone. 'You're just in time,' Mr Maybrick said – in his ordinary clothes now, but wearing a clerical collar. They were standing calmly, but sharing the knowledge that this was the eleventh hour. They were in the compound of a little mission school. 'It's really Muzzafirabad,' Miss Batchelor thought. Her old servant Francis was tolling the bell. They could see hordes of Japanese crossing the golf course, under cover of paper umbrellas. She turned to Mr Maybrick and said, 'We must save a last bullet each,' but when they looked back to the golf course the Japanese had gone and the children were coming to school, summoned by the bell. 'Come along, children,' Barbie said, keeping her voice friendly but authoritative. Francis said: 'The danger has not passed, memsahib.' But she called to everyone, 'It's quite safe now.' They went into the schoolroom, but it was a church again and Mr Maybrick was playing the organ. She sat in an empty pew to give thanks for their deliverance. 'And it was extraordinary,' she said, whenever she told the dream. 'I've never felt so much at peace. I think it was really a dream about poor Edwina Crane. I went to Muzzafirabad just after she'd left. That was a long time ago – 1914 actually. They were tremendously proud of her there. She really *did* save the mission from rioters, she just stood in the doorway, with all the children safe inside, and told them to go away and not bother her. And they obeyed. The children used to show me where she had stood, and I felt I'd never live up to *their* special idea of a mission teacher. I think it was really a dream to tell me that Edwina *is* at peace, in spite of that awful business of her setting fire to herself, in 1942.'

*

And presently, when Teddie was dead, a dream came to trouble Sarah. In the dream they were saying goodbye to him and even he knew that he would never come back. He had a look on his face that expressed the most extraordinarily complete awareness of the place he was going to. The look made him beautiful. They were all stunned by it and by the knowledge that his presence was some kind of trick, because he was already gone. 'Of course, Sarah, it'll be up to you really,' he said, just before he left them. They had to fight their way through a group of Teddie's friends and avoid the figure of the prostrated woman in the white saree, and after that Sarah was running alone through a deserted street. When she got home her father was waiting. 'I suppose you did your best,' he always seemed to say although his lips never actually moved. In this dream she was intermittently being made love to by a man who never spoke to her. Who is that man? people asked her – her mother or father, or someone who happened to pass by. Oh, I don't know, she said. There was a superior kind of mystery about the man.

The dream had begun a few days after they had the news that Teddie was killed. The news was signalled from Comilla to Calcutta and from Calcutta to Area Headquarters in Pankot where it was intercepted by an alert signals corporal who knew Corporal Layton, and liked her for not being standoffish with non-commissioned men, and thought it best to have a word with someone else before the message went by dispatch-rider to the Pankot Rifles lines where all the Laytons' mail was sent. And so at 10.45 on an

[311

April morning Sarah was told by General Rankin that there was some bad news he thought it best to tell her privately so that she and her mother could work out how best to break it to her sister. She remembered the time, 10.45, because when General Rankin sat down he no longer obstructed her view of the clock behind his desk. He had made her sit directly she came in and did not sit himself until he had told her about Teddie and reassured himself that she was going to take it with reasonable composure. To one side of the clock there was the map with tell-tale clusters of flags around Imphal and Kohima. She thought of Teddie as permanently pinned, part of the map.

'Is your mother at home or will she be out shopping?' the General asked.

'They're both at Rose Cottage. I think there's bridge.'

The romantic period of Susan's pregnancy had ended. She was showing. Before long, she said, she would be showing very badly. The grace and favour bungalow stood virtually unprotected from the military gaze in the lines of the Pankot Rifles. She had complained for several weeks that it was like living in a barracks. Now she felt she was showing too much to spend the day happily at the club and had acquired a liking for resting on the veranda at the back of Aunt Mabel's, knitting and crocheting and gazing across the flower-filled garden to the Pankot hills, while her mother played bridge inside with Miss Batchelor and whoever else could be persuaded to forsake the club and the well-stocked bar, and gusty invasions of male company.

Hearing that Susan and her mother were at Rose Cottage the General nodded. Mrs Rankin had played there on two occasions recently and it was scarcely a week since a hint had been dropped to Sarah that her mother's losses were unpaid up. In the midst of this new catastrophe the little debt remained as a source of vague irritation and restraint between the Laytons and the Rankins, not to be forgotten but temporarily overlooked.

'You'd better go up there and get your mother on her own if you can,' Rankin said. 'I'll tell the transport people to provide you with a car, and I'll have a word with your section commander. Your mother may need you at home for a day or two I shouldn't wonder.' He paused. 'What a terrible, terrible thing.'

He went over to a cabinet, poured a small measure of brandy into a glass.

312]

'Drink this. It's Hennessy three star, not country.'

She drank it down. She hated brandy. The smell reminded her of hospitals.

'Who looks after Susan?' Rankin asked, as if he too had been reminded. 'Beames or young Travers?'

'Dr Travers.'

'You may feel or your mother may feel he should be there when Susan is told. Meanwhile I'll ring my wife. We'll all do what we can.'

'Thank you,' she said and put the glass on his desk. 'I'd better go now.' She put the signal in her pocket. 'I think I ought to go by tonga. If I turn up in a car Susan may wonder and get alarmed before we're ready to say anything.'

'Would you like my wife to go with you? She'll be at the club. You could pick her up on your way.'

Ten rupees was what her mother owed. 'It's very kind of you,' she said, 'but it's not as if Mother and Susan are alone.'

'Wait a few minutes before you go. You've had a shock.'

'No, it's better like this. I mean better than just the telegram arriving.'

He saw her to the door. In the outer office the aide who had taken Captain Bishop's place opened the other door for her and accompanied her down the long arcaded veranda. He went with her all the way to the gravelled forecourt and out beyond the sentries who slapped the butts of their rifles. He hailed one of the tongas that stood lined up in the roadway. The sun was very hot, but the air was crisp; the famous Pankot air that always carried a promise of exhilaration and could be cold at night in winter so that fires were lit at four o'clock. Area Headquarters lay midway between the bazaar and the Governor's summer residence. Between these two were the golf course and the club. It was uphill, and the plumed horse took the slope at a nodding walk, jingling its bells and sometimes breaking wind. She remembered Barbie Batchelor's dream. She watched the road slipping by beneath her feet, her back to horse and driver and stable smell – a smell that was part of the smell of Pankot, the whole panorama of which was widening and deepening as the tonga gained height, disappearing as the road curved from the straight into the first of the bends on the hill on whose farther slope Rose Cottage lay with views to all the hills and valleys of the district her grandfather had ridden and her father had walked. Down on her left now was the golf course, come back into view, and, briefly visible, the bungalow where her father and Aunt Mabel lived after the First World War. More distantly she could see the familiar huts and old brick buildings of the Pankot Rifles depot, and the roof, among trees, of the grace and favour bungalow. Another bend in the road and the tonga, momentarily on the straight again, bowled past the flower-strewn embankment and then the open gateway of the club, giving a glimpse of white stucco columns and bright green lawns. Another turn and they were past the closed iron gates of the long driveway that corkscrewed up to the deserted summer residence. Climbing again now, slowly, past openings of private dwellings posted with familiar names: Millfoy, Rhoda, The Larches, Burleigh House, Sandy Lodge. At the top – Rose Cottage.

'Thairo,' she called, but the driver had already stopped. She got down, hidden from view by the high embankment. She wondered whether she should keep the tonga waiting, but decided not, gave him two rupees to save argument and turned into the steep little drive that was flanked by rockeries. Aunt Mabel was cutting roses, basket in arm, secateurs in hand, wearing old brogues, woollen stockings and a shapeless green tweed skirt. As a concession to the sun she had on a collarless sleeveless blouse, bright orange, that exposed her brown, old woman's mottled arms and neck. On her head there was a wide-brimmed pink cotton hat. These days you had to be careful not to come upon her too suddenly. The deafness that Sarah's mother thought of as assumed to match a mood had become more serious than that. But while Sarah was still several yards distant, her aunt turned. After a moment she put the secateurs in her basket and set it down on the grass, came to Sarah and took hold of her left arm, cocked her head to hear whatever it was Sarah had come at this unexpected time of day to say.

'Susan mustn't see me yet. Can you get Mother out here somehow?'

'What's wrong?'

'Teddie's been killed.'

Mabel's expression did not alter. After a moment she let go of Sarah's arm, then touched it again as a mark of reassurance, turned, picked up the basket and went inside. Sarah followed. The veranda at the front of Rose Cottage was narrow. It was cluttered with pots of flowering shrubs. The famous views were all at the back where the garden sloped to a wire fence, below which the land became precipitous. The cottage was one of the oldest in Pankot, built before the fashion came for building in a style more reminiscent of home. Stuccoed, whitewashed, with square columns on the verandas and high-ceilinged rooms inside, it was a piece of old Anglo-India, a bungalow with a large square entrance hall. The hall was panelled. Upon the polished wood Mabel's brass and copper shone. The bowls of flowers gave off a deep and dusty scent, and Sarah, standing in the doorway, half-closed her eyes and imagined the drone of bees on a summer's day at home in England, which she had thought of as Pankot in miniature. But England was far away and Pankot was miniature itself. Rose Cottage was not big enough to contain Susan's loss and the gestures of sorrow that presently must be made. They would be offered and the whole of Susan's loss and other people's sorrow would balloon and Pankot would not be able to contain it. She could not hear any voices. She turned away from the hall and stood on the veranda, amazed at the bright colours of flowers in the sunlight and the antics of a pair of butterflies whom Teddie's death had not affected. She waited for her mother to come out. At this time of day she would be in her first drinks of the day state: languid but mettlesome, neither to be loved nor criticized, and requiring an explanation she would not ask for in so many words and which Sarah in this case could not give.

She heard her mother's footsteps.

Mrs Layton was frowning, puzzled by and impatient of an interruption. The frown meant that Aunt Mabel had not said why Sarah had come. That Mabel had said nothing was too characteristic to be called unfair. Quickly Sarah began to formulate words. There's awfully bad news, Mother. But that wouldn't do at all. Bad news could be about her father. Shot while trying to escape. Killed by a disease made worse by malnutrition; or dead of lost hope or broken heart.

She said, 'Teddie's been killed,' and reached in her pocket, gave the crumpled signal form to her mother who took it, read it, went inside and sat on a hard hall chair and read it again. Mabel came out of the living-room followed by Barbie Batchelor, Mrs Fosdick and Mrs Paynton. They gathered round Mrs Layton. Becoming aware of them, Mrs Layton looked up from the telegram and said, 'Teddie's been killed.'

Sarah went past them into the living-room. Cigarette smoke still hung in the area of the abandoned bridge-table. Here again there were bowls and vases of flowers and deep overstuffed chairs, and a sofa dressed in flowered cretonne. At the far end the french windows were open on to the veranda. She could see the upholstered cane lounging chair and Susan's bare feet crossed at the ankles in an attitude that suggested deep repose of all the body. Her sister's drowsiness and fleshy calm made the veranda momentarily unapproachable. But she had assured herself no movement inside the house had penetrated that quiet, upset that delicate contemplation of a world without trouble.

She went back into the hall. They were talking in low voices. Her mother still sat. She had the fingers of one hand pressed lightly against her forehead. Miss Batchelor was leaning over her, supporting her back with an arm, but the support was unnecessary. Her mother's back was stiff. She caught Sarah's eye. And Sarah knew. It was she, Sarah, who must find a way of breaking the news to Susan, and the way she found would probably be clumsy, in which case Susan might forgive her but never forget.

She said to Aunt Mabel, 'I'm going out to try and tell Susan now. I think someone should ring Dr Travers in case she takes it badly.'

To make Aunt Mabel hear she spoke clearly. The others turned. She had sounded hard but reliable. Such a combination was understood. If no member of the Layton family had been up to it one of them would have taken charge in just that way. Without waiting for Aunt Mabel's reply she went back into the living-room, edged past the chairs round the bridge-table and stepped out on to the paved veranda. Susan was asleep. A faint perspiration was visible on her upper lip. Her swollen belly tautened the cotton smock and the skirt of the smock was rucked up above her bare knees. The rest of her looked too fragile for the burden of disfiguration, but in her sleep she was smiling. There was a faint upward lift to each corner of the moist closed lips.

Sarah could not wake her up and destroy such happiness. She sat on a near-by chair, watching her sister for the slightest sign that she was waking, and a ridiculous notion came to her that Susan should go on for ever dreaming and smiling and she go on sitting: in this silly uniform (she thought) with sleeves rolled up like a soldier's, but showing the white chevrons, and wearing sensible regulation shoes. One of her lisle stockings had a snag near the ankle. She wet a finger and applied it. It would do no good. It never did. The scent from the garden and from the ranges of hills where pine trees grew, oozing aromatic gums, came in waves with the faint breeze that here – even on the stillest day – could be felt on the cheek. Her father said that at eye level from the veranda of Rose Cottage the closest ground was five miles distant as the crow flew. He had worked it out with map and compass, sitting where she was sitting. That was the time he taught her to orientate a map with the lie of the land and take bearings to determine a six-point reference on the grid. He never taught Susan such things. But I am a grown woman, she told herself, not a leggy girl learning the tricks he would have taught the son he never had. In a letter at Christmas Colonel Layton said of Teddie, whose photograph they had sent, 'That son-in-law of mine looks all right. Not quite like seeing him in the flesh, but that will come, DV. Meanwhile I heartily approve and send my love to them both, and to you, Millie, and of course to Sarah.' Of course. Of course. She glanced back at Susan and saw under the book that lay open on the floor, pages down, a block of writing paper and the edge of an envelope that would contain the last letter Teddie wrote, the last she had received at least, to which she had not quite summoned the energy to reply, and so had put it by, to doze, and write later, beginning after lunch, and ending after tea, giving it then to Mabel's old servant Aziz to take down to the post.

She heard a faint sound and looked over her shoulder. Aunt Mabel was standing behind her, watching Susan too. She had never been able to tell what Aunt Mabel was thinking and now that true deafness was setting in even the old look of her sometimes watching you with inward curiosity about what you were thinking and why you were thinking it seldom appeared on the old but unwrinkled face. Her mother once said Mabel had no wrinkles because she cared for nothing and nobody, not even herself, and was never worried or concerned like an ordinary human being.

From the hall came the ring of the telephone. Mabel did not hear it. She moved to the balustrade and began to tend some of the flowers that were growing in pots and hanging baskets. Don't wake, Sarah told her sister. The telephone was promptly answered. She guessed the caller was Mrs Rankin. Mrs Rankin would be relieved that Mildred wasn't alone, but had Mrs Paynton and Mrs Fosdick to support her. In Mrs Rankin's book Mrs Fosdick and Mrs Paynton would count. And Sarah knew that she herself would count. While intending almost the opposite she was growing into a young pillar of the Anglo-Indian community. When they got back from the wedding she had been restless. It had been as if with Susan safely married her role of elder daughter had been taken from her. A married woman took precedence over a spinster. Sensing a release and a challenge she told herself: I must go to the war; and inquired about a transfer to the nursing services, which would take her as close to the war as a girl could get; closer than her clerking would ever take her. When she heard of it her mother made no comment; it was Mrs Rankin who took her aside and said, 'My dear, you mustn't think of it. It seems unfair because you're young, and want to do your bit, more than your bit if you can, but here's where it's going to be done. Have you thought of how much more your mother will need you if Susan has a baby?' And a week later Susan announced that this indeed was what she was going to do. Neither Sarah nor her mother ever said anything again about the war Sarah could not go to, but between them now, in addition to the silences that hinted at need there were these new silences that were like a recollection of intended betrayal, silences of accusation, silences in which Sarah felt herself charged with having attempted to escape from her responsibilities, caring nothing for her mother, being jealous of her sister and forgetful of her father whose peace of mind depended on a certain picture of them holding a fort together. But these were charges she sometimes made against herself and needed no look in her mother's eye, no set of her mother's still lips, to remind her of.

She leaned back in the chair, turning her head to keep the silent watch: on Susan sleeping and smiling, and on Aunt Mabel taking dead heads off an azalea to give strength to buds not yet open. But that only worked with plants. The bud of Susan's belly wouldn't wax stronger with the cutting off of Teddie. Or would it? The image was grotesque but it had come and would not go away. It was merged with another, an image of a shapeless mindless hunger consuming Susan, consuming all of them, feeding on loss, on happiness and sorrow alike, rendering all human ambition exquisitely pointless because the hunger was enough in itself.

Don't wake, she told Susan again, and closed her eyes to contribute to the persuasive arguments of the heat and scent and the siren whispers of the air. She opened them abruptly because Susan had stirred, shifted her legs and turned her head so that now she faced Sarah. After a while with eyes still closed she raised her right arm and made extra shade for her face with the crook of the elbow, then seemed to fall asleep again, but the weight of her own arm disturbed her, and her waking thoughts were more solemn than her sleeping ones. Unsmiling now she half lifted the lids of her eyes and observed Sarah through the fringes of her lashes and the shadow of her elbow. Sarah looked away. Presently she heard another movement – the sound perhaps of Susan lifting her arm to disperse the shadow, raising her head a bit to confirm the reality of Sarah's presence. A moment later Susan asked in a sleepy voice:

'Is it lunch-time already?'

Her eyes were shut again. She had moved her arm and made a pillow of both hands for her face.

'No. I've come back early.'

At the far end of the veranda Mabel stood watching, alerted by the movements Susan had made. She had kept an eye open. Sarah was grateful. In spite of the marked withdrawal from other people, when a real pinch came – Sarah had always thought so – Mabel could be relied on. She was a point of reference. You could not embrace her but you could lean against her and if you ever did so perhaps you would find that she was a shelter too, because she stood firm, and cast a shadow.

'Why have you come back early?' Susan asked, long after Sarah thought she'd dozed off again. And then, 'Anyway, what is the time?' Susan had stopped wearing her watch. She had read somewhere that mothers-to-be shouldn't allow themselves to be distracted by artificial divisions of time. Sarah looked at her own wrist. Was it only thirty-five minutes?

'Eleven-twenty.'

She glanced back at Susan and watched the eyes open yet again. They conveyed a slight annoyance.

'Have you come on badly, or something?'

Sarah shook her head. Since Susan had stopped coming on herself she either pretended not to know when Sarah had a period or spoke of it as if it threatened to disrupt her own routine. So Sarah thought. But perhaps she had become self-conscious and read into Susan's manner what she felt about them herself: that hers were the menstrual flows of a virgin, sour little seepages such as Barbie Batchelor had presumably sustained for a good thirty years of her unreproductive life.

She said, 'No,' and then, seeing an opportunity, added, 'It's not that.' She found herself studying the snag in her stocking again, and automatically wetted her finger, dabbed it, found inspiration from the firm contact. 'Let's help Aunt Mabel with the flowers.' She had an idea that Susan ought to be standing, that it would be bad for her to be told what she had to be told, lying as she was.

She stood up. Susan watched her and then looked round and noticed her aunt standing at the balustrade, attending to the flowers and yet not attending to them.

'Why should we do that?' she asked, but fully awake now, returning her right arm to its crooked position above her head, looking at Aunt Mabel who, Sarah saw, remained still, resisting any temptation to dissociate herself from the situation that was arising.

'Come on,' Sarah said, 'you'll get as big as a house if you lie around all day. You ought to take much more exercise.'

'I am as big as a house, and I've done my exercise.'

'Well, I'm going to push the back of your chair up anyway. You always lie out on it much too flat.' She went round behind and heaved the levered back higher.

'Oh, Sarah, no. What on earth are you doing?'

'Sitting you up.' She readjusted the holding rod. Her arms were trembling. She came round to the front of the chair. 'I'd better lower the foot. Then you'll be almost respectable.' She knelt, and did as she had warned. When she had finished she continued kneeling. She said, 'Sorry. Have I made you awfully uncomfortable?'

Her sister was leaning forward, her hands clasped to the chair arms, her legs slightly apart with the smock ridden farther up from her knees. She was not displeased by the attention but puzzled by its suddenness and the absence of any immediately clear reason for it. Now she leant back, but kept her grip on the arms.

'What have they done, given you a day off?'

'Sort of.'

Susan waited.

'Well?'

Sarah reached for one of Susan's hands.

'Something's happened, which I have to tell you.'

The hand lay beneath hers, quite unresponsive.

'I don't know how to, but I've got to. I think I can only say it straight. It's about Teddie '

She paused, deliberately, to let it sink in. When she believed that it had she went on:

'The signal came this morning and they stopped it being sent over because they knew I was on duty. The signal says – it says that Teddie's been killed. So that's what we have to start believing because there can't be any doubt. If there were any doubt it wouldn't say that, but it does, and I'm sorry, sorry.'

Now she took both of Susan's hands. But they were pulled away. 'No,' Susan said.

She stared down at Sarah.

'No.'

Mrs Fosdick came, and her mother, and Mrs Paynton, then Miss Batchelor. 'No,' she said, rejecting them all, jerking herself away from each touch of a hand on her arm or shoulder. 'No. No. No.'

She kicked out with one foot, as if kicking Sarah away. Sarah got up and the others closed in, filling the gap. They surrounded her completely. 'No,' Sarah heard her say again; but her voice was muffled now, as if she had covered her face.

Sarah went down the steps into the garden. At the end of the garden there was a place – a pergola dense with briar rose, and behind it a fir where there would be shade from the hot yellow light. As she went she heard a sound that made her stop: a drawn-out shriek, a desolate cry of anguish. When she reached the shade behind the pergola and under the fir she stood with her arms folded, and then sat and wondered whether Susan's cry had crossed the five measured miles to the other side of the valley, and wept – for what exactly she did not know – and it was over very quickly. She dried her eyes and did not want to be alone any longer. She got up, left the shade and reapproached the house with the sun heavy on her neck and heating her scalp. The situation was familiar. It had all happened before – people on a veranda and herself returning to join them. How many cycles had they lived through then, how many times had the news of Teddie's death been broken? How many times had Susan been taken indoors – almost dragged, stiffly resistant – in her mother's arms, while Mrs Fosdick and Mrs Paynton stood like silent supervisors of an ancient ritual concerning women's grief? Aunt Mabel had sat down, with the basket of dead heads on her lap.

'Are you all right, Aunty?' she asked, bending over her.

'Yes, thank you.'

'Can I get you anything?'

'No, thank you.'

'Let me take those.' She touched the handle of the basket but Aunt Mabel held on.

'Tell your mother she and Susan can have my room for the night if they would like that. I don't advise it, but Aziz can rig up extra beds and I can pig in with Barbie. You can have the little spare if they decide to stay.'

'Thanks, but I'll try and get them home.'

Mabel gazed up at her, then nodded. Sarah left her and joined Mrs Paynton and Mrs Fosdick who had gone into the sitting-room. There was no sound from anywhere in the house.

'They're in Barbie's room,' Mrs Paynton said, keeping her voice low. 'You mustn't be hurt, Sarah.'

'No,' said Mrs Fosdick. 'She didn't mean it, hitting out at you like that.'

'I wasn't hurt.'

A message had been left at Dr Travers's. Isobel Rankin had phoned and offered to look after Susan and her mother at Flagstaff House. Everyone would do everything they could. It was difficult to tell how Susan was taking it. She hadn't cried yet. But there had been that sound. Sarah guessed that the sound had shaken them. It wasn't the kind of sound a Layton made. The servants had heard it. The sound was shocking, Sarah thought, to everyone but her. They would have preferred her sister to cry, quietly, in the privacy of her room. Well there, in her mother's arms, she could have wept to her heart's content and earned their eager sympathy. God knew they weren't hard women; but there was something intemperate, savage, about a grief that went unaccompanied by a decent flow of tears. They all three stood in the room that Barbie Batchelor had made cosy with chintz and cretonne. Miss Batchelor came back. Her tall thin body, iron-grey short-cropped hair and unhealthy yellow face – a network of lines and wrinkles – suddenly struck Sarah as ridiculous. Missionary India had dried her out. There was nothing left of Barbie Batchelor.

'She's just sitting there,' Miss Batchelor said. 'She won't answer us and she won't lie down on the bed. I feel that if only she would lie down it would be all right.' She hesitated. 'It's not like Susan. Not like Susan at all. Poor Mildred can't get through to her, and one feels so useless. One feels so useless.'

Surprisingly Miss Batchelor herself burst into tears, and sat heavily in one of the cretonne-covered chairs. No one in Pankot had ever seen Barbie Batchelor cry. She had come a few years ago, in retirement from the Missions and in answer to the advertisement old Mabel Layton put in the Ranpur papers for a single woman to share. Only once in her time in Pankot had she come into any sort of prominence, and that was at the time of the August riots down in the plains in 1942. She had cried: 'I know her!' when they read out the reports of the attack on the superintendent of the protestant mission schools in Mayapore, Edwina Crane, who, travelling from Dibrapur back to her headquarters, had seen her Indian companion murdered in front of her eyes and then been knocked senseless by the same mob and had her car burnt out; been found, later, holding the dead man's hand, sitting on the roadside in the pouring rain. 'I know her!' Miss Batchelor cried, and wrote, but had no reply, which was no surprise when eventually it was heard that Edwina Crane had gone very queer as the result of her terrible experience, and died by her own hand, setting fire to herself in a garden shed. 'Oh, poor Miss Crane,' Miss Batchelor was heard to say then. But she had not cried. 'I've always been useless, useless to everybody, how many of those little Indian children really loved God and came to Jesus?' Miss Batchelor said. They soothed her with murmurs of, 'Now don't be silly, how can you say that? There must be hundreds who are grateful to you.'

Sarah felt a suffocating claustrophobia, a tense need to destroy, and run, find air and light.

The claustrophobia was the beginning of the dream she was presently to have, where they were saying goodbye to Teddie, where she herself was running and being made love to by a man whose face she couldn't see and whom nobody seemed to know. He was there and then not there, then there again. He had a great, an insatiable, desire for her but it did not enslave her. He was a happy man and she was happy with him, not jealously possessive. He existed outside the area of claustrophobia, entered it and left it at random, without difficulty. He came to her because she could not go to him. A climax was never reached by either of them, but that did not spoil their pleasure. Disrupted as it was their loving had assurance. There was always the promise of a climax.

•

'She wants to go home,' young Travers said when he came out of Barbie Batchelor's room, where Susan was. He was not young, only younger than Beames, the civil surgeon to the station. 'And I think that's best, so I'll take her in the car with Mrs Layton.' She had refused a sedative. She had not lain down. She had hardly spoken. She did not speak in the car. When they reached home she went straight to her room. She lay on the bed then, while Sarah and her mother saw to the shutters and drew the curtains. She said, no, there was nothing she wanted, only for them to have their lunch and not bother with anything for her. She would be all right in a while.

The front compound of the grace and favour bungalow had a low wall and looked directly across the road to the back of the bleak Pankot Rifles mess, a rambling L-shaped structure, only partially concealed by trees. The Layton dining-room and master-bedroom had views on to this. At the back there were two other bedrooms and the sitting-room and these had kinder views on to an attempted garden – a square of lawn, a wall. Behind the wall were the servants' quarters. The bedrooms – Susan's and Sarah's – were small. They interconnected. They shared a bathroom that was reached from the back veranda. The black labrador, Panther, who had been a puppy when the girls came out in 1939, had mourned the absence of Colonel Layton, then attached himself to Susan, and these days marked the veranda outside her bedroom as his special territory. He whimpered at her door and Sarah told Mahmud to take him to the kitchen compound and try to keep him there. She told Mahmud what had happened. Mahmud was not one of Sarah's childhood memories but he had been in her father's service for many years, almost ten. When he went, pulling the protesting Panther, she knew that the circumstances of the family's mourning were complete. Sorrow would fill the house and compound with a kind of formality and even the dog would quieten. She went to look for her mother and found her wandering aimlessly in her bedroom with a glass in her hand which, with a wholly uncharacteristic gesture, she abruptly tried to hide, covering it with the palm of her other hand. The telephone rang in the hall. Sarah went to answer it.

Returning, she said, 'It was the padre's wife. She wanted to come round now, but I put her off until this evening.'

Her mother must have emptied the glass and put it away, out of sight. 'I never cared much for Teddie, you know,' she said suddenly.

She was sitting erect, almost on the edge of the old PWD arm-chair, rubbing one bare elbow. 'So I can't pretend to be bowled over exactly. And I don't think Susan ever really loved him. She was very secretive about the honeymoon. At least she was with me. Did she say anything to you?'

'No.' This direct approach disturbed and embarrassed her.

'I shouldn't think Teddie was very – experienced. Not that that's terribly important. Although it is if there's a lack of consideration too. And that's how he struck me, as likely to be inexperienced and inconsiderate. I'd always hoped that Muzzy Guide friend of his, Tony Bishop, would cut him out. But he never even tried. I don't think he cared for Teddie much either or Teddie's attitudes. The one thing they had in common was a regiment.'

'We'd better eat,' Sarah said.

'There's some cold chicken and salad. Tell Mahmud to get up a tray for her. She can't not eat.'

But she did not eat. The telephone kept ringing through lunch, and afterwards the chits began to arrive. Mahmud was sent to Jalal-ud-din's to stock up on tick with country gin and bottles of lemon and lime, and cashew nuts, for the expected invasion of callers. They began to arrive from five onwards: Isobel Rankin, Maisie Trehearne, the wife of Colonel Trehearne who commanded the Pankot Rifles Depot, the Adjutant, old Captain Coley, whose wife had not survived the Quetta earhquake and who himself had not risen since because his ambition did not survive either; Lucy Smalley, Mrs Beames, Carol and Christine Beames who worked at Area Headquarters with Sarah; Dicky Beauvais, deputizing for the most recent batch of Susan's pre-showing grass-widow gallants, young officers who came ostensibly to claim the company of the unmarried sister but had tended to end up fetching things for Susan.

They came, spoke in low tones, and went one by one or two by two. The last to come were Dr Travers and the Reverend Arthur Peplow with his wife Clarissa to both of whom Dr Travers had given a lift; and only the doctor and the chaplain entered Susan's room, Travers first, and then Peplow, after Travers came out and pronounced her well enough and wanting to have a word with him.

'She has asked for a Memorial Service,' Peplow told them ten minutes later, accepting a gimlet, 'and I think that very suitable. I shall be very happy to arrange it.'

'Not happy, darling,' said Mrs Peplow, who was always correcting his way of putting things.

'Of course not. Happy to be of use; the circumstances are sad enough. I think on Saturday week, so that I can announce it next Sunday at matins and evensong. If you agree, Mrs Layton.'

'If it's what Susan wants.'

And Susan wanted it. She only referred to it once, the day after, when she asked her mother to send for the durzi and tell him to bring bolts of whatever he had in grey – silk and chiffon. 'It's for the service,' she said. 'I shan't wear black. And grey will always come in.' She drew the design herself, basing it on one of her smocks which the durzi had already made up. She chose a silk for the smock foundation, a chiffon for the outer drapes which she had the durzi cut to hang full and loose; and in it she hardly showed at all, but stood in the shade of the veranda – while the tailor knelt with pins in mouth and chalk in hand – a white-faced grey-clad little ghost. For her veil she made over a circlet of blue velvet and pale blue velvet flowers and hung it with soft grey net. A grey suède handbag, gloves and shoes, were the only other expense – and these would come in too.

And she made an impression, yes, an impression, walking unsupported by but next to her mother, up the aisle of the church in which she had been christened, with Sarah coming along behind, in uniform. The whole station was represented, the pews were packed. In the days preceding the memorial service Pankot had become conscious of a need and of an occasion coming that would satisfy it. At its centre, Susan, veiled, revealed what that need was, moved them to an intensity of determination to fulfil it; to reaffirm. They lifted their voices high to sing, Lord, While Afar our Brothers Fight, Thy Church United Lifts Her Prayer; and lowered them to a grave and tender note of fervent understanding when they came to the third verse:

> For wives and mothers sore distress'd,
> For all who wait in silent fear,
> For homes bereaved which gave their best,
> For hearts now desolate and drear
> O God of Comfort, hear our cry,
> And in the darkest hour draw nigh.

But the last two lines were sung in mounting passion because the verse stirred them to a sense of what was owed to people like the Laytons. In India hadn't the Laytons always given of their best? In those two young girls, the one sad in grey, the other brave in khaki, there ran the blood of Muirs and Laytons and there were those two names on headstones in the churchyard, stones so old now that the names could only be read with difficulty. A time would come – the congregation felt it, as it were a wind driving them before it so that they had to cling hard not to be scattered – when all their names and history would pass into that same dark.

After the hymn Mr Peplow read the 23rd Psalm and as he finished General Rankin went to the lectern and read from Corinthians: *Behold I show you a mystery, We shall not all sleep.* He read well until he reached the passage: O death where is thy sting? O grave where is thy Victory? when his voice became flat with self-consciousness. When he returned to his seat Mr Peplow said, very simply, 'Let us Pray.' They knelt and prayed for the deliverance from evil and the coming of the kingdom, for the whole state of Christ's church militant here on earth, for their sovereign George; and – after a pause – for the quiet repose of the soul of Edward Arthur David Bingham.

After the second lesson (*Man that is born of a woman hath but a short time to live*) which was read by Colonel Trehearne in his high, light, lilting voice, they rose to their feet again and sang 'Abide with Me', and it was remarked by those nearest to her that when they came to the opening lines of the last verse, *Hold Thou Thy Cross before my closing eyes; Shine through the gloom and point me to the skies,* Susan lowered her head and after the Amen sat down very quickly, with her head still bowed. She stayed like this throughout Mr Peplow's short address. He spoke of their sympathy for the young widow of a brave officer whom many of them had known, and remembered clearly for his cheerfulness, his kindly disposition. He had no doubt that Edward Bingham's was the kind of cheerfulness that adversity would not have diminished and it was this picture of him, young, smiling and in the prime of life that they must carry away with them. It would be a gallant soldier's best memorial.

He then spoke of the name Bingham, of the father who, like the son, had served in a famous regiment, and of the marriage only a short time ago of the younger Bingham into a family whose history of service to India went even further back. He did not need

[327

(he said) to speak at length about such things, for in this congregation the meaning of such service was fully understood and never had the meaning been clearer or the need to serve more pressing than now. This young officer had died, not in a foreign land, but on Indian soil, fighting off an enemy who had brought untold misery to the simple peoples of Burma and Malaya and would bring it to the Indians too if at what seemed like the eleventh hour we failed. But to fail, surely, was not possible, and already the tide was turning. Perhaps this time next year we should see the forces of evil and destruction swept into the sea, Burma regained, Malaya relieved, and India safe from threat, free to turn again to the ways of peace. The victory would not be without cost, but men such as he whom they had prayed this morning in remembrance of would, he hoped, not have died in vain. They were troubled times they had lived through, were living through, and yet had to face, and it was not only for victory to their arms they had to pray but for God to grant wisdom to those in whose hands chiefly lay the future happiness and progress of the great sub-continent, with all its complex problems and manifold differences of caste and creed and race. He asked them to join him presently in a minute of silent prayer, for the repose of the gallant dead, for the safety of the soldiers of India and Britain fighting – even as they sat there – shoulder to shoulder on the eastern frontier, for the peace and blessing of God upon the bereaved, and for wisdom in the councils of the world.

He left the pulpit and when he sank to his knees in front of the altar the congregation followed suit in their pews, prayed their prayers and thought their thoughts. It was said that on the eastern frontier the soldiers of India and Britain fighting shoulder to shoulder had found among their enemy Indian soldiers once captured by the Japanese but now fighting for them. The thought was bitter. Somewhere at the back of the church a coin, got ready for the collection, dropped on the tiled floor, but it marked the silence even more heavily and in itself conveyed an assurance of anxious, charitable intention. Rising once more Mr Peplow announced the last hymn, No 437, 'For All the Saints, Who from their labours rest'. The collection was for the Red Cross. Four officers from area headquarters solemnly stalked the pews and were rewarded with the chink of coins and crackle of notes in the woven bags they offered on long wooden rods. As the congregation broke into the penultimate verse, 'But lo! there breaks a yet more glorious day', they delivered the collection to Mr Peplow, waited until he had raised it in humble offering and thanks, and then about-turned and regained their seats in time to join in:

> From earth's wide bounds, from ocean's farthest coast,
> Through gates of pearl streams in the countless host,
> Singing to Father, Son and Holy Ghost.
> Allelulia.

Once more they knelt, for the blessing, and rose to restrained chords from the invisible organ, played by Mr Maybrick, the retired tea planter; and waited while, accompanied by Mr Peplow, the Laytons left. After a decent interval, they began to crowd the aisles, their faces stiff with dignity, automatically taking or giving precedence, so that the Rankins were the first to arrive in the porch where Mr Peplow stood holding one of Susan's hands in both of his. He let her go so that Isobel Rankin could embrace her, which she did, lightly, making a token kiss of the air near one veiled cheek and murmuring, 'It was a beautiful service, I hope you felt that.' Susan murmured in return and put out her hand to take the one offered by General Rankin to whom she said, in a low but firm voice:

'Thank you for reading the lesson so clearly, and for everything.'

The General nodded, touched – Sarah saw – that Susan should think of thanking him at all. Presently the Rankins went, with subdued farewells, and others took their place. Dicky Beauvais touched Sarah's shoulder and said, 'I'll ring you later. Where'll you be?' She told him they were going on to lunch at Rose Cottage and only had to wait for Barbie Batchelor so that they could all go up together in the car General Rankin had lent them for the occasion. He touched his cap and went. Sarah was away from the porch now and shielded her eyes from the sun, and then Miss Batchelor was upon her, grinning but blowing her nose. The others emerged from the porch. Mr Peplow accompanied them down the gravel path that led in a curve through the hummocky graveyard – downward, because the church stood, among pine trees and cypress, on an eminence.

At Rose Cottage Susan went with Barbie into Barbie's room to change into the flowered smock and sandals that had been brought up by Mahmud earlier in the day. Barbie came out and told them Susan had asked for lunch on a tray. She would eat it out on the veranda.

[329

'It's been such a strain for her,' Barbie said. 'I don't think she feels up to talking. I'll tell Aziz and then I think the form is for us all to go in and eat.'

They did so. There were curried eggs and rice. Afterwards Mabel and Barbie went to their rooms and her mother to the spare, for the ritual of sleep. Sarah went out on to the veranda. Susan had had her tray. She was resting on the same chair and in the same position Sarah had found her in ten days before. Sarah sat down, completing the pattern, presently turned her head and saw that Susan was watching her.

'What did Dicky Beauvais say?' she asked.

'Only that he'd ring.'

A pause.

'Is that what you're waiting for?'

Sarah looked away, towards the five-mile hill.

'No, Susan. I'm not waiting for anything.'

A pause.

'You're very lucky.'

'Why lucky?'

'Not to be waiting.' Susan's eyes were shut again. Gently, as if withdrawing into sleep, she turned her head into her folded hands.

At first Sarah did not notice the change in the rhythm of her sister's breathing; but then became conscious of it: conscious that the pauses between the rise and fall were unusually long, the rise and fall unnaturally abrupt. Sarah got up, went close, and understood what was happening. She reached out to touch Susan's head, but was afraid to. Close like this she could hear the suffocating attempts to deny the outlet for a pent-up misery. But what kind of misery? She could not tell. She thought: You have the courage of ten like me. And knelt, leaning on her hip, clasping one ankle, to wait and try to convey to Susan that she was there if wanted. And after a while, still making that sound as if she were suffocating, Susan took one hand away from her face, groped for contact and held on, moving her head from side to side behind the hand that covered it, as if she would wear it down to the skull and Sarah's shoulder to the bone, to relieve her agony.

'There's no one here,' Sarah murmured. 'Let it come out.'

'I can't,' Susan said. Her voice was almost unrecognizable, a hoarse moan below the breath, but emphatic in its conviction. 'I can't. I've got to hang on.'

330]

Sarah bent her head until her cheek rested on the tense knuckles. 'Yes,' she said. 'Yes, if you want.'

'Then it may be all right. I thought the service would help it all come back. But it didn't. It didn't, and I don't know how to face it without. I don't know how to face it.'

She pulled her hand away and flung herself round so that she was on her back; and lay like that, with her eyes shut, turning her head from side to side, pressing down on her swollen belly with both hands.

'At the service I prayed for the baby to die. I want him to die because I don't know how to face it alone. How can I face it with Teddie never never coming back? I didn't want the baby, but it pleased him so, and he wrote and wrote about it, and I could face it like that. But I can't face it alone. I can't bear it alone.'

'You won't be alone, Su —'

'But I am. I am alone.'

Abruptly she sat up, doubled herself over her folded arms and began to move her body in a tight rocking motion. 'Just like I was before, just as I've always been, just as if I'd never tried. But I did. I did try. I did try.'

'What did you try —?'

'You wouldn't understand. How could you? You're not like me. Whatever you do and wherever you go you'll always be yourself. But what am I? What am I? Why – there's nothing to me at all. Nothing. Nothing at all.'

Sarah sat quite still, watching that rocking motion, held by it, and by the revelation, what seemed to be the revelation, of what had lain behind the game that seemed to have ended, the game of Susan playing Susan. Susan nothing? Susan alone? She pondered the meaning of: Whatever you do and wherever you go you'll always be yourself: and recognized their truth. She was herself because her sense of self, her consciousness of individuality was tenacious, grindingly resistant to temptations to surrender it in exchange for a share in that collective illusion of a world morally untroubled, convinced of its capacity to find just solutions for every problem that confronted it, a world where everything was accepted as finally defined, a world that thought it knew what human beings were.

But it did not know what Susan was. In grey and on her knees; yes, it knew that Susan; and it knew Susan in white with the wind catching her veil, or standing at a carriage window flushed and smiling and taking a last sniff at a bunch of flowers before throwing them in that bride's gesture which proved a readiness to share her luck and fortune. It did not know her in a coloured smock, rocking to and fro, and had no answer to her cry that she was nothing.

It did not know her and had no answer and Sarah did not know her either – not as Susan – but with something of a shock recognized in the girl crouched on the chair a sibling whose pretty face and winning ways had been, after all, perhaps, only a fearful armour against the terrors of the night, a shield that was not visible to her but deluded others into believing her protected. What else had they been deluded by? By everything, perhaps, but most of all by the signs and portents of self-absorption, that apparent trick and talent for creating a world around her of which she was the organizing determinedly happy centre. It had not been that at all. There had been no secret garden, but only Susan crying to be let in and building the likeness of it for herself because she believed the secret garden was the place they all inhabited, and she could not bear the thought that she alone walked in a limbo of strange and melancholy desires.

Shifting her weight Sarah reached and put her arms round her sister.

'You do amount to something, and you're really not alone,' she said, and Susan turned into the embrace, with the weird sound of someone inwardly recognizing and inarticulately acknowledging refuge.

II

SEVERAL IMAGES converge. That woman in the *burkha*, glimpsed in Ranpur, making her way to the mosque through the street of the moneylenders: one merely chanced upon her and noted the smell of Chanel No 5; but – walking unhurriedly, in that enfolding garment – she defies her prosaic environment of time and place. She can be pictured years before, not in Ranpur but in Pankot, making her way along a section of the bazaar, like a ghost condemned to walk in a certain place, so many steps, presenting to the world a front, a proof of her existence, silently calling attention to herself; always appearing and disappearing in the same places, as though the route, as well as her presence, is significant.

There was such a woman in the dream Sarah had, but she was in widow's white, not purdah; and did not walk but remained prostrate. Yet, in the recurrence, in the uncertainty as to real intention, similarities existed. The whole of Sarah's dream was like the woman in the *burkha*. It came and went and stayed in her mind, so that sometimes, in daylight, awake, the visions of the dream would transpose themselves and she would find herself leaving Jalal-ud-din's and encountering, through the eyes of the woman who usually begged alms outside, this other woman, the one in white, lying in the dust, seeking for a mercy no one was capable of showing. For Sarah there came a time when the whole of that summer became inextricably entangled, as if, at this point, converging strands of circumstances met and intermingled, but did not cohere; and woven into them were the patterns of her dream, and Barbie's dream, and the tale from the hills that had sent young Morland in his sleep to an unexpected death by drowning. She found it difficult later to remember things in the order they happened. There was a sense in which they became interchangeable.

For instance: did she fancy she saw Lady Manners in the bazaar before the old lady strangely announced her presence in Pankot (strangely because having announced it she remained resolutely in a purdah of her own)? Or had Lady Manners re-entered her sleeping and waking consciousness before she made her presence known, so that the glimpse Sarah thought she had of her, leaving Jalal-ud-din's in the company of a distinguished-looking Indian woman, seemed like some special manifestation rather than a visual confirmation of a presence that was the subject of common gossip? And what came first? Lady Manners or the letter that revived the other image of the stone thrown into the car taking poor Teddie and his best man to the wedding? And when, why, was it first suggested that Susan was dangerously withdrawn and the tale was resurrected of Poppy Browning's daughter who, bearing her first child three months after being told her husband had died in the Quetta earthquake, promptly smothered it?

The most logical sequence would be one in which the letter reviving the image of the stone came first, because this might be seen as having had an effect on Susan that set people talking about Poppy Browning's daughter and the business of the smothered child; and as having had the effect, as well, of reminding Pankot of the affair in the Bibighar Gardens in advance of Lady Manners's arrival, so that the arrival had the special poignancy Sarah seemed to remember as attaching to it.

*

There had been many letters: from all over India, from people who had seen Teddie's death gazetted or the notice in the *Times of India*. Most were addressed to Mrs Layton and she set about answering them with an industriousness that Sarah fancied was in part therapeutic, in part self-indulgent. All through the mornings, and on many an evening, Mrs Layton sat at the oak bureau in the grace and favour living-room, writing, writing. Page after page. There was apparently no end to the store of words, the flood of words. And she became more directly communicative. She discussed the letters with Sarah. She drank less.

There were also letters to originate: to Aunt Lydia in Bayswater, to Colonel Layton in Germany, to that uncle of Teddie's in Shropshire whom the marriage had relegated from his old status of next-of-kin and of whose nephew's death on active service it had therefore become Susan's or Mrs Layton's duty to inform him. The Shropshire uncle had promised a wedding present after the war; it seemed doubtful now that Susan would ever get it; he had not given an impression of a generous nature. There were letters to send to Aunt Fenny too – now left Delhi for Calcutta where Uncle Arthur had at last acquired a job [a strange-sounding kind] that carried the pip and crown of a Lieutenant-Colonelcy: the first to tell Fenny of Susan's loss and the second to put her off coming up, as she offered.

There were expected letters; one each for them from Tony Bishop who, but for the jaundice, would have been Teddie's best man, and who now worked in Bombay. There were unexpected letters, a formal note of condolence from the Nawab of Mirat to Susan and a less formal letter to Mrs Layton from Count Bronowsky who said that the Nawab was deeply affected to hear of the death in action of the husband of the charming girl to whom and to whose family he had had the privilege and pleasure of extending some small hospitality the previous year. He wanted the Laytons to know that they were welcome at any time, now or in the future, to stay as his guests again, at the palace, or in the summer palace in Nanoora. 'How kind,' Mrs Layton murmured, 'but quite out of the

334]

question,' and wrote to thank the Nawab and his wazir, and explained that Susan was awaiting the birth of her baby.

Susan detached herself from the business of the letters. She asked her mother and Sarah to open them, answer for her, and keep by any of those they thought she might look at later. She specified only one exception to this rule. And this was the letter for which they waited. It came (Sarah thought later, unable quite to recall the order of things) in a batch of mail on the Sunday of the week following the Memorial Service. The flimsy envelope, addressed to Susan, was franked by a field post office, and attested for the censor by an officer whose rank alone was legible.

'I think this is it,' Mrs Layton said. She handed the envelope to Sarah who was helping with lists and priorities. Susan was at the back, playing with Panther, throwing a ball from the veranda and waiting at the balustrade while he went to retrieve it. They could hear the scuttering sound of the dog's pads and claws as it hurled itself down the steps and, after an interval, hurled itself back up them again to drop the ball with a *puck* at Susan's feet, panting from the exertion, and with the pleasure of having a mistress who again took notice of him.

Sarah handed the envelope back. 'It must be.' She looked round, alerted to a change in the rhythm of the game by the dog's anxious whimper. Susan was standing by the open window, watching them. 'It's come, hasn't it?' she asked.

Mrs Layton held the envelope out. 'We think so. Here you are, darling. You'll want to take it away.'

Susan came over, took the letter and went back to the veranda. They heard Panther growl and Susan say to him, 'Oh, all right, just once more.' She must have thrown the ball then. The dog scuttered away. Mrs Layton opened another letter. 'It's from Agnes Ritchie in Lahore,' she told Sarah. 'Put her on B list.'

Sarah entered Agnes Ritchie's name in the B column of her list and when her mother gave her the letter put it with others in the B folder. Susan must have thrown the ball into the bushes of bougainvillaea. It was some time before they heard the dog return. Ball in mouth, it came into the living-room, looked round and went out again. They heard then, faintly, from the far end of the veranda, the scraping of its claws on the closed door of Susan's room. In a while this sound of insistence died away. Sarah got up and went outside. The labrador raised its head and glanced at her. The ball was held securely between its extended paws.

'Come on, Panther,' she said, 'I'll throw your ball for you.'

But the dog rested its head again and waited.

*

Mrs Rankin rang and spoke to Mrs Layton about the Red Cross aid committee meeting, Mrs Trehearne sent a chit about the British Other Ranks Hospital Welfare and Troops Entertainments committee. Dicky Beauvais came round and asked Sarah for tennis at five with supper and pictures to follow. Mahmud complained that the dhobi had failed to turn up and asked permission to go into the lines and if necessary into the bazaar to find him. Distantly they heard the bells of St John's announcing matins, and closer, the strains of the regimental band of the Pankot Rifles at practice in the grounds of the officers' mess. The crows swooped and squawked. It was an ordinary Sunday morning. But an hour after she had taken the letter Susan was still in her bedroom, secluded with her evidence of war.

'I've done enough,' Mrs Layton said. 'I'm going to wash my hair.' She gave Sarah the pile of envelopes, the result of the morning's spate, and went into her room, calling for Minnie, Mahmud's widowed niece who helped him run things by taking care of the intimate details of a household of women. The call for Minnie roused the dog. It went padding past the window, making for the source of this evidence of renewed activity. Sarah finished stamping the envelopes, went into the entrance hall and left them on the brass tray where Mahmud would find them on his return from his quest for the lost dhobi. She went into her own room. Minnie had made the bed, tied the laundry into a sheet and pinned Sarah's list to it. The connecting door into Susan's room was closed and she could not hear her sister moving.

She tapped, then opened the door. Susan was sitting on the bed with an album on her knee which Sarah recognized as the one containing the wedding photographs and press cuttings. The letter was on the bedside-table, propped between the table-lamp and a framed picture of Teddie – Susan's favourite because it showed him looking serious, with the mere ghost of a smile.

'Mother's washing her hair and I thought I'd do mine,' Sarah explained. 'You don't want the bathroom for ten minutes, do you?'

Susan shook her head.

'Was it a letter about Teddie?'

'Yes.' She put the album down, picked up the letter and began to read it but seemed to give up half-way. She offered the sheet of buff army paper to Sarah.

'Dear Mrs Bingham, Since it was with me that your husband worked most closely it is, I think, my duty – a very sad one – to offer you on behalf of his divisional commander and fellow officers, deep sympathy in the loss you have sustained by his death, of which you will by now have received official notification. He died as a result of wounds, having gone forward, under orders, with instructions to the commander of a subordinate formation then in contact with the enemy and under heavy pressure. With him at the time was Captain Merrick, whom you met in Mirat of course. Captain Merrick, although himself wounded – and at risk of his own life – rendered the utmost assistance to your husband, and stayed with him until the arrival of medical aid. Captain Merrick told the medical officer that your husband had not been conscious, and it may be some relief to you to know, therefore, that he did not suffer. Captain Merrick has now been evacuated to a base hospital and the Divisional Commander has been pleased to submit a report, in the form of a recommendation, in respect of Captain Merrick's action. Teddie – as most of us knew him here – ever cheerful and devoted to his task, is sadly missed by all of us. Those of us who met you, your mother and your sister, on the occasion of your wedding in Mirat, all send our special personal sympathies. Yours sincerely, Patrick Selby-Smith, Lt.-Colonel.

Sarah returned the letter to its place by Teddie's portrait. Susan was going through the album again.

'I've never noticed it before,' she said, 'but there seems to be only one picture of him.'

'Of Colonel Selby-Smith?'

'No, of Captain Merrick. This is him, isn't it? It's really only half a face.'

Sarah sat on the bed next to her sister and studied the photograph. It was taken at the pillared entrance of the Mirat Gymkhana Club a moment or so before they left for the railway station. It showed Teddie with his plastered cheek turned from the camera and looking down at Susan who stood with her feet neatly together, in a tailored linen suit, wearing a little pill-box hat and holding the bouquet. Behind them on the steps, partly shadowed, were Aunt Fenny and her mother, Uncle Arthur and Colonel and Mrs Hobhouse. Behind these was the group of largely anonymous officers of whom she only recognized Ronald Merrick. Merrick was not looking into the camera but down on to Uncle Arthur's neck. In that little crowd of grinning young men he looked remote, humourless; but younger – she thought – than she remembered him looking in full light, under the sun. The camera and the shadows had smoothed out lines and not recorded the weathered texture of the skin. As a youth, at home, with his fair hair and blue eyes – she was sure they were blue – he must have seemed to those near to him comely and full of promise. 'She didn't care,' he had said, when talking that evening about Miss Manners, 'what your parents were or what sort of school you went to.' He must have been conscious of them himself, though, and Sarah wondered about them, about the ambition that had driven him and the capacity that had enabled him to overcome what she supposed would count as disadvantages if you compared them with the advantages of a man like Teddie Bingham. She had never written to Captain Merrick, but then he had never written to her. Once – or was it twice? – he had sent his regards to them all through Teddie, perhaps more often than Teddie remembered to say. She wondered how literally he had taken what she recalled now as a promise to write sometimes. She had thought the request for letters part of the attempt he seemed to make to convey to others an idea that he was a man rather alone in the world, a man whose background and experience set him somewhat apart but gave him reserves of power to withstand what other men might feel as solitariness. She remembered how they had sat on the terrace the last time she saw him, waiting for the fireflies to come out, and how as the light faded Captain Merrick's body had resisted that diminishing effect, had intensified, thickened, impinged; and how she felt that if she had reached out and touched him then he could have carried the frail weight, the fleeting sensation, of her fingers on his arm or hand or shoulder into those areas of danger that co-existed with those of the impenetrable comfort that surrounded her, protected her, and barred her exit. He had appalled her, she had not trusted him, although why that was so she did not know clearly. He had stood under the light that lit his face and his need, and his implacable desire to be approached; and offered his hand. He still impinged; what he had done or tried to do for Teddie, did not seem to alter – except in a curious way to emphasize – her picture of him as a man obsessed by self-awareness; but the request for letters might have been genuine.

'Yes, that's Ronald Merrick,' she said. 'Are you sure it's the only one?' She turned the pages of the album. It struck her as disturbingly significant of some kind of failing in all of them that he should have been missed out of the main wedding groups, that none of them had noticed his absence at the time, nor remarked it later when the proofs were chosen and the enlargements made. 'Yes, I remember,' she said, turning back to the one photograph in which he was represented. 'Aunt Fenny couldn't find your hat-box and he went to look for it and then immediately he'd gone there was the fuss about getting the pictures taken while the Nawab was still in the garden.'

'I didn't even know my hat-box was lost,' Susan said, 'but I suppose you'd call that typical.'

'Perhaps he didn't want his picture taken.'

'Oh, everyone likes their picture taken.'

'He may have thought of it being in *The Onlooker* and people recognizing him as the policeman in the Manners case.'

Susan considered this. She smoothed the photograph with one finger as if feeling for an invisible pattern she thought must be there, in the grain of the paper. She said, suddenly, 'Teddie was terribly upset. About that I mean. I don't think he ever forgave him. But I must, mustn't I? I mean I must write and thank him for trying to help Teddie. It's the right thing. Especially the right thing when he's not what Aunt Fenny calls one of us.' She smiled, as to herself, and continued smoothing the surface of the photograph. 'I think I envy him. Not being one of us. Because I don't know what we are, do you, Sarah?' She closed the album abruptly. 'The letter doesn't say which hospital or how badly wounded he is, but if it's a base hospital he must be pretty bad, mustn't he? If I enclose a letter for him when I write to Colonel Selby-Smith it would get sent back to wherever he is, wouldn't it?'

'Yes, that would be best.'

'I should write, shouldn't I?'

'It would be a kind thing to do.'

'Oh, not kind. I don't know kind. I don't know anything. I'm relying on you to say.' She was staring at the letter. 'I need help. I need help from someone like you, who knows.'

'Knows what?'

'What's right, and wrong.'

'Help with the letter?'

'Not just the letter. Everything.' She folded the letter and gave it to Sarah. 'Will you show it to Mother for me?'

'I will, but it would be nice if you showed it.'

'I know.' She was upright on the edge of the bed smoothing the counterpane now. 'But I'd rather not.'

'Why?'

'Mother didn't like Teddie. She didn't want me to marry him. She never said so, but it was obvious. She didn't really want me to marry anyone until Daddy comes back. She wants everything to be in abeyance, doesn't she? – because for her everything is. Everything – especially things about men and women. She didn't talk to me, you know.'

'Talk to you?'

'She made Aunt Fenny do it. Or anyway Aunt Fenny volunteered and Mother let her. I don't think that was right, do you?'

After a moment Sarah said, 'Was there anything you didn't know?'

'Oh, it isn't that. It was that Mother let Aunt Fenny. It made me feel she didn't care enough to make sure herself that I knew about the things I had to let Teddie do. She didn't want any of it to happen, so for her it wasn't happening. But at the time it just seemed to me to prove she didn't care, that nobody cared really.'

Sarah felt cold. Again she did not speak for a moment or two. Then she asked, 'Is that how you thought about it? That making love was just something you had to let Teddie do?'

Susan stopped the smoothing. 'I don't know. I didn't think about it much. All that was on the other side.'

'The other side? The other side of what?'

Sarah saw that her sister's cheeks had become flushed. She seemed, simultaneously, to become conscious of the warmth herself and brought her hands up and held them to her face. She no longer wore the engagement ring: only the plain gold band which had a thick old-fashioned look about it as if it might have been Teddie's mother's – the one relic of a life unhappily ended in Mandalay – although he had never said it was.

'I seem to have lost the knack,' Susan said.

'The knack of what?'

'Of hiding what I really feel. I'm out in the open. Like when you lift a stone and there's something underneath running in circles.'

'Oh, Susan.'

But she felt the truth, the pity of it, and was afraid. The wan hand of a casual premonition had stroked her neck.

Susan looked at her and, as if seeing the hand that Sarah only felt, at once covered her eyes and bowed her head. From under her palms her voice came muffled.

'I used to feel like a drawing that anyone who wanted to could come along and rub out.'

'That's nonsense.'

Susan uncovered her face and looked at Sarah, surveying – Sarah felt – her outline and density. She did not say: No one could ever rub you out. But such a judgement, held suddenly by Sarah of herself, briefly lit her sister's expression – calm, unenvious – without quietening the hectic flush that had reappeared after days of absence.

'No, it's not nonsense.' She looked down at her lap and her now folded hands. 'I felt it even when we were children in Ranpur and here, up in Pankot. I think it must have been something to do with the way Mummy and Daddy, everyone, were always talking about *home*, when we go home, when you go home. I knew "home" was where people lived and I had this idea that in spirit I must be already there and that this explained why in Ranpur and Pankot I was just a drawing people could rub out. But when we got home it wasn't any better. It was worse. I wasn't there either. I wanted to tell someone but there was only you I could talk to and when I looked at you I felt you'd never understand because you didn't look and never looked like someone people could rub out. Do you remember that awful summer? The summer they all came home and great-grandpa died? Well, I looked at them and felt no, they hadn't come home, that they could be rubbed out too and that perhaps I fitted in at last. So I longed to come out again, longed and longed for it. When we did come out we weren't kids any more. I wasn't frightened of India as I was as a kid. But everyone seemed real again and I knew I still didn't fit in because there wasn't anything to me, except my name and what I look like. It's all I had, it's all I have, and it amounts to nothing. But I knew I had to make do with it and I tried, I did try to make it amount to something.'

'I never knew you were frightened.'

'Oh yes. I think I was very frightened. I don't know why exactly. But I was always trying to get to the other side, the side where you and everyone else were, and weren't frightened. It was a sort of wall. Like the one there.' She nodded towards the closed window where Panther had tried to get in and Sarah glanced in that direction, saw that the wall she meant was the one at the end of the patch of garden that hid the servants' quarters. 'Was there a wall like that in the garden at Kabul road?'

'Yes.'

'Dividing the servants from us?'

'Yes.'

'I know I was frightened of the servants. No one else seemed to be. I suppose that was part of it. On the other side of the wall it was very frightening but only frightening to me and I expect I was ashamed and had this idea that if only I could get over I'd be like everyone else.'

'Is that what you wanted? To be like everyone else?'

'Oh, I think so. We do as children. I think that's what I wanted. Of course when we came out again I wasn't frightened any more, I thought of it more as wanting to make a life for myself that would add up just like everyone else's life seemed to add up. I mean everyone seemed so sure, so awfully sure, and I wasn't. I wasn't sure at all. I thought, if only I could make a life for myself, a life like theirs, a life everyone would recognize as a life, then no one could come along and rub me out, no one would try. Marrying Teddie was part of it, the best part, even though I didn't really love him.'

'I wondered,' Sarah said.

'Everybody wondered, didn't they? Well, that's the answer. I didn't. I thought I was in love a score of times, but I knew I wasn't really, not inside where it's supposed to matter, and *that* frightened me too. It proved there wasn't anything inside, but I didn't want to go on being alone. I can remember it as clear as clear, the day I thought, why wait? Why wait for something that's never going

342]

to happen? I'm not equipped. Something's been left out. And I was always good at hiding what I felt, so I thought well, I'll get away with it and nobody will ever know. Whoever I marry will never know. And there was poor Teddie. He walked straight into it, didn't he? I married him because I quite liked him and I thought there probably wasn't much to him either. But I think there was. Yes, I think there was. He almost made me feel there might be something to me, in time. But he had a rotten honeymoon. Rotten.'

She turned, looked straight at Sarah and said:

'Not because I was scared or because he didn't *try* to make things different, but because I'd nothing to give him. That's why he was so pleased when I wrote and told him about the baby. He'd married a girl with nothing to her, but she'd given him something to make up for it. And having it to give him could have made *me* something, couldn't it? Who do I give the baby to now, Sarah? There isn't anybody. And I've nothing for it, except myself. And it's odd, awfully odd, but now when I think about what any of us could give it I can't see the answer.'

She hesitated, but held herself very still, and for a few seconds a half-formed picture came to trouble Sarah of Susan as a child holding herself like that, with the gritty surface of a faded red brick wall dark behind the halo of light on her hair; but the picture would not come more vividly or significantly to life and she could not say whether it was an Indian or an English memory.

'No,' Susan repeated. 'I try and try but I can't see the answer. I suppose the trouble is that people like us were finished years ago, and we know it, but pretend not to and go on as if we thought we still mattered.' Again she hesitated, then, looking full at Sarah again, asked, 'Why are we finished, Sarah? Why don't we matter?'

Because, Sarah thought, silently replying, we don't really believe in it any more. Not really believe. Not in the way I expect grandfather Layton believed — grandfather and those Muirs and Laytons at rest, at peace, fulfilled, sleeping under the hummocky graves, bone of India's bone; and our not believing seems like a betrayal of them, so we can't any longer look each other in the eye and feel good, feel that even the good things some of us might do have anything to them that will be worth remembering. So we hate each other, but daren't speak about it, and hate whatever lies nearest to hand, the country, the people in it, our own changing history that we are part of.

But she could not say this to Susan. Instead she asked, 'Why do you say *we*? *We* may be finished or not matter, or whatever it is. But you matter. I matter.' She wished she could believe it with the simple directness with which she said it. 'There's too much of it. Too much "we". Us. One of us. Oh I agree – one of us, I don't know what *we* are any longer, either. Stop thinking like that. You're a person, not a crowd.'

Again Susan studied her, calmly, but not – Sarah decided – un-enviously, although the degree of heat generated by envy was slight, and said, 'How self-assured you are,' in a tone that reminded her – as a blow might remind – of that afternoon on the houseboat in Srinagar when she had looked at that old woman and heard herself say, 'What a lot you know.' What a lot you know. How self-assured you are. But I am not, not, not. Had *she* not been, that old fragile poised little lady, one of whose hands (she suddenly re-called) rested casually with faded Edwardian elegance on the little pearl buttons of a cream pleated blouse? Well, no, perhaps she had known nothing either, and been certain of nothing except that the years of belief were over and those of disbelief begun.

Sarah shook her head.

'I'm not self-assured at all. But I do know this – the baby matters too.' She meant, but did not say, that Susan had a duty to it. She did not want to use the word. There had been, still was, altogether too much talk of duty, almost none of love.

'Yes, I know,' Susan said. 'Everything must be done that can be. And there's something I've been meaning to ask you. Mother said that if you do it, Aunty Mabel will agree.'

'If I do what?'

'Ask her. About the christening clothes.'

'What do I have to ask about the christening clothes?'

'Whether she'll lend them.'

'What christening clothes are those?'

'Yours. Mine got lost or something. But she still has yours. Barbie told me. She saw them in one of Aunty Mabel's presses when Aziz was doing it out.'

'How did Barbie know they were mine?'

'She asked Aunty Mabel. And that's what Aunty Mabel said. And Mother told me she remembered Aunty Mabel was given your christening gown because it was made up mostly of lace that had belonged to Aunty Mabel's first husband's mother, and of course

344]

Aunty Mabel never had any children so the lace wasn't used and she wanted it to be used for you.' Susan paused. 'I thought perhaps you knew. Hasn't Aunty Mabel ever taken it out and shown you and said, 'Look, this is what you were christened in?''

'No, never.'

'I thought perhaps it might have been a secret you had with her.'

'I never knew Aunty Mabel and I had any secrets. Wasn't the gown used for you too?'

'No. I had something modern, so Mummy said. And it got lost, or didn't last. Not like the lace. I'd like it if the baby could wear the gown you were christened in.'

'I'll ask Aunty Mabel. But it might be old and a bit smelly.'

'No. Barbie said it was beautiful. And that Aunty Mabel must have taken special care of it. There's something else I have to ask. I mean about the christening. Will you be godmother? Mother says Aunt Fenny will expect to be asked, but I don't want that.'

'I shouldn't make a very good one.' Sarah hesitated. 'I don't believe in it.'

To say this she had averted her eyes and in her mind was an image of Aunty Mabel kneeling by a press (as she had never seen her kneel) and holding (as she had never seen her hold) the mysterious gown, inspecting it for signs of age and wear as though it were a relic the god in whom Sarah did not believe had charged her to preserve against the revival of an almost forgotten rite. And glancing back at Susan she thought she saw the convulsive flicker of an ancient terror on the plumped-out but still pretty face.

'I know. But if anything happened to me you'd look after the baby, wouldn't you?'

'Nothing's going to happen to you.'

'But if it *did*.'

'Well, there are plenty of good orphanages.'

'Oh, Sarah – not even as a joke.'

'Then don't ask silly questions. Of course the baby would be looked after.'

'That's not what I'm saying, not what I'm asking. Looked after, looked after. I'm asking if *you'd* look after it, not just to say it would be looked after.'

'Something might happen to me too.'

It was unkind, she thought, the effect that embarrassment had. Of course she would look after the baby.

Susan turned her head, seemed to stare at Teddie's picture. She said, 'Yes, something might happen to you. It will. You'll get married. You'd want your own children. Not mine and Teddie's.'

'You'll get married too.'

'Oh no. Not just to give the child a father. Not again, like that, without really loving. And how can I learn that?'

'You'll love the baby.'

'Shall I?' Susan faced her again.

'When you've got the baby it will be all right, and after a while someone like Dicky Beauvais will ask you to marry him.'

'Not someone like Dicky Beauvais.'

She made it sound as if one phase of her life had ended.

'No, all right. But someone.'

'I shouldn't want to be taken pity on and that's what it would be I expect. Poor Teddie Bingham's widow, a child herself really, how will she manage?' Again she glanced at her dead husband's portrait, searching perhaps for something in his hallowed face that showed not pity but compassion for those he had, without meaning to, left behind to manage as they might.

'I think,' she said, 'that after all it would be better if you wrote to Captain Merrick for me. You could thank him so much more kindly, make him understand how much the Laytons are *beholden* to him for what he tried to do for Teddie. Whatever it was. Whatever it was.' She frowned, getting it seemed no clearer picture from the picture of Teddie of the unwanted gift he had made her of his death; and Sarah – catching the frown, considering the tone and rhythm of that repeated qualification, *whatever it was* – became aware of an element of doubt about the death that had entered for both of them.

'Well if you prefer it,' she said and then wondered: But what shall I say? and felt a little surge of resistance to the idea of saying anything, as though the act of writing would count as a surrender, proof that in the end he had succeeded in making her approach him – as herself, for herself, and as a Layton, for the Laytons.

'You could say I'm not fully recovered from the shock,' Susan went on, 'and tell him about the baby. Remind him, rather. He must have known about the baby. Teddie must have told them all about the baby. I expect they made one of those men's jokes about it. Ragged Teddie I mean, about him becoming a father. Perhaps he won't want reminding, but you'd better mention it, use it as one of the things that excuses me from writing to him myself. But I want him to know, I do want him to know that I am beholden.'

It was a word that apparently fascinated her. Spoken, it created, almost, a cloistered air of peace, of withdrawal from the fierce currents of an angry shock-infested world; it did not lay balm to the little wound of doubt, but the wound nagged less. Beholden, beholden. It was transcendental, selfless, forgiving.

'Who knows,' Susan asked, turning to Sarah with that kind of expression on her face, 'perhaps he's lying somewhere, feeling it, feeling it badly, that he was bad luck for Teddie. Last time it was only a stone, this time I suppose it was a shell or bullets, but they were together again. I want to find out. I think I want to know. I think I want to know because I owe it to Teddie to know what happened, otherwise it's just like someone going out alone. But Captain Merrick will know, then he can tell me. Then Teddie may know I know. Do you think —' but she broke off and had to be prompted.

'Do I think what?'

'Do you think it would be nice if we asked Captain Merrick to be godfather?'

'No, I don't.'

'Why not?'

'I don't know. I just don't think it would be.'

'You mean perhaps he doesn't believe in it either. But he did perform a Christian act, didn't he, and it's that that counts, not going to church and making a fuss. It says in the letter, rendered the utmost assistance in spite of being wounded, rendered the utmost assistance and stayed with Teddie until the arrival of medical aid. He was trying to save Teddie's life. Not just for Teddie's sake, but for the baby's probably, and mine too. So I think we ought to ask, and not care what people like Aunt Fenny would think.'

'What would people like Aunt Fenny think?'

'They might think he wasn't suitable, a suitable sort of person.'

'Because he isn't one of us?'

'Yes.'

But, Sarah thought, remembering the night of the fireflies, in a way he is, is, is one of us; the dark side, the arcane side. But at once recollected the question she had asked herself on that occasion: Why should I question his sincerity?

Her resistance ebbed and yet still, as she said, 'Well I shouldn't worry about what Aunt Fenny might say' – thereby implying her

approval of the way being opened to god-relationship with him –
she felt the backlash of that strange dismay which the thought, the
remembered impact, and the new notion of him as the dark side of
their history filled her with; and he became at once inseparable from
the image of the woman in white, of someone – anyone – who
found it necessary to plead with him for an alleviation of suffering
of which – if only unintentionally – he had been the cause.

'It can be done by proxy, can't it?' Susan was saying. 'If he
agrees. He can be godfather without actually being at the christening.'

'Yes, I think so.'

'And it might help him to get better, to know we wanted him for
that. Teddie said he used to be sorry for Captain Merrick before all
that bother he caused at the wedding. He never got any letters, or
almost never. I think that's as much the reason Teddie asked him
to be best man as the fact that they shared quarters. Teddie was very
upset about the stone. But he had a tender heart.'

'Well, and so have you.'

'Oh, no.' She looked down at her hands. 'I have no heart at all.'
Again she looked up. 'Will you do that for me, Sarah, then? Write
for me and find out where he is?'

'Yes, I'll do that.'

But there was no need for that particular letter. The day following there was a note from Captain Merrick himself; a note to
Sarah, which Sarah showed to Susan. And when Susan had read it
she cried out because she was convinced from certain signs and
portents in the note that Captain Merrick no longer had the use of
eyes or limbs.

•

143 British Military Hospital
AFPO 12
17 May 1944

Dear Miss Layton,

By now I expect you will have been told that Teddie was killed,
just three weeks ago, but in case there has been some error or delay
I've thought it wiser to write to you and not to Susan. Perhaps I
would have done so in any case. I'm not very good at expressing
myself on paper and would find it difficult to write a letter to her.

You will find the right words to convey my feelings to her, I am certain, feelings of sympathy and, I suppose, helplessness in the face of what I know to her must be, for the moment, overwhelmingly sad circumstances. I am as you can see from the address and perhaps the handwriting which is that of one of the nursing sisters here, *hors de combat*, but my improvement is, I am told – and feel – steadily satisfactory. Perhaps someone from the formation has already told Susan this, but in case not – I must tell you that I was with Teddie at the time. That of the two of us it should have been I who came out of it strikes me as supremely illogical – for there was Teddie with everything to live for, and I – comparatively – with something less than that. It should have been the other way round that it happened. Yes, indeed it should.

I am to undergo some more surgery, not here but in Calcutta, so they tell me, and after that can look forward to a period of convalescence and then some sick leave by which time it will have been settled about the future. I should be grateful, of course, to have news, some assurance about your sister's state of mind and health, if you could spare a moment to drop me a line (care of this place – it would be forwarded – I go within a day or two possibly). That business lies a bit heavily. All sorts of things go through my mind. I wish I could speak of them more directly to you. Meanwhile my kind regards to you both, and to your mother. I hope you have had recent good news of your father. Sincerely yours, (for) Ronald Merrick (S.P., QAIMNS).

'You could go and see him,' Susan said. 'You could stay with Aunt Fenny and go and see him when they take him to Calcutta.'

'Aunt Fenny could do that.'

'No, not Aunt Fenny. You. He didn't like Aunt Fenny. He didn't like me either. But he liked you. And it's you he's written to. He wants to talk to you.'

After this Susan relapsed into silence. She sat most of that day on the veranda, staring at the red brick wall, while Panther lay beside her, guarding her from those invisible demons which dumb animals perceive as ever-present in human sorrow and abstraction. And long before it began to be said in Pankot that Susan Layton had become dangerously withdrawn (so that among those who remembered, the name and history of Poppy Browning's daughter began to be spoken of) the servants who lived behind that wall observed this fact for themselves and recalled the fateful augury of the monstrous birth high up in the remote hills. In secret places about the bunga-low garden they disposed offerings of milk to quench the thirst, and flowers to appease with sweet perfumes the uncertain temper, of both good and evil spirits.

*

At the entrance to Flagstaff House there was a narrow open-fronted wooden hut, almost the duplicate of the sentry box that stood inside the gateway, but sheltering a book, not a man. The book was chained to the shelf on which it rested. A pencil, also chained, lay in the groove formed in the middle by the open leaves. Every evening a servant came down the drive, unchained the book, took it back to the house and left it on a table in the entrance hall. In the morning the book was returned to the hut. As well as the book there was a small wooden box with a slot cut in its lid, wide enough to take a visiting card. The box, too, was taken every evening into the house and returned next day. The book and the box were the means by which a visitor to or someone newly stationed in Pankot made an official call on the Area Commander. In the old days the call had been obligatory but nowadays a sig-nature in the book or a card in the box was an indication of the presence in (or departure from) Pankot of someone to whom the old forms were still important or who knew them to be considered important to Flagstaff House and felt that to displease its incum-bents was not a dignified thing to do.

It was in the book that Lady Manners announced her presence, one day towards the end of May – Lady Manners, or her ghost, or someone playing a joke, for no address was given beyond the bleak indication of permanent residence, Rawalpindi; no one in Pankot had seen her or knew where she could be staying, and the sentries who had been on duty between 9 a.m. and 5 p.m. could not recall, with the degree of certainty Isobel Rankin hoped for when having them questioned by the steward, anyone reaching the gate on foot, by car, by tonga who had not entered but had gone to the book, signed and departed and who answered a description suited to the name, the rank, the whole condition which Mrs Rankin had in her mind as definitive of that unhappy woman.

Well, the servants would know, anyone's servants would know. But they did not, or pretended they did not, and so great an incidence of pretence was unlikely enough to confirm their denials. Where, then? Clearly not on the Pankot side of Pankot, the side, the real side, reached by taking that right-hand fork from the bazaar that led – gradually – to those majestic heights on which stood the summer residence which Lady Manners had once had the freedom of, all those years ago, longer than anyone now on station including old Mabel Layton, who had not bought Rose Cottage until a year in the thirties when the Manners régime was over, could remember; and which now – this season – once again stood empty. So, then, the other side, where English people never went. Certainly, yes, that would be like her, to come to Pankot and seclude herself among those who belonged to the other side. In Pankot these days there were several Indian officers, and some of them had wives (fragile, shy creatures whom Isobel Rankin took pains with) and they might know. But did not. It was a mystery. And why (if she were truly there and it was no joke, no spirit-mark – that signature) had she signed at all? And had she come alone, or with an entourage? Where was the child? Was the signature a form of apology, a first hesitant step back into the good opinion of her race? Or the opposite of that?

And it was strange, Pankot thought, or if not strange certainly not uninteresting, that two of the marginal actors in the comedy or tragedy of the Bibighar Gardens affair (and it depended what mood you were in, which label seemed the more apt) should impinge simultaneously on the consciousness of sensible people who thought it would have been nicer to forget that it had ever happened: Lady Manners who had stood by and let her niece give birth and then taken the revoltingly conceived child to her bosom, and Captain Merrick who was said to have done his duty and had no thanks and now lay wounded as a result of some attempt – the actual details were not clear – to help poor Susan Bingham's husband, the day he was killed in action.

That story of the stone, which Mrs Layton had brought back from Mirat (referring to it casually, as if a stone were thrown at every wedding); the odd little circumstance of Teddie Bingham's scratch best man turning out to be who he was; and the revelation that Merrick had been sent to a backwater after the failure of the police to establish guilt in the Manners case, and then been allowed to enter the army: these burgeoned under the warmth of approbation felt for a man who had stayed with a dying brother officer,

until the stone itself became a symbol of martyrdom they all understood because they felt they shared it; and so, entering their consciousness, Merrick entered Pankot and was, for as long as interest
in him lasted, part of the old hill station, at the still centre of its
awareness of what was meant by the secret pass-phrase: one of us.
One of us. And it did not matter that he was known, thought to be,
not quite that by right. He had become it by example.

'Of course he was in love with her,' Barbie said – and it was
through Barbie's more intimate knowledge and compulsive interpretation of things that were known casually to the Laytons that
there filtered those elements of incidental intelligence which, even
if their accuracy could not be proven, gave the facts the dark, pon-
derable glow of living issues. Yes, he had been in love with the
Manners girl, but she had preferred that Indian, and she more
than anyone else must have been to blame for the fact that he and
his fellow-conspirators were never tried, never brought properly to
book. She hadn't been able to stop them going to prison, but she
had destroyed the case which had been built up so efficiently and
swiftly by Mr Merrick. And obviously he had suffered for that, been
made to pay for it, as men were made to pay. He had been sent to
Sundernagar, just as though he was in disgrace. She had ruined his
career. Well, she was dead, and one must not speak ill of the dead,
and perhaps before she died she had regretted her infatuation. 'And
I do not,' Barbie said, 'well, as a Christian how could I, feel as
strongly as some about the child. We are all God's children. But
that child has not been brought to God.' Old missionary zeal shone
on her ruined parchment face, and there was a picture to be had
by anyone present when she spoke like this, of Barbie storming
down the hill to seek old Lady Manners out and fill her with so
much dread of the Lord that she would go penitent with the child
in her arms to Mr Peplow; although what he would do if she did
had to remain in the shadow of a half conjecture, the child having
no known father, a heathen name, Parvati (which Barbie remembered because that was the name of Siva's consort), and being dark-
skinned into the bargain (so it was said), in witness of the original
sin of its conception.

'No, I wouldn't,' Sarah said, parrying by direct denial Barbie's
question whether she would recognize Lady Manners if she saw
her. She wondered if her mother had let something be known after
all, about her impulsive action in Srinagar.

352]

'But last year you were so close, your mother said.'

'A hundred yards.'

'You must have had a glimpse?'

'Yes, a glimpse.'

It was evening. They moved in the garden among Aunt Mabel's roses, waiting her return from one of the solitary walks she took, stoutly shod; a deaf old woman climbing steep hills, in silence.

Suddenly Barbie said, 'Who is Gillian Waller?'

'I don't know. Why?'

'I thought she might be a relation. Mabel mentions her.'

'Without saying who she is?'

'I mean in her sleep.' Barbie looked embarrassed. 'I go in you know. To make sure. She's become forgetful. Of the light. Her book. She falls asleep with her spectacles on. One is so afraid of danger. Breakage. A splinter in the eye. And on cold nights in winter of insufficient warmth, sitting up asleep not properly covered.'

'You tuck her up.'

'She doesn't know, but you see I owe her. I'm grateful. And I'm a light sleeper myself. The slightest sound wakes me. Of course in the old days in remote parts one felt vigilance laid on one almost by God as a duty and it's become a habit. I sleep best between two and four. I don't need much and I like to be sure. About *her*. I anticipated a *lonely* retirement, you know, most of us do, in the missions. Well, she knew that. She'd seen some of us, growing old and keeping cheerful and doing it on our own. So. Well, that's it. And recently she's become very restless. And then this talking. Well, muttering. Gillian Waller. As if whoever that is, is on her mind. I'm afraid to ask. I hate to seem to pry. She's such a self-contained person. When I first came to Rose Cottage she terrified me. I've always been a great talker. Talk, talk. God is listening, Mr Cleghorn used to say when I caught him out *not*. He was Muzzafirabad, head of the mission there when I took over from Edwina Crane and worried so because they adored her, and I was older than she. It made me talk the more. Talk, Talk. It laps against her. I thought: she'll never stand it. And that made me talk harder. Waves and waves of my talking. Well, she's an edifice and I came to realize it didn't trouble her. She still likes to see me talk even if she can't catch all the words. Rock of ages. The sea pounds and pounds. There are people like that. She's one. Is Susan more cheerful?'

'Not cheerful, but holding on.'

'To what?' Barbie took Sarah's arm. 'To what?' And then, before Sarah could answer, asked, 'Who was Poppy Browning?'

'Poppy Browning? I don't know. Has Aunt Mabel talked about a Poppy Browning too?'

'No. It was gossip I overheard. Would you say that Susan is dangerously withdrawn?'

Sarah stopped, examined a red rose, bent her head to take its scent and again felt the touch of that casual premonition on the back of her neck, so that it seemed to her that she was arrested, suspended, between an uncertain future and a fading history that had something to do with bending her head like this to a bunch of sweet-smelling flowers: not those which Susan threw and she, Sarah, caught, but those there was evidence in an old photograph of her holding on the day of Aunt Fenny's wedding, while Aunty Mabel, half-shadowed by a wide-brimmed hat, stood: an edifice, rock of ages.

'We endure,' she told Barbie. 'We're built for it. In a strange way we're built for it.' But was Susan? She faced Barbie. 'Is that what you overheard? People saying she's withdrawn?'

'Dangerously withdrawn. They stopped when they saw me. Mrs Fosdick, Mrs Paynton, Lucy Smalley. It was Lucy Smalley who was saying – "Yes, the last time I saw her I couldn't help but be reminded of Poppy Browning's daughter." Then they changed the subject.'

'Just talk then, Barbie, not serious concern. Otherwise they'd have roped you in. You're practically part of the family. You'd be the ideal person for someone really worried about Susan to have a word with.'

'Oh I wish,' Barbie said, holding Sarah's arm tight, then letting it go, abruptly, '– but I can't. Go with you. My old headquarters are in Calcutta, you know.'

*

Barbie's ministrations to Aunt Mabel were unobtrusive. She made herself scarce while Sarah followed Mabel along the rear veranda, holding the cradle-basket for the new crop of dead heads. The light had nearly gone. From inside Barbie touched the switch that turned on the globes on the veranda.

'When are you going then?' Mabel asked.

'Tomorrow.'

Mabel nodded, finished attending to the azalea.

'Where will you stay?'

'I rang Aunt Fenny. She'll put me up for a couple of nights.'

'I thought they lived in Delhi.'

'They moved to Calcutta in January.'

They went on to the next flower. Sarah said:

'I wanted to ask you something. Something special.' It was hard to speak up and still soften the blunt edges of a request. 'I wanted to ask you about an old christening gown.'

The capable old hands continued without pause, caressing, turning, searching, nipping; preserving the strength of the plant, coaxing it to vigour and ripe old age with the removal of those decayed relics of its former flowering. I am asking, Sarah thought, to take something like that from her, as well. And wondered if the same thought had occurred, shot home, a sharp wound swiftly healed by acceptance of its necessity – because without speaking Mabel suddenly turned and went inside, leaving Sarah alone there with the basket. There was silence inside the house but presently Barbie came to the french window and beckoned.

'She's in her room and wants you to go in.'

Sarah put the basket down by the chair that was Susan's favourite and followed Barbie through into the hall. The door of Mabel's room, which Sarah had seldom entered, stood open. She tapped, quite loudly. Mabel was on her knees by the open press at the foot of the bed, laying back folds of tissue paper – the same gestures, in exaggerated form, that she used to part foliage to expose the withered blooms on hidden stalks. She turned the last fold, wordlessly exposed the handiwork of a vanished generation. From a distance it was, as Sarah had predicted, yellowed, and perhaps close-to would be brittle-looking; but when she knelt and placed her hand between the lace and the fine lawn that lay beneath it the lace came alive against the pinkness of her skin.

'It's French,' Aunt Mabel said. 'If you like you can let Susan have it.'

'I didn't know about it,' Sarah replied. 'And it's for you to say.' She hesitated. 'It's exquisite.'

There were sprigs of lavender whose scent mixed with those of sandalwood. Around the hem of the lawn undergarment was a half-inch border of seed pearls. She marvelled at the industry gone into decoration that would not be noticed when the gown was worn. On that day, yes, that one day anyway, wearing this she had looked beautiful.

'My first husband's mother was French,' Mabel said. 'When we married he took me there, to see them. His mother's family. We sailed back to India from Marseilles. I never saw them again.'

'And they gave you the lace?'

'No, his mother gave me that in London. I never saw her again either. She was very handsome. He got his looks from her. And his courage. She was dying but we didn't know. She kept it from us. She saw he was happy.'

Sarah moved her hand under the lace. Astonishing. There was a motif of butterflies. They were alive, fluttering above her moving hand.

'It was an old château. Very old.'

'Where her family lived?'

'Yes. There was a tower.' A pause. 'She lived there. An old woman making lace. She was blind. She'd made lace all her life. I think she was a poor relation or an old retainer. I showed them this lace, this piece. His mother gave it to me – for a christening. And they said, It's Claudine's. Come and see her. Claudine made it, you can tell from the butterflies. So we climbed the tower and went into the room right at the top where she lived and worked. She ran her fingers over the lace, and put her hand under it like you're doing and said, "*Ah, oui, pauvre papillon. C'est un de mes prisonniers.*" And then something I didn't understand but which they told me meant her heart bled for the butterflies because they could never fly out of the prison of the lace and make love in the sunshine. She could feel the sunshine on her hands but her hands wove nothing but a prison for God's most delicate creatures.' A pause. 'I asked them to tell her that real butterflies might play in the sunshine but only lived for a day. It was rather silly and sentimental, but she smiled and nodded and took it as a compliment because she knew I was very young and didn't understand.'

Gently Sarah withdrew her hand. The butterflies were still. She thought of the christening to come and of herself standing, perhaps by the side of Ronald Merrick, making vows in the name of a child swaddled in this lace, and knew that she did not want it used for such a purpose, for that occasion. She knew, but could not have explained.

'Please take it,' Mabel said. 'Anyway, I've meant that you should have it one day.'

Sarah began folding the tissue. She shook her head. 'I'm awfully grateful, but I think it should stay here.'

'No, take it,' Mabel repeated. She completed the folding of the gown into the tissue, lifted and held it so that, involuntarily, Sarah raised both hands to receive it. 'It's yours. It says so in my Will. But take it now. I've no use for it. Things shouldn't be kept if they can't be put to use.' She got slowly but quite steadily to her feet, leaving Sarah kneeling, holding the bulked-up tissue. Their glances met, and held. Then, as she turned her head and began to move away, Mabel said:

'You are very young too, but I expect you understand better than I did at your age.'

•

The tonga was still waiting and the driver was lighting his lamps. She told him to drive down to the bazaar, to Jalal-ud-din's. As well as the christening gown Mabel had given her two hundred rupees to help, she said, with her fare and expenses. 'But they've wangled a travel warrant for me,' Sarah had protested, 'and even given me a movement order to make it look as if I'm on official business.' General Rankin, no less than other right-thinking people in Pankot, approved of Sarah Layton's mission. 'Well, it will help with bills,' Mabel had said, 'I expect your mother owes some.'

Between Rose Cottage and the club there was no other traffic. In early June, before the coming of the summer rain, even the Pankot air lost its bite. The heat of the day lingered on into the dark. She longed for rain. Susan's baby would be born in the early weeks of the rain. The mornings would be misty and on days when there was no rain the hills would be vivid green. She sat in the back of the slow-going tonga, holding the parcel, and fancied she could feel the slight pulsation, the flickering of tiny white wings. She became aware of the quietness of the road, its look of desertion, and remembered Barbie's dream of her gallant ride to St John's and her own dream that began with Teddie, who knew where he was going and struck them dumb because of that.

[357

But at the club entrance there were other tongas and from there down the long stretch to the bazaar, with the golf course on her right, and on her left the bungalows that skirted the foot of Central Hill, dominated by the churches of St John's and St Edward's, they passed others, and a military truck, a taxi or two, and presently there were the lights that marked the beginning of the bazaar.

She got down at the tonga stand, told the driver to wait because she wanted him to take her on down to the Pankot Rifles lines. The shops were open, some of them brightly lit so that the few street lamps were paled to nothing. But it was not an hour for civil shopping. Groups of British soldiers eyed her but let her pass without comment, knowing she was not for them. The corporal's chevrons on her sleeves could never trick them into believing otherwise. A white girl was an officer's girl, and probably an officer's daughter. A chokra trotted by her side, offering his services as a little beast of burden. He waited outside Gulab Singh Sahib's pharmacy while she went in and bought toothpaste and toothbrush to use in Calcutta and, as an afterthought, a bottle of toilet water to sweeten the journey. She paid what they owed and wondered where the line was drawn between necessity and luxury, the high cost of living and extravagance; and, outside, gave the three little parcels to the chokra but refused his offer to carry the parcel of tissue and lace.

'Jalal-ud-din's,' she told him and turned towards the store, walking down the arcaded frontage of Pankot's European-style shops; and saw her – the beggar woman who, for Sarah, had become interchangeable as a suppliant figure with the woman in the white saree. And afterwards, because she had concentrated on the figure of the beggar woman, recalled that embarrassing and distressing scene on Mirat station and Merrick's remote face, his muttered rejection of her plea in the same tongue the woman spoke in, she was unsure, as unsure as she was ashamed; unsure that the elderly white woman, half-hidden by a distinguished-looking middle-aged Indian woman, in the act of bending, climbing into a car through a door held open by an Indian driver, whose bulk almost immediately cut her off, was the woman from the houseboat; ashamed because the glimpse she had, the conviction that the woman was Lady Manners, caused her automatically to stop, half turn away, to avoid anything in the nature of a direct physical confrontation, as if – so – she might make up for an earlier impulsive action, eradicate it, rub it out, and identify herself with a collective conspiracy. She was

358]

ashamed to remember the way she stood, awkwardly poised, persuasively conveying in every exaggerated histrionic gesture and change of expression the portrait of a girl who feared she had left something behind at Gulab Singh Sahib's; so that the chokra, concerned, held up the three packages, inviting her to count. Then he pointed to the package she held herself, as though he thought some fit of absent-mindedness had caused her momentarily not to realize that she held it.

She smiled and nodded and faced towards Jalal-ud-din's again, the shame already warming her face; but there was no sign of the car. It had gone swiftly, silently, no doubt turning the corner of the inverted V to take the steep road into West Hill where people like the Laytons never went. She turned again, retraced her steps to the tonga stand and there gave the chokra his anna.

III

'NOW TELL ME,' Aunt Fenny said, 'what have you really come for?'

The flat was air-conditioned. Perhaps that shadow of professional neglect which Uncle Arthur had always seemed to work under had not lifted; but at least he appeared to have reached the point of contact with the earth of its dark rainbow, and found a crock of fairy gold: the flat, its high view far above the roofs of old aristocratic houses, the like of which he had never secured for his and Aunt Fenny's personal use; and a war-time sinecure which, so far as Sarah could make out, involved him in giving lectures of a paramilitary nature to young officers, on the structure of Indian military and civilian administration. He was, she gathered, seconded to a branch of welfare and education which had its eye on the capacity some of these young Englishmen might show for identifying themselves with the problems of a country with which the war alone had brought them in contact. Behind the lectures was a blandishment: Stay on, stay on. 'We give them a picture, you know,' Colonel Grace said, 'of what it's really like in peace-time, eradicate some of those impressions they have, that we're a load of blimps, sitting on our fannies under punkahs and shouting Koi Hai.' To counteract all that they gave them the stuff. The real stuff. Sarah nodded, and the young men – three of those in question – smiled easily. According to Aunt Fenny the flat was usually fuller even than Sarah had found it of Uncle Arthur's 'chaps'. He had conceived it part of the duties of the department he headed to bring the chaps home, or have them call, in groups, swapping the scratch amenities of the temporary mess out at the place where the courses were held, for the more considerable ones of a genuine Anglo-Indian *pied-à-terre*, where they could imbibe, at breakfast, tiffin or dinner, those lessons that went deeper than any mere chat from a rostrum ever could. There had been no British intake into the ICS since the war began and the Indian army was dense with emergency officers of all kinds who had never thought of making a career of arms, least of all in India. Among them, surely, were a few who would get the call, see the vision, understand the hard realities of imperial service and feel the urge to match themselves to them?

'They're mostly what Arthur calls in abeyance,' Fenny told Sarah as she showed her her room – a comfortable little white-walled box, as cold as a refrigerator, with the bulging grey Bengal monsoon sky – which Sarah had never seen in her life before – filling the hermetically sealed window. Overnight from Ranpur she had ridden into the June rain. It would not reach Pankot for a while yet. She felt, from this alone, that she had travelled into another world, so that it amazed her that it was ever possible to make the mistake of thinking of India as one country.

'What kind of abeyance?' (She was thinking of her mother.)

'Oh, you know, between postings, or getting better from jaundice, or just among the crowd that get stuck in depots and training establishments and apply for courses to stop themselves going barmy. We don't get many who are *born* slackers. At least Arthur doesn't bring them back here. Of course they're not usually quite our kind of people' – (Sarah nodded, again, gravely) – 'but then we're a bit of a dying species, aren't we, pet? And they're mostly nice cheerful chaps, and some of them *are* from good homes, and it's usually that kind who are seriously thinking of staying on after the war. Arthur's a great success with them – I think because he responds to them. He feels they genuinely want to know about India and what it's meant to the standard of life they enjoy back home and take so much for granted.'

'I expect you're a success with them too, Aunt Fenny.'

'Oh, I am! Do you know why? Because I'm happy. Isn't it gorgeous —?' She indicated not the room so much as the flat the room was a cold, rather remote, unlived-in part of. 'To be cool. Oh, to be cool.' There had been a time, surely, when Aunt Fenny had dismissed the more modern aspects of twentieth century Anglo-Indian life as unwelcome signs of things going to the dogs. Sarah smiled. She herself preferred to be less cool, but it was nice to see Aunt Fenny enjoying something. This morning the lines of disapproval that fixed the mouth were like marks of an old illness, like smallpox, that had left no other trace. But it was at the moment Sarah was thinking this that Fenny stopped being happy about the flat and reverted to her older, probing, rather suspicious self.

'Now tell me, what have you really come for?'

Sarah told her. When she finished Aunt Fenny said, 'But, pet, couldn't I have done it for you and saved you all this trouble and expense?'

'They gave me a rail warrant.' She hesitated, observed Aunt Fenny's invisible hackles tremble with the effort she was making not to let them rise, and added, 'Susan has this idea he's lost a limb or his eyesight, and that if anyone goes to see him and then writes to her they might not tell her the truth, out of kindness.'

'But I could have seen him and then come up to Pankot.'

'That would have been expense and trouble for you and you could still have kept the facts from her out of kindness. I think she wanted it to be me because she believes she could see through it if I kept anything back.'

Aunt Fenny smiled, touched Sarah's arm.

'Do I detect six of one and half a dozen of another? I mean he took a bit of a shine to you in Mirat. Was it mutual?'

Sarah looked away, unable to take the opportunity to make Aunt Fenny feel less excluded from the question of Captain Merrick's bodily state of health. 'No, not at all. Anyway, I don't think he took a shine. I'm not really looking forward to it, but it seems to be important to Susan, and I'd like to get it over with as soon as possible. Do you think if I turned up this morning they'd let me see him?'

'You'll do no such thing. You'll tuck down here for the rest of the morning and catch up with some sleep. I'll ring the hospital and see what can be arranged for early evening or late afternoon, then you can have a relaxed day, see Mr Merrick at about five o'clock and come back here in time for drinks. Some of the boys are coming in for dinner. Do you really have to go back tomorrow?'

'Yes, I've booked my sleeper from Ranpur to Pankot for to-morrow night.'

'The old midnight special?'

'Yes.'

'So you'll have to be on the midday from Cal to get the con-nexion? What about a reservation? It's not easy at such short notice.'

'Oh, I'll squeeze in. It's not difficult if you don't want a berth. Someone with a berth to Delhi will let me sit in. We get to Ranpur about nine in the evening, long before anyone wants to have their bed made up.'

'Yes, well, all the same I'll ask your uncle to pull some rank. He'll enjoy that. He's just like a boy about being able to say it's Colonel Grace speaking. But get your head down for now, pet. I can tell you didn't have a berth last night. Was it ghastly?'

'No, fun really. I sat up all night with some nurses who were on their way to Shillong.' And envied them, going to the war it seems I can never go to. We played cards and drank rather a lot of gin. And I listened while they discussed men in general and in par-ticular the two officers who tried to get off with the two prettiest girls and had to be firmly ejected from the carriage when the train stopped at Benares. I fell asleep, near Dhanbad. The taste of the journey is still in my mouth.

She sat on the bed and at once knew how tired she was. Over-excited. Like a child. She was aware of Aunt Fenny stooping to unlace her shoes for her. She protested but it was done just the same. Weightless, her legs lifted easily on to the bed. Curtains were drawn. Comforted by all this evidence of family devotion and the softness of the pillow under her head, she fell asleep.

*

Before the taxi reached the Officers' wing of the military hospital the rain stopped. She arrived in bright sunshine and, mounting the steps to the pillared entrance, took off Aunt Fenny's heavy-duty macintosh. She had changed from uniform into mufti — a plain cotton dress whose lightness she was glad of in a humidity that was higher than she had ever experienced. After she had spoken to the English corporal at the desk and been asked to wait she sat and smoked, but the cigarette was damp. She dropped it, unfinished, into the sand-tray. The corporal answered the telephone, then spoke to a colleague whose uniform bore no chevrons. The private came across.

'Miss Layton for Captain Merrick?'

She nodded, followed him out of the reception hall into a corridor where there were lifts. The smell of ether-meth was settling on her stomach. She felt slightly faint. The private gave instructions to the Indian lift attendant then said to her, 'Sister Prior'll meet you at the top.' She thanked him, noticed – and was sorry for the embarrassment they must cause him – the septic spots on cheek and chin, vivid under the glare of the lift lights. He did not meet her glance. He smelt strongly of cheap hair oil. The attendant closed the mesh gates. Slowly they ascended. The letter from Ronald Merrick had been signed by a nurse in the QAIMNS. But she could not remember the initials. Had it been P for Prior? No. It might have been P, but not for Prior because the letter had come from Comilla. There had been no letter from Calcutta.

The lift stopped and the attendant opened the gates. She thanked him and stepped on to the landing. The smell was stronger than ever. A window gave a view of trees and light to a table with flowers on it and chairs for waiting. But she was the only visitor. There was no sign of Sister Prior; the corridors left and right of the waiting-room were empty. Had the lift man let her out on the wrong floor? Or the boy with the pimples misheard the corporal? She went to the window and stared at the trees and the view between them and the vast *maidan* beyond which was the low-lying clutter of the city. A door shut somewhere along one of the corridors, and presently she heard the sound of a woman's footsteps. She turned, waited, and in a moment the woman entered the waiting-room area: a girl, rather, no older than herself, with dark hair rolled under a neat cap.

'Miss Layton? I'm Sister Prior.' She put out her hand, which Sarah took. The overall scrutiny she was under did not escape her. She wondered whether Sister Prior was the sort who would fall in love with a patient – in love with Merrick, for instance – and be jealously possessive of him. But she had scarcely had time.

'Am I upsetting regular visiting hours?' Sarah asked. Her hand had been let go of rather suddenly.

'That's all right. The message from your – uncle? Colonel —?'

'Colonel Grace.'

'Grace. Well, he said you'd come a long way.'

But Sister Prior made no move. They eyed each other levelly. The same height, Sarah thought, as well as the same age.

'I didn't quite get the relationship. You *are* a relative, aren't you?'

'No.'

'Well, I thought it was odd. I'd always understood he had none. I mean none at home let alone out here. But matron was under the impression from Colonel Grace there was a family connexion.'

'I expect he mentioned my sister. Captain Merrick was best man at her wedding.' She paused, intending not to explain further, but found herself doing so. 'I'm really here on her behalf. We had a letter from him when he was in Comilla.'

'Yes, I see. I haven't told him you're coming. I thought I wouldn't in case you didn't turn up and he was disappointed. But I'll go and tell him now. If I just say Miss Layton will that be enough?'

'Enough, but a bit of a surprise. I live in Pankot.'

'Where?'

'It's a hill station north of Ranpur.'

'Oh. Yes, you have come a long way, haven't you? Is your sister in Calcutta, too?'

'She couldn't travel.'

'Isn't she well?'

'She's having a baby. It's due in three weeks.'

'I see. I hope you don't mind my asking all these questions. Ronald is rather a special case with us. He's been wonderfully brave. But we think terribly lonely. Do you know anything about his family?'

'No, nothing.'

'His record shows his next-of-kin as a cousin of some sort. Both his parents died before the war. I think it was a late marriage. I mean they were quite old. And he has no brothers and sisters, and then of course he's never married himself. And until we heard from Colonel Grace today we were under the impression he had no close friends. I mean the only letters he gets are the official sort. And since he's been here he's never asked me to write a personal letter to anyone, so I've been wondering, I mean how you knew where he was.'

'He wrote us from Comilla and said he was being transferred to

Calcutta. Someone on General Rankin's staff at Pankot checked for us and got the hospital in Comilla to send us a signal where we could contact him. My sister's concerned rather specially. Captain Merrick was wounded at the same time her husband was killed.'

'Oh, I'm sorry. About her husband.'

Sister Prior had not once let her glance fall away. Sarah felt her own fixed by it. 'I'm sure he'll be glad to see you, and I do appreciate your coming such a very long way, but I hope you won't find it necessary to ask him too many questions on your sister's behalf. We try not to let them dwell too much on what happened.'

'I haven't come to ask questions. I've come mainly to tell him how grateful my sister is for what he tried to do to help her husband, in spite of being wounded himself. We don't know exactly what it was he did do, and I'm sure he won't talk about it even if I ask, but it was something that led the divisional commander to send in a recommendation.'

'A recommendation?'

'Yes.'

'You mean for a decoration?'

'Yes.'

'Does he know that?'

'Probably not.'

'I hope you won't mention it.'

'I won't mention it.'

'I suppose decorations serve some sort of purpose. I never see what, myself. But then I've seen too much of what earning them involves. I always think a thumping great cheque would fill the bill better. What can you do with a medal except stick it on their chests and leave them to stick it in a drawer? I expect that shocks you. With an uncle who's a colonel.'

'My father's a colonel too.' About to add: And it doesn't shock me: she changed her mind and said instead, 'I'll wait here while you break the news to Captain Merrick that I've called to see him.'

Sister Prior nodded. A smile – of distant irony – momentarily broadened her pretty lips. Sarah turned, embattled behind the barriers of her class and traditions because the girl had challenged her to stand up for them. Hearing Sister Prior's retreating footsteps she realized the opportunity to prepare herself for whatever it was she had to face in Ronald Merrick's room had gone. Perhaps in any case it would have been deliberately withheld. The sight

[365

might be shocking, and it might please Sister Prior to watch how she took it. She lit another of the damp cigarettes, gathered her things together: Aunt Fenny's macintosh, the box of fruit, the carton of two hundred Three Castles cigarettes packed in four round tins of fifty each. She wished to be ready to go with Sister Prior directly she returned. But the minutes ticked by. It was nearly five o'clock. Occasionally there were footsteps in the corridors, and the sound of doors opened and closed. Voices, once. And the rising clank and whisper of the lift. At five o'clock a dark-skinned Anglo-Indian nurse appeared, coming from the direction Sister Prior had taken.

'Miss Layton? Captain Merrick will see you now.'

She followed the girl down the corridor. Reaching a door numbered 27, which bore beneath a circular observation window a card in a metal frame in which was written in black ink, Captain R. Merrick, the girl tapped, opened and said, 'Miss Layton to see you, Captain Merrick,' and stood aside. Entering, Sarah halted abruptly, shocked to see him on his feet and coming towards her, aided by a stick, dragging the weight of one plastered leg – until, coming to her senses, she saw that the man was not Merrick but a tall burly fellow who smiled and said, 'He's all yours. Ignore me. I was just visiting.' Automatically she smiled in return and looking beyond him saw Merrick in the bed by the window – or anyway a figure lying there, propped by pillows. A complex of bandage and gauze around the head, like a white helmet, left only the features and a narrow area of the cheeks exposed. The sheet that covered his body was laid over a semi-circular frame. She could see nothing of him except the small exposed area of the face and blue-pyjamaed chest and shoulders. His arms were under the arch of the sheet. His head was inclined a little to one side. He was looking at her. As she moved towards him she heard the door shut.

She said, 'Hello, Ronald,' and was then at the bedside. The down-draught from a fan whirling gently above held the sheet pressed against the frame. She could see the pattern of the mesh. She had an unpleasant idea that there was nothing beneath the frame, that what she could see was somehow all that was left of him, although she knew that was not possible. Embarrassed, she switched her glance quickly back to his face, determined to hold it there. He looked younger than she remembered, younger even than in that one and only photograph, as if pain had smoothed out

366]

his face and brought a glow of innocence to his complexion. She could not see his chin, but the upper lip was shaved. She wondered how he managed. And then remembered Sister Prior.

'I've brought you some fruit and cigarettes. I hope that's all right. I remembered you smoked.' She put the packages on the bed-side-table which was empty except for an invalid teapot from which she imagined he was given water. She glanced at him again as she did so, and saw him swallow. Perhaps he had difficulty with his voice. His eyes were closed now, but as she moved round to sit on the chair at the other side of the bed he opened them and watched her. Yes, they were blue. Extraordinarily blue. He swallowed again.

'I'm sorry,' he said, 'I thought Sister Prior was playing some kind of practical joke, or that I was funny in the head because she's not really the joking kind. How is Susan?'

'She's fine. She sent her love. And Mother of course. And Aunt Fenny. She and Uncle Arthur are in Calcutta now. She'll come and see you in a day or two. She asked me to be sure to find out if there's anything you need.'

'That's very kind of her. And kind of you. Are you in Calcutta long?'

'No, I go back tomorrow.'

'To Pankot?'

She nodded.

He said, 'Do smoke. There are some in the drawer.'

'Can I light one for you?'

'I'm afraid it involves more than that. I can't hold anything yet.'

She lit a cigarette from her own case, then – overcoming the reluctance she felt to do so – a mixture of embarrassment and faint revulsion – she stood, leaned forward and held the cigarette near his lips. He moved his head to help her place the tip in his mouth.

'I'm afraid they're very damp.'

He released the cigarette, let his head back on to the pillow and blew out slowly, without inhaling. After a moment's hesitation she inhaled from the cigarette herself. The sharing of the cigarette was an unexpected intimacy. For a while they smoked alternately.

'Your hands,' he said, 'smell so much nicer than Sister Prior's. She's a bit of a dragon.'

'A very pretty dragon.'

'You think so?'

'Don't you?'

'A man in hospital's no judge. All the nurses look pretty, but it's their hands and throats and elbows that count in the end. Sister Prior has very cold hands and red elbows. I'm not sure she hasn't got goitre too. The fact is she depresses me a bit. Sister Pawle in Comilla was much more like it. She's the one who wrote that letter for me. I was beginning to wonder whether it reached you. But this is miles better. Miles, miles better. And thanks for just turning up. You get used to taking the days as they come and it's better not to look forward to anything that isn't routine. But when you've gone I'll have something special to look back on, and count by, that I wasn't expecting.'

She held the cigarette for him but he shut his eyes briefly and thanked her, said he'd had enough. He couldn't actually stop smoking, but it did make him a bit dizzy. Sister Prior was slowly breaking him of the habit.

'What time do you go back tomorrow?' he asked.

'I ought to catch the midday train.'

'Then I shan't see you again.'

'I could come tomorrow morning. Would you like me to?'

His eyes were shut again.

'Oh, I should like it. But they wouldn't. They have other plans for me tomorrow. It's a good thing you turned up today.'

She waited for an explanation. When it seemed there wasn't to be one she asked him directly, 'Is it the surgery you mentioned in your letter?'

He nodded. He opened his eyes but didn't look at her. 'They were going to do it sooner. But I didn't travel as well as they expected. They made me feel like a bottle of wine when they said that. That I hadn't travelled well.'

'Did they fly you out?'

'Yes, it was fun. I've never flown in my life before, until all this. They flew me out of Imphal first, and then from Comilla. I've clocked up about three hours, I think. On my back though. It's an odd feeling flying on your back. You think of yourself as totally invulnerable. Well, you do taking off and in the air. Landing's a bit of a jolt. The chap who was in here when you arrived pranged on Dum-Dum a couple of weeks ago, coming in from Agartala. Extraordinary. The plane was a write-off, but he only bust a leg.'

She said after a while, 'Do you want to tell me about tomorrow, about what they're doing?'

He turned his head towards her, as if to study the depth of her interest.

'Oh, they'll poke about and come up with something and tell me afterwards. And don't be fooled. I look as weak as a kitten, I know, but I'm full of beans under this dopey exterior. Otherwise they wouldn't be doing it yet.'

'What time are they doing it?'

'Nine o'clock. Unless there's an emergency. I mean, not me. Someone else. I'm not a priority. Don't worry. I'm all right.'

'If I rang at about midday I expect they'd tell me how it went.'

'Yes, I'm sure they would.'

'Then I'll do that.'

'Thank you.' A pause. 'Teddie told me Susan was having a baby. He was very proud.'

'It's due next month. In about three weeks.'

He said, 'I expect she hopes it will be a boy.'

'I don't think she minds.'

Again he shut his eyes. 'What do you say?' he asked. 'She was such a happy girl. It's the happy people who are hardest hit when something like that happens. Teddie was a happy sort of man, too. They seemed made for each other. Well, I suppose that kind of happiness means there's a basic resilience, and that when she's got over the shock she'll come up smiling. Although —'

'Although what?'

'She struck me as happy in the way a little girl is. Perhaps that's a protection too. It interested me, the difference between you both.'

He brought the sentence to an abrupt end. She felt the full-stop. They had entered a zone of silence. For a moment she imagined he had fallen asleep, exhausted by the visit and unable to cope with the demands it made on him. Perhaps he was already under sedation, in preparation for whatever they were going to do to him in the morning. She felt a stirring of morbid curiosity, the beginning of a distasteful urge to draw the sheet away and observe the condition of his legs and abdomen, and arms from elbow downwards.

'I expect there are things you both want to know.'

She glanced up quickly.

'I hope my letter didn't worry you,' he added. 'Did you show it to Susan?'

'Yes, I did.' She hesitated. 'It did worry us a bit.'

'I'm sorry. Did anyone ever write to her from the division?'

'She had one the day before from Colonel Selby-Smith, so she knew you and Teddie had been together when it happened. He said you'd helped him. That's one of the reasons I'm here, to tell you how grateful she is. Well, all of us. And of course she's looking for reassurance, that you're all right, or going to be. The letter from Colonel Selby-Smith seemed to hint that what you tried to do to help Teddie made things worse for you. What worried us about your letter was that it had to be dictated.'

'Yes, I see.'

She waited, expecting an explanation, or a comment; the reassurance that she could take back to Susan. When it did not come it was, perversely, not concern for him – which might have filled her – but renewed reluctance to be drawn towards him which she felt; and this seemed to empty her. She thought, almost abruptly: He lacks a particular quality, the quality of candour; there is a point, an important point, at which it becomes difficult to deal with him. He isn't shut off. It isn't that. He's open, wide open, and he wants me to enter, to ask him about the legs I can't see, the forearms I can't see, the obscene mystery beneath the white helmet of bandages. But I won't. They, or their absence, their mystery – these I find appalling as well. It's unfair, perhaps inhuman of me. On the other hand, it can't be inhuman because I feel it, and I belong to the species, I'm a fully paid up member.

He had turned away, aware – possibly – that the purely physical equation of their eyes, meeting, lacked a value. When he began speaking she wondered whether the way in was being widened; salted, like the way in to a dangerous, derelict mine. She found herself exerting pressure on the ground with the soles of her feet and on her chair with the small of her back.

'I thought it might be something else that worried you,' he said, 'that thing I said about the business lying heavily and wanting to talk about it. Get it off my chest. As if I had some sort of confession to make.'

'Have you, Ronald?'

He turned again, stared at her. He smiled slightly.

'Well, we all have, I suppose. The fact is I feel responsible. Perhaps there's something about me that attracts disaster, not for myself, but for others. Do you think that's possible? That someone can be bad luck?'

'Perhaps.'

'I was the worst best man Teddie could have chosen. Remember me saying that? That night I came to say goodbye and found you watching fireflies?'

'Waiting for them. Yes, I do remember.'

'You denied I was the worst, but that didn't fool me. Teddie wasn't fooled either. When I saw him again he'd cooled off. I could see him putting distance between us. Oh, I'm sure there's something in it. You find you have – a victim. You haven't chosen him. But that's what he is. Afterwards he haunts you, just as if he were on your conscience. The irony is that you don't really have him there. You can question your conscience and come out with a clean bill. But he sticks, just the same. Teddie sticks. And that has a certain irony in it. I'm sorry. I'm making it worse. I mean, giving you more cause to worry, not less.'

'It was Susan who worried. But just about you and how you really are and how much of what is wrong is due to your staying and looking after Teddie.'

'Staying?'

'She was told you stayed with him until the arrival of medical aid.'

'I suppose that was one way of putting it, but there wasn't any alternative. Well, make that clear to her. We were both up the creek. The question is why? Whose creek?'

He closed his eyes again, and this time it occurred to her that closing them was deliberate, part of a total effect he was seeking to make. His voice was quite strong; it showed no real sign of fatigue.

'You see, I ask myself, continually ask myself, whatever fault it may have been of his, would it have happened if I hadn't been with him? And the answer is no. It wouldn't. It was the stone all over again. The stone that hit the car. Only this time it wasn't a stone. And of course it wasn't thrown at me. Everything about it was different, but the same. In effect.'

She said, 'You're imagining it. You ought to forget it and concentrate on getting better.'

He lay for a while, not speaking, not looking.

'No,' he said suddenly, so that she was almost startled. 'One doesn't get better by not facing it. Besides, I was fond of him. I may have envied him too. You know how it is. He had all the attributes, didn't he? The game. Playing it. I mean really believing that it was. Astonishing, because it's not a game, is it? Unless you play it, then I suppose that's what it becomes. I keep on telling myself that it was playing the game that killed him, so that his death becomes a kind of joke. Only I can't see it. To me it was just a mess that he wouldn't have got into without me.'

He turned again and watched her.

'I'm telling you, not Susan. I couldn't tell Susan. For her I'd play the game myself. But with you it isn't necessary, is it?'

'No, it's not necessary.'

'Anyway, you'd see through it. I lack the attributes. You notice things like that, but I feel you don't mind, that it doesn't matter to you that I'm not — not like Teddie. It mattered to Teddie. It made him over-meticulous about the rules. He was trying to point the difference between us. He never quite forgave me for what happened at the wedding. He didn't say much, but he made me feel — intended to make me feel — that I'd done something not quite — pukka — getting involved in that sort of thing, accepting the intimacy he offered when he asked me to be best man but failing to tell him just who he was inviting intimacy with. It was the sort of situation you couldn't actually say was wrong. All you could say was it wouldn't have happened if, for instance, I'd been a Muzzy Guide — wouldn't have happened then because a fellow-officer in the true sense of the word wouldn't have any — what? Areas of professional secrecy? He wasn't blaming me. He saw how reasonable it was for me not to go round saying, Look, I'm the police officer in the Manners case, and I get threatening anonymous notes, and any day someone might chuck a stone at me and involve me and whoever I'm with in an embarrassing public scene. Yes, he saw that. All the same he resented *being* involved. He saw it as an unnecessary vulgarity, one that marked the difference between my world and his. He recognized that these two worlds had to meet, I mean in war-time, but that didn't mean he had to like it or encourage the intimacy to continue. We had one brief talk after he'd got back from Nanoora and joined the General and the advance party in the training area we went to, and of course he said all the right things, that I had absolutely nothing to apologize for or explain; but after that he never mentioned Mirat to me again. When I say he told me about Susan having a baby, that isn't strictly true. He told someone else, and it came up in mess — as a cause for general congratulation. Well, you know. One makes a sort of

372]

joke about it. It was quite a night. We were pushing the boat out because the orders had just come from Corps to move the division down into the field. They were all a bit high. Which is partly why Teddie let it out, that he was going to be a father. And that was the night I really knew that he did resent having got mixed up socially with a chap who wasn't a Muzzy Guide or its equivalent. He was laughing at the things the others said to him. But when I congratulated him and asked him to give you and Susan my kind regards he became frigidly polite.'

'You're exaggerating. Teddie wasn't like that.' But she guessed that Teddie had been. 'Anyway, he sent on your kind regards.'

'Oh, but he would. He said "Yes of course. I'll do that." And that was his *word*. The frigidness and politeness were due to him turning it over in his mind first, whether he should agree or say "No, I think not if you don't mind, Merrick".'

'You make him sound terribly old-fashioned.'

'He was.' A pause. 'He believed in the old-fashioned virtues. The junior officers in a war-time divisional HQ are a pretty hybrid bunch. They divide, you know, into the amateurs and the professionals. But there's a paradox, because the professionals are invariably the temporary chaps like me. The amateurs are the permanent men like Teddie, who see it as a game. But even among *them* Teddie stood out as an anachronism. He had old-fashioned convictions. So did a lot of them. But in Teddie you felt he had the courage that was supposed to go with them. And when I look at it squarely, it was having that kind of courage that killed him. But he died an amateur. He should have had a horse.'

'The Muzzy Guides used to.'

'I know.'

Again he closed his eyes.

She said, 'What do you mean, he died an amateur?'

'I'll tell you, but I don't want you to tell Susan.'

'I can't promise not to.'

He smiled, but kept his eyes shut.

She said, 'She may prefer to know he died that way.'

'Yes,' he said presently. 'In its way it had a certain gallantry.' He paused, opened his eyes, glanced at her. 'You know about the Jiffs?'

'Jiffs?'

'They're what we call Indian soldiers who were once prisoners of the Japanese in Burma and Malaya, chaps who turned coat and formed themselves into army formations to help the enemy. There were a lot of them in that attempt the Japanese made to invade India through Imphal.'

'Yes, I've heard of them. Were there really a lot?'

'I'm afraid so. And officers like Teddie took it to heart. They couldn't believe Indian soldiers who'd eaten the king's salt and been proud to serve in the army generation after generation could be suborned like that, buy their way out of prison camp by turning coat, come armed hand in hand with the Japs to fight their own countrymen, fight the very officers who had trained them, cared for them and earned their respect. Well, you know. The regimental mystique. It goes deep. Teddie was always afraid of finding there were old Muzzy Guides among them. And of course that's what he did find. If Teddie had been the crying kind, I think he'd have cried. That would have been better, if he'd accepted the fact, had a good cry, then shrugged his shoulders and said, Well, that's life, once they were good soldiers, now they're traitors, shoot the lot.' Merrick hesitated. 'A lot *were* being shot. Our own soldiers despised them. They were a pretty poor bunch, badly led, badly equipped. And I suppose underneath the feeling artificially inspired by their propaganda – that they were the real patriots, fighting for India's independence – they were, deep down, bent with shame. The Japanese despised them too. They seldom used them in a truly combatant role and left them in the lurch time after time. Anyway, that's the picture we were getting, and we were also getting a picture of our own troops, Indian and British, killing them off rather than taking prisoners. That wasn't what we wanted. The whole thing of the Jiffs became rather my special pigeon in divisional intelligence. And I was trying to get a different picture. I wanted prisoners. Prisoners who would talk, talk about the whole thing, recruitment back in Malaya and Burma, inducements, pressures, promises. Which Indian officers had gone for the thing and which had only been sheep. When it came to the question of Indian King's commissioned officers who had joined the Jiffs, Teddie preserved a sort of tight-lipped silence. He made you feel an officer who turned traitor was probably best dead anyway, unmentionable, quite unspeakable. And perhaps not really a shock, because to him an educated Indian meant a political Indian. But the sepoys, NCOs and VCOs were a different matter. It's those he would have cried for. All those chaps whose fathers served before them, and had medals, and little chits from old commanding officers. Sometimes he said a lot of them probably joined so as to get back on their own side, and that in any major confrontation the Jiffs would come over and help kick the Japanese in the teeth. He became obsessed with the whole question. He seldom talked of anything else, to me anyway, because the Jiffs were my pigeon, and in a subtle way he used the Jiffs, his views on them, and mine, to point up the differences between us. Do you know what distinguishes the amateur?'

Sarah shook her head.

'The affection he has for his task, its end, its means and everyone who's involved with him in it. Most professional soldiers are amateurs. They love their men, their equipment, their regiments. In a special way they love their enemies too. It's common to most walks of life, isn't it? To fall in love with the means as well as the end of an occupation?'

'You think that's wrong?'

'Yes, I think it is. It's a confusion. It dilutes the purity of an act. It blinds you to the truth of a situation. It hedges everything about with a mystique. One should not be confused in this way.'

'Are you never confused, Ronald?'

'I am – frequently confused. But I do try to act, unemotionally. I do try for a certain professional detachment.'

'It's funny,' she said, 'I should have said you were actually quite an emotional person. Underneath. And that it sometimes runs you into trouble.'

He was watching her, but she detected nothing in his expression except – and this so suddenly that she felt she had observed it the moment that it fell on him – a curious serenity. 'Well, of course, you're right,' he said. 'I've certainly run into trouble in my time. It's one thing to try to act unemotionally and quite another thing to do so. No act is performed without a decision being made to perform it. I suppose emotion goes into a decision, especially into a major decision. My decision to get out of the police and into the army was an emotional one, wasn't it? Just like the one I made as a boy, to try to get into the Indian Police. But I don't think I was ever an amateur, either as a copper or a soldier. I had no affection for the job, in either case. But I did the job. I tried not to be confused. That was the difference between Teddie and me – the *real* difference, not the one that had to do with the fact that Teddie was a

Muzzy Guide and I was, well, what I am – a boy from an elementary school who won a scholarship to a better one and found it difficult later not to be a bit ashamed of his parents, and very much ashamed of his grandparents. But any difference that Teddie saw in our attitudes, he'd always put down to the fact that I wasn't the same class. You can't disguise it, can you? It comes out in subtle ways, even when you've learned the things to say and how to say them. It comes out in not knowing the places or the people your kind of people know, it comes out in the lack of points of common contact. People like me carry around with them the vacuum of their own anonymous history, and there comes a moment when a fellow like Teddie looks at us and honestly believes we lack a vital gift as well, some sort of sense of inborn decency that's not our fault but makes us not quite trustworthy. I'm sorry. I'm not speaking ill of him. That's what he thought. And that's why he was killed. I'm only trying to make it clear, make this background clear. He was killed trying to show me how a thing should be done, because he didn't trust me to do it right. Well, it was his own fault – but remove me from the situation and it wouldn't have happened.'

'What situation?'

He closed his eyes again and turned his head away. 'What situation? It was a simpler one than – another I remember. It began with a fellow called Mohammed Baksh. A Jiff. He was captured by a patrol from one of the companies of the British battalion of the Brigade that was probing forward on our right flank. Overnight things had become terribly confused and by morning the British battalion had found itself out on a limb. The advance of the Indian battalion on their left had been held up and it looked as if the British battalion might get cut off or have its flank turned. They were astride a road in hill country and we hadn't got a clear picture of the enemy's strength, or of where the major enemy attack was likely to come from. And this particular Brigadier was suffering from a bout of jitters, he was jumpy about losing his British battalion and wanted to pull them back, but the General had other ideas, of pushing another battalion forward astride the road and deploying both battalions to encircle whatever enemy units there were in the immediate vicinity. But he didn't want to issue the order without personal contact with the Brigadier. He decided to visit the Brigade and get things moving from there, unless he judged the

Brigadier's on-the-spot appreciation had something to be said for it, or he thought him incapable of pressing forward immediately with the right sort of enthusiasm. He took Teddie with him. And at the last moment he turned to me and told me to go with them to make sure the Brigade Intelligence Officer had a complete picture of what we knew, and to assess on the spot anything he might be able to add that would be new to us.' A pause. 'We went in two jeeps. There were three in the General's. The General, Teddie, and the Indian driver, two in mine, myself and my driver. Teddie drove the other jeep. He loved driving. A jeep particularly. And the driver liked sitting perched at the back, with a Sten gun. It was a lovely morning. Bright and crisp. During the day of course it got very hot. Have you ever been in Manipur?'

'No.'

'On the plain itself, around Imphal, it's like northern India up in the North-west Frontier, around Abbotabad; much the same view of hills and mountains. We were south of there, in the foot-hills. The road was pretty rough. Steep wooded banks one side, pretty long wooded drops the other – well, for much of its course. You flattened out every so often, when you went through a village. We reached the Brigade headquarters round about eight-thirty a.m. I wasn't in on the talk that went on between the Brigadier and General. I was with the Brigade Intelligence Officer and he'd just had the IO of the British battalion on the wireless, reporting that patrols had picked up this fellow Mohammed Baksh of the Jiffs. So far he hadn't given any information. They said he looked half-starved and had probably deserted several days before. I wasn't so sure. The picture I had was that most of the Jiffs looked pretty exhausted. They didn't have the stamina of the Japanese. The whole force had crossed the Chindwin and come through hill jungle. The Japanese are old hands at that. Advance first and worry about your lines of communications and supplies afterwards. That's their tech-nique. It worked in Burma and Malaya, but it didn't work this time because we were ready for it. That's why the General wanted to push the other battalion forward. He guessed that the Indian battalion on the left of the British was misinterpreting the strength of the opposition they'd met in the night. I realized it was im-portant to know more about this Jiff fellow. If all that stood in the way of the British battalion was a Jiff formation, then the General could perform his containing operation easily.'

'Didn't the British battalion know what was in front of them?'

'No, they'd reached their objective, and the only reason for the pause was their discovery that their left flank was unprotected, because the Indian battalion hadn't kept pace. The Indians were stuck about two miles back, apparently contained by a Japanese force of at least battalion strength. But the General thought that if the Indian battalion was pinned down by the Japanese, so were the Japanese by the Indians, a sort of tactical stalemate, and since the British battalion was astride the road the initiative was still very much with the Brigade. The British battalion had sent patrols forward, of course, but found nothing except this stray Jiff and their patrols reported no apparent threat to their flank or rear. Down there, you know, it isn't country you can stand and get a view of. You have to probe it more or less yard by yard. But they had found the Jiff, and I wondered whether the fact that he hadn't given any information was because he spoke no English and the IO of the British battalion spoke hardly any Urdu. I asked the Brigade IO what was happening about Baksh. He said he'd asked the battalion to send him back but the answer had been, Come and get him, we can't spare either the transport or the men just to look after a Jiff.'

He stopped, said, 'I'm sorry. Would you help me drink from that contraption on the table?'

She rose, went round by the bed for the teapot and held it for him.

'Thanks.'

'Would you like to share another cigarette?'

'No, but you have one. I enjoy the smell.'

As she lit one she remembered having said much the same thing to him, the night of the fireflies.

'Just then,' he went on, 'the General and the Brigadier came out from their conference. I could see there had been a flaming row. The Brig was about ten years the senior man and was all for caution because men's lives were at stake, the lives of men he loved. The General on the other hand was all for modern ideas of dash, surprise, throwing away the book, using your equipment to its optimum limit, loving the whole impersonal power-game of move and counter-move.' A pause. 'They were both amateurs because they were both hot-headed. They were trying to make a lyric out of a situation that was merely prosaic. It only seemed problematical because we lacked information. But because it seemed problematical all this free emotional rein was given to the business of its solution. Well, there you are. If there are things you don't know, you call the gap in your knowledge a mystery and fill it in with a wholly emotional answer. That morning it struck me as supremely silly because, do you know, there wasn't a single sound of warfare anywhere. It was quite still. Sylvan almost – with the sunlight coming through the trees. A phrase came into my mind. The sweet indifference of man's environment to his problems. Pathetic fallacy or no, I really felt it, an indifference to us that amounted to contempt. The Brig had installed himself in an old bungalow, probably a traveller's resthouse. There was a village near by but the people had fled. The Brigade transport was harboured in a kind of glade – command truck, signals truck. Well, you can probably picture it, just like a Brigade command post on a field exercise. I was never able to get the picture of an exercise out of my mind, even when stuff was flying. There's something fundamentally childish about the arrangements for armed conflict. And there they were, the General and the Brigadier, both red in the face, and Teddie looking pink and embarrassed. They went over to the command truck. The IO was still with me. I told him that if I could get the General's permission I'd go and collect that Jiff myself, and see what I could get out of him. The IO was all for it, glad not to be bothered with such a minor detail. I went to the command truck and saw that something had just happened to put the General back in a good temper. The CO of the Indian battalion had been on the radio. They now realized they'd got the Japanese into a pocket and had decided that the Japanese force wasn't much more than company strength. It meant the Indians could mop the Japs up, complete their advance and make contact with the British battalion. The General asked me if there was anything new on my side, so I told him about the Jiff and that I'd like to go up and try and get him to talk and in any case bring him back. He said, "Yes, you do that, and make sure they understand the operational picture." '

Again he closed his eyes, and said nothing for a while, as if conjuring the image of that morning. But she knew, instinctively, what was coming. Something Teddie had said that marked the beginning of the fatal occasion.

'Of course the operational picture was Teddie's side, not mine, but there was nothing about this picture that a G.3 I. couldn't tell the battalion commander just as clearly as a G.3 Ops could. But Teddie said, "I'll do that, sir, I'll go with him." And the General was in a good enough mood to agree. If he'd thought about it clearly he would have said no. It was absurd, two divisional staff officers going off to a forward battalion to collect one miserable prisoner and to confirm verbally operational information that the CO would get over the radio anyway. But there we were, doing just that, as a result of the General's euphoria following the solution to his problem, but chiefly because of Teddie's obsession, his belief that I was not the man to deal with an Indian soldier who had turned coat. I didn't understand, I didn't have the touch or the sense of the traditions that were involved. Teddie thought he did. The Jiff was the only reason Teddie volunteered to go.

'But before we set off something else happened that gave him a better reason. I suppose we were about five minutes, checking with the Brigade IO, making sure of the location and route. We were about to leave when we were called back. I thought the General had changed his mind, but it wasn't that. Division had been on. The whole operational picture had changed. The division had been drawn into what amounted in military terms to a blind alley. On the map it was advancing roughly south-west to oppose a threat from that quarter, but the major threat was now seen to be south to south-east. In less difficult country it would just have been a question of swinging round in the hope of cutting the advancing force in two, but it's difficult to swing across the grain of hills like that. The reserve Brigade was the only one of the three not faced with that problem. But I won't bore you with tactics. It's enough for you to know there was a bit of a flap, and that this trip of Teddie's and mine was suddenly much more important to both the General and the Brigadier. The Brigadier was already on the radio to the CO of the British battalion, telling him to send a company back to support the Indians who were going in to clear this pocket of Japanese, make sure they didn't break through on to the road, but he wanted definite information about the Jiffs. He wanted to make sure there were no Jiff units waiting their chance to come in and command the road when our own troops swung away from it. He told the CO I was coming along, that the two of us were coming, one to help sort out the Jiff situation and relieve them of the prisoner and the other to put them in the picture as the General now saw it.

'So off we went, in my jeep, the two of us and the driver. There were only three miles to go. That company of the British battalion must have moved. We met them debussing and scattering into the hill on our left. When we got to the battalion we found the head-quarters bivouacked just beyond a village, commanding the junction of the road and a track that led off down into a valley on the right. The junction had been their objective the previous night. They had a company in the jungle between the road and the track and another company in the jungle on the left of the road. The whole thing was terribly brisk and businesslike, that is it was until you realized that there were probably no enemy ahead. The CO was one of those cheery types with a wide moustache and a scarf in his neck – navy blue with white polka dots. We found him sitting on a shooting stick, drinking coffee. He had two spare mugs ready and got his batman filling them when he saw us coming. The complete host. At pains to appear quite unflappable.

'I let Teddie talk first. When he'd finished the CO just nodded, made one or two marks on his map and said, "Well, I could have told them that. There's nothing down the road, except perhaps some stray Jiffs and if they're all like the one we've got they're no problem." He sent for the IO then and told him to take me to the mule-lines where they had the Jiff under guard. Teddie began to follow but the CO called him back. The IO was a pleasant boy. He spoke French and German and had learned some Japanese, but he admitted his Urdu didn't extend much beyond what private soldiers who came out to India in the old days used to pick up in the barracks and bazaars. The only thing he'd got out of Mohammed Baksh was his name. He wasn't even sure whether Baksh had been an Indian prisoner of war or an Indian civilian in Malaya or Burma.

'But when I saw him I was pretty certain he'd been a soldier. He was squatting on his hunkers, under a tree, guarded by a young soldier on mule-lines picket, and directly he saw us coming he got to his feet and stood at attention, and stared straight ahead in that way old soldiers have, never quite meeting your eye unless you ask a personal question. He hadn't learned that as a civilian. He was a mess, though. Dirty, unshaven, undernourished. His uniform had nearly had it. I started firing questions at him. Name, age, what village he was born in, what year he had joined, what regiment, whether he had any relatives serving in the army, whether his

[381

parents were alive, and what his father was. All very quickly, not waiting for the answers, but asking him nothing about the Jiffs or the Japanese or how he'd been captured. I wanted to start him thinking about his home. He'd probably not seen it for two or three years, and coming back to Indian soil could have made him pretty homesick. Then I started asking the questions again, but this time waited for answers. The family questions first, the name of his village, what his father did, was his father still alive? He said he didn't know about his father and I could see the question had got him. It was then that Teddie appeared and that was the signal for Baksh to shut up like a clam, just when I thought I'd begun to break him.

'I decided to leave the personal things aside for a bit and started asking questions about the past few days. Teddie's Urdu wasn't all that hot. He kept asking me what I'd said, and putting in questions of his own, if Baksh had been in the Indian Army, what regiment, who'd been his old commanding officer. The chap got very confused and nervous, looking at Teddie, but not quite at Teddie, at one part of Teddie. It took me a while to get it. That he couldn't keep his eyes off Teddie's regimental flash. And then I realized what was eating him and said, Baksh, you're an old soldier of this officer's regiment, aren't you? He stared at me and then sort of collapsed. Teddie rounded on me, wanted to know what I'd said, so I told him. I said Baksh had once been a Muzzy Guide. He said I was making it up, he didn't believe it. No sepoy of the Muzzy Guides would ever turn coat, he'd rather die. He said there'd been one battalion in Burma and one in Malaya, that he knew every man in the Burma battalion, which had been his own, and all the officers of the one in Malaya. If Baksh was a Muzzy Guide he'd have been in the Malaya battalion. He told me to ask him the name of the Commanding Officer. Well I did so, and Baksh just shook his head and for a moment I thought perhaps Teddie was right, but I kept on asking him and in the end he said, "Hostein Sahib, Hostein Sahib." I thought well, that proved it, Teddie *was* right. The Muzzy Guides wouldn't have an Indian CO. But Teddie said, "Hostein Sahib was what they called Colonel Hastings", and stared at me as if we'd uncovered something terribly sinister, so sinister it was unbelievable. He asked Baksh what happened to Hostein Sahib. The answer was that none of them had seen either Hastings or any of the other officers since the night the battalion, or what was left of it, went into the bag, south of Kuala Lumpur. The Indian soldiers and their British officers had been separated by their Japanese captors. There was a rumour that Hostein Sahib had been shot, then another that he was in a camp up-country, on the Siam border. The Indian officer who came to talk to them later, in Singapore, said Hostein Sahib and the others officers had had plans to get away by themselves to Sumatra and leave the sepoys and NCOs behind, but being captured by the Japanese had stopped it. None of the sepoys believed this, and for weeks they'd refused to listen to men like the Indian officer who came and went in a Japanese staff car and was on friendly terms with the Japanese camp commander.

'What he was trying to do was get them to join the Indian National Army. Baksh said he was a Sikh called Ranjit Singh. He told them he'd been captured up in Ipoh, that the British officers in his regiment had all tried to save their own skins and left him commanding a rearguard action. He'd been a lieutenant. Now he was a major. He used to visit them two or three times a week and tell them about the free Indian Government that was being formed and which it was the duty of every patriotic Indian soldier to support by joining the new Indian Army that would march to Delhi and drive the British out. He said the Japanese were not India's enemy, only enemies of the British. Why pine away in the prison camps which British cowardice and inefficiency had driven brave men into? The British had always excused their imperialism by pointing out that their presence in India was a guarantee of freedom from invasion. But they hadn't kept the Japanese out of Burma and Malaya. The Japanese were freeing all Asia from the white man's yoke and self-respecting Indians couldn't just sit by and let another nation do their job for them.

'Baksh said that after several weeks other officers came, including a couple of Muslims who told them the whole of India was rising against the white imperialists and that men in the army back here were turning against their officers. I expect that would have been around August in forty-two. Some of Baksh's fellow-prisoners began to believe these tales and after a bit were taken out of camp and came back later in INA uniform, said how well they were treated and helped to recruit the rest. He said, "We were forced, Sahib – one man was tortured by an Indian officer because he refused to take the new oath. We didn't know what was true and what was not. We saw white sahibs working on the roads, like coolies. The world was turned upside down." '

Merrick paused.

'That was the kind of information I was after, I mean about the pressures and the officers responsible. There'll be a day of reckoning I suppose. God knows what will happen to all those chaps. The strength of the INA is three divisions. That's a lot of officers and a lot of men. A lot of sentences of death. Too many. It won't happen. I suppose we might hang Subhas Chandra Bose, who's at the head of the whole thing, but for the rest I expect it'll be a question of weeding out the hawks from the doves, tracking down those who've had their own men tortured. Baksh told me what they did to this chap who tried to stand out against them. It's too revolting to repeat.'

He closed his eyes, but when he continued his voice was still strong.

'I asked Baksh to describe what had led to his capture that morning and he told us that two days earlier the Japanese had ordered the officer commanding their unit to establish a listening post to keep watch on the track – the one that led down into the valley, and Baksh and two other men, both ex-Muzzafirabad Guides like himself – had been chosen. Their unit was in a village about three miles south of the junction and the listening post was established in the jungle about a mile ahead of the village in a place where they could look down and get a good view of quite a long stretch of the track. Patrols were to visit the listening post every two hours, but if they saw anything going on one of the three men was to go back and report. Baksh said it was a stupid arrangement, the kind of thing they found themselves doing because the Japanese seldom gave them a proper job. Anyway they spent the whole day watching the track and reporting to the patrols. They thought they'd be ordered back when it got dark, but when the last patrol reached them the leader said he hadn't had any orders to leave the post unmanned. He'd see about it when he got back and in any case send up a hot meal. They'd been on iron rations all day, with only water to drink. But nothing happened. They didn't dare desert the post or even have one man go back and see what was up because their officer, Lieutenant Karim, was always on at them about obeying orders to the letter and showing themselves the equal of the Japanese in endurance and discipline. Karim had been a Jemadar in one of the Punjabi regiments. He'd adopted the Japanese method of clapping soldiers when he was angry.

'So there they were, according to Baksh, stuck all night on the hillside. When it got light they expected the patrol to turn up, but it never did. They had no food left and only very little water. They drew lots for which of them would go back when the sun had been up a couple of hours, and Baksh was the unlucky one. He expected Karim would beat him up.

'When he got back to the village he found it deserted. The unit had gone. It didn't surprise him because the Japanese were always ordering them to move at a moment's notice, usually in the middle of the night. He said it didn't even surprise him that Lieutenant Karim had packed and gone without thinking about the three men at the listening post, and that the patrol leader who'd promised to send a hot meal had forgotten all about them. He said, "In the jungle our doubts returned, each man was only thinking of himself. There was no good spirit in us." Well, it sounded plausible, and Teddie believed it. So did the young IO. I wasn't wholly convinced. I kept an open mind, whether he was telling the truth or trying to cover up the fact that he was a deserter or a spy. He said he scouted around, filled the water bottles from the stream they'd been using, and found some tins of food carelessly left behind, then went back to the post. When they'd eaten they decided to go back to the village thinking by now someone must have noticed their absence and they'd be sent for. In the village they tried to work out which direction the unit had gone. They were afraid of the Japanese appearing and treating them as deserters, or of some of the villagers returning and taking revenge on them for things the Japanese had done. I asked him then how large this unit was. He said it was about half company strength, and had been detached from an INA battalion for special duties, but he didn't know what the special duties were because apart from advancing up the road behind a company of Japanese they hadn't done anything. I wasn't so sure about that either, but I asked him to go on with his story. He said he and the two others had begun to quarrel. One man wanted to go back to the listening post, another wanted to stay hidden in the village and Baksh wanted to scout back along the road in the direction they'd come from a couple of nights before. So they drew lots again, and Baksh won. They tracked back for a couple of miles, keeping to the jungle along the side of the road, and found nothing. He said it was as if God had waved his hand and caused all the soldiers of their own and the Japanese armies to disappear. They went back to the village and on to the listening post. The two others suggested they should go down into the valley. They were sure their unit must have been sent in that direction. Why else should the track leading down into the valley have been kept a watch on? Baksh said there was no point in sending troops into the valley. There was nothing there except the surrounding hills. The road and the high ground on the other side of it were the only features of military value. They'd advanced along the road towards the village. In his opinion their troops had fanned out into the hills, not into the valley. He said they should cross the road and explore the hills, or stay where they were. In one case they'd at least be showing common sense and initiative, in the other obeying the last order received. If they went down into the valley they'd only be acting foolishly. They had a midday meal at the listening post and because they'd hardly slept at all the night before and were tired and hungry they decided to stay put and take it in turns, two men keeping watch and the other one sleeping. He said, "We had no strength left, Sahib, and no spirit. Through no fault of our own we had become deserters and were thinking and doing like that." It was agreed that at dusk they'd go back to the village. Baksh was the last to sleep. He said he woke when it was dark and found the others had gone. They had taken the rest of the food. He went to the village but knew they'd gone down into the valley and that they felt as he was feeling, that the end of the road had been reached and there was nothing for it now but capture by British or Indian troops. He slept in one of the deserted huts and woke during the night because of the sound of firing from the direction of the hill on the other side of the road. At least, he thought that was where it came from. It didn't sound close. When he woke again it was light. The firing had stopped but there were two British soldiers prodding him with their rifles. He was glad it was over. Now, he said, he would be shot, and knew he deserved death for being disloyal to the uniform of his father and fathers before him.' A pause. 'He broke down and wept and begged Teddie to shoot him then and there. That young IO was terribly embarrassed. Oddly enough Teddie wasn't. He held the man's shoulder and shook him a bit and said, "You're still a soldier. Act like one. You've done very wrong, but I am still your father and mother."

386]

The old formula. But Teddie meant it. He really meant it. In spite of what that man had done he felt it was his duty to do his best for him. And I suppose he felt compassion.'

'Did you?' Sarah asked. 'Did you feel that too, Ronald?'

'No. To me Baksh was merely a source of information. I had no feelings about the man himself. He'd made a choice. It hadn't worked out well The law says he should be punished. Well, it happens all the time. You choose, you act, you pay or get paid. That's how I see it. Do you disapprove?'

'I can't, can I?' she said, then added, 'It's true after all. You pay or get paid. Although perhaps there are situations in which it's better for you to pay, more satisfying.' She thought: To the soul, whatever that is, more satisfying to the soul, if you know the choice was wrong. But what do I mean, *wrong*?

'Most people prefer to be paid. We're always looking for rewards. And Baksh got his. So did Teddie. It was a ridiculous scene in its way. It seemed to me to have nothing to do with the reality of what was actually happening. He knelt down and put his head on Teddie's boots, and that didn't embarrass Teddie either. I think it moved him. Very deeply. As if something he'd always believed in and put his trust in had been proved. He pulled Baksh to his feet, quite gently, and then they stared at each other. Measuring up. To each other, and to some standard of, well, what worked, what was possible about conduct. And Baksh gradually reassumed that old soldier look of not looking except into a middle-distance he wasn't even seeing. And Teddie nodded and said, "I remember Hostein Sahib, in Muzzafirabad. My name is Bingham, Bingham. Remember my name." It was a promise that didn't need explaining in so many words. They both understood that Teddie intended to do his best for him. The man felt he belonged again. You could see that. He might be court-martialled and shot, or imprisoned, but even in front of a firing-squad he would belong to the system that was executing him. I suppose it was months since he'd felt he belonged anywhere. It's extraordinary the lengths people will go to to convince themselves that they belong.'

He turned his head slightly and watched her, then said:

'Just then we heard firing on the hill. The Indians were going in to clear that pocket of Japanese, with the company from the British battalion in support. The IO looked at his watch and asked me to question Baksh about the kind of arms this Jiff unit had and whether he thought it possible after all that they'd gone down into the valley and holed out there. The answer was that they had a mortar, a couple of machine guns. The rest carried rifles. They hadn't much spare ammunition. He looked back in the direction of the firing and then in the direction of the valley. I think we all got the same idea at once, that the Jiffs *had* gone into the valley and that they should have opposed the advance of the British battalion during the night or were supposed to harry the battalion once it was seen to have occupied the road junction. The firing on the hill might be their signal to attack. But a unit of only half-company strength was an absurdly small force. If Baksh hadn't lied about the strength, the Jiffs might have gone into the valley to join a Japanese force already holed out there. The IO said he'd better go and have a word with the old man, but before he'd gone more than a yard or so we heard the old man calling to him. I asked Baksh if he'd lied about the strength of the Jiff force. I suggested he'd lied from start to finish. He wouldn't answer me, but just looked dumbly at Teddie. Teddie said, "Leave the poor devil alone." But he asked a question himself. He asked the names of Baksh's two ex-Muzzy Guide companions from the listening post.' A pause. 'Aziz Khan and Fariqua Khan.' A pause. 'I expect I'll always remember them. The names. Not the men. We never saw the men.

'Presently I left Teddie to it and went to find the CO. There was the question of the valley, and who might be in it. If he intended to have a closer look I thought it worth staying for another half-hour. Not more. I'd done the job I came to do, so had Teddie. I knew we ought to be getting back to division and taking Baksh with us. I found the CO at the junction. Up along the road men were coming out of the jungle on either side. He told me he'd been ordered back about a mile and to leave a road block at the junction until the battalion from the reserve Brigade sent a company forward to man it. The little skirmish on the hill was nearly over and he was to move on through the hills, south-east. That was in line with the revised picture we'd had from division. I asked what he thought about the possibility of there being Jiffs or Japanese in the valley. He said the company manning the road block could deal with them, if there were any. Then he said I'd better get moving. He meant we were in the way. We were. Well, you can imagine, a battalion suddenly on the move. I went back to the mule-lines to get Teddie and Baksh. But they weren't there.

The mules were being loaded and led out and I couldn't tell which of the men had been on guard, but the one I spoke to said the IO and the Jiff and the other staff officer had gone down by what he called the short cut. I went back to where we'd left the jeep. It wasn't there either. Neither was the driver. It took me a couple of minutes to find the IO. He seemed surprised to see me. He said he thought I'd gone with Captain Bingham and the Jiff-type to see if the other two Jiffs were anywhere around. When he saw I'd no idea what he was talking about he told me how when he went back to the mule-lines, by the short cut, he found Teddie alone with Baksh. Teddie told him Baksh thought the other two ex-Muzzy Guides were in the valley and would be looking for an opportunity to give themselves up, especially to a Muzzy Guide officer. The IO had said, Well, we're pulling out, take a look if you must, it's all yours. When he asked where I was Teddie said I'd gone down to the road and that he'd pick me up there. Perhaps he intended to. I don't know. At the time I could only think he'd gone off his head and I'm afraid I said as much to the IO. I'm sorry. I think it counted against Teddie afterwards. The IO asked me if I thought the Jiff was trying something on. I said I didn't know, but I wanted him back.

'Sometimes, you know, I lie here and and realize I'd probably be all in one piece still if that young IO had been pigheaded or scared of his CO, if he'd said, "Well, it's your funeral," and gone about his own business. But he was the eager-beaver type. He took me to a jeep parked off the road and told me to jump in, he'd take me down the track. The jeep belonged to the CO but he wouldn't be needing it, not where the battalion was going. He meant for the march into the hills. What transport the battalion had apart from the mules would go back to the Brigade pool. He called out to a sergeant to tell the CO there might be something going on down in the valley and he was going to take a look and in any case check that the company in the woods between the road and the track were pulling out in good order. Then we set off and turned into the track. Men were coming out on to it from the jungle and marching up it in single file. When we got round the first bend we saw Teddie about half a mile ahead. He was in the driver's seat, going quite slowly, and Baksh was in the back with the driver beside him. You couldn't tell at that distance how alert the driver was, or if he had Baksh well covered with his Sten gun. There was a shallow

[389

ravine on our right, with a ridge beyond it, but Teddie was at a point where the ravine came to an end and there was a neck of flattish ground between the track and the ridge, most of it jungle, but making a fairly easy connexion between the ridge and the track. Farther on the ground obviously fell away quite steeply into the valley. When we saw Teddie stop the IO said, "I think he's only taking a quick look-see. He won't find them there, we've patrolled all that." All the same Teddie stopped and a second or so later we heard him, quite clearly. Calling to them. Aziz Khan. Fariqua Khan. Aziz Khan, Fariqua Khan. It was as if Teddie himself gave the signal. There was a single rifle shot and not more than a second or two later an explosion in the woods on our left and then another one bang on the track between us and Teddie's jeep, and then more or less continuously, one after the other in the wood. The company that had been located there and were still in there, moving out section by section, were being mortared from the ridge over on the right and there was more than one mortar, which meant Baksh had lied or there were some Japanese there too.

'I hand it to that young IO. The temptation was to get out of the jeep and dive for cover but he merely swore and started swinging round. The track was narrow, it needed a three-point turn. We were swung round with the wheels an inch or two from the ravine before I realized he meant to drive back up the hill. I remember shouting at him, "What are you doing? Didn't you see?" I don't think he had seen. He shouted back for me to hang on, but I jumped out and said I must get him. I don't think he understood what I was on about. He realized later but at the time he probably thought I didn't relish running the gauntlet back up the track, and was going to ground in the wood, or perhaps he wasn't thinking at all, just acting instinctively, getting back himself as quick as he could to where he was supposed to be and would be needed. The men who'd been marching up the track had scattered. I saw a couple of them leaning against the bank holding their faces. It was a sort of pandemonium. I registered it, but not as someone who had to do anything about it. I was thinking primarily of the other jeep and of what I'd seen in the first few seconds, between the rifle shot, the first mortar bomb explosion and the second one that fell slap on the track. I saw three things. I saw Teddie duck, or appear to duck. I saw the driver pitch over on top of him, as if he'd been hit. And I saw Baksh staring at them, then jumping clear and running

390]

on to that neck of flat ground. Then I couldn't see anything because of the explosion on the track itself.

'And I don't remember anything awfully clearly between jumping out of the IO's jeep and reaching Teddie's. I think I ran down the track until I reached the mortar-bomb crater and that the sight of it acted as a warning signal. I must have gone up into the wood then and run the rest of the way under cover. I do seem to remember some difficult going, and falling, picking myself up again. I know it was a sudden shock to find that the jeep was burning and that the driver was on the ground, not slumped over Teddie any longer, and that Teddie wasn't slumped forward but sideways. It wasn't at all how I'd last seen it. I realized another mortar bomb had fallen a few yards in front of the jeep and that the force of the explosion had hurled the driver off Teddie and also flung Teddie to one side. I don't know about the fire. I think the spare petrol cans had been hit and gone up. I don't really remember going up to the jeep, only being there, pulling Teddie out, trying to get a hold. I must have been hunched forward, protecting my face, reaching in and getting him by the waist or an arm. I don't remember being shot at, or know whether it was then, or when I got him out and dragged him into the wood, or when I had to go back and get the driver and drag him in too. I do remember there wasn't any sign of Baksh. They found him later. Dead of course. The other Jiffs must have shot him. They or the Japanese. It turned out there were Japanese as well.'

She thought: I don't know, I don't know, where that kind of courage comes from or why or what its purpose is, but I know it has a purpose. It's a kind of madness, a sublime insanity which even Ronald who's experienced it can't explain. He wanted to diminish Teddie for me but Teddie isn't diminished. He began to diminish himself, but now he isn't diminished either. For a moment they are both larger than life. Teddie calling stupidly for those men, and Ronald stupidly risking death to try and save him. And that's how I shall remember them. Without understanding why it makes them larger.

His eyes were shut again, had been for some moments, and that impediment in his throat was troubling him. He swallowed and said:

'I thought at first Teddie was dead too, but I'm afraid he wasn't, neither was the driver but the driver wasn't burnt. Teddie was.'

'But he was unconscious?'

'Not all the time.'

'Colonel Selby-Smith wrote that you said Teddie was unconscious and hadn't suffered.'

'Let Susan go on thinking that.' A pause. 'I got them both off the track and as far into the wood as I could manage. The driver's Sten gun was still in the jeep so I only had my revolver, and Teddie's of course, but I thought it was probably all up with the three of us anyway, either from another mortar bomb or from the bunch of Jiffs I expected any moment to come down from the ridge. I think it was becoming aware of that possibility that made me notice my left arm was numb, but I couldn't see any blood or any sign of having been hit. The arm and – other things – made it difficult to do anything about the field-dressings and I couldn't see where Teddie had been hit either. I had him on his back and didn't want to turn him over. It's odd, about – damage to people. I thought the driver was dying, that no one could be such a mess and survive. I thought it would be Teddie who might survive, although I hoped he wouldn't.' A pause. 'He would have been terribly disfigured.'

She waited, then said:

'You don't need to tell me anything you don't like talking about, Ronald. I'd rather you didn't because I couldn't repeat it to Susan, and if I know it she'll see I'm keeping something back. And then she'll worry even more.' She hesitated. 'And you haven't told me anything about you, about what's wrong or what they've got to do to you.'

'Oh, nothing wrong they can't put right. I was burnt a bit. Shot up a bit. But in a few weeks I'll be back on my feet, which I suppose is something.'

She remembered the line from his letter: *There was Teddie with everything to live for and I – comparatively – with something less than that.* It no longer seemed like an affectation but a bare statement of the truth. She would have liked to get him to explain but felt that the explanation was there, in front of her, and in her mind – secreted in all the dark corners of her recollections of her brief encounters with him, and with his reputation.

She said, 'Was it a long time before you got any help?'

'It seemed long. I think it was an hour. A bit more. But after a while I felt quite safe because I realized the Jiffs wouldn't expose themselves to our own direct fire by coming on to the track. They might try to cross it, and of course they'd come on to it if they thought they'd got the battalion pinned down, but somehow I assumed they'd do neither. It never struck me there might be larger forces coming up from the valley. There weren't, but I'm glad I didn't worry about it. I'm trying to make you see that staying there with Teddie and the driver wasn't the death-and-glory thing people might make out.' A pause. 'It was the snuggest place to be when you think of it. And there's this other thing. If all this is a confession of some sort, this is what it's about, what I see about it now, I mean when lying thinking, going back, analysing it. I want you to know. So that you understand the difference, the difference between Teddie and me, and why I say he died an amateur. He went down there for the *regiment*. I told you there was a touch of old-fashioned gallantry in it. All that paternalist business really meant something to him. *Man-bap.* I am your father and your mother. It would have been great if he'd gone down there and called as he did and if they'd come out, hanging their heads, and surrendered to him, trusting in the code, the old code. That's what he wanted. I don't mean there was anything vain or self-seeking about it. He wasn't doing it for himself or for them. He did it for the regiment. He risked everything for it, his own life, the driver's life, Baksh's life, his job. So much. So much it's incalculable. Who knows, his going down there might have looked to that bunch of Jiffs and Japs, who'd been clever enough to get so near without being seen, like the beginning of an advance into the valley. It could have triggered the whole thing off. But in any case he was putting the regiment above his job. If it had come off he could have become one of those people a regiment remembers, celebrates, as part of their legend. Teddie Bingham? By jove, yes, but that was before your time. There were these poor misguided fellows from a Muzzy Guides battalion that got cut to pieces in Malaya back in '41–'42 and had gone into the bag and been forced to join a bunch of renegades we called Jiffs. A lot of them came up with the Japs when they crossed into Indian territory early in '44. Our own chaps shot them out of hand if they had the chance, and there weren't many prisoners until this Muzzy Guide gave himself up, a chap called Mohammed Baksh. Young Bingham was a divisional staff officer at that time, but once a Muzzy always a Muzzy. He'd gone forward with a message from the General to the CO of a battalion that was in danger of being cut off and saw Baksh. Well, directly Baksh saw him the fellow went to pieces, and begged young Bingham to shoot him for his act of treachery, but young Bingham made him stand like a man and talked to him as if he were his own erring son, made him feel he still belonged. "Are there any others with you?" Bingham asked and Baksh said yes, two, both from his old battalion, starved, wretched, hiding out, too afraid to surrender. Well, there was stuff flying but young Bingham never hesitated. "Come on," he said, "show me where," and off they went right into the thick of it and when they got near the place where Baksh had left the other two Bingham said, "What are their names?" Aziz Khan and Fariqua Khan. Brothers I think they were. So what does young Bingham do? He stands up straight where anyone could see him and pick him off and calls out to them, ordering them to return to duty as soldiers of the Muzzy Guides. And, by jove, in a couple of minutes out they came and back he marched them. He didn't even take their rifles away.'

Presently Merrick said:

'But of course it didn't come off and nobody will ever tell the tale like that. And anyway that kind of tale has had its day. Is that why it didn't come off?'

'There's your tale,' Sarah said.

'Oh no, mine was a professional action.' He looked at her and again she thought she detected in his expression that curious serenity. 'It's only amateurs who create legends. There's nothing memorable about doing a job. I said mine was a professional act. I didn't go to save Teddie. I went to get Mohammed Baksh. I want you to accept that, and the fact that when it came to it I didn't have the courage to go looking for him. I pulled Teddie out because I was afraid of what people would say if I left him to fry.' A pause. 'I don't mean that all this went consciously through my mind, but in retrospect I see no other interpretation.' A pause. 'Do you?'

Do I? (she asked herself). Yes, I see a man who was in love with those legends, that way of life, all those things that from a distance seemed to distinguish people like us from people of his own kind, people he knew better. I see a man still in love with them but who has chosen to live outside in the cold because he couldn't get in to warm his hands at this hearth with its dying fire. And it is strange because I long to exchange the creeping cold for a chill reality but feel in my bones that my kind of cold would not be his kind, just as the warmth I knew as a child was different from the warmth he always imagined. I don't understand the distinction he makes between what he calls amateur and what he calls professional, but feel it's a distinction he's made to heal a wound. After all, there are only people, tasks, myths and truth. And truth is a fire few of us get scorched by. Perhaps it's an imaginary flame, and can't be made by rubbing two sticks together.

She said, 'Some people would have been more afraid of pulling Teddie out than of what people would say if he'd been left there. And I don't think you risked your life just to get Mohammed Baksh.'

'No?'

'You went down there without thinking why you went, Ronald. I mean when the shooting had started. You saw they were in trouble and needed help. What you call the game only looks like a game to people who aren't in the team. I'm sorry but even if it's only as twelfth man you're a member of the team after all, aren't you?'

He smiled, turned his head so that he need not look at her. He said, 'You are, when it comes to it, very much the Colonel's daughter, I'm afraid.'

'I was born that way.'

She waited. He did not respond. Again she felt the pressure of his willing her to enter and explore the mysterious areas of his obsession. To counteract it she considered other mysteries, or anyway questions that remained unanswered: the outcome of the battle, whether it had ever been proven that Baksh had lied, and why; what other prisoners were taken and, more grotesquely, the circumstances of his vigil, with Teddie burnt but not unconscious all the time, and himself in some unexplained condition of numbness which perhaps wore off before the time was up.

'Did the driver come through?' she asked. He nodded. 'And Teddie – was Teddie aware of what you'd done?'

'I don't know. I don't think so. If you could use a word like expression in a case like that I'd say his was one of blank amazement. He never made a sound. I'm not sure he could see me. But his eyes moved. At one time I thought he'd gone, but his heart was still beating. I'm sorry. I shouldn't tell you things like that. Burning's a terrible thing. I was glad when they told me he'd had a bullet lodged in his back. I suppose the fire had cauterized the wound. At the time I thought he was only dying from burns.' He looked round at her again. 'Sitting with him reminded me of the last thing I did as DSP Mayapore, just before I was – transferred to Sundernagar. There was an English mission school superintendent living there who committed suicide. Suttee, as a matter of fact.'

'Oh – do you mean Miss Crane?'

'You knew her?'

'No, but the woman my aunt lives with was in the missions. She often talks about her. Edwina Crane.'

'That's her. Edwina Crane. A funny old bird. She'd been around for years but no one knew her at all well except I suppose the Indian children in the schools. If she had any friends they were Indians and half-castes. So it was ironic, because she was the first person from Mayapore to get hurt in the August riots. She was on her way back from a place called Dibrapur with an Indian teacher. A mob stopped them and murdered the teacher, beat her up and burned her car out. We had her in hospital the evening all that other business happened in the Bibighar. She'd been found sitting on the roadside in the pouring rain holding the dead Indian's hand. You couldn't get much out of her. She was half-delirious when I saw her and couldn't remember anything. When she got better I think she was already off her head. Melancholia. I heard she'd resigned from the mission and wasn't seeing anybody. Then she did this dramatic thing, dressed herself in Indian clothes, locked herself in a shed in her garden and burnt herself to death. A symbolic act, I suppose. She must have felt the India she knew had died, so like a good widow she made a funeral pyre. I had to go along there, poke about among her things, and question her old servant. There wasn't much to find, she hadn't left a note. But in a chest I turned up an old picture of Queen Victoria receiving tribute, a very stylized thing, with the old lady sitting on a throne under clouds and angels, and Indians of all kinds gathering round her like children. *Man-bap.* I am your father and mother. And in another place I found the little plate that had been taken off the frame. The picture must have been a gift in recognition of some special service years before. It went something like, To Edwina Crane, for her courage. The mission was in Muzzafirabad. Oh and it dated back years – I think before the First World War. But sitting there with Teddie made it all seem to connect, I mean connect what she had done all that time ago in Muzzafirabad and what he had just done, or tried to do. And then there was the other similarity – death by fire.'

He smiled at her. 'I think that made me feel – what you said. I mean for a moment there I was an amateur myself. I fell for it, really fell for it, the whole thing, the idea that there really was this possibility. Devotion. Sacrifice. Self-denial. A cause, an obligation. A code of conduct, a sort of final moral definition, I mean definition of us, what we're here for – people living among each other, in an environment some sort of God created. The whole impossible nonsensical dream.'

She waited. He had turned his head away again and when the silence continued unbroken the notion that he could have fallen asleep exhausted, nudged – but did not dislodge – the firmer belief she had that everything he said and did was rooted in acute awareness of himself as someone central to an occasion. And suddenly she had a vivid image of him on the platform of Mirat cantonment station, central to an earlier occasion that had been well marked by victims, although on that day, the day of the wedding, only the woman in the white saree had actually been present. But it was the significance of that lonely supplication that now struck her, for the first time, and recreated Bibighar in her mind as an occasion that continued, could not be ruled off as over, done with. Always, before, she had seen the white-clad figure as representative of an old misfortune that had left its mark; a sadness in a stranger's heart, an unknown and so unrecognizable grief; and it was only now, observing the faced-away figure of the man the woman had approached as if he were someone capable of granting an alleviation, that she understood the continuing nature of the misfortune, realized that the boy whom the woman pleaded for must, then at least, still have been paying a price, however far distant away in time had been the occasion of his fault, if there had ever been fault.

A new disturbing element of uncertainty stirred her. It caused her to press again with her feet on the floor and with the small of her back into the uncomfortable upright chair, so powerful was that sensation of not wishing to be drawn towards that central point of reference that was in Merrick, that *was* Merrick. She felt deprived of speech and then saw that this was a protection. Briefly she was adjured to silence by an exquisite tautening of nerves that promised, if only they could snap, to leave her vividly possessed by an absolute, an exemplary, understanding of what had been only partially revealed to her by that incident on the station.

But the moment passed. She was still possessed merely by unanswered questions. What was new and disturbing apart from her realization that the boy had still been paying for his fault, was the shadow of permanent misfortune she saw as fallen on him with the girl's death. Had the girl before, or her aunt since, attempted to reduce the price he paid, might still be paying? Or had a net enclosed him, so subtly, irrevocably, that nothing they could try to do would help? And was Merrick alone responsible for that? Was it these victims, not Teddie, who now lay like a weight on that conscience of his which he said he could examine but give a clean bill to? Perhaps that was the way in to him, to become his victim and then to haunt his conscience. But if so, it seemed to her that it was an approach without access at the end. There was, for some reason, no way into him at all, and all the people whom he chose as victims lay scattered on his threshold.

She thought: You are, yes, our dark side, the arcane side. You reveal something that is sad about us, as if out here we had built a mansion without doors and windows, with no way in and no way out. All India lies on our doorstep and cannot enter to warm us or be warmed. We live in holes and crevices of the crumbling stone, no longer sheltered by the carapace of our history which is leaving us behind. And one day we shall lie exposed, in our tender skins. You, as well as us.

It was extraordinary how like each other they were, and at the same time rigidly divided by an antagonism she believed was mutual. She could not bear the thought of this man clinging through a god-relationship to the family she loved, honoured, felt a strange irritated anguish for. He would, through that relationship, attach himself like lichen to a wall, the crumbling stone of the blind house that was doomed to become a ruin. At least, she cried to herself, let it be as noble a ruin as it can; and then laughed at her absurd pride, the fastidious distaste of this Colonel's daughter for a man she had decided, for no clear reason, she could not trust. And there was this problem too: that she had given her word to Susan that she would ask him.

She opened her mouth, but could not say it. She spoke the first words that came into her head.

'Did you ever know old Lady Manners, as well as her niece?' And then remembered Aunt Fenny had already asked him that, the day of the wedding, and been told he didn't.

He turned his head towards her.

'No. Why?'

'I thought you might have. She's in Pankot.'

'Oh?' He waited. She did not explain. 'Is she well?'

'We don't know. None of us has actually seen her.' Did he look relieved? 'She signed the book at Flagstaff House.'

'Does she still have the child?'

'We don't know that either.'

'I see. Is Pankot such a large place, then?'

'She must be living on the west side. The Indian side. It's rather a mystery, why she signed the book.' She wondered what he would say if she told him now the story of what she had done in Srinagar. The white ward seemed full of shadows and echoes of departed voices. 'Incidentally,' she heard herself say, 'talking about children, before I go, I have a question from Susan,' and hesitated, struggling again with her reluctance and her sense of duty. 'She wonders whether you'd like to be one of the godfathers.' She knew her voice was flattened by a cold formality. The same lack of enthusiasm must show in her face. Guilt pricked her. She might just as well have left the duty unperformed as perform it so badly.

'How very kind of her,' he said. He glanced away as if to turn the possibility over in his mind. She wondered if he felt the dead weight that had descended, the weight of the right-thing, like a stone pressing them down, sapping their strength. With one simple remark he threw the weight off. 'But in all the circumstances it wouldn't be suitable, would it?' His glance returned, penetrating, implacable. She knew relief, felt only a small remorse. She was at a loss to understand what it was about him that so appalled her.

'Are you to be godmother?'

She nodded.

He smiled faintly. She noted for the first time what it was that was so unusual about the blueness of his eyes. It was a blueness she realized she associated with the eyes of dolls: a demanding but un-seeing blue, incapable either of acceptance or rejection. If the pillows were taken away, if he were lain flat, would they close and be in-capable of opening until with inquisitive fingers you swung the delicately balanced lids up for a glimpse of those little mirrors with their grave but startling illusion of response?

'Well,' he said, 'you don't believe in it either, do you? But tell her – tell her I was touched and very grateful.'

'Is your not believing in it the only reason?'

She was denied an answer. The door swung open. 'I'm sorry, Miss Layton,' Sister Prior said, advancing towards the bed – trim, capable and asexually attractive – 'I'm told your uncle's come to fetch you. I'm afraid I wasn't able to let him up. Fact is I'm going to turn you out. How are we?'

'We are well,' Merrick said.

'Are you sure my uncle's here? It wasn't arranged.'

'Quite sure. Unless there are two Colonel Graces.'

'I think there's only one. I'll say goodbye, then, Ronald. I expect Aunt Fenny will be round in a day or two. Is there anything special you'd like her to bring you?'

'I don't think they're on the market.'

'What's that?'

'Nothing. Just my little joke. And thank you. Thank you for coming.'

'I'll ring tomorrow before I leave.'

'Well,' Sister Prior interrupted, 'tomorrow won't be at all a good day to ring us, will it, Captain Merrick?'

'No, Sister Prior. I suppose it won't.'

'The day after,' Sister Prior suggested.

'I shall be in Pankot the day after – I thought of ringing before I left.'

'Oh well, your uncle can keep in touch. I'm sorry to hustle you, but we have our little duties.'

Sarah laughed. Sister Prior in the ward, in front of her patient, was quite a different person from the one in the waiting-room. She did not like either, but preferred the bitterness to the professional coyness. She turned to Merrick.

'I'll write to you from Pankot.'

'Will you?'

The reply, meant – she believed – to shatter her, seemed to bounce off her. Never before had she been so conscious of the thickness of skin that was part of her inheritance. But consciousness of it at once began to thin it down. He had not meant, perhaps, to remind her of the earlier unkept promise, but had spoken involuntarily, out of genuine hope but lack of real expectation.

'Of course,' she said and then, determinedly, subtly stressing his Christian name because as yet he had not called her Sarah, she ended, 'Goodbye, Ronald.'

'Goodbye,' he said. For an instant there was a repetition of that difficulty with the throat. 'Goodbye,' he said again, and closed his eyes, as if he knew he had been played with long enough.

*

In the corridor Sister Prior said, 'He's marvellous, isn't he? You simply wouldn't know he's constantly in pain. He fights taking drugs. Is he a religious man?'

'Religious? No, I don't think so.'

'I ask because there are sects that think pain is something you have to bear. With Ronald we have to get up to all sorts of tricks. But the odd thing is him thinking he's not been drugged has the effect you'd expect if he actually wasn't.'

Sister Prior pressed the button to summon the lift. The Bengal sky beyond the window of the waiting-alcove was sodden with rain and cloud and evening. Below, waiting, was Uncle Arthur on whom fortune had smiled at last.

'Of course,' Sister Prior was saying – and this, surely, was a third persona? – the talkative, informed and uniformed bouncer? – 'it's all to the good that he's not over-dependent. He'll come through tomorrow that much better.'

The lift arrived. Sister Prior waited while the attendant clanged back the gates. Entering, Sarah placed her hand so that the gates should not be shut and the descent begin, and it all be over without having come to its logical end.

'I'm sorry,' she said, 'but we know nothing and he wouldn't say.'

'Oh, I realized that. And you ought to know, oughtn't you? The left arm.'

'The left arm?'

'They took the hand off in Comilla. Tomorrow we have to take off from just above the elbow. Third degree burns and a bullet in the upper arm and one in the forearm. The right arm's a mess too, but we can save that. His face will be scarred for life but his hair will grow again, of course. He might even look human without the bandages.'

As if stung Sarah removed her hand from the gates and Sister Prior took her opportunity and slammed them shut. The lift lurched and began to go down. You bitch, she shouted silently. You bloody, bloody bitch. And wondered, presently (as the lift arrived and she smiled automatically in reply to fat old Uncle Arthur's

[401

brick-red grin behind the mesh – strayed like a Cheshire cat into the infirm and unstable world of suffering), whether she meant herself or Sister Prior.

IV

'WE'VE GONE in,' Uncle Arthur had said. 'We landed in Normandy this morning and established a beachhead. Your mother will be bucked, won't she? I'd lay odds on your father being home by Christmas. We thought we'd have a special drink to that.'

In the vestibule, watched by the sergeant and the orderly with pimples, he introduced her to the officer he had brought with him – one of the men, she imagined, who was to enjoy or suffer dinner with the course leader and his wife and whose evening was probably further disorientated by being asked to help collect the niece who had visited a patient in the military hospital.

'This is Major Clark. For some reason utterly escapes me I think he's sometimes known as Nobby. He was only a Captain a couple of months ago when he had to sit and suffer my interminable spouting. Decent of him to come back and visit us. My niece Sarah Layton. Be a good fellow and whistle the driver up.'

As Clark went out into the porticoed entrance she was aware of a broadness of back, a compactness of body, a physical wholeness. No burns, no bullets, no severance.

'How was young what's-his-name?'

'All right. Considering.'

'Good. Tell us all about it presently. I rang your aunt from the daftar. She said to see if I could pick you up. She's wondering if she should ring your mother.'

'Why should she do that?'

'To make sure she's heard.'

'Heard what?'

'The good news. But she's bound to have. I say, are you all right?'

'Yes, thank you.' She smiled. Her face felt made of elastic.

'It's these places. The smell gets on your tummy. Come on, the gharry's here.'

The gharry was Uncle Arthur's staff car. Clark saw them into the back and sat himself next to the driver. As they turned into the road the rain fell. Lightning scarred the horizon.

'When are you off then?' Uncle Arthur inquired, raising his voice to be heard above the sluicing rain and the long, trundling, skittle ball rolls of converging thunder. But it was Clark he'd spoken to.

'First thing in the morning.'

Clark sat with one arm along the back of the seat, his back wedged in the corner of the seat and the door, so that he could talk and be talked to, see and be seen. Vaguely she registered the voice, the intonation, the air of ease, the appraisal she was under. She looked out of the window, scarcely listened to their conversation. They came out into Chowringhee, a place of lights and bicycles and trams. The window was misting up. The city lights hastened the approaching dark. With the edge of her palm she cleared a view for herself and felt like a child intent on observing, from a position of safety and comfort, an alien and dangerous magic.

'Well, what d'you think of the second city of the Empire?' Uncle Arthur asked. 'It's her first visit,' he explained, not waiting for an answer, something she usually thought of as a failing in other people but as a virtue in him. His lack of curiosity had always made him easy to get on with. It was, she supposed, a wholly avuncular virtue, common to that species. She thought that in its unpossessive uninvolved affection there might be felt something of the granite-rock of always available love. Should she weep – and for a few seconds, alarmingly, she felt like doing so – he would be desperately embarrassed but inarticulately sound, a speechless comfort. 'You should have been here a couple of months ago. Major Clark would have shown you the ins and outs. Wouldn't you?'

'Would I, sir?'

'Well, dammit, Clark, you had a reputation. I doubt he ever got to bed before dawn. But no one would have guessed. Always looked as fresh as a daisy.'

She glanced at Uncle Arthur, realized he had already had a sun-downer to celebrate that distant inaudible barrage of invasion, or had not quite recovered from a sumptuous lunch; and, catching Clark's eye, saw his judgement or knowledge corresponded with her own. There was, on his rather ugly face, an opacity, a semi-revelation of vanity and of amusement at someone else's expense which she did not understand and did not like. She thought of herself as pinned by its calculated directness. And looked back at the streaming window, burning with a ludicrous little sense of in-justice that he should exist, unmarked, to pass silent comments on

Uncle Arthur who seemed to find him engaging and anyway gave him lifts and invitations, good counsel and reports presumably; carried him into the circle of her safety that rested for the moment in the existence of Aunt Fenny in Calcutta; and there, in Pankot, dark, silent and undisturbed by rain or rumours of war and amputation – in Susan and her mother – and far, far away, beyond the streaming window, in the still centre of her father's patience and yearning for release and a quiet passage through the night.

She had not recognized the road. The driver's turn into the forecourt of the apartments was unexpected. She felt the curious flattening of inquiring spirit the traveller suffers from, knowing himself without occupation or investment in the fortunes of a strange city. Sandwiched between Uncle Arthur and Major Clark (who, she noted, smelt of some aromatic substance, an aggressive exudation of his naked body beneath the thin cellular cotton of his khaki bush-shirt) she thought of the lift as taking her from one level of non-experience to another. It came to her that like Ronald Merrick she did not travel well, and then that she was whole and, unlike Susan, unbeholden. I do not, she thought, no I do not, give a damn. The Furies were riding across an uninhabited sky, to their own and no one else's destruction. The real world was a tame, repetitious place: one part of it, when you really looked, was much like another, a chemical accident, a mine of raw material for the creation of random artefacts to house and warm or satisfy the need for sensual pleasure or creature comfort. The lift was one such. It jerked to a stop.

'No, a drink first and a bath second,' she told Aunt Fenny who was abroad in the flat in housecoat, slippers and tidy chiffon turban, midway in her preparations for the evening: a revelation to Major Clarke of intimate domestic detail which Sarah put down as a further sign that Aunt Fenny had entered the new age, in which old Flagstaff House values were shrewdly to be readjusted as an insurance against the extinction of those who had held them. Gimlet and cigarette in hand and for a moment alone, Sarah was conscious of belonging to a class engaged in small, continual acts whose purpose was survival through partial sharing in an evolution which, of all the family, only Aunt Lydia back in Bayswater had anticipated and closely witnessed the process of. It was a survival of exiles. Their enemy was light, not dark, the light of their own kind, of their own people at home from whom they had been too long cut off so that, returning there briefly, a deep and holy silence wrapped them and caused them to observe what was real as miniature. In India they had been betrayed by an illusion of topographical vastness into sins of pride that were foreign to their insular, pygmy natures. From the high window of this concrete monstrosity you could see the tragedy and the comic grandeur of tin-pot roofs, disguised at street level by those neo-classical façades which perversely illustrated the vanished age of reason. What reason? My history (Sarah thought, drinking her sweet gimlet, then drawing on her bitter cigarette), my history, rendered down to a colonnaded front, an architectural perfection of form and balance in the set and size of a window, and to a smoky resentment in my blood, a foolish contrivance for happiness in my heart against the evidence that tells me I never have been happy and can't be while I live here. It's time we were gone. Gone. Every last wise, stupid, cruel, fond or foolish one of us.

She turned from contemplation of the rooftops, aroused by the sounds of more of Uncle Arthur's chaps arriving – among whom she sensed the presence of the next generation of her jailers. To avoid immediate confrontation she brushed past Major Clark who had been standing there as if about to speak and told Aunt Fenny – who was giving orders to the white-clad servant – that she'd finish her drink in the bath.

'I'll come in while you're dressing. I want to hear everything,' Fenny said. 'I've only got to slip into something and I'm ready. Have you anything pretty to wear? Iris Braithwaite from downstairs hopes to come, and perhaps Dora Pedley. They're always got up to kill. But the little party's for you, pet. Afterwards the boys will probably take you dancing or to the flicks, so do your best —' this last in almost a whisper, on the threshold of Sarah's room whose door she held open.

'Well I can't do more than my best, Aunt Fenny.'

'My dear, I'd forgotten. You look done up. Was it bad?'

'They're cutting off his arm.'

'Oh, no.'

The bath was already drawn. She rang the bell and, when he answered, gave her glass to the bearer and told him to bring it back refilled. She shivered in the bleak atmosphere of the air-conditioned room, gratefully entered the steam and humidity of the bathroom to undress in more familiar discomfort. Naked, she put

[405

on her shabby bathrobe and felt caressed, but stubborn in her refusal to succumb to a small passion for personal belongings. For a minute or so, back in the ice-box of the bedroom, she sat, smoked, combed out her hopeless hair and drank the second gimlet, smoothed cleansing cream on to her incorruptible Layton face. So uncomely was it (in her eyes) that a wave of pity for it released a succeeding wave of erotic desire to have it loved, it and all her body – untouched beneath the robe Barbie Batchelor had helped her choose the sensible material for. She went and lay in the bath, the tumbler on its edge, within reach, and wondered what else might be in reach.

No, I don't, she repeated, I don't give a damn. But knew she did. Even for Aziz Khan and Fariqua Khan for whose names she had already conjured faces, and – considering them now, their staring eyes and speechless open mouths (as if aghast at the injustice of no more than condign punishment) – she formulated questions: *Why really did Teddie interfere? What made him so anxious to be present when Ronald Merrick tried to get information out of captured Indian soldiers? Had he witnessed an earlier interrogation? Or was it merely, as Merrick seemed to suggest, because he had grown not to trust him over anything?* When the water had cooled below the point of comfort she got out, wrapped herself in one of Aunt Fenny's new-age towels – which was as big as a tent, as soft as down, fit only for a woman in love – and dried herself quickly as if to avoid contamination; but remained swathed for a few moments longer before substituting the shabby robe that had strayed with her from shabby Pankot.

The air-conditioning enveloped her as she passed from bathroom to bedroom. She felt like a clinical specimen captured and cosseted for some kind of experiment which Aunt Fenny, who knocked and entered, had already undergone and emerged from triumphantly, qualified to conduct on others.

'I've brought nothing long,' Sarah said. Fenny had on an emerald-green dinner gown.

'It doesn't matter. Mrs Braithwaite's just phoned to say Iris has gippy-tum and since they're over at the Pedleys it means Dora won't come either. So, pet, you'll be the only pebble on the beach. Now tell me about poor Mr Merrick.'

Sarah told her as much as it was necessary for her to know. When she had finished Fenny said, 'Why not stay a day or two longer? I mean if you could stand it. I'm sure it would cheer him up to see you again. He won't want to be bothered by me. Besides, I never know what to say to people in a bad way. I don't think I could. I've always been a terrible coward about illness. Arthur says that when he has only a cold even, I act as if I don't love him any more. I can't explain it but other people's physical troubles seem to strike me dumb. If you stay on a day or two and see him over the worst I promise I'll really put the red carpet out for him afterwards. I'm good at jollying people along.'

'Why?' Sarah exclaimed, pausing in the midst of applying foundation cream. 'Why should there be a red carpet? Why should we start getting involved at all?'

Aunt Fenny's face, reflected behind her own in the mirror, looked momentarily blank.

'Well, pet, you know the answer better than I do, I imagine. It's you who came all the way down here to see him.'

'For Susan.'

Fenny smiled. 'Only for Susan?'

'Yes.'

'Are you sure?'

'Yes, I'm sure. Why?'

'Well, he was awfully attentive in Mirat. I thought you might be a bit gone on him.'

'How could I be? He's not our class.'

The irony, she saw, was lost on Fenny.

'No. But he's made something of himself and that sort of thing doesn't matter like it used to, does it? I mean people say it's what a man does and is in himself that counts and I think that's true.'

'Am I really so unattractive, Aunty? A board-school boy with a brain and a gentlemanly veneer, and only one arm? Couldn't I do better than that?'

'Oh, Sarah.' Fenny flushed. 'Well, I was only thinking of you being happy. I thought you might be attracted to him and trying to hide your feelings because of what the rest of us might say. None of the things that are against him would matter to me if you did love him. I'd back you up, honestly, right to the hilt. So do you? Do you, pet?'

'As a matter of fact he appals me.' She finished her unrewarding work with the cosmetic, stared at her own face and at the reflection of poor Aunt Fenny's which now seemed as bereft as her own. 'And it would be wrong to run away with the idea that he liked Teddie, by the way.'

After a bit Fenny said, 'I shan't ask you why you say that. I'll just accept it. But I will ask you this. I've wanted to for ages. Were you in love with Teddie? Did it hurt to lose him to Susan?'

'No. I wasn't in love with Teddie either.' She got up from the stool and went to the white-painted fitted wardrobe, took out the dress she had brought as best. Its absurd nice-young-girl look touched nerves that caused alternate chills of irritation and desolation. Removing the robe and standing for a few seconds in her underwear, acutely self-conscious under Fenny's appraisal of her figure, she put the dress on, hastily but reluctantly, like some kind of outgrown but necessary disguise that fooled nobody any longer. She recalled, from somewhere, but did not immediately connect it to the day of the wedding, taking a dress off and feeling she had entered an area of light. Dealing deftly with the simple buttons and the hook and eye of the kind she always chose – on the large side because she had no patience and seldom any help – she said, 'You see, Aunt Fenny, I don't know what it means when people use that word. But thanks for worrying about me. Just don't, that's all. I've met men I'm attracted to and some of them have been attracted back. That's simple enough. But this other thing, love, love, that's never happened. If it has I never knew it, so it must be over-rated. It must be a bit of a sell.'

'Well,' Fenny said, more brightly, 'that's all right then, isn't it? You've got it all to come. One thing's absolutely certain. You won't be in love and not know it.'

'Did you know it, Aunt Fenny? Did you?'

Fenny's smile contracted, but did not disappear.

'Several times I thought I did, once I knew.'

'You were lucky, then.'

'No, pet. Not lucky. It wasn't Arthur.'

'I'm sorry.'

'Now you must never be sorry. No, never. Ninety-nine per cent of life is compromise. It's part of the contract. I've been perfectly happy. I won't say content. Contentment's a different thing. I think I've reached the stage where I could honestly say if I didn't still think of myself as a young woman, well, I *am*, that I've had a good life. Nothing marvellous has ever happened to me, but nothing bad either. I don't suppose I've done a great deal of good anywhere but

408]

I hope no one could say I've ever done any real harm. When I pop off there won't be a thing you could put your finger on to prove, you know, that I'd done more than earn my keep. It's not much, but even that takes a bit of doing, and it's about the most the majority of us can expect of ourselves.'

'I know.'

'Well, smile for me to show that you do.'

Sarah smiled.

'And if you come here I'll tell you my secret.' Sarah went. She sat on the bed and suffered the warm weight of Aunt Fenny's well-nourished hand on her own chill bony arm. 'It's not a secret to your mother. Has she never told you?' Sarah shook her head. 'I'm not surprised. Families are funny things. They have far more secrets from each other than you'd think likely, don't they? We know a lot about our friends, but not much about our kith and kin.' She paused, but she was still smiling. She said, 'The secret is that I adored your father.'

'My father?'

'But adored him. Not from afar, either, but he only had eyes for Millie. He thought me silly and empty-headed, a terrible little flirt and never took me the least bit seriously. He still doesn't. If I said to him now, John, do you know I loved you madly, he'd think it was a joke because he never noticed then and has never noticed since. In fact only Millie noticed and even she's forgotten just *what* she noticed. So have I, in a way, you know, in the way you do when it's all so long ago. But you see, pet, even now, I mean but even now, perhaps especially now, because it's ages since I've seen him, if he walked into this room my heart would take a funny little turn. Just for a second. Then, bump, back to reality because there never was and couldn't be anything between us. If there had been, if he'd felt the same, well even if we'd never married I'd never be able to say as I do that nothing marvellous has ever happened to me, but he didn't, so it wasn't marvellous. But it *was* this thing you say you don't know about, and it's not just physical attraction. And if it ever happens to you, you mark my words, you'll jolly well know.'

Sarah, who had stared for a while at her own clasped hands, glanced up. She found it difficult to take her aunt as seriously as she probably deserved. Like Sarah's mother and father, Fenny belonged to a generation of men and women – the last one there might ever be – who seemed to have been warmed in their formative years by the virtues of self-assurance and moral certainty; what, she supposed, she used to think of as a perpetual light, one that shone (thinking of Aunt Lydia) on their radical as well as conservative notions of what one was in the world to do. And weren't these things illusion of a kind? And this love, which Fenny said was not just physical attraction, an illusion too? Sex she understood, and even a grand passion because that, presumably, was a compound of physical desire, envy, jealousy and possessiveness. But love of the kind Fenny had described, the kind she herself and no doubt Susan had grown up to believe in as right and acceptable, now seemed to her like one more standard of human behaviour that needed that same climate of self-assurance and moral certainty in which to flourish; like all the other flowers of modest, quiet perfection which Susan had imagined grew on the other side of the wall, in the secret garden.

'Susan —' she began.

'What about Susan, pet?' Then, like Uncle Arthur, without waiting: 'I was thinking of Susan, too, of when we saw her and Teddie off at the station on their way to Nanoora.'

'Were you? Why, Auntie?'

'Because of a similar occasion, when we saw your father and mother off on *their* honeymoon. I coped with it awfully well. Later there was a family joke about it. They said I was so busy being the centre of attraction for all the young officers who came down to wave them off that I hardly had time to wave to them myself. In Mirat I watched you so closely, pet, because it brought it all back to me. I knew something had made you unhappy and I wondered if you were feeling the same about Susan whisking Teddie away as I felt about Millie whisking John. You looked so sad.'

'I wasn't sad.'

'Truly?'

'Truly.'

'Then everything's all right. Now.' A squeeze of the arm. 'Finish making yourself look pretty and come in as soon as you can. And do think over what I said. I mean about staying for a bit, just so that you can enjoy yourself, and meet a few new faces. I'm sure General Rankin will turn a blind eye to a few days absence, and your mother can do without you very well. Just for once. Heaven knows when the baby comes you'll all be at sixes and

410]

sevens, so take advantage now, pet.' She hesitated. 'I know it's been
difficult, for many reasons. In the old days coming out to India was
a tremendous lark. All you've had is this dreary war and – and
what it's done to people.' People like my mother, you mean, Sarah
thought. 'When your father gets home and realizes how much
you've done to help your mother and Su, he'll be very proud of
you, but awfully upset to know how little fun you've had.'

As if on cue the silence beyond the closed door was broken by a
peal of men's laughter. Her aunt made a funny face. 'There you
are,' she said. 'If you leave them too long they start telling each
other horrid stories. Men simply aren't serious creatures at all,
they make a joke of everything. I'd better go and keep them in
order. What a shame Jimmy Clark's only here until tomorrow, he
was one of Arthur's most promising chaps on the course and is such
a nice man, but then he was at your father's old school. They're
sending him down to do some special training in something rather
hush-hush in Ceylon. He's only thirty but Arthur say's he'll probably end up a lieutenant-colonel if the war goes on another year,
which it probably won't. He's got an emergency commission but we
think he's the kind of man who may want to stay on in the army
either here or at home. Incidentally, he's been asking all about you.'

Fenny rose, gave Sarah what was meant as a reassuring pat.
Sarah smiled up at her, feeling it incumbent on her to remain where
she was, like a tense little chrysalis from which – in the ten or
fifteen minutes of privacy that were left to her and encouraged by
homilies and the dutiful desire to shake off all those dark and
gloomy images of the world as a repository only of occasions and
conditions of despair – she would emerge as the tough little butter-
fly of Aunt Fenny's affectionate imagination.

*

'No,' Aunt Fenny said, 'tonight the ladies will *not* withdraw. At
least not for more than a few minutes. There are only two of us
and frankly, Arthur, the walls in this flat are too thin for mutual
comfort.' The chaps, cheered by cocktails, an Anglo-Indian curry,
two bottles of South African hock and the expectation of brandy or
liqueurs, laughed dutifully. There were six of them, including
Jimmy Clark who sat on Sarah's right. On her left, at the head of
the table, was her Uncle Arthur, deep in but chin above his cups.

Opposite her, on Uncle Arthur's left, was a pale-faced young officer with a lick of hair who had begun the evening with what she had detected as intellectual reservations but who was now, long before its ending, apparently entranced and well on his way to what she knew men called being as pissed as a newt. Why a newt? She had kept newts one summer at Grandfather's, in a deep square blue Mackintosh's toffee tin and all she could recall was that the water turned sallow and the newts had died. Perhaps that was it. Sallowness, and death by drowning, like Mr Morland in his dream.

'We'll all withdraw and meet next door for coffee and what's-it. Have you boys decided how you'll finish up the evening? There's Ingrid Bergman and Gary Cooper at the New Empire.'

'Send not,' the pale young officer intoned, 'to ask for whom the bell tolls. It tolls for thee. I've seen it, it's rotten.'

'And unless you've booked there isn't a chance,' another man said.

'Well, Arthur and I are going on to the Purvises,' Fenny announced. 'We thought you young people might make up a party of your own. I'm sorry Iris and Dora couldn't come because then you might have preferred to stay here and dance to the gramophone. There's plenty to drink and bits to eat if you get peckish later, so do stay if you'd prefer to, or all go out somewhere. You can talk it over with coffee. It'll be in in just a few minutes.'

Catching Sarah's eye she nodded and rose. Noisily they followed suit. Major Clark helped Sarah with her chair.

In the living-room Fenny said, 'The thing is, pet, just to fall in with what they decide and not express a preference. Men much prefer the helpless happy type. My bet is they'll plump for the Grand Hotel. It's an officers' hostel these days and they feel at home there. They might mix in with another party. Don't be too put out or standoffish if you find yourself in a gang that includes chichis. Boys like these from home think we treat girls like that awfully badly, and perhaps we do. They laugh at them too, but feel sorry for them, and can't bear it when English girls turn up their noses. But you're not like that, pet, are you? You'll have a lovely time. It's quite a thing for them to *have* an English girl, and they'll adore just being seen there turning up with you. And, pet, there's safety in numbers. Well, listen to me. Birds and bees. I shan't start worrying about you until long after midnight. Jimmy Clark will look after you. He'll know exactly why I put him next to you.'

'Who are the Purvises?'

'Oh just some rather dreary civil types Arthur has to keep in with. They're having a bridge party – Indians, not cards – and want to muster forces for after dinner when it gets tense and embarrassing because everybody's said everything twice.'

'I've never been to a bridge party.'

'Think yourself lucky. It's part of the price you pay when you get posted to a place like this. Let's powder our noses and get moving with the coffee. Some of them *need* it.' She hesitated, apparently struck by a conscientious thought. 'Oh dear. Ought I to let you? I *am* responsible for you to your mother, aren't I?'

'I've been out with tipsy boys before.'

'But it's different here. Calcutta's not Pankot and some of them are tipsy already. Well, one of them is.'

'I don't think we need worry about him.'

Fenny stared at her. A slight flush came and went. 'Don't we? Heavens.' She smiled. 'What can you know about such things? Well, anyway. Come on. Powder noses and into the breach.'

*

The Purvises' bridge party was an official affair so Aunt Fenny and Uncle Arthur used the staff car. They dropped Sarah and Major Clark at the entrance to the Grand Hotel. A following taxi brought the five others. Between the departure of car and arrival of taxi, Clark – shooing away small boys and bent beggars – said, 'Be sure to tell me the moment you've had enough. It can get pretty rackety in here. It may not be quite up your street.'

'Oh, I don't know. Why not?'

'Well, I should say rather, it's not much up mine.'

'That didn't seem to be Uncle Arthur's impression earlier.'

'No.' She felt him glance down at her – not far down; he wasn't tall. She caught sight of the taxi that was bringing the others. 'It wouldn't be the first wrong one he's had. Let's go in. It's a hell of a long walk. They'll soon catch up.'

The long walk was through a shopping arcade. At the end of it was the reception hall. Near by a band thumped; a sound Susan once described as only a degree or so less fascinating than the sound of men *en masse*, waiting in the ante-room of a mess for you to arrive on ladies' night. Bands attracted Sarah too, but hearing this one prodded her alive to the fact that under a wakeful surface, artificially stimulated by plenty to drink and too much chatter, she was exhausted. Was it only yesterday at this time that the train had left Ranpur? She smiled cheerfully at the other five, as they came up, and went in the midst of them through a lounge full of wicker chairs and tables, every one occupied, predominantly by men in uniform, and out on to a broad terrace where a band played to an almost empty floor, under a temporary rainy-season roof. In the dry, presumably, you could dance under the stars. Bearers moved tables together and arranged chairs. About to sit she felt herself held.

Clark said, 'I only dance when there's plenty of room and other people can see, so now's your chance.' He took her on to the floor. A quick-step. An over-familiar tune. Susan would know its name. For the first few moments she felt a pleasure at discovering he danced well and that she could follow. But after one and a half circuits of the floor the old problem arose. She had never been much good at talking and dancing together. The two duties seemed incompatible. She tried to recall what questions she had asked him at dinner. Not many. Dinner had centred mainly on conversation dominated by Uncle Arthur. She said the first thing that came into her head.

'Aunt Fenny tells me you were at Chillingborough.'

He nodded. They were not dancing close, but the realization that he never took his eyes off her was almost as inhibiting as that overclose proximity men occasionally attempted and sometimes embarrassingly established.

'It's Daddy's old school,' she said.

'I know. I hope he survived the experience.'

'Yes, I think so.' She did not know what else to say.

'Good, I survived it too.'

A turn or so.

'Have you been in India long?'

'Six months.'

She wondered whether to him that was a short or long time. 'Aunt Fenny said you were in the desert.'

'Mostly a euphemism for Cairo. But yes, I was for a time in what's called the desert.' A pause. 'Shall I ask the questions now and give you a rest?' She glanced up. His smile was remote. His

414]

skin, close to, had a coarseness of texture which she felt she ought to dislike, but didn't. 'How was your boy-friend?'

'My boy-friend?'

'The chap you took goodies to.'

But just then the band stopped on an up-beat and a clash of cymbals.

He shepherded her to the table. A bearer was unloading glasses and bottles from a tray. Only three of the five other men were sitting there.

'Isn't it on the early side for dropping out?' Clark asked. The one with a blond moustache said, 'No one's dropped out.' The others agreed. She thought: They don't like Clark: and recollected that he was a stranger to them. Perhaps they assumed from Clark's proprietary attitude that his earlier connexion with Colonel and Mrs Grace was of a more intimate kind than their own and gave him rights in her which her aunt and uncle accorded formal recognition. It might not even be obvious to them that until today she and Clark had never met. She felt like saying something that would make the position clear, and was conscience-stricken by the fact that in spite of introductions she was uncertain of their names. To the blond moustached one who asked her what she would drink (Freddie? She would have to listen more closely) she said, 'Do you get kicked out if you only want coffee?' He said something about letting them try and coffee it was but what about having something with it, for instance a sticky green? To please him she agreed before the penny dropped that he meant *crème de menthe*. The order was given, the music started up and Freddie (or was he Tony? Why were men so often called by their diminutives?) said 'May I?' and was on his feet as if he had recognized his possible sole opportunity. She responded automatically and was in his arms, waltzing, before she admitted to herself that dancing with the blond-moustached man was the last thing she had wanted to do. She had noticed the heavy perspiration while sitting at the table. Mercifully he kept his distance, but his hands were wet. Susan said heavy sweat was the sign of a beer drinker which was why British Other Ranks perspired worse than officers.

'Mrs Grace told me you've come miles to visit someone at the BMH.'

'Well, just from Pankot.'

'Where's that?'

She told him.

'I was there myself last month. The B M H I mean, not Pankot. Nothing romantic though. Appendix. These days they give you a spinal. Interesting looking up at the ceiling and sort of half feeling it all going on.'

'It must have been awful.'

'Oh, I don't know. Interesting. Looking up at the ceiling.'

She felt for him. Obviously he found dancing and talking incompatible too. She came out with it. 'I've met so many people tonight I've got the names mixed up.'

'Leonard.'

'Mine's Sarah.'

'I know. Just now I nearly made an awful bloomer. At home I've got a Labrador dog called Sarah. Well, I mean she's a she-dog. I nearly said, like you do when you're thinking of something to say, "I've got a dog named after you." I stopped myself in time but then my mind went blank.' Their ankles made fleeting contact. 'Sorry.'

She smiled. 'Where's home?'

'Shropshire. I'm a Shropshire lad. There are poems about it, but I've never read them.'

'What are you, a farmer?'

'How did you guess?'

An image of Mr Birtwhistle's fields and Mr Birtwhistle's cows imposed itself behind Leonard's corn-stook hair and fiery, dripping face.

'I'm not really a farmer though. My father is.'

'It's a reserved occupation, isn't it?'

'Could be. But I'd only just gone in with him, and Dad's not so old. He's got Italian prisoners working for him. Says they're all right. I'm not missed. Well, not for that.'

'Will you go back to farming?'

'Expect so.' A pause. 'Your uncle makes India sound fascinating, though,' he added dutifully. They exchanged rather solemn glances. 'I suppose,' he said, 'you've lived here most of your life.'

'I went home to school. It works out about half and half.'

'Would you recommend it? Living in India?'

'Why, are you thinking about it?'

'Well, it sounds all right, responsible job, lots of servants. Your uncle says it will be years before the Indians can do without us entirely. Up in the Punjab I went round one of those experimental agricultural stations and I thought then there's a job I could do. A chap from England who knows a bit about farming looks at India generally and thinks he's back in the middle ages. I mean I don't know anything about politics or government or commerce, but I do know a bit about land. Some of the things you see make your hair stand on end. But then when I think of settling down here and getting married and having kids I don't think I'd like it much. I mean sending the kids back home wouldn't be my idea of having a family. Am I wrong?'

'I don't know.' She considered. 'I'd hate never to have been home. I'd feel I'd missed something important that I was entitled to, the thing that makes me English. You go back to claim an inheritance. Then if you have children of your own you send them back to claim theirs. It's part of the sacrifice parents have to make.'

'I couldn't make it. Even knowing that if I had a daughter, as well as a dog called Sarah, she might turn out like you if I did.'

She glanced up at him and felt his presence as a homely kindly man some girl other than herself would be fortunate to love and settle down with.

'But then,' he added, 'I don't think you're typical. Young mem-sahibs usually scare me to death.'

She laughed; but for the rest of the waltz they both seemed to find it difficult again to think of anything to say. As he led her back to the table he said, 'Are you really going back tomorrow?'

'I should.'

'You mean there's a chance not? That film at the New Empire isn't rotten. I could sit through it again any day. But perhaps you've seen it too?'

'Oh, in Pankot we never get anything new.'

'May I ring you then, in the morning? You'll know by then, won't you, what you've decided?'

'Yes.'

'Then I'll ring you. At ten o'clock.' He delivered her up to Major Clark. On her section of the table there was coffee and brandy. 'I hope you don't mind,' Clark said. 'I changed the order because I didn't think you looked like a girl who drank sticky green.' The chairs had been moved, too. She and Clark were now subtly isolated from the others. There were still two absentees. They arrived as the band started up again – the pale officer who had been tipsy and now looked paler than ever and the dark-haired boy whom

[417

she was pretty sure was Tony. As they approached the table Clark whispered to her, 'Let's dance again. I'll tell you why presently.'

A foxtrot. She hated foxtrots. She longed just to sit and drink her coffee, but went back on the floor. Clark said, 'That man's been sick. They ought to send him home.'

'He was all right at dinner.'

'Not really. And the air's hit him. I've suggested to the others he ought not to stay.'

She looked in the direction of the table. The man in question was supporting his head in his hands. Two of the others were leaning towards him. The dark-haired boy had his hand on his back. It looked as if they were encouraging him to call it a day and leave while the going was good, before she and Clark returned to the table. Leonard sat watching with his arms on the table, dissociating himself from the argument. There were now more dancers, the floor was quite crowded. Her view was cut off. Clark said, 'When this dance is finished would you do something for me?'

'What?'

'Go to the powder-room. I'll show you where it is. I'll come back for you in about ten minutes. It shouldn't take longer.'

'I don't mind him being a bit high.'

He looked down at her.

'I mind. So would you if he stayed. So would he tomorrow. He's not just high. He's over the edge. He'll end up crying probably. Don't you think so? Don't you think he's the crying type?'

'I don't know.'

'Well I assure you he is.' A pause. 'I'd be grateful if you'd do as I suggest.' He smiled. This time there was no trace of remoteness. She felt exposed to a sudden, inexplicable but encouraging warmth. Leaving go as the music ended, guided back through the doors between terrace and lounge, she was conscious of his body and of her own under its control and protection. Her elbow was held. 'This way.'

'Ten minutes,' he said a few paces from a door. 'I'll be here. If I'm not, go back in and give me another five. Don't stand outside, unless you don't mind being pestered by strangers.'

*

She stayed in the powder-room for a quarter of an hour. Two

Anglo-Indian girls came in. Her presence seemed to inhibit them. They talked in low voices but she caught the lilt which, if their skins were light enough, helped girls like these to pass themselves off as natives of Cardiff and Swansea. She wondered what she would find to say to them if they joined the party. She stayed at the mirror until they had gone and then, coming out, found him waiting.

She said, 'I thought I'd give it the five extra minutes.'

'I'm afraid even ten was too many, so there's a change of plan.' He took her arm and led her into the lounge with the wicker chairs and tables and noisy men, and through into the arcade towards the street.

'What's happened?'

'I'll explain in a minute.'

Again he shooed boys and beggars. A taxi door was held open by one of the hotel bearers. She entered, understanding that he had sent the man to make sure of one.

The man's 'Salaam, Sahib,' marked the passing of baksheesh. Clark spoke to the driver but she did not hear what he said. He might have given Aunt Fenny's address. He joined her. The taxi moved.

'What did you mean, ten was too many?'

'Just that. He wouldn't budge. And the others were no particular help. I'm sorry.' He offered her a cigarette. Automatically, although not wanting it, she took one. 'It's a dreary place anyway. But then it's all most of them have. I'll show you something better. Unless you want to go home. It's only ten-thirty, though.'

After he had lit her cigarette she gazed through the window at a dark sea, the *maidan* side of Chowringhee.

'See those lights way across?' he asked. 'That's where I first met you.'

'Oh.' She looked. 'You're not really telling me the truth, are you?'

'I think so. Yes. That's the BMH.'

'I mean about why we've left the others.'

'I promised your aunt I'd see you came to no harm, Miss Layton.'

After a while she said, 'My name's Sarah,' and turned to look at him in the odd, distorting lights that flickered in and out of the cab. She thought: It's about now he'll make a pass. But he didn't. He simply stared back at her. She said, 'Where are we going?'

'Across the so-called bridge.'

'What does that mean?'

'You'll see.'

What she saw was that in the politest possible way she had been abducted, that he had never had any intention of sharing her with the others, would have found a way of ditching them even if the pale officer had been sober. It would have taken a bit longer but the end would have been the same. She supposed she should feel flattered as well as annoyed. Perhaps that was what she felt, that or too tired to care much how she spent the rest of the evening.

As if he had followed her reasoning and wished to reassure her he said, 'I'll take you home if you'd prefer that,' but put his hand on hers in what she judged a pretence of consideration meant quite otherwise, meant in fact to have the effect it did, which was to leave her, when the touch was withdrawn, deprived of the source of a faint and therefore unsatisfactory physical response. 'The trouble is,' he said, 'if your aunt finds you there when she gets back she'll know the evening went wrong. That fellow doesn't deserve it but the less said about it all the better. Don't you agree? You and I are both leaving Cal tomorrow but they've got another week under your uncle's eye. I wouldn't want any of them to go back to their units with an adverse report, would you?'

'No.'

'I don't mean we should pretend the party never broke up or that you and I never went off somewhere else, but your aunt and uncle needn't be told why. If one of the others lets it out, that's their funeral. Now,' he ended, and touched her hand again, 'let's forget it and enjoy ourselves. This is the real Calcutta. I'm told this time last year these streets were littered with the corpses of people who came in to try and escape the famine. You have to hope the taxi doesn't conk out, they'd probably cut our throats and chuck us into the Hooghly.'

The taxi had increased speed. The road was ill-lit, a squalid urban area. Shrouded figures lay huddled under lean-to shelters and under arcades. Above, there were tenements. After a while the taxi took a road to the left, over a humped-back bridge. The darkness was now stabbed by the beams of the headlamps.

'All clear,' Clark said, 'we've passed the danger zone.'

The road became kuttcha. There were trees, then open spaces; clutches of houses came and went. 'All round here, in the old days, you'd find a lot of rich Indian merchants. But it's gone down. Don't let it depress you, though. We're not going slumming.'

They drove for another ten minutes, reached a crossroads marked by stalls and huts. Crossing another humped-back bridge the driver had to brake sharply to avoid a stray water-buffalo.

'That's India,' Clark commented. 'The internal combustion engine in confrontation with a creature evolved from the primeval slime.' Ahead there was a low stucco wall. They turned into it and through a gateway. She had an impression of a tall, rather narrow house, with many lighted windows. They drew up at an open doorway. When the engine died she heard the music of sitar, tablas and tamboura. He opened the door on his side, which was next the entrance, and helped her out.

'Walk right up and wait,' he said, 'I have to be persuasive.'

She climbed the few steps, smelling incense, but did not cross the threshold into the narrow hall in which she had a glimpse of curtained doorways guarded by a sleepy Buddha and agile Indian Gods cast in bronze. She watched Clark bargaining with the driver, persuading him either to stay or return at a specified hour, and felt calm, which was odd, because standing made her realize that almost imperceptibly she was trembling, as if in the grip of a faint rigor. He came up the steps smiling vividly. 'Fixed,' he said, and harboured her in his right arm, leading her in. An Indian servant had come through one of the curtained doorways. Clark said, 'I've left a taxi-wallah out there, Billy. Try and see he doesn't get bored or go away, but don't give him anything stronger than beer.'

The man signified agreement. Clark led her through one set of curtains into a square room equipped like a bar. The music was coming from the room beyond.

'It's a free house,' he said, going behind a semicircular counter. 'So what'll you have, brandy? You never got to drink that other one, but this is better, Three Star. I'll make it long.' He popped a soda bottle, poured and came back out with two well-filled glasses. 'Cheers.' She answered by raising her glass. 'The house belongs to an Indian woman called Mira. While the music's on we just creep in and sit like mice.' Again he took her elbow, guided her through another curtained doorway into a room that surprised her by its length. Ceiling fans whirled sluggishly, wafting unfamiliar perfumes. A standard lamp at the far end illuminated a carpeted daïs on which the instrumentalists sat cross-legged. The rest of the room was unlit, but she clearly made out among the clutter of divans and couches men and women who sat with their faces towards the source of light. Clark took her on tiptoe to an unoccupied sofa against the wall just inside the doorway. A few feet in front of it a solitary Indian woman sat on cushions. She glanced round, seemed to smile, but returned her attention quickly to the music.

Sarah sat. Clark leant close to her and whispered, 'It's Pyari on the sitar.' She nodded, but only vaguely registered the name as one she might have heard mentioned as that of a famous man. She was never sure how much she liked Indian music or whether she agreed with the general opinion of the people she knew that it was a noise that showed more than anything else the hopelessness of attempting to understand the people who made it. She had an instinctive feeling, though, that even if it was not really what she understood as music it was being performed with great virtuosity. The sitar looked more capable of playing Pyari than he, an ordinary human being with only so many fingers, of playing it. His struggles were immense but must be paying off, judging by the extraordinary ripples of sound. The tablas were smacked with matching agility by a round little man with a bald copper-coloured head. In the background a statuesque woman produced a resonant whining accompaniment on the upright tamboura.

Sarah sipped her brandy and soda. An evening of Indian culture was the last thing she had expected a man like Clark to offer her, but she was hopeful that, unresponsive to it as she was, the music would go on for some time because when it stopped she would find herself out of place, not knowing what to say to the woman who reclined so elegantly on cushions. She guessed that Indians like these laughed at English people like her. Again Clark leaned towards her and whispered, 'The woman on the couch down on the left in the spangled saree's a Maharanee, but she's suing for divorce. The elderly Englishman next to her had a distinguished career in the ICS. He's currently acting as her private legal adviser and escort while she's in Calcutta, but I don't imagine it goes further than that. That young white boy in mufti whose head he's fondling looks like an AB from a ship of His Majesty's Navy.'

Sarah glanced from the Maharanee to the man and stared, at first fascinated and then repelled by the hand that clutched, let go, and clutched again at the dark hair of a young man who sat at his feet uncomplaining. Clark whispered, 'It's one way for boys like that to see a few of the bright lights when they come ashore, and go back on board with a gold cigarette case like the officers have.'

The Maharanee turned, spoke to the retired civil servant, smiled and put her hand briefly on his free one, ignoring the boy and the older man's attentions to him. Sarah looked back at the musicians, and drank more brandy, felt hollow, embarrassed that in a roomful of Indians two Englishmen should so behave themselves. But the embarrassment was incoherent, less real than the curiosity which made not looking at them a conscious effort, a disciplinary exercise in tact that was also intended to display, for Clark's benefit, false proof of her inurement to all quirks of human taste and to evidence of their open satisfaction. She thought Clark had her under scrutiny. She resisted the impulse to find out, but a movement from him convinced her she had been right and that he was deliberately putting her through a test; but whether it was intended to confirm the presence of a physical aptitude or the absence of a moral quality, she did not know.

She decided to face it directly, and looked at him. He was, as she expected, now watching the musicians. His right arm rested on the back of the sofa. The hand – relaxed but too vigorously formed to look limp – hung a few inches away from her shoulder. His face, in profile, just touched by light, as it might be far back in the auditorium of a theatre with the play in progress, reflected the same quality of assertiveness and self-possession. She turned her head again, towards Pyari.

The music sounded as if it had reached a climax and would end abruptly; which it did. The applause was remarkably loud for such a thinly-scattered audience. She set her glass down and joined in, for politeness. The musicians abandoned their instruments and made *namaste*. Light entered the room at several points as servants rung curtains back and came in with trays.

The Indian woman on the cushions turned round.

'Jimmy, the movement control telephoned. The plane leaves for Colombo half an hour earlier than they originally told you.'

'Thanks, Mira. By the way, I've brought someone along to hear Pyari. Her name's Sarah.'

Sarah murmured hello. The Indian woman nodded, addressed Clark again almost immediately.

'Pyari's in good form, isn't he? They've asked him at Government House. Did you hear?'

'No? Will he go?'

'What do you think? He said he might send one of his third-year pupils because the people there wouldn't know the difference. But none of his pupils wanted to go either, even as a joke, unless he let them hide a bomb in the sitar. He said, "Why should we ruin a good instrument?" So that was that.'

Clark laughed, ignoring the fact that the joke was partly on Sarah. A bearer approached, offering *pan*. Sarah shook her head.

'You should,' he recommended, taking one and beginning to chew. 'It cleanses the blood. Haven't you ever eaten *pan*?'

'I did as a child.'

'Have another drink instead then.'

She surrendered her glass. She had emptied it, nervously. The Indian woman got gracefully to her feet and went farther down the room to talk to a man and woman who sat with their arms round each other.

'Mira's a stunner, isn't she?' Clark said.

'Yes. Beautiful.'

'She keeps a husband in drink and pays all his gambling debts and hotel bills, and his mistress's clothes and jewellery accounts.'

'Does she? Why?'

'Why not? She's so rich she can't count it. Anyway, she likes his mistress. They used to be lovers themselves, but she's mad about the Maharanee now, and as that's quite mutual everything in the garden's lovely. You can always tell. When Mira's crossed she shuts herself up in her rooms for days on end. But one way and another this party's been going on since the day before yesterday. So I gather. I only got in this morning. She's probably paying Pyari a thousand chips for the music, so why should he perform at Government House for nothing? Not that he would anyway. He's very anti-government because they've never done anything to encourage the arts. Most of his students confuse art with politics, so he makes political gestures every so often as part of his duties as a good *guru*, but he couldn't care less about politics himself. In fact' – he looked round the room – 'no one here could. Politics are for the poor and the bourgeois middle class. Most of these people have fortunes stashed away in banks in Lisbon and Zürich. The existence of well-to-do little neutral countries is a pointer to what global war is really all about, or haven't you noticed?'

The bearer returned with drinks.

'I expect you wonder how I got to know this place,' Clark continued. 'Mira has friends in Cairo. They wrote her when they knew I was coming to India. So whenever I come in to Calcutta this is my unofficial address, which explains why your Uncle Arthur had that odd idea I was always out on the tiles. I expect somebody reported to him my bed was never slept in. I mean the one in the quaint monkish little quarters they gave me when I got myself sent on that course he runs. But as I was such a bright boy he obviously turned a blind eye.'

'Yes, I see.' She sipped the new, much stronger, brandy and soda, looked at him and asked, 'Has Mira got friends in Ceylon too?'

'We both have.'

'Then you'll be nice and comfortable.'

'It's one of my aims in life. Isn't it one of yours?'

She stared at her glass and, after a moment's hesitation, allowed the absurd truth to enter like a chill draught through all the ill-fitting doors of her inherited prejudices and superstitions. 'I suppose I've never given it much thought.'

'I guessed you hadn't.' He hesitated. 'But you're refreshingly honest. I thought I wasn't mistaken. That honour-of-the-regiment exterior is paper-thin, isn't it?'

Yes, she thought, pitifully thin; but its thinness was less pitiful than the fact that it was there and could be seen and was the only exterior, the only skin she had. She felt her hand taken, and this time held on to.

'I wonder why?' he asked. 'Didn't the second injection take?'

'The second injection of what?'

'India and the honour-of-the-regiment. It's usually fatal, surely? I mean isn't the first one bad enough? Growing up with all the other po-faced kids in a sort of ghastly non-stop performance of Where The Rainbow Ends? Then having to trot back for a time to a little island that's gone down because it's become full of vulgar money-grubbers and people without standards and all sorts of jacks-in-office trying to paint out the pink parts of the map?'

She smiled, but said, 'I suppose that's how it looks. It's only half the truth.'

'What's the other half?'

She moved her hand from under his. She hated simplifications, especially those to which her own ideas of the complex nature of reality might be reduced. He did not reclaim contact.

[425

'Extraordinary, isn't it,' he said, 'that the people in this country who feel most like foreigners to each other are English people who've just arrived and the ones who have been here for several years. Last Christmas, after I left here, I was up in 'Pindi staying with a friend of a friend back home who's been out here for about ten years. And there they were, the man, the wife, and two of the po-faced kids, and right from the beginning we felt towards each other like I suppose those people do who suffer from that odd racial prejudice thing, as if in spite of our being the *same* colour and class, one of us was black, me, and the others white, them. We were tremendously polite but simply had nothing to say to each other. I felt I'd met a family who'd been preserved by some sort of perpetual Edwardian sunlight that got trapped between the Indian Ocean and the Arabian Sea round about the turn of the century. Of course, having gone straight there from Mira's I was prepared to believe I'd struck something unusual. I hadn't, though, had I? It makes me want to say, Where have you all been? Come back. All is forgiven.'

She was still smiling. She said, 'Come back where? Forgiven by whom, and for what?'

But he was, after all, quite serious. 'I suppose one of the things you need to be forgiven for is deluding the Indians as well as yourselves into thinking that the values of 1911 are still current at home.'

'Why 1911?'

'Wasn't that the year of the Delhi Durbar? *Post*-Edwardian I grant you, but anything before 1900 would be a journalist's exaggeration and anything after 1914–18 quite irrelevant. And when I say deluding Indians I don't mean people of the kind you see in this room, I mean the kind who take you seriously, and that includes chaps like Gandhi and Nehru. Actually I hate the word Westernized, it's used so loosely. You could say Mira's Westernized, but she's modern West and that means a fair slice of modern East as well. Nehru and that lot, all the liberal-upper and bourgeois middle-class of India, they're one hundred per cent old-fashioned West. And it's all as dead as yesterday, isn't it? You ought to bury the body, or expose it to the vultures like the Parsees do. It didn't survive the Great War. It makes an awful smell. Of course there are still pockets of the stink at home, your kind of people go back to them and I was educated at one. Highly unsuccessfully. They went in a lot at Chillingborough for future colonial administrators,

426]

didn't they? They were even planning to have an Indian boy there
— one who wasn't a Maharajah's son. He came round with his dad
during my last term to have a look-see at one of the traditional
founts of all liberal-imperial wisdom, and I thought, the poor little
sod, he thinks this is where his future gets handed to him and un-
wrapped like a slab of chocolate. But he probably hadn't got a
future.'

'Hadn't he?'

'As a tomb-attendant? I expect he's a sub-divisional officer now
and wondering whether to stay in the executive or transfer to the
judiciary. His deputy commissioner is more likely to be an Indian
than an Englishman but the work he does and the attitudes that go
with it will be the same as they were forty years ago when some
pink-faced boy from Wiltshire sat under the same punkah and
wrote manly letters home to his mother.'

'What do you do for a living?'

'You mean in peace-time. The answer's the same in war or
peace. I live.'

'On air?'

'No. I make money too.'

'At what?'

'At what? Do for a living? It's awfully unimportant, isn't it?
Strip the guff from any job and what have you got? A way of
making money. And please don't say, "Somebody has to run
things." I know they do. Running things means making them pay.
I run things to the extent I make things pay. To me a Viceroy is
about as important or unimportant as a company secretary who
drafts the annual report for the shareholders to tell them what the
board's been up to. Your board's made a lousy job of running things
out here. The place is a goldmine, but it's stiff with unemployed
BAs and people who die in the streets of hunger. That's a legacy
from all those blue-eyed Bible thumpers and noble neo-classicists
who came out here because they couldn't stand the commercial pace
back home. You had a perfectly good thing going in that old merchant trading company who used to run things until the industrial
revolution. What you wanted then was a bevy of steely-eyed brass
founders and men of iron who'd have ground the faces of the
Indian peasants in the dirt, sweated a few million to death and
dragged India yelling into the nineteenth century. Instead of which
you got the people who didn't like the smoke and the dark satanic

mills because that sort of thing was vulgar, and after them you got the people who didn't like it because of the inhumanity that went with it. What you didn't get was the damned smoke. And that's the trouble. The Indian empire's been composed exclusively of English people who said No. Out here you've always had the negative side, the reactionaries and the counter-revolutionaries, but you've never had the bloody revolution. That's why an Indian urban dweller's life expectation is still thirty-five and why people die of starvation while the band plays at Government House, and Pyari plays the sitar at Mira's. Well, at home after the war we'll cut your empire adrift without the slightest compunction. It's a time-expired sore, a suppurating mess. From the point of view of people who really run things it's like a leg that you look at one morning and realize is too far gone in gangrene to be worth saving. Limping's better. It's going to be up to the Indians to grow a body from the limb. Of course most of them will make the mistake of thinking their independent body-politic is a whole, walking body. And at home we'll pretend we've fulfilled a moral obligation by giving it back to them. But that won't be the reason. We'll get rid of it because it doesn't pay and it's too late to make it pay. Give the war another year, the one in Europe anyway, and the one with Japan another year. Say summer 1946. You can expect a general election in England in the summer of 1946 at the latest, and the socialists will get in because the common soldier and the factory worker will put them in. Lopping off India is an article of faith with the socialists but when they see that keeping it doesn't pay they'll lop it double-quick. Who wants India's starving millions as one of what we'll all call our post-war problems?'

'Are you a socialist?'

'Good Lord, no. I'm what you'd call a low Tory, if you could call me anything at all.'

'Why are you so sure the socialists would win an election? Won't Mr Churchill's reputation count for anything?'

He laughed, and turned the question.

'Why do women always call him Mr Churchill? It makes him sound like a vicar who's been invited to judge the home-made calves-foot jelly. But the answer's yes, of course, his name *will* count. For everything patriotic, proud, victorious and time-expired. I don't suppose you've talked much to common British soldiers, have you? The fellows you refer to as BORs? You ought to. Ask

428]

them what they think of life out here, I mean the national service wallahs, not the regulars. Then you'll know. If there's one thing war shows the man in the street it's the difference between himself and the officer-caste. Back home it's obvious enough but on foreign service he feels it like a kick in the teeth. I'll tell you what your BOR in Deolali or your cockney motor mechanic with the Desert Rats or your Brummagem door-to-door salesman with Wingate in Burma thinks. He thinks, "All right, mate. Have it cushy whenever you can and be a Boy Scout while the shit flies. Get on winning the war your lot started. I'll even give you a cheer at the end. And when you've got the whole stinking mess sorted out, be a good lad and bugger off, out of my sight, out of my government and out of my bloody life. But for ever." And what goes for the officer-caste goes for Churchill. Your poor blighter of a BOR thinks it's all real, you see. He hears the popping of corks in the officers' tents and goes back to his mug of tea or stale NAAFI beer with murder in his heart knowing everything would be all right if he could guzzle brandy, or if the Colonel had to choke on a mug of tea with bromide in it to stop him feeling randy. He thinks his own lot ought to run things because there are more of his lot drinking tea with bromide in it than there are what he calls la-di-dah poofs swigging brandy and getting hot for women they won't know how to poke.'

With an effort Sarah kept her eyes coolly on a level with his. She understood that the test and his use of gutter-slang, were part of a process of seduction. He would use different methods with different women. The words he chose for her and the whole grava-men of his argument were calculated to expose her as someone for whom, primarily, he felt contempt. He wanted her on her mettle. Or in embarrassed confusion. Or weak and defeated. She was not sure which.

'Go on,' she said.

He laughed, again reached for her hand and grasped it hard. 'You're quite a girl, Sarah Layton.'

'No,' she said, 'I'm not quite a girl. I'm this one,' and was aware of having jerked him into unexpected recognition of her as a person and not a type. She told this from his heavy hand which became, for a second or two, uncharacteristically inert.

'He's on the ball in one sense, your BOR,' Clark continued. 'The brandy's real enough and so's the tea and bromide. His mistake

[429

comes in thinking the difference between them has some kind of moral significance and proves his rights as a human being have been infringed. But what he calls his rights as a human being start where his honest sensations stop, don't they? His honest sensations tell him to knock the Colonel down and pinch his brandy, but he's scared to do that and begins nursing a grievance and inventing a right, the right to a fair share. But when you cut out the moral claptrap your *fair* share of anything is what you're strong enough to grab. Or would you prefer the word earn? In practice it comes to the same thing. Your fair share is what you take. Don't you agree?'

Did she? She felt as if the effort she had put into facing up to him had reduced her power of concentration, that somehow she had missed some of the words and that her sudden inability to answer exposed for both of them the real reason why she sat there, unprotesting. With a gesture half-affectionate, half-mocking, he moved his hand and placed the knuckles behind her ear, ruffling her hair. Understanding that it would amuse him to see her shrink from such contact, she deliberately – but slowly – changed the angle of her head and body to force disengagement. The hand moved away, only to rest again on her bare neck.

'You're very tense,' he said. 'Did your visit to the hospital upset you?'

'I expect so.'

'Is he a bit of a mess, then, this fellow you went to see?'

'They're amputating his arm.'

'Oh. Yes, that *is* bad, isn't it? But it explains one thing that puzzled me. The fact that you appeared to take such an instant dislike to me. It means you must have noticed me and that the dislike was merely a transference of the physical revulsion you felt for the poor blighter they're going to cut up. It's quite common. Amputation *is* revolting, but a woman especially won't accept that it is until she sees someone she likes the look of, then she thinks, "You're disgustingly whole, why have you got two arms, blast you?" Or legs, or whatever it is the chap she used to like hasn't got any longer.'

'But I didn't like him.'

'No?' The hand on her neck moved an inch or so. 'You came an awfully long way to see him then, but I'll accept that and I don't think it makes any difference. The revulsion was there. You took it out on me. Shall I tell you something?'

430]

'What?'

'You're not so tense now.'

It was true. Her body had become capable of controlled and fluid movement: a new feeling that added to her confidence and for which she felt indebted to him in a way she could not explain, except by acknowledging that it flowed from his hand. His eyes and line of cheek, lit obliquely, gave his face — now fully turned towards her — an irony which she thought she understood.

'You're still a virgin, of course, aren't you?'

The shocking directness of the statement caused her to jerk her glance away. She felt that he had hit her. Presently, she said, as clearly and levelly as she could, 'Yes, I'm still a virgin-of-course,' and by doing so arrested the retreat of warmth. But she could not bring herself to face him. For a while she was conscious of his continued observation and of the way her body was becoming increasingly dependent on the support of his hand for whatever air it had of self-possession. When he removed his hand and placed it momentarily on hers before removing it entirely, it seemed to her like a valedictory gesture, an acknowledgement of her as the person she had made him see behind the paper-thin exterior; the girl he had stalked, attacked, and tried to shock into a predictable herd-reaction. But when he took his hand away she felt he took that real self too and left her with nothing but her shell. She sat, coldly bereft, and then wondered if he had taken anything, had seen instead what she herself could not see, but began to have intimations of; that the shell was all there was because she had rejected all the things that had once filled it, and had not replaced them. One by one they had gone, the beliefs, affections and expectations of her childhood: but when? She stared across the room at the carpeted daïs where the unattended instruments lay and felt herself unattended too. Perhaps at her christening certain spectres had come like unbidden guests, spectres of that extinction-through-exile that awaited Muirs and Laytons and all their kind, and stolen away unseen, having cursed or blessed her with an awareness of their presence which would dog her footsteps and fill her mind, until, bit by bit, as she was bidden, she had cast out of herself all her inheritance and was left in possession — as it were of a relic — of a shell whose emptiness was the proof for future generations of where the fault had lain and why there could have been no other end, even for her. Perhaps especially not for her, because once —

hunched on a window-seat – she had drawn her root and branch and ringed her Indian family proudly in red. Perhaps it had been a condition of the christening gift that what she discarded bit by bit should be discarded as proudly as it had once been put on, so that the possibility of looking for substitutes to ensure survival was excluded. If you went down you went down and the proudest way was not to go down fighting for eroded values but, simply, with them, however little you were responsible for them. Those values were your shell as well, what you were left with after you had rejected their substance. The shell was unalterable.

He said, 'I seem to have discovered the chink in your armour. But are you annnoyed with me for asking, or because you have to admit you are? Or is it a bit of both? I can't believe it's that you're plain old-fashioned shocked or embarrassed. And you don't look like a girl who thinks a man should automatically assume the absence of a wedding ring on the hand of a well-brought-up young lady means she's saving it up for Mr Right. Or am I wrong?'

They were questions she could not answer except from a fund of outworn stock replies such as he would only receive with a gently derisive pretence of not having anticipated. The alternative was silence; which she chose.

'In any case,' he said, 'clearly I must apologize.'

The hand rested again on the back of her neck. The warmth flowed back in, revealing the one unchanging purpose to which she could be put, even as a shell. Her nipples hardened in simulation of giving suck, but she continued to stare at the daïs. There was sudden movement in the room. The man who had played the tablas had come back in. A girl accompanied him.

'Mira *is* doing us proud,' he whispered, leaning close. 'It's Lakshmi Kripalani. She sings, in case you didn't know.'

She nodded, more in acknowledgement of his breath's faint palpations of her ear than of the words spoken. Mira was approaching. The Maharanee had also risen and was coming in her wake, but continued on towards the curtained doorway. Mira came to the sofa and leaned forward and spoke to her, excluding Clark.

'They'll be playing again soon. I'd better show you where you can freshen up.'

Clark removed his hand, relieved her of the unfinished glass of brandy.

'It's a good idea,' he said. 'They might go on for an hour. It depends on how inventive they're feeling. I'll keep this warm for you.'

Sarah got up with the half-formed intention of telling him that an hour was too long, that she should go home because they both had an early start to the day ahead; but she could not summon the determination. She followed Mira into the bar, through into the hall, then a passage, and up a staircase that turned twice. They came out on to a gallery whose barred windows were unshuttered and admitted the warm mulchy smell of the Bengal night. The gallery turned at right angles and continued along the length of the side of the house. Light came from naked bulbs fixed into sockets in the gallery roof. The Indians sometimes had a crude, uncluttered attitude towards electricity, Sarah thought. So often the bulb was accepted as a decoration in itself. Mira wore no chola under the dark saree. The elastic of a brassiere showed. At the end of the gallery she turned in at an open door. Sarah followed and paused – astonished at the room's opulence. A double bed, raised on a wide but shallow daïs and enclosed by a white mosquito net hung high and centrally so that the effect was of a regal canopy, was its main focus. The gossamer net shivered under the gentle changing pressures of air wafted by two revolving ceiling fans. The daïs was covered in white carpet and the bedcovers were of creamy white satin. The furniture was satin-walnut. Mira, still without speaking, had walked to a door, opened it and switched on a light.

'There's probably everything you want. If not, just ring and one of the girls will come.'

A fragrance, a chill; the bathroom was air-conditioned. It was larger than her bedroom at Pankot and marble-floored, with sheep-skin rugs. Above the semi-sunken bath gilt faucets projected from marble green tiles. At one end of the bath pink frosted glass screened off the shower.

She looked at Mira, fearing her, chilled by her, but ready to praise what belonged to her. But Mira seemed quite indifferent and held the door open as if anxious to be gone. 'Thank you,' Sarah said, and went past her. The door was closed. The lavatory was in an adjoining cubicle. The cistern was the modern kind with a levered handle. It flushed quietly and immediately. In the pedestal wash-basin, piping hot water flowed. Back in the bathroom she sat on a luxurious stool with curved gilt claw legs and a padded green velvet seat. The legs of the marble-topped table matched the legs of the stool. She studied herself in an immense mirror; a flattering one. Glancing at the array of bottles and sprays and jars she opened her handbag with misgivings about the quality of its contents but determined to use nothing that didn't belong to her, and then was held by a delayed reaction. Her eye had caught objects that struck her as incongruous. Among the scents, lotions and other items in a toilet battery of wholly feminine connexion were two wood-backed bristle hair-brushes and a leather case. The zip was half undone. She reached out, zipped further, then completely, and lifted the cover, stared at the contents – four gold-plated containers and a matching safety razor.

She turned round, considered the bathroom, searching it for other clues to masculine occupation without much idea of what to look for, and noticed in one corner a bin with a padded seat that obviously lifted. She turned back to the mirror and went to work with powder from her compact, occasionally glancing at the bin's reflection. A dab of lipstick completed her repair operations. She shut her handbag. The click echoed. She sat for a while and felt in need of some show of kindness, such as Aunt Fenny had made, taking her shoes off, making her rest, and again remembered that she had not slept properly for two days; three, if she counted the night she last slept in Pankot, disturbed by a gift of lace, a meeting avoided, and expectation of new ground and a long journey. She looked at her watch. Eleven-thirty. Less than six hours since she had said Goodbye, Ronald, and got in return a goodbye that was not coupled with the blessing and absolution of her name.

Her name – she got up from the stool – her formidable, bony, yearning name – and walked to and opened the bin; stared down at the soiled expensive briefs, those meshes of mysterious and complex cellular imprisonment. She closed the lid, knowing that both bath and bedroom were tainted by his casual presence and the ludicrous talent he had for casual contemptuous excitation.

I am sensible now – she decided – after Pyari has played I shall go home, alone if necessary. She reached for door-handle and light-switch, intending to flick the one after opening the other, but when she opened the door a whole field of darkness faced her. She stood arrested by it and by the notion that darkness always contained dangers and presences.

Instinctively, but without conviction, she blamed Mira, who had apparently not even left the door open between bedroom and

434]

gallery. There would have been light enough then. Momentarily she was without a sense of direction. She felt along one wall, searching for another switch. Her elongated shadow probed the slant of bathroom light across the floor and up a blank wall. There was no switch. But she had her bearings. The five-mile hill, the five-mile door. Over there, she told herself; and was rewarded then by the suddenly visible pale strip of light marking the boundary of bedroom and gallery. She walked towards it, and stopped.

'You're going the wrong way,' he said. 'I'm over here.'

His voice came from behind, from some intensely organized, centralized point of reference. Turning towards it she was dazzled by the light from the decoy bathroom. The bed was darkly shadowed by one of the bathroom walls, which jutted into the room.

'You seem startled. Weren't you expecting me?'

'No.'

She turned and walked towards the slit of light, anticipated the driven-home look and the absent key. She jerked the handle. The absurdity of the handle's obedient but unfunctional mobility nullified her attempt to convey composure. Nothing looked sillier than trying to open a door the person watching you knew you knew was locked. She turned back, facing that equally absurd dark central point of reference.

'That's a pity,' he said. 'I thought you understood we had an appointment. Mira did, so you mustn't worry about our absence causing comment. Is it the dark that puts you off? I thought you'd prefer it. At first, anyway.'

'We have no appointment. Please turn the lights on and open the door.'

As she spoke she realized that her eyes had become more used to the dark areas beyond the shaft of light coming from the bathroom. There was a slow rhythmic movement and in the second before the restored bedside lamp reversed the negative image into a positive one she detected the stretched arm, sensed the manipulative action of his hand on the switch, and understood from the spare density of his form that he was naked.

He was seated on the edge of the bed, staring back at her across a still extended arm, caught and held in the ageless classic pose of a figure from some Renaissance ceiling. The shock he gave her was that of astonishment that in the flesh a man could look as he had been depicted for centuries in stone and paint. Lowering the arm he exposed a sculptured chest.

'Are you sure you want the door opened?'

'Yes.'

'The key's here on the table. I've also been thoughtful enough to bring our glasses. Have I miscalculated? I don't often, but it wouldn't be the first time. It's an occupational hazard of the male. You get a few more slaps in the face than you deserve, but you also get your screws, so you can't complain. Are you quite sure you don't want to lose that cherry?'

'Quite sure. I'll give you a minute to unlock the door.'

She moved, making for the bathroom. Casually, he got up and was there ahead of her. She stood still. Naked, the earlier and only slight advantage he had in height was further diminished. In her high heels she eyed him almost levelly, but her manifest disadvantage in strength and weight was pressed home on her as if by an actual pressure of his limbs. She turned, sat on a padded satin-covered chair. Doing so disclosed to her the shameful fact that she was trembling. She faced him again, deliberately. She observed him dispassionately, from head to foot. Having quartered him she looked again to her front and said, 'I've seen you now, so may I go?'

'That wasn't the object of undressing. I turned the light off, remember? The only reason I'm like this is that making a pass at a girl and getting her hot and then introducing the devastatingly practical note of pausing to take your clothes off always strikes me as highly comic. When a man wants a screw he ought not to beat about the bush. It's different for girls because their clothes can come off so gracefully. Have I really wasted my time?'

'Yes.'

'Well, that's an occupational hazard too.'

There was a pause. Presently he crossed her line of vision. When he reached the bed he felt under the mosquito net and drew something out. Blue material. His pyjama trousers. He put them on. The bunched tops of the trousers thickened his waist slightly. He lit a cigarette, then brought their glasses of brandy over. He put them on the floor, went back to the table for an ashtray, returned and sat on the floor himself, and gazed up at her.

'You're not really plain, are you? In fact you're quite pretty. And you've got thin shoulders. In the buff I expect your breasts

436]

look much more prominent.' He put his head on one side, considering her. 'But your hips are a shade too narrow. I bet you've got a hard little bottom. What I like best about you though is you never say anything too obvious. I know the dialogue that can go with this particular situation by heart and it gets pretty boring. So that's what I like best. Your not saying anything obvious and your Colonel's daughter's guts. It makes an unusual combination.' He drank, indicated her own glass. 'Drink up. It'll do you good. I never screw them when they're pissed so you're quite safe. I mean don't *not* drink because you think I'd take advantage if you had too much. But I don't suppose you ever have too much, do you? That's another point in your favour. Your aunt told me you have a thin time at home because your mother drinks. It's embarrassing, isn't it? My father drank a lot. He used to cry too. Does your mother cry? What she ought to do is give up drinking and find some young officer who'll screw her whenever she wants and bow out without making a fuss when the Colonel comes home. After all, that would be better for the Colonel, wouldn't it? To come home to a placid, loving woman, instead of a neurotic alcoholic who gets her screws out of bottles.'

'Like your father?'

'Yes, like him.'

'And what did *your* mother do for screws?'

'Oh, Mother was never hard up. She went in for handsome chauffeurs. When I was eighteen I put my foot down, though, and insisted that even if the chauffeurs went to bed with her they still had to call me either Master James, or Sir.'

'And did they?'

'Yes, but I expect it cost her an extra small fortune at the men's shops in Bond Street.' He smiled. 'Go on. You're doing very well. For one awful moment I thought you were going to say something like "Kindly leave my mother and father out of this." I hope you're not too cross with Aunt Fenny, by the way. She was only trying to paint a little picture of you that would bring out my protective instincts. She said more than she intended, but that was my fault.'

'I realized that.'

'Do all your family view you with the same mixture of alarm and affection as she does?'

'Probably.'

'Why are you shivering?'

'Because I find it difficult to control myself.'

'And you feel you must? What do you find difficult to control? Your temper?'

'Yes.'

For the first time since coming to sit on the floor he freed her from her self-imposed obligation not to let her glance waver. He looked down at his glass and for a moment she escaped into the safe oblivion of private darkness. When she opened her eyes again he was watching her. She said, 'I'd be glad if you'd open the door now. If the taxi's still waiting I can go home without putting you to any trouble. If it's not I'm afraid you'll have to organize one. I don't know where we are.'

'Don't worry about the taxi. You're forgetting I promised Aunt Fenny you'd come to no harm.'

'She's my Aunt Fenny, not yours.'

The comfortable angle of his head and trunk, the casual, easy, disposition of his limbs created confusing images in her mind of strength and languor and confident patience. They were confusing because she herself felt she had come to the end of a tether.

He took his hand from his glass, stubbed his cigarette and rose. She anticipated a physical attack on her, but he did not make it. Instead he went back to the bedside table, picked up the key and returned. He resumed his former position on the floor, tossed the key two or three times like a coin, then placed it on the floor between them.

'*My* key for *your* Aunt Fenny,' he said. 'I pay the forfeit and keep Aunt Fenny. There's not much going on in her, but what goes on is tough as old boots. I like that. If she were five years younger and I were five years older we'd screw. She knows it. In that cosy closed-in little corner of her bird-brain mind where the real Aunt Fenny lives she knows it, just as she knows in the same cosy little corner that asking me to look after you was the most risky thing she could do if you wanted to hang on to that cherry of yours. Obviously what she really thinks is that you ought to get rid of it. Which means she thinks the same as I do, only with her the thought's subconscious. I'll tell you another thing. You're tougher than she is. Far tougher than you probably realize. With you the toughness goes an awfully long way in because you haven't got a bird-brain. It thinks. Potentially you're worth twenty Aunt Fennys.

But the thinking and the toughness aren't worth a bag of peanuts if you lack joy And that's what Aunt Fenny has that you haven't. Joy. Not much. She's too shallow to have much of anything, but I bet you she was a scorcher as a girl. I bet she went for joy first and let the thinking and toughness come later, and that means that in her late middle-age she still remembers how to get a kick out of life. It doesn't really matter which way round you do it, if you do it both ways. But why not do it both ways from the start? Isn't that sensible? Isn't the place already overcrowded with people who have thought for so long they've forgotten how to be happy, or with people who've spent so long trying to be happy they haven't had time to think, so end up not knowing what happiness is? For pete's sake, Sarah Layton, you don't know anything about joy at all, do you?'

'No,' she said. 'No, I don't,' and reached for the key and then, stupidly, lost sight of it because her eyes had responded – as if of their own accord – to a humiliation, an unidentifiable yearning, and a dim recollection of an empty gesture that had something to do with wrenching the reins of a horse and wheeling to confront imaginable but infinitely remote possibilities of profound contentment. She felt the metal of the key under her fingers and the flesh-shock of his hand on her knuckles.

'You're crying,' he said. 'Why? Because you really want me to make love to you? I couldn't promise that. Not love. You couldn't either, could you? Not with me. If you liked we could pretend that it was love but it wouldn't be honest and your honesty is part of what attracts me. You don't belong, do you? And the trouble is you know it, but I suppose while your father's away you feel you have to pretend you do belong, for his sake.'

'No,' she said. 'I do belong. That's what I know. That's the trouble. Please take your hand away.'

He did so. She grasped the key. It weighed nothing. What it would open was a prison of a kind.

'Wait,' he said. He got up, went to the far side of the bed. Through the net she saw blurred pictures of a stranger dressing. There was a superior kind of mystery about him. In her dream there had been no problems, no threat of violence. She had surrendered to him casually. The absence of a climax struck the one familiar note; that and an awareness of her father's unspeaking presence, his silent criticism of her failure to hold back for him the tide of changing circumstances, her failure to hold in trust days he had lost which belonged to him; days that must, to him, be an incalculably dear proportion of those few left in which the once perpetual-seeming light would shine on undisturbed by the brighter, honest, light whose heat would burn the old one to a shadow.

The stranger came from behind the net and stood for a moment watching her. Who is that man? people asked her in the dream. And her reply had always been, Oh, I don't know. She had never been convinced that she spoke the truth, but in any case now knew the answer. Who is that man? Why, one of us, one of the people we really are.

'Well,' he said, 'shall we go, Sarah Layton?' He came closer. 'If so you ought to bathe your eyes. My Aunt Fenny would think the worst had happened if she saw you now.'

She was holding the key in one hand and her handbag in the other. The blurred opaque image of his face cleared. Presently he bent forward, grasped the exposed end of the key and carefully took it from her. He held out his other hand and, when she did not move, reached further and touched the strap of the handbag, then grasped it. Her own grip loosened. She felt the smooth strip of leather slide from her fingers and watched him stand back, holding the two things she had surrendered and which he now seemed to be showing her, waiting for some kind of confirmation that she understood he had them. He transferred the key to the hand with which he held the handbag then stooped and picked up the ashtray and, with his free hand, their glasses, holding them from the insides, rim to rim, between thumb and fingers. He went to the bedside-table, placed the glasses and the ashtray by the lamp and, after a moment's hesitation, placed the handbag there as well. Still holding the key he went over to the door and inserted it in the lock but did not turn it. He came back and stood in front of her in further brief consideration and then went over to the bedside-table again and switched the lamp off so that the room was as it had been at the beginning of their encounter. The shaft of light from the bathroom stretched across the floor, separating them until he emerged from the shadow on the other side of it and crossed over on to her side, and squatted. He touched her right ankle, gently lifted and eased the shoe from her foot and then the shoe from the other foot, and placed the shoes neatly together on one side of the

440]

chair. The hand in which she had held the key was cupped and taken, and then the other, and both carried and held to his face, so that it seemed she had reached out and put her hands on his cheeks with a gesture of adoration. She closed her eyes, exploring the illusion of possession which such an adoration might create between two people and was then aware that her hands were no longer held except by the desire to explore. Her own head was taken. For a while they stayed so, enacting the tenderness of silent lovers, and then slowly bending her head she allowed him to deal with the old maid's hook and eye.

V

HIS HAND was on her arm gentling her from sleep and in the second or two before she woke she knew the sweet relief of this evidence that she had only dreamt the scene in which Aunt Fenny told her Susan was in premature labour brought on by shock; and that the reality was this warm quiescence with which her body came back to life and consciousness, flesh to flesh with the body of the man who had penetrated it, liberated it, and was waking it again from profound rest so that it might enclose and be enclosed and go again, rapt, to the edge of feeling.

'I'm sorry,' the voice said. 'But we're nearly there.' A strange, unbelievable, soundless splintering; an extraordinary convolution of time and space. Her eyes opened and she saw the woman whose name was Mrs Roper. 'We're coming into Ranpur, Miss Layton. I'm sorry to disturb you.'

She pulled herself upright, understanding completely where she was and yet not understanding it at all, but she knew she was indebted to Mrs Roper and to Mrs Roper's friend, Mrs Perryman, and that this was because they had let her share the coupé and had even had the top bunk lowered so that she could rest properly. She knew from the lights in the ceiling, close to her head, that it was night, whereas it had been day when the bunk was lowered. Her uniform was crumpled.

'Can you manage, my dear?'

Mrs Roper's head scarcely came to the level of the bunk. The fans whisked the stray ends of her grey hair which was set in a way that suggested Mrs Roper remembered she was pretty as a girl. Mrs

Roper's husband had been a Forestry Officer in Burma. He sent her back to India in 1941 and as she hadn't heard a word since the Japanese invasion she believed he was hiding out with one of the hill-tribes who had been their friends. Mrs Perryman's hair was brassy-blonde. Her husband had been in the medical service and died of cholera in 1939. She took in paying-guests, one of whom was Mrs Roper. They had been staying with Mrs Roper's brother's family on leave at Ootacamund and were on their way back to Simla, having returned by way of Calcutta to visit a friend of Mrs Perryman's whose husband was in jute. It was their first holiday since the beginning of the war, and they had saved for it, presumably. But they had not mentioned money.

Sarah knew all these things about them because they had talked incessantly from midday when the train left Howrah station until an hour after lunch. They had talked for kindly reasons because Uncle Arthur had taken them on one side to thank them for letting her share the coupé and to ask them to look after her because her great-Aunt, of whom she had been very fond, had died suddenly in Pankot and the shock had sent her sister into premature labour. She swung round on the bunk and was held by a reaction in her blood-stream, unexpected but familiar. Sound and sight became miniature, far away. From behind brass screens she heard Mrs Roper say, 'Now don't rush. I just thought you'd want plenty of time because we only stay in Ranpur ten minutes.'

With her foot she felt for the top of the nest of steps, far down in the distorted well of the coupé, and finding them, made the descent.

'You've had a nice long sleep. We nodded off too. Now don't bother about us. Is there anything we can do?'

'No thank you, Mrs Roper. I'm fine.'

'Leave the bunk. Directly we've had dinner Mrs Perryman and I are going to tuck down.'

In the cubicle she bathed her face in slow-running tepid water. There were specks of soot. The train was going over points, intersection after intersection. She steadied herself on the handgrip and confronted her mirror image. Did it show? Could anyone tell? That she had entered, like other women? Yes; to her it showed; vividly; more vividly than her anxiety for Susan, more strongly than the grief cushioned by disbelief that she felt for Aunty Mabel who walked in and out of her mind, condemned by a memory to go on performing the task to which so many hours of her last days had been stubbornly devoted; more strongly than the concern for her mother who had been alone to cope and for her father for whom Aunty Mabel was now an irretrievable part of a time she had been unable to hold back for him. She did not know why she should have wanted to hold it back. She did not even know she had tried to until she saw that it had gone. She had failed but she had entered. She had entered her body's grace.

Mrs Roper personally selected the coolie to carry Sarah's single suitcase. Thirty years of experience had given her an eye, she said; an eye for the kind of coolie an unaccompanied white girl could rely on not to intimidate her into paying him more than he deserved, and to make sure, in such a case as this, that the transfer from one train to another was smoothly accomplished.

'Shouldn't we find an escort for you?' Mrs Perryman asked. 'There must be at least one young officer on the platform we could whistle up.'

But Sarah was already at the open door of the carriage and there were nearly two hours to go before the train for Pankot left Ranpur. 'I'll go to the restaurant and then to the waiting-room if necessary. I'll be perfectly all right. Thank you for all your kindness.' She shook hands with them and stepped down. The platform was crowded. She saw bearers threading their way through with loaded trays, and called up to Mrs Roper that their meals were coming. Then she waved and followed the elderly coolie who had her suitcase on his head. Her childhood delight in travelling at night was still a potent force. She had always loved the noise, the risk, of railway stations. The journey to Calcutta was the first she had ever made alone. The case, hovering at eye level – and as bodies interposed themselves between her and its bearer looking as if it moved of its own accord without support – was a symbol of childhood's end. It struck her how curious an object a suitcase was. To it you consigned those few essential portable things that bore the invisible marks of your private possession of them; but the case itself was destined to live most of its useful life under the public gaze and in the hands of strangers.

At the door of the station restaurant the coolie halted. The turbanned head, which earned him an anna for all that it could carry at any one time, was set in a rigid thrust-up position that gave his eyes, under wrinkled, hooded lids, a preoccupied, anxious look.

She changed her mind about going to the restaurant first. The Pankot train would be waiting at its special platform. She could look for her reservation and, if she were lucky, get the compartment opened and have a tray sent in. She gave the coolie instructions and once more followed him, to the end of the main platform, to the point where two subsidiary tracks came in to a bay, to sets of buffers, with a platform separating them. On one track there were three lit coaches, one of them painted blue and white, colours she had never seen before, and on the other the Pankot train, which she recognized because of the coaches: old-fashioned, squarer-cut, and with decorative flourishes in the woodwork. There were a few people on the platform, among them two Indian police, and a station official with a white topee. The Pankot train was in darkness. Some way along the platform under a lamp, a group of private soldiers were playing cards. Men off leave or on posting; perhaps both kinds. Tomorrow night they would be playing cards or writing home at the regimental institute and perhaps Mrs Fosdick or Mrs Paynton would be among the women who manned the tea-urns. She felt the first lick of a wave of nostalgia for the Pankot hills, but fought it down because upon its ripples grief could ride in. She spoke to the Indian in the white topee. No, the train was not ready yet. No, he did not have the key to unlock the compartments. But he went with her, looking with a torch for that strange advertisement of her name, noted and written on a piece of card by someone she would never see and placed in its metal bracket on the side of the carriage by someone she might see but never know.

Closer to the group of card-players this other card was found. A coupé. The discovery gave her childish pleasure, as did the fact that there was no name on the card but her own. Miss Layton. She would sleep undisturbed. She turned to the patient coolie and used the old old words of command. *Idhar thairo. Idhar thairo.* Stay here. Stay here. Dutifully he lowered the case and then squatted beside it as though it were a child he had carried far, out of some ancient servitude which he himself still had the habit of but hoped not to entrust with the other burden of the genes; and would not, for the genes of the case were hers, not his.

'What's that blue and white carriage?' she asked the man in the white topee.

'Oh, that is private. It belongs to a maharajah.'

'Which maharajah?'

'I do not know. There are so many.'

She thanked him for finding her compartment and walked back towards the restaurant, anticipating light and noise. This platform was sour and gloomy. Clark's words came back to her. 'A tomb-attendant?' Ahead of her a man was getting out of the blue and white carriage, a man in a white suit and panama hat. He had a stick and took the descent carefully. She noticed him because he might be the maharajah but quickly realized he could not be. The lamp on the platform revealed the fact that he was a European. He took out a cigarette case. He had got out of the carriage to smoke. Perhaps the maharajah was inside and did not like him smoking. He glanced at her, but concerned himself again with his cigarette, as if quite uninterested in her presence. He was oblivious of the fact that she had entered. Had entered. To him, perhaps, all women were assumed to have entered. Into their bodies' grace.

But beyond him she hesitated and turned. Her action caused him to look in her direction, with his one available eye. The other was the blind buffed eye of a nocturnal animal. She retraced her steps.

'Count Bronowsky?'

Already he had lifted his hat, but it was clear to her he did not recognize her, and for a moment she was afraid she had spoken to a man who looked like Bronowsky but was not. He said, 'Yes, I am Count Bronowsky.'

'I'm Sarah Layton. We stayed at the guest house last October when my sister was married.'

'Miss Layton? Well, forgive me. Why didn't I recognize you? But I know. It's the uniform. I see indeed it is you.' He held out his hand and, when she gave him hers, carried it with an old man's courtesy to his lips and then held on to it. His accent, which she did not remember having remarked in Mirat struck her as comic, exaggerated. She had a sense of charade which probably emanated from him because she had had it on the morning of the wedding when he joined the group on the lawn of the Mirat Gymkhana club; a sense of charade, of puppet-show; of dolls manipulated to a point just short of climax.

'Nawab Sahib and I were so very distressed to hear of Captain Bingham's death,' he said. How clever still to remember Teddie's name; but then the old wazir could count a memory for names among his many – obviously many – talents. He had remembered Merrick's too.

'It was kind of you to write. Have you been staying in Ranpur?'
She assumed that like herself he was on the point of departure.

'No, not staying.' He let her hand go. 'Have you?'

'I'm only changing trains. I've just got in from Calcutta.'

'That train is going to Pankot?'

'It is at midnight. I came along to make sure my booking was fixed. Now I'm going to have some supper.'

'In the restaurant?'

'Yes. It's still open.'

'And you are alone?' She nodded. 'My dear Miss Layton, I cannot allow it. We can do better for you than that. In the restaurant you will wait for twenty minutes for something badly cooked, I'm quite sure of it. And then you will not sleep a wink, and what dire consequences might ensue from entering such a place unaccompanied I do not know.' He took her arm, holding hat and stick and unlit cigarette in his other hand, and began to guide her to the steps of the Nawab's coach.

'But —'

'But I am inviting you. On behalf of Nawab Sahib, who is not here by the way. I invite you into more compatible surroundings. Besides, apart from my own pleasure there is that of a handsome young Englishman who is already bored by my company but too well bred to show it. Only his sense of duty persuades him to sit and listen to me as if every word I speak is of importance to him. And Ahmed will be here presently. You remember Ahmed? You rode horses together. Do you like champagne? Of course you like champagne. With perhaps some caviar. And some cold game pie. Or smoked ham with melon. When Nawab Sahib is not in the coach it is possible for me to indulge a taste for smoked ham. The champagne is from my personal pre-war stock. I have been eking it out this past year but the Allied invasion of France encourages me to hope for fresh consignments before too long. You know the story of the true princess?'

'The one who needed twelve mattresses?'

'That is she. But even through twelve mattresses she felt the discomfort of one little pea from the pod. How can I let you suffer the discomfort of entering a public restaurant?'

'Well, I'm used to it. But thank you.'

The way in was like the entrance to a Pullman coach, but a thickness of carpet at once pointed a private superiority. The door that led into the main interior was closed and she waited until Bronowsky had negotiated the steps and joined her. His lameness, like his accent, was new to her. Perhaps it was only noticeable when he had something more agile to perform than walking. He opened the door on to a saloon of red and gold – a travelling throne-room such as she imagined the last Tsar Nicholas would have felt at home in. There were tables lit by crimson-shaded lamps, gilt chairs with crimson backs and seats, footstools, and salon sofas. At the far end an open doorway, hung with looped velvet curtains, gave a view of a dining-table set with a snowy white cloth and decked for a buffet.

As they went in the man Count Bronowsky had forewarned her of looked up from the document he was reading. Her arrival obviously suprised him and to get up he had first to secure the document to the briefcase on which he had been resting it, and un-cross his legs. An army officer, he was wearing best KD.

'Allow me to introduce Captain Rowan,' Bronowsky said. 'This is Miss Layton whom I have just rescued from going alone to the restaurant. Nawab Sahib and I had the pleasure of her company at the Palace guest house last year on the occasion of her sister's marriage.'

Rowan nodded. Sarah thought she would not describe him as handsome. Her main impression of him was of a man, perhaps a little younger than Clark, who would be extremely difficult to get to know. There was something in the careful way in which he had overcome his surprise, temporarily withdrawn his interest from the document, and risen, still in possession of it and of the briefcase, that suggested a controlled expenditure of energy, a distrust of any kind of instant reaction, a firm belief in the importance of keeping reserves of whatever particular capacities he had. She judged that probably they were considerable.

A steward appeared in the doorway of the dining saloon. 'First,' Bronowsky said, 'champagne. We were going to wait for Ahmed, but only as a puritanical exercise in self-discipline. With champagne there should always be a sense of occasion, which you have kindly supplied. Come, sit. Do you smoke?' He offered her a silver box of pink cigarettes with gold tips. When they were settled he went on: 'I myself smoke only in the evenings, and then I'm afraid I smoke too many, but these are mild. My introduction to smoking was of a most unusual nature in that I was chastised by my father not *for* smoking but for showing an aversion for tobacco which he thought unmanly. All through one summer, when we were in the country, and I but sixteen, I was made to sit opposite him in his study at ten o'clock each morning and smoke a cigar under threat of a beating from my English tutor should I but turn a paler shade of pale. The fact that my tutor would not have hurt a fly and that I knew the threat no more than a threat, mere bombast, on the part of a man for whose moral cowardice I had the greatest contempt, did not diminish my valiant struggles to disguise my nausea. It became, you understand, a point of honour to smoke the disgusting thing to the bitter end and retire – apparently in good order. But my repugnance for cigar-tobacco has never left me. That winter, in St Petersburg, I took a perverse fancy for the gold-tipped cigarettes smoked by the lady who frequently visited us. I should perhaps explain that my mother died when I was ten. I would steal one of these cigarettes from this lady's handbag whenever I had the opportunity. She kept them in a tortoiseshell case. I remember the case quite clearly, the smooth feel of it in my fingers. And having stolen one I would smoke it after I had gone to bed delighting in the fact that I had stolen it from her and that, unwomanly as smoking was considered at that time, these particular cigarettes looked revoltingly effeminate. Hence my life-long habit – gold-tipped cigarettes, preferably pink, and after sunset. In such small ways we preserve the memories of our youth and remain to that extent forever young. What memories, Miss Layton – or I should say, what habits that will become memories do you think you will still celebrate when you are my age?'

'I don't know, but I'm sure there are some.'

'With girls perhaps it is different. They grow up and marry and have children of their own and everything from their own childhood is put by. Perhaps this is sad because much later what was put by as done with and forgotten may come back to plague them with an intense nostalgia. Their children grow up and go away and all the years a woman devotes to them are as if they have never been. Women are more courageous than men though. Perhaps they accept that their life's work, I mean in the biological sense, is very quickly over. But a man and his career, that is different. His career is the whole of his life. He can afford to introduce notes of absurdity. Perhaps he needs to. His body undergoes no biological change, his life is not divided in that way, nothing physically dramatic happens to him. He never carries his own creature inside him, the poor man has to make do with the one he was born as. Perhaps this explains why he cherishes the memory of its different stages of growth and hangs on to them, in the hope of seeing something whole.'

The champagne cork popped. They were all three silent witnesses of the ritual of pouring. The steward wore white gloves. He handed the glasses on a silver tray. Bronowsky said, 'Captain Rowan, I had not intended tonight to introduce a personal note, but there was a private reason for the champagne and Miss Layton's gift of her company prompts me to share my secret with you both. Today is my seventieth birthday, and I have a toast.' He grinned. 'As an Englishman you will probably appreciate it more than Nawab Sahib would – who touchingly remembered the day and sent me a telegram this morning from Nanoora.' He raised his glass. ' "It is little I repair to the matches of the Southron folk, Though my own red roses there may blow; It is little I repair to the matches of the Southron folk, Though the red roses crest the caps, I know. For the field is full of shades as I near the shadowy coast, And a ghostly batsman plays to the bowling of a ghost, And I look through my tears on a soundless clapping host, As the run-stealers flicker to and fro, To and fro; O my Hornby and my Barlow long ago!" '

He raised his glass still higher, then lowered it and drank; and, when they followed suit (both – Sarah thought – rather put off their strokes by the unexpectedness of the occasion and the obscure, indeed incongruous, connexion between the words and the man who spoke them) Bronowsky went on: 'The poem was explained to me by the charming boy from whom I learnt it in 1919, but I fear my own private interpretation is the one that remains with me. He was just eighteen and his parents had sent him from England to stay with a French family who were holidaying on the Italian Riviera. He learned, or was supposed to learn, French conversation from them. I, a poor Russian *émigré*, was hired to teach him the language's grammar and syntactical complexities, not I fear successfully because he fell madly in love with the Spanish maid of a neighbouring family. His other interest, his only other interest, was cricket. He came to me one day and said, Monsieur Bronowsky, please teach me a French poem. Well, I knew why. I had seen them together, holding hands and staring into each other's eyes, quite dumb, because the girl really only spoke her own language and what little

French they might have exchanged quite deserted him the moment he was in her adorable presence. "But if she speaks only Spanish," I said to him, "what purpose will a French poem serve? Why not recite to her in English?" He said he'd thought of that but he only knew one poem, which happened not to be suitable. I begged him to let me be the judge of that and made him recite it. I was extraordinarily moved and told him to repeat it to her in just the same manner, but perhaps a little slower and with slightly more expression. I also got him to write it down for me.'

'And was it successful?' Sarah asked. 'I mean with the Spanish maid?'

'Alas. He found her that same afternoon holding hands with a fisher-lad. He told me of this disaster when he came for his evening lesson. He was stunned, well, you could see it, but also well controlled, in the way of the English. He went home very soon after that in order, so he said, to get in some more cricket before the summer ended. You could tell he was quite finished with women. At least for a week or so.'

'What a sad story,' Sarah said.

'Isn't it? I'm delighted you see that it is sad as well as comic. And I've always thought how much that flirtatious young lady's memories were impoverished by the chance she missed to have her hand held and her ears simultaneously enchanted by a poem she would not have understood a word of but could hardly have failed to know was spoken from the heart. You see he felt quite romantic about cricket, and so long as she didn't know what the poem was about, it was the perfect vehicle for him to express one passion through the medium of another. She would have heard the rhymes, and the slow alliterative and repetitive cadences which seem to be holding on to memories to stop them slipping too soon away. She would have heard the strange hard burr of a northern language, softly spoken, and so different from the loudly spoken languages of the south, which the sun seems to have melted so that they flow ever quickly onwards, with hardly a pause, like time itself. Above all, how could she not have detected the note of pride ringing through the lamentation! Oh, if I had been she, no doubt I would have positively swooned away.'

'Anyway,' Rowan said, 'congratulations. Your own journey south has been capped by conspicuous successes.'

'Ah,' Bronowsky exclaimed. 'I have understanding companions.

Thank you. Steward. More champagne. Miss Layton, what news of your father?'

'We haven't heard for some time, but we believe he's well.'

'And he'll be home soon, surely? And your mother and sister? Particularly your sister?'

'Yes, they're both well.' She would not intrude her anxiety. Or her grief.

'And what took you to Calcutta, alone?'

'My aunt lives there now.'

'Ah yes, I recall. Mrs Grace? And your uncle who gave you away? They are both in Calcutta?' She nodded. 'And the officer who was best man, Captain Merrick, have you had news of him?'

She hesitated, again reluctant to introduce a sombre subject on the old man's birthday. In any case he was probably only being polite.

'He interested me considerably,' Bronowsky went on, as if prompting her. 'I thought him an unusual man.'

'Actually it was to visit him in the hospital that I went to Calcutta.'

'Really? What is wrong with him?'

'He was rather badly wounded at the same time Captain Bingham was killed. My sister was anxious to find out if there was anything we could do because she was told he'd tried to help Teddie. There's been a recommendation. I mean for a decoration.'

'Yes,' Bronowsky said after a moment's thought. 'Courage. He had physical courage. You could see that. I'm distressed to hear he was wounded. How badly?'

'He's lost an arm. He pulled Teddie out of a blazing truck while they were under fire.'

'Ah.' A pause. 'Yes. Which arm?'

'The left.'

A pause. 'Then that is something. I observed him picking up bits of confetti, also stubbing a cigarette. He was right-handed.' He turned to Rowan. 'You may remember the man we're speaking of. Merrick?'

'No. I don't think so.'

'I don't mean you would remember him personally. He went into the army from the Indian Police. He figured rather prominently in that case involving an English girl, in Mayapore in 1942. The Bibighar.'

Rowan was drawing on his cigarette. He nodded. 'Oh yes. That case.'

'He was District Superintendent. In Mirat I had a long and interesting talk to him and found him still utterly convinced that the men he arrested were truly guilty. I myself and I suppose most people since have come to the conclusion they couldn't have been. It would have been understandable if Merrick had begun to waver in his opinion – unless you accept that he left the police temporarily under a cloud and he harboured a grudge. But he had tried for years to get into the army. He was a very ordinary man on the surface but underneath, I suspect, a man of unusual talents. Are those boys still in prison?'

'Which boys are those?'

'The ones arrested, not tried, but detained, as politicals.'

'I'm afraid I don't know, Count.'

'I hope they are not forgotten and just being left to rot. The provincial authorities have an obligation in this matter, surely.'

'I'm sure they are not just forgotten.'

'The Indians remember. Unfortunately not only Indians of the right sort. There is a venerable gentleman of Mayapore who last year visited Mirat and engaged in some tortuous processes of intimidation. The stone – Miss Layton, you recall the stone – was almost certainly thrown at the instigation of this slippery customer. He is one of those on whom we keep a watchful eye. I am told he has recently left Mayapore, but I am not told where he has gone, or why. Forgive me, it is an uncheerful subject, and Miss Layton must eat. We shan't wait for Ahmed. In any case he's probably only going to be interested in the champagne.'

Rowan looked at his watch and Bronowsky, who was rising, touched his arm. 'We shall be able to leave on the scheduled time. Ahmed will see to it. Come.' He led them to the dining saloon. Two stewards removed covers from the waiting dishes.

●

'I must go, I'm afraid,' Sarah said, putting down her coffee cup. Her watch showed twenty minutes to midnight and for some time now she had been nervously aware of mounting activity on the platform. Once she had parted the crimson velvet curtains that covered the window she sat near and had seen more soldiers, and officers directing them; Indian families with mounds of roped luggage, some of the women in purdah. The lights were on in the Pankot train but the view was too oblique for her to make out her patient coolie, who would still be waiting.

'Another five minutes,' Bronowsky pleaded. He had regaled them with more champagne and talk of pre-1914 Russia and post-1918 Europe, but for the last ten minutes she had been too conscious of the narrowing gap between the minute and hour hands of her wrist-watch to take in much of what he said. She believed that Captain Rowan was similarly preoccupied, but disguising it better. Occasionally he glanced at her as if to say: I know how you feel, but don't worry.

'If I stay another five minutes I shall never want to go, and I've got my compartment to get unlocked.'

Bronowsky put down his glass. 'Then I mustn't be selfish. But Ahmed will be disappointed. He often talks about you.' They all three stood. He took her hand and kissed it. 'Thank you for my birthday present. You will return to Mirat? One day, very soon?'

'Yes. I should like to,' she said, and realized quite suddenly that she meant it, and knowing how unlikely it was that she would ever go again, felt a wrench at parting that was out of all proportion to the real loss or lack of expectation. She turned to Rowan.

'Goodbye, Captain Rowan.'

He took her hand, but not in farewell. 'I'll see you to your compartment,' he said, but Bronowsky intervened, insisted that this was a privilege he claimed for himself. She thought Rowan's face betrayed a momentary blankness, as if the refusal by Bronowsky of his offer to accompany her had made it necessary for him to dismiss from his mind some line of thought or plan of action he had wished to pursue; but since they had only just met and were unlikely ever to meet again, she knew she must be mistaken. But the impression remained, after they had said goodbye and while Bronowsky was handing her down on to the platform. Once down it vanished to the back of her mind, driven there by surprise.

'Why, they've cordoned us off,' she said.

'It saves us from being boarded and from constant explanations that we are not a public conveyance,' he said, and guided her inside the cordon of ropes that held the crowds away from the three coaches, to a point where a policeman was on duty. Originally there had been only two policemen. There were four or five now.

The policeman let them through. She felt she would have understood the cordoning off and the presence of police if the Nawab had been travelling. But he was in Nanoora. She had assumed from some of the things said by Bronowsky and Rowan in the past hour and a half that Bronowsky was going to Nanoora too.

She glanced up the platform. They were level now with the front of the first of the three coaches which a locomotive was slowly approaching.

'There is our engine,' the Count said, pointing with his stick. He walked on her left, holding her left elbow. 'We are due to leave at half past midnight, so we must hope Ahmed isn't much longer delayed. If we fail to leave at twelve-thirty the railway people can't fit us in to their schedule again until two a.m. That is your coolie attracting our attention. Now, where is an inspector to unlock your compartment? The fellow over there in the white topee?' Bronowsky waved his stick. The coolie humped the suitcase and stood with that same upward-strained rigidity of neck and head.

It was the same kind of topee but a different man under it, and he had the key. He unlocked, entered and switched on lights and fans, and the coolie climbed up and deposited the bag, returned, touching his turban. She had two rupees ready but Bronowsky restrained her and gave the old man a folded note, which looked like five and must have been because after he salaamed he did not go away but waited near by as if accepting an obligation to see that the train carried her safely out of his hands and into those of God.

In the compartment adjacent to hers three young subalterns who looked like new postings from an OTS eyed her curiously, no doubt assuming that the elderly man with the eye-patch and ebony cane was her father, a sahib of the old school. No, she wanted to say to them, it's not as you think you see it. What you see is a trick, everything here is a trick. She turned to Bronowsky, feeling for questions.

'Have you a blanket and things like that?' he asked before she could speak.

'Yes, they're in my case.'

'And you haven't left the key of the case behind in Calcutta?'

She laughed, looked in her handbag and reassured him. The questions eluded her. 'Please don't stay, Count Bronowsky,' she said, and held her hand out. 'Thank you for a marvellous supper and for rescuing me from the restaurant. And – Happy Birthday.'

454]

He took her hand, but was silent for a while, looking down at her through his one eye.

'How self-contained you are! I don't remember that when you were in Mirat. But of course we did not exchange many words and you were somewhat overshadowed by the occasion. A bride is always the centre of attraction. But Ahmed noticed you. He affects not to be susceptible to the charms of white ladies. But after you had gone I observed how on many mornings he rode across the waste-ground opposite my house and retraced exactly the course you had taken together, stopping under the same trees, cantering along the same stretch.' He smiled. 'I am confessing, aren't I? That I watched you from the window of my bedroom. I did, but not intentionally. I caught sight of you by chance, but was held by the spectacle. I was amused to see he was doing as he had warned, the night before, when he told me he was to take you riding. He said: Oh! I shall keep my distance, I shall keep my place. It was a joke, of course. Not a bitter one. He has great objectivity, perhaps too much. He is somewhat like an actor who knows every line in a play and plays his part to perfection but cannot light the character up from in-side, so with him it is always a part. Well here is Ahmed Kasim, he says, committed to go riding with this English girl. What is expected, what does the world say? Yes, of course. Five paces be-hind. How amusing! Only he is perhaps less amused than he would have us think. You understand?'

'I understand, yes.'

'You understand what I am saying, but not why I am saying it. To tell you the truth I am not sure. It's probably the champagne. On the other hand, unlike the majority of people I am the opposite of tongue-tied by railway stations and scenes of departure. It must be due to a fear implanted in my mind years ago that even the simplest goodbye may turn out to be for ever and leave you with a feeling of remorse for big and little things you left unsaid. Not that you should ever say everything. Perhaps I am talking to stop you asking those questions you want to ask which I can't answer. I must beg forgiveness. I am only adding to the mystery. But mysteries are no bad thing, especially for the young. They warm the powers of perception and in themselves can be quite beautiful.'

A warning whistle blew. Bronowsky gripped her hand more firmly, reassuring her there was still time – far more for her than for him. 'But don't misinterpret. That picture you have in your mind now, of Ahmed retracing the course you took across the waste-ground. I did not intend a romantic allusion. I said he had great objectivity. He is a spectator, an observer, and when the need arises he can take a part, but not with his heart in it because he doesn't know what part he wants to play or, if he has an inkling, he doesn't see where it fits in. He's indifferent to all the passions that most arouse people in this country. I suppose with a family like his that's lived, breathed and thought nothing but politics it's not unnatural. But in India it's rare. And because it's rare he thinks of it as a disease peculiar to him. He said to me once: "My mother tells me to think hard about something my father once wrote to her – We are looking for a country. But when I think about it I can only make the comment that the country's here, and so am I, and shouldn't we stop squabbling over it and start living in it? What does it really matter who runs it, or who believes in Allah, or Christ, or the avatars of Hindu mythology, or who has a dark face and who has a light?" '

'Yes,' Sarah said, 'What does it matter?'

Bronowsky considered her, and for the first time she noticed how concentrated, how single-minded, a one-eyed man had to be, how deprived he was of the tragi-comic human right to laugh on one side of his face and cry on the other, like the king in the fairy tale. She felt pierced, as if by a singularity of purpose and intent. But that was a mystery too. Perhaps it was beautiful. She did not know. In a few minutes the chance to know would have gone, would have joined the sad jumble of all the other limited chances which (panic-stricken by the thought that the train would suddenly be gone without her), she felt everyone was given.

'He told me about his father's letter and his reactions to it some time *after* you rode together, after you had left Mirat.'

The whistle blew again.

'And you see, he had never spoken to me so frankly before. And I remembered those solitary rides he took, which I did – I must confess – see at first in a superficially romantic light. But now when I look at that picture of him over and over re-enacting that morning ride, I seem to see him trying to recapture something. Some moment he missed, or did not seize, and only understood later was significant.'

'Yes,' she said, 'there was a moment.'

'Tell me.'

'I can't. It wasn't clear. It was to do with the way he kept behind.'
'Something you said?'
'No. Didn't you see?'
'Beyond the nullah, when you galloped, you were outside my range. Two blurred specks. But coming back I thought you once had difficulty with your horse.'
'Not difficulty. I tricked him. I closed the gap. Just for a moment.'
'And then?'
'That was all. He waited for me to ride on.'
The third whistle. 'Thank you, Miss Layton,' he said. 'Now – you had better take your seat, but don't close the door. My steward has some extra luggage for you.' Looking behind she found the steward waiting with a small hamper held to his chest. 'Come.' He handed her up. She stood back and let the steward come in and place the hamper on the floor. When he left the compartment Bronowsky closed the door. She stood at the lowered window. 'There is some champagne,' he said, raising his voice, 'for a christening, which if my arithmetic is correct will take place in the quite near future. But there are also a few things for you to nibble if you get hungry. Shut the windows tight, lock the door and lower the blinds. And if you are in trouble knock loudly on the wall between you and the young officers next door who have been watching with very understandable interest. When next you write to Captain Merrick please remember me to him and tell him I recall our conversation. He will know what I mean.'
'Yes, I will. And thank you again.'
'Now. Please pander to an old man and an old Russian superstition. The circumstances are wrong but the gesture may overcome them. Just sit quietly for a moment, as one always should before setting out on a journey.'
She sat and exchanged smiles with him through the window. Presently the whistle sounded again – a sustained and urgent note. She got up. When she reached the window of the door the train was moving. Bronowsky stayed motionless – his panama hat held to his breast – but gliding away from her, becoming partially obscured by groups of people who slid past as if the platform were being pulled backwards by some strange law of lateral gravity. As the view of the station expanded she saw distantly the three coaches of the Nawab's private train, marooned under dwindling

points of illumination. She thought, but could not be sure, that two figures were passing through the cordon, a man and a woman in purdah; but the glimpse was scarcely a glimpse; perhaps a brief hallucinatory image switched by her eye from one part of the platform to another.

When she had closed windows and meshes and lowered blinds, secured locks, it was twenty-four hours since she had entered her body's grace. She made up her bed with sheet and blanket, blew up her air pillow, but then sat, tracing the red and green tartan pattern of the pillow's cover with her right forefinger. Why red and green? Why tartan? She held the pillow to her, then lay down, letting it cushion her head.

Are you happy? he asked. I'm content. Then we're friends? Not friends. Enemies? No, not enemies – strangers still. Shall we make love again? She turned her head into the pillow, wanting him because she knew no other man. The pain of wanting was exquisite. She opened her mouth to receive an image of his but found only the warm flesh of her own hand that was not cunning or quick enough to hold back days or rescue a single firefly from all those that rode the night emitting signals of distress; the signal lights of souls gathering like migrant birds for a long journey because the home they knew had become inhospitable.

She dozed, woke, covered herself with the blanket as an insurance against the chill that would accompany their entry into the hills, but could not summon the resolution to turn off lights and fans. She dozed again, but sleep was held back by an instinct to keep watch on the night's dissembling progress. Ten minutes short of half past two. Going with him now, back into the danger zone. Are you sad? he asked. Just silent. Content and silent, he said, it's a good basis to build on, you will have a good life. And already up there in the hills (these hills) Aunty Mabel had gone, and been quickly buried, as was customary. And who knew whether hers had been a good life? I waited up, Aunt Fenny said, I waited up, pet, your mother rang. It was twenty-four minutes to three. At five it would be thirty-six hours since she had stood waiting for Sister Prior, and since Susan – lying on the veranda of Rose Cottage – had watched Aunty Mabel suddenly put down her basket on the rail between two of the azaleas, and sit, and die, as quietly as she had lived.

AT FOUR Ahmed was woken by one of the stewards; and at half past, wearing a new dark grey tropical suit made up by Bronowsky's tailor, he went along the corridor and tapped at the door of his mother's compartment. She was lying fully dressed on her bunk. On the opposite bunk her maid snored with her back turned to the single light that lit his mother's head.

'Is it time?' Mrs Kasim asked, keeping her voice low.

'Yes, Mother. Don't get up.'

'Have you slept at all?'

'Yes. Is there anything I can get you?'

'No, Ahmed, nothing.'

'You shouldn't have stayed awake.'

She held on to his hand. 'It wasn't difficult. Stay with me until the train stops. But don't let's talk. Poor Farina's exhausted.' He sat on the edge of the bunk. His mother nodded, closed her eyes. 'You look very smart,' she murmured, and gripped his hand more tightly, as if to thank him for taking trouble. Her hair was greyer than it had been even six months ago. He didn't know – had never known – what she really thought. She had always seemed content to echo his father's words. What have you got out of it, he wanted to ask, out of all this struggle and dedication and sacrifice? What have your compensations been? Are they so small that you notice a suit and get comfort from having me sit and say nothing?

After a while it began to worry him that perhaps the train was behind schedule, that he was committed to stay for a long time, uncomfortably perched; but there was now a change in the rhythm of the rapidly moving coach. His mother noticed it too. Deep – too deep – lines of concentration appeared on her forehead. Speed was being lost. Presently they had slowed to that tentative pace which always made Ahmed feel that a train had transformed itself from a mindless piece of careering machinery into a sentient intelligent creature, probing forward through a maze of obstacles.

His mother opened her eyes and leant up on one elbow. 'You had better go.'

He bent for her kiss.

'You've got the letter safely?'

'Yes, Mother, I've got it safely.' He patted his breast pocket.

She watched him until he pulled the door to between them. In the corridor he lit a cigarette. The dining-saloon still savoured of old festivity, too recent to have gone stale; but it seemed to belong to another time. A nodding steward jerked awake as Ahmed passed him. He found Bronowsky awake in the saloon, reading a small leather-bound book, smoking one of his pink cigarettes.

'I have been indulging several of my most private vices,' the Count said, 'wakefulness while the world dreams, the poetry of Pushkin and an unfinished bottle. There is still a glass left. Or would you prefer something stronger? Yes. Steward. Bring Kasim Sahib a large scotch and soda. Or no soda? No soda.'

'Is Captain Rowan up?'

'I hope so. He was woken at four-fifteen. I have kept watch as well. But that's a virtue. Has your mother slept?'

'No. She promises to.'

The scotch was brought. Ahmed took a generous gulp.

'Here,' Bronowsky said, reaching into his pocket. 'I have a present for you.' He offered a clove of garlic. 'Chew it before you reach the Circuit House.'

'Thanks.'

'Take care not to get close to Captain Rowan, though. He would be too polite to turn his head. He's expecting an appointment in the Political Department, he tells me. We talked for a while after you went to bed. I expect Sir George Malcolm has entrusted him with this present business mainly to help him get his hand in. He should do well. He has a talent for finding out what he wants to know without appearing to encourage conversation to rise above the level of casual chat, and for feigning indifference to the information when he gets it.'

'What did he want to know tonight?'

'He was fascinated by Merrick and the stone and Pandit Baba Sahib. His dismissal of Merrick's name as one that meant nothing to him was disingenuous. I'm too old a hand not to react when feigned indifference is set off by an aura of alertness. I sensed it when Miss Layton and I were talking and sensed it again when I told you in front of him about Merrick's loss of an arm. When we were alone he worked skilfully back to the subject. He began by asking me how and where I lost the sight of an eye. But of course I helped him. We are both professionals.'

'Are you warning me not to speak too freely to him? You know

I never do that.' Ahmed smiled, and took another mouthful of the whisky. Had he really got a taste for it yet? He wasn't sure.

'I am giving you, possibly, an example of the discreet way in which the English set to work to re-establish a principle of justice, for their own peace of mind, while attempting to preserve the *status quo* resulting from the breaking of the principle. If Rowan knew of Merrick, which I firmly believe, his pretence otherwise suggests that the files on the six unfortunate detenus in the Manners case have quite recently been on His Excellency's desk. Which means that the detention orders are being reviewed, and possibly that poor Mr Merrick's reputation has suffered a set-back far more serious than the one that saw him packed off to a backwater by a department anxious to keep its mistakes from reaching the ears of more powerful departments which need to ensure that the principles of impartial justice are *seen* to be held sacrosanct. Assuming my interpretation is correct, do you understand Captain Rowan's interest in the recent history of the ex-District Superintendent in Mayapore?'

'No. It's too early in the morning, Count Sahib. And he'll be here in a minute.' The train was still at a crawl, single-mindedly solving the Chinese puzzle of steel links that unfairly confronted it.

'Sometimes, Ahmed, you are so deliberately obtuse that I could send you to bed for a week on bread and water.' The Count paused. 'The reason is – and you would do well to remember it – that Captain Rowan has recognized with the sure instinct of his race, that Mr Merrick's recent history is the key to the preservation of the *status quo*. It has probably already been decided that the six boys are unjustly detained and must be released. That is the principle of justice re-established. But how preserve the *status quo* when clearly a mistake was made by Merrick and compounded by superior authority? On paper your prime scapegoat is Merrick. But how unpleasant to have a scapegoat at all. Imagine the relief with which Captain Rowan will go back to Ranpur and initiate discreet inquiries – with the Governor's approval – into the truth of what he has heard tonight. A citation for bravery in the field and an amputated arm. What luck! It wipes the blot from the escutcheon and solves the problem of Mr Merrick's future civil or military employment. The boys go free, the files are closed, and all is – as they say – as it was before. The one thing the English fear is scandal, I mean private scandal. If Mr Merrick had ever been

[461

asked to account for his actions the outside world would never have heard of it.'

'You think he had actions to account for?'

'Undoubtedly.'

The train jerked to a halt. From somewhere beneath and a few feet behind, something clanked. Ahmed went to the window, parted the curtains and saw pools of diffused light on cinders, and under one of the standards that shed the light a limousine from the palace and an army truck. He pulled the curtain to, drained his glass and looked at Bronowsky.

'*Courage, mon ami,*' Bronowsky said, '*le diable est mort.*'

Ahmed repeated the words to himself, to translate them. He smiled. 'Is he?' he asked.

They waited for Rowan.

*

Eventually they were beyond the town. The windows of the limousine were lowered half-way. Sheet lightning spasmodically lit the night sky and the barren landscape.

'It's very close,' Rowan said. 'With any luck it'll be raining tomorrow.'

Ahmed agreed that with any luck it would, and mentally put up his guard. But where could a civilized exchange about the weather lead except to a mutual recognition that they had nothing to say that would destroy their all too ready-made images of each other? Rowan – the archetypal Englishman, unemphatic in speech and gesture but warmed inside no doubt by the belief that what he did would have its modest place in the margins of history; and himself, younger son of a veteran Congress Muslim, the son who failed and got packed off to kick his heels in one of the old princely states where he could embarrass no one; known to drink and to womanize, to be indifferent to politics, a potential wastrel and living proof of the continuing validity of the classic formula of misfortune that could afflict respected parents.

'Is there any point you think we ought to discuss before we arrive?' Rowan asked.

'No, everything is clear.' Clearer to him, he thought, than perhaps Rowan realized; although it would be wrong to make too firm an assumption on that score. He felt in his pocket for the clove of garlic and self-consciously carried it to his mouth. Rowan gave him a quick glance, as a guard would who had to bring a prisoner to a place of interrogation and keep alert for attempts at suicide. The car rode the unrepaired tarmac more evenly than the truck ahead in whose canvas-roofed interior two British military policemen sat stoic under the hypnosis of the twin sources of pursuing light.

Abruptly the gap between truck and limousine shortened.

'We're there, I think,' Rowan said. The truck turned across a culvert that separated the road from the eroded landscape. The limousine followed. They were in a compound that had no walls. There were lights on in the Circuit House. Figures moved on the veranda. There were two other vehicles parked. Getting out of the limousine Ahmed surveyed the land beyond the compound, but the night was black and there was no view of the fort. He followed Rowan on to the veranda. Rowan shook hands with an Englishman in civilian clothes and with one in the uniform of the civil police, but when he turned, wishing to make introductions, Ahmed said, 'I'll wait down there, if you don't mind,' and walked to a place where a chair and a table were set, and took up his position.

Presently Rowan joined him. 'Don't you wish to meet the Divisional Commissioner?'

'Not just now, unless it's essential.'

'Very well,' Rowan said, and left him.

Very well. It was one of the English phrases Ahmed had never understood. Rowan and the others would probably interpret his withdrawal and isolation as a sulky attempt to show them that after all he had a patriotic nature. They could not know that he isolated himself to preserve for as long as possible his sense of detachment from the issues of a situation not of his own devising.

And after a while there was a light, far off; gone as soon as seen; but his muscles had tensed, as though to force his body to leap up and stretch an arm to glean the light before it was extinguished. But he continued to sit still and it was a long time before the light reappeared, moving and unmistakable, a mile down the road and coming at speed.

He got up and stood by the veranda rail, then went to the head of the steps, ignoring Rowan whose shadow fell aslant the floor from the open doorway. He heard Rowan go back in and say something to the others. The approaching car slowed, turned in

across the culvert. He was dazzled by the abrupt glare of the head-
lights and the lingering penumbra as they were doused. An officer
got out of the front passenger seat and opened the near door at the
back. Ahmed felt his way down the steps.

An old man emerged, grasped the young officer's arm and
slowly straightened. Light from the veranda revealed sunken
eyes wide open with the shock of transition to a strange environment. With his free hand the old man shaded them.

'Ahmed? Ahmed? Is that you?' The voice did not belong to the
old man. It was his father's voice. The officer stood away and
Ahmed felt his left arm taken in both the old man's hands.

'Ahmed?'

'Yes, Father.'

'Your mother, Ahmed. Your mother. What news of your
mother?'

'She's well, you'll see her very soon.'

'They let the Mahatma out. Poor Kasturba was dead.'

'I know. But there's nothing like that.'

'Then God is good to me.' He clung to him. Ahmed felt him
trembling. The officer had turned his back.

'Come and sit,' Ahmed said.

Presently the old man released him and stood back, looking sus-
piciously towards the house. 'Who is there?'

'An officer on the Governor's staff and two others I don't know.'

'So many people? But there is a room where I can be alone?'

'We can talk on the veranda.'

'No. Please ask for a room. I must be alone for a few minutes,
then we must talk. After that I will see them. Not before. Ask this
officer to go and tell them.'

'I'll go myself. Wait here.'

The room he entered was barely furnished. Rowan and the
others were standing round a deal table. He spoke to Rowan,
ignoring the Commissioner and the policeman.

'My father asks for a room where he can be alone for a while.'

Rowan turned to the Commissioner. 'Is there another room, sir?'

'There's one at the end, where Mr Kasim was sitting. It's not
locked.'

'Is it for devotional use?' Rowan asked, looking in Ahmed's
direction.

'Apparently no one at the Fort bothered to reassure him my

464]

mother was neither ill nor dying. He's been expecting to hear the worst. So he's not yet ready to talk to anyone.'

'The Fort commander would have had the minimum instructions necessary, but I regret any worry he's been caused.' Again he spoke to the Commissioner. 'I think it would be better if we made this room available to Mr Kasim and wait in the other one ourselves. Is there a way to it other than along the veranda?'

The Commissioner mumbled and led them out through a back door. Ahmed waited until the sounds they made were no longer audible, then went back to his father. He found him sitting in the car. He helped him out and up the steps. Inside the room, in the glare of the light, the physical toll exacted by nearly two years in prison was fully revealed. The long-skirted high-necked coat that had once shown up a comfortable thickness of body, hung loosely. The flesh of the thickened jowls was fallen, the fringe of hair was wholly grey. The white cap of Congress seemed too big. The hawk-like nose had a hungry questing look.

'I'll leave this with you, Father.' He gave him the envelope which contained his mother's letter. 'It's from Mother. She wrote it a few hours ago.'

'Is she near by?'

'Not far. Let me know when you want me.'

For the first time since entering the room his father looked at him.

'No, I am all right. Stay here. We must talk. You are taller. And broader. How long has it been?'

'Nearly three years.'

'You have your full growth. You quite dwarf me. Quite dwarf me.'

The moment was over then. In the few seconds sitting in the car his father had recovered and put back up the barriers.

'They told me nothing until five o'clock yesterday, and then only to pack my things and get a few hours sleep. Am I free, or on my way to another jail?'

'You are free,' Ahmed said; but he had hesitated.

'On what conditions? Is there an amnesty? No – don't answer. Let me read your mother's letter. Sit down.' His father sat at the table. Ahmed chose a seat near the door, which was still open. The room was very warm. The fan was not working. Unhurriedly his father brought out his spectacle case and put the spectacles on. A

[465

slight tremor of the hands was the only sign that his composure was incomplete. The letter was very short but he lingered over it with the concentration Ahmed remembered as characteristic. Briefs, minutes, resolutions, correspondence: they had all been subjected to this slow searching analysis. Why does he take so long? Ahmed had once asked. His mother replied: He reads between the lines.

Kasim folded the letter and put it back in the envelope. He took his spectacles off, returned them to the case and the case to his pocket.

'Your mother says she hopes I will agree but that I'm not to be swayed by emotional or private considerations. You had better tell me what I'm being asked to agree to. All I gather otherwise is that she is on her way to Nanoora to stay with my kinsman, the Nawab, and that this could be the scene of our immediate reunion. I too am invited to Mirat?

'Yes.'

'As a guest of the Nawab?'

'Yes. They call it – under his protection.'

'I see.' Kasim sat back. 'While in the sovereign state of Mirat I would be free to enjoy my rights as a private citizen, providing I did nothing to embarrass my host, which means nothing that incurs the displeasure of the Indian Government. Should I set foot outside the State on the other hand, and go back to Ranpur, then I should probably be rearrested.'

'They haven't said so, Father.'

'They?'

'The Governor in Ranpur.'

'You've seen the Governor?'

'Not personally. Neither has Mother. But he sent representatives. One of them is here tonight.'

'On whose instigation did he send representatives? On the Viceroy's? From newspapers and letters received I gather Wavell is anxious to break the political deadlock of the past two years. Who else is being released into this kind of protection? Nehru?'

'The Viceroy knows, but the initiative's been with Malcolm. It's not a general arrangement.'

'I am the only Congressman of any importance being paroled?'

'Yes, Father. So far as I know, you're the only one.'

'Why?'

The question was snapped. In the past such a tone and such a

whiplash of a word had entangled perjured witnesses and intimidated honest ones. There was no way round the truth.

'Because of my brother.'

A pause.

'There is news of Sayed, then?' Kasim asked calmly.

'Yes.'

'Of his death? He has died in prison camp?'

'No, Father. He's been captured.'

'I know he was captured. He was captured by the Japanese in
Kuala Lumpur in 1942. It is a long time since we had any word.'

But the old man seemed suddenly older. 'We've had word now,'
Ahmed said. His father might never forgive him for saying what
he had to say. Sayed had always been the favourite son, the one
in whom hope had been placed, whose life had not been a source
of disappointment. It should have been Sayed who sat here. The
old man would then not have looked so old. 'Sayed was captured
a month ago in Manipur,' he went on. 'We don't know where he
is except in a prison camp in India with some of the others. Directly
the army knew who he was they told the civil authorities in
Calcutta and those authorities told the authorities in Ranpur.
Malcolm invited Mother to Government House, but didn't say
why. She refused to go so he sent someone to the house. Then she
wrote to me in Mirat. She said she'd suspected for some time that
Sayed had joined the INA. About six months ago she had an
anonymous letter delivered by hand, telling her Sayed sent his love
and would see her soon. I think I know who might have sent it,
but that doesn't matter. And previously one of Mother's friends told
her they thought they'd recognized Sayed's voice on the Japanese
radio.'

'The INA —?'

'The Indian National Army.'

'I know what the initials stand for. I was about to say – the
INA? Sayed?' The old man smiled. 'Captured in Manipur? Yes.
Perhaps a man with this name, Lieutenant Sayed Kasim.'

'He was Major Kasim.'

'There you are then. Prisoners of war don't get promoted.'

'Major is his rank in the INA.'

'Rank? His *rank* in the INA? Is there such a thing? No. Sayed
is not a major in the INA. He is Lieutenant Kasim and his regiment is the Ranpur Rifles. Why have you believed this ridiculous

story? Someone has made a mistake, a ridiculous mistake, as a result of all this feeble propaganda which the British have rightly tried to scotch. Now they are believing it themselves, it seems. The Indian National Army? What can that be? A handful of madmen led by that other madman, Subhas Chandra Bose, who was never any good to Congress. He always had delusions of grandeur. First he escapes from India, then turns up in Berlin and then in Tokyo. He sets up an absurd paper government-in-exile and perhaps a few Indians living in Malaya put on a uniform and help him kowtow to the Japanese, fooling themselves that if the Japanese ever defeat India they will allow Subhas to set up his paper-government in Delhi. But it is all wishful thinking and propaganda, there is no Indian National Army deserving of the name. If a Major Kasim was captured in Manipur he would be some unlucky fellow who foolishly accompanied the Japanese as an observer for Bose. He would not be Sayed. And Sayed would not be fighting and killing Indians. He would not be helping the Japanese to invade his own country.'

'There were thousands of Indians taken prisoner in Burma and Malaya. A lot of them felt they'd been deserted by their British officers. There were tales of a white road out and a black road out.'

'You are speaking up for them? You think your brother is one of them? You are calling your brother a traitor?' Kasim got up, Ahmed felt it obligatory to rise too. But they came no closer to one another. 'You forget that Sayed is an Indian officer. He holds, unless he is dead, the King-Emperor's commission. It was his choice. He was a good officer, the first Indian officer in his chosen regiment. It concerned me that he should choose to take a commission, but then I am a politician. He wished to be a soldier. I said to him once, Do you regret it? He only laughed. In the mess he said they were all equal, that there was only one standard and if you measured up to it you were accepted. To me it all seemed simple and naïve, but Sayed *was* naïve. He was naïve, he could never have made a success of politics, but he did not have it in him to be a traitor. In 1939 he said to me, "You are a minister of state, I am an officer in the Indian army. We are both necessary people." He had no complaints, he encountered no difficulties. It was I who encountered difficulties because a son of mine had taken the King's commission. But I did not see them as difficulties. The world is full of fools who don't see an inch in front of their noses. What kind of independence will it be when we get it if we can't defend it? And how shall we be able to defend it if there aren't boys like Sayed willing to train and discipline themselves faithfully and steadfastly to inherit that side of our national responsibility? What are we living in, a jungle? When the British invited Indians to take the King's commission they were proving what my father called their sincerity. You do not hand your armed forces over to the command of men who will turn it against you. What kind of an army will it be if its officers think of their commissions as meaningless bits of paper? It is a contract, a contract. All of Muslim law is based on the sanctity of contract, of one man's word to another. You must be prepared to suffer and die for it. It is written. It is revealed. It is in our hearts. What are you telling me? That it is not in Sayed's? That he is not a man to keep his contract? That he is an opportunist? A cowardly scoundrel? Without a thought for his own honour or for mine, or his mother's, or for yours? Are you telling me this is the kind of India I have gone to prison for? If you are, you had better leave me here. I do not know that kind of India. I do not know that kind of man. He is not Sayed. He is not my son.'

'We've had a letter, Father. He's written to Mother.'

'A forgery.'

'He says you will help him.'

'Does he?'

'Eventually there'll be court-martials.'

'Will there?'

'In his letter he says he refused to join until they told him you'd been arrested.'

'Well?'

'He asked us to give you his love. He's sorry he failed.'

'Failed?'

'Failed to complete the march on Delhi.'

His father's mouth was working. 'The march on Delhi? What is that? Some city on the moon? Or do you march nowadays on your own capital? He thinks perhaps the Moghul empire still exists and has been ravaged by barbarians? And that I languish in some medieval dungeon, clanking my chains, crying out to my son to muster an army and ride to my rescue? God save me from such a deliverance. I would fear for my life. Such a son would strike me down. He would drag me from prison and have me trampled to death. I don't accept his love. I don't listen to his apology.'

The old man's voice had strengthened and risen to the pitch that had swayed juries, brought order to a noisy Legislative Assembly and sent ministers scuttling at midnight through the corridors of the Secretariat. Ahmed closed the door. The action calmed him and hardened his resolution. He could not escape involvement. He had to speak out.

'I've closed the door because it would be better if they don't hear. There *is* an Indian National Army and it isn't just a few madmen. It would suit the British very well if every Congressman said what you've just said. But do you think they will? A dozen Indian officers helping the Japanese would have no political significance. The British could shoot them for treachery and no one would need to raise a finger in protest. But hundreds of officers and thousands of men do have political significance. Whatever the members of your party feel individually, collectively you're going to have to stand by them, because the ordinary Indian won't see any difference between men like these who grabbed rifles and marched up through Burma with the Japanese and men who said the Indians had no quarrel with the Japanese and called on the whole country to sabotage the British war effort. Except that the young men who grabbed rifles and marched will look more heroic than the old men who went to jail and suffered nothing but personal inconvenience.'

'Then I had better go back and continue in that relatively comfortable state of personal inconvenience.'

'You can't go back, Father. They won't let you. I know Mother talks about hoping you'll agree, but she's got into the habit of thinking you have a choice, and knows you'd choose what you see as the honourable way. But the plain fact is they're chucking you out of the Fort. They pretend it's a compassionate release and men like the Governor may actually feel sorry for you. He obviously knew you well enough to guess you'd feel disgraced, and not proud, about Sayed. But if he knows you as well as that, the kindest thing would have been to keep you in prison, because being in prison is your one current public badge of honour, isn't it?'

'You have never thought so!' the old man cried. 'You have always been ashamed. Why? Do you think I have not been ashamed too? You think it is a matter of pride to look out of a window and know that this is as much as you will be allowed to see of the world? No! It is not a badge of honour, it is one of humiliation. But there are circumstances in which you weigh one humiliation against another, and choose. I have chosen many times before and I can choose again.'

Kasim sat. He took the white cap off and placed it on the table.

'No, Father. You can't choose. At least I don't think so.'

'You don't think so. We'll see. Let them take me forcibly to Mirat. But then let them stop me returning to Ranpur.'

'To do what? Something that will force them to arrest you again? What sort of thing will that be? They only arrested you last time because of your loyalty to the Congress. Wouldn't most of your time be spent persuading your friends and the wives of your colleagues who are still in prison that your release isn't a reward for making a deal with the Governor, or with Jinnah? When a man comes out of political detention and there's no amnesty to explain it his friends want to know why.'

'There is always the truth.'

'About Sayed? What will you do? Talk to your Congress friends as you've talked to me? Call Sayed a traitor? You might just as well write your letter of resignation now, and apply to Jinnah for membership of the League. Not that Jinnah would touch you with a barge-pole if you took that line with him. He'll have to call Sayed a patriot too, if he values his career as a future minister.'

Kasim looked up from contemplation of the cap. The sunken eyes glittered. 'To whom have you been talking? Obviously not your mother. To these representatives of Government? To my feeble-minded kinsman, the Nawab? To that European paederast, that émigré Wazir?'

'I've talked to all of them, but not about this.'

'No?'

Kasim looked again at the cap. 'Then I must apologize for having underestimated you. I had assumed your dissociation from the kind of affairs that have been the central concern of my life was a mask for your failure to understand them. But your assessment of my present position is shrewd, and I am indebted to you for bothering to open my eyes to it. Since one of my sons turns out to be a deserter and a traitor, it is some compensation to realize that the other one is not stupid, as I thought.'

Ahmed glanced down at the floor. He supposed he had invited it. It was only fair that his father should hurt him too. But when he looked up again he found his father's eyes closed and head bent forward. For a long time neither of them spoke. It was his father who broke the silence.

'I am sorry. You did not deserve that. Forgive me. And you have come all this way to meet me. In prison you forget that time doesn't stand still, that circumstances change and that without your knowing it you yourself are carried forward with them. It is a shock to come out and discover it. It is difficult to adjust. I must thank you for perhaps having saved me from too hastily making impractical or anachronistic gestures.'

He put his hands on the table, folded, attempting an illusion of unimpaired competence and capacity. But Ahmed guessed that the hands clasped one another to disguise evidence of a sudden and frightening lack of confidence.

'Presently,' the ex-chief minister said, 'you must call in these patient English officials, but there are a few points I wish to be clear on first. Was it the Governor or the Nawab who suggested I should be released from the Fort and sent to Mirat?'

'The Governor, through his representative. Mother asked me to find out if the Nawab would agree.'

'Then we need not concern ourselves with the Nawab's or his Wazir's motives, but only bear in mind what future political advantage they may see accruing from their generosity. Secondly. What reasons did the Governor give for making the suggestion?'

'None. At least, not in so many words, but the connexion was clear enough, I suppose. The representative told Mother the news about Sayed and then said that the Governor had taken advice —'

'Advice?'

'The inference was that there had been a discussion with the Viceroy. The Governor said he'd be prepared to release you into the protection of anyone acceptable to both sides, and suggested the Nawab. He promised Mother that if she got the Nawab's approval the release would be arranged immediately.'

'But —?'

'There weren't any buts. Except for the condition of secrecy until the release had taken place. The Government will then report it as due to a concern for your health.'

'*My* health?'

'From their point of view it must be more acceptable that way round. I imagine they don't want an epidemic of Congress wives with fatal illnesses certified as authentic by Congress-minded doctors.'

'You miss the point that the Governor imagines it is also more acceptable from my point of view. He offers me an alibi that might stand me in good stead later on when my less fortunate colleagues are released.'

'No, Father. I hadn't missed that point.' He hesitated. 'There's one other thing, the Governor said that arrangements could be made for you to talk to Sayed.'

They stared at one another.

'And this is all?' Kasim asked suddenly, ignoring Ahmed's last remark. 'Nothing is said about the expected duration of my illness, nor about the conditions in which I am to live?'

'You'll have a private suite of rooms in the summer palace in Nanoora. We'll drive first to Mirat. The Nawab's private train will be waiting there for us. Mother is on it. So is Bronowsky. The Nawab's at the summer palace.'

'Which of course is heavily guarded.'

'Not heavily.'

'But where nevertheless I shall be incommunicado. I hope Bronowsky understands that Nanoora will suffer from a slight increase in the population in the form of inquisitive newspapermen anxious for every scrap of information they can pick up or invent about my state of health and mind?'

'He's going to issue bulletins. You won't be pestered.'

'You mean I shan't be allowed to be pestered. Well – my kinsman the Nawab of Mirat will be a more considerate jailer than Government, and in this matter you are right, I have no choice. But I am still their prisoner and this time your mother joins me. It is a sacrifice she will willingly make, but it is one I would have spared her. Do you understand that, Ahmed?'

'Yes, I think so.' He waited, but his father seemed to have no more to say. He was staring at the white cap again. 'Shall I go and tell them you're ready?' The old man nodded, but when Ahmed was about to open the door he was stopped by the sound of the voice continuing.

'What have you been trying to tell me?'

Ahmed turned round.

'That I should bow to the inevitable as I bow to this new humiliation? That I should prepare myself to play along with the crowd

[473

and so ensure my political future? Or that I should acknowledge defeat and retire from politics and grow onions to ward off the chills of old age? Have you ever tasted onions that flourish in the dry weather on mugs of shaving water begged from the prison barber on every second day? It is an interesting flavour. Perhaps it is only in the imagination that one tastes soap. But then the imagination of an ageing man is severely limited and prey to all kinds of quaint illusions and expectations.'

Kasim looked up. 'Unfortunately,' the old man said, 'we have only one life to live and we are granted only one notion of what makes it worth living. It isn't easy to write that notion off as mistaken or the life we live in pursuit of it as wasted.'

'I know.'

'Do you? You will. But not yet. You're young and your life is all before you.'

Yes, but what kind of life? Ahmed wondered. The life he lived now wasn't his own because he lived it in the dense shadows of his father's life and of the lives of men like him. He longed to grope his way out and cast a shadow of his own. The longing was so intense that his blood stirred. It was as if a voice inside him cried out: Rebel! Rebel!

But rebel against what? In India only one kind of rebellion was possible, and that kind had become an old man's game. They had played it a long time and it wasn't over yet. The game and the men had grown old together and India had grown old with them.

'Well?' Kasim asked. 'What are you waiting for? Go and fetch them, or are you going to explain what you've been trying to tell me? Which of the two alternatives you think I should choose?'

Ahmed hesitated. The game had gone wrong but his father had always played it honourably. No doubt he would do so to the end. What was sad was the fact that his father was not looking for a country for himsef but for his sons, and they could never inhabit it because a country was a state of mind and a man could properly exist only in his own. In his father's India, the India his father *was*, Ahmed felt himself an exile; but an exile from where he didn't know. His mind was not clear enough to penetrate the shadows of other men's beliefs which lay across it; and before these beliefs – so sure and positive, so vigorously upheld by words of challenge and acts of sacrifice – he felt stupidly unformed and incoherent. Perhaps it was a beginning of coherence for him to

474]

have understood the nature of his father's problem, and to have spoken out. But farther than that he could not go. Could not? Should not, rather. The problem was his father's, not his; and the hands the problem was in were safe enough. The old man would never compromise. Neither would he give up the fight. The sight of him sitting there, waiting to confront three men he thought of as his country's oppressors, moved Ahmed to despair and melancholy pride. The bizarre notion struck him that if only there were a mirror in the room he would take it down from the wall and put it on the table and say: 'There's the India you're eating out your heart looking for.' In the shape of his father's prison-diminished body, he felt for such an India an undemanding, a boundless love, and for an instant in his own heart and bones he understood his father's youthful longing and commitment and how it had never truly been fulfilled, and had never been corrupted, so that even in an old man's body it shone like something new and untried and full of promise.

But there was something missing; and knowing what it was and how he could cover up his silence and indecision and at the same time convey to his father something of what he felt he went to the table, picked up the white Congress cap and offered it.

'You've forgotten this,' he said. 'They pretend to laugh at it, but of course they're afraid of it really. If they see it on the table they might come to the wrong conclusion.'

His father stared at the cap, then bent his head. Ahmed put the cap on for him, gave it a jaunty tilt. His father's hands touched his, seeking to impose an adjustment. 'No, straight,' he said. 'And firm,' and muttered something which Ahmed only partly caught.

But outside, on the veranda, he caught the whole of it. The sky was lighter and the Fort stood immense and dark and implacable; mercilessly near. 'Straight and firm,' his father had said – 'like a crown of thorns.'

Epilogue

AND AFTER all it seemed that Susan had held somewhere in the back of her mind a memory of the day she once told Sarah she had forgotten: the day Dost Mohammed made a little circle of kerosene-soaked cotton-waste, set light to it and then opened a circular tin, shook it, and dropped the small black scorpion into the centre of the ring of fire. Poised, belligerent, the armoured insect moved stiffly, quickly – stabbing its arched tail, once, twice, three times. Sarah felt the heat on her face and drew back. When the flames died down the scorpion was still. Dost Mohammed touched it gingerly with a twig and then, getting no response, scooped the body into the tin.

'Is it whole?' Susan asked. For a while she had this strange idea that it couldn't be because it had been born nearly a month too soon. She received the child in her arms reluctantly, fearing that even at this stage one of them might destroy the other; or, failing this, that she would find some vestigial trace or growth which a few more weeks' gestation would have taken care of. What will you call him? people asked. 'I don't know,' she said. 'A name is so important. How can I choose an important thing like that entirely on my own?'

Susan had had a bad time. 'But,' Mrs Layton said, 'she was a brick.' And so it was generally agreed. A brick. Like her mother. Among those who knew the Laytons only one person withheld praise of the way in which Mildred Layton had coped in Sarah's absence and this was Barbie who maintained a tight-lipped, red-eyed silence, and made preparations for departure from a place of refuge that had not proved permanent. Perhaps it was to Mr Maybrick that she spoke confidentially and through Mr Maybrick that a story gained subterranean currency that Mildred Layton had ridden roughshod over her suggestion that Mabel had wanted to be buried in St Luke's cemetery in Ranpur, next to her second husband, and not in the cemetery of St John's. Had Mabel ever

476]

expressed such a preference? Perhaps she had, but only to Barbie, and there was nothing in the Will to confirm it. Even if there had been, who could blame Mildred for the hasty arrangements made to inter her stepmother-in-law's body in Pankot within twenty-four hours of the old woman's sudden death? What else could she have done, with Susan in labour brought on by the shock of witnessing that death, alone, on the veranda of Rose Cottage? The expense, the inconvenience (the sheer horror, if you liked) of packing the old woman with ice and transporting her to Ranpur would have been intolerable, and it was more important to help a new life into the world than to be certain that the remains of a spent one were buried in a place one had only an old maid's word had been the place desired by the departed.

And so Mabel Layton had gone to her last resting place in the late afternoon of the day following her death. There were mounds of flowers on the grave to make up for the thin scattering of people who managed to get away for the service. Mrs Layton's flurried presence was noted and respected. She would have been forgiven for not attending because Susan still lay in a room of the Pankot nursing home, as yet undelivered. Her mother had spent the night there and would return directly the funeral was over to spend another night, if need be. Was it, people wondered, a false alarm? It would be quite understandable, if so. It was a terrible thing for a young girl so far advanced in pregnancy to find herself sitting on a veranda with a dead woman. It would have been better if there had been some warning, if old Mabel had cried out or fallen or at least shown signs of being unwell; instead of which she had simply stopped tending the plants on the balustrade and sat down in a chair close to the one Susan was lying on, and given up the ghost. Well, she was an old woman and it was a good way to go; but not good for Susan who had only gradually become puzzled and then alarmed by the angle of the old woman's head. 'Are you awake, Aunty Mabel?' she asked, raising her voice because of the deafness. And, three hours later, when Rose Cottage was almost empty again of all the people Susan had sensibly and courageously helped to summon, her mother found her in the little spare, with her hands pressed to her abdomen and her eyes wide with terror and incomprehension.

'It can't have,' she said, when Dr Travers told her twenty minutes later that her labour seemed to have begun. 'It can't be. It isn't time. The baby isn't finished.' For thirty-three hours she lay in a room of the nursing home which Isobel Rankin had seen was made available – a lovely room, marked down on the official lists as exclusive to the wives of officers of senior field rank. And at five o'clock in the morning – as Sarah slept fitfully on the train from Ranpur, keeping watch on the night's progress (and Ahmed Kasim sat on the veranda of the Circuit House near Premanagar, keeping a different kind of watch) – Susan was delivered of a boy who looked absurdly, touchingly, like Teddie.

'It doesn't matter,' Susan said when Sarah told her Mr Merrick was grateful but felt he couldn't accept. 'I'm going to ask General Rankin, but there have to be two godfathers for a boy so you'd better ask Dicky. At least he's got two arms.' It was the only thing she ever said that showed how little or much she had taken in of Sarah's story about Teddie's death and Merrick's action and misfortune; but thereafter she began to show a tender devotion to the child which Dr Travers said was a sign of her having come through, of her confounding those Jeremiahs who once talked about her as being dangerously withdrawn like the daughter of a woman called Poppy Browning. Who said that? Mrs Layton demanded, not having heard the rumour but remembering Poppy Browning well enough from the old days in Lahore. Miss Batchelor had mentioned it, Dr Travers thought. 'That woman!' Mrs Layton cried; and another nail was driven into Barbie's coffin.

On the day before Barbie quit Rose Cottage for temporary sanctuary with the Peplows, Sarah found her wandering in the garden with Mabel's cradle-basket and Mabel's secateurs. 'I should have kept my mouth shut,' she said, 'I mean about St Luke's in Ranpur. But she *did* wish it. She *told* me. Quite clearly. Last year. I suggested we should go down to Ranpur to do some Christmas shopping but she said, Oh I shall never go back to Ranpur, at least not until I'm buried. I thought your mother knew all about it but was forgetting it in all the rush and confusion. But there you are. I've opened my mouth once too often. Rose Cottage is yours now, and it's not as if I expected to stay on or have longer than a week or two to make other arrangements if Mabel died before I did. What hurts is being misunderstood and leaving a place I've been happy in, under a cloud. I know it was unfair to you, my being here. If I hadn't been, there'd just have been room for you and Susan and your mother. I said so to Mabel. More than once.

Oughtn't I to go, Mabel? I said. After all I'm not family, and they're not comfortable down there in the grace and favour. But she wouldn't hear of it. I don't know why. She lived a life of her own, didn't she? I never knew what she was thinking. It sometimes seemed to me she'd *found* herself, I mean her true self, and just wanted to be alone but have someone who would talk to her. Heaven knows I did that. Well, it's all over now. I've written to the Mission. I thought I might do some voluntary work. There are people starving and dying, aren't there? There must be something I can do, even if it's only laying out bodies. I shouldn't want paying. I've got my pension and the little annuity she's left me. Not that I'm happy about that. Nor is your mother, I shouldn't wonder.'

'You mustn't think that, Barbie. You made Aunty Mabel's last years very pleasant. It's the only way she could repay you. And we've still got plenty. We're well off now.'

Barbie looked round the garden. Mabel's presence was like a scent. 'Shall you be happy here, all of you?'

'I don't know. I don't know at all, Barbie.'

'Will she marry Captain Beauvais?'

'Susan?'

'People think so. They say the child should have a father. I'd encourage it if I were you. If she doesn't marry again you'll never get away.' Suddenly Barbie flushed and grasped Sarah's arm. 'That's what you want, isn't it? To get away. But some people are made to live and others are made to help them. If you stay you'll end up like that, like me. Worse probably because all this' – she released Sarah's arm and made a broad gesture at the garden and the hills – 'it's coming to an end somehow, isn't it? Very soon.'

Abruptly Barbie left her and Sarah did not see her again until the morning of the christening when she sat alone in a pew near the altar while Sarah and Dicky, General and Mrs Rankin, and Sarah's mother, stood at the font and Mr Peplow received the new Edward Arthur David Bingham as a lively member of Holy Church. The baptism was hurried, almost furtive; and when it was over the Rankins went their way and the Laytons went theirs. There was no party but Dicky went back with Sarah and her mother to the grace and favour bungalow where the business of packing private possessions into crates for the move to Rose Cottage had been interrupted the day before. The child was placed in the care of Minnie who had been promoted to the position of ayah and had already notably

[479

proved her worth; but it was Sarah who dealt with the milk and the bottle and the rubber teat while Minnie watched, anxious to learn but so far unsuccessful in persuading the child to accept this substitute for his mother's breast.

In the afternoon Dicky drove Sarah to the nursing home – a week to the day and almost to the hour that he had driven Susan home from there with the child in her arms. He did not go in and Sarah told him she would get a tonga home. 'Shall I come and see you tonight?' he asked. She did not want him but thought it might be better, if only for her mother's sake, to have someone in the house to whom both of them could talk. 'Yes,' she said, 'come in time for drinks.'

'I do hope you find her better,' he said. 'Oh, I do hope so.' He turned away and Sarah went in. Twenty minutes later, escorted, she entered the room where Susan was, which was not a pretty room at all. There were bars at the window. Susan sat on an upright chair, hands folded on her lap, watching the gently falling rain and smiling. Another chair was placed near by and on this Sarah took up her position and waited until Susan slowly turned her head and looked at her.

'Hello, Su. I've come to see if there's anything you want.'

How pretty you look, Sarah thought. Pretty and happy. No, more than happy, profoundly content, totally withdrawn. You've found your way in. Why should that cause us pain and sorrow? Why should it hurt to think that you don't recognize me? Or only recognize me as someone belonging to a world that's become unreal to you and isn't to be compared with the one you've always imagined and imagine now, and smile at because you feel its protection all round you like a warmth?

Now you look back at the window, through the bars which you don't see. The little flush on your cheeks which used to look hectic no longer does so; it's a flush of pleasure and the smile is a smile of happiness, almost of beatitude. Why do we call it sickness? And pray for you to come back to us? When you come back you may remember what you did or tried to do, and why. And we are selfish enough to want you to remember and tell us because we're not people who will accept mysteries if we think there are explanations to be had.

But you scare us. We sense from the darkness in you the darkness in ourselves, a darkness and a death wish. Neither is admissible.

We chase that illusion of perpetual light. But there's no such thing. What light there is, when it comes, comes harshly and unexpectedly and in it we look extraordinarily ugly and incapable.

She glanced round and spoke in a whisper to the young psychiatrist who stood waiting with Dr Travers. 'May I touch her?' The man nodded. Sarah had no faith in him; not because he was young – that was a good thing – but because his work was exclusively with men. She leaned forward.

'Susan? It's me – Sarah.'

But Susan did not look at her again and Sarah shrank from touching her. She did not want to intrude or disrupt the pattern of her sister's absorption. After a while she said, 'Goodbye, Susan. I'll see you again tomorrow,' but the words went unheeded or unheard and she rose and went with the doctors to the door. 'Can you keep her here?' she asked. Travers said they hoped so. The alternative – as Mrs Layton so much feared – was a place in Ranpur. But the patient was very quiet. It was probably only a passing phase. Travers said he could have sworn that a week ago her attitude to the child was normal; maternally loving and possessive.

It wasn't normal, Sarah wanted to say, but none of them had seen it; except Mahmoud's widowed niece, Minnie; and it had not been her place to say but only to watch and learn and be on her guard, and make offerings to the old tribal gods of the hills, which it seemed she and the other servants had got into a habit of doing, secretly, to ward off a rumoured evil of monstrous birth, and which she now continued to do because so far as Minnie was concerned the affliction which she had detected in the young memsahib's devotion to the child was of divine origin, as all madness was, a sign of God's special concern and interest.

Sarah waited until the rain stopped, then left the nursing home and took the first tonga in the line. 'To St John's,' she told the tonga-wallah. She did not want to be alone with her mother. When they reached the church she asked the man to wait and went into the churchyard, past the hummocky graves – old lichen-eaten crosses aslant in long wet grass. She took the path round the south side of the church, to the newer part of the cemetery and stood at Aunt Mabel's grave with its mounds of withered wreaths. Her own little posy, gathered from the garden of Rose Cottage after the funeral, was withered too. The ink had run on the cards, leaving ghostly traces of anonymous remembrances. *Ah, oui. Elle est une*

[481

de Mes prisonnières. That too had been a nail in poor Barbie's coffin because she had told Susan about the butterflies in the lace. Had she been listening or had Mabel repeated the story to her after Sarah had gone? No matter. 'Little prisoner, little prisoner. Shall I free you? Shall I free you?' Susan had said, touching the baby's cheek with her finger. But even that had passed them by as no more than a tender admonition.

Sarah left the graveside and on impulse went into the church through the south door which Mr Peplow always left open during the hours of daylight. She sat in a front pew and after a while had the curious feeling that she was not alone. Little prisoner, little prisoner, shall I free you? Is that what she had meant to do? And was it only yesterday that, finding herself alone with the servants in the grace and favour bungalow while Sarah was at the office and her mother at Rose Cottage measuring curtains, Susan had sent Mahmoud to the bazaar for blue ribbons and then sent Minnie after him to tell him white, not blue?

Uneasy, Sarah looked behind her but saw no one and turned back to her contemplation of the image of her sister's madness; but in the stillness she heard from outside the church the squeaking sound of a motor-car or taxi coming to a halt and then, after a second or two, the short note of summons on its horn; and presently, much closer, the unmistakable sound of footsteps on tiles, within the body of the church. She turned again. A woman in an old-fashioned veiled topee was coming down the aisle towards the altar, making for the south door; a woman who must have been there all the time on the darker side of the nave, and whom Sarah recognized. At the end of the aisle the woman genuflected, supporting herself with one hand on the end of the pew.

Why, what a lot you know, Sarah told her silently, what a lot, what a terrible, terrible lot. But now I know some of it too, and know that this kind of knowing isn't knowing but bowing my head, as you are bowing yours, under the weight of it.

The woman came towards her, one hand held to her breast clutching a cross that wasn't there except in the form of pleats and buttons. Level with her the woman hesitated. Sarah could make out little of the face through the veil, but smiled because she felt beholden, as Susan would have said. The woman said nothing but half raised a hand in a gesture that stopped short both of greeting and farewell, and then went out through the south door to the waiting transport. And when she had gone Sarah moved, stumbling over the cassocks, wanting to ask, to ask; but just what she didn't know. She hesitated too, and was lost. Outside, rounding the buttressed corner of the church she saw the old woman opening the lych-gate, began to run, and stopped. The rain was falling again; gentle rain. All the hills of Pankot were green and soft. She ran down the gravel pathway, past the graves of Muirs and Laytons, understanding that this was part of her dream, the running and the absence of an end to the journey. When she got to the road the car was gone.

Little prisoner, shall I free you? Divine intervention! Well, Minnie had understood and not gone beyond the gate in Mahmoud's wake, to change an order for blue ribbons, but crept cautiously back to the end of the veranda where she had been sorting bundles of laundry for the dhobi, and where Susan Mem was dressing the baby in the lace he was to wear on the morrow, talking to him in her strange guttural tongue.

Divine intervention; odd, alien custom. Which? How could Minnie know? All she could do was watch and wait. After a while the dressing was over. The mother hugged the child to her and then walked out into the bright sunshine of the rainfree afternoon, across the patch of grass towards the wall that hid the servants' quarters. There, for many days, Mahmoud had lit bonfires to destroy the accumulation of unwanted years. And there Susan placed the child on the grass, took the ready-to-hand tin of kerosene and sprinkled a wide circle around it. For a time Minnie stared, fascinated, believing herself a hidden witness of a secret initiation. But when Susan Mem set fire to the kerosene and the flames leapt, arcing their way round in a geometrical perfection, Minnie snatched a sheet from the dhobi's bundle and ran, threw the sheet on to the flames, entered the circle and picked the child up and carried it to safety.

She stood some way off. Susan Mem had not moved. She knelt and watched the flames dying and did not appear to notice the trampled sheet or the fact that the child was no longer there. The grass was too wet for the flames to catch hold. Only the spirit burned, and left a scorched smouldering ring.

'Pankot Rifles Depot *ki taraf jao*,' Sarah told the tonga-wallah who snapped his whip and clicked his tongue. They bowled down the lane from St John's, from the eminence towards the valley. As they went past the nursing home which was set far back from the road in wooded grounds Sarah leant her head against the canopy and imagined herself Susan, leaning her head against the bars that separated her from the window pane. She closed her eyes as perhaps Susan was doing, even now, and after a while felt the quietness of her own happiness and grace welling up inside her; and smiled, ignoring the rain that seemed to be falling on her face.